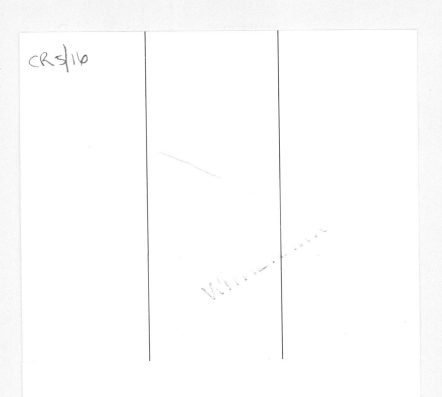

PLEASE RETURN TO THE ABOVE LIBRARY OR ANY OTHER ABERDEEN
CITY LIBRARY, ON OR BEFORE THE DUE DATE. TO RENEW, PLEASE
QUOTE THE DUE DATE AND THE BARCODE NUMBER.

 Aberdeen City Council
Library & Information Services

John Katzenbach has written eight previous novels, including the Edgar Award-nominated *In the Heat of the Summer*, *The Shadow Man* (another Edgar nominee), and *The Analyst*. John Katzenbach has been a criminal court reporter for the *Miami Herald* and *Miami News* and a featured writer for the *Herald's Tropic* magazine. He lives in western Massachusetts.

THE MADMAN'S TALE

When a young female trainee is found brutally murdered in the Nurses' Station of the Western State Mental Hospital, Massachusetts, one inmate claims to have seen the killer, whom he will describe only as The Angel. Twenty years later, Francis Petrel, once a patient there, writes his account of the murder and its investigation on the walls of his tiny apartment. As he goes deeper and deeper into his story, his own madness returns. He remembers being co-opted into the investigation by Lucy Jones, a driven young profiler. Together they faced the same conundrum: how does one find a cold-blooded killer masquerading as mad in a world populated by the deranged?

Books by John Katzenbach
Published by The House of Ulverscroft:

THE ANALYST

JOHN KATZENBACH

THE
MADMAN'S
TALE

Complete and Unabridged

CHARNWOOD
Leicester

First published in Great Britain in 2004 by
Bantam Press
a division of Transworld Publishers
London

First Charnwood Edition
published 2005
by arrangement with
Transworld Publishers, a division of
The Random House Group Limited
London

British Library CIP Data

Katzenbach, John
    The madman's tale.—Large print ed.—
Charnwood library series
    1. Murder—Investigation—Fiction
    2. Mentally ill—Fiction 3. Suspense fiction
    4. Large type books
    I. Title
    813.5′4 [F]

    ISBN 1–84395–666–7

Published by
F. A. Thorpe (Publishing)
Anstey, Leicestershire

Set by Words & Graphics Ltd.
Anstey, Leicestershire
Printed and bound in Great Britain by
T. J. International Ltd., Padstow, Cornwall

This book is printed on acid-free paper

For Ray, who helped to tell this tale
more than he will ever know.

Part One

THE UNRELIABLE NARRATOR

1

I can no longer hear my voices, so I am a little lost. My suspicion is they would know far better how to tell this story. At least they would have opinions and suggestions and definite ideas as to what should go first and what should go last and what should go in the middle. They would inform me when to add detail, when to omit extraneous information, what was important and what was trivial. After so much time slipping past, I am not particularly good at remembering these things myself and could certainly use their help. A great many events took place, and it is hard for me to know precisely where to put what. And sometimes I'm unsure that incidents I clearly remember actually did happen. A memory that seems one instant to be as solid as stone, the next seems as vaporous as a mist above the river. That's one of the major problems with being crazy: you're just naturally uncertain about things.

For a long time, I thought it all began with a death and ended with a death, a little like a nice set of bookends, but now I'm less positive. Perhaps what truly put all those moments in motion all those years back when I was young and truly mad was something far smaller or more elusive, like a hidden jealousy or an unseen anger, or much larger and louder, like the positions of the stars in the heavens or the forces of the ocean tides and the inexorable spin of the earth. I do know that some people died, and I was a lucky child not to join them, which was one of the last observations my voices made, before they abruptly disappeared from my side.

Instead, what I get now instead of their whispered words are medications to quiet their noises. Once a day

I dutifully take a psychotropic, which is an oval-shaped, eggshell blue pill and which makes my mouth so dry that when I speak I sound like a wheezing old man after too many cigarettes or maybe some parched deserter from the Foreign Legion who has crossed the Sahara and is begging for a drink of water. This is followed immediately by a foul-tasting and bitter mood-elevator to combat the occasional blackhearted and suicidal depression I am constantly being told by my social worker that I am likely to tumble into at just about any minute regardless of how I actually do feel. In truth, I think I could walk into her office and click up my heels in pure joy and exaltation over the positive course of my life, and she would still ask me whether I had taken my daily dosage. This heartless little pill makes me both constipated and bloated with excess water, sort of like having a blood pressure cuff wrapped around my midsection instead of my left arm, and then pumped up tight. So I need to take a diuretic and then a laxative to alleviate these symptoms. Of course, the diuretic gives me a screaming migraine headache, like someone especially cruel and nasty is taking a hammer to my forehead, so there are codeine-laced painkillers to deal with that little side effect as I race to the toilet to resolve the other. And every two weeks I get a powerful antipsychotic agent in a shot by going to the local health clinic and dropping my pants for the nurse there who always smiles in precisely the same fashion and asks me in exactly the same tone of voice how I am that day, to which I reply 'Just fine' whether I am or not, because it is pretty obvious to me, even through the various fogs of madness, a little bit of cynicism and drugs, that she doesn't really give a damn one way or the other, but still considers it part of her job to take note of my reassurance. The problem is the antipsychotic, which prevents me from all sorts of evil or despicable behavior, or so they like to tell me, also gives me a bit of palsy in my hands, making them shake as if I was some nervously dishonest taxpayer confronting an accountant from the IRS. It also makes the corners of my mouth twitch slightly, so I need to take a muscle relaxant to prevent my face from freezing into a permanent scare-the-neighborhood-kids mask. All these concoctions zip around willy-nilly through my veins, assaulting various innocent and probably completely befuddled organs on their way to calming the irresponsible electrical impulses that crackle about in my brain like so many unruly teenagers. Sometimes I feel like my imagination is similar to a wayward domino that has suddenly lost its balance, first teetering back and forth and then tumbling against all the other forces in my body, triggering a great linked chain reaction of pieces haphazardly falling *click click click* around inside of me.

It was easier, by far, when I was still a young man and all I had to do was listen to the voices. They weren't even all that bad, most of the time. Usually, they were faint, like fading echoes across a valley, or maybe like whispers you would hear between children sharing secrets in the back of a playroom, although when things grew tense, their volume increased rapidly. And generally, my voices weren't all that demanding. They were more, well, suggestions. Advice. Probing questions. A little nagging, sometimes, like a spinster great-aunt who no one knows precisely what to do with at a holiday dinner, but is nevertheless included in the festivities and occasionally blurts out something rude or nonsensical or politically incorrect, but is mostly ignored.

In a way, the voices were company, especially at the many times I had no friends.

I did have two friends, once, and they were a part of the story. Once I thought they were the biggest part, but I am no longer so sure.

Now, some of the other people I met during what I

like to think of as my truly mad years had it far worse than I. Their voices shouted out orders like so many unseen Marine drill sergeants, the sort that wear those dark brown green wide-brimmed hats perched just above their eyebrows, so that their shaved skulls are visible from the rear. Step lively! Do this! Do that!

Or worse: Kill yourself.

Or even worse: Kill someone else.

The voices that shrieked at those folks came from God or Jesus or Mohammad or the neighbor's dog or their long-dead great-uncle or extraterrestrials or maybe a chorus of archangels or perhaps a choir of demons. These voices would be insistent and demanding and utterly without compromise and I got so that I could recognize in the tautness that these people would wear in their eyes, the tension that tightened their muscles, that they were hearing something quite loud and insistent, and it rarely promised any good. At moments like those, I would simply walk away, and wait near the entranceway or on the opposite side of the dayroom, because something altogether unfortunate was likely to happen. It was a little like a detail I remembered from grade school, one of those odd facts that stay with you: In the event of an earthquake, the best place to hide is in a doorway, because the arched structure of the opening is architecturally stronger than a wall, and less likely to collapse on your head. So when I saw the turbulence in one of my fellow patients become volcanic, I would find the arch where I thought the best chance of surviving lay. And once there, I could listen to my own voices, which generally seemed to watch out for me, more often than not warning me when to make tracks and hide. They had a curiously self-preservative streak to them, and if I hadn't been so stupidly obvious in replying out loud to them when I was young and they first joined my side, I probably never would have been diagnosed and shipped off in the first place, as I was.

But that is part of the story, although not the greatest part by any means, but still, I miss them in an odd way, for now I am mostly lonely.

It is a very hard thing, in this time of ours, to be mad and middle-aged.

Or ex-mad, as long as I keep taking the pills.

My days are now spent in search of motion. I don't like to be sedentary for too long. So I walk, fast-paced, a quick march around the town, from parks to shopping areas, to industrial sections, watching and observing, but keeping myself on the move. Or else I seek out events where there is a waterfall of movement in my view, like a high school football or basketball game, or even a youth soccer game. If there is something busy going on in front of me, then I can take a rest. Otherwise, I keep my feet going — five, six, seven or more hours per day. A daily marathon that wears through the soles of my shoes, and keeps me lean and sinewy. In the winter, I beg unwieldy, clunky boots from the Salvation Army. The rest of the year, I wear running shoes that I get from the local sports store. Every few months the owner kindly slides me a pair of some discontinued model, size twelve, to replace the ones that have been sidewalked into tatters upon my feet.

In the early spring, after the first melt-out of ice, I march my way up to the Falls, where there is a fish ladder, and I daily volunteer to monitor the return of salmon to the Connecticut River watershed. This requires me to watch endless gallons of water flow through the dam, and occasionally spot a fish climbing against the current, driven by great instincts to return to where it was itself spawned — where, in that greatest of all mysteries, it will in its own turn, spawn and then die. I admire the salmon, because I can appreciate what it is like to be driven by forces others cannot see or feel or hear and to feel the imperative of a duty that is greater than oneself. Psychotic fish. After years of gallivanting about most pleasantly in the great wide ocean, they hear a mighty fish-voice deep inside them resonating and that insists they head on this impossible journey toward their own death. Perfect. I like to think of the salmon as if they are as mad as I once was. When I see one, I make a pencil notation on a form the state Wildlife Service provides me and sometimes whisper a quiet greeting: Hello, my brother. Welcome to the society of the crazed.

There is a trick to spotting the fish, because they are sleek and silver-sided from their travels in the salt of the ocean so many scores of miles away. It is a shimmering presence in the glistening water, invisible to the uneducated eye, almost as if a ghostly force has entered the small window where I keep watch. I get so I can almost feel the arrival of a salmon before it actually appears at the base of the ladder. It is satisfying to count the fish, even though hours can pass without one arriving and there are never enough of them to please the wildlife folks, who stare at the charts of returnees and shake their heads in frustration. But the benefits of my ability to spot them translates into other advantages. It was my boss at the Wildlife Service who called the local police and informed them I was completely harmless, although I always wondered how he deduced that and have my sincere doubts as to its overall truthfulness. So I am tolerated at the football games and other events, and now, really, if not precisely welcomed in this little, former mill town, at least I am accepted. My routine isn't questioned, and I am seen less as crazy and more as eccentric, which, I have learned over the years is a safe enough status to maintain.

I live in a small one-bedroom apartment paid for by a state subsidy. My place is furnished in what I call sidewalk-abandoned modern. My clothes come from the Salvation Army or from either of my two younger sisters, who live a couple of towns away, and occasionally, bothered by some odd guilt that I don't really understand, feel the need to try to do something for me by raiding their husbands' closets. They purchased me a secondhand television that I seldom watch and a radio I infrequently listen to. Every few weeks they will visit, bringing slightly congealed home-cooked meals in plastic containers and we spend a little time talking together awkwardly, mostly about my elderly parents, who don't care to see me much anymore, for I am a reminder of lost hopes and the bitterness that life can deliver so unexpectedly. I accept this, and try to keep my distance. My sisters make sure the heat and electric bills are paid. They make certain that I remember to cash the meager checks that arrive from various government aid agencies. They double-check to make absolutely sure that I have taken all my medications. Sometimes they cry, I think, to see how close to despair that I live, but this is their perception, not mine, for, in actuality, I'm pretty comfortable. Being insane gives one an interesting take on life. It certainly makes you more accepting of certain lots that befall you, except for those times when the medications wear a bit thin, and then I can get pretty exercised and angry at the way life has treated me.

But for the most part, I am, if not happy, at least understanding.

And there are some intriguing sidelights to my existence, not the least of which is how much of a student I have become of life in this little town. You would be surprised how much I learn in my daily travels. If I keep my eyes open and ears cocked, I pick up all sorts of little slivers of knowledge. Over the years, since I was released from the hospital, after all the things that were going to happen there did happen, I have used what I learned, which is: to be observant. Pounding out my daily travels, I come to know who's having a tawdry little affair with which neighbor, whose husband is leaving home, who drinks too much, who beats their children. I can tell which businesses are struggling, and who has come into some money from a dead parent or lucky lottery ticket. I discover which teenager hopes for a college football or basketball scholarship, and which teenager will be shipped off for a few months to visit some distant aunt and perhaps deal with a surprise pregnancy. I have come to know which cops will cut you a break, and which are quick with the nightstick or the ticket book, depending on the transgression. And there are all sorts of littler observations, as well, ones that come with who I am and who I've become — for example the lady hairdresser who signals me at the end of the day to come in and cuts my hair so that I am more presentable during my daily travels, and then slips me an extra five dollars from her day's tips, or the manager of the local McDonald's who spots me pacing past, and runs after me with a bag filled with burgers and fries and has come to know that I am partial to vanilla shakes, not chocolate. Being mad and walking abroad is the clearest window on human nature; it is a little like watching the town flow along like the water cascading past the fish ladder window.

And it isn't as if I am useless. I once spotted a factory door ajar at a time it was always closed and locked, and found a policeman, who took all the credit for the burglary that he interrupted. But the police did give me a certificate when I got the license plate of a hit-and-run driver who knocked a bicyclist senseless one spring afternoon. And in something awkwardly close to the takes-one-to-know-one category, as I cruised past a park where children were playing one fall weekend, I spotted a man — and I knew as soon as I saw him, hanging by the entranceway, that something was completely wrong. Once my voices would have noticed him, and they would have shouted out a warning, but this time I took it upon myself to mention him to the young preschool teacher I knew who was reading a woman's magazine on the bench ten yards from the sandbox and swing set and not quite paying enough attention to her charges. It turned out the man was recently released and had been registered just that morning as a sex offender.

This time, I didn't get a certificate, but the teacher had the children paint me a colorful picture of themselves at play, and they wrote a thank-you across it in that wondrously crazy script that children have before we burden them with reason and opinions. I carried the picture back to my little apartment and placed it on the wall above my bed, where it is now. I have a musty brown life, and it reminds me of the colors I might have experienced if I hadn't stumbled onto the path that had brought me here.

That, then, more or less, is the sum of my existence, as it is now. A man on the fringe of the sane world.

And, I suspect I would have simply passed the remainder of my days this way, and never really bothered to tell what I know about all those events I witnessed had I not received the letter from the state.

It was suspiciously thick and had my name typed on the outside. Amid the usual pile of grocery store flyers and discount coupons, it stood out dramatically. You don't get much personal mail when you live as isolated a life as I do, so when something out of the ordinary arrives, it seems to glow with the need to be examined. I threw the useless papers away and tore this open, curiosity pricked. The first thing I noticed was that they got my name right.

Dear Mr. Francis X. Petrel:

It started well enough. The trouble with having a first name that one shares with the opposite sex, is that it breeds confusion. It is not uncommon for me to get form letters from the Medicare people concerned that they have no record of the results of my latest pap smear, and have I had myself checked for breast cancer? I have given up trying to correct these misguided computers.

The Committee to Preserve the Western State Hospital has identified you as one of the last patients to be released from the institution before its doors were permanently closed some twenty years ago. As you may know, there is a movement under way to turn part of the hospital grounds into a museum, while releasing the remainder for development. As part of that effort, the Committee is sponsoring a daylong 'examination' of the hospital, its history, the important role it played in this state, and the current approach to treatment of the mentally ill. We invite you to join in the upcoming day. There are seminars, speeches, and entertainment planned. A tentative event program is enclosed. If you can attend, please contact the person below at your earliest convenience.

I glanced down at the name and number whose title was Planning Board Cochairperson. Then I flipped to the enclosure, which was a list of activities planned for the day. These included, as the letter said, some speeches by politicians whose names I recognized, right up to the lieutenant governor and the State Senate Minority leader. There would be discussion groups, headed up by doctors and social historians from several of the nearby colleges and universities. One item caught my eye: a session entitled 'The Reality of the Hospital Experience — A Presentation.' This was followed by the name of someone I thought I might remember from my own days in the hospital. The celebration was then to finish off with a musical interlude by a chamber orchestra.

I put the invitation down on a table and stared at it

for a moment. My first instinct was to toss it with the rest of the day's trash, but I did not. I picked it up again, read through it a second time, and then went and sat on a rickety chair in a corner of the room, assessing the question that had been posed. I knew people were forever going to reunions. Pearl Harbor or D-Day veterans get together. High school classmates show up after a decade or two to examine expanding waistlines, balding pates, or augmented breasts. Colleges use reunions as a way of extorting funds from misty-eyed graduates, who go stumbling around the old ivy-decked halls recalling only the good moments and forgetting the bad. Reunions are a constant part of the normal world. Folks are always trying to relive times that in their memory were better than they really were, rekindle emotions that in truth far best belong in their past.

Not me. One of the by-products of my state of mind is a devotion to looking ahead. The past is a runaway jumble of dangerous and painful memories. Why would I want to go back?

And yet, I hesitated. I found myself staring at the invitation with a fascination that seemed to flower within me. Although the Western State Hospital was only an hour's ride away, I had never returned there in any of the years after my release. I doubted anyone who'd spent a single minute behind those doors had.

I looked down at my hand and saw that it was shaking slightly. Perhaps my medications were wearing thin. Again, I told myself to toss the letter in the wastebasket and then take off across town. This was dangerous. Unsettling. It threatened the very careful existence that I had stitched together. Walk fast, I told myself. Travel quickly. Pace out your normal routine, because it is your salvation. Put this behind you. I started to do exactly that, then stopped.

Instead, I reached out for the phone and punched in the numbers for the chairperson. I waited through two rings, then heard a voice:

'Hello?'

'Mrs. Robinson-Smythe, please,' I said a little too briskly.

'This is her secretary. Who is calling?'

'My name is Francis Xavier Petrel . . . '

'Oh, Mr. Petrel, you must be calling about the Western State day . . . '

'That's correct,' I said. 'I'll be there.'

'That's great. Now let me just put you through . . . '

But I hung up the phone, almost scared of my own impulsiveness. I was out the door and pounding the pavement as fast as I could, before I had a chance to change my mind. I wondered, as the yards of concrete sidewalk and black macadam highway passed beneath my soles and the storefronts and houses of my town went unnoticed by my eyes, if my voices would have told me to go. Or not.

★   ★   ★

It was an unseasonably hot day, even for late May. I had to transfer buses three times before reaching the city, and each time it seemed that the mingling of hot air and diesel engine fumes had grown worse. The stink greater. The humidity higher. At each stop I told myself that it was completely wrong to go back, but then refused to take my own advice and kept going.

The hospital was on the outskirts of a small typically New England college town which sported equal numbers of bookshops, pizzerias, Chinese restaurants, and low-cost clothing stores with a military bent. There was a slightly iconoclastic character to some of the businesses, however — like the bookstore that specialized in self-help and spiritual growth tomes, where the clerk behind the counter looked like someone who had read every book offered on the shelves and

14

hadn't found any that helped, or the sushi bar that looked a bit bedraggled, and the sort of place where the fellow slicing the raw fish was likely to be named Tex or Paddy and speak with a drawl or a brogue. The heat of the day seemed to emanate from the sidewalk beneath my feet, radiant warmth like a space heater in winter that has only one setting: hot as hell. The small of my back was sticking unpleasantly to the one white dress shirt I owned, and I would have loosened my tie were I not afraid that I wouldn't be able to straighten it again. I wore the only suit I possessed: a blue wool go-to-a-funeral suit that I had purchased secondhand in anticipation of my parents' deaths, but they had, as yet, managed to stubbornly cling to breath, and so this was the first occasion I'd ever worn it. I definitely thought it would be a good suit to be buried in, because it would undoubtedly keep my remains warm in the cold earth. By the time I was midway up the hill toward the hospital grounds, I was already vowing that it would be the last time I ever consciously put it on, no matter how infuriated my sisters would be when I showed up at the wake they had planned for our parents in shorts and an outrageously loud Hawaiian print shirt. But what could they truly say? After all, I'm the crazy one in the family. A built-in excuse for all sorts of behavior.

In a great, curious joke of construction, the Western State Hospital was built on the top of a hill, overlooking the campus of a famous women's college. The hospital buildings mimicked the college, lots of ivy and brick and white framed windows in rectangular three- and four-story dormitories, laid out in quadrangles with benches and stands of small elm trees. I always suspected that the same architects were involved in both projects, and the hospital contractor simply stole materials from the college. From the sky, a passing crow would have assumed that the hospital and the college were more or less the same place. The same bird would have failed to see how different the two campuses were until one stepped inside each building. Then he would have seen the differences.

The physical line of demarcation was a single-lane black macadam road, not even adorned with a sidewalk, that curved up one side of the hill, and a riding corral on the other, where the even better-heeled students among the already well-heeled, exercised their horses. I saw that the stables and the jumps were still where they had been when I'd last seen them twenty years earlier. A solitary horse and rider were going through their paces, circling endlessly around the oval beneath the early summer sun, then accelerating into the jumps. A Möbius strip of action. I could hear the harsh breathing of the animal as it labored in the heat and see a long blond ponytail protruding from beneath the rider's black helmet. Her shirt was black with sweat, and the horse's flanks glistened. Both seemed oblivious to the activity taking place above them, farther up the hill. I walked past, heading to where I saw a bright yellow-striped tent had been erected, just inside the tall brick wall and iron gate to the hospital. A printed sign said REGISTRATION.

A large, overly well-intentioned lady behind a card table outfitted me with a name tag, pinning it to my suit coat with a flourish. She also equipped me with a folder that contained reprints of numerous newspaper articles detailing the development plans for the old hospital grounds: condos and luxury homes because the land had a view of the valley and the river in the distance. I thought that was odd. In all the time I spent there, I could never remember seeing the blue band of the river in any distant vision. Of course, I might have thought it was an hallucination, anyway. There was also a brief history of the hospital and some grainy, black-and-white photographs of patients being treated or passing the time in the dayrooms. I scanned the pictures for faces I recalled, including my own, but saw no one I recognized, except that I recognized everyone. We were all the same, once. Shuffling about in various states of dress and medication.

The folder contained a program for the day's activities, and I saw a number of people heading in to what I remembered was the main administration building. The lecture scheduled for that time block was a presentation, by a history professor, entitled 'The Cultural Significance of the Western State Hospital.' Considering that we inmates were limited to the grounds, and more often than not, locked in the dormitories, I wondered what he would find to talk about. I recognized the lieutenant governor, surrounded by several aides, shaking hands with other politicians as he walked through the door. He was smiling, but I couldn't recall anyone else ever smiling when they were escorted into that building. It was the place you were first taken, and where you were processed. There was also a warning in large block letters at the bottom of the program, stating that many of the hospital's buildings were in significant states of disrepair, and dangerous to enter. The warning requested that visitors limit themselves to the administration building and to the quadrangles for safety purposes.

I took a few steps toward the line of people heading into the lecture, then stopped. I watched the crowd dwindle, as the building devoured them. Then I turned, and walked quickly across the quadrangle.

It was a pretty simple realization that struck me: I wasn't there to hear a speech.

It did not take me long to find my old building. I could have walked the paths with my eyes closed.

The metal grates that covered the windows had rusted, the iron burnished by time and dirt. One hung like a broken wing from a single brace. The brick exterior had faded, too, dulled to an earthy brown color.

The shoots of ivy that were springing forth green with the season seemed to cling with little energy to the walls, untended, wild. The shrubbery that used to adorn the entranceway had died, and the large double doors that led into the building hung loosely from cracked and splintered jambs. The name of the building, carved into a gray granite slab on the corner, much like a tombstone, had suffered as well: someone had chipped away at the stone, so that the only letters I could make out were MHERST. The A that had begun the title was now a jagged scar.

All the housing units had been named after — in some person's cosmic sense of irony — famous colleges and universities. There had been Harvard, Yale, and Princeton, Williams and Wesleyan, Smith and Mount Holyoke and Wellesley, and, of course, mine, which was Amherst. The building named for the town and the college, which in turn had been named after a British soldier, Lord Jeffrey Amherst, whose original claim to fame had been heartlessly equipping rebellious Indian tribes with blankets infected with smallpox. His gifts managed to swiftly accomplish what bullets, trinkets, and negotiations could not.

There was a sign nailed to the door, and I walked up to read it. The first word was DANGER, written in large print. Then there was some blah-blah-blah legalese from the county building inspector, which amounted to an official condemnation of the building. It was followed, in equally large letters: NO UNAUTHORIZED ENTRY.

I thought this was interesting. Once it had seemed to those who occupied the building that we were the ones being condemned. It had never occurred to any of us that the walls, bars, and locks that made up our lives would one day face the same status.

It appeared, as well, that someone else had refused to obey the admonishment. The door locks had been worked over with a crowbar, a device that lacks subtlety, and the doors were ajar. I reached out and pulled hard, and with a creaking noise, the entranceway slid open.

A musty smell filled the first corridor. There was a pile of empty wine and beer bottles in the corner, which, I guessed, explained the nature of the other visitors to the building: high school kids searching for a place to drink away from spying parental eyes. The walls were streaked with dirt and odd graffiti slogans in different hues of spray paint. One said BAD BOYS RULE! I supposed so. Pipes had ripped through the ceilings, dripping fetid dark water onto the linoleum floors. Debris and trash, dust and dirt filled each corner. Mixed with the flat smell of age and disuse was the distinct odor of human waste. I took a few steps forward, but had to stop. A sheet of wallboard had pulled away and fallen across the corridor blocking the path. I saw the center stairs to my left, which led to the upper floors, but they were littered with even more refuse. I wanted to walk through the dayroom, off to my left, and I wanted to see the treatment rooms, which lined the first floor. I also wanted to see the upper floor cells, where we were locked up when we struggled with our medications or our madness, and the dormitory bunk rooms, where we slept like unhappy campers in rows of steel beds. But the stairway looked unstable, as if it would sway and collapse under my weight if I tried to climb it.

I am not sure how long I remained inside, squatted down, bent over, listening to the echoes of all that I had once seen and heard. Just as when I was a patient, time seemed less urgent, less compelling, as if the second hand on my watch slowed to a crawl, and the minutes passed reluctantly.

Ghosts of memory stalked me. I could see faces, hear sounds. Tastes and smells of madness and neglect came back in a steady tidal rush. I listened to my past, as it swirled about me.

19

When the heat of recollection finally overcame me, I rose stiffly and slowly exited the building. I walked over to a bench in the quadrangle beneath a tree, and sat down, turning my face back to what had once been home. I felt exhausted and breathed in the fresh air with effort, more tired in that moment than I was after any of my usual sorties around my hometown. I did not turn away, until I heard some footsteps on the pathway behind me.

A short, portly man, a little older than I, with thinned-out, slicked-down black hair streaked with silver, was hurrying toward where I was sitting. He wore a wide smile, but a little anxiousness in his eyes, and when I faced him, he made a furtive wave.

'I thought I would find you here,' he said, wheezing with the effort and the heat. 'I saw your name on the registration list.'

He stopped a few feet away, suddenly tentative.

'Hello, C-Bird,' he said.

I stood and held out my hand. 'Bonjour Napoleon,' I replied. 'No one has called me by that name in many, many years.'

He grasped my hand. His was a little sweaty with exertion and had a palsied weakness to the grip. That would be the result of his medications. But the smile remained. 'Me, neither,' he said.

'I saw your real name on the program,' I told him. 'You're going to give a speech?'

He nodded. 'I don't know about getting up in front of all those people,' he said. 'But my treating physician is one of the movers and shakers in the hospital redevelopment plan and it was all his idea. He said it would be good therapy. A solid demonstration of the golden road to total recovery.'

I hesitated, then asked, 'What do you think?'

Napoleon sat down on the bench. 'I think he's the crazy one,' he said, breaking into a slightly manic giggle, a high-pitched sound that joined nervousness and joy at once and that I remembered from our time together. 'Of course, it helps that everyone still believes you're completely crazy, because then you can't really embarrass yourself too badly,' he added, and I grinned along with him. That was the sort of observation only someone who had spent time in a mental hospital would make. I sat back down next to him and we both stared over at the Amherst Building. After a moment or two, he sighed. 'Did you go inside?'

'Yes. It's a mess. Ready for the wrecker's ball.'

'I thought the same back when we were there. And everyone thought it was the best place to be. At least that's what they told me when I was processed in. State-of-the-art mental health facility. The best way to treat the mentally ill in a residential setting. What a lie.'

He caught his breath, then added, 'A damn lie.'

Now it was my turn to nod in agreement.

'Is that what you will tell them. In the speech, I mean.'

He shook his head. 'I don't think that's what they want to hear. I think it makes more sense to tell them nice things. Positive things. I'm planning a series of raging falsehoods.'

I thought about this for a moment, then smiled. 'That might be a sign of mental health,' I said.

Napoleon laughed. 'I hope you're right.'

We were both silent for a few seconds, then, in a wistful tone, he whispered, 'I'm not going to tell them about the killings. And not a word about the Fireman or the lady investigator that came to visit or anything that happened at the end.' He looked up at the Amherst Building, then added, 'It would really be your story to tell, anyway.'

I didn't reply.

Napoleon was quiet for a moment, then he asked me, 'Do you think about what happened?'

I shook my head, but we both understood this was a falsehood. 'I dream about it, sometimes,' I told him. 'But it's hard to remember what was real and what wasn't.'

'That makes sense,' he said. 'You know one thing that bothered me,' he added slowly, 'I never knew where they buried the people. The people who died while they were here. I mean, one minute they were in the dayroom or hanging in the hallways along with everyone else, and the next they might be dead, but what then? Did you ever know?'

'Yes,' I said, after a moment or two. 'They had a little makeshift graveyard over at the edge of the hospital, back toward the woods behind administration and Harvard. It was behind the little garden. I think now it's part of a youth soccer field.'

Napoleon wiped his forehead. 'I'm glad to know that,' he said. 'I always wondered. Now I know.'

Again we were quiet for a few seconds, then he said, 'You know what I hated learning. Afterward and everything, when we were released and put into outpatient clinics and getting all the treatment and all the newer drugs. You know what I hated?'

'What?'

'That the delusion that I'd clung to so hard for so many years wasn't just a delusion, but it wasn't even a special delusion. That I wasn't the only person to have fantasies that I was the reincarnation of a French emperor. In fact, I bet Paris is chockablock filled with them. I hated that understanding. In my delusional state, I was special. Unique. And now, I'm just an ordinary guy who has to take pills and whose hands shake all the time and who can't really hold anything more than the simplest job and whose family probably wishes would find a way to disappear. I wonder what the French word for *poof!* is.'

I thought about this, then told him, 'Well, personally,

22

for whatever it's worth, I always had the impression that you were a damn fine French emperor. Cliché or not. And if it had really been you ordering troops around at Waterloo, why hell, you would have won.'

He giggled a sound of release. 'C-Bird, all of us always knew that you were better at paying attention to the world around us than anyone else. People liked you, even if we were all deluded and crazy.'

'That's nice to hear.'

'What about the Fireman. He was your friend. Whatever happened to him? Afterward, I mean.'

I paused, then answered: 'He got out. He straightened out all his problems, moved to the South, and made a lot of money. Had a family. Big house. Big car. Very successful all around. Last I heard, he was heading up some charitable foundation. Happy and healthy.'

Napoleon nodded. 'I can believe it. And the woman who came to investigate? Did she go with him?'

'No. She went on to a judgeship. All sorts of honors. She had a wonderful life.'

'I knew it. You could just tell.'

Of course, this was all a lie.

He looked down at his watch. 'I need to get back. Get ready for my great moment. Wish me luck.'

'Good luck,' I said.

'It's good seeing you again,' Napoleon added. 'I hope your life goes okay.'

'You, too,' I said. 'You look good.'

'Really? I doubt it. I doubt very many of us look good. But that's okay. Thanks for saying it.'

He stood and I joined him. We both looked back at the Amherst Building.

'I'll be happy when they tear it down,' Napoleon said with a sudden burst of bitterness. 'It was a dangerous, evil place and not much good happened there.'

23

Then he turned back to me. 'C-Bird, you were there. You saw it all. You tell everyone.'

'Who would listen?'

'Someone might. Write the story. You can do it.'

'Some stories should be left unwritten,' I said.

Napoleon shrugged his rounded shoulders. 'If you write it, then it will be real. If all it does is stay in our memories, then it's like it never happened. Like it was some dream. Or hallucination thought up by all of us madmen. No one trusts us when we say something. But if you write it down, well, that gives it some substance. Makes it all true enough.'

I shook my head. 'The trouble with being mad,' I said, 'was it was real hard to tell what was true and what wasn't. That doesn't change, just because we can take enough pills to scrape along now in the world with all the others.'

Napoleon smiled. 'You're right,' he said. 'But maybe not, too. I don't know. I just know that you could tell it and maybe a few people would believe it, and that's a good enough thing. No one ever believed us, back then. Even when we took the medications, no one ever believed us.'

He looked at his watch again, and shifted his feet nervously.

'You should get back,' I said.

'I must get back,' he repeated.

We stood awkwardly until he finally turned, and walked away. About midway down the path, Napoleon turned, and gave me the same unsure little wave that he had when he'd first spotted me. 'Tell it,' he called. Then he turned and walked quickly away, a little ducklike in his style. I could see that his hands were shaking again.

★   ★   ★

It was after dark when I finally quick marched up the sidewalk to my apartment, and climbed the stairs and locked myself into the safety of the small space. A nervous fatigue seemed to pulse through my veins, carried along the bloodstream with the red cells and the white cells. Seeing Napoleon and hearing myself called by the nickname that I'd received when I first went to the hospital startled emotions within me. I thought hard about taking some pills. I knew I had some that were designed to calm me, should I get overly excited. But I did not. 'Tell the story,' he'd said to me. 'How?' I said out loud in the quiet of my own home.

The room echoed around me.

'You can't tell it,' I said to myself.

Then I asked the question: Why not?

I had some pens and pencils, but no paper.

Then an idea came to me. For a second, I wondered whether it was one of my voices, returning, filling my ear with a quick suggestion and modest command. I stopped, listening carefully, trying to pluck the unmistakable tones of my familiar guides from the street sounds that penetrated past the laboring of my old window air conditioning unit. But they were elusive. I didn't know whether they were there, or not. But uncertainty was something I had grown accustomed to.

I took a slightly worn and scratched table chair and placed it against the side of the wall deep in the corner of the room. I didn't have any paper, I told myself. But what I did have were white-painted walls unadorned by posters or art or anything.

Balancing myself on the seat, I could reach almost to the ceiling. I gripped a pencil in my hand and leaned forward. Then I wrote quickly, in a tiny, pinched, but legible script:

Francis Xavier Petrel arrived in tears at the Western State Hospital in the back of an ambulance. It was raining hard, darkness was falling rapidly, and his arms and legs were cuffed and restrained. He was twenty-one years old and more scared than he'd ever been in his entire short, and to that point, relatively uneventful life . . .

2

Francis Xavier Petrel arrived in tears at the Western State Hospital in the back of an ambulance. It was raining hard, darkness was falling rapidly, and his arms and legs were cuffed and restrained. He was twenty-one years old and more scared than he'd ever been in his short, and to that point, relatively uneventful life.

The two men who had driven him to the hospital had mostly kept their mouths closed during the ride, except to mutter complaints about the unseasonable weather, or make caustic remarks about the other drivers on the roads, none of whom seemed to meet the standards of excellence that they jointly held. The ambulance had bumped along the roadway at a moderate speed, flashing lights and urgency both ignored. There was something of dull routine in the way the two men had acted, as if the trip to the hospital was nothing more than a way-stop in the midst of an oppressively normal, decidedly boring day. One man occasionally slurped from a soda can, making a smacking noise with his lips. The other whistled snatches of popular songs. The first sported Elvis sideburns. The second had a bushy lion's mane of hair.

It might have been a trivial journey for the two attendants, but to the young man rigid with tension in the back, his breathing coming in short sprinter's spurts, it was nothing of the sort. Every sound, every sensation seemed to signal something to him, each more terrifying and more threatening than the next. The beat of the windshield wipers was like some deep jungle drum playing a roll of doom. The humming of the tires against the slick road surface was a siren's song of despair. Even the noise of his own labored wind seemed to echo, as if he were encased in a tomb. The restraints dug into his flesh, and he opened his mouth to scream for help, but could not make the right sound. All that emerged was a gargling burst of despair. One thought penetrated the symphony of discord — that if he survived the day, he was likely to never have a worse one.

When the ambulance shuddered to a halt in front of the hospital entrance, he heard one of his voices crying out over the stew of fear: *They will kill you here, if you are not careful*.

The ambulance drivers seemed oblivious to the imminent danger. They opened the doors to the vehicle with a crash, and indelicately pulled Francis out on a gurney. He could feel cold raindrops slapping against his face, mingling with a nervous sweat on his forehead, as the two men wheeled him through a wide set of doors into a world of harshly bright and unforgiving lights. They pushed him down a corridor, gurney wheels squealing against the linoleum, and at first all he could see, as it slid past, was the gray pockmarked ceiling. He was aware that there were other people in the corridor, but he was too scared to turn and face them. Instead, he kept his eyes fixed on the sound-proofing above him, counting the number of light fixtures that he rolled beneath. When he reached four, the two men stopped.

He was aware that some other people had stepped to the front of the gurney. In the space just beyond his head, he heard some words spoken: 'Okay, guys. We'll take him from here.'

Then a massive, round, black face, sporting a wide row of uneven, grinning teeth suddenly appeared above him. The face was above an orderly's white jacket that seemed, at first glance, to be several sizes too small.

'All right, Mister Francis Xavier Petrel, you ain't gonna cause us no trouble now, are you?' The man had a slightly singsong tenor to his words, so that they came out with equal parts of menace and amusement. Francis did not know what to reply.

A second black face abruptly hovered into his sight on the other side of the gurney, also leaning into the air above him, and this other man said, 'I don't think this boy here is going to be any sort of hassle. Not in the tiniest little bit. Are you, Mister Petrel?' He, too, spoke with a soft Southern-tinged accent.

A voice shouted in his ear: *Tell them no!*

He tried to shake his head, but had trouble moving his neck. 'I won't be a problem,' he choked out. The words seemed as raw as the day, but he was glad to hear he could speak. This reassured him a bit. He'd been afraid, throughout the day, that somehow he was going to lose the ability to communicate at all.

'Okay, then, Mister Petrel. We going to get you up off the gurney. Then we going to sit down, nice and easy in a wheelchair. You got that? Ain't gonna be loosing those cuffs on your hands and feet quite yet, though. That's gonna come after you speak to the doctor. Maybe he gives you a little something to calm you right down. Chill you right out. Nice and easy now. Sit up, swing those legs forward.'

Do what you're told!

He did what he was told.

The motion made him dizzy, and he seemed to sway for a second. He felt a huge hand grab his shoulder to steady him. He turned and saw that the first orderly was immense, well over six and a half feet tall and probably close to three hundred pounds. He had massively muscled arms, and legs that were like barrels. His partner, the other black man, was a wiry, thin man, dwarfed by his partner. He had a small goatee, and a bushy Afro haircut that failed to add much stature to his modest height. Together, the two men steered him into a waiting wheelchair.

'Okay,' said the little one. 'Now we're going to take

you in to see the doc. Don't you worry none. Things may seem nasty-wrong and bad and lousy right now, but they gonna get better soon enough. You can take that to the bank.'

He didn't believe this. Not a word.

The two orderlies steered him forward, into a small waiting room. There was a secretary behind a gray steel desk, who looked up as the procession came through the doorway. She seemed an imposing, prim woman, on the wrong side of middle age, dressed in a tight blue suit, hair teased a bit too much, eyeliner a little too prominent, lip gloss slightly overdone, giving her a contradictory sort of appearance, a demeanor that seemed to Francis Petrel to be half librarian and half streetwalker. 'This must be Mr. Petrel,' she said brusquely to the two black orderlies, although it was instantly obvious to Francis that she didn't expect an answer, because she already knew it. 'Take him straight in. The doctor is expecting him.'

He was pushed through another door, into a different office. This was a slightly nicer space, with two windows on the back wall that overlooked a courtyard. He could see a large oak tree swaying in the wind pushed up by the rainstorm. And, beyond the tree, he could see other buildings, all in brick, with slate black rooflines that seemed to blend with the gloom of the sky above. In front of the windows was an imposing large wooden desk. There was a shelf of books in one corner, and some overstuffed chairs and a deep red oriental carpet resting on top of the institutional gray rug that covered the floor, creating a small sitting area off to Francis's right. There was a photograph of the governor next to a portrait of President Carter on the wall. Francis took it in as rapidly as possible, his head swiveling about. But his eyes quickly came to rest upon a small man, who rose from behind the desk, as he came into the room.

'Hello, Mister Petrel. I am Doctor Gulptilil,' he said

briskly, voice high-pitched, almost like a child's.

The doctor was overweight and round, especially in the shoulders and the stomach, bulbous like a child's party balloon that had been squeezed into a shape. He was either Indian or Pakistani. He had a bright red silk tie fastened tightly around his neck, and sported a luminous white shirt, but his ill-fitting gray suit was slightly frayed at the cuffs. He appeared to be the sort of man who lost interest in his appearance about midway through the process of dressing in the morning. He wore thick, black-rimmed glasses, and his hair was slicked back and curled over his collar. Francis had difficulty telling whether he was young or old. He noticed that the doctor liked to punctuate every word with a wave of his hand, so that his speech became a conductor's movement with his baton, directing the orchestra in front.

'Hello,' Francis said tentatively.

Be careful what you say! One of his voices shouted.

'Do you know why you are here?' the doctor asked. He seemed genuinely curious.

'I'm not at all sure,' Francis replied.

Doctor Gulptilil looked down at a file and examined a sheet of paper.

'You've apparently rather scared some people,' he said slowly. 'And they seem to think you are in need of some help.' He had a slight British accent, just a touch of an Anglicism that had probably been eroded by years in the United States. It was warm in the room, and one of the radiators beneath the window hissed.

Francis nodded. 'That was a mistake,' he said. 'I didn't mean it. Things just got a little out of control. An accident, really. Really no more than a mistake in judgment. I'd like to go home, now. I'm sorry. I promise to be better. Much better. It was all just an error. Nothing meant by it. Not really. I apologize.'

The doctor nodded, but didn't precisely reply to what Francis had said.

'Are you hearing voices, now?' he asked.

Tell him no!

'No.'

'You're not?'

'No.'

Tell him you don't know what he's talking about! Tell him you've never heard any voices!

'I don't exactly know what you mean by voices,' Francis said.

That's good!

'I mean do you hear things spoken to you by people who are not physically present? Or perhaps, you hear things that others cannot hear.'

Francis shook his head rapidly.

'That would be crazy,' he said. He was gaining a little confidence.

The doctor examined the sheet in front of him, then once again raised his eyes toward Francis. 'So, on these many occasions when your family members have observed you speaking to no one in particular, why was that?'

Francis shifted in his seat, considering the question. 'Perhaps they are mistaken?' he said, uncertainty sliding back into his voice.

'I don't think so,' answered the doctor.

'I don't have many friends,' Francis said cautiously. 'Not in school, not in the neighborhood. Other kids tend to leave me alone. So I end up talking to myself a lot. Perhaps that's what they observed.'

The doctor nodded. 'Just talking to yourself?'

'Yes. That's right,' Francis said. He relaxed just a little more.

That's good. That's good. Just be careful.

The doctor glanced at his sheets of paper a second time. He wore a small smile on his face. 'I talk to myself, sometimes, as well,' he said.

'Well. There you have it,' Francis replied. He shivered a little and felt a curious flow of warmth and cold, as if the damp and raw weather outside had managed to follow him in, and had overcome the radiator's fervent pumping heat.

' . . . But when I speak with myself, it is not a conversation, Mister Petrel. It is more a reminder, like 'Don't forget to pick up a gallon of milk . . . ' or an admonition, such as, 'Ouch!' or 'Damn!' or, I must admit, sometimes words even worse. I do not carry on full back and forth, questions and replies with someone who is not present. And this, I fear, is what your family reports you have been doing for some many years now.'

Be careful of this one!

'They said that?' Francis replied, slyly. 'How unusual.'

The doctor shook his head. 'Less so than you might think, Mister Petrel.'

He walked around the desk so that he closed the distance between the two of them, ending up by perching himself on the edge of the desk, directly across from where Francis stayed confined in the wheelchair, limited certainly by the cuffs on his hands and legs, but equally by the presence of the two attendants, neither of whom had moved or spoken, but who hovered directly behind him.

'Perhaps we will return in a moment to these conversations you have, Mister Petrel,' Doctor Gulptilil said. 'For I do not fully understand how you can have them without hearing something in return and this genuinely concerns me, Mister Petrel.'

He is dangerous, Francis! He's clever and doesn't mean any good. Watch what you say!

Francis nodded his head, then realized that the doctor might have seen this. He stiffened in the wheelchair, and saw Doctor Gulptilil make a notation on the sheet of paper with a ballpoint pen.

'Let us try a different direction, then, for the moment, Mister Petrel,' the doctor continued. 'Today was a difficult day, was it not?'

'Yes,' Francis said. Then he guessed that he'd better expand on that statement, because the doctor remained silent, and fixed him with a penetrating glance. 'I had an argument. With my mother and father.'

'An argument? Yes. Incidentally, Mister Petrel, can you tell me what the date is?'

'The date?'

'Correct. The date of this argument you had today.'

He thought hard for a moment. Then he looked outside again, and saw the tree bending beneath the wind, moving spastically, as if its limbs were being jerked and manipulated by some unseen puppeteer. There were some buds just forming on the ends of the branches, and so he did some calculations in his head. He concentrated hard, hoping that one of the voices might know the answer to the question, but they were, as was their irritating habit, suddenly quite silent. He glanced about the room, hoping to spot a calendar, or perhaps some other sign that might help him, but saw nothing, and returned his eyes to the window, watching the tree move. When he turned back to the doctor, he saw that the round man seemed to be patiently awaiting his response, as if several minutes had passed since he was asked the question. Francis breathed in sharply.

'I'm sorry . . . ,' he started.

'You were distracted?' the doctor asked.

'I apologize,' Francis said.

'It seemed,' the doctor said slowly, 'that you were elsewhere for some time. Do these episodes happen frequently?'

Tell him no!

'No. Not at all.'

'Really? I'm surprised. Regardless, Mister Petrel, you were to tell me something . . . '

34

'You had a question?' Francis asked. He was angry with himself for losing the train of their conversation.

'The date, Mister Petrel?'

'I believe it is the fifteenth of March,' Francis said steadily.

'Ah, the ides of March. A time of famous betrayals. Alas, no.' The doctor shook his head. 'But close, Mister Petrel. And the year?'

He did some more calculations in his head. He knew he was twenty-one and that he'd had his birthday a month earlier, and so he guessed, 'Nineteen seventy-nine.'

'Good,' Doctor Gulptilil replied. 'Excellent. And what day is it?'

'What day?'

'What day of the week, Mister Petrel?'

'It is . . . ' Again he paused. 'Saturday.'

'No. Sorry. Today is Wednesday. Can you remember that for me?'

'Yes. Wednesday. Of course.'

The doctor rubbed his chin with his hand. 'And now we return to this morning, with your family. It was a little more than an argument, wasn't it, Mister Petrel?'

No! It was the same as always!

'I didn't think it was that unusual . . . '

The doctor looked up, a slight measure of surprise on his face. 'Really? How curious, Mister Petrel. Because the report that I have obtained from the local police claims that you threatened your two sisters, and then announced that you were intending to kill yourself. That life wasn't worth living and that you hated everyone. And then, when confronted by your father, you further threatened him, and your mother, as well, if not with an attack, then with something equally dangerous. You said you wanted the whole world to go away. I believe those were your exact words. Go away. And the report further contends, Mister Petrel, that you went into the kitchen

35

in the house you share with your parents and your two younger sisters, and that you seized a large kitchen knife, which you brandished in their direction in such a fashion that they believed that you intended to attack them with the weapon before you finally threw it so that it stuck into the wall. And, then, additionally, when police officers arrived at the house, that you locked yourself in your room and refused to exit, but could be heard speaking loudly inside, in argument, when there was no one present in the room with you. They had to break the door down, didn't they? And lastly, that you fought against the policemen and the ambulance attendants who arrived to help you, requiring one of them to need treatment himself. Is that a brief summary of today's events, Mister Petrel?'

'Yes,' he replied glumly. 'I'm sorry about the officer. It was a lucky punch that caught him above the eye. There was a lot of blood.'

'Unlucky, perhaps,' Doctor Gulptilil said, 'both for you and him.'

Francis nodded.

'Now, perhaps you could enlighten me as to why these things happened this day, Mister Petrel.'

Tell him nothing! Every word you speak will be thrown back at you!

Francis again gazed out the window, searching the horizon. He hated the word *why*. It had dogged him his entire life. Francis, why can't you make friends? Why can't you get along with your sisters? Why can't you throw a ball straight or stay calm in class. Why can't you pay attention when your teacher speaks to you? Or the scoutmaster. Or the parish priest. Or the neighbors. Why do you always hide away from the others every day? Why are you different, Francis, when all we want is for you to be the same? Why can't you hold a job? Why can't you go to school? Why can't you join the Army? Why can't you behave? Why can't you be loved?

36

'My parents believe I need to make something of myself. That was what caused the argument.'

'You are aware, Mister Petrel, that you score very highly on all tests? Remarkably high, curiously enough. So perhaps their hopes for you are not unfounded?'

'I suppose so.'

'Then why did you argue?'

'A conversation like that never seems as reasonable as we're making it sound now,' Francis replied. This brought a smile to Doctor Gulptilil's face.

'Ah, Mister Petrel, I suspect you are correct about that. But I fail to see how this discussion escalated so dramatically.'

'My father was determined.'

'You struck him, did you not?'

Don't admit to anything! He hit you first! Say that!

'He hit me first,' Francis dutifully responded.

Doctor Gulptilil made another notation on a sheet of paper. Francis shifted about. The doctor looked up at him.

'What are you writing?' Francis asked.

'Does it matter?'

'Yes. I want to know what you are writing.'

Don't let him snow you! Find out what he's writing! It won't be anything good!

'These are just some notes about our conversation,' the doctor said.

'I think you should show me what you're writing down,' Francis said. 'I think I have the right to know what it is you're writing down.'

Keep at it!

The doctor said nothing, so Francis continued, 'I'm here, I've answered your questions, and now I have one. Why are you writing things about me without showing me? That's not fair.'

Francis shifted in his wheelchair and pulled against the bonds that restrained him. He could feel the warmth of the room building, as if the heat had suddenly spiked. He strained hard for a moment, trying to free himself, but was unsuccessful. He took a deep breath and slumped back into his seat.

'You are agitated?' the doctor asked, after a few silent moments had passed. This was a question that didn't really need an answer, because the truth was so obvious.

'It's just not fair,' Francis said, trying to instill calm back into his own words.

'Fairness is important to you?'

'Yes. Of course.'

'Yes, perhaps Mister Petrel, you are correct about that.'

Again the two men were quiet. Francis could hear the radiator hissing again and then thought that perhaps it was the breathing of the two attendants, who had not budged from behind him throughout the interview. Then he wondered whether one of his voices might be trying to get his attention, whispering something to him so low that it was hard for him to hear, and he bent forward slightly, as if trying to hear.

'Are you often impatient when things don't go your way, Mister Petrel?'

'Isn't everyone?'

'Do you think you should hurt people when things don't go the way you would like them?'

'No.'

'But you get angry?'

'Everyone gets angry sometimes.'

'Ah, Mister Petrel, on that point you are absolutely correct. It is, however, a critical question as to how we react to our anger when it arises, is it not? I think we should speak again.' The doctor had leaned forward, trying to inject some familiarity in his demeanor. 'Yes, I think some additional conversations will be in order. Would that be acceptable to you, Mister Petrel?'

He didn't reply. It was a little like the doctor's voice

38

had faded, as if someone had turned the volume down on the doctor, or as if his words were being transmitted over a great distance.

'May I call you Francis?' the doctor asked.

Again, he did not respond. He did not trust his voice, for it was beginning to mix together with a swelling of emotions within his chest.

Doctor Gulptilil watched him for an instant, then asked, 'Say, Francis do you recall what it was that I asked you to remember, earlier in our talk?'

This question seemed to bring him back to the room. He looked up at the doctor, who wore a slyly inquisitive look on his face.

'What?'

'I asked you to remember something.'

'I don't recall.' Francis snapped his reply.

The doctor nodded his head slightly. 'But perhaps, you could remind me, then what day of the week it is . . .'

'What day?'

'Yes.'

'Is it important?'

'Let us imagine that it is.'

'Are you sure you asked me this earlier?' Francis said, stalling for time. But this simple fact suddenly seemed elusive, as if concealed behind a cloud within him.

'Yes,' Doctor Gulptilil said. 'I'm quite sure. What day is it?'

Francis thought hard, battling against the anxiety that abruptly crowded past all his other thoughts. Again he paused, hoping that one of the voices might come to his aid, but again, they had fallen silent.

'I believe it is Saturday,' Francis said cautiously. He said each word slowly, tentatively.

'Are you sure?'

'Yes.' But this word fell out of his mouth with little conviction.

'Do you not recall me telling you earlier it was Wednesday?'

'No. That would be a mistake. It is Saturday.' Francis could feel his head spinning, as if the doctor's questions were forcing him to run in ever-concentric circles.

'I think not,' said the doctor, 'But it is of no importance. You will be staying with us for some time, Francis, and we will have another opportunity to speak of these things. I'm certain that in the future you will remember things better.'

'I don't want to stay,' Francis replied quickly. He could feel a sudden sense of panic, mingling with despair, instantly welling up within him. 'I want to go home. Really, I believe they are expecting me, and it is close to dinnertime, and my parents and my sisters, they all want everyone home for dinner. That's the rule in the house, you see. You need to be there by six, hands and face washed clean. No dirty clothes if you've been playing outside. Ready to say grace. We have a blessing before we eat. We always do. It's my job some days to say the blessing. We need to thank God for putting the food on the table. I believe today it's my turn — yes, I'm sure of it — so I need to be there, and I can't be late.'

He could feel tears stinging at his eyes, and he could hear sobs choking some of his words. These things were happening to a mirror image of himself, and not quite him, but himself slightly apart and distant from the real him. He struggled hard to make all these parts of himself come together and focus as one, but it was difficult.

'Perhaps,' Doctor Gulptilil said gently, 'you might have a question or two for me?'

'Why can't I go home?' Francis coughed the question out between tears.

'Because people are frightened for you, Francis, and because you frighten people.'

'What sort of place is this?'

'It's a place where we will help you,' the doctor said. *Liar! Liar! Liar!*

Doctor Gulptilil looked up at the two attendants and spoke next to them. 'Mister Moses, will you and your brother please take Mister Petrel to the Amherst Building. I have written out a scrip for some medication and some additional instructions for the nurses there. He should get at least thirty-six, perhaps more, hours of observation before they consider shifting him into the open ward.' He handed the clipboard across to the smaller of the two men flanking Francis, who nodded his response.

'Whatever you say, Doc,' the attendant said.

'Sure thing, Doc,' his huge partner replied, stepping behind the wheelchair, grasping the handles and rapidly spinning Francis around. The motion made him suddenly dizzy, and he choked back on the sobs that were filling his chest. 'Don't you be so scared, Mister Petrel. Things gonna be okay soon enough. We're gonna take good care of you,' the large man whispered.

Francis did not believe him.

He was wheeled back through the office, into the waiting room, tears streaming down his cheeks, his hands quivering against the cuffs. He twisted in the chair, trying to get the attention of either the large or the small attendant, his voice cracking with a combination of fear and an unbridled sadness. 'Please,' he said, piteously, 'I want to go home. They're expecting me. That's where I want to be. Please take me home.'

The smaller attendant had his face set, as if the pleas coming from Francis were hard for him to hear. He placed his hand on Francis's shoulder and repeated, 'You gonna be okay, now, hear me. It's gonna be okay. Shush now . . . ' He spoke as he might to a baby.

Sobs wracked Francis's body, emanating from deep within him. The prim secretary looked up from her seat behind the desk with an impatient and unforgiving look on her face. 'Quiet down!' she ordered Francis. He swallowed back another sob, coughing.

As he did so, he looked across the room and saw two uniformed state troopers, wearing gray tunics and blue riding pants above polished knee-high brown boots. They were both strapping, tall, taut pictures of discipline, with close-cropped hair and their curved and cocked officers' hats held stiffly at their sides. Each wore a glistening leather Sam Browne belt, polished to a reflective shine, and a holstered revolver high on their waist. But it was the man that they flanked that quickly attracted Francis's attention.

He was shorter than the troopers, but solidly built. Francis would have guessed his age to be in his late twenties or early thirties. He stood in a languid, relaxed fashion, his hands cuffed in front of him, but the language of his body seemed to diminish the nature of the restraints, rendering them less restrictive and more as if they were merely an inconvenience. He wore a loose-fitting single-piece navy blue jumpsuit with the title MCI-BOSTON stitched in yellow above the left hand chest pocket and a pair of old, worn running shoes that were missing their laces. He had longish brown hair, that poked out from beneath the edges of a sweat-stained Boston Red Sox baseball cap, and a two-day shadow of a beard. But what struck Francis first and foremost were the man's eyes, for they darted about, far more alert and observant than the leisurely pose he maintained, taking many things in as rapidly as possible. The eyes carried something deep, which Francis noticed immediately, even through his own anguish. He could not put a word to it instantly, but it was as if the man had seen something immensely, ineffably sad that lurked just beyond the horizon of his vision, so that whatever he saw, or heard or witnessed was colored by this hidden hurt. The eyes came to fix on Francis, and the man managed a small, sympathetic smile, that seemed to speak directly to Francis.

'Are you okay, fella?' he asked. Each word was tinged with a slight Boston-Irish accent. 'Are things that rough?'

Francis shook his head. 'I want to go home, but they say I have to stay here,' he answered. And then piteously, and spontaneously, he asked, 'Can you help me, please?'

The man bent down slightly, toward Francis. 'I suspect there are more than a few folks here who would wish to go home and cannot. Myself presently included in that category.'

Francis looked up at the man. He did not know precisely why, but the calm tones the man used helped to settle him. 'Can you help me?' Francis blurted out, repeating himself.

The man smiled, a mingling of insouciance and sadness. 'I don't know what I can do,' he said, 'but I will do what I can.'

'Promise?' Francis asked suddenly.

'All right,' the man said. 'I promise.'

Francis leaned back in the chair, closing his own eyes for a second. 'Thank you,' he whispered.

The secretary interrupted the conversation with a sharply punctuated command directed to the smaller of the two black attendants. 'Mister Moses. This gentleman . . . ' she gestured toward the man in the jumpsuit, 'is Mister . . . ' then she hesitated slightly, before continuing seemingly purposefully not using his name, ' . . . the gentleman that we spoke about earlier. The troopers will accompany him in to see the doctor, but please return promptly to escort him to his new accommodations . . . ' this word was spoken with a slight edge of sarcasm, ' . . . as soon as you get Mister Petrel settled over at Amherst. They are expecting him.'

'Yes, ma'am,' the larger brother said, as if it was his

turn to speak, although the woman's comments had been directed toward the smaller of the two men. 'Whatever you say, that's what we'll be doing.'

The man in the jumpsuit looked down at Francis again. 'What's your name?' he asked.

'Francis Petrel,' he replied.

The man in the jumpsuit smiled. 'Petrel is a nice name. It's a small seabird, you know, common to Cape Cod. They are the birds you see flying just above the waves on summer afternoons, dipping in and out of the spray. Beautiful animals. White wings that beat fast one second, then glide and soar effortlessly the next. They must have keen eyes to be able to spot a sand eel or a pogy in the surf. A poet's bird, to be sure. Can you fly like that, Mister Petrel?'

Francis shook his head.

'Ah,' the man in the jumpsuit said. 'Well, perhaps you should learn. Especially if you're going to be locked up in this delightful place for too long.'

'Be quiet!' one of the troopers interjected with a gruffness that made the man smile. He glanced over at the trooper and said, 'Or you will do what?'

The trooper didn't reply to this, although his face reddened slightly and the man turned back to Francis, ignoring the command. 'Francis Petrel. Francis C-bird. I like that better. You take things easy, Francis C-Bird, and I will see you again before too long. That's a promise.'

Francis was unable to respond, but felt a slight sense of encouragement in the man's words. For the first time since that horrible morning had begun with so many loud voices, shouts and recriminations, he felt as if he wasn't completely alone. It was a little like the harsh noise and constant racket that had been filling his ears all day had diminished, like a radio's blaring volume turned down slightly. He could hear some of his voices murmuring approval in the background, which relaxed him a bit more. But he did not have time to dwell on this thought, for he was abruptly wheeled out of the office, into the corridor, and the door shut resoundingly behind him. A cold draft made him shudder and reminded him that as of that moment all that he had once known of life had been changed and all that he was to know was elusive and hidden from him. He had to bite down on his lower lip to keep the tears from returning, swallowing hard to remain quiet and let himself be diligently steered away from the reception area and deep into the core of the Western State Hospital.

3

Limp morning light was just sliding over the neighboring rooftops, insinuating its way into my sparse little apartment home. I stood in front of the wall and saw all the words I'd written the previous night crawling down a single long column. My handwriting was pinched tight, as if nervous. The words were arranged in wavering lines, a little like a field of wheat as a breath of warm wind passes over. I asked myself: Was I truly that scared, the day I arrived at the hospital? The answer to that was easy: Yes. And far worse than I had written. Memory often blurs pain. The mother forgets the agony of childbirth when the baby is placed in her arms, the soldier no longer remembers the pain of his wounds when the general pins the medal on his chest and the band strikes up some martial tune. Did I tell the truth about what I saw? Did I get the small details right? Did it happen quite the way I remembered it?

I seized the pencil, dropped to my knees on the floor to the spot where I'd ended my first night at the wall. I hesitated, then wrote:

> *It was at least forty-eight hours later that Francis Petrel awakened in a dingy gray padded cell, tightly encased in a straitjacket, his heart racing, his tongue thick, thirsting for a drink of something cold and some companionship . . .*

It was at least forty-eight hours later that Francis Petrel awakened in a dingy gray padded cell, tightly encased in a straitjacket, his heart racing, his tongue thick, thirsting for a drink of something cold and some companionship. He lay rigidly on the steel cot and thin

46

dark-stained mattress of the isolation room, staring up past the burlap-colored padded walls, to the ceiling, doing a modest inventory of his person and his surroundings. He wiggled his toes, ran his tongue over parched lips, and counted each beat of his pulse until he could detect a slowing. The drugs he'd been injected with made him feel entombed, or at least blanketed with some thick, syrupy substance. There was a single glowing white lightbulb encased in a wire screen high above him, far beyond his reach, and the glare hurt his eyes. He knew he should be hungry, but wasn't. He pulled against the restraints, and knew instantly that was futile. He decided he should call out for help, but first he whispered to himself: Are you still here?

For a moment, there was silence.

Then he heard several voices, all speaking at once, all faint, as if muffled by a pillow: *We're here. We're all still here.*

This reassured him.

You need to keep us hidden, Francis.

He nodded to himself. This appeared obvious. He felt a contradictory set of criteria within himself, almost like a mathematician who sees a complicated equation on a chalkboard that could have several possible answers. The voices that guided him had also landed him in the current fix and there was little doubt in his mind that he needed to keep them concealed at all times, if he ever hoped to get out of the Western State Hospital. As he assessed this dilemma, he could hear the familiar sounds of all the people who traveled in his imagination agreeing with him. These voices all had personalities: a voice of demand, a voice of discipline, a voice of concession, a voice of concern, a voice that warned, a voice that soothed, a voice of doubt, and a voice of decision. They all owned tones and topics; he had grown to know when to expect one or the other, depending upon the situation around him. Since the angry confrontation with his folks, and the police and ambulance had been summoned, the voices had all clamored for attention. But now he had to continue to strain to hear them, which made him furrow his brow with concentration.

It was, in a way, he thought, part of getting himself organized.

Francis remained on the bed uncomfortably for another hour, feeling the closeness of the narrow room, until a small porthole in the only door opened with a scraping noise. From where he lay, he was able to see by lifting himself up like an athlete doing a stomach crunch, a difficult position to hold for more than a few seconds, because of the straitjacket. He did see first one eye, then another, peering in at him, and he managed a weak: 'Hello?'

No one responded and the porthole slammed shut.

It was another thirty minutes by his reckoning before the porthole opened again. He tried another *hello* and this one seemed to work, because seconds later he heard the sound of a key being worked in the lock. The door scraped open and he saw the larger of the two black attendants, pushing his way into the cell. The man was smiling, as if caught in the midst of a joke, and he nodded at Francis not unpleasantly. 'How you doing this morning Mr. Petrel?' he asked brightly. 'You get some sleep? You hungry?'

'I need something to drink,' Francis croaked.

The attendant nodded. 'That's the medications they gave you. Make your tongue all thick, kinda like it be all swollen, huh?'

Francis nodded. The attendant retreated to the corridor, then returned with a plastic cup of water. He sat on the side of the cot and held Francis up like a sickly child, letting him gulp at the liquid. It was lukewarm, almost brackish, with a slight metallic taste, but at that moment, just the mere sense of it pouring

48

down his throat, and the pressure of the man's arm holding him, reassured Francis more than he had ever expected. The attendant must have realized this, because he quietly said, 'It gonna be all right, Mr. Petrel. Mr. C-Bird. That what that other new man called you, and I'm thinking that's a fine name to go by. This place a little rough at first, take some getting used to, but you gonna be just fine. I can tell.'

He lowered Francis back to the bed, and added, 'The doctor gonna come in to see you now.'

A few seconds later, Francis saw Doctor Gulptilil's round form hovering in the doorway. The doctor smiled, and asked, in his slight singsong-accented voice, 'Mr. Petrel. How are you this morning?'

'I'm all right,' Francis said. He didn't know really what else he could say. And, at the same time, he could hear the echoing of his voices, telling him to be extremely careful. Again, they were not nearly as loud as they could be, almost as if they were shouting commands to him from across some wide chasm.

'Do you remember where you are?' the doctor asked.

Francis nodded. 'I'm in a hospital.'

'Yes,' the doctor said with a smile. 'That is not difficult to surmise. But do you recall which one? And how it was that you arrived here?'

Francis did. The mere act of answering questions lifted some of the fog he felt was obscuring his vision. 'It is the Western State Hospital,' he said. 'And I arrived in an ambulance after having some argument with my parents.'

'Very good. And do you recall what month it is? And the year?'

'It is still March, I believe. And 1979.'

'Excellent.' The doctor seemed genuinely pleased. 'A little more oriented, I would suspect. I think today we will be able to remove you from isolation and restraint, and begin to integrate you into the general population. This is as I'd hoped.'

'I would like to go home now,' Francis said.

'I am sorry, Mister Petrel. That isn't yet possible.'

'I don't think I want to stay here,' Francis said. Some of the quavering which had marked his voice the day he'd arrived threatened to reemerge.

'It is for your own good,' the doctor replied. Francis doubted that. He knew he wasn't so crazy to be unable to see that it was clearly for other people's good, not his. He didn't say this out loud.

'Why can't I go home?' he asked. 'I haven't done anything wrong.'

'Do you recall the kitchen knife? And your threatening words?'

Francis shook his head. 'It was a misunderstanding,' he said.

Doctor Gulptilil smiled. 'Of course it was. But you're going to be with us until we come to the realization that we cannot go around threatening people.'

'I promise I won't.'

'Thank you, Mister Petrel. But a promise isn't quite adequate under the current circumstances. I must be persuaded. Utterly persuaded, alas. The medications you have been given will help you. As you continue to take them, the cumulative effect they have will increase your command of your situation and help you to readjust. Then, perhaps, we can discuss returning to society and some more constructive role.'

He spoke this last sentence slowly, then added, 'And what do your voices think of your presence here?'

Francis knew enough to shake his head. 'I don't hear any voices,' he insisted. Deep within him he heard a chorus of assent.

The doctor smiled again, showing slightly uneven rows of white teeth. 'Ah, Mister Petrel, again, I'm not completely sure that I believe you. Still' — the doctor hesitated — 'I think that you can succeed in the general population. Mister Moses here will show you around and fill you in on the rules. The rules are important, Mister Petrel. There are not many, but they are critical. Obeying the rules, becoming a constructive member of our little world here, these are signs of mental health. The more you can do to show me that you can function successfully here, the closer you will step each passing day toward returning home. Do you understand that equation, Mister Petrel?'

Francis nodded vigorously.

'There are activities. There are group sessions. From time to time, there will be some private sessions with myself. Then there are the rules. All these things, taken together, create possibilities. If you cannot adjust, then, I fear, your stay here will be long, and often unpleasant . . . '

He gestured at the isolation cell. 'This room, for example' — and he pointed at the straitjacket — 'these devices, and others, remain options. They always remain options. But avoiding them is critical, Mister Petrel. Critical to your return to mental health. Am I being quite clear about this?'

'Yes,' Francis said. 'Fit in. Obey the rules.' He repeated this inwardly to himself, like a mantra or a prayer.

'Precisely. Excellent. Do you not see, already we have made progress? Be encouraged, Mister Petrel. And take advantage of what the hospital has to offer.' The doctor rose up. He nodded at the attendant. 'All right, Mister Moses. You can release Mister Petrel. And then, please, escort him through the dormitory, get him some clothing, and show him the activities room.'

'Yes sir,' the attendant snapped off with a military crispness.

Doctor Gulptilil waddled off through the door to the isolation room, and the attendant went about the task of unsnapping the bonds of the straitjacket, then unwrapping the sleeves from around Francis, until he finally came free. Francis stretched awkwardly, and rubbed his arms, as if to restore some energy and life to the limbs that had been locked so tightly. He placed his feet on the floor and stood unsteadily, feeling a sensation of dizziness overcome him. The attendant must have noticed, for a huge hand grasped his shoulder, preventing Francis from stumbling forward. Francis felt a little like a baby taking his first step, only without the same sense of joy and accomplishment, equipped only with doubt and fear.

He followed Mister Moses down the corridor on the fourth floor of the Amherst Building. There were a half-dozen six-by-nine padded cells arranged in a row, each with a double-locking system and portholes for observation. He could not tell whether they were occupied or not, except in one case, when they must have made some sound passing by, and from behind a locked door he heard a cascade of muted obscenities that dissolved into a long, painful shriek. A mixture of agony and hatred. He hurried to keep pace with the immense attendant, who didn't seem fazed in the slightest by the otherworldly noise, and who kept up an impressive banter about the layout of the building, the hospital, and its history, as he passed through a set of double doors, leading down a wide, central stairway. Francis only vaguely remembered ascending those steps two days earlier, in what seemed to him to be a distant, and increasingly elusive past, when everything in what he had thought of his life was totally different.

The building's design seemed to Francis to be every bit as crazy as its occupants. The upper floors held offices that abutted storage rooms and isolation cells. The first and second floors held wide-open dormitory-style rooms, crowded with simple steel framed beds, with an occasional footlocker for possessions. Inside the dormitory rooms there were cramped bathrooms and showers, with multiple stalls that he immediately saw delivered little in the way of privacy. There were other bathrooms off the corridors, spaced up and down the floor with MEN or WOMEN marked on the doors. In a concession to modesty, the women were housed on the north end of the corridor, the men on the south. A large nursing station divided the two areas. It was confined by wire mesh screens and a locked steel door. Francis saw that all the doors had two, sometimes three double deadbolt locks on them, all operated from the exterior. Once locked, he noticed, there was no way for anyone inside to unlock the door, unless they had a key.

The ground floor was shared by a large, open area, which Francis was told was the primary dayroom, and a cafeteria and kitchen large enough to fix meals and feed the Amherst Building's residents three times each day. There were also several smaller rooms, which he gathered were devoted to group therapy sessions. These dotted the ground floor. There were windows everywhere, which filled the Amherst Building with light, but every window had a locked wire mesh screen on the outside, so that the daylight that filtered into the building penetrated past bars tossing odd gridlike shadows on the slick, polished floors or the glowing white painted walls. There were doors seemingly placed willy-nilly throughout the building that sometimes were locked, requiring Mr. Moses to pull out a massive key chain from his belt, but other times were left open, so that they simply pushed through unimpeded. Francis could not immediately detect what the governing principles were for locking the doors.

It was, he thought, a most curious jail.

They were confined, but not imprisoned. Restrained but not handcuffed.

Like Mr. Moses and his smaller brother, whom they passed in the hallway, the nurses and the attendants wore white outfits. An occasional physician, or doctor's aide, social worker or psychologist passed them by. These civilians wore either sports coats and slacks, or jeans. They almost all, Francis noted, carried manila envelopes, clipboards, and brown folders under their arms, and they all seemed to walk the corridors with a sense of direction and purpose, as if by having a specific task in hand, they were able to separate themselves from the general population of the Amherst Building.

Francis's fellow patients crowded the halls. There were knots of people, pressed together, while others stood aggressively alone. Many eyed him warily, as he passed. Some ignored him. No one smiled at him. He barely had time to observe his surroundings as he kept pace with the quick march that Mr. Moses adopted. And, what he saw of the other patients was a sort of motley, haphazard collection of folks of all ages and sizes. Hair that seemed to explode from scalps, beards that hung wildly down like the people in old, faded photographs from a century earlier. It seemed a place of contradictions. There were wild eyes everywhere that fastened upon him and measured him as he passed by, and then in contrast, muted looks, and faces that turned to the wall and avoided connection. Words and snatches of conversation surrounded him, sometimes spoken to others, sometimes spoken to inner selves. Clothing seemed to be an afterthought; some people wore loose-fitting hospital gowns and pajamas, others dressed in more regular street garb. Some wore long bathrobes or housecoats, others jeans and paisley shirts. It was all a little disjointed, a little out of whack, as if the colors were unsure what matched what, or the sizes were just off, shirts too loose, pants too tight or too short. Mismatched socks. Stripes conjoined with checks. There was a pungent smell of cigarette smoke virtually everywhere.

'Too many folks,' Mr. Moses said, as they approached

a nursing station. 'Got beds for two hundred maybe. But got nearly three hundred peoples crowded in. You'd think they'd figured that part out, but no, not yet.'

Francis didn't reply.

'Got a bed for you, though,' Mr. Moses added. At the nursing station, Mr. Moses stopped. 'You gonna be A-OK. Hello, ladies,' he said. Two white-clad nurses behind the wire mesh, turned toward him. 'You looking ever so sweet and beautiful this fine morning.'

One was old, with graying hair and a well-lined, pinched face, but who still managed a smile. The other was a stocky black woman, far younger than her companion, who snorted her reply like a woman who had heard nice words that amounted to false promises more than once. 'You always talking so sweet, but what it be you need this time around?' This was said in a mock-gruff tone, that caused both women to crack smiles.

'Why, ladies, I'm always looking only to bring a little joy and happiness into your lives,' he said. 'What more?'

The nurses laughed out loud. 'Ain't no man ever not looking for something,' the black nurse said. The white nurse quickly added, 'Sweetheart, that's the God's truth.'

Mr. Moses also laughed, while Francis suddenly stood awkwardly, unsure what he was to do. 'Ladies, may I be presenting you with Mister Francis Petrel, who be staying with us. Mister C-Bird, this fine young lady be Miss Wright, and her lovely companion, there, be Miss Winchell.' He handed over a clipboard. 'The doctor listed out some meds for this boy. Look to be pretty much the usual.'

He turned to Francis and said, 'What you think, Mister C-Bird? You think the doc maybe prescribed a cup of hot coffee in the morning and a nice cold beer and a plate filled with fried chicken and cornbread at the end of the day? You think that's what the doctor ordered?'

Francis must have looked surprised, because the attendant quickly added, 'I'm just having some fun with you. Don't mean nothing.'

The nurses looked over the chart, then placed it along with a stack of others on a corner of their desk. The older one, Miss Winchell, reached below a counter and brought forth a small, cheap plaid cloth suitcase. 'Mister Petrel, this was left for you by your family.'

She passed it through an opening in the wire mesh, turning to the attendant, saying, 'I've already searched it.'

Francis took the suitcase and fought back the urge to burst into tears. He had recognized it instantly. It was a bag he'd been given as a gift one Christmas morning, when he was young, and because he'd never actually traveled anywhere, he'd always used for storage whenever he wanted to keep something special, or something unusual. A sort of portable secret place for the items collected during childhood, because each small item was, in its own way, a sort of journey in itself. A pine cone collected one fall; a set of toy soldiers, a book of children's verse never returned to the local library. His hands quivered slightly as they ran across the fake leather edging on the satchel, and he touched the handle. The zipper on the bag was open, and he saw that everything that the bag had once held had been removed, replaced with some clothes from his drawers at home. He knew instantly that everything that he'd accumulated in that bag had been emptied out and discarded. It was as if his parents had packed what little they thought of his life into the small luggage, and sent it to him to send him on his way. He could feel his lower lip trembling, and he felt completely and utterly alone.

The nurses passed a second gathering of items through the wire. These included some rough sheets and a pillowcase, a threadbare army surplus olive drab wool blanket, a bathrobe much like the ones he'd already seen on some patients, and some pajamas, again like those he'd already seen. He placed these on top of the suitcase and lifted both in front of him.

Mr. Moses nodded. 'All right, I'll show you your bed. Get your stuff squared away. Then what have we got for Mister C-Bird, ladies?'

Again, one of the nurses checked the chart. 'Lunch at noon. Then he's free until a group session in Room 101 at three with Mister Evans. He comes back here at four thirty for free time. Dinner at six o'clock. Medications at seven. That's it.'

'You get all that, Mister C-Bird?'

Francis nodded. He didn't trust his own voice. He could hear, echoing deep within him, orders to comply, keep quiet, and stay alert. He followed Mr. Moses through a door into a large room with some thirty to forty beds lined up in rows. All the beds were made up, except one, not far from the door. There were a half dozen men lying on beds, either asleep, or staring up into the ceiling, who barely looked in his direction as he entered the room.

Mr. Moses helped him to make the bed and stow his few clothes in a footlocker. There was room for the tiny suitcase, as well, and it disappeared into the empty space. It took less than five minutes to square him away.

'Well, that's it,' Mr. Moses said.

'What happens to me now?' Francis asked.

The attendant smiled a little wistfully. 'Now, C-Bird, what you got to do is get yourself better.'

Francis nodded. 'How?'

'That the big question, C-Bird. You gone have to figure that out for yourself.'

'What should I do?' Francis asked.

The attendant leaned down toward him. 'Just keep to yourself. This place can get a bit rough, sometimes. You got to figure out everybody else, and give 'em what space they need. Don't be trying to make friends too fast, C-Bird. Just keep your mouth shut and follow the rules. You need help, you talk to me or my brother, or one of the nurses, and we'll try to see you straight.'

'But what are the rules?' Francis said.

The large attendant turned and pointed at a sign posted high on the wall.

NO SMOKING IN SLEEPING ROOM
NO LOUD NOISES
NO TALKING AFTER 9 PM
RESPECT OTHERS
RESPECT OTHER PEOPLE'S PROPERTY

When he finished reading through twice, Francis turned. He wasn't sure where to go or what to do. He sat down on the edge of his bed.

Across the room, one of the men who had been lying down staring at the ceiling, feigning sleep, abruptly stood up. He was very tall, well over six and one half feet, with a sunken chest, and thin, bony arms that protruded from beneath a tattered sweatshirt with the logo of the New England Patriots on it, and stovepipe legs that jutted from lime green surgical scrubs that were six inches too short. The sweatshirt sleeves had been sliced off just below the shoulders. He was far older than Francis, and wore stringy gray-tinged hair in a matted clump that fell to his shoulders. His eyes were suddenly wide, as if half-frightened and half-furious. The man instantly lifted one cadaverous hand and pointed directly at Francis.

'Stop it!' he shouted out. 'Stop it, now!'

Francis shrank back slightly. 'Stop what?'

'Just stop! I can tell! You cannot fool me! I knew it as soon as you came in! Stop it!'

'I don't know what I'm doing,' Francis replied meekly.

By now the tall man was waving both arms in the air as if trying to clear cobwebs from his path. His voice was rising with each step he took across the room, 'Stop it! Stop it! I can see through you! You can't do it to me!'

Francis looked around for somewhere to run, or to hide, but he was hemmed in by the man lurching toward him and the back wall of the room. The few other men in the dormitory were still asleep, or ignoring what was happening.

The man seemed to have stretched in size, growing in ferocity with every stride. 'I know! I could tell! From the moment you walked in! Stop now!'

Francis felt frozen with confusion. Inwardly, his voices were all screaming in a cascade of conflicted advice: *Run! Run! He's going to hurt us! Hide!* His head pivoted around, trying to see how he could escape the tall man's onslaught. He tried to will his muscles to work, at least rise up from the bed, but, instead, he shrank backward, almost cowering.

'If you will not stop, then it's up to me to stop you!' the man shouted. He seemed to be preparing himself for an assault.

Francis lifted his arms to fend off the attack.

The tall man gargled out some sort of gathered war cry, lifted himself up, puffing out his sunken chest and waving his arms above his head. Seemed ready to leap on Francis, when another voice sliced across the room.

'Lanky! Stop there!'

The tall man hesitated, then turned in the direction of the voice.

'Just stop right there!'

Francis was still huddled back against the wall, and he couldn't see who was speaking until the tall man turned around.

'What are you doing?'

'But it's him,' the man said to whomever had come into the dormitory. He seemed, in that moment, to have shrunk in size.

'No, it's not!' came the reply.

And then Francis saw that the man fast approaching was the same man he'd met in his first minutes in the hospital.

'Leave him alone!'

'But it's him! I could tell as soon as I saw him!'

'That's what you said to me when I first showed up. That's what you say to every new person who comes into the hospital.'

This made the tall man hesitate.

'I do?' he asked.

'Yes.'

'I still think it's him,' said the tall man, but oddly, most of the passion had fled from his voice, replaced by questions and some doubt. 'I'm pretty sure,' he added. 'He absolutely could be, I'll say that.' Despite the conviction contained in the words, the tenor of the voice was filled with uncertainty.

'But why?' said the man. 'Why are you so sure?'

'It was just, when he came in, it seemed so obvious, I was watching, and then . . . ' The tall man's voice tailed off, fading. 'Maybe I'm wrong.'

'I think you're genuinely mistaken.'

'You do?'

'I do.'

The other man came forward. He was grinning now. He stepped past the tall man.

'Well, C-Bird, I see you're all settled in.'

Francis nodded.

The man turned to the tall man. 'Lanky, this is C-Bird. I met him the other day in the administration building. He's not the person you think he is any more than I was the other day when you first spotted me. I can assure you of that.'

60

'How can you be so certain?' the tall man asked.

'Well, I saw him come in, and I saw his chart, and I promise you, if he was the son of Satan sent here to do evil inside the hospital, there would have been a notation on it, because it had all the other particulars. Hometown. Family. Address. Age. You name it, it was there. Nothing about being the Antichrist.'

'Satan is the great deceiver. His son would be equally clever. Probably be able to hide himself. Even from Gulp-a-pill.'

'Ah, possibly. But there were policemen with me, and they would have been trained to spot the son of Satan. They would have had flyers and handouts, and those pictures like they have on the walls at the post office, you know what I'm saying? I doubt even the son of Satan could have hidden from a pair of state troopers.'

The tall man listened intently to this explanation. Then he turned to Francis.

'I'm sorry. I was apparently mistaken. I can see now that you are not the person I have been on the lookout for. Please accept my sincerest apologies. Vigilance is really our only defense against evil. You have to be so careful, you know, day in, day out, hour after hour. It's exhausting, but utterly necessary . . . '

Francis finally managed to crawl off the bed and stand up. 'Yes. Of course,' he said. 'It's perfectly okay.'

The tall man reached out and shook Francis's hand, pumping it enthusiastically.

'I'm delighted to make your acquaintance, C-Bird. You are generous. And clearly well mannered. I'm sincerely sorry if I scared you.'

To Francis the tall man suddenly seemed far less frightening. He simply seemed old, tattered, a little like an out-of-date magazine that has been left on a table for far too long.

The tall man shrugged. 'They call me Lanky,' he said. 'I'm here most of the time.'

61

Francis nodded. 'I'm . . .'

The other man interrupted. 'C-Bird. No one seems to use their real name in here.'

Lanky moved his head up and down rapidly. 'The Fireman's right, C-Bird. Nicknames and abbreviations and the such.'

Then he pivoted, and quickly marched back across the room, and tossed himself down on his bed, staring back up at the ceiling.

'He doesn't seem to be a bad fellow, and I think in reality, which is a poor word to use in this fine place, I believe he's actually pretty harmless,' the Fireman said. 'He did exactly the same to me the other day, shouting and pointing and acting like he was going to take me on single-handedly, thus protecting society from the arrival of the Antichrist, or the Son of Satan or whomever. Any odd demon that might accidentally land here. He does that to everyone who enters whom he doesn't recognize. And it's not altogether crazy, too, if you think about it. There seems to be a significant amount of evil around in this world, and it has to be coming from somewhere, I'm guessing. Might as well stay vigilant, like he says, even here.'

'Thank you, anyway,' Francis said. He was calming down, a little like a child who thought he was lost, but somehow spots a landmark, that gives him a sense of location. 'But I don't know your name . . .'

'I don't have a name any longer,' the man said. This was spoken with just the slightest touch of sadness around the edge, replaced swiftly by a wry half smile that was tinged with some sort of regret.

'How can you not have a name?' Francis asked.

'I've had to give it up. It's what landed me here.'

This made little sense to Francis. The man shook his head, amused. 'I'm sorry. People have started calling me the Fireman, because that is what I was before I arrived at the hospital. Put out fires.'

'But . . .'

'Well, once my friends called me Peter. So, Peter the Fireman, that will have to do for you Francis C-Bird.'

'All right,' Francis replied.

'I think you'll discover that the naming system here, makes it a little easier. Now you've met Lanky, which is as obvious a nickname for someone who looks like he does as one could possibly have. And you've been introduced to the Moses brothers, except everyone calls them Big Black and Little Black, which, again, seems like appropriate casting. And Gulp-a-pill, which is easier to say and far more accurate given his approach to treatment than the doctor's real name. And who else have you run into?'

'The nurses outside behind the bars, Miss . . .'

'Ah, Miss Wrong and Miss Watchful?'

'Wright and Winchell.'

'Correct. And there are other nurses as well, like Nurse Mitchell, who is Nurse Bitch-All and Nurse Smith, who is Nurse Bones because she looks a little like Lanky, there, and Short Blond, who seems quite beautiful. There's a social worker named Evans — called Mister Evil — whom you're going to meet soon enough, because he's more or less in charge of this dormitory. And Gulp-a-pill's nasty secretary's name is Miss Lewis, but someone dubbed her Miss Luscious, which she apparently hates, but can't do anything about, because it has stuck to her as tightly as those sweaters she likes to wear. She seems to be a real piece of work. It might all seem very confusing, but you'll get it all straight in a couple of days.'

Francis took a quick look around, then he whispered, 'Are all the people in here crazy?'

The Fireman shook his head. 'It's a hospital for crazy folks, C-Bird, but not everyone is. Some are just old, and senile, which makes them seem a little odd. Some are retarded, so they're slow on the uptake, but precisely what got them landed here is a mystery to me. Some folks seem merely depressed. Others are hearing voices. Do you hear voices, C-Bird?'

Francis was unsure how to answer. It seemed as if deep within him there was a debate going on; he could hear arguments suddenly swinging back and forth, like so many electric currents between poles.

'I don't want to say,' Francis replied hesitantly.

The Fireman nodded. 'Some things it's best to keep to oneself.'

He put his arm around Francis for a moment, steering him toward the exit door.

'Come on,' he said. 'I'll show you what there is of our home.'

'Do you hear voices, Peter?' Francis asked.

The Fireman shook his head. 'Nope.'

'You don't?'

'No. But it might be a good thing if I did,' he replied. He was smiling as he spoke, just the slightest touch at the corners of his mouth, in a way that Francis would come to recognize soon enough, that seemed to mirror much about the Fireman, for he was the sort of person who seemed to see both sadness and humor in things that others would see as merely moments.

'Are you crazy?' Francis asked.

Again the Fireman smiled, this time letting out a little laugh. 'Are you crazy, C-Bird?'

Francis took a deep breath. 'I might be,' he said. 'I don't know.'

The Fireman shook his head. 'I don't think so, C-Bird. Didn't think so when I first saw you, either. At least, not too crazy. Maybe a little crazy, but what's wrong with that?'

Francis nodded. This reassured him. 'But what about you?' he continued.

The Fireman hesitated, before replying.

'I'm something far worse,' he said slowly. 'That's why

64

I'm here. They're supposed to find out what's wrong with me.'

'What's worse than being crazy?' Francis asked.

The Fireman coughed once. 'Well,' he said, 'I guess there's no harm. You'll find out sooner or later. I kill people.'

And with those words, he led Francis out into the corridor of the hospital.

4

And that was it, I suppose.

Big Black told me not to make friends, to be cautious, to keep to myself, and obey the rules, and I did my very best to follow everything he advised except that first admonition, and, when I look back, I wonder if he wasn't right about that, as well. But madness is also truly about the worst sorts of loneliness, and I was both mad and alone, and so when Peter the Fireman took me aside, I welcomed his friendship along the descending road into the world of the Western State Hospital, and I did not ask him what he meant when he said those words, although I guessed that I would find out soon enough because the hospital was a place where everyone had secrets but few of them were kept close.

My younger sister questioned me once, long after I was released, what was the worst aspect of the hospital, and after much consideration, I told her: the routine. The hospital existed as a system of small disjointed moments that amounted to nothing, that were established merely to get Monday to Tuesday, and Tuesday to Wednesday and so on, week after week, month after month. Everyone at the hospital had been committed by allegedly well-meaning relatives, or the cold and inefficient social services system, after a perfunctory judicial hearing where we often weren't present, under thirty- or sixty-day orders. But we learned quick enough that these phony deadlines were as much delusions as were the voices we heard, for the hospital could renew the court orders as long as a determination was made that you continued to be a threat to yourself or to others, which, in our mad states, seemingly was always the determination. So, a thirty-day commitment order could easily become a twenty-year stay. A simple downhill path, marching steadily from psychosis to senility. Shortly after our arrival we all learned that we were a little bit like aging munitions, being stored out of sight, deteriorating with every passing moment, rusting and becoming increasingly less stable.

The first thing one recognized at the Western State Hospital was the biggest lie of them all — that no one was truly trying to help you get better, no one was actually trying to help you go home. A lot was said, and a lot was done, ostensibly to help you readjust to society, but these were mostly shows and fictions, like the release hearings that were held from time to time. The hospital was like tar on the road. It stuck you in place. A famous poet once quite elegantly and naively wrote that home was the place where they always took you in. Maybe for poets, but not for madmen. The hospital was about keeping you out of the sane world's eyes. We were all bound by medications that dulled the senses, stymied the voices, but never did completely away with anything hallucinatory, so that vibrant delusions still echoed and resounded throughout the corridors. But what was truly evil about our lives was how quickly we all came to accept those delusions. After a few days in the hospital, it didn't bother me when little Napoleon would stand next to my bed and start talking energetically of troop movements at Waterloo, and how if only the British squares had cracked under the assault of his cavalry, or Blücher had been delayed upon the road, or had The Old Guard not withered under the hail of grapeshot and musketry, how all of Europe would have been changed forever. I was never exactly sure that Napoleon actually thought he was the emperor of France, though at moments he behaved that way, or whether he simply obsessed with all these things because he was a small man, shunted away in a loony bin with the rest of us, and he more than anything wanted to signify something in life.

All of us mad folks did; it was our greatest hope and dream, we wanted to be something. What afflicted us was the elusiveness in achieving that goal, and so, instead we substituted delusion. On my floor alone, there were a half-dozen Jesuses, or at least folks who insisted they could communicate with Him directly, one Mohammad who fell to his knees three times a day, praying to Mecca, although he was often pointed in the wrong direction, a couple of George Washingtons or assorted other presidents, from Lincoln and Jefferson right up to LBJ and Tricky Dick, and more than a few folks, like the truly harmless but occasionally terrifying Lanky, who were on the lookout for signs of Satan or any of his minions. There were folks obsessed with germs, people terrified of unseen bacteria floating in the air, others who believed that every bolt of lightning during a thunderstorm was aimed directly at them, and so they cowered in the corners. There were patients who said nothing, spending days on end in total silence, and others who blasted obscenities right and left. Some washed their hands twenty or thirty times per day, others never bathed. We were an army of compulsions and obsessions, delusions and despairs. One of the men that I came to like was called Newsman. He wandered the hallways like some present day town crier, spouting headlines, an encyclopedia of current events. At least, in his own mad way, he kept us connected to the outside world, and reminded us that events were taking place beyond the walls of the hospital. And there was even one famously overweight woman, who occupied hours playing a mean game of Ping-Pong in the dayroom, but who spent most of her time considering the issues connected with being the direct reincarnation of Cleopatra. Sometimes, however, Cleo only thought she was Elizabeth Taylor in the movie. One way or the other, she could quote virtually every line from the film, even Richard Burton's, or the entirety of Shakespeare's play, as she slammed another winner past whoever dared play the game against her.

When I think back, it all seems so ridiculous, I think I should laugh out loud.

But it wasn't. It was a place of unspeakable pain.

That is what the people who have never been mad cannot understand. How much every delusion hurts. How reality just seems beyond one's grasp. A world of desperation and frustration. Sisyphus and his boulder would have fit in well at the Western State Hospital.

I went to my daily group sessions with Mister Evans, whom we called Mister Evil. A wiry psychiatric social worker with a sunken chest and an imperious attitude that seemed to suggest that he was somehow superior because he went home at the end of the day, and we did not, which we resented, but which was unfortunately the truest kind of superiority. In these sessions, we were encouraged to speak openly about why we were in the hospital, and what we would do when we were released.

Everyone lied. Wonderful, unbridled, optimistic, runaway, enthusiastic lies.

Except Peter the Fireman, who rarely contributed. He sat beside me politely listening to whatever fantastic fiction either I or one of the others came up with, about getting a regular job, or returning to school, or maybe joining an uplifting program that might serve to help others afflicted as we were. All these conversations were lies with one singular and hopeless desire at their core: to appear to be normal. Or, at least normal enough to be allowed to go home.

At the start I sometimes wondered if there hadn't been some private but very tenuous agreement between the two men, because Mister Evil never called on Peter the Fireman to add something to the discussion, even when it turned away from ourselves and our troubles into something interesting, like current events such as the hostage crisis, unrest in the inner cities, or the Red Sox aspirations for the upcoming year — all subjects that the Fireman knew a great deal about. There was some malevolence the two men shared, but one was patient, the other administrator, and at the beginning it was hidden away.

In an odd way, I very shortly came to think as if I was on some desperate expedition to the farthest, most desolate regions of the earth, cut off from civilization, traveling deeper and farther away from all that was familiar into uncharted lands. Harsh lands.

And soon to be harsher, still.

The wall beckoned me, even as the phone in the corner of the kitchen started to ring. I knew it would be one of my sisters, calling to find out how I was, which was, of course, the way I always am, and, I presume, the way I always will be. So, I ignored it.

★   ★   ★

Within a few weeks, what remained of the winter seemed to have retreated in sullen defeat, and Francis moved down a corridor at the hospital, searching for something to do. A woman to his right was mumbling something plaintive about lost babies, and rocking herself back and forth, holding her arms in front of her as if they contained something precious, when they did not. Ahead of him, an old man in pajamas, with wrinkled skin and a shock of unruly silver hair, stared forlornly at a stark white wall, until Little Black came along and gently turned him by the shoulders, so that he was now staring out a barred window. The repositioning with its new vista brought a smile to the old man's face and Little Black patted the man on the arm, reassuring him, then ambled over toward Francis.

'C-Bird, how you doing today?'

'I'm okay, Mister Moses. Just slightly bored.'

'They are watching soap operas in the dayroom.'

'Those shows don't do much for me.'

'You don't get behind that C-Bird? Start in to wondering just what's gonna happen to all those folks with all those strange lives. Lots of twists and turns and mystery that keeps folks tuning in. That don't interest you?'

'I suppose it should, Mister Moses, but I don't know. It just doesn't seem real to me.'

'Well, there's also some people playing some cards. Some board games, too.'

Francis shook his head.

'Play a game of Ping-Pong with Cleo, maybe?'

Francis smiled and continued to shake his head. 'What, Mister Moses, you think I'm so crazy I'd take her on?'

This comment made Little Black laugh out loud. 'No, C-Bird. Not even you that crazy,' he replied.

'Can I get an outdoor slip?' Francis asked abruptly.

Little Black looked at his wristwatch. 'I got some folks going outside this afternoon. Maybe plant some flowers on this fine day. Take a little walk. Get some of that fresh air. You go see Mister Evans, he fix you up, maybe. It's okay with me.'

Francis found Mister Evil outside his office, standing in the corridor deep in conversation with Doctor Gulp-a-pill. The two men seemed animated, gesturing back and forth, arguing vehemently, but it was a curious sort of argument, for the more intense it seemed to get, the lower and softer their voices became, so that eventually, as Francis hovered nearby, the two men were hissing back and forth like a pair of snakes confronting each other. The two men seemed oblivious to everyone in the hallway, for more than a few other inmates joined Francis, shuffling about, moving right and left, waiting for an opening. Francis finally heard Gulp-a-pill say

71

angrily, 'Well, we simply cannot have this sort of lapse, not for a moment. I hope for your sakes they show up soon,' only to have Mister Evil respond, 'Well, they've obviously been misplaced, or maybe stolen, and I'm not to blame for that. We will keep searching, that's the best I can do.' Gulp-a-pill nodded, but his face was set in a curious anger. 'You do that,' he said. 'And I hope they're discovered sooner rather than later. Make sure you inform Security, and have them provide you with a new set. But this is a serious breach of the rules.' And then the small Indian abruptly turned and walked away without acknowledging the presence of any of the others, except for one man, who sidled up to the doctor, but was dismissed with a wave before he could speak. Mister Evans turned toward the others, and was equally irritated: 'What? What do you want?'

His very tone caused one woman to instantly snatch a sob from her chest, and another old man to shake his head negatively, and stumble off down the corridor, speaking to himself, more comfortable with whatever conversation he could have with no one, than the one he could have with the angry social worker.

Francis, however, hesitated. The voices of caution inside his head shouted: *Leave! Leave now!* but Francis paused, and after a moment, mustered up enough courage to say, 'I would like an outdoor pass. Mister Moses is taking some people out to the grounds this afternoon, and I'd like to go with them. He said it would be okay.'

'You want to go out?'

'Yes. Please.'

'Why do you want to go out, Petrel? What is it about the great out-of-doors that seems to be attractive to you?' Francis could not tell whether he was mocking him directly, or merely making fun of the idea of stepping beyond the front door of the Amherst Building.

'It's a nice day. Like the first nice day in a long time. The sun is shining and it's warm. Fresh air.'

'And you think that is better than what is offered here, inside?'

'I didn't say that, Mister Evans. It's just springtime, and I wanted to go out.'

Mister Evil shook his head. 'I think you mean to try to run away, Francis. Escape. I think you believe that you can duck away from Little Black when his back is turned, climb the ivy and vault the wall, then run down the hill past the college before someone spots your flight and catch a bus that will take you away from here. Any bus, you don't care, because any place is better than here; that's what I think you mean to do,' he said. His tone had an edgy, aggressive note.

Francis instantly replied, 'No, no, no, I just want to go to the garden.'

'You say that,' Mister Evil continued, 'but how do I know that you are telling me the truth? How can I trust you, C-Bird? What will you do that makes me believe that you are telling me the truth?'

Francis had no idea how to reply. He did not know how anyone could prove that a promise made was truthful, other than by behaving that way. 'I just want to go outside,' Francis said. 'I haven't been outside since I got here.'

'Do you think you deserve the privilege of going outside? What have you done to earn that, Francis?'

'I don't know,' Francis said. 'I didn't know I had to earn it. I just want to go outside.'

'What do your voices tell you, C-Bird?'

Francis took a small step back, for his voices were all shouting, distant, yet clear, instructions to get away from the psychologist as fast as he could, but Francis persisted, in rare defiance of the internal racket. 'I don't hear any voices, Mister Evans. I just wanted to go outside. That's all. I don't want to escape. I don't want to take a bus somewhere. I just want some fresh air.'

Evans nodded, but locked his lips into a sneer at the same time. 'I don't believe you,' he said, but he pulled a small pad from his shirt pocket and wrote a few words on it. 'Give this to Mister Moses,' he said. 'Permission to go outside granted. But don't be late for our afternoon group session.'

★ ★ ★

Francis found Little Black smoking a cigarette by the nursing station, where he was flirting with the pair on duty. Nurse Wrong was there, and a younger woman, a new nurse-trainee — called Short Blond because she wore her hair cropped close to her head in a pixielike style that contradicted the bouffant do's of the other staff nurses, who were all a little older, and a little more committed to the sags and wrinkles of middle age. Short Blond was young and thin and wiry, with a boylike physique hidden behind the white nursing outfit. Her skin was pale, almost translucent, and seemed to glow softly beneath the overhead lights of the hospital. She had a slight, hard-to-hear voice that seemed to slide into whispers when she was nervous, which, as best as the patients could tell, was often. Large noisy groups made her anxious, and she struggled when the nursing station was swarmed at the hours medications were dispensed. These were always tense times, with folks jostling back and forth, trying to get up to the wire-enclosed window, where the pills were arranged in small paper cups with patients' names written on them. She had trouble getting the patients into lines, getting them to be quiet, and she especially had trouble when some pushing and shoving took place, which was often enough. Short Blond did much better when she was alone with a patient, and her reedy, small voice didn't have to battle with many. Francis liked her,

74

because, at least in part, she wasn't that much older than he was, but mainly because he thought her voice was soothing, and reminded him of his own mother's years earlier, when she would read to him at night. For a moment, he tried to remember when she had stopped doing that, because the memory seemed suddenly far distant, almost as if it were history, rather than recollection.

'You get the permission slip, C-Bird?' Little Black asked.

'Right here.' He handed it over and looked up and saw Peter the Fireman walking down the corridor. 'Peter!' Francis called, 'I got permission to go outside. Why don't you go see Mister Evil, and see if you can come, too.'

Peter the Fireman walked up quickly. He smiled but shook his head. 'No can do, C-Bird,' he said. 'Against the rules.' He glanced over at Little Black, who was nodding in agreement.

'Sorry,' the attendant said. 'The Fireman's right. Not him.'

'Why not?' Francis asked.

'Because,' the Fireman said quietly, slowly, 'that's my arrangement here. Not beyond any of the locked doors.'

'I don't understand,' Francis said.

'It's part of the court order putting me here,' the Fireman continued. His voice seemed tinged with regret. 'Ninety days of observation. Assessment. Psychological determination. Tests where they hold up an inkblot and I'm supposed to say it looks like two people having sex. Gulp-a-pill and Mister Evil ask, and I answer, and they write it down and one of these days it goes back to the court. But I'm not allowed past any locked doors. Everybody's in prison, sort of, C-Bird. Mine is just a little more restricted than yours.'

Little Black added, 'It ain't a big thing, C-Bird. There's plenty of folks here who never get to go out.

75

Depends on what you did that got you here. Of course, there's plenty, too, who don't want to go out, either, but could, if they only asked. They just never do ask.'

Francis understood, but didn't understand, both at the same time. He looked over at the Fireman. 'It doesn't seem fair,' he said.

'I don't think the concept of fair was truly one that anyone really had in mind, C-Bird. But I agreed, and so, that's the way it is. I stay put. Meet with Doctor Gulp-a-pill twice a week. Attend sessions with Mister Evil. Let them watch me. See, even now, while we're talking, Little Black here and Short Blond and Miss Wrong are all watching me and listening to what I say, and just about anything they observe might end up in the report that Gulp-a-pill is going to write up for the court. So, I pretty much need to mind my p's and q's and watch what I say, because no telling what might become the key consideration. Isn't that right, Mister Moses?'

Little Black nodded. Francis found it all to be oddly detached, as if they were speaking about someone else, not the person standing in front of him. 'When you speak like that,' he said, 'it doesn't sound like you're crazy.'

This comment made Peter the Fireman smile wryly, one side of his mouth lifting up, giving him a slightly lopsided, but genuinely bemused look. 'Oh my gosh,' he said. 'That's terrible. Terrible.' He made a slight choking sound deep in his throat. 'I should be even more careful then,' he said. 'Because crazy is what I need to be.'

This made no sense to Francis. For a man who was being watched, Peter seemed relatively unconcerned, which was in opposition to many of the paranoids in the hospital, who believed they were constantly being observed, when they weren't, but took evasive steps nevertheless. Of course, they believed it was the FBI or the CIA or perhaps the KGB or extraterrestrials who were doing the watching, which made their circumstances significantly different. Francis watched the Fireman turn and head off through the dayroom doors, and thought that even when he whistled, or perhaps added some obvious jauntiness to his step, it only served to make whatever saddened him all that much more obvious.

★ ★ ★

The warm sun hit Francis's face. Big Black had joined his brother to lead the expedition, one at the front and one at the rear, keeping the dozen patients making the journey through the hospital grounds in single file. Lanky had come along, muttering about being on the lookout, as vigilant as always, and Cleo, who spent some time staring at the ground, and peering at the dirt beneath every bush and shrub, hoping, as she said to anyone who noticed her behavior, to spot an adder. Francis guessed that an ordinary garter snake would nicely serve the serpent part of the bill, but not the suicide part. There were several older women who walked very slowly and a couple of older men, and three middle-aged male patients, all of whom fit into the bedraggled, nondescript category that marked folks who had been assimilated into the hospital routine for years. They wore flip-flop sandals or work boots — and pajama tops beneath frayed and threadbare woolen sweaters or sweatshirts, none of which seemed to quite fit or match, which was the norm for the hospital. A couple of the men had sullen, angry expressions on their faces, as if the sunlight that seemed to caress their faces with warmth infuriated them in some internal way that defied understanding. It was, Francis thought, what made the hospital such an unsettling place. A day that should have brought relaxed laughter instead inspired quiet rage.

The two attendants kept to a leisurely pace as they moved through the hospital grounds toward the rear of the complex, where there was a small garden. A picnic table that had been through a rough winter, its surface warped and scarred by the weather, held some boxes of seeds and a red child's play bucket with a few trowels and hand shovels arranged within. There was an aluminum watering pail and a hose attached to a single faucet that rose up on a lone pipe directly from the ground. Within a few seconds, Big Black and Little Black had the outdoor group on their hands and knees in the swatch of dirt, raking and tilling with the small hand tools, preparing the earth for planting. Francis kept at this for a few moments, then he looked up.

Beyond the garden was another piece of ground, a long rectangle enclosed by an old wooden picket fence that had once been painted white, but had faded over time to a dull gray. Weeds and unkempt grasses pushed up in tufts through the hardscrabble earth. He guessed that it was a cemetery of sorts, because there were two faded granite headstones, each slightly out of kilter, so that they looked like uneven teeth in a child's mouth. Then behind the back picket fence was a line of trees, planted closely together to form a natural barrier and obscure a metal link fence.

Then he glanced around, back toward the hospital itself. To his left, partially obscured by a dormitory, was the power plant, with a smokestack that released a thin plume of white smoke into the blue sky. Hidden under the ground, leading to all the buildings, were tunnels with heating ducts. He could see some sheds, with equipment stored to their sides. The remaining buildings looked much the same, brick and ivy, with slate gray rooflines. Most were designed to hold patients, but one had been converted to a dormitory for nurse-trainees, and several others redesigned into duplex apartments where some of the younger psychiatric residents and their families stayed. These were discernible because they had telltale children's toys scattered about in front, and one had a sandbox. Near the administration building there was also a security building, where the hospital's guard staff checked in and out. He took note that the administration building had a wing with an auditorium, where, he guessed staff meetings and lectures were given. But all in all, there was a depressing similarity to the complex. It was hard to discern precisely what the designer's layout had meant to suggest, for the buildings had a haphazard arrangement that defied rational planning. Two would be right next to each other, but a third would be angled away. It was almost as if they had been slapped down into space without any sense of order.

The front of the hospital complex was enclosed by a tall redbrick wall, with an ornate black wrought-iron entranceway. He couldn't see a sign out front, but he doubted there would be one, anyway. If one approached the hospital, he guessed, one already knew what it was, and what it was for, so a sign would have been redundant.

He stared at the wall and tried to measure it with his eyes. He thought the wall at least ten to twelve feet high. The wall was replaced on the sides, and on the back end of the hospital by chain-link fencing, which was rusted in many spots and topped with strands of rusted barbed wire. In addition to the garden, there was an exercise area, a swatch of black macadam, which had a basketball hoop at one end and a volleyball net in the center, but both these items were bent and broken, blackened by disuse and lack of care. He couldn't imagine anyone using either.

'What you looking at C-Bird?' Little Black asked.

'The hospital,' Francis replied. 'I just didn't know how big it was.'

'Many, too many, here now,' Little Black said quietly. 'Every dormitory filled to bursting. Beds jammed up close together. People with nothing to do, just hanging in the hallways. Not enough games. Not enough therapy. Just everybody in here getting real close together. That ain't good.'

Francis looked over at the huge gate that he'd passed through on his first day at the hospital. It was wide open.

'They lock it at night,' Little Black said, anticipating his question.

'Mister Evans thought I was going to try to run away,' Francis said.

Little Black shook his head and smiled. 'People always think that's what the folks here will do, but it don't happen,' he said. 'Even Mister Evil, he's been here a couple of years, but he should know better.'

'Why not?' Francis asked. 'Why don't people try to run away?'

Little Black sighed. 'You know the answer to that C-Bird. It ain't about fences, and it ain't about locked doors, although we got plenty of those. There's lotsa ways to keep a person locked up. You think about it. But the best way of all doesn't have anything to do with drugs or deadbolt locks, C-Bird. It's that hardly anybody in here has some place to run to. With no place to go, nobody goes. It's that simple.'

With that, he turned away and tried to help Cleo with her seeds. She hadn't dug the furrows deep enough or wide enough. She showed some frustration on her face, until Little Black reminded her that servants spread flower petals in her path, when her namesake entered Rome. This made her pause, and then redouble her efforts, until Cleo was digging and scraping through the moldy, gravelly ground with a determination that seemed genuinely profound. Cleo was a large woman, who wore brightly colored smocks that billowed around her, concealing her extensive bulk. She wheezed often, smoked too much, and wore her dark hair in scraggly streams down around her shoulders. When she walked, she seemed to lurch back and forth, like a rudderless ship blown off course by high winds and choppy waves. But Francis knew she was transformed, when she took up a Ping-Pong paddle, shedding her unwieldy size almost magically, and becoming svelte, catlike, and quick.

He looked back over at the gate, and then to his fellow patients and slowly began to grasp what Little Black had been saying. One of the older men was having trouble with his trowel; it was shaking hard in a palsied hand. Another had become distracted, and was staring up at a raucous crow perched in a nearby tree.

Deep inside him, he heard one of his voices speak sullenly, repeating what Little Black had told him, as if to underscore each word: *No one runs, because no one has any place to run to. And neither do you, Francis.*

Then a chorus of assent.

For a moment, Francis spun about, his head pivoting wildly. For in that second, beneath the sunlight and the mild spring breezes, his hands already caked with dirt from the garden, he saw what could be his future. And it terrified him more than anything that had happened so far. He could see that his life was a slippery thin rope, and he needed to grasp hold of it. It was the worst feeling he had ever had. He knew he was mad, and knew, just as surely, that he couldn't be. And, in that second, he realized, he had to find something that would keep him sane. Or make him appear to be sane.

Francis breathed in hard. He did not think this would be easy.

And, as if to underline the problem, within him his voices argued loudly, making a racket. He tried to quiet them, but this was difficult. It took a few moments for them all to reduce their volume so that he could make

81

some sense out of what they were saying. Francis glanced over at the other patients, and saw that a couple of them were eyeing him closely. He must have been mumbling something out loud, as he'd tried to impose order on the assembly within him. But neither Big Black nor his brother seemed to have noticed the sudden struggle that had engaged him.

Lanky had, however. He had been working on some dirt a few feet away, and he lurched over to Francis's side.

'You'll be okay, C-Bird,' he said, his voice cracking a little with some emotion that abruptly seemed to be spinning a bit out of control. 'We all will. As long as we keep up our guard, and keep a weather eye out. Got to keep close watch,' he continued. 'And don't turn your back for a minute. It's all around us, and it could happen any time. We have to be prepared. Like Boy Scouts. Ready for it when it comes.' The tall man seemed more agitated and desperate than usual.

Francis thought he knew what Lanky was speaking about, but then understood that it could be almost anything, but most likely concerned a satanic presence on earth. Lanky had a curious manner, where he could slide from manic to almost gentle in the course of seconds. One instant, he would be all arms and angles, moving like a marionette, strings being pulled by unseen forces, and the next diminished, where his height made him seem no more threatening than a lamppost. Francis nodded, took a few seeds from a package and pushed them into the dirt.

Big Black rose up and shook his white attendant's outfit clean of dirt. 'Okay, folks,' he said cheerily, 'gonna spray this place with some water and head on in.' He looked over at Francis, and asked, 'C-Bird, what did you plant?'

Francis looked down at the seed package and said, 'Roses. Red ones. Pretty to look at, but hard to handle.

They've got thorns.' Then he got up, got into line with the others, and marched back toward the dormitory. He tried to drink in and store up as much fresh air as he could, for he feared it might be some time before he got out again.

★   ★   ★

Whatever had caused Lanky to loosen his already weak grip on the day, persisted at the group session that afternoon. They gathered, as usual, in one of the odd rooms inside Amherst, a little like a small classroom, with twenty or so gray metal folding chairs arranged in a rough circle. Francis liked to position himself where he could stare out past the bars on the window if the conversation got boring. Mister Evil had brought in that morning's paper to spur a discussion on current events, but it only seemed to agitate the tall man even more. He sat across from where Francis perched next to Peter the Fireman, shifting about constantly in his chair, as Mister Evil turned to Newsman to recite the day's headlines. This the patient did extravagantly, his voice rising and falling with each reading. There was little good news. The hostage crisis in Iran continued relentlessly. A protest in San Francisco had turned violent, with a number of arrests and tear gas deployed by helmeted police officers. In both Paris and Rome, anti-American demonstrators had burned flags and effigies of Uncle Sam before running wild in the streets. In London, authorities had used water cannon against similar protestors. The Dow Jones Industrial Average had taken a beating and there had been a riot in a prison in Arizona that hadn't been quelled without grisly injury to both inmates and guards. In Boston, police were still puzzled by several homicides that had taken place during the prior year, and reported no new leads in the cases which involved young women being abducted and molested, before being killed. A three-car accident on Route 91 outside Greenfield had claimed a pair of lives, and a lawsuit had been filed by an environmental group accusing a large local employer of dumping untreated waste into the Connecticut River.

Every time Newsman paused in his reading, and Mister Evil launched into an effort to discuss any of these stories, or others, all discouragingly similar, Lanky nodded his head vigorously and started mumbling, 'There! See. That's what I mean!' It was a little like being in some bizarre revivalist church. Evans ignored these statements, trying to engage the other members of the group in some sort of give-and-take conversation.

Peter the Fireman, however, took notice. He abruptly turned to Lanky and asked him directly, 'Big Guy, what's wrong?'

Lanky's voice quavered, as he spoke: 'Don't you see, Peter? The signs are everywhere! Unrest, hatred, war, killing . . . ' He abruptly turned to Evans and asked, 'Isn't there some story in the paper about famine, as well?'

Mister Evil hesitated, and Newsman gleefully said, 'Sudanese Struggle with Crop Failure. Drought and Starvation Cause Refugee Crisis. The *New York Times*.'

'Hundreds dead?' Lanky asked.

'Yes. In all likelihood,' Mister Evans replied. 'Perhaps even more.'

Lanky nodded vigorously, his head bobbing up and down. 'I've seen the pictures before. Little babies with their bellies swollen and spindly little legs and eyes sunken back all hollow and hopeless. And disease, that's always with us, right alongside famine. Don't even need to read Revelations all that carefully to recognize what's happening. All the signs.' He leaned back abruptly in his steel folding chair, took a single long glance outside the barred window that opened on the hospital grounds, as if assessing the final light of the day, and said, 'There is no doubt that Satan's presence is here. Close by. Look at all that is happening in the world. Bad news everywhere you look. Who else could be responsible?'

With that, he folded his arms in front of him. He was suddenly breathing hard, and small droplets of sweat had formed on his forehead, as if each thought that reverberated within him took a great effort to control. The rest of the dozen members of the group were fixed in their chairs, no one moving, their eyes locked on the tall man, as he struggled with the fears that buffeted around within him.

Mister Evil noticed this, and abruptly steered the topic away from Lanky's obsession. 'Let's turn to the sports section,' he said. The cheeriness in his voice was transparent, almost insulting.

But Peter the Fireman persisted. 'No,' he spoke with an edge of anger in his words. 'No. I don't want to talk about baseball or basketball or the local high school teams. I think we ought to talk about the world around us. And I think Lanky's truly onto something. All there is outside these doors is awful. Hatred and murder and killing. Where does it come from? Who's doing it? Who's good anymore? Maybe it isn't because Satan is here, like Lanky believes. Maybe it's because we've all turned for the worse, and he doesn't even need to be here, because we're doing all his work for him.'

Mr. Evans stared hard at Peter the Fireman. His gaze had narrowed. 'I think you have an interesting opinion,' he said slowly, measuring his words in an understated cold fashion, 'but you exaggerate things. Regardless, I don't think it has much to do with the purposes of this group. We're here to explore ways to rejoin society. Not reasons to hide from it, even if things out in the world aren't quite the way we might like them to be. Nor do I think it serves a purpose when we indulge our delusions, or lend any credence to them.' These last words were directed both at Peter and Lanky equally.

Peter the Fireman's face was set. He started to speak, then stopped.

But into that sudden void, Lanky stepped. His voice was quivering, on the verge of tears. 'If we are to blame for all that is happening, then there's no hope for any of us. None.'

This was said with such unbridled despair that several of the other people in the session, who had been quiet until then, immediately muffled cries. One old man started to tear up, and a woman wearing a pink ruffled housecoat, far too much mascara on her eyes, and tufted white bunny rabbit slippers cut loose with a sob. 'Oh, that's sad,' she said. 'That's so sad.'

Francis watched the social worker, as he tried to regain control over the session. 'The world is the way the world has always been,' he said. 'It's our own part in it that concerns us here.'

It was the wrong thing to say, because Lanky jumped to his feet. He was waving his arms suddenly above his head, much the way he had when Francis had first encountered him. 'But that's it!' he cried, startling some of the more timid members of the group. 'Evil is everywhere! We must find a way to keep it out! We must band together. Form committees. Have watchdog groups. We must organize! Coordinate! Make a plan. Raise defenses. Guard the walls. We've got to work hard to keep it out of the hospital!' He took a deep breath, and pivoted, searching out all the members of the group session with his eyes.

Several heads nodded in unison. This made sense.

'We can keep evil out,' Lanky said. 'But only if we're vigilant.'

Then, his body still shaking with the effort speaking out had taken, he sat back down, and once again folded his arms across his chest retreating into silence.

Mr. Evans glared at Peter the Fireman, as if he was to

blame for Lanky's outburst. 'So,' he said slowly, 'Peter. Tell us. Do you think if we're to keep Satan outside these walls, perhaps then we should all be going to church on a regular basis?'

Peter the Fireman stiffened in his seat.

'No,' he said slowly, 'I don't think — '

'Shouldn't we be praying? Going to services. Saying our Hail Mary's and Our Father's and Perfect Acts of Contrition. Taking communion on every Sunday? Shouldn't we be confessing our sins on a near constant basis?'

Peter the Fireman's voice grew low and very quiet. 'Those things might make you feel better. But I don't believe — '

But Mr. Evans interrupted him a second time. 'Oh, I'm sorry,' he said, an edgy cynicism in each word. 'Going to church and all sorts of organized religious activities would be highly inappropriate for the Fireman, wouldn't they? Because the Fireman, well, you have a problem with churches, right?'

Peter shifted in his seat. Francis could see a slippery fury behind his eyes, which he had never seen before.

'Not churches. A church. And I had a problem. But I solved it, didn't I, Mister Evans?'

The two men stared at each other for a second, then Evans said, 'Yes. I suppose you did. And see where it has landed you.'

★　★　★

At dinner, things seemed to grow worse for Lanky.

The meal that night was creamed chicken, which was mostly a thick, grayish cream and not much chicken, with peas that had been boiled into a state where whatever claim they might once have had on being a vegetable had evaporated in the heat of the stove, and hard baked potatoes that had the same consistency as

87

frozen, except that they were as hot as coals taken from the bottom of a fire. The tall man sat alone, at a corner table, while the other residents of the building jammed into seats at the other tables, trying to give him space. One or two residents had tried to join him at the start of the dinner, but Lanky had waved them away furiously, growling a bit like an old dog disturbed from its sleep.

The usual buzz of conversation seemed muted, the ordinary clatter of dishes and trays seemed softer. There were several tables set aside for the elderly, senile patients, who needed assistance, but even the hovering, attentive busywork of feeding them, or aiding the catatonics who stared blankly ahead, barely aware that they were being fed, seemed quieter, more subdued. From where he was seated, chewing unhappily on the tasteless meal, Francis could see that all the attendants in the dining room kept tossing glances at Lanky, trying to keep an eye on him, as they went about the business of taking care of the others. At one point Gulp-a-pill put in an appearance, spent a few moments intently observing Lanky before speaking rapidly with Evans. Before he left, Gulp-a-pill wrote out a scrip, which he handed to another nurse.

Lanky seemed oblivious to the attention he was drawing.

He was talking rapidly to himself, arguing back and forth, as he pushed the food on his plate about into a rapidly congealing mess. He gulped at a glass of water, gestured once or twice wildly, pointing at the air in front of him, his bony index finger jabbing the space, as if punching the chest of no one in front of him as he made a dramatic point to no one who was there. Then, just as rapidly, he would lower his face, and stare at his food, and return to mumbling to himself.

It was near dessert, squares of lime green Jell-O, when Lanky finally looked up, as if suddenly aware of where he was. He spun about in his seat, a look of surprise and astonishment on his face. His wiry gray hair, which usually fell in slimy rings to his shoulders, now seemed electrically charged, like a Saturday morning cartoon character whose finger is pushed into a light socket, except this was not a joke and no one was laughing. His eyes were wide and wild with fear, much like they had been when Francis first encountered the older man, but multiplied, as if accelerated by passion. Francis saw them search rapidly around the room, and then fasten on Short Blond, who was only a little ways away from where Lanky was seated, trying to help an elderly woman through her dinner, cutting each slimy morsel of chicken into small bites, then lifting them to her mouth as if she were a baby in a highchair.

Lanky pushed back sharply from his seat, sending the chair clattering to the floor. In the same motion, he lifted his cadaverous finger and began pointing it at the young nurse-trainee.

'You!' he cried out furiously.

Short Blond looked up, confused. For a second she pointed at herself, and Francis could see her mouth the word, 'Me?' She didn't move from where she was seated. Francis thought that this was probably her limited training. Any veteran of the hospital would have reacted much more swiftly.

'You!' he cried again. 'It must be you!'

From the far side of the dining room, both Little Black and his brother started moving rapidly across the space. But the rows of tables and chairs and the crowd of patients, made their course filled with obstacles, and slowed their pace. Short Blond rose to her feet, staring at Lanky, who was now striding toward her quickly, finger outstretched, pointing directly at her. She recoiled slightly, backing up toward the wall.

'It's you, I know it!' he cried. 'You're the new one! You're the one that hasn't been checked! It's you, it must be! Evil! Evil! We've let her through the door! Get away! Get away! Everyone be careful! No telling what she might do!'

His frantic warnings seemed to imply to the other patients that Short Blond was diseased or explosive. Throughout the dining room, people shrank back in sudden fear.

Short Blond retreated to the nearest wall and held up her hand. Francis could see the edge of panic in her eyes as the old man steadily descended upon her, arms flapping like bird wings.

He started to wave the other patients away, his voice rising in pitch and fury, 'Don't worry! I'll protect us!'

Big Black was now pushing tables and chairs aside, and Little Black vaulted one patient, who had fallen to his knees in some indistinct terror of his own. Francis could see Mister Evil sweeping in their direction, and Nurse Wrong and another nurse also moving through the tangle of patients, all of whom were knotting together, unsure whether to flee or to watch.

'It's you!' Lanky shouted as he reached the nurse-trainee, and towered menacingly above her.

'It's not!' Short Blond screamed in her high-pitched, reedy voice.

'It is!' Lanky yelled back.

'Lanky! Stop there!' Little Black shouted. Big Black was closing fast, his own face set in an obsidian mask of determination.

'It isn't, it isn't!' Short Blond said, cowering, sliding down the wall.

And then, with Big Black and Mister Evil still yards away, there was a momentary silence. Lanky rose up, stretching toward the ceiling, as if he was going to throw himself down upon Short Blond. Francis heard Peter the Fireman cry out from nearby, but he wasn't sure where, 'Lanky don't! Stop right now!'

And, to Francis's surprise, the big man did.

He looked down at Short Blond and a quizzical look

came over his face, almost as if he was inspecting test results from an experiment that didn't precisely show what the scientist thought they should. His face took on a skewed, curious expression. Much more quietly, he gazed at Short Blond, and asked, almost politely, 'Are you sure?'

'Yes, yes, yes,' she choked, 'I'm sure!'

He stared at her closely. 'I'm confused,' he said sadly. It was a deflation of immediate and immense proportions. One second, he'd been this avenging force, gathered as if for assault, then in a microsecond, he was childlike and small, diminished by a storm of doubts.

In that moment, Big Black finally reached Lanky's side, and roughly grabbed the tall man by the arms, pinning them back. 'What the hell are you doing!' he demanded angrily. Little Black was only a stride behind, and he stepped into the space between the patient and the nurse-trainee. 'Step back!' he insisted, a command that was obeyed instantly, because his immense brother jerked Lanky rearward.

'I could be wrong,' Lanky said, shaking his head. 'It seemed so clear, at first. Then it changed. Just all of a sudden, it changed. I'm just not sure.'

The tall man turned his head to Big Black, craning his ostrichlike neck. Doubt and sadness filled his voice. 'I thought it had to be her, you see. It had to be. She's the newest. She hasn't been here at all long. A new-comer, to be sure. And we have to be so careful not to let evil inside the walls. We have to be vigilant at all times. I'm sorry,' he said, turning as Short Blond rose to her feet, trying to regain her own composure. 'I was so sure.' He looked at her hard again, and his eyes narrowed.

'I'm just still not sure,' he said stiffly. 'It could be. She could be lying to me. Satan's assistants are expert liars. They are deceivers, each and every one of them. It's easy for them to make someone seem innocent, when they're really not.'

Now his voice lacked rage and doubt.

Short Blond stepped away from the group, keeping her eyes warily on where Lanky was being held by Big Black. Evans had finally managed to cross the room and join the tangle of people, and he was speaking directly to Little Black. 'See that he gets a sedative tonight. Fifty milligrams of Nembutal, IV, at medication time. Maybe we should put him in isolation for the night, as well.'

Lanky was still eyeing Short Blond, when he heard the word *isolation*. He spun toward Mister Evil and shook his head vehemently. 'No, no, I'm okay, really, I am, I was just doing my job, really. I won't be a problem, I promise . . . ' His voice trailed off.

'We'll see,' said Evans. 'See how he responds to the sedative.'

'I'll be fine,' Lanky insisted. 'Really. I won't be a problem. Not at all. Please don't put me into isolation.'

Evans turned to Short Blond. 'You can take a break,' he said. But the slender nurse-trainee shook her head.

'I'm okay,' she replied, mustering some bravery in her words, and went back to feeding the elderly woman in the wheelchair. Francis noted that Lanky was still staring in Short Blond's direction, his unwavering gaze marked with what he took for uncertainty, but, later, realized could be many different emotions.

★   ★   ★

The usual evening crowd pushed and complained at medication time that night. Short Blond was behind the wire mesh of the nurses' station, helping to distribute the pills, but the other, older and more experienced nurses took the lead in handing out the evening concoctions. A few voices were raised in complaint, and one man started crying when another pushed him aside, but it seemed to Francis that the outburst at dinner had rendered most of the Amherst residents if not exactly speechless, at least subdued. He thought to himself that the hospital was all about balances. Medications balanced out the madness; age and confinement balanced out energy and ideas. Everyone in the hospital accepted a certain routine, he thought, where space and action were limited and defined and regimented. Even the occasional jostling and arguing, like nightly at medication time, was all part of an elaborate insane minuet, as codified as a Renaissance dance step.

He saw Lanky enter the area in front of the nurses' station, accompanied by Big Black. The tall man was shaking his head, and Francis heard him complain, 'I'm okay, I'm okay. I don't need anything extra to calm me down . . . '

But Big Black's face had lost the easygoing edge it usually wore, and Francis overheard him say calmly, 'Lanky, you gotta do this nice and easy-like, because otherwise we're gonna have to put you in a jacket and lock you up in isolation for the night, and I know you don't want that. So take yourself a deep breath and roll up your sleeve and don't fight something that shouldn't be fought.'

Lanky nodded, complacent in that moment, although Francis saw that he eyed Short Blond, working at the rear of the station, warily. Whatever doubts Lanky had about Short Blond's capacity to be a child of Satan, it was clear to Francis that they had not been resolved by medication or persuasion. The tall man seemed to quiver from head to toe with anxiety. But he did not fight Nurse Bones, who approached him with a hypodermic dripping with medication, and who swiped his arm with alcohol and stiffly plunged the needle into Lanky's skin. Francis thought it must have hurt, but Lanky showed no signs of discomfort. He stole a final long look at Short Blond, before allowing Big Black to lead him away, back to the dormitory room.

5

Outside my apartment the evening traffic had increased. I could hear diesel sounds from heavy trucks, the occasional blare of a car's horn and the constant hum of wheels against pavement. Night comes slowly in the summertime, insinuating itself like a mean thought on a happy occasion. Streaky shadows find the alleys first, then start creeping through yards and across sidewalks, up the sides of buildings, and slithering snakelike through windows, or taking purchase in the branches of shade trees until finally darkness seizes hold. Madness, I often thought, was a little like the night, because of the different ways in different years it spread itself over my heart and my imagination, sometimes harshly and quickly, other times slowly, subtly, so that I barely knew it was taking over.

I tried to think: Had I ever known a darker night, than that one at the Western State Hospital? Or a night filled with more madness?

I went to the sink, filled a glass with water, took a gulp, and thought: I've left out the stench. It was a combination of human waste battling against undiluted cleansers. The stink of urine versus the smell of disinfectant. Like babies, so many old and senile patients had no control over their bowels, so the hospital reeked of accidents. To combat this, every corridor had at least two storage rooms equipped with rags, mops, and buckets filled with the harshest of chemical cleaning agents. It sometimes seemed as if there was someone constantly swabbing down a floor somewhere or another. The lye-based cleaners were fiercely powerful, they burned your eyes when they hit the linoleum floor, and made breathing hard, as if something was clawing at your lungs.

It was hard to anticipate when these accidents would happen. In a normal world, I suppose, one could more or less regularly identify the stresses or fears that might prompt a loss of control by some ancient person, and take steps to reduce those occurrences. It would take a little logic, a little sensitivity, and some planning and foresight. Not a big deal. But in the hospital, where all the stresses and fears that ricocheted around the hallways were so unplanned, and stemmed from so many haphazard thoughts, the idea of anticipation and avoidance was pretty much impossible.

So, instead, we had buckets and powerful cleaners.

And, because of the frequency that nurses and attendants were called upon to use these items, the storage rooms were rarely locked up. They were supposed to be, of course, but like so many things at the Western State Hospital, the reality of the rules gave way to a madness-defined practicality.

What else did I remember about that night? Did it rain? Did the wind blow?

What I recalled, instead, were the sounds.

In the Amherst Building there were nearly three hundred patients crowded into a facility originally designed for about one third that number. On any given night a few people might have been moved into one of the isolation cells up on the fourth floor that Lanky had been threatened with. The beds were jammed up next to each other, so that there was only a few inches of space between each sleeping patient. Along one side of the dorm room, there were some grimy windows. These were barred, and provided a little ventilation, although the men in the bunks beneath them frequently closed them up tight, because they were scared of what might be on the other side.

The nighttime was a symphony of distress.

Snoring, coughing, gurgling noises mingled with

nightmares. People spoke in their dreams, to family and friends who weren't there, to Gods who ignored their prayers, to demons that tormented them. People cried constantly, weeping endlessly through the darkest hours. Everyone slept, no one rested.

We were locked in with all the loneliness that night brings.

Perhaps it was the moonlight streaming through the barred windows that kept me flittering between sleep and wakefulness that night. Perhaps I was still unsettled over what had taken place during the day. Perhaps my voices were restless. I have thought about it often, for I am still not sure what kept me in that awkward stage between alertness and unconsciousness throughout the dark hours. Peter the Fireman was groaning in his sleep, tossing about fitfully in the bunk next to mine. The night was hard for him; during the daytime, he was able to maintain a reasonableness that seemed out of place in the hospital. But at night something gnawed steadily away within him. And, as I faded back and forth between these states of anxiety, I remember seeing Lanky, several bunks distant, sitting up, legs folded like a red Indian at some tribal council, staring out across the room. I recall thinking that the tranquilizer that they gave him hadn't done the job, for by all rights he should have been pitched into a dark, dreamless, drug-induced sleep. But whatever the impulses that had so electrified him earlier, they were easily battling the tranquilizer, and instead, he sat, mumbling to himself, gesturing with his hands like a conductor who couldn't quite get the symphony to play at the right tempo.

That was how I remembered him, that night, as I slipped in and out of consciousness myself, right to the moment I had felt a hand on my shoulder, shaking me awake. That was the moment, I thought. Start right there.

And so, I took the pencil and wrote:

96

Francis slept in fits and starts until he was awakened by an insistent shaking that seemed to drag him abruptly from some other unsettled place and instantly reminded him where he was. He blinked open his eyes, but before they adjusted to the dark, he could hear Lanky's voice, whispering softly, but energetically, filled with a childish excitement and pleasure, saying, 'We're safe, C-Bird. We're safe!'

Francis slept in fits and starts until he was awakened by an insistent shaking that seemed to drag him abruptly from some other unsettled place and instantly reminded him where he was. He blinked open his eyes, but before they adjusted to the dark, he could hear Lanky's voice, whispering softly, but energetically, filled with a childish excitement and pleasure, saying, 'We're safe, C-Bird. We're safe!'

The tall man was perched like some winged dinosaur, on the edge of the bed. In the moonlight that filtered past the window bars, Francis could see a wild look of joy and relief on the man's face.

'Safe from what, Lanky?' Francis asked, although as soon as he asked the question, he realized he knew the answer.

'From evil,' Lanky replied. He wrapped his arms around himself, hugging his own body. Then, in a second motion, he lifted his left hand and put it to his face, placing his forehead in his hand, as if the pressure of his palm and fingers could hold back some of the thoughts and ideas that were springing forth so zealously.

When Lanky took his hand away from his forehead, it seemed to Francis that it left behind a mark, almost like soot. It was hard to see in the wan light that sliced the dormitory room. Lanky must have felt something, as well, because he suddenly looked down at his fingers quizzically.

97

Francis sat upright in the bed. 'Lanky!' he whispered. 'What has happened?'

Before the tall man could respond, Francis heard a hissing sound. It was Peter the Fireman, who had awakened, and had swung his legs over the edge of the bunk, and was craning toward them. 'Lanky, tell us now! What has happened?' Peter insisted, also keeping his voice as low as possible. 'But be quiet. Don't wake up any of the others.'

The tall man bent his head slightly, agreeing. But his words came out in an excited, almost joyous rush. Relief and release flooded his words. 'It was a vision, Peter. It must have been an angel, sent right directly to me. C-Bird, this vision came straight to my side, right here to tell me . . . '

'Tell you what?' Francis asked quietly.

'Tell me I was right. Right all along. Evil had tried to follow us here, C-Bird. Evil was right here in the hospital alongside of all of us. But that evil has been destroyed, and now we're safe.'

He breathed out slowly, then added, 'Thank goodness.'

Francis didn't know what to make of what Lanky had said, but Peter the Fireman moved over and sat at the tall man's side. 'This vision — it came here? In this room?' he asked.

'Right to my bedside. We embraced like brothers.'

'The vision touched you?'

'Yes. It was as real as you or me, Peter. I could feel its life right next my own. Like our hearts were beating in unison. Except it was magical, too, C-Bird.'

Peter the Fireman nodded. Then he reached out slowly and touched Lanky's forehead, where the soot marks remained. For a second, Peter rubbed his fingers together.

'Did you see the vision come in through the door, or did it drop down from someplace above?' he asked slowly, first motioning toward the dormitory entrance-way, then up to the ceiling.

Lanky shook his head. 'No. It just arrived, just one second, right by my bed. It seemed as if it was all bathed in light as if directly from heaven. But I couldn't exactly see its face. Almost like it was cloaked. It must have been an angel,' he said. 'C-Bird, think of it. An angel right here. Right here in this room. In our hospital. Helping to protect us.'

Francis said nothing, but Peter the Fireman nodded, his own head bent slightly. He lifted his fingers to his nostrils and whiffed strongly. He seemed to be startled by what he smelled, and he took in a sharp breath of air. For a moment, the Fireman paused, looking around the room. Then he spoke in low, direct words, his voice carrying all the authority that it could, giving orders like a military commander with the enemy close by and danger in every shadow.

'Lanky. Go back to your bed, and wait there until C-Bird and I come back. Don't say anything to anybody. Absolute silence, got that?'

Lanky started to speak, then hesitated. 'Okay,' he said slowly. 'But we're safe. We're all safe. Don't you think the others will want to know?'

'Let's make absolutely sure, before we get their hopes up,' Peter said. This seemed to make sense, because Lanky nodded again. He rose and maneuvered back to his bunk. He turned and held up his index finger, the universal signal for silence, when he got there. Peter seemed to smile at him, then whispered, 'C-Bird, come with me, right now. And be quiet!' Each word he spoke seemed taut with some undefined tension that Francis couldn't quite fathom.

Without looking back, Peter the Fireman began to creep gingerly between the bunks, moving stealthily in the meager spaces that separated the sleeping men. He slid past the toilet, where a little bit of harsh light sliced under the doorway, heading toward the sole door to the dormitory. A few of the men stirred, one man seemed to half rise as they crept past his bunk, but Peter merely shushed him smoothly as they went by, and the man shifted about with a low groan, changing sides and then descending back into sleep.

When he reached the door, he looked back and saw Lanky, once again, sitting cross-legged on the bunk. The tall man saw them and waved before he lay back down.

As Peter the Fireman reached for the door, Francis joined his side. 'The door's locked,' Francis said. 'They lock it every night.'

'Tonight,' Peter said slowly, 'it isn't locked.' And then, by way of proof, he reached out, grasped the handle and turned it. The door pushed open with a small swooshing noise. 'Come on, C-Bird,' he said.

The corridor was darkened for the night, with only an occasional weak light shedding small glowing arcs across the floor. Francis was taken aback momentarily by the silence. Usually the hallways of the Amherst Building were jammed with people, sitting, standing, walking, smoking, talking to themselves, talking to people not there, maybe even talking to one another. The hallways were like the veins of the hospital, constantly pumping blood and energy to each central organ. He'd never seen them empty. The sensation of being alone on the corridor was unsettling. The Fireman, however, didn't seem concerned. He was staring down toward the middle of the hallway, where the nurses' station was marked by a single, faded desktop light, a small glow of yellow. From where they stood, the station seemed empty.

Peter took a single step forward, then stared down at the floor. He dropped down to a knee and gingerly touched a splotch of dark color, much as he had the soot on Lanky's face. Again, he lifted his finger to his nose. Then, without saying a word, he pointed, gesturing for Francis to take note.

Francis wasn't precisely sure what he was supposed to see, but he was paying close attention to everything Peter the Fireman did. The two of them continued to creep down the hallway toward the nursing station, but stopped midway, opposite one of the storage closets.

Francis peered through the weak light, and saw that the nursing station was indeed empty. This confused him, because he had always assumed there was at least one person on duty there round-the-clock. The Fireman, however, was staring down at the floor by the door to the closet. He pointed at a large splotch that marred the linoleum.

'What is it?' Francis asked.

Peter the Fireman sighed. 'More trouble than you've ever known,' he said. 'Francis, whatever is behind this door, don't shout. Especially don't scream. Just bite your tongue and don't say a word. And don't touch a thing. Can you do that for me, C-Bird? Can I count on you?'

Francis grunted a yes, which was difficult. He could feel the blood pumping in his chest, echoing in his ears, all adrenaline and anxiety. In that second, he realized that he hadn't heard a word from any of his voices, not since Lanky had first shaken him awake.

Peter moved cautiously to the storage room door. He pulled his T-shirt out of his pajama pants and covered his hand with the loose end as he reached for the handle. Then he opened the door slowly.

The room gaped in front of them, pitch-black. Peter stepped forward very slowly and reached inside where there was a light switch on the side of the wall.

The sudden glare of light was like a sword stroke.

For a second, perhaps even less, Francis was blinded.

He heard Peter the Fireman choke out a single, harsh obscenity.

Francis craned forward, looking into the storage room past Peter the Fireman. And then he gasped, abrupt fear and shock slamming him like a gust of hurricane wind. He recoiled from what he saw, taking a step backward and feeling like every breath he inhaled was steam-hot. He tried to say something, but even an 'Oh, my God . . . ' came out like a deep, disconnected groan.

On the floor in the center of the storage room, lay Short Blond.

Or the person who had been Short Blond.

She was nearly naked, her nurse's uniform seemingly sliced from her body and discarded in a corner. Her undergarments were still on her body, but pushed out of the way, so that her breasts and sex were exposed. She lay crumpled on her side, almost curled up in a fetal position except that one leg was drawn up, the other extended, a great lake of deep maroon blood beneath her head and chest. Streaks of red had dripped down across her pasty white skin. One arm had been stuffed sharply under the body, the other was extended, like a person waving to someone distant, and rested in a pool of blood. Her hair was matted, almost wet, and much of her skin glistened oddly, reflecting the harsh glare from the storage room light. A nearby bucket of cleaning materials had been knocked over and the stench of cleaning fluid and disinfectant stormed their nostrils. Peter the Firemen bent down toward the body, but then stopped short of feeling for a pulse when both he and Francis saw that Short Blond's throat had been sliced, a huge, gaping red and black wound that must have drained her life in seconds.

Peter the Fireman stepped back into the hallway, next to Francis. He took in a long, slow breath, then exhaled slowly, whistling slightly as the wind passed his clenched teeth.

'Look carefully, C-Bird,' he said cautiously. 'Look at everything carefully. Try to remember everything we see here tonight. Can you do that for me, C-Bird? Be the second pair of eyes that records and registers everything here?'

Francis nodded slowly. His eyes tracked Peter the Fireman, as the man stepped back into the storage room and wordlessly started to point at things. First the gash that cruelly marred her throat, then the overturned bucket and the clothing sliced and tossed aside. He pointed at a visor of blood on Short Blond's forehead, parallel lines that dripped toward her eyes. Francis could not imagine how they had gotten there. Peter the Fireman, lingered momentarily, as he pointed at the marks, then he started to maneuver carefully in the small space, his index finger pointing out each quadrant of the room, each element of the scene, like a teacher with a pointer rapping it impatiently on a blackboard to gain the attention of his dull-witted class. Francis followed it all, printing it like a photographer's assistant on his memory.

Peter lingered longest pointing at Short Blond's hand, extended out from the body. Francis saw suddenly that it appeared that the tips of four of her fingers were missing, as if they'd been sliced off and removed. He stared at the mutilation and realized his breath was coming in short spasms.

'What do you see, C-Bird?' Peter the Fireman finally asked.

Francis stared at the dead woman. 'I see Short Blond,' he said. 'Poor Lanky. Poor, poor Lanky. He must have thought truly he was killing evil.'

'You think Lanky did this?' he asked, shaking his head. 'Look closer,' Peter the Fireman repeated. 'Then tell me what you see.'

Francis gazed almost hypnotically at the body on the floor. He locked on the young woman's face, and was almost overcome with a mingling of fear, excitement, and a distant emptiness. He realized that he had never seen a dead person before, not close up. He did remember going to a great-aunt's funeral, when he was young, and being gripped tightly by the hand by his mother, who had steered him past an open coffin, muttering to him all the time to say nothing and do nothing and behave, for she was afraid somehow that Francis would draw attention to them all by some inappropriate act. But he hadn't, nor had he really been able to see the great-aunt in the coffin. All he could remember was this white porcelain profile, seen only momentarily, like something spotted through the window of a speeding car, as he was shunted past. He didn't think that was the same. What he saw of Short Blond was far different. It was dying at its absolute worst, he realized. 'I see death,' Francis whispered.

Peter the Fireman nodded. 'Yes, indeed,' he said. 'Death. And a nasty one, at that. But you know what else I see?' He spoke slowly, as if measuring each word on some internal scale.

'What?' Francis asked cautiously.

'I see a message,' the Fireman replied.

Then, with an almost crushing sense of sadness, he added, 'And Francis, evil hasn't been killed. It is right here among us and is as alive as you or I.' Then he stepped back into the corridor and quietly added, 'Now we need to call for help.'

6

Sometimes I dream about what I saw.

Sometimes I realize that I am no longer dreaming, but I am wide-awake and it is a memory imprinted like the raised outline of a fossil in my past, which is far worse. I can still see Short Blond in my mind's eye, perfectly framed, like in one of the pictures that the police came and took later that night. But I suspect the police photographs weren't nearly as artistic as my memory's vision. I recollect her form a little like some lesser Renaissance painter's vivid but journalistically inaccurate imagination of a martyred saint's death.

What I remember is this . . . Her skin was porcelain white and perfectly clear, her face was set in a beatified repose. All it lacked was a glowing halo around her head. Death as a little more than an inconvenience, a mere momentary bit of distasteful and uncomfortable pain on the inevitable, delicious, and glorious road to heaven. Of course, in reality (which is a word I have learned to use as infrequently as possible) it was nothing of the sort. Her skin was streaked with vibrant dark blood, her clothes were ripped and torn, the slice in her throat gaped like a mocking smile and her face was wide-eyed and twisted in shock and disbelief. A gargoyle of death. Murder at its most hideous. I stepped back from the doorway to the storage closet that night filled with any number of vibrating, unsettling fears. To be that close to violence is the same as having one's heart suddenly scraped raw by sandpaper.

I didn't know her much in life. I would come to know her much better in death.

When Peter the Fireman turned away from the body and the blood and all the big and little signs of murder,

I had no idea what was about to happen. He must have had a much more precise notion, because he immediately admonished me once again not to touch anything, to keep my hands in my pockets, and to keep my opinions to myself.

'C-Bird,' he'd said, 'in a short amount of time people are going to start asking questions. Really nasty questions. And they may ask these questions in a most unpleasant fashion. They may say they just want information, but trust me, they're not about helping anyone but themselves. Keep your answers short and to the point and don't volunteer anything beyond what you have seen and heard this night. Do you understand that?'

'Yes,' I'd said, but I really had little idea what I was agreeing to. 'Poor Lanky,' I repeated once again.

Peter the Fireman had nodded. 'Poor Lanky is right. But not for the reasons you think. He's about to get a real up close and personal look at evil, after all. Maybe we all are.'

He and I walked down the corridor to the empty nurses' station. Our bare feet made little slapping sounds against the floor. The wire gate entranceway that should have been locked was swinging open. There were a few papers scattered around the floor but these could have tumbled off the desk when someone simply moved too quickly. Or they might have been swept to the floor in the midst of a brief struggle. It was hard to tell. There were two other signs that something had happened there: The locked cabinet that contained medications was wide open, and a few plastic pill containers littered the floor and the sturdy black telephone on the nurses' station desk was off its hook. Peter pointed at both these observations, just as he had earlier as we had surveyed the storage closet. Then he reached down and replaced the receiver, then immediately picked it back up to get a dial tone. He pushed zero, to connect himself with hospital security.

'Security? There has been an incident in Amherst,' he said briskly. 'Better come quickly.' Then he abruptly disconnected the line and waited for another dial tone. This time he punched in 911. A second later, he calmly said, 'Good evening. I want to inform you that there has been a homicide in the Amherst Building at the Western State Hospital in the area adjacent to the first-floor nursing station.' He paused, and then added, 'No, I'm not giving my name. I've just told you all you need to know at this point: the nature of the incident and the location. The rest should be pretty damn apparent when you get here. You will need crime scene specialists, detectives, and the county coroner's office. I would also suspect you should hurry up.' Then he hung up. He turned to me and said, with just a slight wry touch and perhaps a little more than interest, 'Things are about to get truly exciting.'

That is what I remember. On my wall, I wrote:

Francis had no idea the extent of the chaos about to break above his head like a thunder burst at the end of a hot summer afternoon . . .

Francis had no idea the extent of the chaos about to break above his head like a thunder burst at the end of a hot summer afternoon. The closest he'd ever been to a crime up to that point was what he had unfortunately created all by himself when all his voices had shrieked at him and his world had turned upside down, and he had blown up and threatened his parents and his sisters and ultimately himself with the kitchen knife, the act which landed him in the hospital. He tried to think about what he'd seen and what it meant, but it seemed as if it was just beyond the reach of contemplation and more in the realm of shock. He became aware of his voices speaking in muted, but nervous fashion, deep within his head. All

107

words of fear. For a moment he looked about wildly, and wondered whether he should just sneak back to his bed and wait, but then he couldn't move. Muscles seemed to fail him, and he felt a little like someone caught in a strong current, being tugged inexorably along. He and Peter waited by the nurses' station, and within a few seconds he heard the distinctive noise of hurrying footsteps and a fumbling of keys in the locked front door. After a moment, the door flew open and two hospital security personnel burst through. They each carried flashlights and long, black nightsticks. They were dressed in matching gray work outfits that seemed more the color of fog. Outlined for just an instant in the doorway, the two men seemed to blend with the wan light of the hospital corridor. They moved swiftly toward the two patients.

'Why are you out of the dormitory?' the first guard asked, brandishing his club. 'You're not supposed to be out,' he added unnecessarily. Then he demanded, 'Where's the nurse on duty?'

The other security guard had moved into a supporting position, braced to assault if Francis and Peter the Fireman proved to be a threat. 'Did you call Security?' he asked sharply. And then he repeated the same question as his partner. 'Where's the nurse on duty?'

Peter simply jerked his thumb back toward the closet. 'Down there,' he said.

The first guard, a heavyset man with Marine Corps shorn hair and a neck that hung in fatty folds over his far-too-tight collar, pointed at Francis and Peter with his nightstick. 'Neither of you two move, got that?' He turned to his partner, and said, 'Either of these two guys moves a muscle, you let them have it.' The partner, a wiry, bantam-sized man with a lopsided grin, removed a canister of spray Mace from his utility belt. And then the thickset guard moved quickly down the hallway, wheezing slightly with the press of exertion. He had a wide-beamed flashlight in his left hand, and his baton in the right. The arc of light carved moving slices from the gray hallway as he moved forward. Francis saw that the security guard jerked open the storage door without using the same precautions that Peter had.

For a moment, he stood, frozen, his jaw dropping. Then he grunted and said, 'Jesus Christ!' as he reeled backward seconds after the flashlight's beam illuminated the nurse's body. Then, almost as quickly, he jumped forward. From where they were standing, they saw the guard put his hand on Short Blond's shoulder and turn the body so that he could try to feel for a pulse.

'Don't do that,' Peter said quietly. 'You're disturbing the crime scene.'

The smaller guard had paled, although he hadn't yet fully seen the extent of hard death that lay inside the storage room. His voice was high-pitched with anxiety, and he shouted, 'Just shut up, you fucking loonies! Shut up!'

The large guard lurched back again, and turned, wild-eyed with shock, toward Francis and Peter the Fireman. He was muttering obscenities. 'Don't either of you move! Don't fucking move!' he said furiously. He stepped toward them, slipping in one of the pools of blood that Peter had been so cautious to avoid. Then he raced back and grasped Francis by the arm and spun him around, slamming him against the wire of the nursing station, frantically pushing his face into the mesh. In virtually the same motion, he savagely crashed the back of Francis's legs with the nightstick, bringing him tumbling forward and falling to his knees. Pain like an explosion of white phosphorous burst behind Francis's eyes, and he gasped sharply, seizing air that seemed filled with needles. For a moment, his vision spun about dizzily, and he thought he might pass out.

Then, as he regained his wind, the force of the blow receded, leaving only a dull, throbbing bruise on his memory. The smaller guard rapidly followed suit, spinning Peter the Fireman about and smashing the small of his back with the nightstick, which had the same effect, dropping him to his knees with a rasping breath. Both men were immediately handcuffed, and then knocked flat to the floor. Francis could smell the unpleasant odor of the disinfectant that was constantly used to swab the corridor. 'Fucking loonies,' the security guard repeated. Then he pushed into the nursing station and dialed a number. He waited a second for someone on the other end to pick up, then said, 'Doctor, this is Maxwell in Security. We have big trouble over in Amherst. You'd better get over here right away.' He hesitated, then said, obviously in answer to a question, 'A pair of inmates have killed a nurse.'

'Hey!' Francis said, 'we haven't — ' but his denial was cut off by a sharp kick into his thigh from the smaller man. He bit back his tongue and chewed on his lip. He had been spun around, and couldn't see Peter the Fireman. He wanted to twist in that direction, but also didn't want to get kicked again, so he held his position, as he heard the sound of a siren cutting through the outside darkness, growing stronger with each passing second. It was blaring as it pulled to a halt in front of Amherst, then faded like an evil thought.

'Who called the cops?' the smaller guard asked.

'We did,' said Peter.

'Jesus Christ,' the guard said. He kicked at Francis a second time.

He aimed his foot and drew it back for a third blow, and Francis braced for the pain, but the guard didn't follow through. Instead he suddenly blurted out, 'Hey! What're you think you're doing!'

He said the question as if it were an order, no inquiry behind the sentiment, only a demand. Francis managed to turn his head slightly, and saw that Napoleon and a couple of others from the dormitory had pushed the door open, and were standing hesitantly in the entranceway to the corridor, unsure whether they could come out. The noise from the sirens must have awakened everyone, Francis realized. In the same moment, the main light switch was thrown, and the hallway burst into light. From the south side of the building, Francis suddenly could hear high-pitched, wailing cries, and someone began to slam on the locked door to the women's dormitory. The steel plates and deadbolt locks held the door fast, but the noise was like a bass drum, echoing down the hallway.

'Goddamn it!' the guard with the Marine haircut shouted. 'You!' He was pointing his nightstick at Napoleon and the other timid, but curious men who'd stepped out of the sleeping area. 'Back inside! Now!' He ran toward them holding his arm out like a traffic cop giving directions, brandishing his nightstick at the same time. Francis could see the men retreat in fear, and the guard slammed himself into the door, pushing it closed and then locking it tightly. He turned, and then skidded, as his foot slipped in one of the dark splotches of blood that marred the corridor. The door drumming from the women's side picked up in intensity, and Francis heard two other voices coming from behind his head.

'What the hell's going on here?'

'What're you doing?'

He turned again, and could just catch sight beyond where Peter the Fireman was stretched out on the floor, of two uniformed police officers. One of the men was reaching for his weapon, not drawing it, but nervously unsnapping the flap that held it in place.

'We got a report of a homicide?' one of the uniformed officers asked. Then, without waiting for a response, he must have seen some of the blood in the corridor, for he stepped forward, past the nursing station, over to the door to the storage room. Francis tracked the policeman with his eyes, and saw the man stop short outside the door. Unlike the hospital guards, however, the policeman said nothing. He simply stared in, almost, in that second, like so many of the hospital patients who stared off into space, seeing whatever it was they wanted to see, or needed to see, but which wasn't what was in front of them.

From that moment it seemed that things happened quickly and slowly, both at the same time. It was, to Francis, as if time somehow had lost its grip on the progress of the night, and that its orderly processing of the dark hours past midnight was disrupted and thrown into disarray. Before too long, he was shunted off to a treatment room down the corridor from where crime scene technicians were setting up shop and photographers were clicking off frames of pictures. Each time their flash went off it was like a lightning strike on some distant horizon and it caused the cries and turmoil in the locked dormitories among the patients to redouble in tension. At first he was unceremoniously slammed into a seat by the smaller of the two security guards and left alone. Then two detectives in plain clothes and Doctor Gulptilil came in to see him after a few minutes. He was still in his nightclothes and handcuffed, and uncomfortably seated in a stiff wooden desk chair. Francis presumed that Peter the Fireman was in similar circumstances in an adjacent room, but he couldn't be sure. He wished he didn't have to face the policemen by himself.

The two detectives wore suits that seemed slightly rumpled and ill fitting. They had close-cropped haircuts and hard jawlines, and neither man wore any sense of softness in his eyes, or the manner in which he spoke. They were of similar heights and builds and Francis thought he would probably mix them up if he were to ever meet them again. He didn't really hear their names, when they introduced themselves, because he was looking over toward Doctor Gulptilil for reassurance. The doctor, however, perched himself against one wall, and saying nothing after admonishing Francis to tell the detectives the truth. One of the two policemen sidled up next to the doctor, and leaned beside him against the wall, while the other half sat on a desk in front of Francis. One leg swung in the air almost jauntily, but the policeman sat so that his black holster and steel blue pistol, worn on his belt, were obvious. The man had a slightly lopsided smile, which made almost everything he said appear dishonest.

'So, Mister Petrel,' the detective asked, 'why were you out in the corridor after lights-out?'

Francis hesitated, remembered what Peter the Fireman had told him, and then launched into a brief recounting of being awakened by Lanky, and then following Peter out into the hallway, and subsequently discovering Short Blond's body. The detective nodded, then shook his head.

'That dormitory door is locked, Mister Petrel. It's locked every night.' The detective stole a quick glance at Doctor Gulptilil, who nodded vigorously in assent.

'It wasn't locked tonight.'

'I'm not sure I believe you.'

Francis did not know how to respond.

The policeman paused, letting some silence creep around the room and making Francis nervous. 'Tell me, Mister Petrel. Okay if I call you Francis?'

Francis nodded.

' . . . Okay then, Franny, you're a young guy. You ever have sex with a woman before tonight?'

Francis reeled back in the chair. 'Tonight?' he asked.

'Yeah,' the detective continued. 'I mean, before tonight when you had sex with the nurse. Did you ever have relations with any girl?'

113

Francis was genuinely confused. Voices thundered in his ears, shouting all sorts of contradictory messages. He looked over toward Doctor Gulptilil trying to see if he could see the tumult that was taking place within him. But the doctor had moved into a shadow, and it was hard for Francis to see his face.

'No,' Francis said, hesitancy marred the word.

'No, what? Never? A good-looking guy like you? That must have been pretty frustrating. Especially when you got turned down, I'll bet. And that nurse, she wasn't all that much older than you, was she? Must have made you pretty angry when she turned you down.'

'No,' Francis said again. 'That's not right.'

'She didn't turn you down?'

'No, no, no,' Francis said.

'You mean you're telling me she agreed to have sex, and then killed herself?'

'No,' he repeated. 'You have it all wrong.'

'Right. Sure.' The detective looked over at his partner. 'So, she didn't agree to have sex, and then you killed her? Is that the way it went?'

'No, you're wrong again.'

'Franny, you've got me all confused. You say you're out in a corridor past a locked door when you shouldn't be, and there's a raped and dead nurse-trainee, and you just happen to be there? Why it doesn't make any sense. Don't you think you could be a little more helpful here?'

'I don't know,' Francis responded.

'What don't you know? How to help out? Why just tell me what happened when the nurse turned you down. How hard is that? Then it will all make sense to everyone, and we can wrap this up tonight.'

'Yes. Or no,' Francis said.

'I'll tell you another way it makes sense: If you and your buddy got together and decided to sneak out and pay the nurse a little nighttime visit, and then things didn't exactly go the way you planned. Look, Franny, just level with me, okay? Let's just agree on one thing, all right?'

'What's that?' Francis asked tentatively. He could hear the cracks in his voice.

'You just tell me the truth, okay?'

Francis nodded.

'Good,' said the detective. He continued in a low, soft, seductive voice, almost as if each word spoken could only be heard by Francis, that they were speaking some language only they knew. The other policeman and Doctor Gulp-a-pill seemed to evaporate from the small room, as the detective continued speaking, sirenlike, enticing, making it seem as if the only possible interpretation was his. 'Now the only way I can see this happening is maybe a little bit of an accident, huh? Maybe she kinda led you and the other guy on. Maybe you thought she was going to be a little friendlier than she turned out to be. A little misunderstanding. That's all. You thought she meant one thing, and she thought, well, she meant another. And then things got out of hand, right? So, really, it was all an accident, right? And look, Franny, no one is going to blame you all that much. I mean, after all, you're here. And you've already been diagnosed as being a little crazy, so this is pretty much in the same ballpark, right? Have I got it down now, Franny?'

Francis took a deep breath. 'Not in the slightest,' he said sharply. For a moment he wondered if denying the detective's persuasive tones wasn't the bravest thing he'd ever done.

The detective stood up quickly, shook his head once, and glanced at his partner. This other policeman seemed to vault the room in a single stride, slamming his fist against the table violently, abruptly lowering his face to Francis's so that the spittle and spray from his screamed words fell all over him.

'Goddamn it! You fucking Looney Tune! You killed her and we know it! Stop fucking around and tell us the truth or I will beat the shit out of you!'

Francis recoiled, pushing the chair back, trying to gain some space, but the detective grabbed him by the shirt and slammed him forward. In the same motion, he jammed Francis's head down, smashing it against the tabletop, dazing him. When he lurched upright, Francis could taste blood on his lips, and could feel it dripping from his nose. He shook his head, trying to regain his senses, only to be sent spinning by a vicious openhanded slap across his cheek. Pain seared his face and soared behind his eyes, and then, almost simultaneously, he felt himself losing his balance, and he fell to the floor. He was dizzy and disoriented, and he wanted something or someone to come help him.

The detective grabbed him, lifted him up as if he were almost weightless, and slammed him back down into the chair.

'Now, damn it to hell, tell us the truth!' He pulled back his hand, readying it to punch Francis again, but held up, as if waiting for a reply.

The blows seemed to have scattered all his voices within him. They were shouting warnings from locations deep within him, hard to hear and hard to make out. It was a little like being in the back of a room filled with strange and unfamiliar people speaking in different languages.

'Tell me!' the detective repeated.

Francis did not reply. Instead, he grasped hold of the chair frame and readied himself for another blow. The detective lifted his hand, then stopped. He made a grunting noise of resignation and stepped back. The first detective stepped forward.

'Franny, Franny,' he said soothingly, 'why are you making my friend here so angry? Can't you just straighten this out tonight, so we can all go home and get to bed. Get things back to normal? Or,' he continued, smiling as he spoke, 'whatever passes for normal around here.'

He leaned forward and lowered his voice conspiratorially. 'Do you know what is happening next door, right now?'

Francis shook his head.

'Your buddy, the other guy who was in on the little party tonight, he's giving you up. That's what's happening.'

'Giving me up?' Francis asked.

'He's blaming you for everything that happened. He's telling the other detectives that it was your idea, and that you were the one who did the rape, and the murder, and that he just watched. He's telling them that he tried to stop you, but that you wouldn't listen to him. He's blaming you for the whole sorry mess.'

Francis considered this for a moment, then shook his head. The detective's suggestion seemed as crazy and impossible as anything else that had happened that night, and he didn't believe it. He ran his tongue over his lip and felt some swelling to go with the salty taste of the blood. 'I told you,' he said weakly. 'I told you what I know.'

The first detective grimaced, as if this response wasn't acceptable, not in the slightest, and made a small hand gesture toward his angry partner. The second detective stepped forward, lowering his face so that he was looking directly into Francis's eyes. Francis shrank back, awaiting another blow, unable to move to defend himself. His vulnerability was total. He squeezed his eyes shut.

But before the blow arrived, he heard the door scrape open.

The interruption seemed to put everything in the room into an odd, slow motion. Francis could see a uniformed officer in the doorway, and both detectives leaning toward him, in muffled conversation. After a moment, it seemed to gain in animation, though the tones stayed low and impossible for Francis to make out. After a moment or two, the first detective shook his head and sighed, making a small sound of disgust, then turned back toward Francis. 'Hey, Franny-boy, tell me this: The guy you said woke you up, the guy you told us about at the start of our little conversation, before you said you headed out into the corridor, that the same guy that attacked the nurse earlier tonight, during dinner? Went after her in front of just about every damn person in this building?'

Francis nodded.

The detective seemed to roll his eyes, and toss his head back in resignation. 'Shit,' he said. 'We're wasting our time here.' He turned toward Doctor Gulptilil, still lurking in the shadows, and angrily asked, 'Why the hell didn't you tell us about that earlier? Is everybody in here flat-out nuts?'

Gulp-a-pill didn't answer.

'Anything else that's fucking of critical importance that you left out, Doc?'

Gulp-a-pill shook his head negatively.

'Sure,' said the detective sarcastically. He gestured at Francis. 'Bring him along.'

Francis was pushed out into the corridor by a uniformed officer. He glanced to his right and saw that another set of policemen had emerged from an adjacent office with Peter the Fireman, who sported a vibrant red and raw contusion near his right eye, but a defiant, angry look that seemed to hold all the policemen in a similar state of contempt. Francis wished he could appear as confident. The first detective suddenly grasped Francis by the arm and spun him slightly, positioning him so that he could see Lanky, handcuffed, flanked by two other policemen. Behind him, far down the hallway, a half-dozen hospital security guards had cornered all the first-floor Amherst Building male patients into a tight knot, away from the spot where some crime scene technicians were photographing and measuring the storage closet. Two paramedics emerged from the pack of policemen with a black body bag placed on top of a white-sheeted gurney, much like the type that Francis had ridden when he'd arrived at the Western State Hospital.

There was a collective groan from the gathering of inmates when they saw the body bag. A few men started crying, and others turned away, as if by averting their gaze they could avoid understanding what happened. Others went rigid at the sight, and a few simply continued doing whatever they were doing, which was mostly weaving and waving, dancing about or staring at the walls. Francis could hear some muttering sounds as they spoke to one another. The women's wing had been quieted, but when the body came out, although they were locked away, they must have sensed something, because the deep pounding on the door resumed momentarily, like a drumroll at a military funeral. Francis looked back at Lanky, whose eyes seemed frozen on the apparition of the nurse's body as it creaked past him on the gurney. In the bright corridor lights, Francis could see deep swaths of maroon blood on the tall man's billowing nightshirt. 'That the guy that woke you up, Franny?' the first detective demanded, his question carrying with it all the authority of a man accustomed to being in charge of things.

Francis nodded.

' . . . And after he woke you up, you went out to the corridor where you found the nurse already dead, right? Then you called Security, right?'

Again Francis nodded. The detective looked over at the policemen standing next to Peter the Fireman, who also bent their heads in agreement. One replied, as if to an unspoken question, 'That's what this guy said, too.'

Lanky seemed to be quivering. His face was pale, and his lower lip shook with fear. He looked down at the handcuffs restraining him, then put his hands together, as if in prayer. He stared across the hallway to Francis and Peter. 'C-Bird,' he said, his voice quavering with every word, his hands pushed forward like a supplicant at a church service, 'Tell them about the Angel. Tell them about the Angel who came in the middle of the night and told me that the evil had been taken care of. We're safe now, tell them, please C-Bird.' His voice gathered a plaintive, lost tone, as if each word he spoke seemed to plummet him further into despair.

The detective instead, suddenly half shouted at Lanky, who shrank back at the force of the questions shot at him like so many sharpened spears or arrows. 'How'd you get that blood on your shirt, old man? How'd you get that nurse's blood on your hands?'

Lanky looked down at his fingers and shook his head. 'I don't know,' he replied. 'Maybe the Angel brought it to me?'

As he was replying, a uniformed officer came walking down the corridor, holding a small plastic bag. At first Francis could not see what it contained, but as the policeman approached, he recognized it as the small, white, three-peaked cap that hospital nurses often wore. Only this one seemed crumpled and the rim was stained in the same color as the streaks on Lanky's nightshirt. The uniformed officer said, 'Look's like he tried to keep a souvenir. Found this underneath his mattress.'

'Did you find the knife?' the detective asked the officer.

The policeman shook his head.

'What about the fingertips?'

Again a negative from the uniformed officer.

The detective seemed to think for a moment, assessing things, then he spun abruptly to face Lanky, who continued to cower against the wall, encircled by officers, all of whom were shorter than he was, but all of whom seemed, in that second, to be larger.

'How'd you get that hat?' the detective demanded of Lanky.

The tall man shook his head. 'I don't know, I don't know,' he cried. 'I didn't get it.'

'It was underneath your mattress. Why did you put it there?'

'I didn't. I didn't.'

'Doesn't make much difference,' the detective replied with a shrug. 'We've got a lot more than we need. Someone read him his rights. We're out of this loony bin right now.'

The policemen started to push and prod Lanky down the hallway. Francis could see panic striking like lightning bolts right throughout the tall man's body. He twitched as if electric current was flooding him, as if each step he was forced to take was on hot coals. 'No, please, I didn't do anything. Please. Oh, evil, evil, it's all around us, please don't take me away, this is my home, please!' As Lanky cried pitifully, despair echoing throughout the corridor, Francis felt his own handcuffs being removed. He looked up, and Lanky caught his eye. 'C-Bird, Peter, please help me,' he called out. Francis could not imagine ever hearing so much pain in so few words. 'Tell them it was an Angel. An Angel came to me in the middle of the night. Tell them. Help me, please.'

And then, with a final shove and push from the collected police officers, Lanky was rushed out the front door of the Amherst Building and swallowed up by what remained of the night.

7

I suppose I slept some that night, but I cannot recall actually closing my eyes.

I can't even remember breathing.

My swollen lip stung, and even after washing up a little, I could still taste blood where the policeman had struck me. My legs were sore from the blow from the security guard's nightstick and my head spun from all that I'd seen. It makes no difference how many years have passed since that night, the number of days that stretch into decades, I can still feel the pain of my encounter with the authorities who thought — even if briefly — that I was the killer. When I lay stiffly on my bunk, it was hard for me to connect Short Blond, who had been alive earlier that day, with the gory figure that was taken away zipped up in a body bag, then probably dumped on some cold steel table, to await a pathologist's scalpel. It remains just as difficult to reconcile today. It was almost as if they were two separate entities, worlds apart, having little, if any, relationship to each other.

My memory is clear: I remained motionless in the darkness, feeling the restless pressure of each passing second, aware that the entire dormitory was unsettled; the usual night noises of unquiet sleep were exaggerated, underscored by a busy nervousness and nasty tension that seemed to layer the tight air in the room like a new coat of paint. Around me, people shifted and twitched, despite the extra course of medications that had been handed out before we were all shuffled back into the room. Chemical quiet. At least, that was what Gulp-a-pill and Mr. Evil and the rest of the staff wanted, but all the fears and anxieties created that night were far beyond even the medications' capabilities. We twisted and turned uneasily, groaning and grunting, crying and sobbing, our feelings taut and raw. We were all afraid of the night that remained, and just as afraid of whatever the morning would bring.

Absent one, of course. Having Lanky so abruptly severed from our little madhouse community seemed to leave a shadow behind. In the days since I'd arrived in the Amherst Building, one or two of the truly old and infirm had died of what were called natural causes, but which could be better summed up in the word neglect or the word abandonment. Occasionally and miraculously someone with a little bit of life left would actually be released. More often, Security had moved someone frantic and unruly or out of control screaming into one of the upstairs isolation cells. But they were likely to return in a couple of days, their medications increased, their shuffling movements a little more pronounced and the twitching in the corners of their faces exaggerated. So disappearances weren't uncommon. But the manner that Lanky had been taken from our side was, and that was what caused our ricocheting emotions as we watched for the first streaks of daylight to slide through the bars on the windows.

I made two grilled cheese sandwiches, filled an only slightly dirty glass with cold tap water, and leaned back against the kitchen counter, munching away. A forgotten cigarette burned in a jammed ashtray a few feet away, and I watched as its slender plume of smoke rose through the stale air of my home.

Peter the Fireman smoked.

I took another bite of the sandwich, then a gulp from the glass of water. When I looked back across the room, he was standing there. He reached down for the stub of my cigarette and lifted it to his lips. 'Ah, back in the hospital one could smoke without guilt,' he said, a little slyly. 'I mean, which was worse: risking cancer or being crazy?'

'Peter,' I said, smiling. 'I haven't seen you in years.'

'Have you missed me, C-Bird?'

I nodded my reply. He shrugged, as if to apologize.

'You're looking good, C-Bird. A little thin, maybe, but you've hardly aged at all.' Then he blew a pair of insouciant smoke rings as he began to look around the room. 'So, this is your place? It's not bad. Things working out, I see.'

'I don't know I'd say they were working out exactly. As best as could be expected, maybe.'

'That's right. That was the unusual thing about being mad, wasn't it, C-Bird? Our expectations got all skewed and changed about. Ordinary things, like holding a job and having a family and getting to go to Little League games on nice summer afternoons, those things got real hard to accomplish. So we revamped, right? Revised and retrenched and reconsidered.'

I grinned. 'Yes, that's right. Like just owning a sofa, that's a big achievement.'

Peter tossed his head back, laughing. 'Sofa ownership and the road to mental health. Sounds like one of the papers that Mister Evil was always working on for his doctorate that never got published.'

Peter continued to look around. 'Got any friends?'

I shook my head. 'Not really.'

'Still hearing voices?'

'A little bit, sometimes. Just echoes, really. Echoes or whispers. The meds they have me on all the damn time pretty much squelch the racket they used to make.'

'The medication can't be all that bad,' Peter said, winking, 'because I'm here.'

This was true.

Peter moved to the kitchen entranceway and looked over at the wall of writing. He moved with the same athletic grace, a kind of highly defined control over his motions that I recalled from hours spent walking through the ward corridors of the Amherst Building. No shuffling or staggering for Peter the Fireman. He looked exactly as he had twenty years earlier, except that the Red Sox baseball cap that he often jauntily wore back then was stuffed into the back pocket of his jeans. But his hair was still full and long, and his smile was just as I remembered it, worn on his face in the same way it would be, if someone had told a joke a few moments earlier, and the humor had lingered. 'How's the story going?' he asked.

'It's coming back.'

He started to say something, then stopped, and stared at the columns of words scribbled on the wall. 'What have you told them about me?' he asked.

'Not enough,' I said. 'But they've probably already figured out that you were never crazy. No voices. No delusions. No bizarre beliefs and lurid thoughts. At least, not crazy like Lanky or Napoleon or Cleo or any of the others. Or even me, for that matter.'

Peter made a little, wry smile.

'Good Catholic lad, big Irish Dorchester second-generation family. A dad who drank too much on Saturday night and a mother who believed in Democrats and the power of prayer. Civil servants, elementary school teachers, cops and soldiers. Regular attendance at Mass on Sunday, followed by Catechism class. A bunch of altar boys. The girls learned step dancing and sang in the choir. The boys went to Latin High and played football. When it came time for the draft, we signed right up. No student deferments for us. And we didn't get to be mentally ill. At least not exactly. Not in that diagnosable, defined way that Gulp-a-pill liked, where he could look up your disorder in the Diagnostic and Statistical Manual and read precisely what sort of treatment plan to come up with. No, in my family, we got to be peculiar. Or eccentric.

125

Or perhaps a little weird, or slightly off base, out of whack or off-kilter.'

'You weren't even all that peculiar, Peter,' I said.

He laughed, a short, amused burst. 'A fireman who deliberately sets a fire? In the church where he was baptized? What would you call that? At least a little strange, huh? A little more than just odd, don't you think?'

I didn't answer. Instead I watched him move through my small apartment. Even if he wasn't really there, it was still good to have company.

'You know what bothered me, sometimes, C-Bird?'

'What?'

'There were so many moments in my life that should have driven me insane. I mean, clear-cut, no-holds-barred, genuinely terrible moments that should have added up to a nice, fine frothing at the mouth madness. Growing up moments. War moments. Death moments. Anger moments. And yet the one that seemed to make the most sense, that had the most clarity to it, was what put me in the hospital.'

He paused, continuing to survey my wall. Then he added, in a low voice, 'When I was barely nine my brother died. He was the one closest to me in age, just a year older, Irish twins was the family joke. But his hair was much lighter than mine, and his skin seemed always pale, like it had been stretched thinner than my own. And I could run, jump, play sports, stay out all day, but he could barely breathe. Asthma and heart troubles and kidneys that barely worked. God wanted him to be special that way, or so I was told. Why God decided that was considered beyond me. So there we were, nine and ten, and we both knew he was dying, and it didn't make any difference to us, we still laughed and joked, and made all the little secrets brothers do. On the day they took him for the last time to the hospital, he told me that I would have to be the boy for the both of us. I wanted so badly to help him. I told my mother that Billy could have my right lung and my heart, that the doctors could give me his, and we'd just trade off for a while. But of course, they didn't do that.'

I listened, and didn't interrupt Peter, because as he spoke, he walked closer to the wall where I'd begun to write our story, but he wasn't reading the words scrawled there, he was telling his own. He took a drag from the cigarette and then continued speaking slowly.

'In Vietnam, C-Bird, did I tell you about the point man who got shot?'

'Yes, Peter. You did.'

'You should put that in what you write. About the point man and my brother who died young. I think they're part of the same story.'

'I'll have to tell them about your nephew and the fire, as well.'

He nodded. 'I knew you would. But not yet. Just tell them about the point man. You know what I remember the most about that day? That it was so damn hot. Not hot like you or I or anyone growing up in New England knew hot. We knew hot like in August, when it was a scorcher, and we went down and swam in the harbor. This was an awful, sickly hot that felt poisonous. We were snaking through the bush single file and the sun was high overhead. The pack on my back felt like it had every item I needed and every care I had in the world packed inside. The bad guys had a simple policy for their snipers, you know. Shoot the guy in front on the point and drop him. Wound him, if you could. Aim for the legs, not the head. At the sound of the shot, everyone else would take cover, except for the medic you see, and that was me. The medic would go for the wounded man. Every time. You know, in training, they told us not to foolishly risk our own lives, but we always went. And then the sniper would try to drop the medic, because he was the one guy in the platoon that everyone

127

owed, and this would bring everyone else out into the open, trying to get to the medic. A remarkably elemental process. How a single shot gives you an opportunity to kill many. So, that was what happened this day, they shot the point man, and I could hear him calling for me. But the platoon leader and two other guys were holding me back. I was short. Less than two weeks in my tour left. So instead, we listened while he bled to death. And that's the way it was reported back at headquarters later, making it seem inevitable. Except it wasn't true. They held me back, and I struggled and complained and pleaded, but all the time I knew that if I wanted, I could break free. That I could go for him, all it would take was a little more effort. And that was what I wouldn't spend. That little extra push. So, instead, we had this little charade in the jungle while a man died. It was the type of situation where what is right is what will be fatal. I didn't go, and no one blamed me, and I lived and went home to Dorchester and the point man died. I didn't even know him all that well. He'd been in the platoon for less than a month. I mean, it wasn't like I was listening to my friend die, C-Bird. He was just someone who was there, and then he cried for help, and kept crying until he couldn't cry any longer because he was dead.'

'He might not have lived, even if you'd reached him.'

Peter nodded, smiling. 'Sure. Right. I told myself that, too.'

He sighed. 'All my life, I had nightmares about people calling for help. And I didn't go.'

'But you became a fireman . . . '

'Easiest way to do penance, C-Bird. Everyone loves the fireman.'

Peter slowly faded from my side. It was midmorning, I remembered, before we got a chance to speak. The Amherst Building was filled with sunlight that sent creases through the thick leftover smell of violent death.

The white walls seemed to glow with intensity. The patients were walking around, doing their regular shuffle and lurch, but a little more gingerly. Moving cautiously, because all of us, even in our mad states, knew that something had happened and sensed that something was still to happen. I looked around and found my pencil.

★   ★   ★

It was midmorning before Francis had a chance to speak with Peter the Fireman. A deceptive, glaring spring sunshine burst past the windows and steel bars, sending explosions of light through the corridors, reflecting off the floor that had been cleaned of all the outward signs of murder. But a residue of death lurked in the stale air of the hospital; patients moved singly or in small groups, silently avoiding the places where murder had left its signs. No one stepped in the spots where the nurse's blood had pooled up. Everyone gave the storage closet a wide berth, as if getting too close to the scene of the crime might somehow rub some of its evil off on them. Voices were muted, conversation was dulled. Patients shuffled a little more slowly, as if the hospital ward had been transformed into a church. Even the delusions that afflicted so many of the inmates seemed quieted, as if for once taking a backseat to a much more real and frightening madness.

Peter, however, had taken up a position in the corridor where he was leaning against the wall, staring directly at the storage room. Every so often his eyes would measure the distance between the spot where the nurse's body was discovered and where she had been first assaulted, in the wire mesh enclosed station in the center of the hallway.

Francis moved toward him slowly. 'What is it?' he asked quietly.

129

Peter the Fireman pursed his lips together, as if concentrating hard. 'Tell me, C-Bird, does any of this make any sense to you?'

Francis started to respond, then hesitated. He leaned up against the wall next to the Fireman and began to look in the same direction. After a moment, he said, 'It's like reading the last chapter of a book first.'

Peter smiled and nodded. 'How so?'

'Well,' Francis said slowly, 'it's all in reverse. Not reverse, like a mirror, but as if we are told the conclusion but not how we got there.'

'Go on, C-Bird.'

Francis felt a kind of energy as his imagination churned with what he'd seen the night before. Within him, he could hear a chorus of assent and encouragement. 'Some things really bother me,' he said. 'Some things I just don't understand.'

'Tell me some of the things,' Peter asked.

'Well, Lanky, for starters. Why would he want to kill Short Blond?'

'He thought she was evil. He tried to assault her in the dining hall earlier.'

'Yes, and then they gave him a shot, which should have calmed him down.'

'But it didn't.'

Francis shook his head. 'I think it did. Not completely, but it did. When I got a shot like that it was like having all the muscles in my body sliced, so that I barely had the energy to lift my eyelids and look out at the world around me. Even if they didn't give Lanky enough, some would have done the job, I think. Because killing Short Blond would take strength. And energy. And more, too, I suppose.'

'More?'

'It would take purpose,' Francis said.

'Go on,' Peter said, nodding his head.

'Well, how does Lanky get out of the dormitory? It

was always locked. And if he did manage to unlock the door to the dormitory, where are the keys? And why, if he did get out, why would he take Short Blond to the storage room. I mean, how does he do that? And then why would he' — Francis hesitated, before selecting the word — '*assault* her? And leave her like he did?'

'He had her blood on his clothes. Her hat was underneath his mattress,' Peter said with a policeman's stolid conclusiveness.

Francis shook his head. 'I don't understand that. That hat. But not the knife that he used to kill her?'

Peter lowered his voice. 'What did Lanky tell us about, when he awakened us?'

'He said an angel came to his side and embraced him.'

Both men were silent. Francis tried to imagine the sensation of the angel stirring Lanky from his nervous sleep. 'I thought he made it up. I thought it was something he just imagined.'

'So did I,' Peter said. 'Now, I don't know.'

He began to stare at the storage closet again. Francis joined in. The longer he stared, the closer he got to the moment. It was, he thought, as if he could almost see Short Blond's last seconds. Peter must have noticed, for he, too, seemed to pale. 'I don't want to think Lanky could do that,' he said. 'It doesn't seem like him at all. Even at his worst, and he certainly was at his scariest yesterday, it still doesn't seem like him. Lanky was about pointing and shouting and being loud. I don't think he was about killing. Certainly not killing in a sneaky, quiet, assassin's type of way.'

'He said evil had to be destroyed. He said it real loud, in front of everyone.'

Peter nodded, but his voice carried disbelief. 'Do you think he could kill someone, C-Bird?'

'I don't know. In a way, I think, under the right circumstances, anyone could be a killer. But I'm just guessing. I've never known a killer before.'

This reply made Peter smile. 'Well, you know me,' he said. 'But I think we should get to know another.'

'Another killer?'

'An Angel,' Peter said.

★ ★ ★

Shortly before the afternoon group session the following day, Francis was approached by Napoleon. The small man had a hesitancy about him, that seemed to speak of indecision, and doubt. He stuttered slightly, words seeming to hang up on the tip of his tongue, reluctant to burst forth for fear of how they would be received. He had the most curious sort of speech impediment, for when he launched himself into history, as it connected to his namesake, then he would be far more clear and precise. The problem was, for anyone listening, to separate the two disparate elements, the thoughts of that day from the speculations about events that had taken place more than 150 years earlier.

'C-Bird?' Napoleon asked, with his customary nervousness.

'What is it, Nappy?' Francis replied. They were hanging on the edge of the dayroom, not actually doing anything but patiently assessing their thoughts, as the folks of the Amherst Building often did.

'Something has really been bothering me,' Napoleon said.

'There's been a lot that's bothered everyone,' Francis responded. Napoleon ran his hands over his chubby cheeks.

'Did you know that no general is considered more brilliant than Bonaparte?' Napoleon said. 'Like Alexander the Great or Julius Caesar or George Washington. I mean, he was someone who shaped the world with his brilliance.'

'Yes. I know that,' Francis said.

'But what I don't understand is why, when he was so roundly considered such a man of genius, does everyone only remembers his defeats?'

'I'm sorry,' Francis said.

'The defeats. Moscow. Trafalgar. Waterloo.'

'I don't know if I can answer that question, Nappy . . . ,' Francis started.

'It's truly bothering me,' he said quickly, 'I mean, why are we remembered for our failures? Why do defeats and retreats mean more than victories? Do you think Gulp-a-pill and Mister Evil ever talk about the progress we make, in group, or with medications? I don't think so. I think they only talk about setbacks and mistakes and all the little signs that we still belong here, instead of the indications that we're getting better and just maybe we ought to be going home.'

Francis nodded. This made some sense.

But the short man continued, his stuttering hesitancy dropping aside. 'I mean, Napoleon remade the map of Europe with his victories. They should be remembered. It really makes me so angry . . . '

'I don't know that there's much you can do about it — ,' Francis started, only to be cut off as the small man leaned forward and lowered his voice.

'It makes me so angry the way Gulp-a-pill and Mister Evil treat me and treat all these historical things that are so important, that I could hardly sleep last night . . . '

This statement got Francis's attention.

'You were awake?'

'I was awake when I heard someone working a key through the door lock.'

'Did you see . . . '

Napoleon shook his head. 'I heard the door swing open, you know, my bunk isn't far away, and I closed my eyes tight, because we are supposed to be asleep, and I didn't want someone to think that I wasn't

133

sleeping when I was supposed to and get my meds increased. So I pretended.'

'Go on,' Francis urged.

Napoleon put his head back, trying to reconstruct what he remembered. 'I was aware that someone went by my bunk. And then, a few minutes later, passed by again, only this time to exit. And I listened for the lock turning, but it never happened. Then, after a little bit, I peeked just a tiny little peek, and I saw you and the Fireman heading out. We're not supposed to go out at night. We're supposed to be in our bunks and fast asleep, so it scared me when you went past, and I tried to go to sleep, but now, I could hear Lanky talking to himself, and that kept me up until the police came and the lights came on and we could see all the terrible things that had happened.'

'So, you didn't see the other person?'

'No. I don't think so. It was dark. I might have looked a little, though.'

'And what did you see?'

'A man in white. That's all.'

'Could you tell how big? Did you see his face?'

Napoleon shook his head again. 'Everyone looks big to me, C-Bird. Even you. And I didn't see his face. When he walked past my bunk, I squeezed my eyes shut and hid my head. I do remember one thing, though. He seemed to be floating. All white and floating.'

The small man took a deep breath. 'Some of the bodies, during the retreat from Moscow, froze so solid that the skin took on the color of ice on a pond. Like gray and white and translucent, all at the same time. Like fog. That was what I remember.'

Francis absorbed what he'd heard, and saw that Mister Evil was walking through the dayroom, signaling the start of their afternoon group session. He also saw Big Black and Little Black maneuvering through the throng of patients. Francis started suddenly, when he

134

noticed that both men wore their white pants and white orderly jackets.

Angels, he thought.

★　★　★

Francis had one other, brief conversation, while heading into the group session. Cleo stepped in front of him, blocking his passage down that corridor to one of the smaller treatment rooms. She swayed back and forth before speaking, a little like a ferryboat nestling into its berth at a dock.

'C-Bird,' she said. 'Do you think Lanky did that to Short Blond?'

Francis shook his head slightly, as if in doubt. 'It doesn't seem to be the sort of thing that Lanky would do,' he said. 'It seems so much worse than he could ever manage.'

Cleo breathed out deeply. Her entire bulk shuddered. 'I thought he was a good man. A little wacky, like the rest of us, confused about things, sometimes, but a good man. I cannot believe that he would do such a bad thing.'

'He had blood on his shirt. And he seemed to have picked out Short Blond and for some reason, he thought she was evil, and this scared him, Cleo. When we get scared, we do things that are unexpected. All of us do. In fact, I'd bet that just about everyone here did something when they got scared, and that's why they're here.'

Cleo nodded in agreement. 'But Lanky seemed different.' Then she shook her head. 'No. That's not right. He seemed the same. And we're all different, and that's what I mean. He was different outside, but in here, he was the same, and what happened, that seemed like an outside thing that seemed to happen inside.'

'Outside?'

'You know, stupid. Outside. Like beyond.' Cleo made a wide, sweeping gesture with her arm, as if to indicate the world beyond the hospital walls.

This made some sense to Francis and he managed a small smile. 'I think I see what you're getting at,' he said.

Cleo leaned forward. 'Something happened last night, in the girls' dormitory. I didn't tell anyone.'

'What?'

'I was awake. Couldn't sleep. Tried going over all the lines of the play, but it didn't work, although usually it does. I mean, go figure. Usually, when I get to Anthony's speech in act two, well, my eyes roll back and I'm snoring like a little baby, except, I don't know if little babies snore, because nobody's ever let me get anywhere near theirs, the nasty bitches — but that's another story.'

'So you couldn't sleep, either.'

'Everyone else was.'

'And?'

'I saw the door open, and a figure come in. I hadn't heard the door key in the lock, my bunk, it's way on the far side, right by the windows, and there was moonlight last night that was hitting my head. Did you know that in the old days, people thought if you went to sleep with the moonlight on your forehead you would wake up crazy? That's where the word lunatic comes from. Maybe it's true, C-Bird. I sleep in the moonlight all the time, and I keep getting crazier and crazier, and no one wants me anymore. I haven't got anybody anywhere to talk to me, and so they put me in here. All by myself. No one to come visit. That doesn't seem fair, does it? I mean some people somewhere should come visit me. I mean, how hard would that be? The bastards. The goddamn bastards.'

'But someone came in to the bunk room?'

'Strange. Yes.' Cleo shook a little bit, quivering. 'No

one ever comes in at night. But this night, someone did. And they stayed a few seconds, and then the door went shut again, and this time, because I was listening hard, I heard the key in the lock.'

'Do you think anybody asleep by the door saw the person?' Francis asked.

Cleo made a face and shook her head. 'I already asked around. Discreetly, you know. No. Lots of people sleeping. It's the meds, you know. Everyone gets knocked right out.'

Then her face flushed and Francis saw the sudden arrival of some tears. 'I *liked* Short Blond,' she said. 'She was always so kind to me. Sometimes she would share lines with me, speak Marc Anthony's part, or maybe the chorus. And I *liked* Lanky, too. He was a gentleman. Opened the door and let the ladies pass through first at dinnertime. Said grace for the whole table. Always called me Miss Cleo, so polite and nice. And he really had all of our interests at heart. Keep evil away. Makes sense.'

She dabbed at her eyes with a handkerchief and then blew her nose. 'Poor Lanky. He was right all along, and no one listened and now look. We need to find some way to help him, because, after all, he was just trying to help all of us. The bastards. The goddamn bastards.'

Then she grabbed Francis by the arm, and made him escort her into the group session.

Mister Evil was arranging steel folding chairs in a circle inside the treatment room. He gestured at Francis to take a couple from where they were stacked beneath a window, and Francis dropped Cleo's arm and crossed the room, as she gingerly lowered herself into one of the seats. He reached down and seized a pair, and was about to turn and bring these back to the center where the group was gathering, when some movement outdoors grabbed his attention. From where he was standing, he could see the main entranceway, the great

137

iron gate that was open, and the drive that went up to the administration building. A large black car was pulling to the front. This, in itself, wasn't all that unusual; cars and ambulances arrived off and on throughout the day. But there was something about this particular one that he could not precisely say, but which grabbed his attention. It was as if it carried urgency.

Francis watched as the car shuddered to a halt. After a second, a tall, dark-skinned woman emerged wearing a long tan raincoat and carrying a black briefcase that matched the long hair that fell about her shoulders. The woman stood, and seemed to survey the entirety of the hospital complex, before burrowing forward, and striding up the stairs with a singleness of purpose that seemed to him to be like an arrow, shot at a target.

8

Organization came slowly and unnaturally to them all. It wasn't, as Francis noted inwardly, as if they were suddenly rowdy or even disruptive, like schoolchildren being called to pay attention to some boring classwork. It was more that the members were restless and nervous simultaneously. They'd all had too little sleep, too many drugs, and far too much excitement, mixed with a significant amount of uncertainty. One older woman who wore her long, stringy gray hair in a tangled cascading explosion on her head kept bursting into tears, which she would rapidly dab away with her sleeve, shake her head, smile, say she was okay, only to burst forth in sobs again after a few seconds. One of the middle-aged men, a hard-eyed former commercial fishing boat sailor with a tattoo of a naked woman on his forearm, wore a furtive, uneasy look, and kept twisting in his seat, checking the door behind him, as if he expected someone to silently slip into the room. People who stuttered, stuttered more. People likely to snap angrily perched on their chairs. Those likely to cry seemed quicker to their teary-eyed destination. Those who were mute descended deeper into silence.

Even Peter the Fireman, whose calmness usually dominated the sessions, had difficulty sitting still, and more than once lit a cigarette and paced the perimeter of the group. He reminded Francis of a boxer in the moments before the bout was scheduled to begin, loosening up in the ring, throwing rights and lefts at imaginary jaws, while his real opponent waited in a distant corner.

Had Francis been a veteran of the mental hospital, he would have recognized a significant tick upwards in the paranoia levels of many of his fellow patients. It was still unarticulated, and like a kettle steadily heating toward a boil, had yet to truly start singing. But it was noticeable, nonetheless, like a bad smell on a hot afternoon. His own voices clamored for attention within him, and it took the usual significant force of will to quiet them. He could feel the muscles in his arms and stomach tightening, as if they could lend assistance to the mental tendons that he was employing to keep his imagination in check.

'I think we should address the events of the other night,' Mr. Evans said slowly. He was wearing reading glasses, which he let slip down on his nose, so that he peered over them, his eyes darting back and forth from patient to patient. Evans was one of those people, Francis thought, who would make a statement that seemed straightforward — like the need to address precisely what was dominating everyone's thoughts — but look as if he meant something utterly different. 'It seems to be on everyone's minds.'

One of the men in the group instantly pulled his shirt up over his head and clamped his hands over his ears. There was some squirming in the seats from the others. No one spoke immediately, and the silence that crept over the group seemed to Francis to be tight, like the wind that filled a sailboat's sails — invisible. After a second, he shattered the quiet by asking, 'Where's Lanky? Where have they taken him? What have they done with him?'

Mr. Evans looked relieved that the first questions were so easily answered. He leaned back on his steel chair and replied, 'Lanky was taken to the county lockup. He's being held in an isolation cell there under twenty-four-hour observation. Doctor Gulptilil went over to see him this morning and to make certain that he's receiving his proper medications in the proper dosages. He's okay. He's a little calmer than he was

140

before the' — he paused — 'incident.'

This statement took the assembly a moment or two to absorb.

It was Cleo who burst forth with the next question. 'Why don't they bring him back here? This is where he belongs. Not in some jail with bars and no sunshine and probably a bunch of criminals. Bastards. Rapists and thieves, I'll bet. And poor Lanky. In the hands of the police. The fascist bastards.'

'Because he's being charged with a crime,' the psychologist said quickly. Francis thought him oddly reluctant to use the word murder.

'But I don't understand something,' Peter the Fireman said in a voice low enough to make everyone in the room turn toward him. 'Lanky is clearly crazy. We all saw how he was struggling, what's the word you like to use . . .'

'Decompensating,' Mister Evil said stiffly.

'A real dumb-ass word,' Cleo said angrily. 'Just a real stupid, dumb-ass, goddamn completely useless bastard of a word.'

'Right,' Peter continued, picking up some speed. 'He was really in the midst of some big moment. I mean, we could all see it, all day, growing worse and nobody did anything to help him. And so he exploded. And he was already here in the hospital for all of his problems, why would they charge him? I mean isn't that pretty much the definition of someone who didn't really know what he was doing?'

Evans nodded, but also bit his lip slightly before answering. 'That's a determination the county prosecutor will have to make. Until then, Lanky stays where he is . . .'

'Well, I think they should bring him back here where his friends are,' Cleo said angrily. 'We're all he knows now. He doesn't have any family except us.'

There was a general murmur of assent.

'Isn't there something we can do?' the woman with the stringy hair asked.

This comment also inspired a round of mumbled agreement.

'Well,' Mister Evil said in a less-than-convincing tone, 'I think we should all continue to address the problems that put us here. By working at getting better, perhaps we can find a way of helping out Lanky.'

Cleo snorted in obvious disgust. 'Goddamn wishy-washy stupid,' she said. 'Idiotic, dumb bastards.' It was a little unclear to Francis precisely whom Cleo was referring to, but he didn't find himself disagreeing with her choice of words. Cleo had an empress's ability to cut to the crux of the matter, in a most condescending and imperious manner. Obscenities began to sprout throughout the group. The room seemed to fill with an unruly noise.

Mister Evil held up his hand, clearly exasperated. 'This sort of angry talk doesn't do Lanky — or any of us — any good,' he said. 'So let's shut it off now.'

He made a dismissive, slicing gesture with his hand. It was the sort of motion that Francis had grown accustomed to seeing from the psychologist, one that underscored once again who was sane and thus, who was alleged to be in control. And, as usual, it had the properly intimidating effect; the group slowly settled back, grumbling, into the steel seats, the small moment heading toward rebelliousness dissipating in the stale air around them. Francis could see that Peter the Fireman was still deep within the moment, however, his forearms crossed in front of him and his brow knitted.

'I think there's not enough angry talk,' he said, finally, not loudly, but with a sense of purpose behind each word. 'And I fail to see how it doesn't do Lanky any good. Who knows what might or might not help him at this point? I think we should be even more vocal in protest.'

Mister Evil spun in his seat. 'You probably would,' he said.

The two men glared at each other for a moment, and Francis saw they were both on the verge of something a little bigger and more physical. Then, almost as swiftly the moment disappeared, because Mister Evil turned away, saying, 'You should keep your opinions to yourself. Where they best belong.'

It was a dismissive statement, and it froze the group.

Francis saw Peter the Fireman considering a response, but in that second's delay, there was a sound at the therapy room door.

All the heads turned as the door swung open. Big Black languidly moved his immense bulk into the room. For a second, he filled the doorway, blocking everyone's vision. Then he was followed by the woman that Francis had seen through the window at the start of the session. She, in turn, was followed by Gulp-a-pill and finally, by Little Black. The two attendants took up sentrylike positions by the door.

'Mister Evans,' Dr. Gulptilil said swiftly, 'I am so sorry to interrupt the session . . . '

'That's okay,' Mister Evil responded. 'We were close to finishing anyway.'

Francis had the radical thought that they were more at the start of something than the finish. However, he didn't really listen to the exchange between the two therapists. His eyes were locked, instead, on the woman standing just between the Moses brothers.

Francis saw many things, it seemed to him, all at once: She was slender and exceptionally tall, perhaps only an inch or so beneath six feet, and he would have put her age at just around thirty. Her skin was a light, cocoa brown, close in shade, he thought, to the oak leaves that were the first to change in the fall and her eyes had a slightly oriental appearance. Her hair dropped in a vibrant black sheen past her shoulders.

She wore a simple tan trench coat, open to reveal a blue business suit. A leather briefcase was clutched in long, delicate fingers, and she stared across the room with a singularity of purpose that would have quieted even the most distraught patient. It was, he thought, almost as if her presence silenced the delusions and fears that occupied each seat.

At first, Francis thought she was the most beautiful woman he had ever seen, and then she turned just slightly, and he saw that the left side of her face was marred by a long, white scar, that creased her eyebrow, jumped over the eye, then raced in a zigzag fashion down her cheek, where it ended at her jaw. The scar had the same effect as a hypnotist's watch; he couldn't pull his eyes away from the jagged line that bisected her face. He wondered for a moment whether it wasn't like looking at some mad artist's work, where overwhelmed by an unexpected perfection, the deranged painter had seized a palette knife and decided to treat his own art with utter cruelty.

The woman stepped forward. 'Which are the two men who found the nurse's body?' she asked. Her voice had a huskiness to it that Francis thought penetrated right through him.

'Peter. Francis,' Doctor Gulptilil said briskly. 'This young woman has driven all the way out here from Boston to ask some questions from you. Would you please accompany us to the office, so that she might question you properly?'

Francis rose, and in that second became aware that Peter the Fireman was staring equally hard at the young woman. 'I know you,' he said, but beneath his voice. As he heard the words, Francis saw the young woman focus on Peter the Fireman's face, and for just an instant, her forehead creased in a sudden touch of recognition. Then, almost as swiftly, it returned to its impassive scarred beauty.

The two men stepped forward, out of the circle of chairs.

'Watch out,' Cleo said abruptly. And then she quoted from her favorite play: 'The bright day is done, and we are for the dark . . . ' There was a momentary silence in the room, and she added, in a hoarse smoky voice, 'Watch out for the bastards. They never mean you any good.'

★   ★   ★

I stepped back from the living room wall and all the words gathered there and thought to myself: There. That's it. We were all in place. Death, I think, sometimes is like an algebraic equation, a long series of x factors and y values, multiplied and divided and added and subtracted until a simple, but awful, answer is arrived upon. Zero. And, at that moment, the formula was in position.

When I first went to the hospital, I was twenty-one, and had never been in love. I had never kissed a girl, not felt the softness of her skin beneath my fingertips. They were a mystery to me, mountaintops as unattainable and unreachable as sanity. Yet they filled my imagination. There were so many secrets: the curve of a breast, the lift of a smile, the small of the back as it arced in sensual motion. I knew nothing, envisioned everything.

So much in my mad life has been beyond my grasp. I suppose I should have somehow expected to fall for the most exotic woman I would ever know. And, I suppose, too, I should have understood that in the single moment, the flashing glance between Peter the Fireman and Lucy Kyoto Jones, that there was much more to be said, and a connection much deeper that would emerge. But I was young, and all I saw was the presence, suddenly, in my little life of the most extraordinary person I had ever set eyes upon. She seemed to glow a little like the lava lamps that were so popular with hippies and students, a constantly melding, twisting form that flowed from one shape to another.

Lucy Kyoto Jones was the product of a union between a black American serviceman and a Japanese-American mother. Her middle name was the city where her mother had been born. Hence the almond-shaped eyes and the cocoa skin. The undergraduate degree from Stanford and Harvard Law part I would come to learn later.

I would come to learn about the scar on her face, later, as well, for the person who put that scar there, and the other one that she wore less obviously deep within her, set her on the course that brought her to the Western State Hospital with questions that were soon to become very unpopular.

One of the things I learned in my maddest years was that one could be in a room, with walls and barred windows and locks on the doors, surrounded by other crazy people, or even stuffed into an isolation cell all alone, but that really wasn't the room one was in at all. The real room that one occupied was constructed by memory, by relationships, by events, by all sorts of unseen forces. Sometimes delusions. Sometimes hallucinations. Sometimes desires. Sometimes dreams and hopes, or ambition. Sometimes anger. That was what was important: to always recognize where the real walls were.

And that was the case then, as we sat in Gulp-a-pill's office.

I looked out the apartment window and saw that it was late. The daylight had fled, replaced by the thickness of the small-town night. I have several clocks in my apartment, all provided by my sisters, who, for some reason I have yet to be able to ascertain, seem to think that I have a near constant and deeply pressing need to always know what time it is. I thought to myself, the words are the only time I need now, so I took a break, smoking a cigarette, and collecting all the clocks from the apartment and unplugging them from the walls, or removing the batteries that ran them, so that they were all stopped. I noticed that they were all paused at more or less the same moment — ten after ten, eleven after ten, thirteen after ten. I picked each clock up and changed both the hour and the minute hands on each, so that there was no longer even a semblance of consistency. Each was stopped at a different moment. This accomplished, I laughed out loud. It was as if I had seized time and freed myself from its constraints.

I remembered how Lucy had sat forward, fixing first Peter, then me, then Peter again with a withering, humorless gaze. I suppose, at first, she meant to impress us with her singleness of purpose. Perhaps she had thought that was how one dealt with crazy folks — in a decisive manner, more or less like one would with a wayward puppy. She demanded, 'I want to know everything about what you saw the other night.'

★   ★   ★

Peter the Fireman hesitated before replying.

'Perhaps you might first tell us, Miss Jones, precisely why you are interested in our recollections? After all, we both made statements to the local police.'

'Why am I interested in the case?' she said briskly. 'There are some details that were brought to my attention shortly after the body was discovered, and after a phone call or two to the local authorities, I felt it of some importance to personally check them out.'

'But that says nothing,' Peter replied, with a small, dismissive gesture of his own. He sat forward on his seat, bending toward the young woman. 'You want to know what we saw, but both C-Bird and I are already nursing bruises from our first encounter with hospital security and the local homicide cops. I suspect we are both fortunate not to be stuffed in some isolation cell at the county jail, having been erroneously accused of a serious crime. So before we agree to help you, why don't you tell us once again why you are so interested — in a bit more detail, please.'

Dr. Gulptilil had a slightly shocked look on his face, as if the notion that a patient might question someone sane was somehow against the rules. 'Peter,' he said stiffly, 'Miss Jones is a prosecuting attorney in Suffolk County. And I think she should be the one asking the questions.'

The Fireman nodded. 'I knew I'd seen you before,' he said quietly to the young woman. 'In a courtroom, probably.'

She looked at him for a moment or two before she answered. 'Sitting across from you, once, for a couple of court sessions. I saw you testify, in the Anderson fire case, maybe two years ago. I was still an assistant handling misdemeanors and DUI's. They wanted some of us to see you get cross-examined.'

Peter smiled. 'I recall that I held up pretty well,' he said. 'I was the one who found where the torch had set the fire. It was pretty clever, you know. Fixing an electrical outlet next to where the flammable material was stored in the warehouse, so that their own product pushed the fire. It took some planning. But then, that's what a good arsonist is all about: planning. It's part of the thrill for them, the construction of the fire. It's how the good ones really get off.'

'That's why they had us come watch,' Lucy said. 'Because they thought you were on your way to becoming the best arson investigator on the Boston force. But things didn't work out, did they?'

'Oh,' Peter said, smiling a little more widely, as if

there was some joke in what Lucy Jones had said, but Francis hadn't heard. 'One could argue that they have, indeed. It really just depends on how you see things. Like justice and what's right and all that. But, really, now my story isn't why you're here, is it Miss Jones?'

'No. The nurse-trainee's murder is.'

Peter stared at Lucy Jones. He glanced over toward Francis, then to Big Black and Little Black, who hung in the back of the room, then finally at Gulp-a-pill, who was sitting a bit uneasily in his seat behind his desk. 'Now why,' Peter said slowly, turning back to Francis, '*why*, C-Bird, would a prosecuting attorney from Boston drop everything she was doing and drive all the way out to the Western State Hospital, to ask questions of a couple of crazy folks about a death that happened well outside her jurisdiction, where a man has already been arrested and charged? Something about that death must have piqued her interest, C-Bird. But what? What could have caused Miss Jones to rush out here so urgently and ask to speak with a couple of Looney Tunes?

Francis looked over at Lucy Jones, whose eyes had centered on Peter the Fireman with a mingled look of intrigue and a recognition that Francis couldn't quite name. After a long moment, she turned to Francis and with a small grin that was skewed slightly in the direction of the scar on her face, asked, 'Well, Mister Petrel . . . can you answer that question?'

Francis thought for a moment. In his imagination, he pictured Short Blond just as they found her. Then he said, 'The body.'

Lucy smiled. 'Yes indeed. Mister Petrel . . . may I call you Francis?'

Francis nodded.

'Then what about the body?'

'Something about it was special.'

'Something about it might have been special,' Lucy

149

Jones continued. She looked over at Peter the Fireman. 'Do you want to jump in here, now?'

'No,' Peter said, crossing his arms in front of him. 'C-Bird is doing just fine. Let him continue.'

She looked back over at Francis. 'And so . . . ?'

Leaning back for an instant, then, just as swiftly pushing himself back forward, Francis thought about what she might be driving at. Images flooded him, of Short Blond, over and over, the way her body was twisted in death, and the manner in which her clothes were arranged. He realized that it was all a puzzle, and a part of it was the beautiful woman sitting across from him. 'The missing joints on her hand,' Francis said abruptly.

Lucy nodded and leaned forward. 'Tell me about that hand,' she said. 'What did it look like to you.'

Doctor Gulptilil stepped in suddenly. 'The police took photographs, Miss Jones. Surely you can inspect those. I fail to see what it is . . . ' But his complaint dissipated, as the woman made a gesture for Francis to continue.

'They looked like someone, the killer, had removed them,' Francis said.

Lucy nodded. 'Now, can you tell me why the man accused, what's his name . . . '

'Lanky,' Peter the Fireman said. His own voice had gained a deeper, more solid tone.

'Yes . . . why this man Lanky, whom you both knew, might have done that?'

'No. No reason.'

'You can think of no reason why he might have marked the young woman in that fashion? Nothing he might have said beforehand? Or the way he'd been behaving. I understand he'd been quite agitated . . . '

'No,' Francis said. 'Nothing about the way Short Blond died fits with what I know of Lanky.'

'I see,' Lucy said, nodding. 'Would you concur with

that statement, Doctor?' She turned to Doctor Gulptilil.

'Absolutely not!' he said forcefully. 'The man's behavior leading up to the killing was exaggerated, very much on edge. And he'd tried to attack her earlier that day. He has had a distinct propensity to threaten violence on numerous occasions in the past, and in his agitated state, he slipped over the edge of restraint, just as the staff feared he might.'

'So, you don't agree with the assessment of these men?'

'No. And the police subsequently found evidence in the area of his bed. And the bloodstains on his nightshirt positively matched those of the murdered nurse.'

'I'm aware of those details,' she said coldly. Lucy Jones turned back to Francis. 'Could you return to the missing tips of the fingers, please, Francis?' she asked, significantly more gently. 'Would you describe precisely what you saw, please?'

'Four joints probably sliced off. Her hand was in a pool of blood.'

Francis lifted his own hand and held it up in front of his face, as if he could see what it would be like to have the tips of his fingers severed.

'If Lanky, your friend, had performed this — '

Peter interrupted. 'He might have done some things. But not that. And certainly not the sexual assault, either.'

'You don't know that!' Doctor Gulptilil said angrily. 'That's pure supposition. And I have seen the same types of mutilations, and I can assure you that they could have been caused by any number of methods. Accident, even. The notion that Lanky was somehow incapable of cutting her hand, or that it happened through some other suspicious means is pure conjecture! I can see where you are heading with this, Miss Jones, and I think the implication is both

151

erroneous and potentially disruptive for the entire hospital!'

'Really?' Lucy said, turning once again toward the psychiatrist. The single word didn't demand an expansion. She paused, then looked over at the two patients. She opened her mouth to ask another question, but Peter interrupted her before the next word came out.

'You know, C-Bird,' he said, speaking to Francis, but staring at Lucy Jones, 'right now I'm guessing that this young woman prosecutor has seen other bodies very much like Short Blond's. And that each one of those other bodies was missing one or more joints from the hand, much like Short Blond was. That would be my guess for the moment.'

Lucy Jones smiled, but it wasn't a smile that contained even the slightest hint of humor. It was, Francis thought, one of those smiles one used to cover up all sorts of feelings. 'That is a good guess, Peter,' she said.

Peter's eyes narrowed further and he sat back, as if thinking hard, before he continued speaking slowly. He directed his words at Francis, but they were truly intended for the woman who sat across from him. 'C-Bird, I'm also thinking that our visitor here is charged, somehow, with finding the man who removed those finger joints from those other women. And that is why she hurried out here and is so eager to speak with us. And you know what else, C-Bird?'

'What, Peter?' Francis asked, although he could sense the answer already.

'I'll wager that at night, deep after midnight, in the complete dark of her room back there in Boston, lying alone in her bed, the sheets all tangled and sweaty, Miss Jones has nightmares about each one of those mutilations and what they might mean.'

Francis said nothing, but looked over at Lucy Jones, who slowly nodded her head.

9

I stepped away from the wall, dropping my pencil to the floor.

My stomach churned with the stress of memory. My throat was dry and I could feel my heart racing. I turned away from the words floating on the dingy white paint in front of me and walked into the small apartment bathroom. I turned on the hot water tap, and then the shower as well, filling the room with a sticky, humid warmth. The heat slid over me, and the world around me began to turn to fog. It was how I remembered those moments in Gulp-a-pill's office, when the real nature of our situation began to take form. The room steamed up, and I could feel an asthmatic shortness of breath, just as I did that day. I looked at my reflection in the mirror. The heat made everything foggy, as if indistinct, lacking edges. It was getting harder to tell whether I was as I was now, getting old, hair thinning, wrinkles forming, or how I was then, when I had my youth and my problems, all wrapped together, my skin and muscles as tight as my imagination. Behind that mirror image of myself were the shelves where all my medications were arrayed. I could feel a palsy in my hands, but worse, a rumbling, earthmoving shaking within me, as if some great seismic shift was taking place on the terrain of my heart. I knew I should take some drugs. Calm myself down. Regain control over my emotions. Quiet all the forces that lurked underneath my skin. I could feel madness trying to grasp my thinking. Like fingernails clawing for purchase on a slope, a little like a climber, who suddenly feels his equilibrium slip, and who teeters for a moment, knowing that a slide will turn into a fall, and if *he cannot grab hold of something, a plummet into oblivion.*

I breathed out superheated air. My mind was scorched.

I could hear Lucy Jones's voice, as she had bent toward Peter and me.

' . . . A nightmare is something you awaken from, Peter,' she had said. 'But thoughts and ideas that remain after its terrors have disappeared are something considerably worse.'

★　★　★

Peter nodded in agreement. 'I am completely familiar with those sorts of waking moments,' he said very quietly, with a stiff formality that curiously seemed to bridge something between them.

It was Doctor Gulptilil who broke into the thoughts that were gathering in that room. 'Look, see here,' he said, with a brisk officiousness, 'I am not at all pleased with the direction that this conversation is heading, Miss Jones. You are suggesting something that is quite difficult to contemplate.'

Lucy Jones turned to the doctor. 'What is it that you believe I'm suggesting?' she asked.

Francis thought to himself: That's the prosecutor within her. Instead of denying or objecting or some other slithering response, she turned the question back on the doctor. Gulp-a-pill, who was no fool even though he often sounded like one, must have recognized the same, the technique not an unfamiliar one for psychiatrists; he squirmed uncomfortably before replying. He was cautious, a good deal of the high-pitched tension had been removed from his voice, so that the unctuous, slightly Anglicized tones of the hospital psychiatric director had returned in force. 'What I believe, Miss Jones, is that you are unwilling to see circumstances that suggest something opposite to what you are wishing. An unfortunate death has taken place. Proper authorities were immediately summoned. The crime scene was professionally inspected. Witnesses interviewed in depth. Evidence was obtained. An arrest made. All this was done according to procedure and according to form. It would seem that it is time, now, to let the judicial process take over and see what is to be determined.'

Lucy nodded, considering her response.

'Doctor, are you familiar with the names of Frederick Abberline and Sir Robert Anderson?'

Gulp-a-pill hesitated, as he mentally examined the two names. Francis could see him flipping through the index of his memory, only to draw a blank. This was the sort of failure that Doctor Gulptilil seemed to hate. He was a man who refused to display any disadvantage, no matter how slight or insignificant. He scowled briefly, pursed his lips, shifted about in his seat, cleared his throat once or twice, then replied by shaking his head. 'No, I am sorry. These two names mean nothing to me. What, pray, is their relevance to this discussion?'

Lucy didn't directly answer this, instead she said, 'Perhaps, Doctor, you would be more familiar with their contemporary. A gentleman known in history as Jack the Ripper?'

Gulptilil's eyes narrowed. 'Of course. He occupies some footnotes in a number of medical and psychiatric texts, primarily due to the undeniable savagery and notoriety of his crimes. The other two names . . . '

'Abberline was the detective assigned to investigate the Whitechapel murders in 1888. Anderson was his supervisor. Are you at all familiar with the events of that time?'

The doctor shrugged. 'Even schoolchildren are familiar in a fashion with the Ripper. There are rhymes and songs, which have given way, I believe to novels and films.'

Lucy continued. 'The crimes dominated the news. Filled the populace with fear. Became something of the standard against which many similar crimes are vetted even today, although, in reality, they were confined to a well-defined area and a highly specific class of victims. The fear they caused was truly out of proportion to their actual impact, as was their impact on history. In London today, you know, you can take a guided bus tour of the murder sites. And there are discussion groups that continue to investigate the crimes. Ripperologists, they are called. Nearly a hundred years later, and people remain morbidly fascinated. Still want to know who Jack truly was . . .'

'This history lesson is designed to do what, Miss Jones? You are making a point, but I believe we are all uncertain what it is.'

Lucy didn't seem concerned by the negative response.

'You know what has always intrigued criminologists about the Ripper crimes, Doctor?'

'No.'

'As suddenly as they started, they stopped.'

'Yes?'

'Like a spigot of terror turned on, then shut off. Click! Just like that.'

'Interesting, but . . .'

'Tell me, Doctor, in your experience, do people who are dominated by sexual compulsion — especially to commit crimes, horrific, ever-increasingly savage crimes of dramatic proportions — do they find ample satisfaction in their acts, and then spontaneously stop?'

'I am not a forensic psychiatrist, Miss Jones,' he said briskly.

'Doctor, in your experience . . .'

Gulptilil shook his head. 'I suspect, Miss Jones,' he

156

said with an arch tone in his voice, 'that you, as well as I, know the answer to that question to be no. They are crimes without ends. A homicidal psychopath doesn't reach an eventual conclusion. At least not internally, although in the literature of such persons there are some who are driven by excessive guilt to take their own lives. These, unfortunately, seem to be in the minority. No, generally speaking, repetitive killers are stopped by some external means.'

'Yes. True enough. Anderson, and we suspect, by proxy, Abberline, privately theorized that there were three possibilities for the cessation of the Ripper crimes in London. Perhaps the killer had emigrated to America — unlikely, but possible — although there are no subsequent records of Ripper-type murders in the States. A second theory: he had died, either at his own hand, or that of another's — which was also not terribly likely. Even in the Victorian era, suicide was not particularly common, and we would have to speculate that the Ripper was tortured by his own fiendishness, and there is no evidence of that. Third, a far more realistic possibility.'

'Which was?'

'That the man known as the Ripper had in fact been incarcerated in a mental hospital. And, unable to talk his way out of bedlam, he was swallowed up and lost forever inside thick walls.'

Lucy paused, then asked, 'How thick are the walls here, Doctor?'

Gulp-a-pill reacted swiftly, pushing himself to his feet. His face was contorted in anger. 'What you are suggesting, Miss Jones, is horrific! Impossible! That some latter-day Ripper is here now, in this hospital!'

'Where better to hide?' she asked quietly.

Gulp-a-pill struggled for composure. 'The notion that a murderer, even a clever one, would be able to conceal his true feelings from the entire staff of professionals here is ludicrous! Perhaps one could in the 1800s, when psychology was in its infancy. But not today! It would take a near constant force of will, and a sophistication and knowledge of human nature far more profound than any patient here is capable of. Your suggestion is simply impossible.' He said these last words with a forcefulness that masked his own fears.

Lucy started to reply, then stopped. Instead, she reached down and grasped her leather briefcase. She rummaged around inside for a moment, then turned to Francis. 'What was it you called the nurse-trainee who was murdered?' she asked quietly.

'Short Blond,' Francis said. Lucy Jones nodded.

'Yes. That would seem right. Her hair was cropped short . . . '

As she spoke, almost musing to herself, she withdrew a manila envelope from her satchel. From this, she removed a series of what Francis instantly saw to be large, eight-by-ten color photographs. She glanced at these, flipping through them on her lap, then she picked one out and tossed it on the desk in front of Gulp-a-pill.

'Eighteen months ago,' she said, as the picture skidded on the wood surface.

Another photograph emerged from the pile. 'Fourteen months ago.'

Then a third fluttered down. 'Ten months ago.'

Francis craned forward, and he saw that each picture was of a young woman. He could see glossy red streaks of blood gathered around the throat of each. He could see clothes stripped and rearranged. He could see eyes open to nothing except horror. They were all Short Blond, and Short Blond was each of them. They were different, yet the same. Francis looked closer, as three more photographs skidded across the desktop. These were close-up pictures of each victim's right hand. And then he saw: One finger joint missing on the hand of the first; two on the second; three on the third.

He tore his eyes away and glanced over at Lucy Jones. Her own eyes had narrowed and her face had set. For a second, Francis thought, she glowed with an intensity that was both red-hot and ice-cold all at once.

She breathed in slowly, and spoke in a quiet, hard voice: 'I will find this man, Doctor.'

Gulp-a-pill was staring down helplessly at the photographs. Francis could see that he was assessing the depth of the situation. After a moment, he reached out and took all the pictures and placed them together, like a card sharp gathering a deck together after it has been shuffled, but knowing full well where the ace of spades was located. He fit them into a single pile and tapped it on the desk to even each edge. Then he handed the photographs back to Lucy. 'Yes,' he said slowly, 'I believe you will. Or, at the very least, make a rigorous attempt.'

Francis did not think that Gulp-a-pill meant one word of what he said. And then he reconsidered; perhaps there were some words that Gulptilil spoke that he did mean, and others that he did not. Determining which was which was a very tricky process.

The doctor returned to his seat and to his composure. For a moment or two he drummed his fingers against the desktop. He looked over at the young prosecutor and raised his bushy black eyebrows, as if anticipating another question.

'I will need your assistance,' Lucy finally said.

Doctor Gulptilil shrugged. 'Of course. That is most obvious. My help, and the help of others, surely. But I think, despite the dramatic similarities between the death we have had here, and the ones you have so theatrically displayed, that you are, in truth, mistaken. I believe our nurse-trainee was unfortunately assaulted by the patient currently in custody and charged with the crime. However, in the interest of justice, of course, I will assist you in whatever method at my disposal, if only to put your mind at rest, Miss Jones.'

Again, Francis thought each word spoken said one thing, but meant another.

'I'm going to stay here until I have some answers,' Lucy said.

Doctor Gulptilil nodded slowly. He smiled humor-lessly. 'Answers are perhaps not something we are particularly good at providing here,' he said slowly. 'Questions, we have in abundance. But resolutions are much harder to come by. And certainly not with the sort of legal precision that I think you will be seeking, Miss Jones. Nevertheless,' he continued, 'we shall make ourselves available, to the best of our ability.'

'To conduct a proper investigation,' Lucy said briskly, 'as you accurately pointed out, I'll need some assistance. And I need access.'

'Let me remind you once again: This is a mental hospital, Miss Jones,' the doctor said quickly. 'Our tasks here are quite distinct from your own. And I imagine, might seem in conflict. Or at least, that potential exists, surely, as you can see. Your presence cannot disrupt the orderly process of the facility. Nor can you be so intrusive as to upset the fragile states of many of the people we treat.'

The doctor paused, then continued with a singsong certainty. 'We will make records available to you, as you wish. But as for the wards and questioning potential witnesses or suspects — well, we are not equipped to help you in that fashion. After all, we are in the daily business of assisting folks stricken with serious and often crippling disease. Our approach is therapeutic, not investigative. We have no one here with the sorts of expertise that I believe you will require . . . '

'That's not true,' Peter the Fireman said under his breath. His words stopped everyone in the room, filling the space around with a dangerous and unsettled quiet. Then he added in a steady, firm voice: 'I do.'

Part Two

A
World
Of
Stories

10

My hand was cramped and sore, as was my existence. I gripped the stub of pencil tightly, as if it were some sort of lifeline tethering me to sanity. Or, perhaps, insanity. It was getting harder for me to tell the one from the other. The words I'd written on the walls surrounding me wavered, like heat plumes above a black strip of highway at noon on a cloudless summer day. Sometimes I thought of the hospital as a special universe, all unto itself, where we were all little planets held in place by great gravitational forces none of us could quite see, orbiting through space on our own paths, yet interdependent, each of us connected, yet separate. It seemed to me that if you gather souls together for almost any reason, in a prison, in an Army or at a professional basketball game, or a Lions' Club meeting, or a Hollywood opening or a union meeting or a school board session, there is a commonality of purpose, a shared link. But that was far less true for all of us, because the only real bond we held in common was a singular desire to be different from what we were, and for many of us, that was a dream that seemed forever unreachable. And, I suppose, for the ones that had been swallowed up by the hospital for years, it was no longer even a preference. There were many of us scared of the outside world and the mysteries that it held, so much so, that we were willing to risk whatever danger breathed inside the walls. We were all islands, with our own stories, thrown together in a location that was quickly becoming less and less safe.

Big Black told me once, when we were standing idly in a corridor in one of those many moments where there was simply nothing to do except wait for something to happen although it rarely did, that the teenage children of the people who worked at the Western State Hospital, who lived on the grounds had a ritual, whenever they had a Saturday night date; they would walk down to the campus of the nearby college to get picked up or dropped off. And, when asked, they would say that their folks were on the staff — but that they would wave toward the school, not up the hill to where we all passed our days and nights. Our madness was their stigma. It was as if they feared catching the diseases we carried. This seemed reasonable to me. Who would want to be like us? Who would want to be associated with our world?

The answer to that was chilling: One person.

The Angel.

I took a deep breath, inhaling, exhaling, letting the hot air whistle between my teeth. It had been many years since I actually permitted myself to think about him. I looked at what I had written and understood that I could not tell all those stories without telling his, as well, and that was deeply unsettling. An old nervousness and an ancient fear crept into my imagination.

And, with that, he entered the room.

Not entering, like a neighbor or a friend, or even like an uninvited guest, with perhaps a knock on the door and a pleasant, if forced, greeting, but like a ghost. The door didn't creak open, a chair wasn't drawn up, introductions weren't made. But he was there, nevertheless. I spun about, first one way, then the other, trying to pick him out of the still air around me, but I could not. He was the color of wind. Voices that I had not heard in many months, voices that had been quieted within me, suddenly began to shout warnings, echoing in my ears, racing through my head. But it was almost as if the message they had for me was being spoken in a foreign language; I no longer knew how to *listen. I had a horrible feeling that something elusive but immensely important was suddenly out of order, and danger very close. So close, that I could feel it breathing against my neck.*

★   ★   ★

There was a momentary silence in the office. A sudden burst of rapid-fire typing penetrated the closed door. Somewhere, deep within the administration building, a distraught patient let out a long, plaintive howl, unforgiving in its intensity; but it faded away, like the cry of a faraway dog. Peter the Fireman slipped forward in his seat, in the same way that an eager child who knows the answer to a teacher's question does.

'That's correct,' Lucy Jones said quietly.

These words only seemed to energize the haphazard quiet.

For a man trained in psychiatry, Doctor Gulptilil prized a certain political shrewdness, perhaps even beyond medical decisions.

Like many physicians of the mind, he had the uncanny ability to step back and survey the moment from a spot emotionally distant, almost as if he were in a guard tower staring down into a yard. To his side, he saw a young woman with some fiercely held belief, and an agenda that was far different from any he might have. She wore scars that seemed to glisten with heat. Across from him, he eyed the patient who was far less insane than any of the others in the hospital and yet, far more lost, with the possible exception of the man the young woman was hunting so diligently — if he truly existed, which was a question Doctor Gulptilil had serious doubts about. He thought the two of them might have a combustibility that could prove troublesome. He also glanced at Francis, and thought suddenly that he was likely to be swept along by the force of the other two, which, he suspected, would not necessarily be a positive thing.

Doctor Gulptilil cleared his throat several times, and shifted about in his seat. He could see the potential for trouble at virtually every turn. Trouble had an explosive quality that he spent much of his time and energy defeating. It was not as if he particularly enjoyed his job as psychiatric director of the hospital, but he came from a tradition of duty, coupled with a near religious commitment to steady work, and working for the state combined many virtues that he considered paramount, not the least of which was a steady weekly paycheck and the benefits that went with it, and none of the significant risk of opening his own office and hanging up a shingle and hoping for a sufficient stream of local neurotics to start making appointments.

He was about to interrupt, when his eyes fell upon a photograph on the corner of his desk. It was a studio-setting portrait of his wife and their two children, a son in elementary school, and a daughter who had just turned fourteen. The picture, taken less than a year earlier, showed his daughter's hair falling in a great black wave over her shoulders and reaching halfway to her waist. This was a traditional sign of beauty for his people, no matter how far removed they were from his native country. When she was little, he would often simply sit and watch, as her mother passed a comb through the cascade of shiny black hair. Those moments had disappeared. In a fit of rebellion a week earlier, the daughter had sneaked off to a local hairdresser and had her hair cropped to a pageboy length, defying both the family tradition and the predominant style of that year. His wife had cried steadily for two days, and he had been forced to deliver a stern lecture which was mostly ignored and a significant punishment which consisted of banning her from any nonschool activities for two months, and limiting her telephone privileges to homework, which prompted an angry outburst of tears and an obscenity or two that surprised him that she even knew. With a start, he realized that all the victims wore short haircuts. Boyish cuts. And they were all noticeably slender, almost as if they wore their femininity reluctantly. His daughter was much the same, still all angles and bony lines, with curves only hinted at. His hand quivered a little, as he considered that detail. He also knew that she resisted his every attempt to limit her travels around the hospital grounds. This knowledge made him bite down momentarily on his lower lip. Fear, he thought abruptly, doesn't belong to psychiatrists; it belongs to the patients. Fear is irrational, and it settles parasitically on the unknown. His profession was about knowledge and the study and steady application of it to all sorts of situations. He tried to dismiss the connective thought, but it left only reluctantly.

'Miss Jones,' he said stiffly, 'precisely what is it you propose?'

Lucy took a deep breath before answering, giving herself a moment to array her thoughts with machine-gun-like precision. 'What I propose is to uncover the man who I believe committed these crimes. These are the murders in three different jurisdictions in the eastern part of the state — followed by the murder that took place here. I believe that the killer remains free, despite the arrest that has been made. What I will need, to prove this, is access to your patient files and the ability to conduct interviews on the wards. In addition' — and it was here that the first hesitation crept into her voice — 'I will need someone who will work at uncovering this individual from the inside.' — she glanced over at Francis — 'Because I think this individual will have anticipated my arrival. And I think his behavior, when he knows I am investigating his presence, is likely to change. I'll need someone able to spot that.'

'Exactly what do you mean by anticipate?' Gulp-a-pill asked.

'I think the person who killed the young nurse-trainee did so in such a manner because he knew two things — that he could easily blame it on another person, the unfortunate fellow you call Lanky; and that someone very much like me would still come searching for him.'

'I beg your pardon . . . '

'He had to know that if investigators of the other crimes were hunting for him, then they would be drawn here, too.'

This revelation created another small silence in the room.

Lucy fixed her eyes on Francis and Peter the Fireman, examining both with a distant, detached gaze. She thought to herself that she could have found far worse candidates for what she had in mind, although she was concerned about the volatility of the one, and the fragility of the other. She also glanced over at the two Moses brothers. Big Black and Little Black were poised in the rear of the room. She guessed that she could enlist them in her plan, as well, although she was unsure if she would be able to control them as efficiently as she could control the two patients.

Doctor Gulptilil shook his head. 'I think you ascribe a criminal sophistication to this fellow — whom I am still uncertain actually exists — that is beyond what we can or should reasonably expect. If you want to get away with a crime, why do you invite someone to look for you? You only raise the potential for being captured and prosecuted.'

'Because killing for him is only a small part of the adventure. At least, that's what I suspect.'

Lucy did not add to this statement, because she did not want to be asked what she feared were the *other* elements of what she called 'the adventure.'

Francis was aware that a moment of some depth had arrived. He could feel strong currents at work in the room, and for an instant had the sensation that he was being pulled into water beyond his touch. His toes stretched forward inadvertently, like a swimmer in the surf, searching in the foam beneath for the bottom.

He knew that Gulp-a-pill no more wanted the prosecutor there than he did the person she believed she was cornering. The hospital was, no matter how mad they all were, still a bureaucracy, and subject to pencil pushers and second-guessers throughout state government. No one, who owes their livelihood to the creaky machinations of the state legislature, wants anything that in any way, shape, or form, rocks the proverbial boat. Francis could see the physician shifting about in his seat, trying to steer his path through what he guessed was a potentially thorny political thicket. If Lucy Jones was correct about who was hiding in the hospital, and Gulptilil refused her access to the hospital records, then Gulp-a-pill opened himself up to all sorts of disasters — if the killer chose to kill again and the press got wind of it.

Francis smiled. He was glad that he wasn't in the medical director's position. As Doctor Gulptilil considered the rather difficult canyon he was in, Francis glanced over at Peter the Fireman. He seemed on edge. Electric. As if he'd been plugged into something and the switch had been turned on. When he did speak, it was low, even, with a singular ferocity.

'Doctor Gulptilil,' Peter said slowly, 'if you do what Miss Jones suggests, and subsequently she is successful at finding this man, then you will get to claim virtually all the credit. If she, and we who help her, fail, then you are unlikely to get any of the blame, for the failure will be of her own making. That will land on her shoulders, and those of the crazy folks who tried to help her.'

After assessing this, the doctor finally nodded.

'What you say, Peter' — he coughed once or twice as he spoke — 'is probably true. It perhaps is not completely fair, but it is true, nevertheless.'

He looked at the gathering. 'This is what I will permit,' he said slowly, but with each word gaining confidence. 'Miss Jones, certainly you can have access to whatever records you need, as long as complete patient confidentiality is maintained. You may also select from whatever group you isolate as suspicious, people to interview. Either myself, or perhaps Mister Evans, will need to be present during any interviews you conduct. That is only fair. The patients — even those who might be suspected of crimes — have some rights. And should any object to being questioned by you, then I will not force them. Or, conversely, will recommend that they be accompanied by a legal advocate. Any medical decisions that might arise from any of those conversations must come from the staff. This is fair?'

'Of course, Doctor,' Lucy replied, perhaps a little rapidly.

'*And*,' the doctor continued, 'I would urge you to move with dispatch. While many of our patients, indeed, the majority, are chronic, with little chance at release without years of attention, a significant portion of the others do become stabilized, medicated, and then do successfully apply to return to home and families. There is no way that I can immediately discern which of these categories your suspect is in, although I might have suspicions.'

Again, Lucy nodded affirmatively.

'In other words,' the doctor said, 'there is no way to determine if he will remain here even for an instant, now that you have arrived. Nor will I stop out-processing patients who are qualified for release, just because you are searching through the hospital. Do you understand? The day-to-day operations of the facility cannot be compromised.'

Again, Lucy looked as if she wanted to say something, but kept her mouth closed.

'Now, as far as enlisting the aid of other patients in your' — he took a long look at Peter the Fireman, and then at Francis — 'inquiries . . . well, I cannot in any official manner condone such a process, even if I were to see its value. But you may do what you wish, informally, of course. I will not stand in your way. Or their way, for that matter. But I cannot allow these patients any special status or extra authority, you understand? Nor can they disrupt their own course of treatment in any manner.'

He looked over at the Fireman, and then paused as he stared at Francis. 'These two gentlemen,' he said, 'you understand that they each have a different status here in the hospital. Nor are the circumstances bringing them here, or the parameters of their stays here, the same. This could cause you some trouble, if you hope to enlist them.'

Lucy waved a hand in the air, as if some precursor to a comment, but then stopped. When she did respond, it was with a stiff formality that seemed to underscore the agreement. 'Of course. I understand completely.'

There was another brief silence, and then Lucy Jones continued: 'It goes without saying, that my reason for being here, and what I hope to accomplish, and how I might achieve that, should remain confidential.'

'Of course. Do you think I would announce that a vicious murderer might remain loose in our hospital?' Gulptilil spoke briskly. 'This would undoubtedly create a panic, and, in some cases, likely set back years of treatment. You must do your investigation as privately as possible, although, I fear, there are likely to be rumors and speculation almost instantaneously. Your mere presence on the wards will create that. Asking questions will engender uncertainty. This is inevitable. And

171

certainly, some of the staff shall have to be informed, to a greater or lesser degree. Alas, that, too, is unavoidable, and how it might affect your inquiries, I am unable to imagine. Still, I wish you luck. And I will also make one of the treatment offices in the Amherst Building, close to the crime scene, available for you to conduct whatever interviews you consider necessary. You need to merely page me or Mister Evans from the nurses' station nearby prior to interrogating any subjects. That will be acceptable?'

Lucy nodded. 'That makes sense.' Then she added, 'Thank you, Doctor. I understand your concerns completely and I will work hard to maintain some secrecy.' She paused, because she realized that it would not be long before the entire hospital — at least those connected enough to reality to care — would understand why she was there. And, she recognized as well, that made her job more urgent. 'I also think, if only for convenience, it might be necessary for me to stay here at the hospital for this period of time.'

The doctor considered this for an instant. For a moment, a quite nasty smile crept in at the corners of his mouth, but was dismissed rapidly. Francis suspected that he was the only one who had seen it. 'Certainly,' he said. 'There is a bedroom available in the nurse-trainees' dormitory.'

Francis realized the doctor did not have to actually identify who its previous occupant had been.

★   ★   ★

Newsman was in the corridor of the Amherst Building when they returned. He smiled as they approached. 'Holyoke Teachers Mull New Union Pact,' he said briskly, '*Springfield Union-News*, page B-1. Hello, C-Bird, what are you doing? Sox Face Weekend Series Against Yankees With Pitching Questions, *Boston*

Globe, page D-1. Are you going to meet with Mister Evil, because he has been looking for you and he doesn't seem very happy. Who's your friend, because she's very pretty and I'd like to meet her.'

Newsman gave a little wave, a little shy grin toward Lucy Jones, then opened up the broadsheet he had stuffed under his arm, walking down the corridor a little like a drunken man, his eyes locked onto the words of the newspaper, his attitude intent on memorizing each word. He passed a pair of men, one old, one middle-aged, dressed in loose-fitting hospital pajamas, neither of whom seemed to have ever brushed or combed his hair in the current decade. Both were standing in the center of the passageway, a few feet away from each other, speaking softly. It was as if the two were conversing, until one took a closer look at their eyes, and realized that each was having a conversation with no one, and certainly not the other, and that each was oblivious to the other's presence. Francis thought for a moment that people like them were part of the architecture of the hospital, as much a presence as furniture, walls, or doors. Cleo liked to call the catatonics *Catos* which, he thought, was probably as good a word as any. He saw a woman walking briskly down the corridor suddenly stop. Then start. Then stop. Then start. Then she giggled and went on her way, trailing a long, pink seersucker housecoat behind her.

'It's not precisely the world you might expect,' he heard Peter the Fireman say.

Lucy was a little wide-eyed.

'Do you know much about madness?' Peter asked.

She shook her head.

'No crazy Aunt Martha or Uncle Fred in your family? No weird Cousin Timmy, who likes to torture small animals? Neighbors, perhaps, that talk to themselves, or who believe that the president is actually a space alien?'

Peter's questions seemed to relax Lucy. She shook

her head. 'I must be lucky,' she said.

'Well, C-Bird can teach you all you'll need to know about being crazy,' Peter answered with a small laugh. 'He's an expert, now, aren't you C-Bird?'

Francis didn't know what to say, so he simply nodded. He watched some unchecked emotions race across the prosecutor's face, and he thought that it is one thing to burst into a place like the Western State Hospital with ideas and suppositions and suspicions, but an altogether different thing to then act upon them. She had the look of someone considering a tall peak before them, a mixture of doubt and confidence.

'So,' Peter continued. 'Where do we start, Miss Jones?'

'Right here,' she said briskly. 'At the crime scene. I need to get a feel for the place where the murder happened. Then I need to get a sense of the hospital, as a whole.'

'A tour?' Francis asked.

'Two tours,' Peter answered. 'One that inspects all this,' and with that, he gestured at the building, 'and a second one that starts to examine this,' and with that, he tapped on the side of his forehead.

Little Black and his brother had accompanied them back to Amherst from the administration building, but had left the three of them while he and Big Black conferred at the nursing station. Big Black then had disappeared into one of the adjacent treatment rooms. Little Black was smiling as he approached the group.

'This,' he said not unpleasantly, 'is a pretty damn unusual set of situations we've got here.' Lucy did not reply and Francis tried to read in the wiry black man's face what it was that he really thought of what was happening. This was, at least initially, impossible. 'My brother went in to get your new office straight, Miss Jones. And I filled in the nurses on duty that you're gonna be here for a couple of days, at the very least.

One of them will show you over to the trainees' dormitory later. And I'm guessing that right about now, Mister Evans is having himself a long and unhappy conversation with the head doc, and that he's going to want to speak with you, too, real soon.'

'Mister Evans is the psychologist in charge?'

'Of this unit. That's right, ma'am.'

'And you don't think he will be pleased by my presence?' She said this with a small, wry smile.

'Not exactly, ma'am,' Little Black responded. 'Something you got to understand about how things are here.'

'What's that?'

'Well, Peter and C-Bird can fill you in as well as I, but, to be short and sweet about it, the hospital is all about getting things to just sail along nice and smooth. Things that are different, things that are out of the ordinary — well, they makes folks upset.'

'The patients?'

'Yes, the patients. And if the patients are upset, then the staff is upset. Staff gets upset, then the administrators get upset. You get the picture? People like things smooth. All people. Crazy folks. Old folks. Young folks. Sane folks. And I'm not thinking you're about making things be smooth at all, Miss Jones. No, I'm guessing that you are all about the exact opposite.'

Little Black said this with a wide grin, as if he found it all amusing. Lucy Jones noted this, lifted her shoulders lightly, and asked, 'And you? And your rather large brother? What do the two of you think?'

At first, Little Black let out a short burst of laughter. 'Just because he's big and I'm small, don't mean we both don't have the same large ideas. No, ma'am. How you think ain't about how you look.' He gestured at the knots of patients moving through the corridor, and Lucy Jones saw the truth in those words. Then the attendant took a short breath and stared at the

175

prosecutor. When he replied, it was in a voice lowered so that only the small group could hear. 'Maybe we both think that something wrong did happen here, and we don't like that, because, if it did, then in a little way, we are to blame, and we are not liking that one little bit, not at all, Miss Jones. So, if a few feathers get ruffled, then we're thinking that ain't such a bad thing.'

'Thank you,' Lucy said.

'Don't thank me quite yet,' Little Black replied. 'You got to remember, when all is said and over and done, me, my brother, the nurses and the doctors and most of the patients, but not all, well, we're gonna still be here, and you're not. And so don't be thanking anyone quite yet. And a whole lot depends on whose feathers are the one's that get the ruffling, if you know what I mean.'

Lucy nodded. 'Point well taken,' she said. She looked up and spoke under her breath, 'And I'm guessing this must be Mister Evans?'

Francis pivoted and saw Mister Evil striding swiftly in their direction. He had a welcoming appearance in his body language, a smile, his arms held wide. Francis did not trust this for an instant.

'Miss Jones,' Evans said quickly, 'let me introduce myself.' There were perfunctory handshakes.

'Did Doctor Gulptilil inform you of the reason for my presence here?' Lucy asked.

'He explained that you have suspicions that perhaps the wrong person was arrested here in the young nurse's murder, a suspicion that I find somewhat laughable. Nevertheless, you are here. This, he told me, was something of a follow-up investigation.'

Lucy eyed the psychologist carefully, aware that his response fell somewhat short of the complete truth, but in a broadly painted sort of way, was accurate. 'So I can count on your help?' she asked.

'Most certainly.'

'Thank you,' she said.

'In fact, perhaps you would like to begin an assessment of the Amherst Building's patient files? We could begin that now. There's still some time before dinner and evening activities.'

'First, I'd like a tour,' she said.

'I can do that now,' he replied.

'I was hoping that the two patients might take me around.'

Mister Evil shook his head. 'I don't think that's such a good idea.'

She did not respond.

'Well,' he continued, puncturing the momentary silence, 'Peter and Francis are, unfortunately, currently restricted to this floor. And outside access for all patients, regardless of their status, is being limited until the anxiety created by the murder and the arrest of Lanky has dissipated. To make things more complicated, your very presence on the unit — well, I hate to say this, but it really prolongs the minicrisis we are experiencing. So for the foreseeable future, we'll be in a heightened security mode. Not precisely unlike a prison lockdown, Miss Jones, but our own version of the same. Movement around the hospital is being curtailed. Until we get the affected patients fully stabilized again.'

Lucy started to respond, but then stopped. Finally, she asked, 'Well, certainly they can show me the crime scene, and this floor, and fill me in on what they saw and what they did, just as they have for the police. That's not too challenging to the rules, is it? And then perhaps you, or one of the Moses brothers can accompany me through the remainder of the building and to the companion units?'

'Of course,' Mister Evil replied. 'A short tour followed by a longer tour. I will make the arrangements.'

Lucy turned back to Peter and Francis. 'Let's just go over that night once more,' she said.

'C-Bird,' Peter said, stepping in front of Mister Evil, 'lead the way.'

The crime scene in the closet had been dutifully swabbed down and cleaned up, and when Lucy opened the door, it stank of recently applied disinfectant, and no longer seemed to Francis to contain any of the evil that he recalled. It was as if a place of utter hellishness had been returned to normalcy, suddenly completely benign. Cleaning fluids, mops, buckets, spare light-bulbs, brooms, stacked sheets, and a coiled hose were all arranged in an orderly fashion on the shelves. The overhead light made the floor glisten, but not with any sign of Short Blond's blood. Francis was slightly taken aback by how clean and routine it all appeared, and he thought for a moment that turning the closet back into a closet was almost as obscene as the act that had taken place there.

Lucy bent down and ran her finger over the place where the body had come to rest, as if, Francis thought, by feeling the cool linoleum floor she could somehow connect with the life that had flowed out in that spot.

'So, she died here?' Lucy said, turning toward Peter. He bent down beside her, and when he did answer, it was in a low, confidential voice.

'Yes. But I think she was already unconscious.'

'Why?'

'Because the stuff that surrounded the body didn't resemble a setting where a fight took place. I think that the cleaning fluids were thrown about to disrupt the crime scene, and to make people think something different about what took place.'

'Why would he douse her body in cleaning fluid?'

'To compromise any forensic evidence he might have left behind.'

Lucy nodded. 'That would make sense.'

Peter looked across at Lucy, saw that she wasn't saying something, rubbed his hand against his chin, then rose up, shaking his head slightly. 'The other cases you're looking at. How was the crime scene in those?'

Lucy Jones smiled, but it was humorless. 'Good question,' she said. 'Hard rain,' she said quietly. 'Thunderstorms. Each killing took place out-of-doors during a rainy period. As best as anyone can figure, the murders happened in one spot, then the corpse was moved to a hidden, but exposed location. Probably preselected. Very difficult for the crime scene analysts. The weather compromised virtually all the physical evidence. Or so I have been told.'

Peter looked around the closet, then stepped back.

'He made his own rain, here.'

Lucy stepped out of the closet as well. She looked down toward the nursing station. 'So, if there was a fight . . . '

'It took place down there.'

For a moment, Lucy's head pivoted about. 'But what about noise?' she asked.

Francis had been quiet up to that point. But with that question, Peter turned to him. 'You tell her, C-Bird.'

Francis flushed, abruptly put on the spot, and his first thought was that he had absolutely no idea, and he opened his mouth to say that, but stopped. Instead, he considered the question for an instant, saw an answer and then replied, 'Two things, Miss Jones. First, all the walls are thickly insulated and all the doors are steel, so it is difficult for sound to penetrate any of them. There's lots of noise here in the hospital, but it is usually muffled. But more important, what good would it do to call for help?'

Deep within him, he heard a rumbling of his own voices. *Tell her!* they shouted. *Tell her what it's like!*

He continued. 'People cry out all the time. They have nightmares. They have fears. They see things or they hear things, or maybe just feel things. Everyone here is accustomed to the noises made by tension, I guess. So, if someone yelled out, 'Help me!'' He paused, then finished: 'It would be no different from any other time someone cried out with more or less the same request. If they yelled out 'Murder!' or simply screamed, it wouldn't be all that much out of the ordinary. And no one ever comes, Miss Jones. No matter how scared you are and how hard it is. In here, your nightmares are your own to handle.'

She looked at him, and in that second she saw that he spoke from experience on that point. She smiled at the young man, and saw that he was rubbing his hands together slightly nervously, but with an eagerness to contribute and she thought suddenly that inside the Western State Hospital there must be all sorts of different types of fears, beyond the one she had come hunting for. She wondered if she would have to come to know all of them. 'Francis,' she said, 'you seem to have a poetic streak. Still, it must be difficult.'

The voices that had been so muted in recent days had raised their own sound to a near shout that seemed to echo through the space behind Francis's eyes. To quiet them, he said, 'It would probably help, Miss Jones, if you understand that while we are all thrown in here together, we are all really alone. More alone than anywhere else, I guess.'

What he truly wanted to say was *more alone that anywhere else in the entire world*.

Lucy looked at him closely. She understood one thing: In the outside world, when someone calls for help, there is a duty for the person who overhears that plea to act. A basic civility, she thought. But in the Western State Hospital, everyone called out, all the time. Everyone needed help, all the time. Ignoring those summons, no matter how desperate and heartfelt, was really just a part of the hospital's daily routine.

She shrugged off a bit of the claustrophobia that descended upon her in that second. She turned to look at Peter, and saw him standing with his arms crossed, but a grin on his face. 'I think,' he said, 'you should see the dormitory where we were asleep when all this happened.'

And, with that, he led her down the corridor, pausing only to point at spots where blood had pooled up. But these, too, had been erased.

'The police,' he said quietly, 'thought all these blood spots were like the trail Lanky left behind. And, they were a mess, because the idiot security guard stepped all over them. He even slipped on one and fell and spread it all over the place.'

'What did you think?' Lucy asked.

'I thought they were a trail, all right. But one that led to him. Not one that he made.'

'He had her blood on his nightclothes.'

'The Angel embraced him.'

'The Angel?'

'That's what he called him. The Angel that came down to his bedside and told him that evil was destroyed.'

'You think . . . '

'What I think, Miss Jones, is pretty obvious.'

He opened the door to the dormitory, and they went inside. Francis pointed out where his bunk was, as did Peter the Fireman. They also showed her Lanky's bed, which had been stripped, and the mattress removed, so that only the steel frame and metal coils remained. The small foot locker that he'd had to hold his few clothes and personal items had also been taken, so that Lanky's modest space in the dormitory now seemed nothing more than a skeleton. Francis saw Lucy note the distances, measuring with her eyes the space between the bunks, the path to the door, the door to the adjacent bathroom. For a moment, he was a little embarrassed showing her where they lived. He was acutely aware, in that moment, how little privacy they had, and, in that

181

crowded room, how much humanity had been stripped away from them. It made him angry, and more than a little self-conscious, as he watched the prosecutor survey the room.

As always, a couple of men lay on their beds, staring up at the ceiling. One man was mumbling to himself, carrying on a discussion of some intensity. Another saw her, then rolled over to watch. Others simply ignored her, lost in whatever series of thoughts occupied them at that moment. But Francis saw Napoleon rise up, and with a grunt, move his portly body across the room as rapidly as possible.

He approached Lucy, and then, with something of a misshapen flourish, bowed. 'We have so few visitors from the world,' he said. 'Especially such beautiful ones. Welcome.'

'Thank you,' she replied.

'Are these two gentlemen filling you in adequately?' he asked.

Lucy smiled. 'Yes. So far, they have been quite accommodating.'

Napoleon looked slightly downcast. 'Ah, well,' he replied, 'that is good. But please, should you require anything, please do not hesitate to ask.' He fumbled about for a moment, patting his hospital garb. 'I seem to have forgotten my business cards,' he said. 'Are you, perhaps, a student of history?'

Lucy shrugged. 'Not particularly. Although I took some European history courses as an undergraduate.'

Napoleon's eyebrows rose. 'And where might that have been?'

'At Stanford,' Lucy Jones replied.

'Then you should comprehend,' Napoleon said, waving a single arm wide, as the other suddenly pressed in on his side. 'Great forces are in play. The world hangs in balance. Moments become frozen in time, as immense seismic convulsions shake humanity. History holds its breath; gods strive on the field. We live in times of huge change. I shudder at the significance of it all.'

'We each do what we can,' Lucy replied.

'Of course,' Napoleon answered, bowing at the waist. 'We all do what is asked of us. We all play a part on history's great stage. The little man can become great. The minor moment looms large. The tiny decision can affect great currents of time.'

Then he leaned forward, whispering, 'Will night fall? Or will the Prussians arrive in time to rescue the Iron Duke?'

'I think,' Lucy said confidently, 'that Blücher arrives in time.'

'Yes,' Napoleon said, almost winking. 'At Waterloo, this was true. But what about today?'

He smiled mysteriously, gave a little wave to Peter and Francis, then turned and walked away.

Peter lifted his shoulders, in a motion of release, with a familiar wry smile on his face. Then he whispered to Francis, 'I'll bet Mister Evil heard every word of that, and that Nappy gets his medications increased tonight.' He spoke quietly, but loud enough so that Lucy Jones could hear, and, Francis suspected, that Mister Evans, who had trailed them into the dormitory, could hear, as well.

'He seems quite friendly,' Lucy said. 'And harmless.'

Mister Evil stepped forward. 'Your assessment is accurate, Miss Jones,' he said briskly. 'That is the case for most everyone here. They mostly do harm to themselves. The problem for us staff is: which have the potential for violence. Who has that capacity reverberating about inside. Sometimes, that is what we look for.'

'That would be what I am here for, as well,' she replied.

'Of course,' Mister Evans said, shifting his eyes over to Peter the Fireman, 'with some, we already have those answers.'

The two men glared at each other, just as they always did. Then Mister Evil reached out and gently took Lucy Jones by the arm, a gesture of old world gallantry that, given their circumstances, seemed to mean something much different. 'Please, Miss Jones,' he said briskly, 'allow me to take you through the remainder of the hospital, although much of it is the same as what you see here. There are afternoon group sessions and activities scheduled, and dinner, as well, and much to do.'

For a second, Lucy seemed about to withdraw from the psychologist. Then she nodded, and replied, 'That would be fine.' But before exiting, she turned to Francis and Peter the Fireman and said, 'I will have some other questions for you later. Or perhaps tomorrow morning. If that is acceptable?'

Both Peter and Francis nodded in acknowledgment.

'I'm not certain that these two can assist you all that well,' Mister Evans said, shaking his head.

'Perhaps they can, perhaps they cannot,' Lucy Jones said. 'That remains to be seen. But one thing is certain, Mister Evans.'

'And what is that?' he asked.

'At the moment, they are the only two people I don't suspect.'

★   ★   ★

Francis had difficulty falling asleep that night. The usual sounds of snoring and whimpering, which were the night chords of the dormitory, made him restless. Or, at least, that is what he thought, until he lay back in his bunk with his eyes open to the ceiling, and he realized that it wasn't the ordinariness of the night that was disruptive, it was all that had taken place during the day. His own voices were calm, but filled with questions, and he wondered whether he would be able to do what

184

it was that was ahead of him. He had never thought of himself as the sort of person who noted detail, who saw meaning in words and actions, the way he thought Peter did, and the way that he knew Lucy Jones did. They seemed to him to be in control of their ideas, which was something he only aspired to. His own thoughts were haphazard, squirrel-like, constantly changing direction, always flitting off one direction or the next, shunted first one way, then the next, driven by forces within him he didn't really understand.

Francis sighed, and half turned in his bunk. It was then that he saw that he wasn't the only one awake. A few feet distant, Peter the Fireman was sitting up on his bed, his back pressed against the wall, knees drawn up in front, so that he could encircle them with his arms, staring out across the room. Francis saw that Peter's eyes were fixed on the far bank of windows, staring past the cross-hatched grid of iron bars and milky glass to the dusky shafts of moonlight and ink black night beyond. Francis wanted to say something, but then he stopped himself, imagining that whatever was driving Peter from sleep that night was some crackling current far too powerful to be interrupted.

11

I could sense the Angel reading every word, but the quiet remained intact. When you are crazy, sometimes, quiet is like a fog, obscuring ordinary, everyday things, familiar sights and sounds, making everything a bit misshapen, mysterious. Like a road often traveled, that because of the odd way fog refracts headlights at night, seems suddenly to bend to the right, when one's brain screams out that in truth, it tracks straight ahead. Madness is like that moment of doubt, when I wouldn't know whether to trust my eyes or my memory, because each seemed to be capable of the same insidious errors. I could feel some sweat on my forehead, and I shook my entire body, a little like a wet dog, trying to free myself of the clammy, desperate sensation that the Angel had brought along with him into my rooms.

'Leave me alone,' I said, any strength or confidence that I had sliding abruptly away. 'Leave me alone! I fought you once!' I shouted. 'I shouldn't have to fight you again!'

My hands were shaking and I wanted to call out for Peter the Fireman. But I knew he was too far away, and I was alone, and so I balled my hands into fists, to prevent the quivering from being too obvious.

As I seized a deep breath, there was a sudden pounding at my front door. The pistol-like blows seemed to burst into the reverie, and I rose up, my head spinning for an instant, until I regained some equilibrium. I crossed the room in a few, quick steps, and approached the door to my apartment.

There was another burst of knocks.

I heard a voice: 'Mister Petrel! Mister Petrel? Are you okay in there?'

186

I leaned my forehead up against the wooden door. It felt cool to the touch, as if I were fevered, and it was made of ice. I slowly sorted through the catalogue of voices I knew. One of my sisters, I would have recognized instantly. I knew it wasn't my parents because they had never come to visit me at my home.

'Mister Petrel! Please answer! Are you okay?'

I smiled. I heard a small H sound preceding the last word.

My neighbor across the hallway is Ramon Santiago, who works for the city sanitation department. He has a wife, Rosalita, and a beautiful baby girl called Esperanza, who seems a most studious child, because she stares out from her perch in her mother's arms with a college-professor's look of attentiveness for the world around her.

'Mister Petrel?'

'I'm okay, Mister Santiago, thank you.'

'Are you sure?' We were speaking through the closed door, and I could sense he was inches distant, right on the other side. 'Please, you should open up. I just want to make sure everything is okay.'

Mister Santiago knocked again, and this time, I reached out and turned the handle of the deadbolt lock, opening the door just a sliver. Our eyes met, and he looked closely at me.

'We heard shouting,' he said. 'It was like somebody was getting ready for a fight.'

'No,' I replied, 'I'm alone.'

'I could hear you talking. Like you was having an argument with somebody. You sure you're okay?'

Ramon Santiago was a slight man, but a couple of years lifting heavy trash containers in the predawn city hours had built up his arms and shoulders. He would be a formidable opponent for anyone, and, I suspected, rarely had to resort to confrontation in order to get his opinions heard.

'No. Thank you, but I'm fine.'

'You don't look so good, Mister Petrel. You feeling sick?'

'I've just been a little stressed out lately. Missed a few meals.'

'You want I should call someone? Maybe one of your sisters?'

I shook my head. 'Please, Mister Santiago, they'd be the last folks I'd want to see.'

He smiled back at me. 'I know. Relatives. Sometimes they can just drive you crazy.' As soon as that word fell from his lips, he looked stricken, as if he'd just insulted me.

I laughed. 'No, you're right. They can. And in my case, they most certainly have. And, I'm guessing, they probably will again, some day. But I'm all right for now.'

He continued to eye me cautiously.

'Still, man, you got me a little worried. You taking your pills okay?'

I shrugged. 'Yes,' I lied. I could tell he didn't believe me. He continued to look closely at me, his eyes fixed on my face, as if he was searching every wrinkle, every line, for something that he would recognize, as if the illness I carried could be identified like some rash on my skin, or jaundice. Without taking his eyes off me, he threw a couple of words back over his shoulder in Spanish, and I saw his wife and their little child, hanging in the entranceway to their apartment. Rosalita looked a little frightened, and she lifted her hand and gave me a little wave. The baby, too, returned my own smile. Then Mister Santiago switched back into English.

'Rosie,' he said, demanding, yet not angrily, 'go fix up Mister Petrel a paper plate with some of that rice and chicken we're having for dinner. He looks like he could use a good solid meal.'

I saw her nod, give me a shy little smile of her own, and disappear inside their apartment. 'Really, Mister Santiago, that's kind of you, but not necessary . . .'

'It's not a problem. Arroz con pollo. Where I come from, Mister Petrel, it fixes just about everything. You sick, you get rice and chicken. You get fired from your job? You get rice and chicken. You got a broken heart?'

' . . . Rice and chicken,' I said, finishing the sentence for him.

'That's one hundred percent right.' We grinned together.

Rosie returned a few seconds later with a paper plate piled high with steaming chicken and fluffy yellow rice. She brought it across the corridor to me and I took it from her, just grazing her hand slightly, and thinking that it had been some time since I'd actually felt another human's touch. 'You don't have to . . . ,' I started again, but both the Santiagos were shaking their heads.

'You sure you don't want me to call somebody? If not your family, how 'bout social services? Or a friend, maybe?'

'Don't have too many friends anymore, Mister Santiago.'

'Ah, Mister Petrel, you got more folks care about you than you think,' he said.

I shook my head again.

'Someone else then?'

'No. Really.'

'You sure you weren't being bothered by somebody? I heard voices raised. Sounds to me like a fight about to be starting . . .'

I smiled, because the truth was that I was being bothered by someone. They just weren't there. I cracked open my door and let him peer inside. 'All alone, I promise,' I said. But I saw his eyes leap across the room and catch a glimpse of the words I was placing

189

on the walls. In that instant, I thought he would say something, but then he stopped. He reached out, and put a hand on my shoulder.

'You need some help, Mister Petrel, you just knock on my door. Anytime. Day or night. You got that?'

'Thank you, Mister Santiago,' I said, nodding my head. 'And thank you for the dinner.'

I closed the door, and took a deep breath, filling my nostrils with the aroma of the food. It seemed suddenly as if it had been days since I'd eaten. Perhaps it had been, although I remembered grilled cheese. But when was that? I found a fork in a drawer and tore into Rosalita's specialty. I wondered whether arroz con pollo, which was good for so many ailments of the spirit, might help my own. To my surprise, each bite seemed to energize me, and as I chewed away, I saw the progress I had made on the wall. Columns of history.

And I realized I was alone again.

He would be back. I had no doubt about that. He was lurking, vaporous, in some space just beyond my reach, and eluding my consciousness. Avoiding me. Avoiding the Santiago family. Avoiding the arroz con pollo. Hiding from my memory. But for the moment, to my great relief, all I had was chicken, rice, and words. I thought to myself: All that talk in Gulp-a-pill's office about keeping things confidential had been nothing but showy emptiness.

★   ★   ★

It did not take long for all the patients and staff to become aware of Lucy Jones's presence in the Amherst Building. It was not merely the way she dressed, in loose dark slacks and sweater, carrying her leather briefcase with an orderliness that defied the more slovenly character of the hospital. Nor was it her height and bearing, or the distinctive scar on her face, that separated her from the regulars. It was more in the way she passed through the corridors, heels clicking on the linoleum floor, with an alertness in her eyes that made it seem as if she was inspecting everything and everyone, and searching for some telltale sign that might lead her in the direction she needed. It was an awareness that wasn't defined by paranoia, visions, or voices. Even the Catos standing in the corners, or leaning up against the walls, or the senile elderly locked into their wheelchairs, all seemingly lost inside their own reveries, or the mentally retarded, who stared dully at almost all that happened around them, seemed to take some strange note that Lucy was driven by forces every bit as powerful as those they all struggled with, but that hers were somehow more appropriate. More connected to the world. So when she paced past them, the patients would follow her with their eyes, not interrupting their murmuring and mumbling, or the shakiness in their hands, but still watching her with an attentiveness that seemed to defy their own illnesses. Even at mealtimes, which she took in the cafeteria with the patients and staff, waiting in line like everyone else for the plates of nondescript, institutionalized food, she was someone apart. She took to sitting at a corner table, where she could look out at the other people in the room, her back to a painted lime green cinder block wall. Occasionally, someone would join her at the table, either Mister Evil, who seemed most interested in everything she was doing, or Big Black or Little Black, who immediately turned any conversation over to sports. Sometimes some of the nursing staff would sit with her, but their stark white uniforms and peaked caps set her even more apart from the regular hospital routine. And when she conversed with one of her companions, she seemed to constantly slip-slide her glance around the room, giving Francis the impression that she was a little like a field hawk soaring on wind currents above them all, looking

191

down, trying to spot some movement in the withered brown stalks of the early New England spring and isolating her prey.

None of the patients sat with her, including, at the start, Francis or Peter the Fireman. This had been Peter's suggestion. He had told her that there was no sense in letting too many folks know that they were working with her, although people would figure it out for themselves before too much time had passed. So, at least for the first days, Francis and Peter ignored her in the dining hall.

Cleo, however, did not.

As Lucy was carrying her tray to the refuse station, the portly patient accosted her.

'I know why you're here!' Cleo said. She was loud, and forcefully accusatory, and had it not been for the usual dinnertime clatter of dishes, trays, and plates, her tone of voice might have grabbed everyone's attention.

'Do you now?' Lucy calmly replied. She stepped past Cleo and began to scrape leftovers from a sturdy white plate into a trash canister.

'Indeed, yes,' Cleo continued with a matter-of-fact tone. 'It is obvious.'

'Really?'

'Yes,' Cleo went on, filled with bluster and the peculiar bravado that madness sometimes has, where it releases all the ordinary brakes on behavior.

'Then perhaps you should tell me what you think.'

'Aha! Of course. You mean to take over Egypt!'

'Egypt?'

'Egypt,' Cleo said, waving her hand to indicate the entire room, motioning in a slightly exasperated fashion at the clarity of it all, which had initially eluded Lucy Jones. 'My Egypt. Followed pretty damn fast by seducing Marc Anthony and Caesar, as well, I wouldn't doubt.'

Cleo harumphed loudly, crossed her arms for a

moment, blocklike in Lucy's path, and then added, as was her usual response to just about everything, 'The bastards. The damn bastards.'

Lucy Jones looked quizzically at her, then shook her head. 'No, in that, you are decidedly mistaken. Egypt is safe in your hands. I would never presume to rival anyone for such a crown, nor for the loves of their life.'

Cleo lowered her hands to her hips and stared at Lucy. 'Why should I believe you?' she demanded.

'You will need to take my word on this.'

The large woman hesitated, then scratched at the twisted mangle of hair she wore on top of her head. 'Are you a person of honesty and integrity?' she asked abruptly.

'I am told that I am,' Lucy replied.

'Gulp-a-pill and Mister Evil would say the same, but I do not trust them.'

'Nor do I,' Lucy said quietly, leaning forward slightly. 'On that count, we can certainly agree.'

'Then, if you do not mean to conquer Egypt, why are you here?' Cleo asked, putting her hands back on her hips, and resuming an aggressively intuitive tone.

'I think there is a traitor in your kingdom,' Lucy said slowly.

'What sort of traitor?'

'The worst sort.'

Cleo nodded. 'This has to do with Lanky's arrest and Short Blond's murder, doesn't it?'

'Yes,' Lucy replied.

'I saw him,' Cleo said. 'Not well, but I saw him. That night.'

'Who? Who did you see?' Lucy asked, suddenly alert, leaning forward.

Cleo smiled catlike, knowingly, then she shrugged. 'If you need my help,' she said, a sudden portrait of haughtiness, her voice dripping with entitlement, 'then you should apply for it in an appropriate fashion, at the correct time, at a proper place.'

With that, Cleo stepped back, and after taking a moment to light a cigarette with a flourish, she spun away, a look of satisfaction on her face. Lucy appeared a little confused, and took a step after her, only to be intercepted by Peter the Fireman, who had carried his tray up to the refuse counter at that moment, although Francis could see that he had barely touched any of his food. He began to scrape his plate, and thrust the utensils through an opening into the cleaning station. As he did this, Francis heard him say to Lucy, 'It's true. She saw the Angel that night. She told us that he entered the women's dormitory, stood there for a moment, then exited, locking the door behind him.'

Lucy Jones nodded. 'Curious behavior,' she said, although even she realized that this particular observation was somewhat useless inside a mental hospital where all the behavior was, at best, curious, and at worse, something truly awful. She looked over at Francis, who had risen and now stood next to them. 'C-Bird, tell me why would someone who has just committed a violent crime, taken the extraordinary trouble to cover up his tracks and worked hard to see that someone else is blamed for the crime and should by all rights want to disappear and hide, enter into a room filled with women who, if any one of them happened to awaken, might remember him?'

Francis shook his head. He wondered to himself: *Could they remember him?* He could hear several of his voices vying within him to answer that question, but he ignored them and instead fixed on Lucy's eyes. She shrugged.

'A riddle,' Lucy said. 'But an answer I'll need sooner or later. Do you think you could get me that answer, Francis?'

He nodded.

She laughed a bit. 'C-Bird has confidence. Good thing,' she said.

And then she led them out into the corridor.

She started to say another thing, but Peter held up his hand. 'C-Bird, don't let anyone else know what Cleo saw.' Then he turned to Lucy Jones. 'When Francis first spoke with her, and she first mentioned that the man we're seeking entered the women's dormitory, she was unable to really provide any sort of coherent description of the Angel. Everyone was pretty upset. Perhaps, now that she has had a little more time to reflect on that night, she might have noticed something important. She likes Francis. I think it might be wise if he went and spoke with her again about the events that night. This would have the added advantage of not drawing any attention to her, because as soon as you start questioning her, people will understand she might have some connection to all this.'

Lucy considered what Peter said, and then nodded. 'That makes some sense. Francis, can you handle that by yourself, and then get back to me?'

Francis said, 'Yes,' but he was unsure of himself, despite what Lucy had said about his confidence. He couldn't remember actually ever questioning someone to try to elicit information.

Newsman wandered past them at that moment, stopping a few feet distant, doing a little balletlike pirouette on the polished floor, his shoes squeaking as he spun, then saying, '*Union-News:* Market plunges in bad economic news.' Then, with a flourish, he spun about again, and tacked down the hallway, a newspaper held out in front of him like a sail.

'If I go talk to Cleo again,' Francis asked, 'what will you do, Peter?'

'What will I do? It's a little more like 'What would I like?' What I would like, C-Bird, is for Miss Jones to be more forthcoming with the files she has brought with her.'

Lucy didn't reply at first, and Peter turned to face her.

'It would help us to have a little better idea of the details that brought you here, if we are to help you while you stay.'

Again, she seemed to hesitate. 'Why do you think — ,' she started, only to have Peter interrupt her. He was smiling, in that offhand way he had, which meant, at least to Francis, that he had found something amusing and slightly unusual, all at once.

'You brought the files with you, for the same reasons that I would have. Or anyone else who was investigating a case that is barely better than a supposition would have. Because you will need to reassure yourself of similarities, at virtually every stage. And, because somewhere, Miss Jones, you have a boss, as well, who is going to want to see some progress quickly. Probably a boss, like all bosses, with a short fuse on his temper, and a highly exaggerated political sense of how his young assistants should be spending their time profitably. So, our first real order of business is to determine common threads, between what went before, in those other killings, and what happened here. So, I think I should see those files.'

Lucy took a deep breath. 'Interestingly enough, Mister Evans asked me for the same thing, this morning, using more or less the same rationale.'

'Great minds must think alike,' Peter said. This was spoken with unconcealed sarcasm.

'I refused his request.'

Peter hesitated, then said, 'That's because you are as yet uncertain whether he is trustworthy.' This, too, was amusing, and he seemed to laugh on the tail end of the sentence.

Lucy smiled. 'More or less precisely what I just told

the lady you call Cleo.'

'But C-Bird and I, well, we are in a different category, are we not?'

'Yes. A pair of innocents. But if I show you these . . . '

'You will anger Mister Evans. Tough.'

Again, Lucy paused, before replying, this time with a hesitancy born of curiosity in her voice. 'Peter,' she said slowly, 'do you care so little about who it is that you piss off? Especially someone whose opinion as to your current mental state could be so critical for your own future . . . '

Peter seemed about to laugh out loud, and ran a hand through his hair, shrugging and then shaking his head with the same off-balance smile. 'The short answer to your questions is *Yes*. I care very little who I piss off. Evans hates me. And whatever I do or say, he's still going to hate me, and it is not because of who I am as much as because of what I did. So I don't really hold out any hope for him to change. Probably not fair for me to ask him to change, either. And, he's probably not alone in the We Hate Peter Club around here, he's just the most obvious, and, I might add, the most obnoxious. Nothing I do is ever going to change that. So, why should I concern myself with him?'

Lucy, too, smiled slightly. It made the scar on her face curve, and Francis thought suddenly that the most curious thing about a blemish as profound as hers was that it made the rest of her beauty all that more substantial.

'I protest too much?' Peter asked, still grinning.

'What is it they say about the Irish?'

'They say a lot. But mainly that we like to hear ourselves speak. This is the most dramatically trite cliché. But, alas, one based on centuries of truth.'

'All right,' Lucy said. 'Francis, why don't you go and see Miss Cleo, while Peter accompanies me to my little office.'

Francis hesitated, and Lucy asked again, 'If that's all right with you?'

He bent his head in agreement. It was a strange sensation, he thought. He indeed wanted to help her, because every time he looked at her, he thought she was more beautiful than before. But he was a little jealous of Peter getting to accompany her, while he had to launch himself after Cleo. His voices, still muted, rumbled within him. But he ignored the noise and after a momentary hesitation, hurried down the corridor toward the dayroom, where he suspected Cleo would be behind the Ping-Pong table, in her customary spot, trying to enlist victims in a game.

★   ★   ★

Francis was correct. Cleo was roosted in the back of the dayroom, by the Ping-Pong table. She had arranged three other patients on the side opposite her, equipping each with a paddle, and showing them a designated area, where they were to respond if her shot landed there. She also demonstrated to each patient how they should crouch down, and grip the paddle, and shift their weight to the balls of their feet in anticipation of action. It was, Francis saw, a miniclinic in how to play the game. And, he guessed, destined for failure. They were all older men, with stringy gray hair and flaccid skin marked by brown age spots. He could see each of them unhappily trying to focus on what they were being told, and struggling with their responsibilities. These simple tasks were magnified in the moment before the game was to begin, and he could also see that the more urgent the need to reply to Cleo's opening Ping-Pong salvo was, the less capable they were of meeting it, no matter how well she had instructed them.

Cleo said 'Ready?' three times, looking each in the eyes, as she prepared to serve the ball.

Each of the opponents reluctantly nodded.

With a flick of the wrist, Cleo launched the ball vertically. Then her paddle came forward with snakelike speed, and knocked it across the table, where it landed once on her side of the table, clicking loudly, then jumping the net, striking the other side, spinning and passing directly between two of the opponents, neither of whom budged in the slightest.

Francis thought Cleo would explode. She reddened, and her upper lip seemed to curl back in anger. But then, just as swiftly the whirlwind of fury dissipated. One of the opponents retrieved the little white ball and tossed it across the table to her. She set it down on the green surface, beneath her own paddle.

'Thanks for the game.' She sighed, replacing all the anger on her face with resignation. 'We'll work on our footwork a little more later.'

The three opponents all looked significantly relieved, and wandered off to distant corners of the room.

The dayroom was crowded as usual, with a bizarre mixture of activities. It was an open, well-lit room, with a bank of steel barred windows on one wall that let in the sunshine, and an occasional mild breeze. The glistening white painted walls seemed to reflect the light and energy in the space. Patients in various forms of dress, ranging from the ubiquitous loose-fitting robes and slippers to jeans and overcoats, milled about the room. There were cheap red and green leather couches and well-worn armchairs spread about the space, and these were occupied by men or women who sat quietly reading, despite the hum of noise that filled the room. At least, they appeared to be reading, but pages turned only infrequently. There were out-of-date magazines and tattered paperback novels on sturdy wooden coffee tables. In two of the corners there were television sets, which each had a passel of regulars gathered around, absorbing the soap operas. The pair of television sets

199

were in dialogue conflict, tuned to different stations, as if the characters on each show were squaring off against the other network. This was a concession to the near daily fights that had sprung up between devotees of one show, versus those favoring a competing show.

Francis continued to look around and saw there were some patients playing board games, like Monopoly or Risk, a couple of chess and checkers games and some patients that played cards. Hearts was the dayroom favorite. Poker had been banned by Gulp-a-pill when cigarettes were used as chips a little too often, and some patients began hoarding them. These were the less crazy ones, or, Francis thought, the people who hadn't checked all connections to the outside world at the door, when they were shipped off to the hospital. He would have put himself in the same category, a distinction all the voices he heard within him agreed with. And then, of course, there were the Catos, just wandering about the space, speaking to no one and everyone, all at once. Some danced. Some shuffled. Some walked briskly back and forth. But all had their own pace, driven by visions so distant that Francis could only guess what they contained. They made him sad, and they frightened him a little, because he feared becoming like them. Sometimes, he thought, on the balance beam of his own life he was closer to them than he was to normal. He considered them doomed.

A thin haze of blue cigarette smoke hovered over everyone. Francis hated the room, and tried as much as possible to avoid it.

It was a place where everyone's out of control thoughts had free rein.

Cleo, of course, ruled the Ping-Pong table and its immediate surroundings.

Her blustery manner and fearsome appearance cowed most of the other patients, including, to some degree, Francis. But, at the same time, he believed she had a liveliness that most of the others lacked, which he enjoyed, and he knew she could be funny, and frequently managed to make others laugh, a valuable and rare quality in the hospital. She spotted him hovering on the edge of the area, and grinned wildly.

'C-Bird! Come to give me some competition?' she asked.

'Only if forced,' Francis said.

'Then I insist. Forcing you. Please . . .'

He walked over and picked up a paddle. 'I need to speak with you about what you saw the other night.'

'The night of the murder? Did the woman prosecutor send you to ask me?'

He nodded.

'It has something to do with the traitor she is searching for?'

'Correct.'

Cleo seemed to think for a moment, then she held up the small white Ping-Pong ball, eyeing it closely. 'Tell you what,' she said. 'You can ask your questions while we play. As long as you keep returning the ball, I'll keep answering your questions. We'll make it into a game within a game.'

'I don't know . . . ,' Francis started, but Cleo dismissed his protest with a nonchalant wave.

'It will be a challenge,' she said.

With that, she flipped the ball into the air and served it toward him. Francis reached across the green table, and punched the ball back. Cleo returned it to him easily, and suddenly a rhythmic clicking filled the space, as the ball went back and forth.

'Have you thought about what you saw that night?' Francis asked, as he stretched forward for his shot.

'Of course,' Cleo replied, easily flicking the ball back toward him. 'And the more I think about it, the more intrigued I get. There is much afoot here in Egypt. Rome, too, has its interests, no?'

'How so?' Francis said, grunting this time, but keeping the ball in play.

'What I saw only took a few seconds,' Cleo said, 'but I think it said a lot.'

'Go on,' Francis said.

Cleo returned the next shot with a little more pace and a little more angle, so that he had to reach to his backhand to get it back, which he did, surprising himself. He saw Cleo grin as she gathered his return and parried it easily. 'Entering the room, and surveying it, after he'd done all that he'd done,' Cleo said, 'indicated to me that he's not really afraid of very much, is he?'

'I don't follow,' Francis said.

'Sure you do,' Cleo replied, this time giving him an easy slow shot down the middle of the table. 'We're all afraid of something, here, aren't we C-Bird? Either afraid of what's inside us, or afraid of what's inside each other, or afraid of what's outside. We're afraid of change. We're afraid of staying the same. We're petrified by anything out of the ordinary, terrified of a change in the routine. Everyone wants to be different, but that's the biggest threat of all. And so, what are we? We live in a world so dangerous that it defies us. Do you follow?'

Everything Cleo said, Francis thought was true. 'What you're saying is we're all captives?'

'Prisoners. Absolutely,' Cleo said. 'Confined by everything. Walls. Medications. Our own thoughts.' This time she hit the ball a little harder, but she kept it within his reach. 'But the man I saw, well, he wasn't was he? Or, if he was, then what he's thinking isn't at all like everyone else, is it?'

Francis knocked the ball into the net. It dribbled back toward him.

'My point,' Cleo said. 'Serve it up.'

Francis plunked the ball across the table, and once again the clicking noise of the ball traveling back and forth filled the room. 'He wasn't afraid,' Francis said, 'when he opened that door to your dormitory . . . '

Cleo caught the ball in midair, stopping the rally. She leaned across the table. 'He has keys,' she said quietly. 'He has keys that can unlock what? The doors in the Amherst Building? Or beyond? Keys that can unlock the other dormitories. Storage areas? How about the offices in the administration building? How about the staff housing, will his keys work on those doors? Can he unlock the front gate, Francis? Can he unlock the front gate and simply walk out of here whenever he wants?'

She put the ball back in play.

He thought for a moment, then said, 'The keys are power, aren't they?'

Click, click went the ball against the table surface. 'Access is always power,' Cleo said, with a sense of finality in her voice. 'The keys say much,' she added. 'I wonder how he obtained them.'

'Why did he come into your room, risking being seen?'

Cleo did not answer for several passes of the ball back and forth above the net, before she said, 'Perhaps because he could.'

Again, Francis considered this, then he asked, 'Are you sure you couldn't recognize him if you saw him again? Have you thought about how tall he was, what his build was like. Anything that might distinguish him. Something to look for . . . '

Cleo shook her head, but then stopped. She took a deep breath, and seemed to concentrate on the game, picking up velocity with each stroke, making the ball fly back and forth across the table. Francis was a bit surprised that he was able to keep pace with her, returning her shots, moving right and left, forehand and backhand, meeting the ball solidly each time. Cleo was smiling, dancing from side to side, her own body moving with balletlike grace that contradicted her bulk.

'But Francis, you and I, we don't have to know his face, to recognize him,' she said after a moment. 'We need only to see that attitude. It would be unique in here. In this place. In our home. No one else will have that look, will they, C-Bird? Because, once we spot that,' she said, 'we'll know precisely what it is we are looking at. True?'

Francis reached out and struck the ball just a little hard. It flew across the table, missing the back line by two inches. With a darting, quick motion, Cleo snatched the ball from the air, before it bounced across the room. 'Just long,' she said. 'But an ambitious shot to try, C-Bird.'

Francis thought: *In a place filled with fears, they were looking for the man who had none.* In a corner of the dayroom, several voices suddenly started shouting. He could hear rage, and he pivoted around. A loud sob, followed by an angry shriek, creased the room. He put the paddle down, and stepped back from the table.

'You're improving, C-Bird,' Cleo cackled, her laugh superimposed on the sounds of the burgeoning fight. 'We should play again.'

★   ★   ★

When Francis reached Lucy's office, he'd had a little time to think about what he'd learned. He found her leaning up against a wall, behind a simple gray steel desk. Her arms were folded in front of her, and she was watching Peter. He was seated, and he had three large manila case files opened on the desktop surface in front of him. Spread about were eight-by-ten glossy color photographs, crime scene maps in stark black-and-white, with arrows and circles and notations, and written forms that were filled out with details. There were coroner's office reports and aerial pictures of the locations. As Francis entered the room, Peter looked up with a look of exasperation.

'Hi, Francis,' he said. 'Any success?'

'Maybe a little,' Francis replied. 'I spoke with Cleo.'

'Could she provide any better description?'

Francis shook his head. He gestured at the piles of documents and pictures. 'That seems like a lot,' he said. He'd never seen the volumes of paperwork customarily associated with a homicide investigation before, and it impressed him.

'Lots that says little,' Peter replied. Lucy nodded her head in agreement.

'But then again, says a lot, too,' Peter added. Lucy made a wry look with her face, as if this particular observation was painful or unsettling.

'I don't understand,' Francis said.

'Well,' Peter began slowly, but picking up momentum, as he spoke, 'what we have are three crimes, all committed in different police jurisdictions, probably, because bodies were moved postmortem, which means that no one precisely has charge of any case, which is always a bureaucratic mess, even when the State Police get involved. And we have victims discovered in various states of decomposition, whose bodies have been exposed to the elements, which makes forensics at best difficult and really well-nigh impossible. And we have crimes, which, as best as one can tell from the detectives' reports, were randomly selected, at least the victims were, because there are few, if any similarities in the women who were killed, other than body type, hair type, and age. Short hair and slender physique. One was a waitress, one was a college student, and one was a secretary. They didn't know each other. They didn't live anywhere near each other. They didn't have anything in particular that linked them together, other than the unfortunate fact that each traveled home alone on various forms of public transportation — you know, subways or buses — and that each had to walk several blocks through darkened streets to get to their apartments. Making them eminently vulnerable.'

'Easy,' Lucy said, 'for a patient man to pick out and stalk.'

Peter hesitated, in that second, as if something Lucy said raised some question within him. Francis could see that some notion was churning about within him, and he was unsure whether to put it to words and speak it out loud. Finally after a few moments had passed, Peter leaned back, and said, 'Different jurisdictions. Different locales. Different agencies. All here together . . . '

'That's right,' Lucy said carefully, as if she was suddenly watching her words.

'Interesting,' Peter replied. Then he leaned forward, back toward the materials on the desktop, surveying the entirety slowly. After a second, he stopped and picked up the three photographs of the victims' right hands. He stared at the mutilated fingers for a moment. 'Souvenirs,' he said briskly. 'That's pretty damn classic.'

'What do you mean?' Francis asked.

'In the studies done on repetitive killers,' Lucy said quietly, 'one common characteristic is the need for the killer to remove something from the victim, so that he can relive the experience later.'

'Remove?'

'A lock of hair. A piece of clothing. A part of the body.'

Francis shuddered. He felt young, in that moment, as young as he'd ever been, and wondered how it was that he knew so little of the world, and Peter and Lucy, who weren't more than eight, maybe ten years older than he was, knew so much. 'But you said it told you a lot, too,' Francis said. 'Like what?'

Peter looked over at Lucy, their eyes linking for a second. Francis eyed the young prosecutor carefully, and thought that his question had somehow crossed some sort of divide. There are moments, he knew, when words assembled and uttered suddenly created bridges

206

and connections, and he suspected this was one of those moments.

'What all this says, Francis,' Peter said, speaking to his friend, but his eyes on the young woman, 'is that Lanky's Angel knows how to commit crimes in a manner that creates immeasurable problems for the folks who would want to stop him. That means that he has some intelligence. And a significant amount of education, at least, in the ways of killing. When you think about it, there are only two ways that crimes get solved, C-Bird. The first, and best way, is when the great mass of evidence gathered at the scene of the crime points inexorably in one direction. Fingerprints, clothing fibers, blood work, and murder weapons that can be traced and maybe even eyewitness testimony. Then these things can be coupled with clear-cut motives, like insurance money, or robbery, or an angry dispute between estranged couples.'

'What's the other way?' Francis asked.

'That's when you uncover a suspect, and then you find ways of linking him to the events.'

'That sounds like it's backward.'

'It is indeed,' Lucy said.

'Is it more difficult?'

Peter sighed. 'Difficult? Yes. That it is. Impossible? No.'

'That's good,' Francis said. He looked at Lucy. 'I would be worried if what we had to do were impossible.'

Peter burst out with a laugh. 'Actually, C-Bird, it's really simply a matter of us using some other means to figure out who the Angel is. We create a list of potential suspects, and then narrow that down until we are more or less certain we know who it is. Or, at the least, have a few names of potential killers. Then we apply what we know about each crime to these suspects. One, I trust, will stand out. And once we see that, it won't be all that hard to put him in proximity to these victims. Things will fall together, we just don't know yet how or what it will be. But there will be something in this mess of papers and reports and evidence that will trap him.'

Francis took in a deep breath. 'What sort of other means are you talking about?' he asked.

Peter grinned. 'Well, my young friend, there's the rub. That's what we need to figure out. There's someone in this place who isn't what everyone thinks he is. He's got a whole different sort of crazy lurking about inside him, C-Bird. And he's got it hidden pretty damn carefully. We just have to figure out who's acting a lie.'

Francis looked at Lucy, who was moving her head up and down.

'That, of course,' she added slowly, 'is more easily said than done.'

12

Sometimes the lines of demarcation between dreams and reality become blurred. Hard for me to tell precisely which is which. I suppose that's why I am supposed to take so much medication, as if reality can be encouraged chemically. Ingest enough milligrams of this or that pill, and the world comes back into focus. This is sadly true, and, for the most part, all those drugs do pretty much what they are supposed to do, in addition to all the other things not so pleasant. And, I guess, it is all in all positive. It just depends on how much value one places on focus.

Currently, I wasn't placing much value on it all.

I slept, I don't know for how many hours, on the floor of my living room. I had taken a pillow and blanket from my bed, and then stretched out beside all my words, reluctant to leave them, almost like an attentive parent, afraid to leave a sickly child at night. The floor was board hard, and my joints complained in protest when I awakened. There was some dawn light slipping into the apartment, like a herald trumpeting in something new, and I rose to my task not precisely refreshed, but at least a little less groggy.

For a moment, or two, I looked about, reassuring myself that I was alone.

The Angel was not far, I knew. He had not fled. That wasn't his style. Nor had he concealed himself behind my shoulder again. My senses were all on edge, despite the few hours' sleep. He was close. He was watching. He was waiting. Somewhere nearby. But the room was empty, at least for the time being, and I felt some relief. The only echoes were my own.

I tried to tell myself to be very careful. In the Western

State Hospital, there had been the three of us arrayed against him. And still it had been an equal contest. Now, here alone in my apartment, I feared that I wasn't capable of the same fight.

I turned to the wall. I remembered asking Peter a question and his response, spoken in an upbeat tone: 'Detective work is about a steady, careful examination of facts. Creative thinking is always welcome, but only within the boundaries of known details.'

I laughed out loud. This time irony overcame me, and I replied, 'But that's not what worked, was it?' Maybe in the real world, especially today, with DNA testing and electronic microscopes and forensic techniques honed by science and technology and screaming modern capabilities, finding the Angel wouldn't have been so tricky. Probably not at all. Put the right substances into a test tube, a little bit of this and a little bit of that, run them through a gas chronometer, apply some space-age technology, get a computer readout and find our man. But back then, in the Western State Hospital, we didn't have any of those things. Not a one.

All we had was ourselves.

⋆   ⋆   ⋆

Inside the Amherst Building alone, there were nearly three hundred male patients. That figure was duplicated in the other housing units, bringing the hospital total to close to 2,100. The female population was slightly less, measuring one hundred and twenty-five in Amherst, and a little over nine hundred in the hospital itself. Nurses, nurse-trainees, attendants, security personnel, psychologists, and psychiatrists brought the number of people at the hospital to well above three thousand. It wasn't the widest world, Francis thought, but it was still a substantial one.

In the days after Lucy Jones's arrival, Francis had taken to examining the other men walking the corridors with a different sort of interest. The idea that one among them was a killer unsettled him, and he found himself pivoting and turning whenever someone closed in on him from behind. He knew this was unreasonable, and knew also that his fears were misplaced. But it was hard for him to erase a sense of constant dread.

He spent a lot of time trying to make eye contact in a place that discouraged it. He was surrounded by all sorts of mental illness, in varying degrees of intensity, and he had no idea how to change the way he looked at all that sickness to spot an entirely different disease. The clamor he felt within himself, from all his voices, added to the nervousness racing about inside his body. He felt a little like he was charged with electrical impulses, all darting about haphazardly, trying to find some location where they might settle. His efforts to rest were frustrated, and Francis felt exhausted.

Peter the Fireman didn't seem quite as hamstrung. In fact, Francis noted, the worse he felt, the better Peter seemed to be. There was more urgency in his voice, and quickness to his step, as he traversed the corridors. Some of the elusive sadness that he'd worn when first he'd arrived at the Western State Hospital had been shunted aside. Peter had energy, which Francis envied, because he had only fear.

But the time spent with Lucy and Peter, in their small office, managed to control even that for him. In the small space, even his voices quieted, and he was able to listen to what they said with relative peace.

The first order of business, as Lucy explained to him, was to create a means of narrowing the number of potential suspects. It was easy enough for her, she said, to go through the hospital records for each patient and determine who was *available* to kill the other victims that she believed were linked to the murder of Short

Blond. She had three other dates, in addition to Short Blond. Each killing had taken place within a few days, or weeks, of the time the bodies were discovered. Clearly, the greatest percentage of hospital inmates were not out on the street during the time frame that all three of the other killings were performed. The long-term patients, especially the elderly, were easy to remove from their process of inspection.

She did not share this initial inquiry with either Doctor Gulptilil or Mister Evans, although Peter and Francis knew what she was doing. This created some tension, when she asked Mister Evil for the Amherst Building records.

'Of course,' he said. 'I keep the primary dossiers in my office in some file cabinets. You can come there and inspect them whenever you like.'

Lucy was standing outside her own office. It was early in the afternoon, and Mister Evil had already come by twice that morning, knocking loudly at her door and asking if he could be of assistance, and to remind Francis and Peter that their regularly scheduled group session was going to take place as usual and that they would be required to be there.

'Now would be good,' she said. She took a step down the hallway, only to be interrupted by Mister Evil.

'Only you,' he said stiffly. 'Not the other two.'

'They're helping me,' she said. 'You know that.'

Mister Evil nodded, in response, but then changed the nod into a vigorous back and forth negative. 'Yes, they might be,' he said slowly. 'That remains to be seen, and, as you well know, I have my doubts. Still doesn't give them the right to examine the confidential files of other patients. There is sensitive, personal information in those dossiers, gleaned from therapeutic sessions, and I cannot permit that information to be examined by other clients of our little hospital, here. That would be unethical on my part and a violation of state laws

212

concerning privacy of records. You should be aware of that, Miss Jones.'

Lucy paused, considering what he'd said. 'I'm sorry,' she replied slowly. 'You are, of course, correct. I simply assumed that the exigencies of the situation might create some leeway on your part.'

He smiled. 'Of course. And I wish to provide you with the widest possible latitude on your wild-goose chase. But I cannot break the law, nor is it fair for you to ask me, or any of the other dormitory supervisors to do so.' Mister Evil wore long brown hair, and wire-rim glasses, giving him a close to scruffy look. To offset this impression, he often wore a tie and a white shirt, although his shoes were always scuffed and worn. It was, Francis thought, a little as if he did not want to be associated either with a world of rebellion or the land of the status quo. Not really wanting to be a part of either put Mister Evil into a difficult spot, he thought.

'Right,' she said. 'I wouldn't want to do that.'

'Especially, because I have yet to see from you any real indication that the mythical person you are pursuing is actually here.'

She did not reply to this at first, only smiling.

'And,' she said, after a short silence had surrounded them unhappily, 'precisely what sort of evidence is it that you'd like me to show you?'

Evans, too, smiled, as if he enjoyed the fencing back and forth. Thrust. Parry. Strike.

'Something other than supposition,' he said. 'Perhaps a witness that was credible, although where you might find one inside a mental hospital presently eludes me . . . ' He said this with a small laugh, as if it was a joke. ' . . . Or perhaps the murder weapon that has, as of now, not been uncovered. Something concrete. Something solid . . . ' Again, he seemed about to act as if this was all a great amusement, just for him. 'Of course, as you've probably figured out, Miss Jones,

213

concrete and *solid* are not concepts particularly suited to our little world, here. You know as well as I, that statistically, the mentally ill are far, far more likely to do harm to themselves than they are to hurt someone else.'

'Perhaps the person I'm seeking isn't exactly what you would call mentally ill,' Lucy said. 'A different category completely.'

'Well,' Evans answered briskly, 'that may be the case. In fact, it is likely. But what we have here, in abundance, are the latter, not the former.'

With that, he gestured, bowing slightly and sweeping his arm in the direction of his own office. 'You would still like to examine the files?' he said.

Lucy turned to Peter and Francis. 'I need to go do this. Get started, at least. I will meet with you later.'

Peter looked angrily at Mister Evans, who did not look back in his direction, but instead, led Lucy Jones down the corridor, dismissing patients who approached him with short, chopping hand motions. It was, Francis thought, a little like a man cutting his way with a machete through the jungle.

'It would be nice,' Peter said, under his breath, 'if it turned out that that son of a bitch was the man we were hunting for. That would really be special, and would make all this time in here incredibly worthwhile.' Then he burst out in a short laugh. 'Ah, well, C-Bird. The world is never that convenient. And you know what they say: 'Beware of getting what you wish for.'' But even as he spoke, he continued to watch Mister Evans as he maneuvered down the hallway. He waited a few moments, and then added, 'I'm going to go speak with Napoleon.' Peter sighed. 'At least, he will have the eighteenth-century perspective on all this.'

Francis would have joined him, but he hesitated, as Peter wheeled and walked swiftly toward the dayroom. In that moment, he saw Big Black leaning up against the wall of the corridor, smoking a cigarette, his white uniform bathed in light that streamed through the windows, so that he glistened. For some reason, the light made Big Black's skin seem even darker, and Francis saw that the attendant had been watching them. He walked over, and the huge man separated himself from the wall, and dropped his smoke to the floor.

'A bad habit,' Big Black said. 'One that is just as likely to kill you as anything else in here. Maybe. Can't be altogether too sure about that, what with all that's been happening. But don't you go and take it up like everybody else in this place, C-Bird. Lots of bad habits in here. And not much to do about them. You try to keep yourself out of bad habits, C-Bird, and you'll find yourself out of here, sooner or later.'

Francis didn't reply. Instead, he watched the attendant stare down the corridor, his eyes fixing on first one patient, then another, but clearly, his real attention somewhere else.

After a moment, Francis asked, 'Why do they hate each other, Mister Moses?'

Big Black did not answer this question directly, other than to say, 'You know, sometimes, down South where I was born, there were these old women who could sense the weather changing. They were the ones who knew when storms were gonna blow in off the water, and especially, during hurricane season, they were forever walking about, sniffing the air, sometimes saying little chants and spells, sometimes throwing bones and seashells on a piece of cloth. A little like witchcraft, I guess, and now that I am an educated man, living in a modern world, C-Bird, I know better than to believe all those spells and incantations. But, trouble was, they were always right. Storm coming, they knew it long before anyone else did. They were the ones got the folks to bring in the livestock, fix the roof of the house, maybe bottle some water, just for the emergency that no one else could see was coming. But which came, all the same. Makes no sense, when you think about it; makes perfectly good sense, if you don't.'

He smiled, and put his hand on Francis's shoulder. 'What you think, C-Bird? You look at those two and the way they act and feel that storm coming on, too?'

'I still don't understand, Mister Moses.'

The large man shook his head. 'Let me say this: Evans, he's got a brother. And maybe what it was that Peter did, maybe that did something to that brother. And so, when Peter came here, Evans made right certain that he was the one in charge of his evaluation. He made sure that Peter knew that whatever it was that Peter wanted, he was going to make damn certain that Peter didn't get it.'

'But that can't be fair,' Francis said.

'Didn't say something was fair, C-Bird. Didn't say nothing about things being fair, the one way or the other. Only said that's maybe some part of that little bit of trouble that's heading bad, isn't it?'

Big Black removed his hand and stuck it in his pocket. As he did so, the chain of keys on his belt jangled.

'Mister Moses, those keys — can you go anywhere in here with them?'

He nodded. 'In here. And in all the other dormitories, too. Unlock doors to Security. Unlock dormitory doors. Even get into the isolation cells, too. Want to go out the front gate, Francis? These will help show you the way.'

'Who has keys like that?'

'Nursing supervisors. Security. Attendants like me and my brother. Main staff.'

'Do they know where all the sets are, at all times?'

'Supposed to. But like everything around here, what they are supposed to do and what really happens might be different things.'

He laughed. 'Now, C-Bird, you starting to ask questions like Miss Jones and Peter, too. He knows how

216

to ask questions. You're learning.'

Francis smiled in reply to the compliment. 'I wonder,' he said, 'if all those sets of keys are accounted for at all times.'

Big Black shook his head. 'Ain't quite asking that question right, C-Bird. Try again.'

'Are any keys missing?'

'Yes. That's the question, isn't it? Yes. Some keys are missing.'

'Has anyone searched for them?'

'Yes. But maybe *search* ain't the right word. People looked in all the real likely places, and then gave up when they didn't find them.'

'Who lost them?'

'Why,' Big Black said with a grin, 'that person would be our very good friend, Mister Evans.'

The huge attendant burst out with another laugh, and as he threw his head back, he spotted his smaller brother heading toward them. 'Hey,' he called out, 'C-Bird is starting to figure things out.'

Francis saw the nurses stationed behind the wire mesh of the station in the middle of the corridor look up, and smile, as if this was something of a joke. Little Black also grinned, as he sauntered up to the two of them. 'You know what, Francis?' he said.

'What's that, Mister Moses?'

'You get the handle on the way this world works,' he spoke, gesturing wildly with his arm to indicate the hospital ward. 'You get a good solid grip on all this, and I'll tell you the truth, figuring out the world outdoors there, right out there past the walls — well, that won't be so hard for you. If you get the chance.'

'How do I get that chance, Mister Moses?'

'Now, ain't that the great question, little brother? That's the great big question gets asked every minute of every day in here. How does a gentleman get that chance. There's ways, C-Bird. There's more than one way, at least. But ain't no simple yes and no rules. Do this. Do that. Get a chance. Nope, don't work precisely that way. You've got to find your own path. You'll get there, C-Bird. Just got to see it when it shows itself. That's the problem, ain't it?'

Francis did not know how to respond, but he thought the older brother undoubtedly wrong. And he didn't think he had any ability to understand any world whatsoever. A few of his voices rumbled deep within him, and he tried to listen to what they were saying, because he suspected they had an opinion or two. But as he concentrated, he saw that both attendants were watching him, taking note of the way his own face wore whatever was inside of him and for a moment, he felt naked, as if his clothing had been ripped from him. So, instead, he smiled as pleasantly as he could, and walked off down the corridor, his footsteps keeping quick pace with all the doubts drumming about within him.

★   ★   ★

Lucy sat behind the desk in Mister Evans's office as he rummaged through one of four file cabinets lined up against one wall. Her eyes were drawn to a photograph on the corner, which was a wedding picture. She saw Evans, his hair a little more closely cropped and combed, wearing a blue pin-striped business suit that still seemed to merely underscore his skinny physique, standing next to a young woman wearing a white gown which only barely concealed a significant pregnancy, and who was wearing a garland of flowers in frizzy brown hair. They were in the middle of a group that ranged in age from very old to very young, and all wore similar smiles, that, on balance, Lucy thought she could accurately describe as forced. In the midst of the wedding party, was a man wearing a priest's flowing robes, which caught the photographer's light in their golden brocade. He had his hand on Evans's shoulder, and, after a slight double take, Lucy recognized a nearly complete resemblance to the psychologist.

'You have a twin?' she asked.

Evans looked up, saw where her eyes were fixed on the photograph, and turned toward her, his arms filled with yellow file folders. 'Runs in the family,' he said. 'My daughters are twins as well.'

Lucy looked around, but failed to see a photograph. He saw the inquisitive survey and added, 'They live with their mother. Suffice it to say we're going through a bit of a rough spot.'

'Sorry to hear that,' she said, although she didn't say that that was no explanation for not having their photo on the wall.

He shrugged. He dumped the files on the desk in front of her. They made a thudding sound.

'When you grow up as a twin, you get accustomed to all the jokes. They are always the same, you know. Two peas in a pod. How do ya tell 'em apart? You guys share the same thoughts and ideas? When one spends all their years knowing that there is a mirror image of oneself asleep in the bunk bed above, it changes one's understanding of the world. Both for the better, and for the worse, as well, Miss Jones.'

'You were identical twins?' she asked, mostly just for conversation, though a single glance at the picture told her the answer to her question.

Mister Evans hesitated before replying, his gaze narrowing, and a distinct ice slipping into his words. 'We were once. No longer.'

She looked at him quizzically.

Evans coughed once, then added: 'Why don't you ask your new friend and detective partner to explain that statement? Because he has that answer a whole lot better than I do. Ask Peter the Fireman, the sort of guy

219

who starts out extinguishing fires, but ends up setting them.'

She did not know how to respond, so instead, she drew the files toward her. Mister Evans took up a seat across from her, leaning back, crossing his legs in a relaxed fashion and watching what she was doing. Lucy did not like the way his glance penetrated the air around her, bulletlike, and she felt uncomfortable with the intensity of his scrutiny. 'Would you like to help?' she asked abruptly. 'What I have in mind is not all that difficult. Initially, I'd simply like to eliminate those men who were here in the hospital when one or another of these three additional killings took place. In other words, if they were here — '

He interrupted her. 'Then they couldn't be out there. That should be an easy matter of comparing dates.'

'Right,' she said.

'Except there are some elements that make it a little harder.'

She paused, then asked, 'What sort of elements?'

Evans rubbed his chin, before answering. 'There are a percentage of patients who have been voluntarily committed to the hospital. They can be signed in and out, on a weekend, for example, by responsible family members. In fact, it is encouraged. So, it is conceivable that someone whose records seem to show that they are a full-time resident here, actually has spent some time outside the walls. Under supervision, of course. Or, at least, allegedly under supervision. Now, that would not be the case for people ordered here by a court. Nor would it be the case for patients that after they arrived, the staff has deemed to be a danger to themselves, or perhaps someone else. If an act of violence got you here, then you wouldn't be released, even for a visit home. Unless, of course, a staff member felt it was an acceptable part of one's therapeutic approach. But this would also depend upon what medications the patient was currently prescribed. Someone can be sent home for overnight with a pill. But not needing an injection. See?'

'I think so.'

'And,' Evans continued, picking up some steam as he spoke, 'we have hearings. We are required to periodically present cases in a quasijudicial proceeding, in effect to justify why someone should be kept here, or, in some cases, released. A public defender comes up from Springfield, and we have a patient advocate, who sits on a panel with Doctor Gulptilil and a guy from the state division of Mental Health Services. A little like a parole board type hearing. Those happen from time to time, as well, and they have an erratic track record.'

'How do you mean *erratic?*'

'People get released because they've been stabilized, and then they're back here in a couple of months after they decompensate. There is an element to treating mental illness which makes it seem very much like a revolving door. Or a treadmill.'

'But the patients you have here in the Amherst Building . . . '

'I don't know whether we have any current patients who have the capacity — both social and mental — to be granted a furlough. Maybe a couple, at best. I don't know that we have any scheduled for hearings. I'd have to check. Furthermore, I don't have a clue about the other buildings. You will have to find my counterparts in each one and check with them.'

'I think we can eliminate the other buildings,' Lucy said briskly. 'After all, the killing of Short Blond took place here, and I suspect the killer is likely here.'

Mister Evans smiled unpleasantly, as if he saw a joke in what she said that wasn't obvious to her. 'Why would you assume that?'

She started to respond, but stopped. 'I merely thought — ,' she started, but he cut her off.

'If this mythical fellow is as clever as you think, then I shouldn't imagine that traveling between buildings late at night was a problem he couldn't overcome.'

'But there is Security patrolling the grounds. Wouldn't they spot anyone moving between buildings?'

'We are, alas, like so many state agencies, understaffed. And Security travels set patterns at regular times, which wouldn't be all that difficult to elude, if one had that inclination. And there are other ways of traveling about unseen.'

Lucy hesitated again, realizing there was a question there that she should ask, and into the momentary pause, Mr. Evans added his opinion: 'Lanky,' he said, with a small, almost nonchalant wave. 'Lanky had motive and opportunity and desire and ended up with the nurse's blood all over him. I fail to see why it is that you want to look so much harder for someone else. I agree that Lanky is, in many regards, a likable fellow. But he was also a paranoid schizophrenic and had a history of violent acts. Especially toward women, whom he often saw as minions of Satan. And, in the days leading up to the crime, his medications had been shown to be inadequate. If you were to review *his* medical records, which the police took with him, you would see an entry from me suggesting that he might have found a way to conceal that he wasn't getting the proper dosages at the daily distribution. In fact, I had ordered that he be started on intravenous injections in upcoming days, because I felt that oral dosages weren't doing the job.'

Again, Lucy did not reply. She wanted to tell Mr. Evans that the mutilation of the nurse's hand alone, in her mind at least, cleared Lanky. But she did not share that observation.

Evans pushed the files toward her. 'Still,' he said, 'if you examine these — and the thousand others in the other buildings — you can eliminate some people. I think I would deemphasize times and dates and concentrate more time on diagnosis. I'd rule out the mentally retarded. And the catatonics who don't respond to either medication or electric shock treatments, because they just don't seem to have the physical capacity to do what you think they did. And the other personality disorders that contraindicate what you're looking for. I'm happy to help by answering any questions you might have. But the hard part — well, that's for you.'

Then he leaned back and watched her, as she drew forward the first dossier, flipped open the jacket, and began to inspect it.

★   ★   ★

Francis leaned up against the wall outside Mister Evil's office, unsure what else to do. It wasn't long before he saw Peter the Fireman sauntering down the corridor, heading to join him. Peter slumped himself up against the wall, and stared toward the door blocking them from where Lucy was poring over patient records. He exhaled slowly, making a whistling sound.

'Did you speak with Napoleon?'

'He wanted to play chess. So I did play a game and he kicked my butt. Still, it's a good game for an investigator to learn.'

'Why is that?'

'Because there are infinite variations on a winning strategy, yet one is still restricted in the moves one can make by the highly specific limitations of each piece on the board. A knight can do this . . . ' He made a forward and sideways gesture with his hand. 'While a bishop can go like so . . . ' He changed to a diagonal slashing motion. 'Do you play, C-Bird?'

Francis shook his head.

'You should learn.'

223

As they spoke, a heavyset, thickly built man who lived in the third floor dormitory lurched to a halt across from them. He wore a look that Francis had come to recognize among many of the retarded people in the hospital. It combined a blankness and an inquisitiveness at the same time, as if the man wanted an answer to something, but knew he could not understand it, which created a state of near constant frustration. There were a number of men in Amherst, and throughout Western State Hospital, like this man, and day in, day out, they frightened Francis as much as any one, because they were on balance, so benign, and yet, capable of sudden, inexplicable aggressiveness. Francis had learned quickly to steer clear of the retarded men. When Francis looked over at him, he opened his eyes wide, and seemed to snarl, as if angry that so much in the world was so far beyond his reach. He made a small gurgling sound, and continued to stare at Peter and Francis intently.

Peter returned the gaze, with an equal ferocity. 'What are you looking at?' he asked.

The man simply gurgled a little louder.

'What do you want?' Peter demanded. He peeled himself from the wall, tensing.

The retarded man emitted a long, grunting sound, like a wild animal squaring off against a rival. He took a step forward, hunching his shoulders. His face contorted, and it seemed to Francis that the limits of the man's imagination made him more terrifying, because all that he possessed, within his meager resources, was rage. And there was no way of determining where it came from. It just erupted, at that moment, in that spot. The retarded man flexed his hands into fists and then swung wildly in the air between them, as if he was punching a vision.

Peter took another step forward, then stopped. 'Don't do it, buddy,' he said.

The man seemed to gather himself for a charge.

Peter repeated, 'It's not worth it.' But as he spoke, he braced himself.

The retarded man took a single additional step toward them, then halted. Still grunting with an internal fury that seemed massive, he suddenly took his fist and slammed it against the side of his own head. The punch resounded down the corridor. Then he followed this, with a second blow, and a third, each one echoing loudly. A small trickle of blood appeared by his ear.

Neither Peter nor Francis moved.

The man let out a cry. It had some of the pitch of victory, some of the tone of anguish. It was hard for Francis to tell whether it was a challenge or a signal.

And, as it resounded down the hall, the man seemed to stop. He let out a sigh, and straightened up. He looked over at Francis and Peter and shook his head, as if clearing something from his vision. His eyebrows knit together abruptly, quizzically, as if some great question had penetrated within him, and in the same revelation, he'd seen the answer. Then he half snarled, half smiled, and abruptly lurched off down the hallway, mumbling to himself.

Francis and Peter watched him move unsteadily away.

'What was that about?' Francis asked, a little shakily.

Peter shook his head. 'That's just it,' he replied softly. 'In here, you just don't know, do you? You just can't tell what has made someone burst like that. Or not. Jesus, Mary, and Joseph, C-Bird. This is the strangest damn place I hope either of us ever has the misfortune to land.'

The two men leaned back up against the wall. Peter seemed stricken by the attack that hadn't happened, as if it had said something to him. 'You know, C-Bird, when I was in Vietnam, I thought that was pretty weird. Strange things were likely to happen all the damn time. Strange and deadly things. But, at least, they had some rhyme and reason to them. I mean, after all, we were

225

there to kill them, and they were there to kill us. Made some perverse logic. And after I came home, and joined the department, sometimes, in a fire, you know things can get pretty dicey. Walls tumbling. Floors giving way. Heat and smoke everywhere. But still, there's some cosmic sense of order to it all. Fire burns in defined patterns, accelerated by certain stuffs, and, when you know what you're doing, you can usually take the right precautions. But this place is something else. It's like everything is on fire all the time. It's like everything is hidden. And booby-trapped.'

'Would you have fought him?'

'Would I have had a choice?'

He looked around at the flow of patients moving throughout the building.

'How does anyone survive in here?' he asked.

Francis didn't have an answer. 'I don't know that we're really supposed to,' he whispered.

Peter nodded, his wry smile suddenly back in place. 'That, my young and crazy friend, might be the most dead-on accurate thing you've ever said.'

13

When Lucy emerged from Mister Evans's office, she carried a legal-size yellow pad of paper in her right hand and a look of significant displeasure on her face. A long, quickly scrawled list of names ran down one side of the top page on the pad. She moved rapidly, as if driven to increase her pace by a sense of dismay. She looked up when she spotted Francis and Peter the Fireman waiting for her, and she gave a little, rueful shake of her head, as she approached them.

'I'd thought, rather foolishly it turns out, that this would simply be a matter of checking dates against hospital records. It's not that simple, primarily because the hospital records are something of a mess, and not centralized. A lot of busywork involved. Damn.'

'Mister Evil wasn't as helpful as he said he might be?' Peter observed archly, asking a question that already had its answer contained within it.

'No. I think that would be a safe assessment,' Lucy replied.

'Well,' Peter said, affecting a mock, slightly British accent that almost managed to sound like Gulp-a-pill, 'I am shocked. Simply shocked . . . '

Lucy continued down the corridor, her pace as rapid as her thoughts.

'So,' Peter asked, 'what were you able to find out?'

'What I learned was that I'm going to have to check every other housing unit, in addition to Amherst. And, beyond that, I'm going to have to find records for every patient that might have had a weekend furlough during the relevant time period. And, further complicating matters, I'm not at all sure that there's any sort of master list, which would make that easier. What I do

227

have is a list of names from this building that more, or less, fit into the range of possibilities. Forty-three names.'

'Did you eliminate some by age?' Peter asked, the jocularity now removed from his voice.

She nodded. 'Yes. That was my first thought, as well. The old-timers, well, no need to question them.'

'I think,' Peter said slowly, as he started to rub his right hand across his cheek, as if by friction, he could loosen some ideas stuck within, 'that we might consider one other important element.'

Lucy looked at him.

'Physicality,' Peter said.

'What do you mean?' Francis asked.

'What I mean is that it requires some strength to commit the crime that we're concerned with. He had to overpower Short Blond, then drag her to the storage room. There were signs of a struggle in the nursing station, so we know that he didn't manage to sneak up behind her and knock her out with some lucky punch. In fact, if I were to guess, he probably looked forward to the struggle.'

Lucy sighed. 'True. The more he beat her, the more he got excited. That would fit what we know of this type of personality.'

Francis shuddered, hoping the others didn't see him. He had a little trouble discussing so coldly and casually some moments that were, he thought, far beyond horror.

'So,' Peter continued, 'we know we're looking for someone with some muscle. That rules out a bunch of people inside here right away, because, although Gulptilil would probably deny it, this place doesn't exactly seem to attract the physically fit. Aren't too many marathon runners and bodybuilders inside here. And we should also reduce the pool of candidates to a range of ages. And then, it seems to me, there is one other area that might help further narrow the list. Diagnosis. Who is here with some significant violence in their past. Who suffers from the type of mental illness that might be expanded to include murder.'

Lucy said, 'My thinking exactly. We come up with a portrait of the man we're seeking, and things will come into focus.' Then she turned to Francis. 'C-Bird, I'm going to need your help in that area.'

Francis bent toward her, eager. 'What do you need?'

'I don't think I understand madness,' she said.

Francis must have looked confused, because she smiled. 'Oh, don't get me wrong. I understand the psychiatric language and the diagnosis criteria and the treatment plans and all the textbook stuff. But what I don't understand is how it all seems from the inside, looking out. I think you can help me in that regard. I need to know who could have done these crimes, and hard evidence is going to be tricky to come by.'

Francis was uncertain, but he said, 'Whatever you need . . .'

Peter, though, was nodding his head, as if he could see something that was obvious to himself and should have been obvious to Lucy, but which still eluded Francis. 'He can do that, I'm sure. He's a natural. A teacher-in-training. Can't you C-Bird?'

'I'll try.' Deep within him, he heard a rumbling, as if there was an argument going on within his inner population, and then, finally, he heard one of his voices insist: *Tell them. It's okay. Tell them what you know.* He hesitated one second, then spoke, feeling as if his words were being directed from sources within. 'There's one thing you should realize,' he said slowly, cautiously. Both Lucy and Peter looked at him, as if they were a little surprised he was joining the conversation.

'What's that?' Lucy asked.

Francis nodded to Peter. 'Peter's right, I guess, about being strong, and right, too, that there aren't a lot of people inside here who would appear to have the physical strength necessary to outfight someone like Short Blond. I mean, that makes sense, I guess. But not completely. If the Angel were hearing voices commanding him to attack Short Blond, and these other women — well, it's not true that he would have to be as strong as Peter suggests. When you hear these things, and the voices are telling you to do something — I mean, really screaming and insistent and without compromise — well, pain, difficulty, strength, all these things become secondary. You simply do what they demand. You overcome. If a voice told you to pick up a car, or a boulder, well, you would do it, or kill yourself trying. So it is not necessarily true when Peter suggests that the Angel is a strong man. He could still be almost anyone, because he could find the necessary strength. The voices would tell him where to find it.'

He paused, and he heard a deep echo within saying *That's right. Good job, Francis.*

Peter looked deeply at Francis, then broke out into a smile. He punched Francis on the arm.

Lucy smiled, too, followed by a long sigh. 'I will keep all that in mind, Francis. Thank you. I think you might be right. It just goes to show that this isn't your ordinary type of investigation. Rules are a bit different inside here, aren't they?'

Francis felt a sense of relief, and was pleased to have contributed something. He pointed at his forehead. 'Rules are different inside here, too,' he said.

Lucy reached out and touched him on the arm. 'I'll keep that in mind.' Then she shook her head. 'Now there's something else I need you guys to find out for me.'

'Anything,' Peter said.

'Evans suggested that there are ways to travel between buildings at night where one can avoid being seen by Security. I'm capable of asking him precisely what he means by this, but I'd like to limit his involvement as much as possible . . . '

'Makes sense to me,' Peter said rapidly. Perhaps a bit too much so, for he gained a sharp look from Lucy.

'Still, I wonder if you can't pursue this from the patients' point of view. Who knows how to get from here to there? How do you do it? What are the risks? And who would want to do it?'

'Do you think the Angel came from another building?'

'I want to find out if he could.'

Peter nodded again. 'I see,' he said. He started to say something, but then stopped. 'We'll find out what we can,' he said after a moment.

'Good,' Lucy said with brisk confidence. 'I'm going off to see Doctor Gulptilil, and pursue the dates and times a little more carefully. I'll get him to escort me to the other units, so that I can come up with a rough list of names from each.'

'You can probably eliminate the men with a diagnosis of mental retardation, as well,' Peter said. 'That will narrow the field. But only severe mental retardation.'

Again she nodded. 'Makes sense. Why don't you two plan on meeting me in my office prior to dinner and we'll compare notes.'

She turned and walked rapidly down the corridor. Francis noticed that the patients who were moving through the same space all stepped aside as she sailed past, shrinking back from her. He thought, at first, that people must be scared of Lucy, which he didn't understand, but then, he realized it was unfamiliarity that scared them. She was sane, and they were not. More, it was what she represented, which was something alien, a person with an existence that stretched beyond the walls. And last, he thought, what was ultimately the most unsettling thing about seeing

231

someone like her within the hospital was that it drove home a sense of uncertainty about the world they all lived in.

Francis looked closely at the faces of some of the patients and realized that there were very few people in that building who really wanted the disruption to their world that Lucy represented. In the Western State Hospital, patients and staff clung to routine, because it was the only way of keeping all the forces that warred within each patient at bay. It was why so many people were stuck there for so many years, because, very swiftly one came to understand what was dangerous. He shook his head. It was all upside down, he thought. The hospital was a place filled with risk, a constantly bubbling cauldron of conflict, anger, and madness; yet, it somehow measured out to be less frightening than the world outside. Lucy was the outside. Francis turned, and saw Peter the Fireman also watching her departure. He could see a sense of frustration in Peter's face. It was a frustration caused by being imprisoned. They were the same, Francis thought, because they both belonged somewhere else.

He was unsure if he also fit into that category.

After a moment, Peter turned and shook his head slightly. 'This is going to be tricky, C-Bird,' he said.

'What do you mean?'

'Well, Lucy thinks this is a no-big-deal question. Something to keep us occupied and focused. But it's a bit more than that.'

Francis looked at Peter, asking him to continue with his eyes.

'As soon as we start asking Lucy's question, someone is going to hear that we're inquisitive. The word will get out, and sooner or later get around to someone who actually does know how to get from building to building after dark, when everyone is supposed to be locked up, drugged out, and asleep. That's the someone we're looking for. That's inevitable. And it will make us vulnerable.'

Peter took a deep breath, and let it out slowly. 'Think about it for a second,' he said, a little bit under his breath. 'We all live in these independent housing units spread about over the hospital grounds. We eat here. We go to sessions here. We have recreation here. We sleep here. And every unit is the same. One after the other, all the same. Little contained worlds, within a bigger, contained world. With very little contact between each unit. I mean, hell, your brother could be right next door, and you wouldn't know it. So, why would anyone want access to another place that was exactly the same as the one he just left, anyway? It's not like we're all a bunch of low-rent South Boston mobsters stuck in Walpole Prison doing life without parole, trying to figure out how to escape. No one here thinks about breaking out, at least, not that I can tell, as yet. So the only reason someone might have for wanting to get from this building to the next is the reason we're investigating. And every time we start to ask a question that will make the Angel think we're onto some element that might reduce the field of suspects, well . . . '

Peter hesitated. 'I don't know that he's ever killed a man. Probably pretty strictly the women we know about.' He let his voice trail off.

★ ★ ★

Big Black and Nurse Wrong set up a painting exercise in the dayroom that afternoon for Mister Evil's regular group session. There was no explanation as to where Evans had disappeared to, and Lucy was out of the Amherst Building as well. The dozen members of the group were all issued large white sheets of thick cotton paper that felt rough to the touch. They were then placed in a loose circle, and given a choice between

233

watercolors and crayons.

Peter looked askance at the whole endeavor, but Francis thought it was a welcome change from sitting in a meeting designed to underscore their madness and contrast it with Mister Evans's sanity, which he had come to think was the sole agenda of the group gatherings. Cleo had an eager look in her face, as if she'd already anticipated what she intended to sketch and Napoleon hummed a little martial music to himself, as he contemplated the blank sheet on his lap, rubbing his fingers along the edge.

Nurse Wrong stepped into the center of the group. She treated all the patients as if they were children, which Francis hated. 'Mister Evans would like all of you to use this time to do a self-portrait,' she said briskly. 'Something that says something, anything, about how you see yourself.'

'I can't do a picture of a tree?' Cleo questioned. She gestured toward the bank of dayroom windows that were filled with refracted light, glistening with the afternoon. Beyond the glass and wire mesh, Francis could see one of the quadrangle trees on the grounds swaying in a light breeze, the springtime weather just ruffling the new green leaves.

'Unless you think of yourself as a tree,' Nurse Wrong replied, stating something so obvious that it was nearly overwhelming.

'A Cleo tree?' Cleo asked. She raised her chunky arm and flexed it like a bodybuilder. 'A very strong tree.'

Francis chose a small tray of watercolors. Blue. Red. Black. Green. Orange. Brown. He had a small paper cup of water that he placed on the floor next to his feet. After a final glance toward Peter, who had suddenly bent over his sheet of paper, and was busily at work, Francis turned to his own blank canvas. He dipped his small brush into the liquid to wet the tip, then into the black paint. He made a long, oval shape on the page and then turned to the task of filling in the features.

In the back of the dayroom, a man faced up against the wall, mumbling steadily, like a person at prayer, interrupting himself only every few minutes to steal a glance in the group's direction, before returning to his conversation. Francis noticed the same retarded man who'd threatened them earlier; he lurched through the room, grunting, occasionally staring in their direction, slapping his fist into his palm repeatedly. Francis turned back to his drawing, and continued to slide the paintbrush gently over the sheet of paper, watching with some satisfaction as a figure grew in the center of the page.

Francis worked intently. He tried to give himself a smile, but it came out crookedly, so that it seemed that half his face was enjoying something, while the other half filled with regret. The eyes stared out at him intently, and he thought he could see beyond them. Francis thought the painted Francis had shoulders perhaps a little too slumped, and a posture that was perhaps too resigned. But this was less important than trying to show that the Francis on the sheet of paper had feelings, had dreams, had desires, had all the emotions that he associated with the outside world.

He did not look up until Nurse Wrong announced there were only a few minutes left in the session.

He glanced to his side and saw that Peter was intently putting the finishing touches on his own picture. It was a pair of hands, gripping bars that stretched from the top of the sheet to the bottom. There was no face, no body, no sense of person whatsoever. Just the fingers wrapped around thick shafts of black that dominated the page.

Nurse Wrong took Francis's painting from his hands and paused to examine it.

Big Black came over and stared over her shoulder at the painting. He broke into a smile. 'Damn, C-Bird,' he said. 'This is some fine work. Boy's got some talent he didn't tell no one about.'

The nurse and the huge attendant moved off, collecting the other patients' work, and Francis found himself standing next to Napoleon. 'Nappy,' he said, quietly, 'how long have you been here?'

'In the hospital?'

'Yes. And in here, in Amherst.' He gestured at the dayroom. Napoleon seemed to think for a moment before responding.

'Two years now, C-Bird, except it could be three, I'm not sure. A long time,' he added sadly. 'A real long time. You lose track. Or maybe it's that they want you to lose track. I'm not sure.'

'You're pretty experienced in how things work around here, aren't you?'

Napoleon bowed slightly, almost gracefully. 'An expertise, alas C-Bird, that I would prefer not to own. But true enough.'

'If I wanted to get from here to one of the other buildings, how would I do it?'

Napoleon looked slightly frightened by the question, he took a single step back, and shook his head. His mouth opened, flustered, and he stammered his reply: 'You don't like it here with us?'

Now it was Francis's turn to shake his head negatively. 'No. I mean late at night. After medication, after lights-out. Suppose I wanted to get to one of the other buildings without being seen, could I do it?'

Napoleon considered the question. 'I don't think so,' he said slowly. 'We're always locked in.'

'But suppose I wasn't locked in . . . '

'We're always locked in.'

'But suppose . . . ,' Francis said again, slightly exasperated by the round man's response.

'This has something to do with Short Blond, doesn't it? And Lanky, too. But Lanky couldn't get out of the dormitory. Except the night Short Blond died, when it was unlocked. I've never heard of the door being left unlocked before. No, you can't get out. No one can. I don't know that I've ever heard someone wanting to.'

'Somebody could. Somebody did. And somebody wanted to. Somebody's got a set of keys.'

Napoleon looked terrified. 'A patient has a set of keys,' he whispered. 'I've never heard of that.'

'I think so,' Francis said.

'That would be wrong, C-Bird. We're not supposed to have keys.' Napoleon shifted his weight from foot to foot, as if the ground beneath the soles of his tattered slippers had grown hot to the touch. 'I think, if you got outside, I mean out of the building, avoiding the security patrol would be pretty easy. I mean, they don't seem like the brightest guys on the planet, do they? And I think they have to clock in at the same locations, at the same time every night, so avoiding them — well, even somebody as crazy as one of us probably could manage it with a little bit of planning . . . ' He giggled slightly, almost losing control, grinning at the radical opinion that the security guards were incompetent. But then his brow knit together closely. 'But that wouldn't be the problem, would it, C-Bird?'

'What do you think the problem would be?' Francis asked.

'Getting back in. The main door, even if you had a key, is right across from the nurses' station. It's the same in every building, isn't it? And even if the nurse or the attendant on duty were asleep at the time, the sound of the door opening would likely awaken them.'

'What about the emergency exits on the side of the building?'

'I think those are barred and nailed shut.'

He shook his head. 'Probably a fire code violation,' he added. 'We ought to ask Peter. I'll bet he knows.'

'Probably. But still, even if you wanted to, you don't

237

think it could be done?'

'There might be some other way. I've just never heard of one in all the time I've been here. And I've never heard of anyone who wanted to get from one place to another, C-Bird. Never. Not once. Why would anyone, when all we want and all we need and all that we could possibly use is right here in this building?'

That was a depressing question, Francis thought. And also untrue, for there was someone who had needs that departed from those that Napoleon was talking about. Francis thought to himself, probably for the first time: What is it the Angel needed?

$$\star \quad \star \quad \star$$

It was Peter who spotted the maintenance man as we walked out of the dayroom. I wondered later if things might have been different if we'd been able to see exactly what he was doing, but we were on our way to talk to Lucy, and that always seemed to be the top priority. Afterward, I spent hours, maybe days, simply contemplating all the congruity of things — as if this or that outcome might have been changed if any of the three of us had been able to see the connectivity that was so important. Sometimes madness is about fixation, dwelling on a single notion. Lanky's obsession with evil. Peter's need for absolution. Lucy's need for justice. They, or course, weren't mad, at least not in the way I knew it, or Gulp-a-pill knew it, or even how Mister Evil knew it. But, in a curious sort of way, needs that are powerful can become a kind of madness unto themselves. The difference is, they're not so easily diagnosable as the madness I had. Still, seeing the maintenance man, a middle-aged fellow, with circles under his eyes, wearing his matching gray shirt and slacks, thick brown work boots, his dark hair streaked with sandy dust, and his clothing marred by black oil residue, should have spoken to us in some odd, subterranean way. He carried his wooden toolbox in a grimy hand, and a dingy rag drooped from his belt. He jingled a little, with his keys striking against the yellow plastic encased flashlight that bounced from a bracket around his waist. He had a satisfied look, the appearance that a man who can suddenly see the end of a long and dirty task might wear, and Peter and I heard him turn to Big Black and Little Black and as he lit a cigarette, say, 'Won't be long now. Almost finished. Damn, what a bitch,' before heading into a storage room at the opposite end of the hallway from where Short Blond's body was taken.

When I think back, I can see so many little things that should have meant something. Little moments that really should have been big moments. A maintenance man. A retarded man. A missing administrator. A man talking to himself. Another man seemingly asleep in a chair. A woman who thought she was the reincarnation of an ancient Egyptian princess. I was young, and I didn't understand that crime is like all the mechanical parts of a transmission. Bolts and nuts, screws and pins, all meshing together to create a self-contained momentum that travels forward, controlled by forces that are a little like the wind; invisible, yet leaving signs in a piece of scrap paper that suddenly takes flight and dashes down the sidewalk, or a tree branch being tugged first one way, then the next, or merely the distant dark storm clouds scudding across an ominous sky. It took me a long time to see that.

Peter knew it, as did Lucy. Perhaps that was what connected them, at least at first. They were alert and constantly watching for all the gears that would tell them where to look for the Angel. But, later, afterward, I thought that what linked them was something more complex. It was that they had arrived at the Western State Hospital at that same moment unaware of what it was that they needed. Both had a great gap within themselves, and the Angel was there to provide the necessary filler.

I sat cross-legged in the center of my living room.

The world around seemed hushed and quiet. Not even a stray sound of a baby crying from the Santiagos' apartment. Beyond the living room window, it was pitch-black. Night thick as a stage curtain. I listened for the noise of traffic, but even that was muted. None of the diesel interruptions of trucks passing by. I looked down at my hands and thought it must be a couple of hours before dawn. Peter once told me that the last darkness of the night before morning was the time when most people died.

It was the Angel's time.

I rose, took my pencil, and began to sketch. Within a few minutes I had Peter as I remembered him. Then I set to drawing Lucy by his side. I wanted to make her beauty pure, so I cheated a little, when it came to lining in the scar on her face. I made it a little smaller than it should have been. In a few more moments I had them with me, and just as I recalled them from those first days. Not how any of us was changed.

*   *   *

Lucy Jones could see no shortcut that might bring her closer to the man she hunted. At least nothing simple and obvious, like a list of patients dramatically and conveniently available to have committed all four murders. So, instead, what she did was allow Doctor Gulptilil to escort her from building to building, and in each she went over the roster of male inmates. She eliminated everyone suffering from dementia bought on by senility, and she was judicious in examining the list of men designated as profoundly retarded. She also struck from her growing list anyone with more than five years in the hospital. This, she conceded inwardly, was only a guess on her part. But she thought that anyone having spent that much time in the hospital was probably so filled with antipsychotic medications, and so constrained by madness, that functioning outside the hospital in even a modestly effective way was probably unlikely. And, she thought, the person who was the Angel had some capabilities in both settings. The more she thought about this, the more persuaded she was that she needed to find someone who could function in both worlds.

To her dismay, she realized she couldn't eliminate staff members. The problem in that arena, would be persuading the medical director to turn over employee files, which she doubted he would do without some evidence suggesting that a doctor, a nurse, or an attendant was somehow connected to the crime. As she walked alongside the small Indian physician, she didn't really listen to him, as he droned on about the values of residential treatment centers for the mentally ill and instead wondered how she could proceed.

In New England, in the late spring, there is an evening murkiness, as if the world is unsure about the state of change from the dank winter months into summer. Warm southern breezes pushed up by upper currents of air, mingle freely with shafts of cold that tumble down from Canada. Both sensations were like unwelcome immigrants, searching for a new home. Around her, she became aware of the shadows that crept forward across the hospital grounds, moving inexorably toward each of the housing units. She felt both hot and cold, a little like being caught up in a fever, sweating hard, but pulling a blanket tight to the chin.

She had more than 250 possible suspects on the succession of lists she had made in each building, and she worried that there were a hundred names that she'd rejected perhaps too quickly. She guessed that there would be another twenty-five or thirty possible suspects among the staff, as well, but she wasn't prepared to head in that direction yet, because she knew it would alienate the medical director, whose help she still needed.

As the two of them approached the Amherst Building, she realized with a start that she hadn't heard any catcalls, or shouts, from the housing buildings they had walked past. Or, perhaps, she had heard them, but failed to react. She took note of this inwardly, and thought how quickly the world of the hospital made the odd become routine.

'I have done a little reading about the sort of man you are pursuing,' Dr. Gulptilil said, as they crossed the quadrangle. Their footsteps clicked against the black macadam of the walkway, and Lucy looked up and saw that the iron gates of the hospital were being rolled shut for the night by a security guard. 'It is interesting how little medical literature is devoted to this murderous phenomena. Very few true studies, alas. There are some profiling efforts under way by police authorities, but in general, the psychological ramifications, diagnosis and treatment plans for the sort of person you are seeking have been generally ignored. In the psychiatric community, you must understand, Miss Jones, we do not like to waste our time with psychopaths.'

'Why is that, Doctor?'

'Because they cannot be treated.'

'At all?'

'No. Not at all. At least, not the classic psychopath. He does not respond to antipsychotic medication, the way a schizophrenic does. Nor, for that matter, a bipolar personality, an obsessive-compulsive, a clinical depressive or any number of diagnoses that we have developed medications for. Ah, now, that is not to say that the

242

psychopath doesn't have identifiable medically recognizable illnesses. Far from it. But their lack of humanity, I suppose that's the best way to put it, places them in a different category, and one that is not well understood. They defy treatment plans, Miss Jones. They are dishonest, manipulative, often dramatically grandiose, and extremely seductive. Their impulses are their own and unchecked by the ordinary conventions of life and morality. Frightening, I must add. Very unsettling individuals when one comes into clinical contact with them. The astute psychiatrist Hervey Cleckley has an interesting book of case studies, which I would be more than happy to lend to you. It is perhaps the definitive work on these sorts of people. But it will make for most distressing reading, Miss Jones, because the conclusions drawn suggest there is little we can do. Clinically speaking, that is.'

Lucy stopped outside the Amherst Building, and the small doctor turned eagerly toward her, bending his head slightly, as if to improve his hearing. A single high-pitched shout creased the air, emanating from one of the adjacent buildings, but they both ignored it.

'How many patients here have been diagnosed as psychopaths?' she asked abruptly.

He shook his head. 'Ah, a question I have anticipated,' he said.

'And the answer is?'

'Someone diagnosed as a psychopath would not be suitable for the treatment plans we have here. They are also not aided by long-term residential care, lengthy courses of psychotropic medication, even some of the more radical programs which we, upon occasion, administer, such as electrical convulsive therapy. Nor are they capable of other traditional forms of treatment, such as psychotherapy or even' — and with this, he giggled slightly in the self-assured manner that he had, which Lucy had already determined to be irritating

243

— 'a course of traditional psychoanalysis. No, Miss Jones, a psychopath does not belong in the Western State Hospital. They do, perhaps, belong in prison, which is generally where you will find them.'

She hesitated, then asked, 'But you're not saying there are none here, are you?'

Doctor Gulptilil smiled, Cheshire catlike, before responding. 'There is no one here with that diagnosis written clearly and unequivocally on their admitting jacket, Miss Jones. There are some where some possible psychopathological tendencies are noted, but these are secondary to a more profound mental illness.'

Lucy grimaced, more than a little angry at the doctor's evasiveness.

Doctor Gulptilil coughed. 'But, of course, Miss Jones, if what you suspect is true, and your visit here is not rooted in error, as so many seem to think, then clearly there is one patient who has been significantly misdiagnosed.'

He reached up, unlocked the front door to Amherst with a key, and then held the door open for her with a small bow and slightly forced gallantry.

14

Lucy headed to her small room on the second floor of the nurse-trainees' dormitory late that evening, darkness surrounding her every step. It was one of the more obscure buildings on the hospital grounds, isolated in a shadowy corner, not far from the power plant with its constant hum and smoke plume, and overlooking the small hospital graveyard. It was as if the dead, haphazardly buried nearby, helped hush the sounds around the building. It was a stiff and square, three-storied, ivy-covered, federal-styled brick house with some imposing white Doric columns outside the front portico, that had been converted fifty years earlier and then reconfigured again in the late Forties and early Sixties, so that whatever remained of its first incarnation as someone's fine and grand hillside home was now merely memory. In two hands, she carried a brown cardboard box jammed with perhaps three dozen patient files, a group with a loosely defined potential, that she had selected from the list of names she was steadily compiling. Included in her selection were the files belonging to both Peter the Fireman and Francis, which she had taken when Mister Evans wasn't paying as much attention as perhaps he should have been. These were to satisfy, she hoped, some lingering curiosity about what had landed her two partners in the mental hospital.

Her overall idea was to start in familiarizing herself with what generally went into the dossiers, and then she would begin to interview patients once she had a firm grasp of what sort of information was already available. She couldn't really immediately see any other approach. There was no physical evidence in her possession that could be pursued — although she was well aware that there was significant physical evidence somewhere. A knife, or some other highly sharpened weapon, like a prison shank or a set of razor-sharp box cutters, she thought. That was carefully hidden. There had to be some other bloody clothes, and perhaps a shoe with its sole still rimmed with the nurse's blood. And somewhere there were the four missing fingertips.

She had telephoned the detectives who had taken Lanky into custody and asked about these. They had been singularly unhelpful. One believed that he had sliced them off, then flushed them down a toilet. A lot of effort to no discernible reason, she thought. The other, without stating it clearly, danced around the suggestion that Lanky had perhaps ingested them. 'After all,' the detective said, 'the guy's crazy as a loon.'

They were not, Lucy thought, particularly interested in considering any alternatives. 'Come on, Miss Jones,' the first detective had said, 'we've got the guy. And a prosecutable case, except for the fact that he's nuts.'

The box of files was heavy and she balanced it on her knee as she pulled open the side door to the dormitory. So far, she thought, she had yet to see some telltale indicators of a kind of behavior that might be examined more closely. Inside the hospital, everyone was strange. It was a world that suspended the ordinary laws of reason. Outside the hospital, there would be some neighbor who noticed some odd behavior. Or a coworker in an office who felt uncomfortable. Perhaps a relative who held unsettled doubts.

That wasn't the case here, she told herself. She had to discover new routes. It was a matter of outwitting the killer she believed hid in the hospital. At that particular game, she was confident of success. It shouldn't, she thought, be all that difficult to outmaneuver a crazy man. Or a man posing as crazy. The problem that existed, she realized with a sense of discouragement, was how she could define the parameters of the game.

Once the rules were in place, she thought, as she dragged herself up the steep stairwell one slow step at a time, feeling the same sort of exhaustion one feels after a long and debilitating illness, she would win. She had been taught to believe that all investigations were ultimately the same, a predictable set piece played out on a well-defined stage. This was true examining the books of some tax-dodging corporation, or finding a bank robber, child pornographer, or scam artist. One item would link to another, and then lead her to a third, until all, or at least enough, of the puzzle was visible. Failed investigations — of which she had yet to be a part — were the accidental result of one of those links being hidden, or obscured, and that absence exploited. She blew out and shrugged. It was critical, she told herself, for her to create the external pressure necessary for the man they had taken to calling the Angel to make some mistakes.

He would do this, she thought coldly.

The first thing was to search the files for small acts of violence. She didn't think that a man capable of the killings she was investigating would be able to completely hide a propensity for anger, even in the hospital confines. There will be some sign, she told herself. An outburst. A threat. An explosion. She just needed to make sure that she recognized it when it raised itself up. In the off-center world of the mental hospital, someone had to have seen something that didn't fit any of the acceptable patterns of behavior.

She was completely confident, as well, that once she began to ask questions, she would see answers. Lucy had great trust in her ability to cross-examine her way to the truth. She did not consider, at that moment, the distinctions between asking a sane person a question and asking a certifiably crazy person the same inquiry.

The stairwell reminded her a little of some of the

dormitories at Harvard. Her footsteps echoed against the concrete risers, and she was abruptly aware that she was alone, in a solitary, confined space. A shaft of awful memory creased through her, and she caught her breath sharply. She exhaled slowly, as if blowing hot air out of her lungs would carry with it the ripples of remembrance that iced over her heart. She looked around wildly, for a moment, thinking *I have been here before* and then, instantly dismissing this fear. There were no windows, and no sound penetrated from the outside. It was the second time that day, she thought, that noise had surprised her. The first time was when she had realized that there was a constant cacophony about the hospital. Groans, shrieks, catcalls, and mutterings. In short order, she had grown accustomed to the constancy of racket. She stopped in her tracks.

Quiet, she said to herself, is as unsettling as a scream.

The echoes faded around her, and she listened to the raspy sound of her own breath. She waited until a complete silence had enveloped her. She leaned over the black iron banister, searching up and down, to make certain she was alone. She could see no one. The stairwell was well lit, and there were no shadows to hide in. She waited another moment or two, trying to shake off a sense of narrowing that overcame her. It was as if the walls had closed in ever so slightly. There was a chill in the stairwell, which made her think that the heating system in the dormitory didn't penetrate to that space, and she shivered, and then thought that was completely wrong, because she could suddenly feel sweat dripping beneath her arms.

Lucy shook her head, as if by force of vigorous motion she could clear the sensation from within her. She attributed the clammy feeling that she could feel in her palms with the hospital and her role in it. She reassured herself that being one of the few completely reasonable persons around was undoubtedly likely to make her feel nervous, and that it was only the accumulation of all that she had seen and felt in her first days in the hospital that had come back to visit her.

Again, exhaling slowly, she scraped her foot against the floor, making a scratching sound, as if to impose a sense of something ordinary and routine in the stairwell.

But the noise she made chilled her.

Memory scorched her, like acid.

Lucy swallowed hard, reminding herself that it was a rule in her heart to not dwell on what had happened to her so many years earlier. There was no profit in revisiting pain, recollecting fear, or reliving a hurt so profound. She reminded herself of the mantra she had adopted after being assaulted: *You only remain a victim, if you allow it*. Inadvertently, she started to lift her hand to her scarred cheek, but was stopped by the bulk of the file box she carried. She could feel where she had been damaged, as if the scar glowed, and she remembered the tightening sensation of the emergency room surgeon's stitches, as he'd pulled the separated flaps of skin back together. A nurse had quietly reassured her, while two detectives, a man and a woman, had waited on the other side of a white floor-to-ceiling curtain, while the physicians tended first to the obvious wounds that bled, and then to the harder wounds, that were internal. It had been the first time she'd heard the words *rape kit*, but not the last, and within a few years, she would have both a professional and personal knowledge of the words. She breathed out again, slowly. The worst night of her life had started in a stairwell much like that one, and then, as quickly as that awful thought arrived, she dismissed it harshly.

I am alone she reminded herself. *I am all alone.*

Gritting her teeth, her ears still edgily sorting through every ancillary sound and noise, she pushed to the doorway, and shouldered her way into the second floor of the dormitory. Her room — Short Blond's former room — was adjacent to the stairwell. Doctor Gulptilil had given her a key, and she set the box down, while she retrieved it from her pocket.

She slipped it into the lock, and then stopped.

Her door was open. It slid forward an inch or two, revealing a strip of darkness around the edges.

She stepped back sharply into the corridor, as if the doorway was electrified.

Her head pivoted right and left, and she bent forward slightly, trying to spot someone else, or hear some telltale sign that told her someone was close by. But her eyes seemed suddenly blind and her hearing deafened. She took a quick measurement of all her senses, and they all answered warnings.

Lucy hesitated, unsure of what to do.

Three years prosecuting cases in the sex crimes unit of the Suffolk County prosecutor's office had taught her much. As she had swiftly risen through the ranks to become the assistant chief of the unit, she had immersed herself in case after case, relentlessly pursuing all the minutia of assault after assault. The constancy of crime had created within her a sort of daily testing mechanism, where each and every little act of her existence was held up against an invisible internal standard: *Is this going to be the small mistake that gives someone an opportunity?* In the larger scheme of things, this meant she was aware that she shouldn't walk alone through a darkened parking lot at night or answer an unexpected knock at her door by opening it. It meant keeping windows locked, being alert and aware and constantly on guard and sometimes it meant carrying the handgun that she was authorized by the prosecutor's office to keep, in her hand. It also meant not repeating the innocent mistakes she herself had made one terrible night when she was a law student.

She bit down on her lip. That weapon was locked in a case inside her bag within the room.

Again she listened, telling herself nothing was amiss, when everything irrational and terrified within her insisted the opposite. She set down the box of patient files, nudging it to the side. The side of caution within her screamed implacably, a din of warning.

She ignored it, and instead, she reached forward for the door handle.

Then, hand on the brass fitting, she stopped.

Had the metal been hot to the touch, she would have failed to notice it.

Breathing out slowly, she stepped back.

She spoke to herself, as if by slowing the speed of consideration, she would give it more weight: *The door was locked and now it is open. What are you about to do?*

Lucy stepped back a second time. Then she abruptly turned, and started walking quickly down the corridor. Her eyes searched right and left, her ears sharpened, listening. She picked up her pace, so that she was nearly running, a fast jog through the carpeted floors, her feet making a muffled sound beneath her. All the other dormitory rooms on that floor were closed, and silent. She reached the end of the hallway, starting to breathe hard, then tossed herself down the stairwell at that end, her shoes beating a drummer's tattoo against the risers. The stairwell was identical to the one at the other end, that she had climbed up a few minutes earlier, empty and echoing. She pushed through a heavy door, and then, for the first time, heard some voices. She moved toward the sound, taking the steps two at a time, and came upon three young women, standing by the first floor front entrance. All wore white nursing outfits beneath cardigan sweaters of different hues, and they looked up, surprised, as Lucy launched herself in their direction.

Gesturing a little wildly, Lucy grabbed some breath and said, 'Excuse me . . . '

The three nurse-trainees stared at her.

' . . . I'm sorry to interrupt your conversation,' she said, 'but I'm Lucy Jones, the prosecutor sent here to . . . '

'We know who you are, Miss Jones, and why you're here,' one of the nurses said. She was a tall black woman, with athletic, broad shoulders and dark hair and matching complexion. 'Is something wrong?'

Lucy nodded, and inhaled before replying, trying to regain some composure. 'I'm not sure,' she said. 'I returned here and found my dormitory door unlocked. I'm sure I left it locked this morning when I went over to the Amherst Building . . . '

'That's not right,' one of the other nurses said. 'Even if building maintenance or the cleaning service went in there, they're supposed to lock up afterward. That's the rule.'

'I'm sorry,' Lucy said, 'but I was alone up there and . . . '

The tall black nurse nodded, in understanding. 'We're all a little jumpy, Miss Jones, even with Lanky's arrest. These sorts of things just don't happen in the hospital. Why don't we three accompany you back to the room and check it out.'

No one had to expand on the phrase *these things* to understand it.

Lucy sighed. 'Thank you,' she said. 'That is kind of you. I would really appreciate it.'

The four women then turned and walked up the stairwell, marching together, a little like a squad of waterbirds paddling across a lake in the early morning. The nurses continued talking, gossiping really, about a couple of the doctors working in the hospital, and making jokes about the weaselly appearance of the latest group of legal advocates who had arrived at the hospital that week for a round of quasijudicial commitment hearings. Lucy led the way, moving rapidly right up to the door.

'I really appreciate this,' she repeated, and then she reached out and grabbed the door handle, twisted it, and pushed.

The door lock stopped her in her tracks. The door ratcheted back and forth, but did not open.

She pushed again.

The nurses looked at her a little oddly.

'It was open,' Lucy said. 'It was definitely open.'

'It seems locked now,' the black nurse said.

'I'm sure it was open. I put my hand on the handle and put in the key and before I turned it the door opened just a little,' Lucy said. Her voice, however, lacked conviction. She was suddenly filled with doubts.

There was a momentary, awkward pause, and then Lucy removed her room key from her pocket, slid it into the lock and opened the door. The three nurses hovered behind her. 'Why don't we go in and make a quick check?' one said.

Lucy pushed the door open, and stepped inside the room. It was dark inside and she flicked the switch for the overhead light. Abruptly the small space lit up. It was a sparse, narrow area, a monklike room with nothing on the walls, a sturdy chest of drawers, a single bed, and a small brown wooden desk and hard backed chair. Her suitcase remained open in the center of the bed, on top of a red corduroy bedspread, which was the only splash of vibrant color in the room. Everything else was either oaken brown, or white, like the walls. As the three nurses watched, Lucy opened the small closet on one wall, and peered inside at its emptiness. Then she walked over to the small bathroom, and checked the shower stall. She even dropped to one knee and checked under the bed, although they could all see that there was no one concealed under there. Lucy rose up, dusted herself off, and turned to the three nurses. 'I'm sorry,' she said. 'I'm quite certain the door was open, and I had the sensation that there was someone in the room waiting for me. I've put you out and . . . '

But all three nurses shook their heads. 'Nothing to apologize for,' the black nurse said.

'I'm not apologizing,' Lucy said sturdily. 'The door was open. Now it's locked.'

But inwardly, Lucy was unsure whether this was true.

The nurses were silent, until the black nurse shrugged and spoke slowly, 'Like I said before, we're all a little jumpy, and it makes more sense to be safe than sorry.'

The others murmured in agreement.

'You okay now?' the nurse asked.

'Yes. Fine. I appreciate your concern,' Lucy said, a little stiffly.

'Well, you need help again, you just find anyone. Don't hesitate. Best to trust your feelings in times like these.'

The nurse didn't elaborate on what she meant by times like these.

Lucy locked the door behind the nurses, as they walked back down the hallway. She was a little embarrassed, as she turned and leaned up against the door, pushing it with her back. She looked around and thought to herself: *You weren't wrong. Someone was here. Someone was waiting.*

She glanced over at her bag. *Or someone was just having a look.* She stepped to the modest collection of clothes and toiletries that she had brought with her and realized, in that second, that something was missing. She didn't know what, but she knew something had been taken from her room.

★   ★   ★

It was you, wasn't it?

Right there, right at that moment, you tried to tell Lucy something important about yourself, and she missed it. It was something critical, and something frightening, far more frightening than anything she felt as she closed that door behind her with a satisfying thud. She was still thinking like a normal person, and that was to her great disadvantage.

★   ★   ★

Peter the Fireman looked across the dormitory room, trying hard to separate the pain of distant memory from the immediate task at hand. Uncertainty marred his thoughts, and he felt the bitterness that indecision can nurture. He thought of himself at the very least as a man of determination and a man of decisiveness, and he was uncomfortable with doubts. He knew it had been impulse which prompted him to volunteer his and C-Bird's services to Lucy Jones, and he was still certain that it had been the correct choice. But his enthusiasm hadn't contemplated failure, and he strained to see a manner in which they could succeed. Everywhere he considered, he saw restraints and prohibitions, and he did not see how they could overcome all those limitations.

In the world of the mental hospital, he considered himself to be the sole pragmatist.

He sighed. It was deep into the night and he was leaning up against the wall, his feet stretched out on the bed, listening to the racket of sleep surrounding him. Even the nighttime knew no respite from pain, he thought. The people in the hospital were unable to flee their troubles, no matter how many narcotics Gulp-a-pill had prescribed. He thought this was what was so insidious about mental illness; that it took so much force of will and depth of treatment to simply get to a position where one could consider trying to get better, that the task seemed almost Herculean for most, and well-nigh impossible for some. He heard one long moan, and almost turned in that direction, but then stopped, because he recognized the author. It saddened him, sometimes, when Francis tossed in his sleep, because he knew the young man didn't really deserve the hurts that emerged unwelcome in the darkness.

He didn't think he fit the same category.

Peter tried to relax, but could not. For a moment, he wondered whether when he closed his eyes, if the same turmoil erupted from his sleep sounds. The difference, he told himself, between him and all the others, including his young friend, was that he was guilty, and they probably were not.

In his nostrils, inexplicably, he could suddenly smell the thick, sweet odor of some indistinct accelerant. The first whiff screamed gasoline, the second, a benzine-based lighter fluid.

He almost shot up in surprise, launching himself out of bed, the sensation was so powerful. His first instinct was to somehow raise the alarm, organize the men, get them out, before the inevitable fire burst forth. In his mind's eye, he suddenly saw streaks of red and yellow flame searching the bedding, the walls, the floor beneath their feet, for fuel. He could sense the deep desperate choking that would inevitably follow, as thick curtains of smoke fell across the stage of the room. The door was locked, as it was every night, and he could hear the panicked men, screaming, calling for help, pounding on the walls. Every muscle in his body tensed, and then, just as rapidly, relaxed, as he breathed in, and he realized the smell flitting through his nose was as much a hallucination as any of those that plagued Francis or Nappy or even the particularly dire ones that had afflicted Lanky.

He sometimes thought that his entire life had been

defined by odors. Beer and whiskey smells that followed his father, mingling freely with the odors of dried sweat and dirt from hard work at some construction site or another. Sometimes, too, his father wore thick diesel smells from fixing the heavy equipment. And burying his head into the large man's chest was to come away with a nose filled with the stale scent of too many of the cigarettes that eventually would kill him. His mother, in contrast, always had a chamomile scent to her, because she battled hard against the harshness of the detergents that she used in the laundry she took in. Sometimes, beneath the heavy smell of the soaps she liked, he could just catch a whiff of the sharp odor of bleach. She wore a far better scent on Sundays, when she was scrubbed, but had spent some time in the kitchen early, baking, so that in her churchgoing finery she combined an earthy, bread-smell, with an insistent cleanliness, as if that was what God would want. Church was stiff clothes beneath the white and gold robes of the altar boy and incense that sometimes made him sneeze. He remembered all those scents, as if they were in the hospital alongside him.

The war had given him a whole new world of odors to remember. Thick jungle smells of vegetation and heat, cordite and white phosphorous from firefights. Clammy smells of smoke and napalm in the distance, that mingled with the claustrophobic smells of the bush that entwined him. He grew accustomed to the smells of blood, vomit, and fecal matter that mixed so often with death. There were exotic cooking smells, in the villages they passed through, and dangerous smells of swamps and flooded fields that they maneuvered past. There was the acrid, familiar smell of marijuana back in the base camps, as well, and the harsh, eye-stinging smell of cleaning fluids used on weapons. It was a place of unfamiliar and unsettling scents.

He had learned, when he returned, that fire had

dozens of different smells at all its different stages and in all its different incarnations. Wood fires were distinct from chemical fires, which had little similarity to fires that gutted concrete. The first licking, tentative burst was different from the moment where it rose up and took flower, and different again from the crackling smell of a fire in control of its own voracious future. And it was all distinct from the heavy odors of charred timbers and twisted metals that followed, when it had been beaten back and defeated. He had known, then, too, the unique odor of exhaustion, as if bone-weary fatigue had a scent all its own. When he had signed up for arson investigator's school, one of the first things they taught him was how to use his nose, because gasoline that was used to start a fire smelled different from kerosene and that smelled different from all the other ways that people created destruction. Some were subtle, with distant, elusive bouquets. Others were obvious and amateurish, demanding attention from the first moment he stepped onto the rubble of whatever remained.

When it had come time to set his own fire, he'd used regular gasoline purchased at a filling station barely a mile away from the church. Purchased with a credit card in his own name. He didn't want anyone to have any doubts as to who authored that particular blaze.

In the semidarkness of the madhouse dormitory, Peter the Fireman shook his head, although in denial of precisely what, he was uncertain. That night he'd controlled his murderous rage, and simply taken everything he'd learned about how to conceal the origin of a fire, everything that was about caution and subtlety, and ignored it. He'd left a trail so obvious that even the most callow investigator would have had no trouble finding him. He had set the fire, then walked through the nave to the vestry, voice raised in warning, but believing that he was alone. He had stopped, as he heard the fire start to move eagerly behind him, and stared up at a stained glass window, that suddenly seemed to glow with life, as it caught the reflection of the fire. He'd crossed himself, just as he'd done a thousand times, then stepped outside, to the front lawn, where he'd waited to see it explode in full flower, and then he'd walked home to wait in the darkness on the front steps of his mother's house for the police to arrive. He knew he had done a good job, and he'd known that even the most dedicated ladder company wouldn't succeed at extinguishing the blaze until it was too late.

What he hadn't known was that the priest whom he had come to hate was inside. On a fold-out cot in the main office, and not, at home in his bed, where he, by all rights and usual behavior, should have been. Sleeping in the arms of a heavy narcotic, no doubt prescribed to him by a physician-parishioner, concerned that the good father looked pale and drawn and that his sermons seemed marred by anxiety. As well they should have been, for he well knew that Peter the Fireman knew what he had done to his little nephew, and knew, as well, that of all the members of the parish, Peter, alone, was likely to do something about it. This had always bothered Peter: There were so many others that the priest could have easily preyed upon, who weren't related to someone who might rise up. Peter wondered, too, if the same drug that had left the priest asleep in his bed while death crackled all around him, was what Gulp-a-pill liked to give the patients in the hospital. He guessed that they were, a symmetry that he thought pleasantly and almost laughably ironic.

Peter whispered out loud, 'What's done is done.'

Then he glanced around, to see if the noise of his words had awakened anyone.

He tried to close his eyes. He knew he needed to sleep, and yet, held no hope that it would bring him any rest.

He blew out in frustration, and swung his feet over

the side of the bunk. Peter told himself to head into the bathroom, get a drink of water. He rubbed his hands across his face, as if he could wipe away some of his memories.

And, as he did this, he had the sudden sensation that he was being watched.

He straightened up abruptly, instantly alert, his eyes immediately darting about the bunk room.

Most of the men were shrouded in shadow. A little light crept into one corner from the bank of windows. He searched back and forth across the rows of unsettled men, but he could see no one awake, and certainly no one staring in his direction. He tried to dismiss the sensation, but could not. It filled his stomach with a nervous energy, as if all the senses he had of sight, and hearing and smell and taste and touch were suddenly screaming warnings to him. He tried to tell himself to calm down, because he was beginning to think that he might just be turning as paranoid as all the men who surrounded him, but as he reassured himself, he just caught a bit of motion out of the corner of his eye.

He pivoted in that direction and for a single second, he saw a face staring in through the small observation window in the entranceway door. Their eyes met, and then, just as abruptly, the face disappeared, dropping from view.

Peter jumped up, and moving fast through the wan darkness, he dodged his way between the sleeping men to the doorway. He thrust his own face up to the thick glass, and peered out into the corridor. He could only see a few feet in either direction, and all he saw was dark emptiness.

He placed his hand on the doorknob and pulled. It was locked.

A great surge of anger and frustration swept over him. He gritted his teeth and believed somewhere deep within himself that he was always destined to find that which he wanted was unreachable, beyond a locked door.

The weak light, the shadowy darkness, the thick glass, all had conspired to prevent Peter from noting even the smallest of details in the face. All he could take away was the ferocity in the eyes that had settled on him. The look had been uncompromising and evil, and, perhaps for the first time, he thought that maybe Lanky was strangely correct in all his protests and entreaties. Something evil had crept unbidden into the hospital, and Peter knew that this evil knew all about him. He tried to tell himself that his understanding this indicated strength. But he suspected that this was perhaps a lie.

15

By the arrival of midday, I was exhausted. Too little sleep. Too many electric thoughts running rippity-zip through my imagination. I sat alone, taking a modest break, cross-legged on the floor, smoking a cigarette. I believed that the shafts of sunlight streaming through the windows, carrying with it the daytime's ration of thickly oppressive valley heat, had chased away the Angel. Like some Gothic novelist's creature, he was a charter member of the night. All the noon sounds of commerce, of people moving about the city, the diesel rumble of a truck or bus, a distant siren from a patrolman's car, the thump of the newspaper deliveryman tossing his bundle to the sidewalk, school children talking loudly as they made their way down the pavement, all conspired to drive him away. He and I both knew that I was far more vulnerable in the silent midnight hours. Night brings doubt. Darkness sows fears. I expected him to return as soon as the sun fled. There's no pill as yet invented that can alleviate the symptoms of loneliness and isolation that the end of the day brings. But in the meantime, I was safe, or, at least as safe as I could reasonably expect. No matter how many locks and bolts I had on my door, they wouldn't keep out my worst fears. This observation made me laugh out loud.

I reviewed the text that had flown from my pencil and thought: I've taken far too many liberties. Peter the Fireman had taken me aside the following morning shortly after breakfast and whispered to me: 'I saw someone. In the main entranceway observation window. Staring in, just like he was looking for one of us. I couldn't sleep, and as I lay there in my bunk I got

262

the sensation that someone was watching me. When I looked up, I saw him.'

'Did you recognize him?' I asked.

'Not a chance.' Peter had shaken his head slowly. 'Just one second, he was there, then, when I swung out of bed, he was gone. I went to the window and looked out, but couldn't see anyone.'

'What about the nurse on duty?'

'I couldn't see her, either.'

'Where was she?'

'I don't know. In the bathroom? Taking a walk? Maybe upstairs, talking with the upstairs nurse on duty? Asleep in her chair?'

'What do you think?' I'd asked, nervousness starting to creep into my voice.

'I'd like to think it was a hallucination. We have lots of those in here.'

'Was it?'

Peter had smiled, and shook his head. 'No such luck.'

'Who do you think it was?'

He laughed, but without much humor and not because there was some pending joke. 'C-Bird, you already know who I think it was.'

I stopped and took a deep breath and bit down on all the echoes within me.

'Why do you think he came to the doorway?'

'He wanted to see us.'

That was what I remembered with complete clarity. I remembered where we were, how we were dressed. Peter had on his Red Sox cap, slightly pushed back from his forehead. I recalled what we ate that morning: Pancakes that tasted like cardboard inundated in thick, sweet syrup that had more to do with some food scientist's chemical concoction than a New England maple tree. I stubbed out my cigarette on the bare apartment floor and chewed over my recollections instead of the food I undoubtedly needed. That was what he had told me. I guessed about all the other stuff. I wasn't swear-on-the-Bible sure that the night before he was trapped in the web of sleeplessness by what he'd done so many months earlier. He didn't directly tell me that was what kept him lying awake in his bunk, so that when the sensation of being watched came over him, he was alert to it. I don't know if I even thought about it back then. But now, years later, I just figured that that was what it had to be. It made sense, of course, because Peter was ensnared in the briar patch of memory. And, before too long, all these things became conflated, and so, to tell his story, and Lucy's and my own, too, as well, I realize that I have to take some liberties. Truth is a slippery thing, and I'm not all that comfortable with it. Nobody mad is. So, if I get it down right, maybe it's wrong. Maybe it's exaggerated. Maybe it didn't happen quite the way I remember it, or else, maybe my memory is so stretched and tortured by so many years of drugs that the truth will forever elude me.

I think it is only poets who romanticize that insanity is somehow liberating, when the opposite is true. Every voice I heard, every fear I felt, every delusion, every compulsion, every little thing that pulled together to create the sad me who was banished from the house where I had grown up and sent off in restraints to the Western State Hospital, none of it had anything in common with freedom or liberation or even being unique in some positive way. The Western State Hospital was just the place where we were kept while we engaged in the construction of our own internal sort of detention.

Not so true for Peter, because he was never as crazy as the rest of us were.

Not true either, for the Angel.

And, in a curious way, Lucy was the bridge between the two of them.

We were still standing outside the dining room,

264

waiting for Lucy to appear. Peter seemed to be thinking hard, replaying in his mind what he'd seen and what had happened the prior night. I watched him as he seemed to pick up every piece of those few moments, lift them into the light and slowly turn them, like an archaeologist might, as he came across some relic, gently blowing the dust of time away. Peter was much the same with observations; it was as if he thought that if he just twisted whatever it was mentally into the right angle, holding it up to the right shaft of light, he would see it for what it truly was.

As I watched him, he turned to me, and said, 'We know this, now: The Angel doesn't live in the dormitory with us. He might be upstairs in the other dormitory room. He might come from another building, although I haven't figured out how, yet. But at least we can exclude our roommates. And we know another thing. He has learned that we are somehow involved in all this, but he doesn't know us, not well enough, and so he is watching.'

I spun about in the corridor.

Cato was leaning up against a wall, eyes fixed on the ceiling beyond us. He might have been listening to Peter. He might have been listening to some hidden voice deep within himself. Impossible to tell. A senile old man, his hospital pajama pants having come loose, wandered past us, drooling slightly around an unshaven jaw, mumbling and staggering, as if he couldn't understand that the reason he was having trouble walking stemmed from the pants dropped around his ankles. And the hulking retarded man, who'd been threatening the other day, lurched past, in the old man's wake, but when he briefly turned toward us, his eyes were filled with fear and gone was all the anger and aggression from the other day. His medications must have been altered, I thought.

'How can we tell who is watching?' I asked. My head

pivoted to the right and left, and I felt a cold shaft slide through me, when I thought that any one of the hundreds of men staring ahead in reverie could actually be assessing and measuring, taking stock of me.

Peter shrugged. 'Well, that's the trick, isn't it. We're the ones doing the searching, but the Angel's the one doing the watching. Just stay alert. Something will come up.'

I looked up and saw Lucy Jones coming through the front entrance to Amherst. She paused to speak with one of the nurses and I saw Big Black amble over to join her. I saw her hand him a couple of manila case files from the top of the overflowing file box that she had carried in and then set down on the glistening floor. Peter and I took a step toward her. But we were interrupted by Newsman, who saw us and skipped up into our path. His eyeglasses were slightly askew on his face, and a shock of hair jumped off his scalp like a rocket ship. His grin was as lopsided as his attitude.

'Bad news, Peter,' he said, although he was smiling, as if that could somehow deflate the information. 'It's always bad news.'

Peter did not reply and Newsman looked a little disappointed bending his head slightly to the side. 'Okay,' he said, slowly. Then he looked down toward Lucy Jones, and he seemed to begin to concentrate hard. It was almost as if the act of remembering took a physical effort. After a few moments straining, he broke into a grin. 'Boston Globe. September 20th, 1977. Local News Section, page 2B: Refusing to Be A Victim; Harvard Law Grad Named Sex Crimes Unit Head.'

Peter stopped. He turned quietly to Newsman. 'How much of the rest do you remember?'

Newsman hesitated again, doing the heavy lifting of searching his memory, then he recited: 'Lucy K. Jones, twenty-eight, a three-year veteran of the traffic and felony divisions, has been named to head up the newly formed Sex Crimes Unit of the Suffolk County Prosecutor's Office, a spokesman announced today. Miss Jones, a 1974 graduate of Harvard Law School will be in charge of handling sexual assaults and coordinate with the homicide division on killings that stem from rapes, the spokesman said.'

Newsman took a breath, then rushed on. 'In an interview, Miss Jones said that she was uniquely qualified for the position, because she had been the victim of an assault during her first year at Harvard. She was driven to join the prosecutor's office, she said, despite numerous offers from corporate law firms, because the man who'd assaulted her had never been arrested. Her perspective on sex crimes, she said, came from an intimate knowledge of the emotional damage an assault can create and the frustration with a criminal justice system ill equipped to deal with these sorts of violent acts. She said she hoped to establish a model unit that other district attorneys around the state and nation can copy . . . '

Newsman hesitated, and then said, 'There was a picture, too. And a little more. I'm trying to remember.'

Peter nodded. 'No follow-up feature in the Lifestyle Section in the next day or so?' he asked quietly.

Again, Newsman scoured his memory. 'No . . . ,' he said slowly. The smaller man grinned, and then, as he always did, immediately wandered off, looking for a copy of that day's newspaper. Peter watched him walk off, then turned back to me. 'Well, that explains one thing and starts to explain others, doesn't it, C-Bird?'

I thought so, but instead of answering the question, responded, 'What?'

'Well, for one thing, the scar on her cheek,' Peter said.

The scar, of course.

I should have paid more attention to the scar.

As I sat in my apartment picturing the white line that

267

straggled down Lucy Jones's face, I repeated the same mistake I'd made so many years earlier. I saw the flaw in her perfect skin and wondered how it had changed her life. I thought to myself that I would have liked to have touched it once.

I lit another cigarette. Acrid smoke spiraled in the still air. I might have sat there, lost in memory, had there not been a series of sharp knocks at my door.

I struggled to my feet in alarm. My train of thought fled, replaced by a sense of nervousness. I stepped toward the entranceway, and then I heard my name called out sharply. 'Francis!' This was followed by another series of blows against the thick wood of the door. 'Francis! Open up! Are you there?'

I stopped, and for a moment considered the curious juxtaposition of the demand: Open up! followed by the query: Are you there? At best backward.

Of course, I recognized the voice. I waited a moment, because I suspected that within a second or two, I would hear another familiar tone.

'Francis, please. Open the door so we can see you . . .'

Sister One and Sister Two. Megan, who was slender and demanding as a child, but grew into the size of a professional linebacker and developed the same temperament, and Colleen, half her bulk and the shy sort who combines a sense of timidity with a dizzy can-you-do-it-for-me-because-I-wouldn't-know-where-to-start incompetence about the simplest things in life. I had no patience for either of them.

'Francis, we know you're in there, and I want you to open this door immediately!'

This was followed by another bang bang bang against the door.

I leaned my forehead up against the hard wood, then pivoted, so that my back was against it, as if I could help block their entrance. After a moment or two, I

268

turned around again, and spoke out loud: 'What do you want?'

Sister One: 'We want you to open up!'

Sister Two: 'We want to make sure you're okay.'

Predictable.

'I'm fine,' I said, lying easily. 'I'm busy right now. Come back some other time.'

'Francis, are you taking your medications? Open up right now!' Megan's voice had all the authority and about the same amount of patience as a Marine Corps drill sergeant on an exceptionally hot day at Parris Island.

'Francis, we're worried about you!' Colleen probably worried about everyone. She worried constantly about me, about her own family, about the folks and her sister, about people she read about in the morning paper, or saw on the news at night, about the mayor and the governor and probably the president as well, and the neighbors or the family down the street from her who seemed to have fallen on hard times. Worrying was her style. She was the sister closest to my elderly and inattentive parents, had been since we were children, always seeking their approval for everything she did and probably everything she even thought.

'I told you,' I said carefully, not raising my voice, but also not opening the door, 'I'm fine. I'm just busy.'

'Busy with what?' Megan asked.

'Just busy with my own project,' I said. I bit down on my lip. That wouldn't work, I thought to myself. Not for an instant. She would just become more insistent because I no doubt pricked her curiosity.

'Project? What sort of project? Did your social worker tell you you could do a project? Francis, open up right now! We drove all the way over here because we're worried about you, and if you don't open up . . .'

She didn't need to finish her threat. I wasn't sure what she would do, but I suspected that whatever it

269

was, it would be worse than opening up. I cracked the door open approximately six inches, and positioned myself in the opening to block them from entering, keeping my hand on the door, ready to slam it shut.

'See? Here I am, in the flesh. None the worse for wear. Just exactly like I was yesterday, the same as I'll be tomorrow.'

The two ladies inspected me carefully. I wished that I had cleaned myself up, made myself a little more presentable before heading to the door. My unshaved cheeks, scraggly, unwashed hair and nicotine-stained fingernails probably gave off the wrong impression. I tried to tuck in my shirt a little, but realized I was only bringing attention to how slovenly I must have appeared. Colleen gasped a bit when she saw me. A bad sign, that. Meanwhile, Megan tried to peer past me, and I guessed that she saw the writing on the living room walls. She started to open her mouth, then stopped, considered what she intended to say, then started again.

'Are you taking your medications?'

'Of course.'

'Are you taking all your medications?' She emphasized each word carefully, as if she was speaking with a particularly slow child.

'Yes.' She was the sort of woman that it was easy to lie to. I didn't even feel all that guilty.

'I'm not sure I believe you, Francis.'

'Believe what you like.'

Bad answer. I kicked myself inwardly.

'Are you hearing voices again?'

'No. Not in the slightest. Whatever gave you that crazy idea?'

'Are you getting anything to eat? Are you sleeping?' This was Colleen speaking. A little less intense, but, on the other hand, a little more probing.

'Three squares per day and a good eight hours per

270

night. In fact, Mrs. Santiago fixed me a nice plate of chicken and rice the other day.' I spoke briskly.

'What are you doing in there?' Megan demanded to know.

'Just taking inventory of my life. Nothing special.'

She shook her head. She didn't believe this, and kept craning her head forward.

'Why won't you let us in?' Colleen asked.

'I have a need for my privacy.'

'You're hearing voices again,' Megan said decisively. 'I can just tell.'

I hesitated, then asked, 'How? Can you hear them, as well?'

This, of course, angered her even more.

'You need to let us in immediately!'

I shook my head. 'I want to be left alone,' I replied. Colleen looked on the verge of tears. 'I just want you to leave me alone. Why are you here, anyway?'

'We told you. We're worried about you,' Colleen said.

'Why? Did someone tell you to worry about me?'

The two sisters stole a look between them and then came back to me. 'No,' Megan said, trying to modulate the insistence of her tone. 'We just haven't heard from you in so long . . . '

I smiled at them. It was nice that now we were all lying.

'I've been busy. If you'd like to make an appointment, well, have your people call my secretary, and I'll try to work you in before Labor Day.'

They didn't even laugh at my joke. I started to close the door, but Megan stepped forward and placed her hand on it, halting its progress. 'What are those words I see?' she demanded, pointing. 'What are you writing?'

'That would be my business, not yours,' I said.

'Are you writing about mother and father? About us? That wouldn't be fair!'

I was a little astonished. My instant diagnosis was that she was more paranoid than I am. 'What is it,' I said slowly, 'that makes you think you are interesting enough to write about?'

And then I closed the door, probably a little too hard, because the slamming sound resonated through the little apartment building like a gunshot.

They knocked again, but I ignored it. When I stepped away, I could hear a widespread murmuring of familiar voices within me congratulating me on what I'd done. They always liked my small displays of defiance and independence. But they were swiftly followed by a distant, echoing sound of mocking laughter, that rose in pitch and erased the familiar sounds. It was a little like a crow's cry, carried on a strong wind, passing invisibly over my head. I shuddered, and shrank down a little, almost as if I could duck beneath a sound.

I knew who it was. 'You can laugh!' I shouted out at the Angel. 'But who else knows what happened?'

★   ★   ★

Francis took a seat across from Lucy's desk, while Peter paced around in the back of the small office. 'So,' the Fireman said with a small amount of impatience, 'Miss Prosecutor, what's the drill?'

Lucy gestured toward some case files. 'I think it is time to start bringing in some patients to talk. Those who have some record of violence.'

Peter nodded, but seemed a little dismayed. 'Surely when you started reading case files you realized that covers just about everybody in here, except the senile and the retarded, and they just might have some violent entries, as well. We need to find some disqualifying characteristics, I think, Miss Jones . . . ,' he started, but she held up her hand.

'Peter, from now on just call me Lucy,' she said. 'And

that way I won't have to call you by your last name — because I know from your file that your identity is supposed to be if not exactly hidden, at least, well, *de-emphasized*, correct? Because of your notoriety in some rather significant parts of the great Commonwealth of Massachusetts. And, I know, as well, that upon arrival here, you made a point of telling Gulptilil that you no longer had a name, an act of disassociation which he interpreted as having some wish to no longer bring some sort of unspecified shame on your large family.'

Peter stopped pacing, and for an instant Francis thought he was going to get angry. One of his voices shouted out *Pay attention!* and he kept his own mouth shut and watched the two of them carefully. Lucy wore a grin, as if she knew she had discomfited Peter, and he had the look of someone trying to come up with the right riposte. After a moment or two, he leaned back against the wall, and smiled, a look that wasn't wholly dissimilar to that worn by Lucy.

'Okay, Lucy,' he said slowly. 'First names are fine. But tell me this, if you will. Don't you think interviewing any patient with a violent past, or even a violent act or two since he arrived here, will ultimately be fruitless? More critically, just how much time do you have, Lucy? How long do you think you can take, coming up with an answer here?'

Lucy's grin fled abruptly. 'Why would you ask that?'

'Because I wonder if your boss back in Boston is fully aware of what you're up to out here.'

Silence filled the small room. Francis was alert to every movement from his companions: the look in the eyes, and behind them, the positioning of arms and shoulders that might indicate subtle differences from the words spoken.

'Why wouldn't you think that I have the full cooperation of my office?'

Peter simply asked, 'Do you?'

Francis saw that Lucy was about to answer one way, then another, and finally a third, before she replied.

'I do and I don't,' she finally said slowly.

'That sounds to me like two different explanations.'

She nodded.

'My presence here is not yet part of an official case file. I believe one should be opened. Others are undecided. Or more accurately, unsure of our jurisdiction. So when I wanted to head out here, just as soon as I heard about Short Blond's killing, there was some contentious debate in my office. The upshot was that I was permitted to go, but not on an official basis, exactly.'

'I'm guessing that those circumstances weren't precisely outlined to Gulptilil.'

'You'd be right about that, Peter.'

He moved about the back of the room again, as if by motion he could add momentum to his thoughts. 'How much time do you need before the hospital administration gets fed up — or your office wants you back?'

'Not long.'

Again, Peter seemed to hesitate, sorting through his observations. Francis thought that Peter saw facts and details in much the same way that a mountain guide did: seeing obstacles as opportunities, measuring achievement sometimes in single steps. 'So,' Peter said, as if he was suddenly speaking to himself, 'Lucy is here, persuaded that a criminal is here, as well, and determined to find him. Because she has a . . . special interest. Right?'

Lucy nodded. 'Right.' Any amusement had fled her face. 'Your days at Western State certainly haven't affected your investigative abilities.'

He shook his head. 'Oh, I think they have,' he said. He didn't say whether this was for the better or for the worse. 'And what might that special interest be?'

After a long pause, Lucy bent her head lower. 'Peter, I don't think we know each other quite well enough. But let me say this: The individual who committed the other three killings managed to get my personal attention by taunting my office.'

'Taunting?'

'Yes. In the you-can't-catch-me vein.'

'You don't want to be more specific?'

'Not right now. These are details that we would hope to use in an eventual prosecution. So — '

Peter interrupted her. 'You don't want to share specifics with a couple of crazy guys.'

She took a deep breath. 'Not any more than you would like to be specific if I asked about how you spread gasoline through that church. And why.'

Both were silent for a moment, again. Then Peter turned to Francis, and said, 'C-Bird, what links all these crimes together? Why these killings?'

Francis realized he was being given a test, and he answered quickly. 'The victim's appearance, for one thing. Age and isolation; they all were in the habit of traveling in a regular fashion by themselves. They were young and they had short hair and slender physiques. They were found in some location, exposed to elements, that was other than where they were killed, which complicates matters for the police. You told me that. And in different jurisdictions, as well, which is another problem. You told me that, too. And they were all mutilated in the same way, progressively. The missing fingers, just like Short Blond.'

Francis took a deep breath. 'Am I right?'

Lucy Jones nodded, and Peter the Fireman smiled. 'Dead-on,' he said. 'We need to be alert, Lucy, because young C-Bird here has a far better memory for detail and observation than anyone gives him credit for.' Then he stopped, seeming to think for a moment. Once again, he started to say one thing, then appeared to change direction at the last moment. 'All right, Lucy. You should keep some information that might help us to yourself. For the time being. What's the drill, then?'

'We have to find a way to find this man,' she said stiffly, but slightly relieved, as if she understood, in that second that Peter meant to ask another question or two that would have turned the conversation in a different direction. Francis couldn't tell if there was gratitude in what she said, but he saw that his two companions were staring tightly at each other, speaking without saying words, as if they both understood something that had slid past Francis in that moment. Francis thought that might be true, but he did observe something else: Peter and Lucy had established some credentials that seemed to him to place both of them on the same plane of existence. Peter was a little less the mental patient, and Lucy a little less the prosecutor, and what they both suddenly were was something more akin to partners.

'The problem is,' Peter said carefully, 'I believe he has already found us.'

16

If Lucy was surprised by what Peter said, she didn't immediately display it.

'What do you mean, exactly?' she asked.

'I'm guessing that the Angel already knows that you are here and, presumably, the why of your presence, as well. I think there aren't quite as many secrets around here as one might like. More accurately, there's a different definition of what constitutes a secret. So I suspect he's fully aware that you're here hunting him, despite Gulptilil and Evans's promises of confidentiality. How long do you suppose those promises lasted? A day? Maybe two? I would wager that just about everyone here who can know, does know. And I would suspect our friend the Angel is alert to the idea that somehow C-Bird and I are helping you.'

'You reach these conclusions precisely how?' Lucy asked slowly. There was a dry and cautious suspiciousness in her voice that Francis noted, but that Peter seemed to ignore.

'Well, it's mostly supposition, of course,' Peter said. 'But one thing leads to another . . . '

'Well,' Lucy said, 'What's the first *one thing*?'

Peter rapidly filled her in on the vision that he'd observed through the window the previous night. As he described what he'd seen, and how quickly he'd moved to the doorway in an effort to catch a better look, he seemed to watch Lucy equally closely, as if to assess her response with some precision. He finished by saying, 'And so, if he knows about us, enough to want to see us, then he knows about you. Hard to tell, but . . . well, there you have it.' He shrugged slightly, but his eyes wore conviction that contradicted his body language.

'What time last night did this happen?' Lucy asked.

'Late. Well after midnight.'

Peter observed her hesitation. 'There's some detail you would like to share?'

Again, Lucy hesitated. Then she said, 'I believe I, too, was visited last night.'

Peter seemed to rock back, slightly alarmed. 'How so?'

Lucy took a breath, then described going back to the nurse-trainees' dormitory and finding her door unlocked, then locked upon her return. Although she was unable to say who, or why, and while she remained convinced that something had been taken, she was unable to say what. Everything seemed to be in place and intact. She had taken the time to inventory her small collection of possessions and could not find anything missing.

'So,' Lucy said briskly, 'as far as I can tell it's all there. Still, I can't shake the sensation that something is gone.'

Peter nodded. 'Perhaps you should double-check. Something obvious would be an article of clothing. Something a little more subtle would be' — he seemed to think hard for a moment — 'some hair from your brush. Or perhaps he took a swipe of your lipstick and ran it down his chest. Or sprayed some perfume on the back of his hand. Something like that.'

Lucy seemed slightly taken aback by that suggestion, and she shifted about in her seat as if it was a little hot, but before she replied, Francis shook his head back and forth vigorously. Peter turned to him, and asked, 'What is it, C-Bird?'

Francis stuttered slightly, as he spoke. 'I don't think you're quite right, Peter,' he said, speaking quietly. 'He doesn't need to take anything. Not clothes or a toothbrush or hair or underwear or perfume or anything that Lucy brought with her, because he's already taken something far bigger, and much more important. She just hasn't seen it quite yet. Maybe because she doesn't want to see it.'

Peter smiled. 'And what would that be, Francis?' he asked slowly, his voice a little low, but filled with an odd pleasure.

Francis's voice quavered slightly as he responded. 'He took her privacy.'

The three of them were quiet for a moment, as Francis's words filled each of them. 'And then something else,' he added cautiously.

'What's that?' Lucy demanded. Her face had reddened slightly, and she'd started to tap the end of a pencil against the surface of the desk.

'Maybe your safety, too,' Francis said.

The weight of silence grew in the small room. Francis felt as if he'd overstepped some boundary with what he had said. Peter and Lucy were both professionals at the process of investigation, and he wasn't, and he was surprised that he'd even had the bravery to say anything, especially something quite as provocative as what he'd suggested. One of his more insistent voices shouted from deep within him *Be quiet! Keep your mouth shut! Don't volunteer! Stay hidden! Stay safe!* He was unsure whether to listen to this voice or not. After a moment, Francis shook his head and said, 'Maybe I'm wrong about this. It just came into my head all of a sudden, and I didn't really think it through . . . '

Lucy held up her hand. 'I think it's a most pertinent observation, C-Bird,' Lucy said, in the slightly academic way that she sometimes adopted. 'And one that I should keep in mind. But what about the second visit of the night, over to the window looking in on you and Peter? What do you make of that moment?'

Francis stole a quick sideways glance at Peter, who nodded and made a small encouraging gesture. 'He could see us anytime, Francis. In the dayroom or at a meal, or even coming and going to a group session. Hell, we're always hanging out in the corridors. He could get a good look at us then. In fact, he probably has. We're just not aware of it. Why risk moving about at night?'

'He probably has watched us during the daytime, Peter, you're right about that,' Francis said slowly. 'But it doesn't mean the same thing to him.'

'How so?'

'Because during the day, he's just another patient.'

'Yes? Sure. But . . . '

'But at night, he can become himself.'

★   ★   ★

Peter spoke first, his voice filled with a kind of admiration. 'So,' he said with a little laugh, 'it turns out that just as I suspected, C-Bird sees.'

Francis shrugged a little and smiled, thinking that he was getting a compliment and recognizing in some deep and unfamiliar recess that he had very rarely ever been paid any sort of compliment during any of his twenty-one years on the planet. Criticism, complaints, and underscoring his obvious and persistent inadequacy had been what he had known on a pretty steady basis up to that point. Peter leaned across and gave him a little punch on the arm. 'You're going to make a terrific cop yet, Francis,' he said. 'A little odd-looking, perhaps, but a dandy one, nevertheless. We'll need to get you a bit more of an Irish brogue, and a much bigger stomach and puffy red cheeks and a nightstick to swing around and a penchant for doughnuts. No, an *addiction* to doughnuts. But we'll get you there, sooner or later.'

Then he turned to Lucy, and said. 'This gives me an idea.'

She, too, was smiling, because, Francis thought, it wasn't hard to find the absurd portrait of the irrepressibly skinny Francis as the burly beat cop fairly amusing. 'An idea would be good, Peter,' she said in reply. 'An idea would be excellent.'

Peter remained quiet, but for a moment he moved his hand in front of him, like a conductor in front of a symphony, or perhaps a mathematician trying out a formula in the air in front of him, lacking a blackboard on which to scribble numbers and equations. Then he pulled up a chair, reversing it, so that he was sitting backward on it, which, Francis thought, gave his posture and his ideas some urgency, as he spoke.

'We have no physical evidence, right? So that's not a road we can take. And we have no help, especially from the local cops who processed the crime scene, investigated the murder, and arrested Lanky, right?'

'Right,' Lucy said. 'Right. And right again.'

'And we don't really believe, despite what Gulp-a-pill and Mister Evil have said, that they're gonna help much, right?'

'Right again. I think it's clear that they're probably trying to decide what approach creates the least problem.'

'True. Not hard to picture the two of them sitting in Gulp-a-pill's office, with Miss Luscious taking notes, doping out the least amount they can do to cover their butts in every conceivable direction. So, in fact, we don't have much going for us right now. In particular, an obvious and fruitful starting point.'

Peter was alive with ideas. Francis could see him electric.

'What is any investigation?' he said rhetorically, looking squarely at Lucy. 'I've done them, you've done them. We take this solid, stolid, sturdy, determined approach. Collect this bit of evidence and add it to that. Build a picture of the crime brick by brick. Every detail of a crime, from inception to conclusion, gets fit into a rational framework to provide an answer. Isn't that what they taught you in the prosecutor's office? So that the steady accumulation of provable items eliminates everyone except the suspect? Those are the rules, right?'

'I know that. You know that. But your point, exactly, is what?'

'What makes you think the Angel doesn't know that, too?'

'Okay. Yes. Probably. And?'

'So, what we need to do is turn everything upside down.'

Lucy looked a little askance. But Francis saw what Peter was driving at.

'What he's saying,' Francis said carefully, 'is we shouldn't play by any rules.'

Peter nodded. 'Here we are, in this mad place, and you know what will be impossible, Lucy?'

She didn't reply.

'What will be impossible is if we try to impose the reasonableness and the organization of the outside world in here. This place is mad, so what we need is an investigation that reflects the world here. One that fits. Tailor what we do to the place we're in. When in Rome, so to speak.'

'And what would be the first step?' Lucy asked. It was clear that she was willing to listen, but not sign on immediately.

'Exactly what you imagined,' Peter said. 'We interrogate people. You question them in here. Start out all nice and official and by the book. And then turn up the pressure. Accuse people unreasonably. Misrepresent what they say. Turn their paranoia back on top of them. Do as much wrong and irresponsible and outrageous as you can. Unsettle everyone. It will make this place stand on its ear. And the more that we disrupt the ordinary process of this hospital, the less likely the Angel will feel safe.'

Lucy nodded. 'It's a plan. Maybe not much of one,

but it's a plan. Although I can't see Gulptilil going along with it.'

'Screw him,' Peter said. 'Of course he won't. And neither will Mister Evil. But don't let that stand in your way.'

She seemed to think hard for a moment, then laughed. 'Why not?' And then she turned to Francis. 'They won't let Peter in on any questioning I do. Too much baggage comes with him. But you're different, Francis. I think you should be the one to sit in. It'll be you and Evans or the big round doctor, himself, because he's demanding someone be there, and those are the ground rules that Gulptilil set. We create enough smoke, and maybe we'll see some fire.'

No one, of course, saw what Francis saw, which were the dangers in this approach. But he kept quiet, shushed all the voices within him who were nervous and filled with doubts, and simply bent his shoulders to the course that was created.

★ ★ ★

Sometimes in the spring, after I'd been released from the Western State Hospital and after I'd settled into my little town, when I went up to the fish ladder to my job helping out the wildlife agency counting returning salmon, I would spot the silvery, shimmering shadows of fish and wonder whether they understood that the act of returning to the place where they were spawned, in order to renew the cycle of existence, was going to cost them their lives. With my notebook in hand, I counted fish, often fighting off the urge to warn them somehow. I wondered whether they had some deep, genetic impulse that informed them that returning home would kill them, or whether it was all a deception that they willingly went along with, the desire to mate being so strong that it covered up the inevitability of death. Or

283

were they like soldiers, given an impossible and obviously fatal command, who decide that sacrifice is more important than life?

My hand would shake, sometimes, as I made marks on my counting sheet. So much death passing by in front of me. We get it all wrong, sometimes. That which seems filled with danger, like the great wide ocean, is actually safe. That which is familiar and recognized, like home, is in truth far more threatening.

Light seemed to fade around me, and I stepped back from the wall, over to the living room window. I could feel the room behind me crowding with memories. There was an evening breeze, just a small breath of warmth. We are all defined by the dark, I thought. Anyone can portray anything in the daylight. But it is only at night, after the world has closed in, that our true selves come out.

I could no longer tell whether I was exhausted or not. Lifting my eyes, I surveyed the room. It was interesting to me to see myself alone and knowing that it wouldn't last. They would all crowd in on me, sooner or later. And the Angel would be back. I shook my head.

Lucy, I remembered abruptly, had drawn up a list of nearly seventy-five names. Those were the men she wanted to see.

★ ★ ★

Lucy drew up a list of some seventy-five inmates from throughout the Western State Hospital that seemed to have the potential for killing within them. They were all men who had shown overt hostility toward women, whether it was blows thrown in a domestic-type dispute, threatening language, or obsessive behavior, where they had focused on a female neighbor or family member, and blamed them for their madness. She still secretly clung to the notion that the murders were, at their core, sex crimes. The current thinking in the criminal justice world was that all sex crimes were crimes of violence first, and sexual release a distant second. It didn't make sense to her to discard everything that she had learned from the moment she had been victimized herself, to the dozens of courtrooms where she had stared across the bar at one man or another, every one of them mirroring in some big or small way, the man who had assaulted her. Her record of convictions was exemplary, and she expected that, despite the obstacles that the mental hospital created, she would succeed once again. Confidence was her calling card.

As she walked across the hospital grounds toward the administration building, she started to draw in her head a portrait of the man she was hunting. Details, such as the physical strength to overwhelm Short Blond, enough youth to be filled with homicidal fervor, enough age so that he was less likely to make rash mistakes. She was persuaded that the man had both a practical knowledge and the sort of innate intelligence that makes certain criminals hard to corner. Her mind churned with all the elements of the crimes that haunted her, and she insisted to herself that when she actually came face-to-face with the right man, she would know him immediately.

The reason for this optimism was the belief she held that the Angel somehow wanted to be known. He would be conceited, she thought, and arrogant, and besting her in this intellectual exercise inside the mental hospital was what he wanted.

She knew this in a way far more profound than Peter or Francis, or for that matter, anyone else at Western State was aware. Several weeks after the second homicide had taken place, the two severed finger joints had been acquired by her office in the most mundane fashion — in the daily mail delivery. The perpetrator had placed them inside a common plastic baggie, sealed up in a tan padded mailer, of the sort available at virtually every office supply store throughout New England. The address on the mailer had been typed on a label, and read simply enough: CHIEF OF SEX CRIMES UNIT.

There had been a single sheet of paper enclosed with the grisly remains. On it had been typed the question: *Looking For These?* and nothing else.

Lucy had been initially confident when the bloody souvenirs had been turned over to forensics. It did not take long to confirm that they belonged to the second victim and that they had been removed postmortem. The typing on the note and the address label were identified as belonging to a 1975 Sears model 1132 electric typewriter. The postmark on the package gave her more hope, because it was narrowed down to the main mail facility in South Boston. In a doggedly efficient style more or less precisely as Peter the Fireman had described, Lucy and two investigators from her office had traced every Sears model 1132 typewriter sold in Massachusetts, New Hampshire, Rhode Island, and Vermont for a six-month period prior to the killing. They had also questioned every postal worker at the mail facility, to see if any could remember handling that particular package. Neither line of inquiry had produced anything resembling a viable lead.

The postal workers had been unhelpful. If a typewriter had been purchased with a check or with a credit card, then Sears had a record. But it was an inexpensive model, and more than a quarter of the machines moved during the time frame had been bought with cash. In addition, the investigators learned that virtually every one of the more than fifty retail outlets in New England had a new model 1132 on display, where it could be tried out. It would have been a relatively simple matter to walk up to a typewriter on a busy Saturday afternoon, stick a piece of paper in the platen, and write whatever one wanted, without drawing the slightest bit of attention to oneself, even from a salesperson.

Lucy had hoped that the man who sent the fingertips would do so again, either with the first victim or the third, but he had not.

It was, she thought, the worst sort of taunting; the message wasn't in the words, or even the body parts, it was in the delivery that could not be traced.

It had also had the unsettling by-product of sending her to the literature of Jack the Ripper, who had carved out a piece of kidney from a prostitute-victim named Catharine Eddowes aka Kate Kelly and sent it to the Metropolitan Police in 1888 with a mocking note, signed with a flourish. That her quarry was familiar with this most celebrated case made her nervous. It told her much, but it took its toll on her imagination, as well. She did not like the notion that she was hunting a person with a sense of history, because this implied some intelligence. Most of the criminals that she had coldly seen off to prison had been noteworthy for their flat-out stupidity. In the Sex Crimes Unit, it was a bit of a given that the forces that drove a man to the particular act would also cause him to be sloppy and forgetful. The ones that struck randomly and with some planning and foresight were significantly harder to find.

These homicides, she thought, in an odd way, defied characterization. Francis had been accurate, when Peter had asked him what linked them together. But she could not help feeling the sensation that there was something other than hair and body type and savagery that prompted the killings, although she knew that fear defied the conventional wisdom.

She was trudging along outside, on one of the pathways between the hospital buildings, her mind lost in thoughts about the man that Peter and Francis had taken to calling the Angel. She ignored the fine day that had arisen around her, shafts of bright sunshine finding new growth on tree branches, warming the world with its promise of better weather. Lucy Jones had the sort of mind that liked to sort and compartmentalize, that enjoyed the rigorous pursuit of detail, and at that moment, it was excluding the temperature, sunlight, and new growth around her, replacing these simple observations with a continual mental gnawing away at the hurdles she faced. Logic and an orderly application of rules and regulations and laws had sustained her throughout her adult life. What Peter had suggested frightened her, although she had been careful not to show that. And, she acknowledged inwardly, it made some sense, because she was a little at a loss as to how else to proceed. It was a plan, she believed, that reflected his own passion, and not one designed in any rational way.

But Lucy thought of herself as a chess player, and this was as good an opening gambit as she could imagine. She reminded herself to remain independent, which was how she imagined she could control events.

As she walked, head down, deep in thought, she suddenly thought she heard her name.

A single, long, drawn out, whistled 'Luuuuuuc-cccyyyy . . . ' that was carried on a mild spring breeze, lingering in the trees that dotted the hospital grounds.

She stopped abruptly, and pivoted about. There was no one on the path behind her. She looked right, then left, and craned her head forward, listening, but the sound had disappeared.

She told herself that she was mistaken. The noise could have been any of a half dozen other sounds, and that the tension in what she was doing had put her on edge and she had misheard what was really just an ordinary cry of some great internal pain or anguish, no different from any of the hundreds that the wind carried through the world of the hospital every day.

288

Then she told herself that this was a lie.

It had been her name.

She turned toward the nearest building, and stared up at the windows. She could see some faces of patients looking idly back in her direction. She slowly turned toward other dormitories. Amherst was in the distance. Williams, Princeton, and Yale were closer. She spun about, searching the impassive brick buildings for some telltale indication. But each building remained silent, as if her attention had turned off the spigot of anxiety and hallucination that so often defined the sounds that emanated from each.

Lucy remained rooted to her spot. After a moment, she heard a cascade of obscenities from one building. This was followed by some angry voices and then a high-pitched scream or two. This was what she expected to hear, and with each sound, she told herself that she had heard something that wasn't there, which, she noted ironically to herself, probably put her in the mainstream of the hospital population. With that thought, she stepped forward, turning her back on every window and every pair of eyes that might have been darkly watching her every step, or might have been staring blankly off into the inviting azure blue sky above. It was impossible to tell which.

17

Peter the Fireman stood in the center of the dining room, holding a tray and surveying the bubbling volcanic activity that surrounded him. Mealtimes in the hospital were an unending series of small skirmishes that were a reflection of the great interior wars that each patient fought. No breakfast, lunch or dinner went by without erupting into some minor incident. Distress was served as regularly as runny scrambled eggs or bland tuna salad.

To his right, he saw an elderly, senile man, grinning maniacally, letting milk dribble down his chin and chest, despite the near constant efforts of a nurse-trainee to prevent him from drowning himself; to his left, two woman were arguing over a bowl of lime green Jell-O. Why there was only one bowl, and two claimants, was the dilemma that Little Black was patiently trying to sort out, although each of the women, who seemed to look almost identical, with scraggly twists of gray hair and pale pink and blue housecoats, appeared eager to come to blows. Neither, it seemed, was in the slightest bit willing to simply walk the ten or twenty paces back to the kitchen entrance and obtain a second bowl of Jell-O. Their high-pitched, shrieking voices melded with the clatter of plates and silverware, and the steamy sheen of heat that came from the kitchen, where the meal was being prepared. After a second, one of the women reached out suddenly, and dashed the bowl of Jell-O across the floor, where the dish shattered like a gunshot.

He moved to his customary table in the corner, where his back would be against the wall. Napoleon was already there, and Peter suspected Francis would be along shortly, although he wasn't sure where the young man was at that moment. He took his seat and suspiciously eyed the plate of noodle casserole in front of him. He had doubts about its provenance.

'So,' Peter asked as he poked at the meal, 'Nappy, tell me this: What would a soldier in the Great Army of the Republic have eaten on a fine day such as this?'

Napoleon had been eagerly attacking the casserole, shoveling forkfuls of the glop into his mouth like a piston-driven machine. Peter's question slowed him, and he paused to consider the issue.

'Bully beef,' he said after a moment, 'which given the sanitary conditions of the times, was pretty dangerous stuff. Or salted pork. Bread, surely. That was a staple, as was hard cheese that one could carry in a rucksack. Red wine, I believe, or water from whatever well or stream was close. If they were foraging, which the soldiers did often, then perhaps they would seize a chicken or a goose from some nearby farm, and cook it on a spit, or boil it.'

'And if they intended to go into battle? A special meal, perhaps?'

'No. Not likely. They were usually hungry, and often, like in Russia, starving. Supplying the army was always a problem.'

Peter held an unrecognizable morsel of what he'd been told was chicken up in front of his face and wondered whether he could go into battle with this particular casserole as his inspiration.

'Tell me, Nappy, do you think you're mad?' he asked abruptly.

The round man paused, a significant portion of oozing noodles stopped in its path about six inches from his mouth, where it hovered, as he considered the question. After a moment, he set the fork down and sighed a response. 'I suppose so, Peter,' he said a little sadly. 'Some days more than others.'

'Tell me a little bit about it,' Peter asked.

Napoleon shook his head, and the remainder of his usual enthusiasm slipped away. 'The medications control the delusion, pretty much. Like today, for example. I know I'm not the emperor. I merely know a lot about the man who was the emperor. And how to run an army. And what happened in 1812. Today, I'm just an ordinary bush-league historian. But tomorrow, I don't know. Maybe I'll fake it when they hand me my medication tonight. You know, tuck it under my tongue and spit it out later. There are some pretty effective sleight of hand tricks that just about everyone learns in here. Or maybe the dosage will be off just a little bit. That happens, too, because the nurses have so many pills to hand out, sometimes they don't pay as much attention as to who gets what as maybe they should. And there you would have it: A really powerful delusion doesn't need much ground to take root and flower.'

Peter thought for a moment, then asked, 'Do you miss it?'

'Miss what?'

'The delusions. When they're gone. Do they make you feel special when you have them, and ordinary when they're erased?'

He smiled. 'Yes. Sometimes. But they sometimes hurt, too, and not merely because you can see how terrifying they are for everyone around you. The fixation becomes so great, that it overwhelms you. It's a little like a rubber band being pulled tighter and tighter within you. You know that eventually it has to break, but every moment that you think it will snap and everything inside you will come loose, it stretches out just a little farther. You should ask C-Bird about that, because I think he understands it better.'

'I will.' Again, Peter hesitated. As he did, he saw Francis moving gingerly across the room to join them. The young man moved in much the same manner that

Peter remembered from days on patrol in Vietnam, unsure whether the very ground he walked upon might be booby-trapped. Francis tacked between arguments and angers, blown a little to the right, and then the left by rage and hallucination, avoiding the shoals of senility or retardation, to finally arrive at the table, where he threw himself into a seat with a small grunt of satisfaction. The dining room was a dangerous passage of troubles, Peter thought.

Francis poked at the fast-congealing mess on his plate.

'They must not want us to get fat,' he said.

'Someone told me that they sprinkle the food with Thorazine,' Napoleon said, leaning forward, whispering conspiratorially. 'That way they know they can keep us all calm and under control.'

Francis glanced over at the two Jell-O-deprived women still screeching at each other. 'Well,' he said, 'I wouldn't believe it, because it doesn't seem to be working all that fantastically.'

'C-Bird,' Peter asked, gesturing modestly toward the two women, 'why do you think they're arguing?'

Francis looked up, hesitated, lifted his shoulders, then replied: 'Jell-O?'

Peter smiled, because this was slightly funny. Then he shook his head. 'No, I can see that. A bowl of lime green Jell-O. I didn't realize it was something worth trading blows over. But why Jell-O? Why now?'

In that second, Francis saw what Peter was really asking. Peter had a way of framing bigger questions within small ones, which was a quality Francis admired, because it displayed, if nothing else, the capacity to think beyond the walls of the Amherst Building. 'It's about having something, Peter,' he said slowly. 'It's about something tangible here where there is so little that we can actually possess. It's not the Jell-O. It's about having the Jell-O. A bowl of Jell-O isn't worth having a fight over. But something that reminds you of who you are, and what you could be, and the world that awaits us, if only we can seize hold of enough little things that will turn us back into humans, well, that's worth fighting for, isn't it?'

Peter paused, considering what Francis had said, and all three of them saw the two women abruptly burst into tears.

Peter's eyes lingered on the pair, and Francis thought that every incident like that must hurt the Fireman deep within his core, because he didn't belong. Francis stole a look over at Napoleon, who shrugged and smiled and happily returned to his mound of food. He belongs, Francis thought. I belong. We all belong, except for Peter, and he must be very afraid, deep inside, that the longer he stays here, the closer he will get to becoming like us. Francis could hear a murmuring of assent deep within him.

★   ★   ★

Gulptilil looked askance at the list of names Lucy had thrust across the desk at him. 'This seems like a substantial cross section of the population here, Miss Jones. Might I ask what your determining criteria were in selecting these patients from the overall clientele?' He sounded stiff and unhelpful with his question, and, when uttered in his warbling, singsong voice, made all the pretentiousness sound a little ridiculous.

'Of course,' Lucy replied. 'Because I couldn't think of a determining factor that was psychological in nature, like a defining disease, I used instead prior incidents of violence toward women. All seventy-five names here have done something which can be construed as hostile to the opposite sex. Some more than others, surely, but they all have that one factor in common.' Lucy spoke just as pompously as the medical director did, an acting

294

quality that she had honed in the prosecutor's office, which often helped her in official situations. There are very few bureaucrats who are not cowed by someone capable of speaking their own language, only better.

Gulptilil looked back at the list, surveying the rows of names, and Lucy wondered whether the doctor was able to assign a face and a file to each. He behaved that way, but she doubted he had that much interest in the actual intimacies of the hospital population. After a moment of two, he sighed.

'Of course, your statement can equally be applied to the gentleman already in custody for the murder,' he said. 'Nevertheless, Miss Jones, I shall do as you request,' he said. 'But I must suggest that this appears to be something of a wild-goose chase.'

'It's a place to start, Doctor.'

'It is also a place to stop,' he replied. 'Which, I fear, is what will happen to your inquiries when you seek information from these men. I imagine that you will find these interviews to be frustrating.'

He smiled, not in a particularly friendly fashion, and added, 'Ah, well, Miss Jones. You would like, I imagine, to get these interviews under way promptly? I will speak with Mister Evans, and perhaps the Moses brothers, who can begin transporting the patients to your office. That way, at least, you can begin to fully encounter the obstacles that you are up against here.'

She knew that Doctor Gulptilil was speaking about the vagaries of mental illness, but what he said could be construed in different ways. She smiled at the medical director and nodded in agreement.

★　★　★

By the time she returned to Amherst, Big Black and Little Black were waiting for her in the corridor by the first-floor nursing station. Peter and Francis were with them, leaning against the wall like a pair of bored teenagers hanging out on a street corner waiting for trouble, although the manner in which Peter's eyes swept back and forth down the corridor, watching every movement and assessing each patient that rambled past, contradicted his languid appearance. She did not immediately see Mister Evans, which, she thought, might be a good thing, given what she was about to ask of them. But that was her first question for the two attendants.

'Where is Evans?'

Big Black grunted. 'He's on his way over from one of the other buildings. Support staff meeting. Should be here any second. The big doc called over and tells us that we're supposed to start escorting people in to see you. You got a list.'

'That's right.'

'Suppose,' Little Black said, 'they aren't quite as eager to come see you. What're we supposed to do then?'

'Don't give them that option. But if they get frantic, or start to lose control — well, I can come to them.'

'And if they still don't want to talk?'

'Let's not anticipate a problem before we know we have one, okay?'

Big Black rolled his eyes a little, but didn't say anything, although it was clear to Francis that much of Big Black's existence at the hospital was about precisely that: anticipating a problem before it arose. His brother let out a slow sigh, and said, 'We'll give it a try. Can't promise exactly how people will react. Never done anything like this in here before. Maybe there won't be any trouble.'

'If they refuse, then they refuse, and we'll figure something else out,' she said. Then she bent forward slightly and lowered her voice a little. 'I have an idea. I wonder if you guys can help me out, and keep it confidential.' She waited as the two brothers immediately eyed each other. Little Black spoke for the two of them.

'Sounds to me like you're about to ask a favor that might get us into trouble.'

Again, Lucy nodded her head. 'Not all that much trouble, I hope.'

Little Black grinned widely, as if he saw a joke in what she said. 'It's always the person doing the asking that thinks whatever it is ain't that big a deal. But, Miss Jones, we're still listening. Not saying yes. Not saying no. Still listening.'

'Instead of you two going to each person and transporting them, I want just one of you to go.'

'Generally, Security thinks should be two guys with any transfer like this. One walking on either side. Those are the hospital rules.'

'Well, let me tell you what I'm getting at,' she said, taking a step closer to the men, so that only that small group might hear her, which was probably unnecessary in the hospital, but more a natural response to the meager conspiracy that Lucy had in mind. 'I'm only modestly optimistic that these interviews will turn up something, and I'm really about to rely on Francis probably far more than he's aware,' she said slowly. The others looked over at the young man quickly, who blushed, as if singled out in class by a teacher he had a crush upon. 'But as Peter pointed out the other day, what we really have here is a lack of hard evidence. I'd like to try to do something about that.'

Both Big Black and Little Black were now listening intently. Peter, as well, took a step forward, narrowing the small group further.

'What I would like,' Lucy continued, 'is while I'm talking with these patients, that their living areas get thoroughly searched. Have either of you ever shaken down a bunk and storage area?'

297

Little Black nodded. 'Of course, Miss Jones. On occasion, that's a part of this fine job.'

Lucy stole a quick glance over at Peter, who seemed to be controlling his desire to speak with some difficulty. 'And,' she added slowly, 'what I'd really like is for Peter to be a part of those searches. Like, in charge.'

The two attendants looked at each other, before Little Black spoke up. 'Peter's got a *No Exit* ticket on his jacket, Miss Jones. What that means is he ain't allowed out of the Amherst Building except on special circumstances. And it would be Doctor Gulptilil or Evans who says what those special circumstances would be. And Evans hasn't let him outside these doors even once.'

'Is he supposed to be a flight risk?' she asked, a little like she would at a bail hearing before a judge.

Little Black shook his head. 'Evans put it on the case file. More like a punishment, really, 'cause he's facing some serious charges back in your part of our fine state. Peter here under a court order to get evaluated, and that *No Exit* on the jacket, it's a part of that evaluation, I'm guessing.'

'Is there a way around it?'

'A way around everything, Miss Jones, if it's important enough.'

Peter had dropped into quiet. Francis saw again that he was anxious to speak, but had the sense to keep his mouth shut. Francis noted that neither Big Black nor his brother had as yet said no to Lucy's request.

'Why you think you need Peter to do this, Miss Jones? Why not just my brother or me?' Little Black asked quietly.

'A couple of reasons,' Lucy said, perhaps a little too rapidly. 'One, as you know, Peter was a fine investigator, and knows how and where to look and what to look for and how to treat any evidence, if we can come up with some. And, because he's been trained in forensic evidence collection, I'm hoping that he will spot something that maybe you or your brother might miss . . . '

Little Black pursed his lips together, a small movement that seemed to acknowledge the truth in what Lucy was saying. She took this as encouragement, and continued. ' . . . And another reason — I'm not sure I want to compromise either you or your brother in all this. Say you come up with something in a search. You're obligated to tell Gulptilil, who will, in turn, then control the evidence. Very likely, it will get lost, or screwed up. Peter *finds* something, quote and unquote, well, he's just another crazy guy in this hospital. He can leave it, tell me about it, then we can obtain a legitimate search warrant. Keep in mind, I'm hoping that there's going to come a time when we're going to need a policeman to come in and make an arrest. I need to preserve some sort of investigative integrity, whatever that is. You see what I'm driving at, here, gentlemen?'

Big Black laughed out loud, although there was no joke pending, except for the concept of *investigative integrity* inside the mental hospital. His brother put his hand to his head. 'Man, Miss Jones, I think you're gonna get us into some heavy duty trouble before all this is finished up.'

Lucy merely smiled at the two men. A wide smile, that showed her teeth and was accompanied by a glistening, welcoming look in her eyes, that spoke of a conspiracy of both need and elegance. Francis noted this, and thought for the first time in his life how hard it is in life to turn down a request from a beautiful woman, which probably wasn't fair, but true nevertheless.

The two attendants were looking at each other. After a second, Little Black shrugged and turned back to Lucy Jones. 'Tell you what, Miss Jones. My brother and I, we'll do what we can. Don't you let Evans or

Gulp-a-pill know 'bout this.' He paused, letting a small silence hover over all of them. 'Peter, you come talk to us in private, maybe we work something out. I got an idea . . . '

Peter the Fireman nodded his head.

'What we supposed to be looking for, anyway?' Big Black asked.

Peter stepped in, to answer this question. 'Bloodstained clothes or shoes. That would be the most obvious thing. Then somewhere there's a knife or some other sort of handmade weapon. Whatever it is, it will have to be sharp as hell because it was used to cut both flesh and bone. And the missing set of keys, because our Angel has a means of getting into locked areas pretty much whenever he seems to have the need, and doors don't seem to mean all that much to him. Anything else that points to a greater knowledge about the crime poor Lanky is in prison for. Or anything that points at the other crimes that have gotten Lucy's attention, from the other part of the state. Like newspaper clippings. Or maybe an item of woman's clothing. I don't know. But I do know there's one thing out there that's still missing and it would be helpful to find,' he said. 'Things, actually.'

'What's that?' Big Black asked.

'Four severed fingertips,' Peter said coldly.

★   ★   ★

Francis shifted about uncomfortably in Lucy's small office, trying to avoid the glare that came his direction from Mister Evans. There was a heavy silence in the room, as if the heater had been left on at the same time that the outdoor temperature soared, creating a sticky, sickly kind of heat. Francis looked over toward Lucy and saw that she was busy with one of the patient files, flipping through pages with scrawled notations,

300

occasionally taking a note or two of her own on a yellow legal pad at her right hand.

'He shouldn't be here, Miss Jones. Despite what assistance you think he will bring, and despite the permission from Doctor Gulptilil, I still think it remains highly inappropriate to involve a patient in this process in any capacity. Certainly any insight that he might have is significantly less educated than any that I or any of the other support staff here in the hospital might incorporate into these proceedings.' Evans managed to sound undeniably pompous, which, Francis thought, wasn't his usual tenor. Generally, Mister Evil had a sarcastic, irritating tone, that underscored the differences between them. Francis suspected that his pretentious large-word and clinical vocabulary was a tone Evans generally adopted in hospital staff meetings. Making oneself *sound* important, Francis realized, wasn't exactly the same thing as *being* important. The usual chorus of agreement stirred within him.

Lucy looked up and simply said, 'Let's see how it works. If it creates a problem, we can always change things around, later.' Then she dipped her head back to the file.

Evans, however, persisted. 'And, while he's in here with us, where is the other one?'

'Peter?' Francis asked.

Again, Lucy lifted her head. 'I've got him doing some of the more menial tasks associated with this inquiry,' she said. 'Even though we remain somewhat informal, there's always some really dull but necessary stuff to do. Given his background, I thought he was extremely suitable.'

This seemed to placate Evans, and Francis thought it was a pretty clever response. Francis realized that maybe when he was a little older he would learn how to say something that wasn't exactly true, without exactly lying at the same time.

There were another few seconds of uncomfortable silence, and then a knock on the door, and it swung open. Big Black was standing there, dwarfing a man Francis recognized from the upstairs dormitory. 'This is Mister Griggs,' Big Black said with a grin. 'On the list. Top of the list.' With his massive hand, he gave the man a small push into the room, then stepped back to the wall, taking up a position where he could watch and listen, arms folded in front of him.

Griggs took a stride into the center of the room, then hesitated. Lucy pointed toward a chair, putting him in a position where Francis and Mister Evil could both watch the man's responses to her questions. He was a wiry, muscled man, middle-aged and balding, with long fingers and a sunken chest, and an asthmatic wheeze that accompanied much of what he said. His eyes darted about the room furtively, giving him the appearance of a squirrel lifting its head to some distant danger. A squirrel with yellowed, uneven teeth and an unsettled disposition. He eyed Lucy with a single, penetrating glance, then relaxed, sticking his legs out with a look of irritation.

'Why am I here?' he asked.

Lucy responded rapidly. 'As you may be aware, there have been some questions raised about the killing of the nurse-trainee in this building in the past weeks. I was hoping that you might shed some light on that incident.' Her voice seemed routine, matter-of-fact, but Francis could see in her posture, and in the way her eyes locked onto the patient, that there was a reason this man had been selected first. Something in his file had given her an edgy kind of hope.

'I don't know anything,' he answered. He shifted about, and waved his hand in the air. 'Can I leave now?'

On the file placed in front of her, Lucy could see words like *bipolar* and *depression* coupled with *antisocial tendencies* and *anger management issues*.

Griggs was a potpourri of problems, she thought. He also had slashed a woman with a razor blade in a bar after buying her a series of drinks and getting turned down when he propositioned her. Then he fought hard against the police that had arrested him, and within days of his arrival at the hospital, had threatened Short Blond and several other female nurses at the hospital with uncertain and unspecified, but undeniably dire punishments whenever they attempted to force him to take medication at night, change the television channel in the dayroom, or stop harassing other patients, which he did on a near daily basis. Each of these incidents had been dutifully documented on his case file. There was also a notation that he had insisted to his public defender that unspecified voices had demanded that he cut the woman in question, a claim that had delivered him to Western State instead of the local jail. An additional entry, in Gulptilil's handwriting, questioned the veracity of the claim. He was, in short, a man filled with rage and lies, which, in Lucy's mind, made him into a prime candidate.

Lucy smiled. 'Of course,' she said. 'So on the night of the homicide — '

Griggs cut her off. 'I was asleep upstairs. Tucked in for the night. Zonked out on whatever the shit they give us.'

Pausing, Lucy glanced at the yellow pad in front of her, before raising her eyes and fixing them on the patient. 'You refused medication that night. There's a note in your file.'

He opened his mouth, started to say one thing, then stopped. 'You ought 'ta know,' he said, 'just because you say you won't take it, it don't mean you get a pass. All it means is that some goon like this one' — he waved at Big Black, and Francis had the distinct impression that Griggs would have used some other epithet, if he hadn't been scared of the massive black man — 'forces you to

303

take it. So I did. Few minutes later, I was off in dreamland.'

'You didn't like the nurse-trainee, did you?'

Griggs grinned. 'Don't like any of 'em. No secret in that.'

'Why is that?'

'They like to lord it over us. Make us do stuff. Like we don't mean anything.'

Griggs used *us* and *we* but Francis didn't think he had any plurality in mind, other than himself.

'Fighting women is easier, isn't it?' Lucy asked.

The patient shrugged. 'You think I could fight him?' he replied, again indicating Big Black.

Lucy didn't answer the man's question, instead, she bent forward slightly. 'You don't like women, do you?'

Griggs snarled, slightly, and spoke in a low-pitched, fierce voice. 'Don't like you much.'

'You like to hurt women, don't you?' Lucy asked.

He burst out in a wheezing laugh, but didn't answer.

Keeping her own voice steady and cold, Lucy then suddenly shifted direction. 'Where were you in November,' she asked abruptly. 'About sixteen months ago.'

'Huh?'

'You heard me.'

'I'm supposed to remember back that far?'

'Is that a problem for you? Because I sure as hell can find out fast enough.'

Griggs shifted about in his seat, gaining a little time. Francis could see the man's mind working hard, as if trying to see some danger through a fog. 'I was working on a construction site in Springfield,' he said. 'Road crew. Bridge repair. Nasty job.'

'Ever been in Concord?' she asked.

'Concord?'

'You heard me.'

'No, I never been in Concord. That's in the whole

304

other part of the state.'

'Your boss on that construction crew, when I call him up, he's not going to tell me that you had access to a company truck, is he? And he's not going to tell me that he sent you on trips to the Boston area?'

Griggs looked a little scared and confused, a momentary flight of doubt. 'No,' he said. 'Other guys got those easy jobs. I worked in the pits.'

Lucy suddenly had one of the crime scene photographs in her hand. Francis saw that it was the body of the second victim. She rose up and leaned across the table and thrust it under Griggs's nose. 'You remember this?' she demanded. 'You remember doing this?'

'No,' he said, his voice losing some more of its bravado. 'Who's that?'

'You tell me.'

'Never seen her before.'

'I think you have.'

'No.'

'You know that road crew you worked on, there's records that show where everyone was each and every day. So proving that you were in Concord's gonna be easy for me. Just like that notation that you didn't get any medication the night the nurse was killed right here. It's just a matter of paperwork, filling in the blanks. Now, try again: Did you do this?'

Griggs shook his head.

'If you could, you would, wouldn't you?'

He shook his head again.

'You're lying to me.'

Griggs seemed to breath in slowly, wheezing, getting a deep, lungful of air. When he did speak, it was with a high-pitched, barely restrained anger. 'I didn't do that to no girl I never seen, and you're lying to me if you think I did.'

'What do you do to women you don't like?'

He smiled sickly. 'I cut 'em.'

Lucy sat back and nodded. 'Like the nurse-trainee?'

Griggs again shook his head. Then he looked across the room, eyeing first Evans, then over at Francis. 'Not going to answer no more questions,' he said. 'You want to charge me with something, then you go ahead and do it.'

'Okay,' Lucy said. 'Then you're finished for now. But maybe we'll talk again.'

Griggs didn't say anything else. He simply rose. He worked some saliva around his mouth, and for a moment Francis thought he was going to spit on Lucy Jones. Big Black must have thought the same, because Griggs took a step forward, only to have the huge attendant's hand descend like a vise grip on his shoulder.

'You finished here, now,' Big Black said calmly. 'Don't do nothing that makes me any angrier than I might already be.'

Griggs shrugged out of the attendant's grasp, and turned. Francis thought he clearly wanted to say something else, but instead, exited after pushing the chair a little, so that it scraped a small ways across the floor. A minor display of defiance.

Lucy ignored this, and started to write some notes down on the yellow legal pad. Mister Evans, too, was writing something down on a small notebook page. Lucy spotted this and said, 'Well, he didn't precisely rule himself out, did he? What are you writing?'

Francis kept quiet, as Evans looked up. He wore a slightly self-satisfied look on his face. 'What am *I* writing?' he asked. 'Well, for starters, a note to myself to adjust Griggs's medications over the next few days. He seemed significantly agitated by your questions, and I would say is likely to act out aggressively, probably toward one of the more vulnerable patients around here. One of the old women, for example. Or perhaps one of the staff. That's equally possible. I can increase some doses over the short term, preventing that anger from manifesting itself.'

Lucy stopped. 'You're going to what?'

'Chill him out for a week or so. Maybe longer.'

Mister Evil hesitated, then added, still keeping the smug tone in his words, 'You know, I could have provided a bit of a shortcut here. You are correct that Griggs refused his medication on the night of the homicide. But that refusal meant that he was given an intravenous injection later that night. See the second notation on the chart? I was there for that, and I supervised the procedure. So, when he says he was asleep when the murder took place, I can assure you he's telling the truth. He was sedated.'

Again, Evans paused, then continued. 'Perhaps there are others you want to question, where I can help in advance?'

Lucy looked up frustrated. Francis could see that she not only hated wasting her time, but hated dealing with the situation in the hospital. He thought, it must be difficult for her, because she had never been in a place like this. Then he realized that very few people with any claim on normalcy had ever been in a place like the hospital.

He bit down on his lip, holding back from saying anything. His mind was churning, fierce images from the interview just completed. Even his voices were remaining quiet within him, because, as he'd listened to the other patient speak, Francis had begun to see things. Not hallucinations. Not delusions. But things about the man speaking. He had seen ridges of fury and hatred, he had seen a sneering delight in the man's eyes as he saw the picture of death. He had seen a man capable of much depravity. But, at the same time, he'd seen a man with a great and terrible weakness inside. A man who would always *want* but would rarely *do*. Not the man they were looking for, because all of Griggs's anger had been so obvious. And Francis knew, right in that second, sitting in that small room, that there would be little obvious about the Angel.

★ ★ ★

At the very moment that Francis was sitting stricken because he had seen things that went beyond the small office where Lucy, Mister Evil, and he had conducted the interview, Peter the Fireman and Little Black were completing their search of the modest living area claimed by the patient Griggs. Peter had discarded his usual outfit, and set aside his beaten Boston Red Sox cap, and was wearing the ubiquitous snow-white slacks and coat of a hospital attendant. The uniform had been Little Black's idea. It was, in some ways, a perfect camouflage inside the hospital; one would have to look twice to see that the person wearing it wasn't really an attendant, but was actually Peter. In a world filled with hallucination and delusion, it would create some doubt. It gave him, he hoped, just enough cover so that he could do the job that Lucy had defined for him, although he knew that if he were to get spotted by Gulp-a-pill or Mister Evil or any of the others who knew him well enough, he would be immediately slammed into an isolation cell, and Little Black would be severely reprimanded. The wiry attendant hadn't been terribly concerned about this, saying 'Unusual circumstances require unusual solutions,' a comment that seemed more sophisticated than Peter would have earlier given him credit for making. Little Black also pointed out that he was the local union's shop steward, and his large brother was the union secretary, which gave them some armor in case they were caught.

The search itself had been utterly fruitless.

It had not taken him long to rifle through the

patient's personal items, stored in an unlocked suitcase beneath the bed. Nor had it been particularly difficult for Peter to run his hands through the bedding, checking the sheets and mattress for anything that might connect the man to the crime. He had moved swiftly through the adjacent area, as well, hunting for any other location where something like a knife could be concealed. It was easy to be efficient; there weren't really all that many spots in the living area that might hide something.

He stood up and shook his head. Little Black wordlessly gestured for the two of them to get back to the place where he'd arranged to meet with his brother.

Peter nodded and took a single step forward, then suddenly pivoted, and looked about the room. As always, there were a couple of men lying on their beds, eyes fixed on the ceiling, lost in some reverie that he could only guess at. One old man was rocking back and forth, crying to himself. A second seemed to have been told some joke, because he had wrapped his arms around himself, and was giggling uncontrollably. Another man, the hulking retarded man that he'd seen before in the corridors, was in the distant corner of the dormitory room, bent over, sitting on the edge of his bed, eyes cast down, staring steadily at the floor. For a moment, the retarded man looked up, across the space, blankly absorbing something, then turning away. Peter could not tell, in that second, whether the man understood that they were searching an area of the room, or not. There was no way to determine what the retarded man comprehended. It was possible, of course, that their actions were simply being ignored, lost in the near total impassivity that enclosed the man. But, Peter realized, it was equally possible that the man had somehow deep in his head dulled by circumstance and daily psychotropic medications, made the connection between the patient taken off to the interview room, and the subsequent search of the area. He didn't know whether this connection would leave the room, or not. But he feared that if the man they were hunting for came to that understanding, his task would be much more difficult. If people in the hospital knew that various areas were being searched, it would have some impact. How much, he was unsure. Peter did not make another critical leap of observation, which would have been that the Angel might want to do something about it, if he learned what Peter was doing.

He looked back at the motley collection of men in the room and wondered whether word would travel quickly across the hospital, or not at all.

To his side, Little Black muttered, 'Come on, Peter. Let's move.'

He nodded, and joined the attendant, pushing rapidly through the dormitory door.

18

Sometime later that day, or maybe after the next, but certainly at some point during the steady procession of mad folks being escorted into Lucy Jones's office, it occurred to me that I had never really been a part of something before.

When I thought about it, I believed it was a curious thing, growing up and understanding in an odd, peripheral, or maybe subterranean way that all sorts of connections were going on all around me — and yet I was destined forever to be excluded. As a child, not being able to join in is a terrible thing. Maybe the worst.

Once I lived on a typical suburban street, lots of one- and two-story, white-painted middle-class homes, with well-trimmed, green front yards with perhaps a row or two of vibrantly colored perennials planted under the windows and an aboveground pool in the back. The school bus stopped twice in our block, to accommodate all the kids. In the afternoons, there was a constant ebb and flow up and down the street, a noisy tidal surge of youth. Boys and girls in jeans frayed at the knees, except on Sundays, when the boys emerged from their homes in blue blazers and stiffly starched white shirts and polyester ties and the girls wore dresses that sported ruffles and frills, but not too many of either. Then we were all collected, along with parents, in the pews of one or another nearby church. It was a typical mix for Western Massachusetts, mostly Catholic, who took the time to discuss whether eating meat on Friday was a sin, with some Episcopalians and Baptists mixed in. There were even a few Jewish families on the block, but they had to drive across town to the synagogue.

It was all so incredibly, overwhelmingly, cosmically typical. Typical block of a typical street, populated by typical families who voted the Democratic ticket and swooned a little over the Kennedys and went to Little League games on warm spring evenings not so much to watch as to talk. Typical dreams. Typical aspirations. Typical in every regard, from the first hours in the morning, to the last hours of the night. Typical fears, typical concerns. Conversations that seemed riveted to normalcy. Even typical secrets hidden behind the typical exteriors. An alcoholic. A wife beater. A closet homosexual. All typical, all the time.

Except, of course, for me.

I was discussed in quiet tones, the same under the voice whispers that were ordinarily reserved for the simply shocking news that a black family had moved in two streets over, or that the mayor had been seen exiting a motel with a woman who was decidedly not his wife.

In all those years, I was never once invited to a birthday party. Never asked to a sleepover. Not once shoved into the back of a station wagon for an off-the-cuff trip to Friendly's for an ice-cream sundae. I never got a phone call at night to gossip about school or sports or who had kissed whom after the seventh grade dance. I never played on a team, sang in a choir, or marched in a band. I never cheered at a Friday night football game in the fall, and I never self-consciously put on an ill-fitting tux and went to a prom. My life was unique because of the absence of all those little things that make up everyone else's normalcy.

I could never tell which I hated more — the elusive world I came from and never could join or the lonely world I was required to live in: Population one, except for the voices.

For so many years, I could hear them calling my name: *Francis! Francis! Francis! Come out!* It was a little like what I would have suspected the children in my block to cry on some warm July evening, when the light faded slowly and the day's heat lingered well past the dinner hour, had they ever done so, which they never did. I suppose, in a way, it's hard to blame them. I don't know if I'd have wanted me to come out and play. And, as I grew older, so did the voices, so that their tones changed, as if they were keeping stride with every year that passed in my life.

All these thoughts must have been coming somewhere from the filmy world between sleep and wakefulness, because I suddenly opened my eyes in my apartment. I must have dozed for a bit, my back thrust up against a blank piece of wall. They were all thoughts that my medications used to stifle. There was a crick in my neck, and I rose unsteadily. Once again, the day had faded around me, and I was alone again, except for memories, ghosts, and the familiar murmurings of those long-suppressed voices. They all seemed quite enthused to have rediscovered a grip on my imagination. In a way, it seemed as if they were awakening alongside me, the way I imagined a real lover would, had I ever had a real lover. In my mind's ear, they clamored for attention, a little bit like a happy crew at a busy auction, making bids on any number of different items.

I stretched nervously and walked over to the window. I looked out at the creeping night strands moving across the city, just as I had done dozens of times before, only this time, I fixated on one shadow, behind a stodgy brick auto parts store down the block. I watched the edge of the shadow spread, and thought it was an eerie thing, that each shadow bore only the most tangential resemblance to the building or tree or fast-walking person that birthed it. It takes a form of its own, evoking its ancestry, but remaining independent. The same, but different. Shadows, I thought, can tell me much about my world. Maybe I was closer to being one of them, than I was to being alive. Then, out of the corner of my eye, I noticed a patrol car moving slowly down my block.

I was suddenly fired with the thought that it was there to check on me. I could feel the two sets of eyes inside the darkened vehicle turned up, moving across the front of the apartment building like sets of spotlights, until they rested directly on my window. I tossed myself to the side, so that I couldn't be seen.

I shrank back, huddled against the wall.

They were here to get me. I knew this, just as surely as I knew that day follows night and that the night follows day. My eyes searched the apartment, trying to find a place to hide. I held my breath. I had the sensation that every heartbeat in my chest echoed like a foghorn. I tried to push myself deeper against the wall, as if it could camouflage me. I could sense the officers outside the door.

But then nothing.

There was no insistent pounding at the door.

No raised voices with that single word Police! that says everything all at once.

Silence surrounded me, and after a second, I leaned forward slightly, craning my head around the window and seeing the street empty in front of me.

No car. No policemen. Just more shadows.

I stopped for a moment. Had it even been there?

I breathed out slowly. When I turned back to the wall, I insisted to myself that nothing was wrong, and that there was nothing to worry about, which reminded me that that was precisely what I'd tried to tell myself all those years earlier in the hospital.

The faces remained in my memory, if sometimes not the names. Slowly, over the course of that day, and the next, Lucy had brought in, one after the other, men that she believed had some of the elements of the profile she was building deep in her own head. Men of anger.

It was, in a way, a crash course in one slice of the humanity that made up the hospital clientele, a cut from the fringe. All sorts of mental illnesses were herded into that room, and seated in the chair in front of her, sometimes with a little nudge from Big Black, sometimes, with no more than a gesture from Lucy and a nod from Mister Evans.

As for myself, I kept quiet and listened.

It was a parade of impossibility. Some of the men were furtive, eyes darting back and forth, evasive in every response to each question. Some seemed terrified, shrinking back in their chairs, sweat leaping onto their foreheads, quaver in their voices, as they seemed pummeled by every question that Lucy posed, no matter how routine, benign, or insignificant. Others were aggressive, instantly raising their voices, shouting in newly encouraged rage, and, on more than one instance slamming their fists on her desktop, filled with righteous indignation and denial. A few were mute, staring blankly across the room, as if each statement that fell from Lucy's mouth, each question that hovered in the air was something rendered on some totally different plane of existence, something that meant nothing in any language that they knew, and so to answer was impossible. Some men responded with gibberish, some with fantasy, some with anger, some with fear. A couple of men stared at the ceiling, and a couple made strangling motions with their hands. Some looked at the crime scene photographs with fear, some with an unsettling fascination. One man instantly confessed, blubbering 'I did it, I did it' over and over again, not allowing Lucy to ask any of the questions that might have indicated that he actually had done it. One man said nothing, but grinned, and dropped his hand into his pants to excite himself until the uniquely discouraging pressure of Big Black's massive grip on his shoulder forced him to stop. Throughout the process,

315

Mister Evil sat at her side, always quick, when the patient had been escorted out by Big Black, to explain why this man or that man was disqualified for this reason or that reason. There was a certain irritating clarity to his approach; it was supposed to be helpful and informative, while, in reality it was obstructive and obfuscating. Mister Evil, I thought, wasn't nearly as clever as he thought, nor as stupid as some of us believed, which was, when I think back upon it, a most dangerous combination.

And throughout the interview process, the most curious thing came over me: I started to see. It was as if I could envision where every pain came from. And how all those accumulated pains had over the years evolved into madness.

I felt a darkness coming over my heart.

My every fiber screamed at me to rise up and run, to get out of that room, that everything I saw and heard and learned was terrible, was information and knowledge I had no right to possess, no need to have, no desire to collect. But I remained frozen, unable to move, as frightened in those moments of myself, as I was of the hard men that came through the door who had all done something terrible.

I wasn't like them. And yet, I was.

★   ★   ★

The first time Peter the Fireman stepped outside the Amherst Building he was almost overcome, and he had to grip the banister to keep from stumbling. Bright sunlight seemed to flood over him, a warm, late spring breeze ruffled his hair, the scent of hibiscus blooming along the pathways filled his nostrils. He hesitated unsteadily on the top step of the stairs leading to the side door, a little drunkenly, or dizzy, as if he'd been spun around for weeks on end inside the building, and this was the first moment when his head wasn't turning. He could hear traffic from the roadway beyond the hospital walls, and off to the side some children playing in the front yard of one of the staff housing units. He listened carefully, and from beyond the happy voices, he picked out the strands of a radio playing. Motown, he thought. Something with a seductively catchy big beat and sirenlike harmonies on the refrain.

Peter was flanked by Little Black and his large brother, but it was the smaller of the two attendants who whispered urgently, 'Peter, you got to keep you head down. Don't let anyone get a good look at you.'

The Fireman was dressed in white duck slacks and short lab coat, like the two attendants, although they wore regulation thick black shoes, and he was shod in high-topped canvas basketball sneakers, and anyone alert to charades would have picked up on that distinction. He nodded, and hunched himself over a little, but it was difficult for him to keep his eyes on the ground for long. It had been too many weeks since he'd actually been outside, and longer still since he'd walked anywhere without the restraints of handcuffs and his past hobbling his steps.

To his right, he could see a small motley group of patients working in the garden, and over on the decrepit black macadam onetime basketball court a half-dozen other patients were simply wandering back and forth around the remains of the volleyball net, while two other attendants smoked cigarettes and kept a vague eye on the shuffling crowd, almost all of whom had their faces lifted to the warm afternoon sunshine. One wiry, middle-aged woman was dancing, just a little, moving her arms in wide gyrations, and striding first to her right, then back to her left, a waltz without rhythm or purpose, but as genteel as some Renaissance court.

They had worked out the system of the search in advance. Little Black had called ahead to the other

317

housing facilities on the interhospital intercom system, and they would enter through the side door, and as Big Black went to get the subject from Lucy's list to take them back to Amherst, Peter and Little Black would process the man's living area. What this had devolved into was Little Black's keeping an eye out for any of the other nurses or attendants, who might be curious, while Peter moved swiftly through whatever pathetically small collection of possessions the man in question had managed to keep. He was very good at this, able to finger his way through clothes and papers and bedding without disrupting much, if anything, moving very rapidly. It was, he'd learned during the first searches in his own building, impossible to keep what he was doing secret from everyone — there was always some patient or another lurking in the corner, perched on his bed, or merely glued to the far wall, where they could safely see out the window and across the room, preventing anyone from sneaking up on them. No limit, Peter thought, more than once, to paranoia in the hospital. The problem was, a man behaving suspiciously in the context of the mental hospital didn't mean the same thing as it did out in the real world. Inside the Western State Hospital, paranoia was the norm, and accepted as a part of the daily routine of the hospital, as regular and expected as meals, fights, and tears.

Big Black saw Peter lifting his eyes up to the sunshine, and he smiled. 'Makes you kinda forget, don't it,' he said quietly. 'Nice day like this.'

Peter nodded.

'Day like this,' the big man continued, 'it don't seem fair to be sick.'

Little Black joined in, unexpectedly. 'You know, Peter, day like this actually makes things worse around here. Makes everyone get this little taste of what they missing. You can smell the world happening, like it's just out there beyond the walls. Cold day. Rainy day. Windy and snowy. Those are the days that everyone just gets up and goes along. Never take any notice. But a beautiful day like this one, right hard on just about everybody.'

Peter didn't reply, until Big Black added, 'Really hard on your little friend. C-Bird still got hopes and dreams. This is the sort of day that is real hard on those, because it makes you see just how far away all those things are.'

'He'll get out,' Peter said. 'And soon, too. There can't be all that much holding him in here.'

Big Black sighed. 'I wish that were true. C-Bird, he's got a world of trouble.'

'Francis?' Peter asked incredulously. 'But he's harmless. Any damn fool can see that. I mean, he probably shouldn't be here at all . . . '

Little Black shook his head, as if indicating that neither what Peter said was true, nor could the Fireman see what they saw, but didn't say anything. Peter stole a glance toward the main entrance to the hospital, with its huge wrought-iron gate and solid brick wall. In prison, he thought, confinement was always an issue of time. The act defined the time. It could be one or two years, or twenty or thirty, but it was always a finite amount, even for those condemned to life, because it was still measured in days, weeks, and months, and eventually, inevitably, there was either a parole board hearing scheduled or death awaiting. That wasn't true for the mental hospital, he realized, because one's stay there was defined by something far more elusive and far more difficult to obtain.

Big Black seemed to be able to guess what Peter was thinking, because he chimed in again, sadness still lurking in his voice. 'Even if he gets hisself a release hearing, he's got a long way to go before they let him out of here.'

'That doesn't make any sense,' Peter said. 'Francis is smart and wouldn't hurt a flea . . . '

'Yeah,' Little Black jumped in, ' . . . and he's still

hearing voices even with the medications and the big doc can't get him to understand why he's here, and Mister Evil don't like him none, though can't see why not. What all that adds up to, Peter, is your friend is gonna be here, and there ain't no hearing gonna be scheduled for him. Not like some of the others here. And sure as hell not like you.'

Peter started to reply, then clamped his mouth shut. They walked on for a moment in silence, as he let the day's warmth try to erase the cold thoughts that the two attendants had chilled him with. Finally, he said, 'You're wrong. You're both wrong. He's going to get out. Go home. I know it.'

'Ain't nobody at his home wants him,' Big Black said.

'Not like you,' Little Black said. 'Everybody wants a piece of the Fireman. You gonna end up somewhere, but it ain't gonna be here.'

'Yeah,' Peter said, bitterly. 'Back in prison. Where I belong. Doing twenty to life.'

Little Black shrugged, as if to say that once again Peter had managed to get something if not precisely wrong, at least skewed slightly. They took a few more strides toward the Williams dormitory.

'Keep your head down,' Little Black said, as they approached the side entrance to Williams.

Peter lowered his head again, and dropped his eyes so that he was staring at the dusty black path they walked. It was difficult, he thought, because every shaft of sunlight that hit his back reminded him of being someplace else, and every breath of warm wind suggested happier times. He stepped forward, insisting to himself that it served no purpose to remember what he had once been, and what he now was, and that he should only look to what he would become. This was hard, he realized, because every time he looked at Lucy he saw a life that might have been his, but which had eluded him, and he thought, not for the first time, that every step he took only brought him a bit closer to some fearsome precipice, where he teetered unsteadily, maintaining his balance only with the most tenuous grip on icy rocks, held in place by thin ropes that were fraying quickly.

★   ★   ★

The man directly across from her smiled blankly but said nothing.

For the second time, Lucy asked, 'Do you remember the nurse-trainee that went by the nickname Short Blond?'

The man rocked forward in the seat and moaned slightly. It was neither a *yes* moan, nor a *no* moan, simply a sound of acknowledgment. At least, Francis would have described the sound as a moan, but that was for lack of any better word, because the man didn't seem discomfited in the slightest, either by the question, the stiff-backed chair or the woman prosecutor sitting across from him. He was a hulking, broad-shouldered man, with hair cropped short and a wide-eyed expression. A small line of spittle was collected at the corner of his mouth, and he rocked to a rhythm that played only in his own ears.

'Will you answer any questions?' Lucy Jones asked, frustration creeping into her voice.

Again, the man remained silent, except for the small creaking noise of the chair he sat upon, as he rocked back and forth. Francis looked down at the man's hands, which were large and gnarled, almost as weathered as an old man's hands, which wasn't at all right, because he thought the silent man was probably not much older than he was. Sometimes Francis thought that inside the mental hospital, the ordinary rules of aging were somehow altered. Young people looked old. Old people looked ancient. Men and women who should have had vitality in every heartbeat, dragged as if the weight of years marred every step, while some who were nearly finished with life had childlike simplicity and needs. For a second, he glanced down at his own hands, as if to check that they were still more or less age appropriate. Then he looked back to the big man's. His hands were connected to massive forearms, and knotted, muscled arms. Every vein that stood out spoke of barely restrained power.

'Is there something wrong?' Lucy asked.

The man gave out another growling, low-pitched grunt, that had little to do with any language Francis had ever heard before he'd arrived at the hospital, but one which he'd grown accustomed to hearing in the dayroom. It was an animal noise, expressing something simple, like hunger or thirst, lacking the edge that it might have, if anger was the basis of the sound.

Evans reached over and took the file away from Lucy Jones, quickly running his eyes over the pages collected inside the folder. 'I don't think interviewing this subject will be profitable,' he said with a smugness that he couldn't hide.

Lucy, a little angry, pivoted toward Mister Evil. 'And why?'

He pointed at a corner of the file. 'There's a diagnosis of profound retardation. You didn't see that?'

'What I saw,' Lucy said coldly, 'was a history of violent acts toward women. Including an incident where he was interrupted in the midst of a sexual assault on a much younger child, and a second instance where he struck someone, landing her in the hospital.'

Evans looked back down at the folder. He nodded. 'Yes, yes,' he said rapidly. 'I see those. But what gets written on a folder is often not a precise recounting of what took place. In this man's case, the young girl was the neighbor's daughter who had frequently played with him in a teasing fashion and who undoubtedly has issues of her own, and whose family opted to not press any charges, and the other case was his own mother, who was pushed during a fight that stemmed from the man's refusal to do some mundane household chore, and hit her head on a table corner, necessitating the trip to the hospital. More a moment where he was unaware how strong he was. I think, as well, that he lacks the sort of keen criminal intelligence that you are searching for, because, and correct me if I'm mistaken, your theory of the murder suggests that the killer is a man of some considerable sophistication.'

Lucy took the folder back out of Evans's hands and looked up at Big Black. 'I think you can take him back to his dormitory now,' she said. 'Mister Evans is correct.'

Big Black stepped forward and took the man by the elbow, lifting him up. The man smiled, and Lucy said, 'Thank you for your time,' not a word of which the man seemed to understand, although the tone and sentiment must have been apparent, because he grinned and made a little wave with one of his hands, before dutifully following Big Black out the door. The pleasant smile he wore never wavered.

Lucy leaned back in her seat and sighed. 'Slow going,' she said.

'I have had my doubts all along,' Mister Evans replied.

Francis could see that Lucy was about to say something, and in that second, he heard two, maybe three of his voices all shouting at once *Tell her! Go ahead and tell her!* and so he leaned forward in his own chair and opened his mouth for the first time in hours.

'It's okay, Lucy,' he said slowly, then picking up some speed. 'That's not the point.'

Mister Evans instantly looked angry that Francis had said anything, as if he'd been interrupted, when he hadn't. Lucy turned toward Francis. 'What do you mean?'

'It's not about what they say,' Francis said. 'I mean, it doesn't make sense, really, whatever questions you might ask, about the night of the killing, or where they were, or if they knew Short Blond, or have they ever been violent in the past. No matter what questions you ask about that night, or even about who they are, it's not really important. Whatever they say, whatever they hear, whatever response they make, not one word will be what you should be listening for.'

As Francis might have guessed, Mister Evans waved his hand dismissively. 'You don't think that anything they say might be important, C-Bird? Because, if not, then what is the purpose of this little exercise?'

Francis shrank back in his chair, a little afraid to contradict Mister Evil. There are some men, he knew, that stored up slights and affronts, and then paid one back at some later time, and Evans was one of them.

'Words,' Francis said slowly, a little quietly. 'Words aren't going to mean anything. We're going to need to speak a different language to find the Angel. A wholly different means of communicating. and one of these people, coming through that door, will be speaking it. We just need to recognize it, when it arrives. We can find it in here,' he continued, speaking cautiously, 'but it won't exactly be what we expect.'

Evans snorted slightly, and then pulled out his notebook, and wrote a small notation down on a lined sheet. Lucy Jones was about to respond to Francis, but she saw this action on the psychologist's part, and instead she turned to him. 'What was that?' she asked, pointing to the notebook.

'Nothing much,' he said.

'Well,' she persisted. 'It had to be something. A reminder to pick up a quart of milk on the way home. A decision to apply for a new job. A maxim, a play on words, a bit of doggerel or poetry. But it was something. What?'

'An observation about our young friend, here,' Evans replied blankly. 'A note to myself that Francis's delusions are still current. As evidenced by what he said, about creating some sort of new language.'

Lucy, instantly angered, was about to reply that she had understood everything Francis had said, but then she stopped herself. She stole a quick glance in Francis's direction and she could see that every word that Mister Evans spoke had scorched itself into his world of fears. Say nothing, she told herself abruptly. You will only make it worse.

Although precisely how things could be worse for Francis, she was a little at a loss to imagine.

'So, who do we have next?' Lucy said instead.

★   ★   ★

'Hey, Fireman!' Little Black said in a slightly lowered voice, but with some added urgency. 'You got to hurry up.' He stared down at his watch, then looked up and tapped the face on his wrist with his index finger. 'We got to get a move on,' he said.

Peter was running his hands through the bedding of one of Lucy's potential suspects, and he looked up a little surprised. 'What's the rush?' he asked.

'Gulp-a-pill,' Little Black said quickly. 'He usually makes his midday rounds pretty damn soon, and I need to get you back over to Amherst and out of those clothes before he starts wandering around the hospital and spots you somewhere you ain't supposed to be, dressed like you ain't supposed to be dressed.'

Peter nodded. He slid his hands under the edges of the bed, palpitating the mattress beneath. One of Peter's fears was that the Angel had managed to slice a section out of a mattress, and then concealed his weapon and

325

his souvenirs inside. It was, Peter thought, what he himself would have done if he'd had any items that he'd wished to hide from attendants or nurses or any other patient with prying eyes.

He felt nothing and shook his head.

'You just about finished?' Little Black asked.

Peter continued working the mattress, probing every shape and lump to make certain that it was what it should be. He saw that the usual sorts of patients were still eyeing him from across the room. Some were intimidated by Little Black, because they cowered in the corner, pressed up against the wall. A few others were sitting vacantly on the edge of their bunks, looking off into a void, as if the world they inhabited was somewhere else.

'Yeah, just about,' Peter mumbled to the attendant, who tapped his watch face again.

The bed was clean, Peter thought. Nothing immediately suspect. There was now only the matter of a quick search of the man's belongings, which were gathered in a foot locker beneath the steel frame of the bed. Peter pulled the locker out. He rifled through, finding nothing more suspect than some socks that were in dire need of laundering. He was about to step back when something caught his eye.

It was a flat white T-shirt, folded up and placed near the bottom of the locker. It was no different from the cheap type sold at discount stores throughout New England and worn by many of the men in the hospital beneath a heavier winter shirt during the colder months. But that wasn't what caught his attention.

The shirt was stained with a huge dark red brown splotch across the chest.

He had seen stains like that before. In his training as an arson investigator. In his time in the jungle in Vietnam.

Peter held the shirt in his hands for a second, rubbing

the fabric beneath his fingers as if he could tell something more by touching it. Little Black was a few feet away and finally insistence crept into his voice. 'Peter, we got to leave now. I don't want to have to do any explaining that I don't have to, and I sure as hell don't want to have to explain nothing to the big doc, if I don't need to.'

'Mister Moses,' Peter said slowly. 'Look at this.'

Little Black stepped forward, so that he could lean over Peter's shoulder. Peter said nothing, but he heard the attendant whistle softly.

'That could be blood there, Peter,' he said after a moment. 'Sure looks like it.'

'That's what I thought,' Peter replied.

'Ain't that one of the things we're supposed to be looking for?' Little Black asked.

'It is, indeed,' Peter replied quietly.

Then he carefully folded the shirt back precisely as it was when he'd discovered it, and slipped it into the same position that it had occupied before he had drawn it forth. He returned the foot locker to its customary spot beneath the bed, hoping that it was positioned as it had been. Then he stood up. 'Let's go,' he said. He glanced over at the small gathering of men across the room from him, but whether they had noticed anything or not was impossible for Peter to tell from the vacant eyes that stared back at him.

19

Peter slid out of the white attendant's uniform in the area just inside the door to the Amherst Building. Little Black took the baggy pants and loose-fitting jacket from him, folded them up and stuffed them beneath his arm, while Peter pulled on a pair of wrinkled jeans. 'I'll stash these,' he said, 'until we're sure Gulptilil has finished his rounds and we can get back to business.' The wiry attendant then looked narrowly at Peter and added, 'You gonna tell Miss Jones about what we saw and where we saw it?'

Peter nodded. 'As soon as Mister Evil steps away from her side.'

Little Black grimaced. 'He'll find out. One way or another. Always does. Sooner or later, man seems to know everything going on around here.'

Peter thought that was an intriguing bit of information but he didn't comment on it.

For an instant, Little Black seemed indecisive. 'So, what we gonna do about a man got a shirt hidden away all stained with blood we don't think is his own?'

'I think we need to keep quiet and keep what we found to ourselves for the time being,' he said. 'At least until Miss Jones decides how she wants to proceed. I think we need to be very careful. After all, the man whose bunk that was is in there talking with her right now.'

'You think she's gonna pick up on something, talking to him?'

'I don't know. We just need to be cautious.'

Little Black nodded in agreement. Peter could see that the attendant was alert to the volatility of the knowledge they had acquired. A single blood-stained

T-shirt, that could cause all sorts of difficulties. Peter ran his hand through his hair, as he considered the situation, recognizing that he needed to be both wary and aggressive. His first thought was technical: How to isolate and proceed against the man who slept in the bunk where he'd made his discovery. There was much to do, he realized, now that he had a genuine suspect. But all his training suggested caution in his approach, even if that contradicted his own nature. He smiled, because he recognized the familiar dilemma that he'd faced throughout his life, the balance between small steps and headlong plunges. He was aware that he was where he was, at least in part, because of a failure to hesitate.

In the corridor outside the office where Lucy was conducting interviews, the larger of the Moses brothers was standing, keeping watch on a patient that rivaled him in size, and perhaps in strength as well, though if this detail concerned Big Black, he didn't show it. The man was rocking back and forth, a little like a truck with its wheels stuck in mud, running through the gears until he found one that would help him to get going. When Big Black spotted Peter and his brother approaching, he nudged the man forward.

'We need to be escorting this gentleman back to Williams,' he said, as they closed distance. Big Black made eye contact with his brother, and added, 'Gulp-a-pill's upstairs, doing rounds on the third floor.'

Peter didn't wait for the attendants to tell him what to do. 'I'll just wait here for Miss Jones,' he said. He pushed himself up against the wall, trying, as he did so, to get a really good assessment of the man Big Black was accompanying. He attempted to look into the man's eyes, to measure his posture, his appearance, as if he could see into his heart. A man that might be a killer.

As Peter slouched nonchalantly, and the trio of patient and attendants stepped past him, he could not resist speaking out loud, but under his breath, a whispered impulse designed for the ears of the man being escorted past: 'Hello Angel,' he said. 'I know who you are.'

Neither of the Moses brothers seemed to overhear his greeting.

Nor did the patient hesitate in the slightest. He merely shuffled along, plodding just behind the Moses brothers, seemingly unaware that he'd been spoken to. He moved a little bit like a man wearing hand and leg restraints, in short choppy steps, although there was nothing actually restricting his motion.

Peter watched the man's broad back disappear through the front door before he lifted himself off the wall and stepped toward the office where Lucy Jones waited. He didn't exactly know what to make of what had just happened.

Before he reached the office, however, Lucy Jones emerged, closely followed by Mister Evil, who was clearly speaking to her in an energetic way, and Francis, who was hanging back, as if to distance himself from the psychologist. Peter could see that C-Bird had a troubled look, as if some thought or some idea had diminished him slightly. He looked lighter. But the young man lifted his head up abruptly, saw Peter approaching, and seemed to recover in that second, immediately moving away from Mister Evil toward Peter. At the same time, Peter saw Gulptilil enter the hallway from the far stairwell, leading a small coterie of staff members. Lots of notepads and pencils, scribbling observations, taking notations. Peter saw Cleo, cigarette dangling from her lower lip, launch herself out of an old and uncomfortable chair, and directly into the medical director's path. She held her ground like some ancient warrior defending the gates of her city.

'Ah, Doctor!' Her voice was just a little shy of being a shout. 'What do you intend to do about the inadequate food portions being served at mealtimes? I don't believe that the state legislature envisioned starving us all to death when they established this place. I have friends who have friends who know people in high places, and they just might have the governor's ear on issues of mental health . . . '

Gulp-a-pill hesitated and turned toward Cleo. The group of interns and resident physicians accompanying him paused, and like a chorus line at a Broadway show, turned in unison. 'Ah, Cleo,' the doctor replied unctuously, mimicking her choice of words. 'I was unaware that there was a problem, and equally unaware that you had complained. But I do not think it necessary to involve the entirety of state government in this matter. I will speak with the kitchen staff and make certain that everyone gets all they need at mealtimes.'

Cleo, however, was just getting started.

'The Ping-Pong paddles are worn,' she continued, picking up some momentum with each word. 'They need replacing. The balls are frequently cracked, thereby rendering them useless and the nets are frayed and held together with string. The table is warped and unsteady. Tell me, Doctor, how is one supposed to improve their game with inferior equipment that doesn't meet even the minimum United States Table Tennis Association standards?'

'Again, I was unaware that this had arisen as a problem. I will examine the recreation budget to see if there are funds for a purchase.'

While this might have placated some, Cleo was far from finished. 'There's far too much noise in the dormitories at night to get a good sleep. Far, far too much. Sleep is critical to one's sense of well-being and overall progress toward health. The Surgeon General recommends at least eight hours per day of uninterrupted sleep. And furthermore, we need more space. Much more space. There are death row prisoners with more living space than we have. The overcrowding is out of control. And we need more toilet paper in the bathrooms. A lot more toilet paper. And . . . ' By now her voice was a cascade of complaints, ' . . . why aren't there more attendants to help people out at night, when we have nightmares? Every night, someone screams for help. Nightmares, nightmares, nightmares. You call and call and cry and no one ever comes. That's wrong, just plain, flat-out goddamn son of a bitch wrong.'

'We, like many state institutions, currently have staffing problems, Cleo,' the doctor responded with a condescending tone. 'I will, of course, register your complaints and your suggestions and see if there's anything we can do. But if the skeleton staff that works the overnight shift were to respond to every cry they overheard, they would be worked to a frazzle within a night or two, Cleo. I'm afraid nightmares are something that we will all have to learn to live with from time to time.'

'That is hardly fair. With all the medications you bastards pump us full of, you ought to be able to find something so folks can sleep without being excessively troubled.' Cleo seemed to inflate herself as she spoke, rising up with a regal haughtiness, a Marie Antoinette of the Amherst Building.

'I will examine the physician's guide for some additional medication,' the doctor lied. 'Are there any more issues that you need addressed?'

Cleo looked a little flustered, a little frustrated, but, then almost as swiftly, this look dissolved into something considerably more sly. 'Yes,' she said briskly. 'I want to know what is happening to poor Lanky.' And then she lifted her arm and pointed at Lucy, who was standing patiently waiting by the side of the corridor. 'And I want to know if she's been able to find the real killer!'

The words echoed in the hallway.

Gulptilil smiled wanly, and answered quietly, 'Lanky continues to remain in solitary confinement, accused of first degree murder. I believe I have explained this to you before. He had a bail hearing, but, as one would expect, none was granted. He has been assigned a public defender, and he continues to get his medications from the hospital. He's still being held in the county jail, pending additional court hearings. I am told his spirits are fine . . .'

'That's a lie,' Cleo said angrily. 'Lanky's probably miserable away from here. This is his home, such as it is, and we are his friends, such as we are. He should be returned here forthwith!' She took a deep breath, and then, sarcastically, mimicked the doctor's words. 'I have told you this before. Why don't you listen to me?'

' . . . And as to your other question,' Gulptilil continued, ignoring Cleo's accusation, 'well, that is better directed to Miss Jones. But she is under no obligation to inform anyone as to what progress she feels she has made. Or *not* made.' The last words were underscored by Gulptilil's acid voice.

Cleo stepped back, muttering something to herself. Gulptilil separated himself from her, and like a scout leader on a hike in the woods, waved the accompanying group of residents to follow him down the corridor. He had only taken a few steps, however, before Cleo burst out, loud, insistent and ringing with accusation, 'I'm watching you, Gulptilil! I can see what's going on! You may fool some of the people around here, but not me!' Then, slightly under her breath, but not enough so that the physicians couldn't hear her, she added, 'You're all bastards.'

The medical director paused, half started to turn back, then obviously thought better of it. Francis could see that his face was set, unsuccessfully trying to hide the discomfort of the moment.

'We're all in danger and you sons of bitches aren't

doing anything about it!' Cleo bellowed.

Then she gave a little giggle, took a long drag on her cigarette, cackled to herself and slumped back down into her seat, where she continued to watch the director move down the corridor, grinning with a self-satisfied look on her face. Holding her cigarette in her hand like a baton, she waved it in the air. A conductor satisfied with the final notes of the orchestral arrangement.

Francis was oddly encouraged by Cleo's bombast. It seemed to him that her outburst had gained the attention of every patient wandering the ward. Whether it meant anything to any of them, Francis could not tell, but he smiled to himself at her meager display of rebelliousness and wished that he had the same confidence to be as demanding. Cleo, for her part, must have sensed Francis's thoughts, because she blew a large elaborate smoke ring into the still corridor air, watched it dissipate, then gave Francis a wink.

Peter sidled into the space next to Francis, must have thought the same, and whispered, 'When the revolution comes, she'll be on the barricades. Hell, she'll probably be leading the rebellion and she's big enough to be a barricade all by herself.'

'What revolution?' Francis asked.

'Don't be so literal, C-bird,' Peter said with a small laugh. 'Think symbolically.'

'That may come easy for the Queen of Egypt,' Francis replied. 'But I don't know about me.' The two of them grinned.

Gulptilil, however, still apparently unamused, approached them. 'Ah, Peter and Francis,' he said, the lilting tones returning to his voice, but with none of the pleasantry ordinarily associated with the lighthearted sound. 'My pair of investigators. And how is your progress?' he asked.

'Slow and steady,' Peter replied. 'That is how I would describe it. But it is really for Miss Jones to determine.'

'Of course. She determines one sort of progress. I, and the others in charge here, are more concerned with a totally different sort of progress, are we not?'

Peter hesitated, then nodded.

'Of course, we are,' Gulptilil said. 'And to that end, this is a fortuitous meeting. Both of you need to come to my office this afternoon. Francis, it is time you and I had a chat about your continuing adjustment. And Peter, you will have a visitor of some significance this afternoon. The Moses brothers will be informed when they arrive, and they will escort you to administration.'

The pear-shaped medical director arched one eyebrow upward, as if curious as to the reactions of each man. He watched both their faces for an unsettling half minute or so, then continued on a few paces, turning to Lucy. 'Miss Jones, good day to you. And have you managed to make inroads in your dilemma?'

'I have managed to eliminate a number of potential suspects.'

'That, I presume, is something you consider valuable?'

She did not reply.

'Well,' Gulptilil continued, 'please keep at it. The sooner we have some conclusions, the better for all involved, I believe. Mister Evans has proven to be of assistance in your inquiries?'

'Of course,' Lucy said rapidly.

Gulptilil then pivoted toward Mister Evil. 'You will keep me posted, as well, as matters develop and the circumstances warrant?' he said.

'Of course,' Evans said. This, Francis thought, was all a bit of bureaucratic playacting. He was certain that Evans was keeping Gulp-a-pill assessed of everything at every point. He assumed that Lucy Jones knew this, as well.

The medical director sighed, and then continued down the corridor, and exited by the main door. After a moment, Evans turned to Lucy Jones, and said, 'Well, I gather we're taking a break now, and I have some paperwork to do.' He, too, exited quickly.

Francis heard someone from the dayroom laugh out loud. High-pitched and mocking, it swirled around the Amherst Building. But when he turned to see where the laughter was coming from, it stopped, fading away invisibly in the shafts of midday sunlight that filtered through the barred windows.

Peter peeled himself from the wall, whispered to Francis, 'Come on,' and approached Lucy. In that moment the Fireman changed abruptly, immediately focused on something other than Cleo and her demands or his pleasure at seeing Gulptilil discomfited. Francis saw that Peter's face was set. He took Lucy Jones by the elbow, turned her around and said, 'I found something I need to tell you about.'

Wordlessly, she nodded, after, Francis thought, measuring the look on Peter's face. The three of them returned to her small office.

'That last man,' Peter said, as they took chairs around the desk, 'what sort of impression did you get speaking to him?'

Lucy arched an eyebrow up. 'The short answer is none,' she said, and then she turned to Francis. 'Isn't that right, Francis?'

He nodded, and she continued: 'The man, while possessing the physical strength and the youth to do some of the things we are considering, is severely retarded. He wasn't able to communicate anything of any importance, mostly just sat there about as dense to what I was asking as imaginable, and Evans thought he should be ruled out. The guy we're looking for has some brains. At least enough to plan his crimes and avoid detection.'

Peter looked a little surprised, then said, 'Evans thought that man should be eliminated as a suspect?'

'He made that point,' Lucy replied.

'Well, that's curious, because I discovered a bloodstained white T-shirt hidden near the bottom of his belongings.'

Lucy rocked back in her seat, initially not saying anything. Francis watched her absorb this information and noted how guarded she became. His own imagination was energized, and after a second, he leaned forward and asked, 'Peter, can you describe what you found? How can you be sure it was what you say?'

It only took Peter a moment or two to fill in a picture for the two of them.

'You are absolutely sure that it was blood?' Lucy finally asked.

'As sure as I can be without lab tests.'

'There was spaghetti for dinner the other night. I'm wondering whether this guy has trouble manipulating utensils. He might have spilled sauce on his chest . . .'

'It wasn't that sort of stain. It was thick, a maroonish brown in color, and was smeared about. Not as if it had been dabbed at, by someone with a damp rag who wanted to clean it up. No, this was something that someone wanted to keep, intact.'

Lucy spoke slowly, 'Like a souvenir? We're looking for someone who wants to keep souvenirs.'

'I suspect,' Peter said, in reply, 'that this had more or less the same effect as a snapshot. For the killer that is. You know, a family goes on vacation and later, they have their pictures developed, and they sit around watching slides of the trip and reliving the memories. My guess is that for our Angel, this shirt would provide much the same thrill and satisfaction. He could hold it up, touch it, and remember. I would imagine that remembering the moment is probably nearly as powerful as the moment itself,' Peter concluded.

Francis could feel a din of voices within him. Conflicting opinions, advice, fear, and unsettled feelings. After a second, he nodded, in agreement with what Peter was saying. But he asked Lucy, 'Was there any indication, in any of the other killings, that anything was taken from the victims, other than the finger joints?'

Lucy, on the verge of responding to what Peter had said, shifted gears, and pivoted toward Francis. She shook her head. 'Not that we could tell. No articles of clothing were missing. At least, not from any inventory of items that we came up with. But that doesn't completely rule it out.'

Francis was troubled by something, but he was unable to say what, and none of his voices were clear and decisive. They echoed contradictory opinions within him, and he did his best to shut them out so that he could concentrate.

Lucy was nervously tapping a pencil on the tabletop. She turned to Peter, and asked, 'Did you find anything else that was incriminating?'

'No.'

'The fingertips?'

'No. And no knife, either. Or the building keys.'

She leaned back, but it was Francis who spoke.

'I think,' he said slowly, 'that what I said earlier is true.' He was a little surprised that he was as forceful as he was. 'Before you came back, Peter. When Evans was here.' It was a little, he thought, as if he was hearing his own voice, but that it was coming from some other Francis, not the Francis that he knew he was, but a different Francis, a Francis that he hoped he someday might be. 'When I said we need to uncover the Angel's language.'

Peter looked at Francis with an intrigued eye, and Lucy bent to his words. Francis hesitated for an instant, ignored a surge of doubt and then said, 'I wonder if this isn't the first lesson in communication.' The others remained quiet, and then he added, 'We just need to find out what he's saying, and why.'

★ ★ ★

For a moment or two, Lucy wondered whether her pursuit of a killer in the hospital might render her mad, as well. But she saw madness as a by-product of frustration, not some organic illness. This was dangerous thinking, she realized, and with a bit of mental weight lifting, dismissed the notion from her head. She had sent Peter and Francis off to eat lunch, while she tried to map out a course of action. Alone, in her small office, she spread the hospital folder of the man she had tried to interview that morning out on her desk. Some things should make sense, she thought. Some connections should be obvious. Some steps should be clear.

She shook her head, as if that might remove the sense of contradiction that overcame her. Now she had a name. A piece of evidence. She had begun successful prosecutions with far less. And, still, she was uneasy. The dossier in front of her should have indicated something persuasive, and yet, it did the opposite. A profoundly retarded man, incapable of answering even the simplest of questions, who had stared across at her seemingly unable to understand anything she asked, had an item in his possession that only the killer would have. This did not add up.

Her first inclination was to send Peter back to take the shirt from the box beneath the man's bed. Any competent crime lab would be able to match the bloodstains against Short Blond's. It was also possible that hair, or fiber evidence was on the shirt, and a microscopic examination might turn up further links between the victim and the assailant. The trouble with simply taking the shirt was that it would be an illegal seizure and probably tossed out by a judge in any subsequent hearing. And there was the curious matter of the lack of the other items that they were searching for. That, too, did not make sense to her.

Lucy had considerable capabilities of concentration. In her short, but meteoric career in the prosecutor's office, she had distinguished herself by being able to see the crimes she investigated in more or less the same way that one watched a movie. In the screen of her imagination, she was able to put details together, so that sooner or later she could envision the entire act. It was what made her so successful. When Lucy came into court, she understood, probably even better than the man she was prosecuting, why and how he'd done what he'd done. It was this quality that made her so formidable. But inside the hospital, she felt adrift. It simply wasn't the same as the criminal world she was accustomed to.

Lucy groaned, frustrated. She stared down at the dossier for the hundredth time, and was about to slam it shut, when there was a tentative knock on the door. She looked up, and it swung open.

Francis was leaning in, poking his head around the corner.

'Hello, Lucy,' he said. 'Can I disturb you?'

'C-Bird, come in,' she said. 'I thought you'd gone to lunch.'

'I did. Or I am. But something occurred to me on the way there, and Peter told me to right away come and tell you.'

'What is that?' Lucy asked, gesturing for the young man to come into the office and seat himself. This Francis did with a clumsy series of motions that seemed to indicate that he was both eager and reluctant.

'The retarded man,' Francis said slowly, 'he didn't seem at all like the sort of person that we're looking for. I mean, some of the other guys that have been in here, who have been ruled out, they seemed, outwardly at least, like much better candidates. Or at least, what we think a candidate should look and sound like.'

Lucy nodded. 'That's what I thought, too. But this one guy — how does he have the shirt?'

Francis seemed to shudder, before replying. 'Because someone wanted us to find it. And someone wanted us to find this man. Someone knew that we were interviewing and searching, and he made the connection between the two events, and so he anticipated what we were going to do, and he planted the shirt.'

Lucy inhaled sharply. This made some sense to her. 'Why would someone drag us to this person?'

'I don't know yet,' Francis said. 'I don't know.'

'I mean,' Lucy continued, 'if you wanted to frame someone for a crime that you'd committed, it would make more sense to plant things on someone whose behavior would be truly suspicious. How can this man's behavior get our interest?'

'I know that, too,' Francis said. 'But this man is different. He's the least likely candidate I think. A brick wall. So there needs to be another reason why he was selected.'

He stood up suddenly, looking skittish, as if a disturbing noise had exploded close by. 'Lucy,' he said slowly, 'there is something about this man that should tell us something. We just need to figure out what it is.'

Lucy grasped the man's hospital folder and held it up. 'Do you think there's something in here that might help us?' she asked.

Francis nodded. 'Maybe. Maybe. I don't know what goes into a folder.'

She thrust it across the desk. 'See what you can see, because I'm drawing a blank.'

Francis reached out and took the folder. He had never actually looked at a hospital file record before, and for a moment he felt as if he were doing something illegal, staring into another patient's life. The existence that all the patients knew about one another was so much defined by the hospital and the day-to-day routine that after a short time confined there, one more or less forgot that the other patients had lives outside the walls. All those elements, of past, of family, of future, were stripped away inside the mental hospital. Francis realized that somewhere there was a file about him, and one about Peter, as well, and that they contained all sorts of information that seemed in that moment terribly distant, as if it had all happened in another existence, at a different time, to a different Francis.

He pored over the retarded man's file.

It was written in clipped and nondescript hospitalese and divided into four sections. The first was background about his home and family; the second contained clinical history, which included height, weight, blood pressure, and the like; the third was course of treatment, outlining various drugs assigned; and the fourth was prognosis. This final section consisted of only five words: *Guarded. Long term care likely.*

There was also a chart that showed that the retarded man had, on more than one occasion, been checked out of the hospital for weekend furloughs to his family.

Francis read about a man who had grown up in a small town not far from Boston and who had only relocated to Western Massachusetts in the year before his hospitalization. He was in his early thirties, and had a sister and two brothers, all of whom tested normal and lived seemingly humdrum lives of exquisite routine. He had first been diagnosed as retarded in grade school and had been in and out of various developmental programs all of his life. No plan had ever stuck.

Francis rocked back in his seat, and quickly saw a simple, deadly situation that resembled a box. A mother and father growing older. A childlike son, larger and less able to be controlled with every passing year. A son who was unable to understand or control impulses or rage. Of sexual interest. Of strength. Siblings who wanted to get away, far away, as fast as possible, unwilling to help.

He could see a little bit of himself in every word. Different, but the same, still.

Francis read through the file once, then again, all the time aware that Lucy was watching his face closely, measuring every reaction that he had to the words on the page.

After a moment, he bit down on his lip. He could feel a little quiver in his hands. He could sense things swirling around him, as if the words on the pages combined with the thoughts in his head to make him dizzy. He felt a surge of danger, and he breathed in sharply, then pushed himself away from the file, sliding it across the desktop to Lucy.

'Do you have any ideas, Francis?' she asked.

'Nothing, really,' he said.

'Nothing jumps out at you?'

He shook his head. But she could see that this was a lie. Francis did have ideas, she realized. He just didn't want to say what they were.

*   *   *

I tried to remember: What scared me the most?

That was one of the moments, that time in Lucy's office. I was beginning to see things. Not hallucinations, like those that rang in my ears and echoed in my head. Those, I was familiar with, and while they might have been irksome and difficult and helped define my madness, I was accustomed to them and their demands and fears and the things they might or might not ask of me at any given moment. After all, they had been with me since I was a child. But what scared me right then was seeing things about the Angel. Who he might be. How he might think. For Peter and Lucy, it wasn't the same. They understood that the Angel was an adversary. A criminal. A target. Someone hiding from

343

them, whom they were empowered to uncover. They had hunted people before, stalked them and brought them to justice, so there was a different context to their pursuit than what I had suddenly surrounding me. In those moments, I had begun to see the Angel as someone like me. Only far worse. He had taken footsteps, and, for the first time, I believed that I was able to retrace them. Placing my own shoe in his well-trod path was something that everything inside me screamed was wrong. But possible.

I wanted to flee. A chorus within me sang loudly that nothing right was happening. My voices were an opera of self-preservation, warning me to get out, get away, to run and hide and save myself.

But how could I? The hospital was locked. The walls were high. The gates were strong. And my own illness barred me from flight.

How could I turn my back on the only two people who had ever thought that I was worth anything?

'That's right, Francis. You couldn't do that.'

I had crept down and huddled in a corner of the living room, staring over at my words, when I heard Peter speak. Relief flooded me, and I pivoted about, searching the room for his presence.

'Peter?' I replied. 'You're back?'

'I didn't really leave. I've been here all along.'

'The Angel was here. I could feel him.'

'He will be back. He's close, Francis. He will get closer still.'

'He's doing what he did before.'

'I know, C-Bird. But you're ready for him this time. I know you are.'

'Help me, Peter,' I whispered. I could feel tears flowering in my throat.

'Oh C-Bird, this time it's your fight.'

'I'm scared, Peter.'

'Of course you are,' he said, with the matter-of-fact

tones that he sometimes used, but always had the quality of being nonjudgmental. 'But that doesn't mean it's hopeless. It only means you need to be careful. Just like before. That hasn't changed. It was your caution, the first time that was critical, wasn't it?'

I stayed in my corner, my eyes darting around the room. He must have seen me, because when I spied him, leaning up against the wall opposite me, he gave a little wave of his hand, and broke into a familiar grin. I could see that he was wearing a bright orange jumpsuit, but it had faded through use and was ripped and torn and smeared with dirt. He held a shiny silver helmet in his hands, and his face was streaked with soot and ash and lines of sweat. He must have seen me staring, because he gave a little laugh, a wave of the hand, and shook his head. 'Sorry about the rough appearance, C-Bird.'

I thought he looked a little older than I remembered, and behind his grin I could see some of the harsh inroads of hurt and trouble. 'Are you okay, Peter?' I asked.

'Of course, Francis. It's just I've been through a lot. So have you. We always wear the clothes that the fates dress us in, don't we, C-Bird? Nothing new about that.'

He turned over to the wall and his eyes ran up and down the columns of words. He nodded in agreement. 'You're making progress,' he said.

'I don't know,' I answered. 'Every word I write seems to make the room get darker.'

Peter sighed, as if to say that he'd anticipated this. 'We've been through a lot of darkness, haven't we, Francis. And some of it together. That's what you're writing about. Just remember, we were there with you, and we're here with you now. Can you keep that in mind, C-Bird?'

'I'll try.'

'Things got a little complicated that day, didn't they?'

345

'Yes. For both of us. And Lucy, too, because of it.'

'Tell it all, Francis,' he said.

I looked over at the wall, and saw where I had left off. When I turned back to Peter, he had disappeared.

20

It was Peter who suggested that Lucy proceed in two distinct directions. The first path, he emphasized, was to not stop interviewing patients. It was critical, Peter said, that no one, either patients or staff, know that they had uncovered a piece of evidence, because precisely what it meant, and where it pointed, was as yet unclear to any of them. But if the news got out, they would lose control over the situation. It was a by-product of the unstable world of the mental hospital, he told her. There was no way of anticipating what unrest, even panic, it might cause among all the fragile personalities that made up the population. This meant, among other things, that the bloody shirt had to be left where it was, and that no outside agencies should be involved, especially the local cops who'd taken Lanky into custody, even if they risked losing it as a piece of evidence down the road. And, he added, people in the Amherst Building were beginning to get accustomed to the steady stream of patients entering from other buildings at the elbow of Big Black in order to be questioned by Lucy, and there might be a way of working that routine into an advantage. The second suggestion Peter had was slightly harder to bring about.

'What we need to do,' he said to Lucy quietly, 'is get that big guy and his things transferred over to Amherst. And we need to do this in a way that doesn't draw much attention to the change.'

Lucy agreed. They were standing in the corridor, static amid the early afternoon ebb and flow of patients through the building, as therapy groups and crafts classes were getting under way. The usual haze of cigarette smoke hung in the still air, and the clattering of feet mingled with the hum of voices. Peter, with Lucy and Francis, seemed to be the only people not moving. Like rocks in a fast-running river, activity bubbled around them. 'Okay,' Lucy said. 'I think that makes sense. He bears watching. But beyond that?'

'I don't know. Not precisely,' Peter replied. 'He's the only suspect we have, and C-Bird here doesn't think he's the real suspect anyway, an observation that I think I subscribe to. But exactly how he fits into the greater scheme of things we're going to need to find out. And the only way to do that — '

' . . . is to keep him close enough to watch. Yes. This makes as much sense as anything,' she said. Then she lifted an eyebrow, as if an idea had occurred to her. 'I think I know what to do. Let me make some arrangements.'

'But quietly,' Peter said. 'Don't let anyone know . . . '

She smiled. 'Peter, I can manage this. Being a prosecutor is all about making things happen in precisely the way you want them to happen.' Then she added, as if to underscore a bit of a joke: 'More or less.' Lucy looked up and saw the Moses brothers making their way down the corridor. She nodded to them. 'Gentlemen, I think we need to get back on track. I wonder if I could have a word with you quietly, before Mister Evans returns from wherever he is.'

'He's over talking with the big doc,' Little Black said cautiously. He turned to Peter and made a little waving gesture with his hand, which was, in effect, a question. Peter nodded.

'I told her,' he said. 'Does anyone else . . . '

'I told my brother,' Little Black said. 'But that's it.'

Big Black edged forward. 'I'm not seeing that dude as the guy we're looking for,' he said stolidly. 'I mean the man can barely feed hisself. Likes to sit around and play with dolls. Maybe watch the television. I don't see him as a murderer, unless you get him so riled up he takes a swing at somebody. Boy is strong. Stronger than he knows.'

'Francis said more or less the same thing,' Peter said.

'C-Bird's got instincts.' Big Black laughed.

'So for the time being, nobody else gets told anything, okay?' Lucy interjected. 'Let's try to keep it that way.'

Little Black shrugged, but rolled his eyes, as if to say that in a place where everyone seemed to be filled with the secrets of their past, keeping a secret about their present was well-nigh impossible. 'We'll try,' he said. 'One other thing. C-Bird, Gulp-a-pill wants to see you now.'

Then the large attendant turned toward Peter. 'You, I'm supposed to get a little later.'

Peter looked intrigued. 'What do you think . . . ,' he started, but both the attendants shook their heads.

'Not speculating,' Little Black said. 'Not yet.'

* * *

While his brother escorted Francis through the main entryway to Amherst en route to Doctor Gulptilil's office, Little Black trailed Peter and Lucy into the interview room. The prosecutor immediately went over to the box of patient files that she had accumulated, and removed the one belonging to the hulking retarded man from the top of the pile. Then she rapidly checked through her handwritten master list of potential suspects, until she found one that she thought would do the trick. She thrust the file across to Little Black, and said, 'This is the guy I want to speak with next.'

He glanced down at the file and nodded. 'I know this man. Short-fused son of a bitch,' he said. Then he stammered in embarrassment. 'Pardon my language, Miss Jones. It's just I had a run-in or two with this guy. He's one of the bad-news types around here.'

'All the better,' she said. 'Considering what I have in mind.'

Little Black looked quizzically at her, and Peter slumped into his seat, smiling. 'Miss Jones seems to have an idea,' he said.

Lucy picked up a pencil and rolled it around her fingers while she examined the patient's file. The man in question was an institutional fixture, having spent much of his life either in prison for a garden-variety of assaults, robberies, and burglaries, or in various mental health facilities, complaining of auditory hallucinations and suffering from manic rages. Some of each, she guessed, were invented. Some were real. What was perhaps most real, of course, was that he had psychopathic, manipulative qualities, which were more or less ideal for what she had in mind. And an explosive anger.

'How has this guy been a problem?' she asked Little Black.

'He's just one of those men, always wants to push the limits, you know what I'm saying? Ask him to move one way, he goes the other. Tell him to be here, he shows up over there. You try to push him a bit, he cries that you're beating him and files a formal complaint with the big doc. Likes to get into the face of other patients, too. Always hassling one or the other. I think he steals stuff from folks behind their backs. Just a sorry excuse for a human all around, if you ask me.'

Lucy said, 'Well, let's bring him in, and see if we can't get him to do what I want.'

Beyond that, however, she wasn't willing to explain, although she noted that Peter seemed to concentrate carefully on what she was saying, and then relax in his chair, as if he perceived something behind what she designed, like a delay switch on a mechanical device. Lucy guessed that this was true, and thought it was a quality that she would probably come to admire. Then, when she considered it a bit further, realized that she had seen several qualities in Peter that she was beginning to admire, which only made her even more curious as to why he was where he was and had done what he had done.

★ ★ ★

Miss Luscious took charge of Francis as soon as Big Black ushered him into the medical director's office. As always, the secretary wore an unfriendly scowl, as if to say that any disruption in the carefully plotted daily routine that she had established with iron-fisted organization was something she personally resented. She handed Big Black a message to meet his brother at the Williams Building, and then she quickly half pushed Francis through the office door, saying, 'You're late. You need to hurry.'

Gulp-a-pill was standing by his window, staring out across one of the quadrangles. He seemed to linger for a moment, keeping watch on whatever he could see. Francis moved into a chair across from the doctor's desk, and stared out the same window, to try to see what the physician found so intriguing. He realized that the only times he'd looked out a window that wasn't barred or grated was in the medical director's office. It made the world look far more benign than it really was.

The doctor turned abruptly. 'A fine day, Francis, don't you think? Spring seems to have taken hold quite firmly.'

'Sometimes, inside where we are, it's hard to get a sense of the season changing,' Francis said. 'There's a lot of grime and dirt on the windows. If we had the windows washed, I bet it would help people's moods.'

Gulptilil nodded. 'This is an excellent suggestion, Francis, and one that displays some insight. I will mention it to the building and grounds workers, see if they can't add some window scrubbing to their duties, although, I suspect, they are overburdened already.'

He sat down behind his desk, gathered himself, and leaned forward, putting his elbows on the surface, lifting his arms to form an inverted V and placing his chin at the juncture of his hands. 'So, Francis, do you know what day it is?' he asked.

Francis answered rapidly. 'Friday.'

'And how is it that you are so sure?'

'Tuna fish and macaroni on the luncheon menu. Standard Friday fare.'

'Yes, and why would that be?'

'In deference to the Catholic patients, I would suspect,' Francis answered. 'Some still feel it necessary to eat fish on Fridays. My own family does. Mass on Sundays. Fish on Fridays. It's the natural order of things.'

'And you?'

'I don't think I'm as religious,' Francis said.

Gulptilil thought this was interesting, but did not follow up on it. 'Do you know the date?' he asked.

Francis shook his head. 'I believe it is either the fifth or sixth of May,' he said. 'I'm sorry. The days seem to blend together in the hospital. And usually I count on Newsman to fill me in on current events, but I haven't seen him today.'

'It is the fifth. Can you remember that for me, please.'

'Yes.'

'And do you recall who is the president of the United States?'

'Carter.'

Gulptilil smiled, but barely moved his chin from its perch on his fingertips. 'And so,' the medical director continued, as if what he were about to say was a logical extension of the prior conversation, 'I have met with Mister Evans, who reports to me that although you have

352

made some progress in socialization and in understanding your illness, and the impact that it has upon yourself and those close to you, that he believes despite your current course of medication that you continue to hear voices belonging to people who are not present, voices that urge you to act in specific fashions, and that you still have fixed and settled delusions about events.'

Francis did not reply, because he did not hear a question. Within him, whispers ricocheted about, but they remained quiet, hard to hear, almost as if they were all afraid that the medical director would be able to hear them as well, if they raised their tones.

'Tell me, Francis,' Gulptilil continued, 'do you think that Mister Evans's assessment is accurate?'

'It's hard to respond,' Francis said. He shifted about a little uncomfortably in his seat, aware, in that second, that any action he made, every word he spoke, every inflection, every mannerism, might be fodder for the doctor's opinion. 'I think Mister Evans automatically considers something that one of us patients says that he disagrees with to be a delusion, and so it is hard to know what to say in answer.'

The medical director smiled, and finally leaned back. 'That is a cogent and organized statement, Francis. Very good.'

For an instant, Francis started to relax, but then, as quickly, he remembered to not trust the doctor, and especially not to trust a compliment tossed his direction. There was a murmuring of assent deep within him. Whenever his voices agreed with him, it gave Francis confidence.

'But Mister Evans is also a professional, Francis, so we should not discount what he says too rapidly. Tell me, how is life in Amherst for you? Do you get along with the other patients? The remainder of the staff? Do you look forward to Mister Evans's therapy sessions? And, tell me, Francis, do you think you are closer to being able to go home? Has your time here so far been, shall we say, *profitable*?'

The doctor moved forward, a slightly predatory motion that Francis recognized. The questions hovering in the air were a minefield, and he needed to be cautious in his replies. 'The dormitory is fine, Doctor, although overcrowded, and I believe I am able to get along with everyone, more or less. It is sometimes difficult to see the value in Mister Evans's therapy sessions, although it is always helpful when the discussion turns to current events, because I sometimes fear that we are too isolated here in the hospital, and that the world's business continues without our engagement in it. And I'd very much like to go home, Doctor, but I'm unsure what it is that I have to prove to you and to my family that will allow me to.'

'None of them,' the doctor said stiffly, 'has deemed it necessary or worthwhile to come visit you, I believe?'

Francis looped some coils of control over emotions that threatened to erupt. 'Not yet, doctor.'

'A phone call, perhaps? A letter or two?'

'No.'

'That must cause you some distress, does it not, Francis?'

He took a deep breath. 'Yes,' he said.

'But you do not feel abandoned?'

Francis was unsure what the right answer was, so he said, 'I'm okay.'

Gulptilil smiled, not the bemused smile, but the snakelike one. 'And you are okay I suspect because you still hear the voices that have been with you for so many years?'

'No,' Francis lied. 'The medication has erased them.'

'But you acknowledge that they have been there in the past?'

Within him, he could hear echoes *no, no, no, don't*

say anything, hide us, Francis!

'I'm just not precisely sure I know what you mean, Doctor,' he replied. He didn't imagine for an instant that this would put the doctor off his pursuit.

Gulptilil waited for several seconds, letting silence flow throughout the room, as if he expected Francis to add something, which he did not.

'Tell me this, Francis. Do you believe that there is a killer loose in the hospital?'

Francis inhaled sharply. He hadn't expected this question, although, he understood, it would have been fair to say that he hadn't expected *any* question. For a moment, he let his eyes race around the room, as if he was looking for a way out. His heart was pounding and all his voices were silent, because they all knew that hidden within the doctor's question were all sorts of important notions, and he had no idea what the right answer would be. He saw the doctor lift an eyebrow quizzically, and Francis knew that delay was as dangerous as anything.

'Yes,' he said slowly.

'You do not believe that this is a delusion and a paranoid one, at that?'

'No,' he said, trying unsuccessfully to not sound hesitant.

The doctor nodded his head. 'And why do you think this?' he asked.

'Miss Jones seems convinced. And so does Peter. And I don't think that Lanky . . .'

Gulptilil held up his hand. 'These details we've discussed before. Tell me, what has changed in the ah, *investigation*, ah, that suggests that you are on the correct path.'

Francis wanted to squirm in his chair but didn't dare to do so. 'Miss Jones is still interviewing potential suspects,' he said. 'I don't believe that she has reached any conclusions yet about any individual, other than some that have been cleared. Mister Evans has helped her with that.'

Gulptilil paused, assessing the answer. 'You would tell me, would you not, Francis?'

'Tell you what, Doctor?'

'If she had made some determination.'

'I'm not sure . . . '

'It would be a sign, at least to me, that you have a much firmer grasp of reality. It would show some progress on your part, I think, if you were able to express yourself on this score. And who knows where that might lead, Francis? Taking charge of reality, why that's an important step on the road to recovery. A very important step and a very important road. And that road would lead to all sorts of changes. Perhaps a visit from your family. Perhaps a furlough home for a weekend. And then, perhaps greater freedoms, still. A road of significant possibility, Francis.'

The doctor bent toward Francis, who remained silent.

'I make myself clear?' he asked.

Francis nodded.

'Good. Then we will make time to speak of these matters again in the next few days, Francis. And, of course, should you think it important to speak to me at any time, about any details or observations you might have, why, my door is always open to you. I will always make the time available. At any time, do you understand?'

'Yes. I believe so.'

'I am pleased with your progress, Francis. And pleased, as well, that we had this talk.'

Francis again remained silent.

The doctor gestured toward the door. 'I believe we are finished for this moment, Francis, and I have to prepare for a rather important visitor. You may let yourself out. My secretary will arrange for someone to escort you back to Amherst.'

Francis pushed himself up out of the chair and took a few tentative strides toward the office door, when he was stopped by Doctor Gulptilil's voice. 'Ah, Francis, I almost forgot. Before you leave, can you tell me what day it is?'

'Friday.'

'And the date.'

'The fifth of May.'

'Excellent. And the name of our distinguished president?'

'Carter.'

'Very good, Francis. I hope we will have an opportunity soon to speak some more.'

And with that, Francis let himself out the door. He didn't dare to look back over his shoulder, to see if the doctor was watching him. But he could feel Gulptilil's eyes boring into his back, right into the place where his neck met his skull. *Get out now!* he heard from deep within his head, and he was eager to oblige.

★   ★   ★

The man seated across from Lucy was wiry and small, a little like a professional horse racing jockey in build. He wore a crooked smile, that seemed to her to bend in the same direction that the man hunched his shoulders, giving him a lopsided appearance. He had stringy black hair that encircled his face in a tangled mass, and blue eyes that glowed with an intensity that was unsettling. Every third breath the man took seemed to emerge in an asthmatic wheeze, which didn't prevent him from lighting one cigarette after the other, so that a smoky haze surrounded his face. Evans coughed once or twice and Big Black retreated to a corner of the office, just close enough, just far enough. Big Black, Lucy thought, seemed to have an instinctive knowledge of distances, almost automatically going to just the right amount for every patient.

She glanced at the file in front of her. 'Mister Harris,' she said. 'I wonder if you might tell me if you recognize any of these people.'

With that, she thrust the crime scene photographs across the desk at the man.

He took each one carefully, spending perhaps a few too many seconds examining each. Then he shook his head. 'Murdered people,' he said with a lingering emphasis on the first word. 'Dead and left in the woods, it looks like. Not my cup of tea.'

'That isn't an answer.'

'No. I don't know them.' His lopsided grin expanded slightly. 'And if I did, would you expect me to admit it?'

Lucy ignored this. 'You have a record of violence,' she said.

'A fight in a bar isn't a murder.'

She looked closely at him.

'Nor is drunk driving. Or beating up some guy who thought he could call me names.'

'Look carefully at that third picture,' she said slowly. 'Do you see the date inscribed on the bottom of the photograph?'

'Yes.'

'Can you tell me your whereabouts during that time?'

'I was here.'

'No, you weren't. Please don't lie to me.'

The man Harris shifted about. 'Then I was in Walpole on some of those bogus charges they like to hit me up with.'

'No, you weren't. I repeat: Don't lie to me.'

Harris shifted about. 'I was down on the Cape. I had a job down there working for a roofing contractor.'

Lucy looked at the file. 'Curious time, wasn't it? You're up on some roof somewhere, claiming to be hearing voices, and at the same time, after hours, all sorts of houses within blocks of where you're working are getting ripped off.'

'Nobody ever filed those charges.'

'That's because you got them to ship you here.'

He smiled again, showing uneven teeth. A slippery, awful man, Lucy thought. But not the man she was hunting. She could sense Evans growing uneasy at her side.

'So,' she said slowly, 'you had nothing to do with any of this?'

'That's right,' Harris said. 'Can I leave now?'

'Yes,' Lucy said. As Harris started to rise, she added: 'As soon as you explain to me why another patient would tell us that you boasted of these killings.'

'What?' Harris said, his voice rising an octave instantly. 'Somebody said I did what?'

'You heard me. So explain why you're boasting in the dormitory, it's Williams, right? Tell me why you would say what you said.'

'I haven't said anything like that! You're crazy!'

'This is a crazy place,' Lucy said slowly. 'Tell me why.'

'I didn't. Who told you this?'

'I'm not at liberty to divulge the source of information.'

'Who?'

'You have made claims that have been overheard in the dormitory where you live. You have been indiscreet, to say the least. I'd like you to explain yourself.'

'When did . . . '

Lucy smiled. 'Just recently. This information only came to us recently. So you are denying saying anything?'

'Yes. It's crazy! Why would I boast about something like that? I don't know what you're driving at, lady, but I haven't killed nobody yet. It don't make sense . . . '

'You think everything in here should make sense?'

'Somebody's lying to you, lady. And somebody wants

359

to get me into trouble.'

Lucy nodded slowly. 'I will take that into consideration,' she said. 'All right. You can leave. We may, however, have to speak again.'

Harris fairly vaulted out of the chair, taking a step forward, which caused Big Black to uncurl from his position, a movement which the slight man couldn't help but notice. It made him stop. 'Son of a bitch,' he said. And then he turned and exited, after stubbing his cigarette butt on the floor beneath his feet.

Evans was red-faced. 'Do you have any idea the trouble those questions might cause?' he demanded. He pointed at the file, slapping his finger down at Harris's diagnosis. 'See what it says, right there. Explosive. Anger management issues. And you provoke him with a bunch of off-the-wall questions that you know won't elicit any response other than fury. I'll bet Harris ends up in an isolation cell before the end of the day, and I'll be in charge of seeing him sedated. Damn! That was simply irresponsible, Miss Jones. And if you're intending to persist with questions that will only serve to disrupt life on the wards, I'll be forced to speak with Doctor Gulptilil about it!'

Lucy pivoted toward Evans. 'Sorry,' she said. 'Thoughtless of me. I'll try to be more circumspect with the next interviews.'

'I need a break,' Evans said, rising angrily. He stormed out of the room.

Lucy, however, felt a sense of satisfaction.

She, too, rose up and stepped out of the office into the corridor. Peter was waiting, wearing a small, elusive smile, as if he understood everything that had taken place outside of his presence. He gave her a small bow, acknowledging that he had seen and heard enough, and admired the ploy she'd come up with on such short notice. But he didn't get the chance to say anything to her because at that moment Big Black emerged from behind the nursing station bars, holding a set of hand and foot cuffs. The chains made a rattling sound that echoed in the corridor. More than one patient wandering through the area saw the attendant, and saw what he held in his hands, and like startled birds taking wing, they swirled out of his path as rapidly as possible.

Peter, however, remained stock-still, waiting.

From a few feet away, Cleo stood up, her immense bulk swaying back and forth as if buffeted by a hurricane wind.

Lucy watched Big Black approach Peter, whisper an apology, and then snap the cuffs on his wrists and attach them around his ankles. She kept her mouth closed.

But as the final restraint clicked shut, a red-faced, infuriated Cleo abruptly shouted out, 'The bastards! The bastards! Don't let them take you away, Peter! We need you!'

Silence hammered the corridor.

'Damn it to hell,' Cleo sang out, 'We *need* you!'

Lucy saw that Peter's face was set, and that all his grinning insouciance had fled. He lifted his hands up, as if testing the limits of the restraints, and she thought she could see a great agony sweep through him, before he turned and passively allowed Big Black to lead him down the corridor hobbled like a wild beast that couldn't be trusted.

21

Peter cautiously shuffled down the hospital pathway at the side of Big Black in the unmistakable loping manner caused by the restraints binding his legs and hands. The huge attendant remained silent, as if embarrassed by the escort duty. He had apologized once to Peter as they stepped outside of the Amherst Building, and then shut up. But he was walking quickly, which prompted Peter to half run to keep up, and forced him to keep his head down, eyes on the black macadam walkway, concentrating on what he was doing so that he would not stumble and fall.

Peter could feel a little of the late afternoon sunlight on his neck, and he managed to lift his head a couple of times to see that shafts of light were streaking over the rows of buildings, as the sunset took grasp of the end of the day. There was a little chill in the air, a familiar reminder that the spring in New England owns a warning to not be overconfident about the advent of summer. Some of the white paint on the window frames glistened, making the barred glass look like heavy-lidded eyes watching his progress across the quadrangle. The cuffs around his hands dug painfully into the flesh of his wrists and he realized that all the exuberance he'd felt when he'd first sneaked out of the Amherst Building in the company of the two brothers to start searching for the Angel, the excitement that had flooded him with every remembered smell and sense, had fled, replaced by a gloom of imprisonment. He did not know what meeting he was being taken to, but he suspected it was significant.

This thought was buttressed by the sight of two black Cadillac limousines parked in the rotary in front of the hospital administration building. They were polished to a reflective sheen.

'What's going on?' Peter whispered to Big Black.

The attendant shook his head. 'They just told me to get the restraints and bring you along real quick. So now you know as much as me.'

'Which is nothing,' Peter said, and the big man nodded in agreement.

He lurched up the stairs behind Big Black and hurried down the hallway to Gulptilil's office. Miss Luscious was waiting behind her secretary's desk, and Peter saw that her familiar scowl had been replaced by a look of discomfort and that she had covered up her usual skintight blouse with a loose-fitting cardigan. 'Hurry up,' she said. 'They've been waiting.' She did not say who *they* were.

The chains jangled with the music of restraint as he hurried forward, and Big Black held the door open for him. Peter shuffled into the room.

He first saw Gulp-a-pill behind his desk. The medical director rose, as Peter entered. There was, as usual, an empty seat in front of the desk. There were also three other men in the room. All wore the black suits and white collars of the clergy. Peter did not recognize two of the men, but the third was a face familiar to any Boston Catholic. The Cardinal was seated to the side, dead center of a couch that was placed along the wall. He had his legs crossed, and he seemed relaxed. One of the other priests was seated next to him, and held a brown leather folder in his hands, a yellow legal-size notepad, and a large, black pen, which he fiddled with nervously. The third priest had been given a seat behind Gulptilil's desk, just to the side of the medical director. He had a sheaf of papers in front of him.

'Ah, Mister Moses, thank you. Please, if you would be so kind, remove the restraints from Peter's hands and legs.'

It took a moment or two for the attendant to do this. Then he stepped back, looking toward the medical director, who gave him a small, dismissive wave. 'Just wait outside for us to call you, won't you please, Mister Moses. I'm sure that there is no need for any additional security to be present during this meeting.' He looked over at Peter and added, 'We are all gentlemen here, are we not?'

Peter did not reply to this. He didn't feel very much like a gentleman in that moment.

Without a word, Big Black turned and left Peter standing alone. Gulptilil gestured toward the chair. 'Be seated, Peter,' he said. 'These men would like to ask you some questions.'

Peter nodded, and sat down heavily, but slid to the front of the chair, poised. He tried to appear confident, but he knew this was unlikely. He could feel a rush of emotions within him, a range from out-and-out hatred to curiosity, and he warned himself to keep whatever he said short and direct. 'I recognize the Cardinal,' Peter said, looking directly at the medical director. 'I have seen his picture on many occasions. But I'm afraid I do not know the other two gentlemen. Do they have names?'

Gulptilil nodded. 'Father Callahan is the Cardinal's personal assistant,' Gulptilil said, indicating the figure seated beside the Cardinal. He was a middle-aged, balding man, with a pair of thick eyeglasses that were pushed tight to his face, and stubby fingers that gripped his pen tightly and drummed against the legal pad. He nodded at Peter, but did not rise to shake hands. 'And the other gentleman is Father Grozdik, who has some questions for you.'

Peter nodded. The priest with the Polish name was much younger, probably close in age to Peter himself. He was lean, athletic, well over six feet tall. His black suit seemed tailored to a narrow waist and he had a languid, feline appearance. His dark hair was worn long, but brushed back from his face, and he had penetrating blue eyes that were lodged on Peter, and had not wavered from him since he'd been escorted into the room. He, too, did not rise, offer his hand, or say anything in greeting, but leaned forward in a eerily predatory fashion. Peter met the man's gaze, then said, 'My guess is that Father Grozdik also has a title. Perhaps he would share that with me.'

'I'm with the Archdiocese's legal office,' he said. The priest had a flat, even voice that betrayed little.

'Perhaps, if the Father's questions are of a legal nature, I should have my attorney present?' Peter said. He formed this as a question purposefully, hoping to read something in the priest's response.

'We were all hoping that you would agree to meet with us informally,' the priest answered.

'That would of course depend on what it is you wish to know,' Peter said. 'Especially, as I note that Father Callahan over there has already begun to take notes.'

The older priest stopped writing in midstroke. He lifted his eyes to the younger priest, who nodded back at him. The Cardinal remained motionless on the couch, watching Peter carefully.

'Do you object?' Father Grozdik asked. 'It might be important at some later point to have a record of this meeting. That would be as much for your protection as ours. And, should nothing come of this, well, then we can always agree to destroy the record. But, if you have an objection . . . ' He let his voice trail off.

'Not yet. Maybe later,' Peter said.

'Good. Then we can proceed.'

'Please do,' Peter said stiffly.

Father Grozdik stared down at his papers, taking his time before continuing. Peter realized instantly that the man had had training in interrogation techniques. He could see this in the patient, settled manner the priest had, arranging his thoughts prior to opening his mouth with a question. Peter guessed the military, and saw a simple procession: Saint Ignatius for high school, then Boston College for undergraduate work. ROTC training at college, a tour of duty overseas with military police, a return to BC Law and more Jesuitical training, then the fast track in the archdiocese. Growing up, he'd known a few like Father Grozdik, who had been placed by virtue of intellect and ambition, on the church's priority list. The only thing out of place, Peter realized, was the Polish name. Not Irish, which he thought was interesting. But, then, in that moment, he realized that his own background was Irish Catholic, as was the Cardinal's and the Cardinal's assistant, and so, a message was being sent by bringing in someone of different ethnic origins. He wasn't precisely sure what advantage this gave the three priests. He guessed that he would find out in short order.

'So, Peter,' the priest began, ' . . . it is acceptable that I call you Peter? I would like to keep this session informal.'

'Of course, Father,' Peter said. He nodded his head. That was clever, he thought. Everyone else had an adult's authority and a status. He only had a first name. He had used the same approach with more than one arsonist that he'd questioned.

'So, Peter,' the priest began again, 'you are here in the hospital for a mental evaluation ordered by the court prior to continuing with the charges against you, is that not correct?'

'Yes. Trying to figure out whether I'm crazy. Too crazy to stand trial.'

'That is because many people who know you believe your actions to be, what? Shall we say 'out of character'? Is that a fair representation?'

'A fireman who sets a fire. A good Catholic boy who

burns down a church. Sure. Out of character is fine with me.'

'And, are you crazy, Peter?'

'No. But that's what most of the folks in here would say if they were asked the same question, so I'm not sure my opinion counts for all that much.'

'What conclusions do you think the staff here have reached so far?'

'I would suspect they are still in the process of accumulating impressions, Father, but that they more or less have reached the same conclusion as I have. They will put it a little more clinically, of course. Say that I'm filled with unresolved angers. Neurotic. Compulsive. Perhaps even antisocial. But that I knew what I was doing, and that I knew it was wrong, and that's the legal standard, more or less, right Father? They must have taught you that at Boston College law, right?'

Father Grozdik smiled and shifted himself slightly in his seat, and then replied humorlessly. 'Yes. Good guess, Peter. Or did you spot the class ring?' He held up his hand and displayed a large, gold ring that caught some light coming through the window. Peter realized that the priest had positioned himself in such a way that the Cardinal could watch Peter's reactions to questions without Peter being able to turn and see how the Cardinal was responding.

'It's a curious matter, isn't it, Peter?' Father Grozdik asked, his voice remaining flat and cold.

'Curious, Father?'

'Perhaps curious is not the correct word, Peter. Intellectually intriguing might be a better way of thinking of the dilemma you are in. Existential, almost. Have you studied psychology much, Peter? Or philosophy, perhaps?'

'No. I studied killing. When I was in the service. How to kill and how to save people from being killed. And after I came home, I studied fires. How to put them out.

And how to set them. Surprisingly, I didn't find these two courses of study to be all that different.'

Father Grozdik smiled and nodded. 'Yes. Peter the Fireman, or so I understand you are called. But surely you are aware that there are some aspects to your situation that transcend simple interpretations.'

'Yes,' Peter said. 'I am aware.'

The priest leaned forward. 'Do you think much about evil, Peter?'

'Evil, Father?'

'Yes. The presence upon this earth of forces that can only best be explained by a sense of evil.'

Peter hesitated, then nodded. 'Yes. I have spent a good deal of time considering it. You can't have traveled to the places I have without being aware that evil has a place in the world.'

'Yes. War and destruction. Certainly these are arenas where evil has a free hand. It interests you? Intellectually, perhaps?'

Peter shrugged, as if to display a certain nonchalance about the questions, but inwardly he was marshaling all his powers of concentration. He did not know in what direction the priest was going to turn the conversation, but he was wary. He kept his mouth shut.

Father Grozdik hesitated, then asked, 'Tell me Peter, what you have done . . . do you consider it evil?'

Peter paused, then said, 'Are you asking for a confession, Father? And I mean the sort of confession that usually requires a Miranda warning. Not a confession booth statement, because I am relatively certain that there is no number of Our Fathers or Hail Marys, there's no perfect act of contrition that would constitute an adequate penance for my behavior.'

Father Grozdik did not smile, nor did he seem particularly unsettled by Peter's response. He was a measured man, very cold and direct, Peter thought, which stood in contrast to the oblique nature of the questions he had. A dangerous man, and a difficult adversary, Peter believed. The problem was, he did not know for certain whether the priest was an adversary. Most likely. But that didn't explain why he was there. 'No, Peter,' the priest said flatly. 'Not either sort of confession. Let me put you at ease on one score . . . ' He said this in a manner that Peter recognized was designed to do the opposite. ' . . . Nothing you say here today is going to be used against you in a court of law.'

'Another court, then, perhaps?' Peter replied, with a slight mocking tone. The priest did not respond to the bait.

'We're all judged ultimately, are we not, Peter?'

'That remains to be seen, doesn't it?'

'As do all the answers to all sorts of mysteries. But evil, Peter . . . '

'All right, Father,' Peter said. 'Then the answer to your first question is yes. I believe that much of what I have done is evil. When you examine it, from one perspective, which would be the Church's perspective, it seems pretty clear. It is why I am here, and why I will go to prison in short order. Probably for the rest of my life. Or damn close to it.'

Father Grozdik seemed to assess this statement, and then he asked, 'But my suspicion, Peter, is that you are not telling me the truth. That no, deep within, you do not think that what you did was truly evil. Or that you think that when you set that fire, you intended to use one evil to erase another. Perhaps that is a bit closer to the truth.'

Peter did not want to reply to this. He let silence fill the room.

The priest bent forward a little. 'Would it not be fair to say that you believe that your actions were wrong, on one moral plane. But right upon another?'

Peter could feel sweat under his arms and forming at the back of his neck.

'I'm not sure I want to be talking about this,' he said.

The priest looked down and examined some papers, flipping through them rapidly until he seemed to find what he was searching for, examine it, then lift his eyes back to Peter with another question. 'Do you recall the first thing you told the police when they arrived at your mother's house? And, I might add, discovered you sitting on a step with your can of gasoline and matches in hand.'

'Actually, I used a lighter.'

'Of course. I stand corrected. And you told them?'

'You seem to have the police report in front of you.'

'Do you recall saying, 'This evens things up,' before they arrested you?'

'I do.'

'Perhaps you could explain that to me.'

'Father Grozdik,' Peter said bluntly. 'I suspect you would not be here if you did not already know the answer to that question.'

The priest seemed to glance sideways, toward the Cardinal, but Peter wasn't able to see what the Cardinal did. He guessed some slight hand motion, or a nod of the head. It was only a small moment, but something turned right then.

'I do, Peter. At least, I believe I do. Tell me this, then, the priest that died in the fire, did you know him?'

'Father Connolly? No. I had never met him. In fact, I didn't really know all that much about him. Except, of course, for one salient detail. I'm afraid that after I returned home from Vietnam, my churchgoing days were, shall we say, limited. You know, Father, you see a lot of cruelty and dying and senselessness, and you start to wonder where God is. Hard to not have a crisis of faith, or however you want to put it.'

'So, you burned down a church and with it a priest . . .'

'I didn't know he was there,' Peter said. 'And I didn't

realize there were others inside, as well. I thought the church was empty. I called out, and knocked on some doors. Just bad luck, I guess. Like I said, I thought it was empty.'

'It wasn't. And, to be frank, Peter, I am not sure I believe you on this score. How hard were those knocks? How loud were your warnings? One man dies, three are injured. Scarred.'

'Yes. And I shall go to prison, as soon as my little sojourn here in the hospital is completed.'

'And you say you didn't know the priest . . . '

'But, Father, I knew of him.'

'And what is it you are saying?'

'How much do you need to know, Father? Perhaps it is not me that you should be speaking to. But my nephew. The altar boy. And maybe a few of his friends — '

Father Grozdik held up his hand, stopping Peter in midsentence. 'We have spoken with a number of parishioners. Much information has come our way, in the aftermath of the fire.'

'Well, then, I suspect you already know that whatever tears were shed over Father Connolly's unfortunate death, they are far fewer than those that have been shed, and still remain to be shed, by my nephew and some of his friends.'

'So you took it upon yourself . . . '

Peter finally felt a surge of rage, familiar, neglected, but rage not unlike what he'd felt when he'd heard his nephew's quavering voice describe what had happened to him. He leaned forward and stared harshly at Father Grozdik and said, 'No one would do anything. I knew that, Father, just as I know that spring follows the winter, and summer precedes the fall. With absolute certainty. So I did what I did because I knew no one else would do anything. Certainly not you and the Cardinal, there. And the police? No chance. You wonder about evil, Father. Well, there's a little less evil in this world now, because I set that fire. And maybe when you add it all up, it was wrong. But maybe, it wasn't either. So, to hell with you, Father, because I don't care. I'm going to leave, now. And when these doctors figure out I'm not crazy, they can send me off to prison and throw away the key, and all will be back in balance, won't it? A perfect equilibrium, Father. A man dies. The man who kills him goes off to prison. Drop the curtain. Every one else can get on with their lives.'

Father Grozdik listened to Peter, and then very calmly said, 'You might not have to go to prison, Peter.'

★   ★   ★

I have often wondered what truly went through Peter's head and heart when he heard those words. Hope? Elation? Or perhaps, fear? He wouldn't tell me, though he did fill in all the details of the conversation with the three priests later that night. I think he left it for me to figure out for myself, because that was Peter's style. Unless one reached a conclusion on their own, it wasn't a conclusion worth reaching. So, when I asked him, he shook his head, and said, 'C-Bird, what do you think?'

Peter had come to the hospital to be evaluated, knowing that the only evaluation that meant anything was the one that he carried within him. Short Blond's killing and the arrival of Lucy Jones had spurred within him a sense that he could balance things out even more. Peter was riding a seesaw of conflicts and emotions, over what he'd heard, and what he'd done, and his whole life had been set into rocklike understandings of how he could even it all out. Smooth over one evil with one good. It was the only way that he could fall asleep at night, and wake up the following day, consumed with the task of making everything right. He was driven forward, constantly trying to find equanimity, always having it elude him. But later, when I thought about it, I believed that neither his waking nor his sleep could ever be free from nightmares.

For me, it was so much simpler. I just wanted to go home. The problem I faced was less defined by the voices I heard, than it was by what I could see. The Angel was no hallucination, the way they were. He was flesh and blood and rage, and I was beginning to see all that. It was a little like a shoreline emerging from the fog, and I was sailing directly toward him. I tried to tell Peter that, but I could not. I don't know why. It seemed as if it would say something about myself that I did not want to say, and so I kept it to myself. At least for the time being.

★　★　★

'I'm not sure I follow, Father,' Peter said, reining in a surge of emotions.

'The Archdiocese has many concerns about this incident, Peter.'

Peter did not immediately reply, although sarcastic words leapt to the tip of his tongue. Father Grozdik peered over at Peter, trying to read his response in the way he balanced on the chair, the tilt of his body, the look in his eyes. Peter thought he was suddenly engaged in the harshest poker game he'd ever experienced.

'Concerns, Father?'

'Yes, precisely. We want to do what is right in this situation, Peter.'

The priest continued to measure Peter's reactions.

'What is right . . . ,' Peter said slowly.

'It is a complicated situation, with many conflicting aspects.'

'I'm not sure that I completely agree, Father. A man was committing acts of, well, a certain depravity. He was, in all likelihood, immune from being called to task

373

for what he had done. And so I, hotheaded, and filled with righteous fervor and anger, took it upon myself to do something about it. All by my lonesome. A vigilante mob of one, you might say, Father. Crimes were committed, Father. Prices were paid. And now, I'm willing to take my punishment.'

'I think it is far more subtle than that, Peter.'

'You can think what you want.'

'Let me ask you this: Did anyone ask you to do what you did?'

'No. On my own. Not even my nephew suggested it, and he was the one who will carry the scars.'

'Do you think he will somehow be made whole again by what you've done?'

Peter shook his head. 'No. Which saddens me.'

'Of course,' Father Grozdik said, speaking rapidly. 'Now, did you tell anyone, afterward, why you had done what you did?'

'Like the police that arrested me?'

'Exactly.'

'No.'

'And here, in this hospital, have you told anyone the reasons behind your actions?'

Peter thought hard for a moment, then said, 'No. But it would seem that more than a few people know the connective why. Maybe not completely why, but know, nonetheless. Crazy people sometimes see things with accuracy, Father. An accuracy that eludes us on the street.'

Father Grozdik bent forward slightly in his seat. Peter had the sense that he was watching a predatory bird circling above a bit of roadkill.

'You saw much combat overseas, did you not?'

'I saw some.'

'Your military records indicate that you spent almost your entire tour of duty in combat areas. And that on more than one occasion you were decorated for your actions. And a Purple Heart, as well, for wounds received.'

'That's true.'

'And you saw people die?'

'I was a medic. Of course.'

'And they died, how? In your arms more than once, I would wager.'

'You would win that bet, Father.'

'And so, you returned and you think this had no impact upon you. Emotionally?'

'I didn't say that.'

'Are you aware of a disease called post-traumatic stress disorder, Peter?'

'No.'

'Doctor Gulptilil could explain it. Once it was simply called battle fatigue, but now it has been given a far more clinical sounding name.'

'You're making a point?'

'It can cause people to act, shall we say as we did at the start, out of character. Especially when they come under sudden and significant stress.'

'I did what I did. End of story.'

'No, Peter,' Father Grozdik said, shaking his head. 'Start of story.'

Both men remained silent for a moment. Peter thought that the priest was probably hoping that he would say something, pitch the conversation forward, but Peter wasn't willing to do that.

'Peter, has anyone informed you of what has happened since your arrest?'

'In what regard, Father?'

'The church you burnt has been razed. The site cleared and prepped. Money has been donated. A great deal of money. Extraordinary generosity. A real coming together of the community. Plans have been drawn up. A bigger, far more beautiful church is planned for the same site, one that will truly express glory and righteousness, Peter. A scholarship fund has been established in Father Connolly's name. There is even talk about a youth center being added to the designs, in his memory, of course.'

Peter opened his mouth slightly. He was speechless.

'The outpouring of love and affection has been truly memorable.'

'I don't know what to say.'

'God works in mysterious ways, does He not, Peter?'

'I'm not altogether sure that God has much to do with this, Father. I'd be a little more comfortable if He wasn't brought into this equation. So, what are you saying?'

'I'm saying, Peter, that a great good is on the verge of being done. Out of the ashes, so to speak. The ashes that you created.'

And there it is, Peter realized. That was why the Cardinal was seated over on the couch watching every motion Peter made. The truth about Father Connolly and his predilection for altar boys was a far smaller truth than the response flowing into the Church. Peter twisted in his seat, and looked directly at the Cardinal.

He nodded his head at Peter, and spoke for the first time. 'A great good, Peter,' he said. 'But one that might be in jeopardy.'

Peter saw that immediately. No youth centers were intentionally named after child molesters.

And the person that threatened it all, was him.

Peter turned back to Father Grozdik. 'You are about to ask something of me, are you not, Father?'

'Not precisely, Peter.'

'Then what is it that you want?'

Father Grozdik placed his lips together in a pursed smile, and Peter instantly realized that he had asked the wrong question in the wrong way, because by asking, Peter had implied that he would do what the priest wanted. 'Ah, Peter,' Father Grozdik said slowly, but with a coldness that surprised even the Fireman. 'What we want . . . what we all want — the hospital, your family, the Church — is for you to get better.'

'Better?'

'To that end, we would like to help.'

'Help?'

'Yes. There is a clinic, a facility, that is leading the way in post-traumatic stress research and treatment. We believe, the Church believes, even your family believes, that you would be far better suited to a stay there, than you would here in Western State.'

'My family?'

'Yes. They seem quite eager to see you get this help.'

Peter wondered what they had been promised. Or threatened. He was angry for an instant, shifted in his seat, then abruptly saddened as he realized that he'd probably solved nothing for any of them, especially his damaged nephew. He wanted to say all this, but stopped himself, and instead, shunted all those thoughts deep within him.

Peter asked instead: 'And where is this facility?'

'It is in Oregon. You can be there within days.'

'Oregon?'

'Yes. A quite beautiful part of that state, or so I'm reliably informed.'

'And the charges against me?'

'A successful completion of the treatment plan would result in the charges being dropped.'

Peter thought hard, then asked, 'And I do what, in return?'

Father Grozdik pitched forward once again. Peter had the sensation that the priest had discussed long before his arrival at Western State precisely how he would reply to that question. Father Grozdik spoke in a low, clear, very slow voice: 'We would expect that you would do nothing and say absolutely nothing today, *or at any time in the future*, that might prevent great and wondrous progress from being made with such enthusiasm.'

These words chilled him and his first response was anger. A great mixture of ice and fire within him. Fury commingled with cold. He managed to control himself with great effort.

'You say you've actually talked this over with my family?' he asked flatly.

'Do you not think that your return here to this state would cause them great anguish, by reminding them of so much, and so many troubled times? Do you not think it would be far better for Peter the Fireman to begin anew, somewhere distant? Do you not think that you owe them the opportunity to get on with their lives, as well, and not to be hounded by terrible memories of such awful events?'

Peter did not reply.

Father Grozdik shuffled the papers on the desktop. Then he said: 'You can have a life, Peter. But we need you to agree. And promptly, for this offer may not remain viable for very long. In many places, many people have made significant sacrifices and difficult arrangements so that this offer can be made to you, Peter.'

Peter's throat was dry. When he did speak, words seemed to squeak past his lips. 'Promptly, you say. Do you mean minutes? Days? A week, a month, a year?'

Father Grozdik smiled again. 'We would like to see you getting the proper treatment within days, Peter. Why prolong barriers to your emotional well-being?'

This question seemingly did not require an answer.

He stood up. 'You will need to tell Doctor Gulptilil of your decision promptly, Peter. We, of course, will not demand you to make it on the spot. I'm sure there is much for you to think about. But it is a fine offer, Peter, and one that will bring much good out of this terrible series of circumstances.'

Peter rose, as well. He looked over at Doctor

Gulptilil. The round Indian physician had kept his mouth shut throughout the conversation. The doctor gestured toward the door, and finally said, 'Peter, you may ask Mister Moses to escort you back to Amherst. Perhaps he can do this without the restraints at this time.'

Peter took a step back, and the doctor added, 'Ah, Peter, when you reach what is so clearly the only possible decision on this matter, simply inform Mister Evans that you wish to speak with me, and then we will get the necessary paperwork for your transfer in order.'

Father Grozdik seemed to stiffen slightly, as he stood beside the doctor, behind the desk. He shook his head. 'Perhaps,' he said cautiously, 'Doctor, we could have Peter deal only with you on this matter. In particular, I believe that Mister Evans, your associate, should not be, shall we say, *involved* in any way, shape, or form.'

Gulp-a-pill looked oddly at the priest, who added, by way of explanation, 'It was his brother, Doctor, who was one of the men injured running into the church in a vain attempt to rescue Father Connolly. Evans's brother is still in the midst of long-term, and considerably painful therapy for burns received that tragic night. I fear your associate might harbor some animosity toward Peter.'

Peter hesitated, thought about one, two, perhaps a dozen responses, but said none of them. He nodded toward the Cardinal, who nodded back, but without a smile, the priest's florid face set in an edge, which told Peter that he was walking on a very thin and desperately narrow precipice.

★ ★ ★

The ground floor corridor in the Amherst Building was crowded with patients. There was a buzz in the hallway, as people spoke to one another or to themselves. It was only when something out of the routine took place that people grew silent, or else made untethered noises that could have been speech. Any change was always dangerous, Francis thought. It frightened him to realize he was growing accustomed to existence at Western State. A sane person, he told himself, accommodates change and welcomes originality. He promised himself to embrace every different thing that he could, to fight off the dependence upon routine. Even his voices echoed agreement within him, as if they, too, could see the dangers in becoming just another face in the hallway.

But, as he told himself this, there was a sudden silence in the corridor. Noise dropped away like a receding wave at the beach. When Francis looked up, he saw the reason: Little Black was leading three men through the center of the hallway toward the first-floor dormitory room. Francis recognized the hulking retarded man, who easily carried a footlocker in both arms, and had a large Raggedy Andy doll stuck under his armpit. The man sported a contusion on his forehead and a slightly swollen lip, but wore a skewed smile, which he delivered to anyone who met his gaze. He grunted, as if making greetings, as he trotted behind Little Black.

The second man was slight, and significantly older, with glasses and thin, wispy white hair. He seemed to be light on his feet, like a dancer, and Francis watched him pirouette down the corridor as if the gathering there was a part of a ballet. The third man was dull-lidded, a little shy of middle age, a little beyond youth, wide in the shoulders, dark-haired and stocky. He plodded forward, as if it was a struggle to keep up with either the retarded man or the Dancer. A Cato, Francis thought at first. Or else damn close to it. But then, when he looked a little closer, he saw the man's black eyes moving furtively back and forth, inspecting the sea of patients parting in front of Little Black's procession. Francis saw the man's eyes narrow, as if what he saw displeased him, and an edge of his mouth turned upward in a doglike snarl. Francis immediately altered his diagnosis, and recognized a man that deserved a wide berth. He carried a brown cardboard box with his meager belongings.

Francis saw Lucy emerge from the office and stand watching the group move toward the dormitory. He caught Little Black's slight nod of his head in her direction, as if to signal her that the disruption that she'd set in motion had succeeded. A disruption that had necessitated the moving of several men from one dormitory to another.

Lucy moved to Francis and whispered to him quickly. 'C-Bird, tag along there, and see that our guy gets into a bunk where you and Peter can keep an eye on him.'

Francis nodded, wanted to say that the retarded man wasn't the man they should be watching, but did not. Instead, Francis peeled himself from the wall and moved down the hallway, which returned to a busy buzz and muted talk as he passed.

He saw Cleo poised near the nursing station, her eyes locked on each of the men as they ambled past her. Francis could see the large woman's mind working, her brow furrowed in examination, one hand lifted, pointing as the three men sailed down the hallway. It seemed to him that she was measuring, and suddenly, in a loud, near-frantic voice, Cleo shouted out: 'You're not welcome here! None of you are!'

But none of the men turned, or broke stride, or showed for a second that they heard or understood anything Cleo said.

She harumphed loudly and made a dismissive gesture with her hand. Francis hurried past her, trying to keep up with Little Black's quick march.

When he entered the dormitory, he saw that the

retarded man was being situated in Lanky's old bunk, while the others were being moved into spaces not far from the wall. He watched as Little Black oversaw making the beds and stowing the belongings, and then took the men on the short tour, which consisted of pointing out the bathroom, the poster of hospital rules that Francis imagined were the same as the dormitory they had been transferred from and informing them that dinner would begin within a few minutes. Then he shrugged and headed out, pausing only to say to Francis, 'Tell Miss Jones that there was a helluva fight over in Williams. The guy she pissed off, went right for the big guy there. It took a couple of attendants to pull him off, and the other two kinda got caught up in it by accident. The other son of a bitch is gonna do a couple of days in a detention and observation cell. Probably gonna get a whole lot shot into him to calm his butt down, too. Let her know it worked out pretty much like she thought it would, except that everyone over in Williams is strung out and upset and it's likely to take a couple of days for everything to settle down over there.'

Then Little Black pushed through the door, and left him alone with the three new men.

Francis watched as the large retarded man sat on the edge of the bed and gave his doll a hug. Then he began to rock back and forth, with a little half grin on his face, as if he was slowly assessing his new surroundings. The Dancer did a little spin, and then went over to the barred window and simply stared out at what remained of the afternoon.

But the third man, the stocky one, spied Francis and seemed to stiffen instantly. For a second, he recoiled. Then he rose up and pointed accusingly at Francis and stepped quickly across the floor, dodging the beds, and right up into Francis's face. He was hissing with rage. 'You must be the one,' the man spat, his voice barely a whisper, but filled with an awful low noise of anger.

'You must be the one! You're the one that's looking for me, aren't you?' Francis did not reply, but pushed himself back tight to the wall. The man lifted a fist and held it beneath Francis's jaw. His eyes flashed fury but it was contradicted by the snakelike sound of his voice, words that filled the space around them like a rattler's warning sound.

'Because I'm the one you're looking for.' He sliced words from the air.

Then, with a nonchalant smile, he pushed past Francis and out the door into the hallway.

22

But I knew, didn't I?

Perhaps not right at that moment, but soon enough.

At first, I was still taken aback, surprised by the vehemence of the admission thrust in my face. I could feel a quiver within me, and all of the voices shouted out warnings and misgivings, contradictory impulses to hide, to follow, but mostly to pay attention to what I understood. Which was of course, that it didn't make sense. Why would the Angel simply walk directly up to me and confess his presence, when he had done so much to conceal who he was? And, if the stocky man wasn't really the Angel, why had he said what he did?

Filled with misgivings, my insides a turmoil of questions and conflicts, I took a deep breath, steadied my nerves and rushed through the dormitory door in order to trail the stocky man out into the corridor, leaving the Dancer and the retarded hulk behind. I watched him as he paused, lighting a cigarette with a dandified flourish, then looking up and surveying the new world that he'd been transferred into. I realized that the landscape of every housing unit was different. Perhaps the architecture was similar, the hallways and offices, dayroom, cafeteria, dormitory spaces, storage closets, stairwells, upstairs isolation cells all following more or less the same pattern, with maybe little design distinctions. But that wasn't the real terrain of each housing unit. The contours and topography were really defined by all the variety of madnesses contained within. And that was what the stocky man hesitated, assessing. I caught another glimpse of his eyes, and I knew that he was a man usually on the verge of an explosion. A man who had little control over all the rages that raced around his bloodstream contending with the Haldol or Prolixin that he was given daily. Our bodies were battlefields of contending armies of psychosis and narcotics, fighting from house for control, and the stocky man seemed to be caught up as much as any of us in that war.

I didn't think the Angel was.

I saw the stocky man push aside an elderly senile fellow, a thin, sickly sort who stumbled and almost fell to the floor and just as nearly burst into tears. The stocky man persisted down the corridor, pausing only to scowl at two women rocking in a corner singing lullabies to baby dolls held in their arms. When a wild-haired, disheveled Cato in loose pajamas and long, flowing housecoat, harmlessly meandered into his path, he screamed at the blank-faced man to move aside, and then continued on, his pace quickening, as if his footsteps could keep the beat defined by his anger. And every step he traveled took him farther, I thought, from the man we were pursuing. I don't think I could have said exactly why but I knew it with a certainty that grew as I followed down the corridor. I could see in my imagination precisely how when the fight broke out in Williams that had been orchestrated by Lucy, the stocky man had been instantly caught up in the trading of blows, and that was why he was transferred to Amherst. An addendum to the incident. He wasn't the sort who could ever idly sit back and watch a conflict unfold, shrinking into a corner, or taking refuge against the wall. He would respond electrically, leap in immediately, regardless of what the cause was, or who was fighting whom, or the why or wherefore of any of it. He just liked a fight, because it allowed him to step away from all the impulses that tormented him, and lose himself in the exquisite anger of trading blows. And then, when he rose, bloodied, his madness wouldn't allow him to wonder why he'd done what he'd done.

Part of his illness, I recognized, was in always drawing attention to himself.

But why had he been so specific, thrusting his face up to mine? 'I'm the man you're looking for'?

In my apartment, I bent forward, leaning my head up against the wall, placing my forehead against the words that I'd written, while I paused, deep within my own memories. The pressure against my temple reminded me a little of a cold compress placed on the skin, trying to reduce a childhood fever. I closed my eyes for an instant, hoping to get a little rest.

But a whisper creased the air. It hissed directly behind me.

'You didn't think I would make it easy for you?'

I didn't turn. I knew that the Angel was both there and not there.

'No,' I said out loud. 'I didn't think you would make it easy. But it took me some time to figure out the truth.'

★   ★   ★

Lucy saw Francis emerge from the dormitory, trailing after another man and not the one that she'd sent him to keep an eye on. She could see that Francis's face was pale, and he seemed to her to be riveted on what he was doing, almost oblivious to the predinner half step, do-si-do square dance of anticipation going on in the crowded corridor. She took a stride in his direction, then stopped, knowing somewhere within her that C-Bird probably had a reasonable grasp on what he was doing.

She lost sight of the two men as they headed into the dayroom, and she began to maneuver toward that room, when she saw Mister Evans steaming down the hallway toward her. He had the wild-eyed look of a dog that has had its well-gnawed bone stolen from him.

'So,' he said angrily, 'I hoped you're pleased. I've got one attendant over at the emergency room with a fractured wrist, and I've had to transfer three patients from Williams and put a fourth in restraints and in isolation for at least twenty-four hours, maybe more. I've got uproar and turmoil in one housing unit, and one of the transfers is probably significantly at risk, because he's had to shift locations after several years. And through no fault of his own. He just got caught up in the fight by accident, but ended up getting threatened. Damn! I hope you can appreciate what a setback this is, and how dangerous it is, especially for the patients who come to accept one thing and are suddenly tossed into another housing unit.'

Lucy looked at him coldly. 'You think I managed all that?'

'I do,' Evans said.

'I must be far more clever than I thought,' she answered sarcastically.

Mister Evil snorted, his face flushed. It was the appearance of a man who doesn't like seeing the carefully balanced world that he controls upset in any fashion, Lucy thought. He started to respond angrily, impetuously, but, then, in a manner that Lucy found unsettling, he managed to gain control, and speak in a far more contained fashion.

'My recollection,' Mister Evil said slowly, 'was that your arrangement here, working in this treatment facility was dependent on a lack of disruption. I seem to remember that you agreed to keep a low profile, and not to get in the way of the treatment plans already in place.'

Lucy did not respond. But she heard what he was implying.

'That's my understanding,' Mister Evil continued. 'But correct me if I'm wrong.'

'No, you're not wrong,' she said, 'I'm sorry. It won't happen again.' These were falsehoods, she knew.

'I'll believe that when I see it,' he said. 'And, I presume, you intend to continue interviewing patients in the morning.'

'I do.'

'Well, we'll see,' he said. And with the thinly veiled threat hovering in the air, Mister Evil turned and started to the front door. He stopped after a couple of strides, when he spotted Big Black accompanying Peter the Fireman. The psychologist immediately saw that Peter wasn't restrained, as he had been earlier. 'Hey!' he called out, waving at Big Black and Peter. 'Hold it right there!'

The huge attendant stopped, turning toward the dormitory head. Peter hesitated, as well.

'Why isn't he in restraints?' Mr. Evans shouted angrily. 'That man is not allowed out of this facility without cuffs on his hands and feet. Those are the rules!'

Big Black shook his head. 'Doctor Gulptilil said it would be okay.'

'What?'

'Doctor Gulptilil — ,' Big Black repeated, only to be cut off.

'I don't believe that. This man is under a court hold. He faces serious assault and manslaughter charges. We have a responsibility . . . '

'That's what he said.'

'Well, I'm going to check on it. Right now.' Evans spun, leaving the two men standing in the corridor, as he blasted toward the front door, first fumbling with his keys, swearing when he thrust the wrong one into the lock, swearing louder when the second one failed to work, and then finally giving up, and lurching off down the corridor toward his office, scattering patients out of his path.

Francis trailed behind the stocky man, as the new resident cut a swath through Amherst. There was something in the way his head was cocked slightly to the side, his lip raised, white teeth displayed, the bend of his shoulders forward and the thickly tattooed forearms swinging at his waist that clearly warned the other patients to steer to one side or the other. A predatory, challenging walk through Amherst. The stocky man took a long look through the dayroom, like a surveyor eyeballing a tract of land. The few remaining patients inside the room shrank to the corners, or buried themselves behind out-of-date magazines, avoiding eye contact. The stocky man seemed to like this, as if he was pleased to see that his bully status was going to be easily established, and he stepped into the center of the room. He didn't seem aware that Francis was following him until he stopped.

'So,' he said in a loud voice, 'I'm here now. Don't anybody try to fuck with me.'

As he projected this, it seemed a little foolish to Francis. And perhaps cowardly, as well. The only folks left in the dayroom were old and obviously infirm, or else lost in some distant and private world. Nobody who might rise to challenge the stocky man was available.

Despite his voices shouting caution within him, Francis took several steps toward the stocky man, who finally grew aware of Francis's presence and spun to face him.

'You!' he said loudly. 'I thought I'd already dealt with you.'

'I want to know what you meant,' Francis said cautiously.

'What I meant?' The man mocked Francis with a singsong voice. 'What I meant? I meant what I said and I said what I meant and that's all there is to it.'

'I don't understand,' Francis said, a little too eager. 'When you said 'I'm the man you're looking for,' what did you mean?'

The man brayed out loud. 'Seems pretty damn obvious, don't it?'

'No,' Francis said cautiously, shaking his head. 'It isn't. Who do you think I'm looking for?'

The stocky man grinned. 'You're looking for one mean mother, that's who. And you've found him. What? Don't you think I can be mean enough for you?' He stepped toward Francis, bunching his hands into fists, bending forward slightly at the waist, cocking his body like the hammer on a pistol.

'How did you know I was looking for you?' Francis persisted, holding his ground despite all the urgent entreaties within him to flee.

'Everyone knows. You and the other guy and the lady from outside. Everyone knows,' the stocky man said cryptically.

There are no secrets, Francis thought. Then he realized that was wrong.

'Who told you?' Francis asked suddenly.

'What?'

'Who told you?'

'What the hell do you mean?'

'Who told you I was looking?' Francis said, his voice rising in pitch and picking up momentum, driven forward by something utterly different from the voices he was so accustomed to, forcing questions out of his mouth when every word increased the danger he was facing. 'Who told you to look for me? Who told you what I looked like? Who told you who I was, who gave you my name? Who was it?'

The stocky man lifted a hand and placed it directly under Francis's jaw. Then he gently touched Francis with the knuckles, as if making a promise. 'That's my business,' he said. 'Not yours. Who I speak to, what I do, that's my business.' Francis saw the stocky man's eyes widen slightly, as if opening to some idea that was elusive. He could sense that any number of volatile elements were mixing in the stocky man's imagination, and somewhere in that explosive concoction was some information that he wanted.

Francis persisted. 'Sure, it's your business,' he said, changing his tone to a slow pace, as if that might help. 'But maybe it's a little bit of mine, as well. I just want to know who it was that told you to single me out and say what you said.'

'No one,' the stocky man replied, lying.

'Yes, someone,' Francis countered. The man's hand dropped away from Francis's face, and he saw electric fear in the stocky man's eyes, hidden beneath rage. It reminded him, in that second, of Lanky, when he fixated on Short Blond, or earlier, when the tall man had fixated on Francis. A total absorption with a single notion, an overwhelming tidal wave of a single sensation, all set loose deep within, in some reach and cavern that even the most potent medication had difficulty penetrating.

'It's my business,' the stocky man persisted.

'The man who told you, he might be the man I'm searching for,' Francis said.

The stocky man shook his head. 'Screw you,' he said. 'I'm not helping you with anything.'

For an instant Francis stood directly across from the stocky man, not willing to move, thinking only that he was close to something and that it would be important for him to find it out, because it would be something concrete that he could take to Lucy Jones. And, in the same moment, he saw the machinery of the stocky man whirling faster and faster, anger, frustration, all the ordinary terrors of being mad coalescing, and in that volcanic moment, Francis suddenly realized that he had pushed something just a bit too far. He took a step backward, but the stocky man followed him.

'I don't like your questions,' the man said low and cold.

'All right, I'm finished,' Francis replied, trying to retreat.

'I don't like your questions and I don't like you. Why did you follow me in here? What are you trying to make me say? What are you going to do to me?'

Each of these questions hammered forth like blows. Francis glanced right and left, trying to spot somewhere to run to, somewhere he might hide, but there were none. The few people in the dayroom had shrunk away, concealing themselves in corners, or else staring at walls or ceiling, anything that might help them to will themselves mentally to some far different place. The stocky man pushed his fist into Francis's chest and knocked him back a stride, slightly off-balance. 'I don't think I like you getting in my face,' he said. 'I don't think I like anything about you.' He pushed again, harder.

'All right,' Francis said, holding up his hand. 'I'll leave you alone.'

The stocky man seemed to tighten in front of Francis, his whole body growing taut and stretched. 'Yeah, that's right,' he said, growling, 'and I'm going to make sure of it.'

Francis saw the fist coming and managed to just lift his forearm enough to deflect some of the blow before it landed on his cheek. For a moment, he saw stars, and he spun back trying to keep his balance, stumbling slightly over a chair. This actually helped him, because it threw the stocky man's second punch astray, so that the left hook whistled just above Francis's nose, close enough so that he could feel its heat. Francis thrust himself backward again, sending the chair slamming across the floor, and the stocky man jumped forward, this time landing another wild blow that caught Francis high on the shoulder. The man's face was red with fury, and his rage made his attack inaccurate. Francis fell back, hitting the floor with a breath-stealing crash, and the stocky man leapt onto him, straddling his chest, looming above him. Francis managed to keep his arms free, and he covered up, and started kicking ineffectually, as the stocky man started to rain wild, freewheeling blows down onto Francis's forearms.

'I'll kill you!' he cried. 'I'll kill you!'

Francis squirmed, shifting right and left, doing his best to avoid the flurry of punches, aware only peripherally that he hadn't really been hit hard, knowing that if the stocky man took even a microsecond to consider the advantages of his assault, he would be twice as deadly.

'Leave me alone!' Francis cried, uselessly.

In the narrow space between his arms, deflecting the attack, Francis saw the stocky man rise up slightly, gather himself, as if suddenly realizing that he needed to organize the assault. The man's face was still flushed, but it suddenly took on a purpose and rationale, as if all the fury collected within him had been channeled into a single flow. Francis closed his eyes, yelled, 'Stop it!' one last helpless time, and realized that he was about to be hurt severely. He shrank back, no longer aware what words he was screaming to make the man stop, knowing only that they meant nothing in the face of the rage steaming toward him.

'I'll kill you!' the stocky man repeated. Francis had little doubt that he meant it.

The stocky man let out a single, guttural cry and Francis tried to avert his head, but, in that second, everything changed. A force like a huge wind slammed into the two of them, crashing together in a frenzied tangle. Fists, muscles, blows, and cries all gathered together, and Francis seemed to spin aside, aware suddenly that the weight of the stocky man was suddenly off of his chest, and that he had been cut free. He rolled over once, then scrambled back to the wall, and saw that the stocky man and Peter were suddenly entwined, knotted together in a pile. Peter had his legs wrapped around the man, and had managed to pin one hand with his own gripped around the man's wrist. Words disappeared in a cacophony of shouts, and they spun together like a top on the ground and Francis saw Peter's face set in a fierce rage of his own, as he twisted the stocky man's arm toward some breaking point. And, in the same moment, another pair of missiles suddenly flashed into Francis's vision, as the white-jacketed Moses brothers launched themselves into the fray. For a moment, there was an orchestra of screaming, shouting anger, and then Big Black managed to grab the stocky man's other arm, while at the same time throwing his own massive forearm across the man's windpipe, while Little Black pulled Peter away, slamming him awkwardly against a couch, while the larger brother wrapped the stocky man in a stifling embrace.

The stocky man screamed obscenities and epithets, choking, spittle flying from his lips, 'Fucking nigger goons! Let me go! Let me go! I ain't done nothing!'

Peter slid back, so that his back was against the couch, his feet out in front of him. Little Black released him, and sprang to his brother's side. The two men expertly twisted the stocky man, so that he was beneath them, hands pinned, legs kicking for a moment, until they, too, stopped.

'Hold him tight,' Francis heard coming from his side. He looked up and saw that Evans, brandishing a hypodermic syringe, was hovering in the doorway. 'Just hold him!' Mister Evil repeated, as he took a bit of alcohol impregnated gauze in one hand, and the needle in the other, and approached the two attendants and the

394

hysterical stocky man, who resumed twisting and struggling and shouting angrily, 'Fuck you! Fuck you! Fuck you!'

Mister Evil swiped a bit of skin and plunged the needle into the man's arm, in a single, well-practiced motion. 'Fuck you!' the man cried again. But it was the final time.

The sedative worked quickly. Francis wasn't sure how many minutes, because he had lost track of the steady passage of time, replacing it with adrenaline and fear. But within a few moments, the stocky man relaxed. Francis saw his wild eyes roll back, and a loose-fitting sort of unconsciousness take over. The Moses brothers relaxed as well, letting their tight grip loosen, and they moved back as the man lay on the ground.

'We'll need a stretcher to transport him to isolation,' Mister Evil said. 'He's going to be out cold in a second.' He pointed at Little Black, who nodded.

The man groaned, twitched, and his feet moved like a dog's that dreams of running. Evans shook his head. 'What a mess,' he said. He looked up, and saw Peter where the Fireman was still lying out on the floor, catching his breath and rubbing his own hand, which had a red bite mark on it. 'You, too,' Evans said, stiffly.

'Me, too, what?' Peter asked.

'Isolation. Twenty-four hours.'

'What? I didn't do anything except pull that son of a bitch off C-Bird.'

Little Black had returned with a folding stretcher and a nurse. He maneuvered over to the stocky man and started to put the drugged patient into a straitjacket. He looked up, as he worked, toward Peter and he shook his head slightly.

'What was I supposed to do? Let that guy beat the shit out of C-Bird?'

'Isolation. Twenty-four hours,' Evans repeated.

'I'm not . . . ,' Peter began.

Evans arched his eyebrows upward. 'Or what? Are you threatening me?'

Peter took a deep breath. 'No. I just object.'

'You know the rules for fighting.'

'He was fighting. I was trying to restrain him.'

Evans stood over Peter and shook his head. 'An intriguing distinction. Isolation. Twenty-four hours. Do you want to go easy, or, perhaps, with a little more trouble?' He held the syringe up for Peter to see. Francis saw that Evans truly wanted Peter to make the wrong choice.

Peter seemed to control a surge of his own anger with great difficulty. Francis saw him grit his teeth together. 'All right,' he said. 'Whatever you say. Isolation. Lead the damn way.'

With that, he struggled up to his feet and dutifully followed Big Black, who, along with his brother, had loaded the stocky man onto the stretcher, and were maneuvering him out the dayroom door.

Evans turned to Francis. 'You've got a bruise on your cheek,' he said. 'Have a nurse take a look at it.'

Then he, too, pushed out of the dayroom, without even glancing at Lucy, who had taken up a position by the door, and who took that moment to fix Francis with a searing, inquisitive look.

★   ★   ★

Later that night, in her tiny room inside the nurse-trainees' dormitory, Lucy sat alone in the dark, trying to see progress in her investigation. Sleep had eluded her, and she had pushed herself up on the bed, back to the wall, staring out, trying to discern familiar shapes in the area around her. Her eyes adjusted slowly to the absence of light, but after a moment she could make out the unmistakable form of the desk, the small table, the bureau, the bedside stand and lamp. She continued to concentrate, and recognized the lump of clothes that she'd tossed haphazardly onto the stiff wooden chair when she'd come in earlier and prepared for bed.

It was, she thought, a mirror of what she was going through. There were things that were familiar, and yet they remained hidden, distorted, concealed by the darkness inside the hospital. She needed to find a way of illuminating evidence, suspects, and theories. She just couldn't see precisely how.

She leaned her head back and believed she'd done much to make a mess of things. At the same time, despite the lack of anything concrete to point to, she felt more persuaded than ever that she was dangerously close to achieving what she had come to the hospital for.

She tried to picture the man she was hunting, but found that just like the shapes in the room, he remained indistinct and elusive. The hospital world simply did not lend itself to easy supposition, she thought. She recalled dozens of moments, where she sat across from a suspect, either in a police interrogation room, or later, in a courtroom, and she had observed all the tiny details, the wrinkles on the man's hands, the furtive look in his eyes, perhaps the manner in which he held his head, all of which blended together into a portrait of someone narrowly defined by guilt and crime. When they sat across from Lucy, it always, she thought, seemed so *obvious*. The men she'd seen through arrest and prosecution had worn the truth of their actions like so many cheap suits of clothes. Unmistakable.

Continuing to stare into the night, she told herself that she had to think more creatively. More obliquely. More subtly. In the world she came from, there had been little doubt in her mind whenever she'd come face-to-face with her quarry. This world was the exact opposite. There was nothing except doubt. And, she wondered, feeling a chill that didn't come from the open window, she might even have been face-to-face with the man she hunted. But here he owned the context.

She lifted her hand to her face and touched her scar. The man who'd attacked her had been a cliché of anonymity. His face had been obscured by a knit ski mask, so that she only saw his dark eyes. He wore black leather gloves on his hands, jeans, and a nondescript pullover parka of the sort available in any number of outdoors equipment stores. On his feet had been Nike running shoes. The few words he spoke were guttural, rough, designed to conceal any accent. He didn't really need to say anything, she remembered. He let the glistening hunting knife that had sliced her face speak for him.

That was something she had thought about hard. In the processing of the event afterward, she had dwelt on this detail, for it spoke to her in an odd way, and had made her wonder if the rape had been less of the purpose of the whole encounter than the disfigurement of her face.

Lucy leaned back, bouncing her head off the wall once or twice, as if the modest blows could loosen some thought from where it was glued within her imagination. She wondered sometimes how it was that her entire life had been altered by the time she'd been assaulted in that dormitory stairwell. How long was it, she asked? Three minutes? Five minutes from start to finish, from the first terrifying sensation when she'd been grabbed, to the sound of his footsteps heading off?

No more than that, surely, she told herself. And everything from that moment on had been changed.

Beneath her fingers, she touched the ridges of the scar. They had retreated, almost blended back even with the rest of her complexion, as the years had passed.

She wondered whether she would ever love again. She doubted it.

It wasn't anything as simple as coming to hate all men for the acts of one. Or being unable to see the distinctions between the men she had come to know and the one who had harmed her. It was more, she thought, as if a place within her had been turned dark, and iced over. She knew that the man who had assaulted her had fueled much of her life and that every time she had pointed accusingly in a court of law at some sallow-faced defendant destined for prison she was slicing slivers of retribution from the world and gathering them to herself. But she doubted that the hole inside her would ever be filled enough.

Her mind slid then to Peter the Fireman. Too much like me, she thought. This made her sad, and unsettled, unable to appreciate that they were both damaged in like fashion, and that should have linked them. Instead she tried to picture him in the isolation room. It was the closest thing to a prison cell the hospital had, and in some ways it was worse. It existed for the sole purpose of eliminating any outside thoughts that might intrude on the patient's world. Gray, stuffed padding covered the walls. The bed was bolted to the floor. A single thin mattress and threadbare blanket. No pillow. No shoelaces. No belt. A toilet that had little water in the bowl to prevent someone from trying to drown themselves in that sad way. She didn't know if Peter would be put into a straitjacket. That would be procedure, and she guessed that Mister Evil would want to see procedure followed. For a moment she wondered how Peter was able to maintain any sanity at all, when just about everything that surrounded him was crazy. She guessed that it took a considerable force of will to constantly remind himself that he did not belong.

That would be painful, she thought.

In that regard, she realized, they were even more alike.

Lucy took a deep breath and told herself that sleep was critical. She needed to be alert in the morning. Something had driven Francis to confront the stocky man, and she didn't know what it was, but suspected it was relevant. She smiled. Francis was proving to be more helpful than she had imagined he would be.

She closed her eyes, and as she shut one dark away with another, she was suddenly aware that she could hear an odd sound, one that was familiar, but unsettling. Her eyes popped open and she recognized the noise as the soft padding sound of footsteps in the carpeted hallway outside her room. She let out a long slow whistle and realized her heart rate had increased, which she instantly told herself was an error. Footsteps weren't that unusual in the nurse-trainees' dormitory. After all, there were different shifts, requiring twenty-four-hour attendance, and this caused the sleep patterns in the dormitory to be erratic.

But as she listened, she thought the footsteps paused outside her door.

She stiffened in the bed, craning her head in the direction of the faint, distinctive sound.

She told herself she was mistaken, and then thought she heard the handle of her door slowly turn.

Lucy instantly turned to the bed stand, and fumbling noisily, managed to click on the bedside lamp. Light flooded the room, and she blinked a couple of times, as her eyes adjusted. In almost the same motion, she threw herself out of the bunk, and stepped across the room, banging into a metal wastebasket, which skittered noisily across the floor. The door had a deadbolt lock, and she saw that it had not moved from the closed position. Crossing the room rapidly, Lucy pushed herself up to the solid wooden door and placed her ear against it.

400

She could hear nothing.

She listened for a sound. Anything that might tell her something; that someone was outside, that someone was fleeing, that she was alone, that she was not.

Silence gripped her as awfully as the noise that had plunged her into alertness.

She waited.

She let seconds slide past her, craning forward.

One minute. Perhaps two.

Through the window open behind her, she suddenly heard some voices passing by beneath. There was a laugh, then it was joined by another.

She turned back to the door. She reached up, threw the deadbolt lock, and with a sudden, swift motion, thrust the door open.

The corridor was empty.

She stepped out and peered to the right and to the left.

She was alone.

Lucy took another deep breath, letting the wind inside her lungs calm her racing heart. She shook her head. *You were always alone* she told herself. *You are letting things get to you.* The hospital was a place of unfamiliar extremes, and being surrounded by so much odd behavior and mental illness had made her jumpy. If she had something to fear, it was far less than whoever it might have been had to fear from her. This sense of bravado reassured her.

Then she retreated again into the room Short Blond had once occupied. She locked the door, and before getting back into bed, arranged the wooden chair so that it was balanced up against the door. Not as much as an additional barrier, because she doubted that would work. But propped in such a way that were the door to open, it would crash to the floor. She took the metal waste-basket and placed that on top, then added to the makeshift tower her small suitcase. She believed that the noise of it all tumbling to the floor would be enough of an early warning to rouse her, no matter how deep her sleep might be.

23

Was that you?

'It was never me. It was always me.'

'You took risks,' I said stiffly, argumentatively. 'You could have played it safe, but you didn't, which was a mistake. I couldn't see that at first, but eventually I saw it for what it was.'

'There was much you didn't see C-Bird.'

'You're not here,' I said slowly, the tone of my words betraying the lack of confidence I felt. 'You're only a memory.'

'Not only am I here,' the Angel hissed, 'but this time I'm here for you.'

I spun about, as if I could confront the voice that harried me. But he was like a shadow, flitting from one dark corner of the room to the next, always elusive, just out of my reach. I reached down and seized an ashtray jammed with butts and twisted cigarette filters, and threw it as hard as I could at the shape. His laughter blended with an explosion of glass, as the ashtray shattered against the wall. I twisted, right, then left, trying to line him up, but the Angel moved too quickly. I shouted at him to stand still, that I wasn't scared of him, to fight fair, all of which sounded a little like a crying child in a playground trying to confront a bully. Each moment felt worse, every second that passed I felt smaller, less capable. Furious, I picked up the wooden stool and threw it hard across the room. It smashed against the frame of the door, gouging out a chunk of painted wood, then dropping to the floor with a thud.

With every second passing, I felt more and more despair. I opened my eyes, searching the room for Peter who might help, but he wasn't there. I tried to picture

Lucy, Big Black, Little Black, or any of the others from the hospital, hoping to enlist someone in my memory who might stand by my side and help me fight.

I was alone, and my solitude was like a blow against my heart.

For a moment, I thought I was lost, then, through the fog of all the noise of madness past and madness to come, I heard a sound that seemed out of place. An insistent banging that seemed, well, un-right. Not exactly wrong, but something different. It took me a few moments to collect myself and understand it for what it was. Someone at my front door.

The Angel blew another chilly breath on the back of my neck.

The knocking persisted. It grew louder, like the volume being turned up.

I cautiously approached the sound.

'Who is it?' I asked. I was no longer completely certain that the noise from the outside world was any more real that the snakelike voice of the Angel, or even Peter's reassuring presence on one of his haphazard visits. Everything was blending together, a soup of confusion.

'Francis Petrel?'

'Who is it?' I repeated.

'It's Mister Klein from the Wellness Center.'

The name seemed vaguely familiar. It had a distant quality, as if it belonged somewhere in the recollections of childhood, not something current. I bent my head to the door, trying to fix a face to the name, and slowly features came into shape in my imagination. A slender, balding man, with thick glasses and a slight lisp, who rubbed his chin nervously near the end of the afternoon, when he grew tired, or else when one of his client patients wasn't making progress. I wasn't sure that he was actually there. I wasn't sure that I could actually hear him. But I knew that somewhere a Mister

Klein actually did exist, that he and I had spoken many times in his too-bright, sparse office, and that there was a slim possibility that this was indeed him.

'What do you want?' I demanded, still standing by the door.

'You've missed your last couple of regularly scheduled therapy appointments. We're concerned about you.'

'Missed my appointments?'

'Yes. And you have medications that need to be monitored. Prescriptions that probably need filling. Would you please open the door?'

'Why are you here for me?'

'I told you,' Mister Klein continued. 'You have been regularly scheduled at the clinic. You have missed appointments. You've never missed appointments before. Not since your release from Western State. People are concerned.'

I shook my head. I knew enough not to open the door.

'I'm fine,' I lied. 'Please leave me alone.'

'You don't sound fine, Francis. You sound stressed. I could hear shouting from inside your apartment when I came up the stairs. It sounded like a fight was going on. Is there someone in there with you?'

'No,' I said. This wasn't exactly true, nor was it exactly false.

'Why won't you open the door and we can talk a little more easily.'

'No.'

'Francis, there's nothing to be afraid of.'

There was everything to be afraid of. 'Leave me alone. I don't want your help.'

'If I leave you alone, will you promise to come to the clinic on your own?'

'When?'

'Today. Tomorrow at the latest.'

'Maybe.'

'That's not much of a promise, Francis.'

'I'll try.'

'I need your word that you will come to the clinic either today or tomorrow and get a full examination.'

'Or what?'

'Francis,' he said patiently, 'do you really need to ask that question?'

Again I placed my head against the door, banging it with my forehead, once, then twice, as if I could chase thoughts and fears out of my thinking. 'You'll send me back to the hospital,' I said cautiously. Very quietly.

'What? I can't hear you.'

'I don't want to go back,' I continued. 'I hated it there. I almost died. I don't want to go back to the hospital.'

'Francis, the hospital is closed. Closed for good. You won't have to return there. No one does.'

'I just can't go back.'

'Francis, why won't you open the door?'

'You're not really there,' I said. 'You're just another dream.'

Mister Klein hesitated, then said, 'Francis, your sisters are worried about you. Many people are worried about you. Why won't you let me take you to the clinic?'

'The clinic isn't real.'

'It is. You know it. You've been there many times before.'

'Go away.'

'Then promise me you will come there on your own.'

I took a deep breath. 'All right. I promise.'

'Say it,' Mister Klein insisted.

'I promise I will come to the clinic.'

'When?'

'Today. Or tomorrow.'

'I have your word?'

'Yes.'

I could feel Mister Klein hesitating again, just beyond the door, as if assessing whether or not to believe me. Finally, after a moment of silence, he said, 'Okay then. I'll accept that. But don't let me down, Francis.'

'I won't.'

'If you let me down, Francis, I will be back.'

This sounded to me like a threat. I sighed deeply. 'I'll be there,' I said.

I listened for the sound of his footsteps retreating down the hallway.

Good, I said to myself, and I scrambled back to the wall of writing. I dismissed Mister Klein from my memory, right alongside hunger, thirst, sleep, and everything else that might intrude on my storytelling.

★　★　★

It was well past midnight, and Francis felt alone in the midst of the harsh breathing and disjointed snoring sounds of the Amherst dormitory. He was in that troubled half sleep, a place between wakefulness and dreams, where the world around him was indistinct, as if its moorings to reality had come loose and it was being tugged back and forth by tides and currents that he could not see.

He was worried about Peter, who was locked in a padded isolation cell at Mister Evil's order, and probably struggling against all sorts of fears along with a straitjacket. Francis remembered his own hours in isolation and shuddered. Restrained and alone, they had filled him with dread. He guessed that it would be just as harsh for Peter, who would probably not even have the questionable advantages of being drugged. Peter had told Francis many times that he wasn't afraid of going to prison, but somehow Francis didn't think that the world of jail, no matter how harsh, equated with an isolation cell at Western State. In the isolation cells, it was as if one spent every second with ghosts of unspeakable pain.

He thought to himself: It is lucky that we are all crazy. Because if we weren't, then this place would make us crazy in pretty quick time.

Francis felt an arrow of despair strike him, as he understood in that second that Peter's grip on reality would, one way or another, open the exit door to the hospital. At the same time he knew how hard it would be for him to gain enough purchase on the slippery, shale rock slope of his imagination to ever persuade Gulptilil or Evans or anyone at Western State to release him. Even if he were to start informing on Lucy Jones and her investigative progress to Gulp-a-pill, as the doctor wanted, he doubted that it would lead to anything other than more nights listening to men moan in torment as they dreamed of terrible things.

Troubled by everything that stalked him in his sleep, struggling with everything that surrounded him when he was awake, Francis closed his eyes and shut out sounds around him, praying that he would get a few hours of dreamless rest before morning.

To his right, a few bunks away, he could hear a sudden thrashing sound, as one of the patients twisted and turned in nightmare. He kept his eyes closed, as if that could shut out whatever personal agony had intruded on some other patient's dreams.

After a moment, the noise receded, and he squeezed his lids together, murmuring to himself, or perhaps listening to a voice say *go to sleep*.

But the next noise he heard was something unfamiliar. A scraping sound.

Followed by a hiss.

Then a voice, followed by the sudden sensation of a hand closing over his eyes.

'Keep your eyes closed, Francis. Just listen, but keep your eyes closed.'

Francis breathed in sharply. A quick inhale of very hot air. His first instinct was to scream, but he bit that back. His body jerked and he started to lift up, only to feel himself pushed by a significant force back on his pillow. He raised a hand to grab at the wrist of the Angel, only to be stopped by the sound of the man's voice.

'Don't move, Francis. Do not open your eyes until I tell you. I know you are awake. I know you can hear every word I say, but wait for my command.'

Francis went rigid on the bed. Beyond the darkness behind his eyes, he could sense a person standing over him. Looming terror and darkness.

'You know who this is, don't you Francis?'

He nodded slowly.

'Francis: If you move, you will die. If you open your eyes, you will die. If you try to scream out, you will die. Do you understand the framework for our little conversation tonight?' The Angel's voice was low, hardly more than a whisper, but it pummeled him like fists. He didn't dare move, even as his own voices screamed at him to run and flee, and as he lay motionless, in a tumult of internal confusion and doubt, the hand over his eyes suddenly evaporated, replaced by something far worse.

'Can you feel this, Francis?' the Angel demanded.

The sensation against his cheek was cold. A flat icy pressure. He didn't move.

'Do you know what that is, Francis?'

'A blade,' Francis whispered his reply.

There was a momentary hesitation, then the low, awful voice continued: 'You know about this knife, Francis?'

He nodded again, but he didn't truly understand the question.

'What do you know, Francis?'

He swallowed hard. His throat was dry. He could feel the blade continuing to press down on his face and he didn't dare to shift position, because he thought it would slice through his skin. He kept his eyes closed, but he was trying to gain a sense of size for the presence beside him. 'I know it's sharp,' Francis said, weakly.

'But how sharp?'

Francis couldn't choke out a reply through a throat suddenly parched for moisture. Instead he groaned slightly.

'Let me answer my own question,' the Angel said, speaking in tones still hardly more than a whisper, but with an echo that reverberated within Francis louder than a scream. 'It is very sharp. Like a straight razor, so that if you even move just the tiniest bit, it will part your flesh. And it is strong, too, Francis, strong enough to slice easily through skin and muscle and even bone. But you know that, don't you Francis, because you already know some of the places where this knife has found a home, don't you?'

'Yes,' Francis croaked.

'Do you think that Short Blond had a real understanding what this knife meant when it bit into her throat?'

Francis didn't know what the man meant, so he remained silent.

There was a small, slithering laugh.

'Think about the question, Francis. I'd like an answer.'

Francis kept his eyes squeezed shut. For a moment, he hoped that the voice was really just a nightmare and that it wasn't truly happening to him, but, even as he wished this, the pressure of the blade against his cheek seemed to increase. In a world filled with hallucination, it was sharp and real.

'I don't know,' Francis choked out.

'You're not using your imagination enough, Francis. In here, that's all we really have, isn't it? Imagination. It might take us in unique and terrible ways, force us to head in nasty and murderous directions, but it's the only thing we really own, isn't it?'

Francis thought this was true. He would have nodded, but he was afraid that any motion would put a scar forever on his face like Lucy's, and so he remained as rigid and still as he could, barely breathing, fighting against muscles that wanted to twitch with terror. 'Yes,' he whispered, his lips barely moving.

'Can you understand just how much *imagination* I have, Francis?'

Again, whatever words he tried to speak in reply were croaked into mere sounds.

'So, what did Short Blond know, Francis? Did she only know pain? Or maybe something deeper, far more terrifying? Did she connect the sensation of the knife cutting through her flesh with the blood that was pouring out and was she able to assess it all, and realize that it was her own life that was disappearing, and her own helplessness that made it all so pathetic?'

'I don't know,' Francis said.

'What about you, Francis? Can you feel how close you are to death?'

Francis couldn't answer. Behind his closed eyes he could only see a red sheet of terror.

'Can you feel your own life hanging by such a thin strand, Francis?'

He knew that he didn't have to answer that question.

'Do you understand that I can take your life this second, Francis?'

'Yes,' Francis said, but he was unaware where he got the strength to speak even that word.

'Do you realize I can take your life in ten seconds. Or thirty seconds, or perhaps I will wait an entire minute, depending upon how much I want to savor the moment. Or perhaps tonight isn't the night at all. Perhaps tomorrow would fit my plans better. Or next week. Or next year. Whenever I want, Francis. You are here, in this bed, in this hospital every night, and you will never know when I might return, will you? Or maybe, I should just do this now, and save myself the meager trouble . . . '

The flat of the knife blade seemed to rotate and for a second the edge touched his skin, and then the flat returned.

'Your life belongs to me,' the Angel continued. 'It's mine to take when I please.'

'What do you want?' Francis asked. He could feel tears welling up behind his tightly squeezed eyelids and his fear finally burst through and his hands at his sides and his legs shook with spasms of terror.

'What do I want?' The man laughed, hissing, still barely a whisper. 'I have what I want for tonight, and am closer to getting everything I want. Much closer.'

Francis could sense the Angel lowering his face to his, so that the two men's lips were only inches apart, like lovers.

'I am close to everything of importance to me, Francis. So close that I am like a shadow on all your heels. I'm like a scent that sticks to you that only a dog can smell. I'm like the answer to a riddle that's just a little too complicated for the likes of you.'

'What do you want me to do?' Francis was nearly begging. It was as if he wanted some sort of task or job that might free him from the Angel's presence.

'Why nothing, Francis. Except to remember our little conversation when you go about your daily business,' the Angel replied.

There was a momentary silence, and then, he continued, 'You may count to ten, and then open your eyes, Francis. Remember what I told you. And incidentally' — the Angel seemed almost gleeful and

412

terrible at the same time — 'I've left a little present for your friend the Fireman and the bitch prosecutor, too.'

'What?'

The Angel lowered his face closer to Francis, so that Francis could actually feel his breath against his skin. 'I like to leave a message. Sometimes, it's in what I take. But this time, it's in what's left behind.'

With that, the pressure on his cheek abruptly disappeared, and he could sense the man rising from the bedside. Francis continued to hold his breath, and then began counting. Slowly, one through ten, before opening his eyes.

It took another few seconds for his eyes to adjust to the dark, but when they did, he lifted his head and turned toward the dormitory door. For a second, the Angel was outlined, glowing, almost luminescent. He was turned, looking at Francis, but Francis was unable to make out any of his features except for a pair of eyes that seemed to burn into him and a glistening white aura that surrounded him like some otherworldly light. Then the vision disappeared, the door thumping shut with a muffled bump, and followed by the unmistakable noise of the lock being turned, which, to Francis, seemed like a lock being shut on all hope and possibility. He shuddered, his entire body quivering uncontrollably as if chilled by a plunge into icy waters and the onset of hypothermia. He remained in his bed, plunging through a darkness of terror and anxiety that had rooted within him, and which seemed to spread unchecked like infection throughout his body, wondering whether he would be able to move when morning light filled the room. His own voices remained quiet, as if they, too, were afraid that Francis suddenly teetered on the edge of some immense cliff of fear, and that should he slip and fall, he would never be able to climb out.

Francis lay still, not sleeping, not moving, throughout the night.

His breathing came in short, shallow spasms. He could feel his fingers twitching.

He did nothing except listen to the sounds around him and the pounding in his own chest. When morning arrived, he suddenly wasn't certain that he could force his limbs to move, wasn't even sure that he could make his eyes wander from the locked position they were in, staring out up into the dormitory ceiling, but seeing only the fear that had visited his bedside. He could feel emotions tripping around within his head, haphazardly slamming into sidewalls, skidding, sliding, racing, runaway, out of control. He no longer was sure that he had the ability to rein them in and gain any grip whatsoever, and, for an instant, he thought in actuality he might have died that night, that the Angel had really cut his throat like he had Short Blond's and that everything he thought and heard and saw now was only a dream, and was some reverie that penetrated the final seconds of his life, that really the world around him was utterly dark, night remained closing in on him, and that his own blood was seeping out steadily, with every heartbeat.

'All right, folks,' he heard from the doorway. 'Time to rise and shine. Breakfast is waiting.' It was Big Black, greeting the dormitory residents in customary fashion.

Around him, people started to groan their ways out of sleep, leaving behind all the troubled dreams and near-nightmares that plagued them, unaware that a real, breathing nightmare had been in their midst.

Francis remained rigid, as if glued to his bunk. His limbs refused commands.

A few men stared down at him, as they stumbled past.

He heard Napoleon say, 'Come on, Francis, let's go to breakfast . . . ' but the round man's voice trailed into nothing as he must have seen the look on Francis's face. 'Francis?' he heard, but he did not reply. 'C-Bird, are you okay?'

Again, he warred within himself. Inside, his voices had started up. They pleaded, they cajoled, they insisted, over and over, *Get up, Francis! Come on, Francis! Rise up! Put your feet on the floor and wake up! Please, Francis, please get up!*

He did not know whether he had the strength. He did not know whether he would ever have the strength again.

'C-Bird? What's wrong?' He heard Napoleon's voice grow worried, nearly plaintive.

He did not reply, but continued to stare up at the ceiling, all the time believing more and more firmly that he was dying. Or perhaps he was already dead, and every word he heard was just the last reverberations of life, accompanying his last few heartbeats.

'Mister Moses! Come here! We need help!' Napoleon seemed suddenly on the verge of tears.

Francis could feel himself spiraling in two opposing directions. One that seemed to thrust him down, one that insisted he soar upward. They battled within him.

Big Black pushed to his side. Francis could hear him ordering the remaining members of Amherst out into the corridor. He bent over Francis's form, looking deep into the younger man's eyes, muttering rapid-fire obscenities. 'Come on, Goddamn it, Francis, get up? What's wrong?'

'Help him,' Napoleon pleaded.

'I'm trying,' Big Black answered. 'Francis, tell me, what's wrong?' He clapped his hands sharply in front of Francis's face, trying to get a reaction. He grasped Francis by the shoulder and shook him hard, but Francis remained stiff on the bunk.

Francis thought that he no longer had any words. He doubted his ability to speak. Things inside him were

415

glazing over, like ice forming on a pond.

The garbled voices redoubled commands, pleading, urging him to respond.

The only thought that penetrated Francis's fear was the single idea that if he didn't move, he would surely become dead. That the nightmare would become true. It was as if the two had blended together. Just as day and night were no longer different, neither was dream and wakefulness. He teetered again, on the edge of consciousness, a part of him urging him to shut it all down, retreat, find safety in the refusal to live, another part pleading with him to step away from the siren's song of the blank, dead world that suddenly beckoned him.

Don't die, Francis!

At first, he thought this was one of his familiar voices speaking to him. Then, in that perilous second, he realized that it was himself.

And so, mustering every minute amount of strength that he had, Francis croaked out words that one second earlier he'd feared were lost to him forever. 'He was here . . . ,' Francis said, like a dying man's last breath, only contradictorily, the mere sound of his voice seemed to energize him.

'Who?' Big Black asked.

'The Angel. He spoke to me.'

The attendant seemed to rock back, then forward.

'Did he hurt you?'

'No. Yes. I can't be sure,' Francis said. Every word seemed to strengthen him. He felt like a man whose fever suddenly broke.

'Can you stand up?' Big Black said.

'I'll try,' Francis replied. With Big Black steadying him, and Napoleon holding out his hands as if he would break any fall, Francis lifted himself up, and pivoted his feet out of bed. He was dizzy for a second as blood rushed out of his head. Then he stood.

'That's good,' Big Black whispered. 'You must have gotten some kinda scare.'

Francis didn't respond. This was obvious.

'You gonna be okay, C-Bird?'

'I hope so.'

'Let's keep all this to ourselves, okay? Talk to Miss Jones and Peter, when he gets out of isolation.'

Francis nodded. Still shaky. He realized that the huge black attendant understood just how close he had come to not being able to get out of that bed ever again. Or falling into one of the blank holes occupied by the catatonic patients, who looked out on a world that existed only for themselves. He took an unsteady step forward, then another, and he felt blood flowing throughout his body and the risks of a greater madness than the one he already owned falling away from him. He could feel his muscles and his heart, all working. His voices cheered, then quieted, as if taking satisfaction in his every movement. He breathed out slowly, like a man who has just avoided being struck by a piece of falling rock. Then he smiled, regaining some of his familiar grin.

'Okay,' Francis said to Napoleon, still holding Big Black's massive forearm to steady himself. 'I think I could use something to eat.'

Both men nodded, and took a step forward, except it was Napoleon who hesitated.

'Who's that?' he asked abruptly.

Francis and Big Black pivoted about, following Napoleon's glance.

They both saw the same thing, at the same moment. Another man had failed to get out of bed that morning. He had gone unnoticed in the attention Napoleon had drawn to Francis. The man lay motionless, a misshapen lump on a steel bunk.

'What the hell,' the huge attendant said, more irritated than anything else.

Francis stepped forward several paces, and saw who it was.

'Hey,' Big Black said loudly, but there was no response.

Francis took a deep breath and then walked across the dormitory room, angling between crowded beds, to the supine man's side.

It was the Dancer. The elderly man who'd been transferred into Amherst the day before. The retarded man's bunkmate.

Francis looked down and saw the man's rigid, stiff limbs. No more flowing, graceful motions listening to music only he could hear, Francis thought.

The Dancer's face was set hard, almost porcelain in appearance. His skin was white, as if he'd been made up to go onstage. His eyes were wide open, as was his mouth. He looked surprised, maybe even shocked, or even more, perhaps terrified at the death that had come for him that night.

24

Peter the Fireman sat cross-legged on the steel bunk in the isolation cell, like a young and impatient Buddha eagerly awaiting enlightenment. He had slept little the previous night, although the padding on the walls and ceiling had muffled most of the sounds of the unit, save the occasional high-pitched scream or disconnected angry shout that emerged from one of the other rooms very much like the one he was confined within. These random cries meant as much to him as animal sounds that echoed through a forest after dark; they bore no obvious logic or purpose except for the person that uttered them. Midway through the long night, Peter had wondered whether the screams that he heard were actually happening, or were more likely sounds that had been issued some time in the past by long-dead patients, and like radio beacons shot into space, were destined to reverberate through eternity into the darkness, never stopping, never ceasing and never finding a home. He felt haunted.

As daylight crept hesitantly into the cell through the small observation portal in the door, Peter pondered the bind he was in. He had no doubt that the offer from the Cardinal was sincere, although that was probably not the correct word, because sincerity didn't seem to have much to do with his situation. The offer simply required him to disappear. Walk away from all the tangible aspects of his life and vanish into a new existence. The only location where his home, his family, his past, would continue to live was in his memory. There would be no returning once he accepted the offer. Who he was, and what he had done, and why he had done it, were all to evaporate from the collective consciousness of the

419

Boston Archdiocese, to be replaced by something new and shiny and with glistening spires that reached heavenward. In his own family, he'd be the brother who died under hushed circumstances, or the uncle who went away, never to return, and, as years passed, his family would come to believe whatever myth the Church helped to create, and who he had been would crumble away.

He assessed his alternatives: prison; MCI Bridgewater; maximum security; lockdowns and beatings. Probably for much of the rest of his life, because the considerable weight of the Archdiocese, which at this moment was pressuring prosecutors to allow him to vanish into a program in Oregon, would shift if he rejected the plan, and come down heavily on him. He knew there would be no other deals.

Peter could hear the distinctive clanging sound of a jail door being closed and hydraulic locks shutting with a whooshing noise. This made him smile, because he thought it about as close as he was likely to get to one of his friend C-Bird's hallucinations, only this one was uniquely his.

For a moment, he remembered poor Lanky, filled with fear and delusion, his grasp on the little life that the hospital provided him dropping away, turning and pleading with Peter and Francis to help him. He wished, in that second, that Lucy could have heard those cries. It seemed to him that throughout his entire life people had been calling to him for help and that every time he'd tried to come to their assistance, no matter how fine his intentions, something had always gone wrong.

Peter could hear some sounds from the corridor beyond the bolted door to the isolation cell, and there was a thudding noise of another door being opened, then slammed shut. He couldn't refuse the Cardinal's offer. And, he couldn't leave Francis and Lucy alone to face the Angel.

He understood, that however he managed it, he had to propel the investigation forward, as rapidly as possible. Time no longer allied itself with him.

Peter looked up at the locked door, as if he expected someone to open it right at that second. But there was no sound, not even from the restless corridor beyond, and he remained seated, trying to check his impatience, thinking that in some small way the situation he was in resembled his whole life. Everywhere he'd been, it was as if there was a locked door preventing him from moving freely.

So he waited for someone to come for him, dropping ever deeper into a canyon walled with contradictions, unsure whether he would be able to climb out.

$$\star \quad \star \quad \star$$

'I see no apparent signs of foul play,' the medical director said stiffly, almost formally.

Doctor Gulptilil was standing next to the Dancer's body where it lay porcelain-toned and death-rigid on the bunk. Mister Evil was at his side, as were two other psychiatrists and a psychologist from other housing units. One of the men, Francis had learned, doubled as the hospital's pathologist, and he was bending closely over the Dancer, inspecting him cautiously. This physician was tall and slender, with a hawk nose and thick glasses and the nervous habit of clearing his throat before saying anything and nodding his head up and down so that his slightly unkempt shock of black hair bobbed, regardless whether he was agreeing or disagreeing. He had a clipboard, with a form on it, and he was taking some notes, jotting them down rapidly as Gulp-a-pill spoke.

'No signs of a beating,' Gulptilil said. 'No external

signs of trauma. No obvious wounds of any note.'

'Sudden heart failure,' the vulturelike doctor said, head moving rapidly. 'I see from his records that he had been treated for a heart condition in the past couple of months.'

Lucy Jones was hovering just behind the doctors. 'Look at his hands,' she said abruptly. 'The nails are torn and bloody. Those could be defensive wounds.'

The doctors all turned to her, but it was Mister Evil that took it upon himself to respond. 'He was caught up in a fight yesterday, as you well know. Really, just a bystander who got drawn into it, when two men slammed into him. Not something he would have participated in, but he struggled to get free from the melee. I suspect that's how his nails were affected.'

'I suppose you would say the same about the scratches on his forearms?'

'Yes.'

'And the way the sheet and blanket are tangled around his feet?'

'Heart attack can be very fast and very painful and he might have twisted about for an instant before being overcome.'

The physicians all murmured in agreement. Gulp-a-pill turned to Lucy.

'Miss Jones,' he said, speaking slowly, patiently, which only underscored how impatient he truly was. 'Death, alas, is not uncommon in the hospital. This unfortunate gentleman was elderly and had been confined here for many years. He had suffered one heart attack in the past, and there is little doubt in my mind that the emotional stress of moving from Williams to Amherst in the past days, coupled with the fight he was caught up in through no fault of his own, and the debilitating effect of substantial courses of medications over the years, all had conspired to weaken his cardiovascular system further. A most normal, to be sure, and not remarkable death, here at Western State. I thank you for your observation . . . '

He spoke, pausing in such a way as to demonstrate that he was actually not thanking her for anything, before continuing. ' . . . But are you not seeking someone who uses a knife, and who somewhat ritualistically defaces the hands of his victims and who, to the best of your knowledge, confines his assaults to young women?'

'Yes,' Lucy replied. 'You are correct.'

'So, this death would not seem to fit the pattern that interests you?'

'Again, Doctor, you are correct.'

'Then, please, allow us to handle this death in routine fashion.'

'You don't call in outside authorities?'

Gulptilil sighed, but again, this only barely concealed his irritation. 'When a patient dies during surgery, does the neurosurgeon call a policeman? This situation is analogous, Miss Jones. We file a report with the state. We hold a mortality conference with the staff. We contact the next of kin, if there are any listed. In some cases, where doubt factors are large, we hand the body over for autopsy. In others, however, we do not. And oftentimes, Miss Jones, because this hospital is the only home and only family that some unfortunate patients have, we are in charge of seeing our dead directly into the grave.'

He shrugged, but again, a movement that spoke of disinterest and nonchalance, hid what Lucy Jones thought was anger.

In the doorway, a crowd of patients gathered, trying to see into the dormitory. Gulptilil glanced at Mister Evil. 'I think this is bordering on the morbid, Mister Evans. Let's clear those folks out and move the fellow over to the morgue.'

'Doctor . . . ,' Lucy started in again, but he cut her

off, and turned, instead to Mister Evil.

'Tell me, Mister Evans, did anyone in this unit awaken last night and observe a struggle? Was there a battle that anyone saw? Were there screams and punches thrown and shouted curses and imprecations? Everything that ordinarily fits into the type of conflict that we are accustomed to?'

'No, Doctor,' Evans replied. 'None whatsoever.'

'A fight to the death, perhaps?'

'No.'

Gulptilil turned to Lucy. 'Certainly, Miss Jones, if there had been a murder, someone in the midst of this room would have awakened and seen or heard something. Absent that, however . . .'

Francis took a half step forward, about to say something, but then stopped.

He glanced over at Big Black, who shook his head slightly. The big attendant was giving good advice, Francis realized. If he described what he'd heard, and the presence that had lurked by his own bedside, it most likely would merely have been considered another hallucination by physicians predisposed to reach that conclusion. *I heard something — but no one else did. I felt something — but no one else noticed. I know a murder took place — but no one else does.* Francis immediately saw the hopelessness of his position. His protest would have been noted and registered in his file as yet a further indication of how far he was from meaningful recovery and the opportunity to get out of the hospital.

Francis held his breath. In the hospital, the Angel's presence was still neither real nor delusion. He knew the Angel understood this. No wonder, Francis thought, to a chorus of assent within him, the killer was confident. *He can get away with anything.*

The question, Francis asked himself, was: *What is it he wants to get away with?*

So he clamped down on his lip, and stared instead at the Dancer. What killed him, Francis wondered? No blood. No marks around the neck. Just a death mask engraved on his features. Probably a pillow held down over the face. Quiet panic. Silent death. A momentary thrashing about and then oblivion. Is that what I heard last night? Francis asked himself. He thought painfully: Yes. I just never opened my eyes to the noise.

The knife that had killed Short Blond, this time had been reserved for him. But the message on the bunk was for all of them. Francis could feel his muscles shuddering. He was still gathering himself together, understanding how close he'd been that night to either real death or being driven into a deeper madness. It was, he thought, as if the two of them went hand in hand, a matched set of unpleasant alternatives.

'I hate these sorts of deaths,' Gulptilil said offhandedly to Mister Evans. 'They upset everyone. See that medications are adjusted for anyone who seems to be unreasonably focused on this event,' the medical director said, throwing a look in Francis's direction. 'I do not want patients dwelling on this death, especially with a release hearing scheduled for later this week.'

'I know what you mean,' Evans said.

Francis, however, suddenly bent toward the doctor's words. He was unsure whether the Dancer's death would prove to be anything more than a curiosity for everyone in the housing unit. But he did know that the news that a release hearing was scheduled for that week would have a dramatic impact on many of the patients. Someone might get out, and hope inside Western State was the half brother of delusion.

He stole one last look at the Dancer and felt an improbable sadness within him. There's a man who got his release unexpectedly, Francis thought.

But within the ebb and flow of fear and sadness that he felt, Francis perceived something else: a juxtaposition of events that he couldn't quite identify, but which gave him a cold suspicion within that worried him.

A gurney was wheeled into the dormitory to remove the Dancer's body. Gulptilil and Mister Evil oversaw the dead man being rolled out of his bunk and placed under a dingy white sheet. Lucy shook her head, watching what she thought might be a crime scene cavalierly eradicated.

Gulptilil turned, and trailing after the body, spotted Francis. He paused, and said, 'Ah, Mister Petrel. I wonder if it might not be time soon for us to have another session.'

Francis knew what the doctor wanted. He nodded, because he didn't know what else to do. But then, in a switch that left the medical director almost open-mouthed in surprise, Francis lifted his arms above his head, and pirouetted about slowly, moving his feet and arms as gracefully and balletlike as he could, in conscious imitation of the dead man's dance to music only he could hear.

Gulptilil tried to interrupt him, suddenly asking, 'Mister Petrel, are you okay?' which Francis thought a most fantastically stupid question, as he simply danced out of the doctor's path.

★   ★   ★

At their regularly scheduled group session that day, the conversation turned to the space program. Newsman had been spouting headlines for the past few days, but there was widespread disbelief amongst the patients at Western State whether any moon walks had actually taken place. Cleo in particular had been defiant, rumbling about government cover-ups and unknown otherworldly dangers, giggling one instant, then growing morose and quiet the next. The swings in her mood seemed obvious to everyone except Mister Evil, who ignored most of the external signs of madness when they reared up. This was his usual approach. He liked to listen, take a note, and then the patient would discover later, when he or she lined up for the evening medication, that their dosage had been adjusted. This had a stifling effect upon much of the conversation, because everyone at the hospital saw the daily medications as so many links of the chain that kept them there.

The Dancer's death wasn't mentioned, although it was on everyone's minds. Short Blond's murder had fascinated and scared them, but the Dancer dying reminded them all of their own mortality, which was a different fear altogether. More than once, patients sitting in the group's loose circle burst out in a laugh, or choked a sob, none of which had anything to do with the course of the conversation, but seemed to erupt spontaneously from some internal thought or another.

Francis thought that Mister Evil was watching him particularly closely. He attributed this to his bizarre behavior earlier that morning.

'What about you, Francis?' Evans asked abruptly, poking at Francis with a question.

'I'm sorry, what about me what?' Francis replied.

'What do you think about astronauts?'

He thought for a moment, then shook his head. 'It's hard to imagine,' he answered.

'What is hard?'

'To be that far away, connected only by computers and radios. No one has ever traveled as far before. That's interesting. It's not the reliance on all the equipment, it's that no adventure ever has been quite like it.'

Mister Evil nodded. 'What about explorers in Africa or the North Pole?'

'They faced elements. Unknown. But astronauts face something different.'

'What's that?'

'Myths,' Francis said. He looked around at all the others, and then asked, 'Where is Peter?'

Mister Evil shifted about. 'Still in isolation,' he said. 'But he should be out soon. Let's get back to the astronauts.'

'They don't exist,' Cleo said. 'But Peter does.'

Then she shook her head. 'Maybe he doesn't,' she said. 'Maybe all this is a dream and we're going to wake up any second.'

An argument broke out then, between Cleo and Napoleon and several others about what really existed and what didn't, and if something took place where you couldn't see it, did it really happen. All of this caused the group to snort and wave their hands excitedly in contradiction and dispute, which Evans allowed to ricochet back and forth. For a moment or two, Francis listened, because, in an odd way, he thought there were some similarities between his position in the hospital and men on their way to space. They were adrift, he thought, the same way he was.

He believed that he had recovered from his fright from the night before, but he had little confidence in his ability to greet the night to come.

He probed his memory for all the words the Angel had spoken, but it was hard for Francis to remember them with the sort of precision that he thought was necessary. Fear, he realized, skews things about. It's like trying to see accurately when staring into a fun house mirror. The image is wavy, indistinct, distorted.

For an instant, he told himself: Stop trying to see the Angel. Start trying to see what the Angel sees.

Deep inside him, voices shouted out in sudden warning. *Stop! Don't do that!*

Francis shifted about in his seat uncomfortably. The voices wouldn't have warned him, if they hadn't seen something important and dangerous. He shook his head slightly, as if to restore his connection to the group that was continuing to argue, and he looked at the others, just as Napoleon was saying, ' . . . Why do we need to go up into space anyway . . . ' and he saw that Cleo was eyeing him from across the circle with a slightly bemused, slightly curious, almost impressed look of attention. She leaned forward in her seat, ignoring Napoleon, which infuriated the small round man, and she quietly said to Francis, 'C-Bird saw something, didn't he?'

Then she cackled, her body quivering with some joke that only she understood, just as Peter stepped into the room.

He immediately waved to the group, and then made a sweeping, formal bow to his fellow patients, like a king's attendant in some sixteenth-century court. Then he grabbed a steel folding chair and pulled himself into the circle.

'None the worse for wear,' he said, as if anticipating the question.

'Peter seems to like isolation,' Cleo said.

'Nobody snores,' Peter replied, which got everyone to grin and chuckle.

'We have been discussing astronauts,' Mister Evil said. 'In the time remaining, I'd like to conclude that discussion.'

'Sure,' Peter said. 'Didn't mean to interrupt anything.'

'Well, fine. Now, does anyone have anything else to add?' Mister Evil turned away from Peter and examined the collected patients. He was met with silence.

Evans let a few seconds pass. 'Anyone?'

Again, the group, so vociferous a few minutes earlier, was quiet. Francis thought that this was like them; that sometimes words flowed from all of them almost unchecked, flooding the air, and other moments, they disappeared, and with almost religious fervor, everyone looked inward. Shifts in mood were commonplace.

'Come on,' Evans said, exasperation creeping into his voice. 'We were making progress a moment or two before we were interrupted. Someone, Cleo?'

She shook her head.

'Newsman?'

For once, he didn't have a headline to spout.

'Francis?'

Francis didn't answer.

'Say something,' Evans said stiffly.

Francis was at a loss and he saw Evans shifting about, his own anger increasing. It was, Francis thought, a matter of control. Mister Evil liked to control everything in the dormitory, and once again Peter had disrupted that power. More than any patient, no matter how rigid with madness they were, none of them could compare with Mister Evans's need to own every moment of the day and night inside the Amherst Building.

'Say something,' Evans repeated, even colder. This was an order.

Francis hurried about within himself, trying to imagine what it was that Mister Evil wanted to hear, but, in reply, he was only able to blurt out: 'I'll never go into space.'

Evans shrugged and snorted, 'Well, of course not . . . ' as if what Francis had said was the silliest thing he'd ever heard.

But Peter, who'd been watching and listening, suddenly leaned forward. 'Why not?' he asked.

Francis turned to the sound of the Fireman's voice. Peter was grinning. 'Why not?' he said again.

Evans looked upset. 'We don't encourage delusions here, Peter,' he snapped.

But Peter, fresh from the padded walls of the isolation cell, ignored him. 'Why not, Francis?' he asked a third time.

Francis waved his hand about, as if to indicate the hospital.

'But C-Bird,' Peter continued, his voice picking up momentum as he spoke, 'why couldn't you be an astronaut? You're young, you're fit, you're smart. You see things that others might fail to notice. You're not conceited and you're brave. I think you'd make a perfect astronaut.'

'But Peter . . . ,' Francis said.

'No buts at all. Why, who's to say that NASA won't decide to send someone crazy into space? I mean who better than one of us? I mean, people would surely believe a crazy spaceman a helluva lot quicker than some military-salute-the-flag type, right? Who's to say they won't decide to send all sorts of folks up into space, and why not one of us? They might send politicians, or scientists or maybe tourists even, someday. Maybe they'll find that when they send a crazy guy up, that floating about in space without gravity to hold us on earth, well, it helps us? Like a science experiment. Maybe . . . '

He paused, taking a breath. Evans started to speak, but before he could, Napoleon hesitantly added, 'Peter might be right. Maybe gravity makes us crazy . . . '

Cleo jumped in. 'Holds us down . . . '

'All that weight right on our shoulders . . . '

'Prevents our thoughts from zooming up and out . . . '

From around the room, patient after patient started to nod in agreement. Suddenly each seemed to find his tongue. There were first murmurs of assent, then abrupt acclaim.

'We could fly. We could float.'

'No one would hold us back.'

'Who would be better explorers than us?'

Around the group, men and women were smiling, agreeing. It was as if in that moment they could

431

suddenly all see themselves as astronauts, hurtling through the heavens, their earthbound cares forgotten and evaporated, as they slipped effortlessly through the great starry void of space. It was wildly attractive, and for a few moments, the group seemed to soar skyward, each member imagining the force of gravity being sliced away from him, experiencing an odd sort of fantasy freedom in those seconds.

Evans seethed. He started to speak, then stopped.

Instead, he tossed an angry glare at Peter, and without a word, stomped from the room.

The group quieted, watching Mister Evil's back. Within seconds, the fog of troubles fell back upon all of them.

Cleo, however, sighed loudly and shook her head. 'I guess it's just you, C-Bird,' she said, briskly. 'You'll have to head to the heavens for all of us.'

★   ★   ★

Dutifully, the group rose, folded up their chairs and placed them against the wall where they belonged, making a rattling, metallic clanking sound as one after the other was lined up. Then, lost in his own thoughts, each member made his way out of the therapy room, back into the main Amherst corridor, blending into the tidal flow of patients that maneuvered up and down the hallway.

Francis grasped Peter by the arm.

'He was here, last night.'

'Who?'

'The Angel.'

'He came back again?'

'Yes. He killed the Dancer but no one wants to believe that and then he held a knife to my face and told me he could kill me or you or anyone he wanted, whenever he wanted.'

'Jesus!' Peter said. Whatever leftover exhilaration Peter had felt at outmaneuvering Mister Evil disappeared, and he bent to every word Francis spoke. 'What else?' he asked.

Francis, hesitantly, trying hard to recall everything that had happened, could feel some of the remainder of fear that still lurked about within him. Telling Peter about the pressure of the blade on his face was harsh. He thought, at first, that it might make himself feel better, but it did not. Instead, it merely redoubled anxiety within him.

'He held it how?' Peter asked.

Francis demonstrated.

'Jesus,' Peter repeated. 'That must have scared the hell out of you, C-Bird.'

Francis nodded, unwilling to say out loud precisely how scared he'd been. But then, in that second, something struck him, and he stopped, his brows knitting as he tried to see through a question that was murky and clouded. Peter saw Francis's sudden consternation, and asked, 'What is it?'

'Peter . . . ,' Francis started, 'you were the investigator once. Why would the Angel hold the knife against my face that way?'

Peter stopped, thinking.

'Shouldn't . . . ' Francis continued, 'shouldn't he hold it against my throat?'

'Yes,' Peter said.

'That way, if I screamed . . . '

'The throat, the jugular vein, the larynx, those are the vulnerable spots. That's how you kill someone with a knife.'

'But he didn't. He held it to my face.'

Peter nodded. 'That's most intriguing,' he said. 'He didn't think you would scream . . . '

'People scream all the time in here. It doesn't mean anything.'

433

'True enough. But he wanted to terrify you.'

'He succeeded,' Francis said.

'Did you get a look . . . '

'He made me keep my eyes closed.'

'How about his voice?'

'I might recognize it, if I heard it again. Especially close up. He hissed, like a snake.'

'Do you think he was trying to conceal it somehow?'

'No. Funny. I don't think so. It was like he didn't care.'

'What else?'

Francis shook his head. 'He was . . . *confident*,' he said cautiously.

Peter and Francis walked out of the therapy room. Lucy was waiting for them midway down the corridor, near the nursing station. They headed toward her, and as they maneuvered through the knots of patients, Peter spotted Little Black, standing not far from the station, a few feet away from Lucy Jones, and he saw the smaller of the two brothers bent over, jotting down something in a large black notebook attached to the metal grate with a modest silver chain, a little like a child's bicycle lock. In that second, he thought of something, and he stepped toward Little Black rapidly, only to have Francis grasp at his arm and stop him.

'What?' Peter said.

Francis looked pale, suddenly, and there was a nervous hesitancy in his voice. 'Peter,' he said slowly. 'Something occurs to me.'

'What's that?'

'If he wasn't scared of speaking to me, that meant he wasn't worried that I might accidentally overhear his voice in some other location. He didn't worry about me recognizing it because he knows there's no chance I'll ever hear it.'

Peter stopped, nodding, and gestured toward Lucy.

'That's interesting, Francis,' he said. 'That's very interesting.'

Francis thought that *interesting* wasn't the word that Peter really meant. Francis pivoted about and thought to himself: *Find silence.*

He noticed a slight quiver in his hand when he thought this, and he realized suddenly that his throat had dried up. There was a noxious taste in his mouth, and he tried to swirl saliva around but he had none. He looked at Lucy, who wore an expression of annoyance; he thought it had little to do with them, but much to do with how the world she had entered so confidently now proved more elusive than she had first guessed.

As the prosecutor approached them, Peter stepped toward Little Black.

'Mister Moses,' he spoke cautiously, 'what are you doing?'

The slender attendant looked up at Peter. 'Just routine,' he said.

'What do you mean?'

'Routine,' Little Black continued. 'Just making some notes in the daily log book.'

'What else goes into that book?'

'Any changes ordered by the head doc, or Mister Evil. Anything out of the ordinary, like a fight or lost keys or a death like the Dancer's. Any switches in the routine. Lots of little, stupid crap, too, Peter. Like when you take your bathroom break at night, and when you check the doors and when you check the sleeping dormitories and any phone calls that come in or anything like I say that just about anybody who works here might think was out of the ordinary. Or you notice, maybe, one patient making progress for some reason or another. That can go in here, too. When you get on station at the start of your shift, you're supposed to check the overnights. And then, before you clock out, you're supposed to make some entry and sign it. Even if it's only a couple of words. This goes on every day. Log book is supposed to make things easier for the next folks that come in, so they're up to date on anything happening.'

'Is there a book like that — '

Little Black interrupted him. 'One on every floor, by every nursing station. Security got their own, too.'

'So, if you had that, you would know, more or less, when things happen. I mean, the routine things?'

'Daily log is important,' Little Black said. 'It keeps track of all sorts of things. Got to have a record of everything that happens in here. It's like a little history book.'

'Who keeps those logs, when they get filled up?'

Little Black shrugged. 'Stored down in the basement somewhere in boxes.'

'But if I were to get a look at one of those, I'd know all sorts of things, wouldn't I?'

'Patients not supposed to see daily log books. It ain't like they're hidden or anything. But they're for the staff.'

'But if I did see one . . . even one that had been retired and put in storage, I'd have some pretty good ideas about when things take place on what sort of schedule, wouldn't I?'

Little Black slowly nodded his head.

Peter continued, but now he was speaking to Lucy Jones. 'For example, I might have a pretty good idea when I could move around the hospital without being detected. And I might know the best time to find Short Blond alone at the first-floor nursing station in the middle of the night and drowsy because she routinely worked a double shift one day each week, wouldn't I? And I'd know, too, that Security had long since been by to check on the doors and maybe gab a little bit and that no one else at all was going to be around, except a bunch of drugged out, sleeping patients, right?'

Little Black didn't have to answer this question. Or any of the others.

'That's how he knows,' Peter said softly. 'He doesn't know absolutely for certain, with military precision, but he knows enough, so that he can guess with a great deal of certainty, and with a little bit of foresight, can wait and pick the right moments.'

Francis thought this was possible. He felt cold inside, because abruptly he began to think that they had just taken a step closer to the Angel, and he had already been too close to the man, and he wasn't sure that he wanted to get that close again to the knife and the voice.

★   ★   ★

Lucy was shaking her head back and forth, and finally said to Peter and Francis, 'I can't put my finger on it exactly, but something is wrong. No, that's not it, it's more that something is right and wrong, both at the same time.'

Peter grinned. 'Ah, Lucy,' he said, almost mocking the way that Gulptilil liked to begin his sentences with an elongated pause, and adopting the Indian physician's lilting accented English. 'Ah, Lucy,' he repeated, 'you make the sort of sense that belongs here in the madhouse. Please continue.'

'This place is getting to me,' she said quietly. 'I think I'm being followed back to the nurse-trainees' dormitory at night. I hear noises by my door that disappear when I get up. I sense that someone has been into my belongings, although there is nothing missing. I keep thinking we're making progress, and yet, I can't point at what it is. I'm beginning to think that I'll start hearing voices any second now.'

For a moment, she turned and looked at Francis, who seemed not to be listening, but was lost in thought. She peered down the corridor and saw Cleo holding forth on some incredibly important issue or another, waving her arms energetically, her voice booming out, not that anything she said made particularly cogent sense. 'Or,' Lucy said, shaking her head, 'I will come to imagine that I'm the reincarnation of some Egyptian princess.'

'That might cause a significant conflict,' Peter replied with a grin.

'You'll survive,' Lucy continued. 'You're not crazy like the rest of these folks. Soon as you get out, you'll be okay. But C-Bird . . . what will happen to him?'

'Bigger questions for Francis,' Peter said, instantly turning glum. 'He needs to prove he isn't crazy, but how do you do that in here? This place is designed to make people more crazy, not less. It makes all the diseases people suffer, like, contagious . . . ,' Peter said, bitterness creeping into his voice. 'It's as if you come in here with a cold, and it turns into strep or bronchitis and then into pneumonia, and finally into some terminal respiratory failure and then they say, 'Well, we did all we could . . . ''

'I need to get out of here,' Lucy said. 'You need to get out of here, too.'

'Correct,' Peter replied, 'But the person who needs out more than anybody is C-Bird, because otherwise, he'll be lost forever.' Peter smiled again, but this was a smile that was merely a blanket thrown over all his sadness. 'It's as if you and I, we elect our own troubles. We choose them in some perverse, neurotic way. Francis, all his troubles were delivered to him. No fault of his own, not like you and me. He's innocent, which is a hell of a lot more than you can say for me.'

Lucy reached out her hand and touched Peter's forearm, as if to buttress the truth in what he said. For a moment, Peter stayed stock-still, like a bird dog on point, his arm almost burning with the sensation of the touch. Then he stepped a little ways back, as if he couldn't stand the pressure. But as he did that, he smiled, and sighed deeply, although he turned his face away from Lucy as he did it, as if, in that second, he couldn't force himself to see what he could see.

'We need to find the Angel,' Peter said. 'And we need to do it right away.'

'I agree,' Lucy said. But then she looked at Peter curiously, because she saw that he meant something beyond the simple encouragement.

'What is it?'

But before he could answer that question, Francis, who had been weighing something inwardly and not paying attention to the others, looked up and approached the two of them. 'I had an idea,' he said hesitantly, 'I don't know, but . . . '

'C-Bird, I need to tell you something . . . ,' Peter started, then he interrupted himself. 'What's your idea?'

'What do you need to tell me?'

'It can wait a little bit,' Peter said. 'But your idea?'

'I was so scared,' Francis began. 'You weren't there, and it was pitch-dark, and that knife was at my cheek. Fear is funny, Peter,' he continued, 'because it rearranges all your thinking so much that you can't see anything else because of it. And I bet Lucy already knows this, but I didn't and it gave me an idea . . . '

'Francis, try to make a little more sense,' Peter said, like he would to a student in an elementary school. Affectionate, but interested.

'Fear like that, it makes you think of only one thing: How scared you are and what's going to happen, and will he come back, and the terrible things he's done and what he might still do, because I knew he could have killed me, and I wanted to descend into some sort of safe place where I could be all alone . . . '

Lucy bent to Francis, because suddenly she saw a glimmer of what he was driving at. 'Go on,' she said.

'But all that fear, it covered up something that I should have seen.'

439

Peter nodded. 'What?'

'The Angel knew you would not be there that night.'

'The log. Or he saw for himself. Or he heard I was being moved to isolation . . . '

'So, the situation was ripe for him to move last night, because he didn't want to try to handle both of us at once, I don't think. I'm kinda guessing here, but it makes some sense to me. Anyway, he had to move last night, because the situation was perfect for him to terrify me . . . '

'Yes,' Lucy said. 'I can see that.'

'And he needed to kill the Dancer. Why?'

'To show us how he could do anything. To underscore the message. We're not safe.' Francis breathed out hard, because the notion that the Dancer was killed simply to make a point truly unsettled him. He couldn't imagine what could drive the Angel forward so dramatically, and then, in the same second, he realized that perhaps he could. This frightened him even more, but he took refuge in the bright light of the midday corridor, and being surrounded by Peter and Lucy. They were competent, and strong, Francis thought, and the Angel was being cautious with them because they weren't mad and weak like he was. He breathed out slowly and continued, 'But these are risks. Do you suppose there was another reason he had to be in that room last night?'

'What sort of reason?'

Francis was almost stuttering, each thought that he had seemed to echo within him, deeper and farther away, as if he was on the edge of some great hole that only promised oblivion. He closed his eyes for a second, and there was a red streak of light behind his lids, almost blinding him. He took his time forming each word, because in that second he saw what was in that room that the Angel needed.

'The retarded man . . . ,' Francis began. 'He had

440

something that belonged to him . . . '

'The bloody shirt.'

'Well, I wonder . . . '

Francis didn't get a chance to finish. He looked up at Peter, who turned to Lucy Jones. They didn't have to agree out loud. Within seconds, the three of them had crossed the corridor and pushed into the dormitory room.

★   ★   ★

They were fortunate that the hulking retarded man was sitting on the edge of his bed, crooning softly to his Raggedy Andy doll. In the back of the dormitory, there were a few other patients, mostly lying about, staring out the window or at the ceiling, disconnected from anything. The retarded man looked up at the three of them and smiled. Lucy pushed forward, taking the lead.

'Hello,' she said. 'Do you remember me?'

He nodded.

'Is that your friend?' she asked.

Again, he nodded.

'And is this where the two of you sleep?'

He patted the mattress, and she sat down at his side. As statuesque as Lucy was, she was still dwarfed by the retarded man, who shifted in his seat to make a little room for her.

'And this is where the two of you live . . . '

Again he grinned and smiled. He seemed to concentrate hard for a moment, and then he haltingly said, 'I live in the big hospital.'

The words tumbled like boulders from his mouth. Each one was misshapen and rock hard, and she imagined that the effort to form each one was a monumental task.

'And this is where you keep your things?' she asked.

Again, his head moved up and down.

'Has anyone tried to hurt you?' she asked.

'Yes,' the retarded man said slowly, as if the single word could be drawn out so that it could say more than simply agreeing. 'I had a fight.'

Lucy took a deep breath, but before she could ask another question, she saw that the retarded man's eyes had filled with some tears.

' . . . I had a fight,' he repeated, and then he added, 'I don't like to fight. My momma told me, no fighting. Never.'

'Your momma is wise,' Lucy said. She had no doubt that the retarded man could do serious damage if he permitted himself to.

'I'm too big,' he said. 'No fighting.'

'Does your friend have a name?' she asked, gesturing toward the doll.

'Andy.'

'I'm Lucy. Can I be your friend, too?'

He nodded and smiled.

'Will you help me with something?'

He knitted his brows together, and she thought he was having trouble understanding, so she said, 'I've lost something.'

He grunted a response, as if to indicate that he, too, had once lost something and that he didn't like it.

'Will you look in your things for me?'

The retarded man hesitated, then shrugged. He reached down under the bed, and with a single hand pulled forward a green, military-style trunk. 'What?' he asked.

'A shirt.'

He handed the Raggedy Andy doll to Lucy carefully, and then undid the clasp on the foot locker. She noted that the trunk wasn't locked. He pulled the lid back and she saw his meager possessions. There were some underwear and socks folded on the top, next to a photograph of the retarded man and his mother. The picture was a few years old, and had a few creases in it, and was frayed around the edges from where it had been handled far too many times. Then beneath that were some jeans and a spare pair of shoes, a couple of sports shirts and a slightly threadbare dark green woolen sweater.

The bloody shirt was missing. Lucy rapidly looked over at Peter, who shook his head.

'Gone,' he said quietly.

She turned back to the retarded man. 'Thank you,' she said. 'You can put your things away now.'

He closed the trunk and shoved it back under the bunk. She handed him back the Raggedy Andy doll.

'Do you have any other friends in here?' she asked, gesturing around the room.

He shook his head. 'All alone,' he said.

'I'll be your friend,' she said, which made him smile, although she realized what a lie this was, which made her feel guilty, in part for the hopelessness of the retarded man, and a little for herself, because she wasn't sure she liked at all having the ability to deceive a person who was little more than a child, and who would only grow older, but never wiser.

★ ★ ★

Back in her office, Lucy sighed. 'Well,' she said, 'I guess the idea that we might actually find a bit of evidence seems to be too much.'

She sounded discouraged, but Peter was more upbeat. 'No, no, we learned something. The idea that the Angel would plant something and then go to the trouble of removing it tells us something about his personality.'

Francis, however, felt his head spinning. He could feel a small quiver in his hands, because within him so much that was usually a turmoil of crosscurrents and

443

murkiness, had an edge of clarity to it. 'Closeness,' he said.

'What?'

'He picked the retarded man for a reason. Because he knew he would be questioned by Lucy. Because he was close enough to be able to plant a piece of evidence on. Because he wasn't someone who would threaten him. Everything the Angel does has a purpose.'

'I think you're right,' Lucy said slowly. 'Because when you think about it, what does this tell us?'

Peter's voice was suddenly cold. 'It tells us that he's not exactly hiding.'

Francis groaned, as if this idea pained him like a blow to the chest. He rocked back and forth, and Peter and Lucy eyed him with concern. For the first time, Peter understood that what was an exercise in intelligence for him and Lucy, an adventure in outsmarting a clever and dedicated killer, was, perhaps, something far more difficult and dangerous for Francis. 'He wants us to search for him,' Francis said, the words bleeding through his lips. 'He enjoys all this.'

'Well, then we've got to end the game,' Peter said.

Francis looked up. 'We have to not do what he expects us to do because he knows. I don't know how or why, but he knows.'

Peter took a deep breath, and for a moment or two, all three of them were quiet, as they chewed over what Francis had said. Peter didn't think that the moment was right, but he could think of no other time that might be more appropriate, and any further delay might make things worse. 'I don't have much time left,' he said quietly. 'Sometime in the next few days, I'm going to be shipped out of here. Forever.'

25

I rolled over on the floor and felt the hardwood surface flush against my cheek as I fought against the sobs that captured my entire body. All of my life I had spiraled from one loneliness to another, and simply recalling the instant in time that I heard Peter the Fireman say that he would be leaving me by myself in Western State plummeted me into a black despair that mimicked the one I felt in the Amherst Building all those years ago. I suppose I had known from the opening second when we had met, that I was bound to be left behind, but still, hearing it firsthand was like a blow to the chest. There are some deep sadnesses that never leave one's heart no matter how many hours slide by, and this was one of those. Writing the words that Peter spoke that afternoon rekindled all the feelings of despair that had been hidden for so many years by so many drugs and treatment plans and therapeutic sessions. My hurt erupted, filling me with a deep gray volcanic ash.

I wailed like a starving child, abandoned in the darkness. My body convulsed with the shock of recollection. Tossed down on the cold floor like a shipwrecked sailor thrown up on a distant, strange shore, I gave into the utter futility of my history and let every failure and flaw find voice in one wracking sob after another, until, exhausted, I finally quieted.

When the awful silence of fatigue filled the air around me, I could just make out a distant mocking laugh, retreating into the shadows. The Angel still hovered nearby, enjoying every filigree of pain I experienced.

I lifted my head and snarled. He remained close. Close enough to touch me, just far enough so that I couldn't grasp him. I could sense the distance narrowing, closing by millimeters with each passing second. That was his style. Hide. Evade. Manipulate. Control. Then, when the moment was ripe, he would pounce. The difference was, this time I was the target.

I gathered myself and struggled to my feet, wiping a sleeve across my tearstained face. Pivoting about, I searched the room.

'Here, C-Bird. Over by the wall.'

But it wasn't the Angel's hissing, murderous voice, it was Peter's.

I spun to the sound. He was sitting on the floor, leaning up against the wall of writing.

He looked tired. No, that's not quite right. He had traveled beyond exhaustion, into a different realm altogether. His jumpsuit was streaked with soot and dirt, and I could see grime on his face, scarred by streaks of sweat. There were rips in his clothes, and his heavy brown work boots were ridged with mud, leaves, and pine needles. He toyed with his silver steel helmet, flipping it back and forth in his hands, spinning it like a child's top. After a moment or two, as he seemed to regain a little bit of his strength and composure, he finally took the helmet and lifted it above his head, tapping it against the wall.

'You're getting there,' he said. 'I guess I really didn't understand how terrified you must have been of the Angel. I could never see coming what you did. It's a good thing one of us was crazy. Or just crazy enough.'

Even with all the filth that covered him, Peter's insouciance still clawed through. I couldn't help but feel a sense of relief. Still, I bent down, crouching just across from him, close enough so that I could reach out and touch him, but I didn't.

'He's here now,' I whispered, cautiously. 'He's listening to us.'

'I know,' Peter said. 'The hell with him.'

'He's come for me, this time. Like he promised back then.'

'I know,' Peter repeated.

'I need your help, Peter,' I said. 'I don't know how to fight him.'

'You didn't know before, but you figured it out,' Peter replied. A little bit of his wide, white grin penetrated past his exhaustion, past all the collected dirt and debris.

'It's different now,' I said. 'Before it was ... ' I hesitated.

'Real?' Peter asked.

I nodded.

'And this isn't?'

I didn't know what to reply.

'Will you help me?' I asked again.

'I don't know that you really need it. But I'll try to do what I can.' Peter wearily gathered himself and slowly rose to his feet. For the first time, I noticed that the backs of his hands were charred raw and bloody. The skin seemed to be loosened, for it hung in flaps from the bones and tendons. He must have seen where my eyes went, because he glanced down and then shrugged. 'Can't do anything about that,' he said. 'It gets worse.'

I didn't ask him to elaborate, because I thought I understood. In the momentary silence that followed, he turned and peered at the wall. He shook his head. 'I'm sorry, C-Bird,' he said quietly. 'I knew it would hurt you, but I didn't really understand how harsh it would be.'

'I was alone,' I said. 'I wonder sometimes if there's anything worse in the whole world.'

Peter smiled. 'There are worse things,' he said. 'But I understand what you mean. I didn't have a choice though, did I?'

Now it was my turn to shake my head. 'No. You had to do what they wanted. And that was your only chance. I understand that.'

'It didn't exactly turn out great for me,' Peter said. He laughed, as if this was a joke, then he shook his head. 'I'm sorry, C-Bird. I didn't want to leave you, but if I'd stayed . . . '

'You would have ended up like me. I understand that, Peter,' I said.

'But I was there for the most important part,' he said. I nodded.

'And so was Lucy.'

Again, I nodded my head in agreement.

'So, we all paid a price, didn't we?' he asked.

In that second, I heard a long, wolflike howl. It was an unearthly sound, filled with anger and revenge. The Angel.

Peter heard it, too. But it didn't frighten him the way it did me.

'He's coming for me, Peter,' I whispered. 'I don't know if I can handle him alone.'

'True enough,' Peter replied. 'One never can be sure of everything. But you know him, C-Bird. You know his strengths; you know his limitations. You knew it all, and it was what we needed once before, wasn't it?' He looked over at the wall of writing. 'Put it down, C-Bird. All the questions. And all the answers.'

He stepped back, as if making a path for me to the next blank spot. I took a deep breath and moved forward. I wasn't aware that Peter faded from my side, as I picked up the stub of pencil, but I did note that the chill from the Angel's breath frosted the room around me, so that I shivered as I wrote:

By the end of the day, Francis was overcome by the sensation that things were taking place that all made sense, but that he couldn't quite see the shape of the stage . . .

By the end of the day, Francis was overcome by the sensation that things were taking place that all made sense, but that he couldn't quite see the shape of the stage. The jumble of ideas that coursed through his imagination were still puzzling to him, complicated no end by the resurgence of his own voices that seemed to be as divisive and as doubting as they had ever been. They formed a knot of confusion within his head, shouting conflicting suggestions and demands, urging him to flee, to hide, to fight back, so frequently and fiercely that he could barely hear other conversations. He still held the belief that everything would become obvious if he simply looked at it through the right microscope.

'Peter, Gulp-a-pill said that there are some release hearings scheduled for this week . . . '

Peter's eyes had arched up. 'That will put people on edge.'

'Why?' Lucy asked.

'Hope,' Peter responded, as if that single word said everything at once. Then he'd looked back at Francis. 'What is it, C-Bird?'

'It seems to me that somehow there's some connection in all this to the dormitory room at Williams,' he said slowly. 'The Angel had to pick out the retarded man, so he had to be familiar with his routine in order to place the shirt there. And he had to figure out that the retarded man would be one of the men Lucy was going to question.'

'Proximity,' Peter said. 'Opportunity to observe. Good point, Francis.'

Lucy nodded, as well. 'I think,' she said, 'that I will get the roster of patients in that dormitory room.'

Francis thought for a moment, then asked, 'Lucy, can you get the list of patients scheduled for release hearings, too?' He kept his voice low, so that no one could hear him.

'Why?'

He shrugged. 'I don't know,' he said. 'But so much seems to be happening and I'm trying to see how it might be connected.'

Lucy nodded, but Francis was unsure whether she actually believed him.

'I'll see if I can get it, as well,' she said, but Francis had the distinct impression that she was saying this to accommodate him, and wasn't seeing any potential connection. She looked over at Peter. 'We could arrange to search the entire room over in Williams. It wouldn't take long, and it might turn up something of value.'

Lucy thought to herself that it was critical to try to maintain the more concrete aspects of the investigation. Lists and suppositions were intriguing, but she was much more comfortable with the sorts of details that people can testify to in courtrooms. The loss of the bloody shirt bothered her far more than she had let on, and she was eager to find some other morsel of hard evidence that could provide the foundation for a case.

Lucy thought again: knife; fingertips; bloody clothes and shoes.

Something had to be somewhere she told herself.

'That might make some sense,' Peter said. He looked over at the prosecutor, and recognized what might be at stake.

Francis, however, was less sure. He thought the Angel would surely have anticipated that maneuver. What they had to come up with, he thought, was something oblique. Something the Angel wouldn't think of. Something skewed and different and more in keeping with where they were, rather than where they wanted to be. The three of them started to head toward Lucy's office, but Francis spotted Big Black over by the nursing station, and he peeled off to speak with the huge attendant. The others continued on, not fully aware, it seemed, that Francis had dropped behind.

Big Black looked up. 'It's early for medication, C-Bird,' he said. 'But I'm guessing that isn't what you want, is it?'

Francis shook his head. 'You believed me, didn't you?'

The attendant glanced around, before answering. 'I sure did, C-Bird. The problem is, it never does any good in here to agree with a patient when the brass thinks something different. You understand, don't you? It wasn't about the truth or not. It's about my job.'

'He might come back. He might come back tonight.'

'He might. I doubt it, though. If he thought killing you was the right thing, C-Bird, he would have done it already.'

Francis agreed with this, although it was one of those observations that was both reassuring and frightening at the same time.

'Mister Moses,' Francis croaked out breathlessly, 'why is it that no one in here wants to help Miss Jones catch this guy?'

Big Black instantly stiffened and shifted about. 'I'm helping, ain't I? My brother, he's helping, too.'

'You know what I mean,' Francis said.

Big Black nodded. 'That I do, C-Bird. That I do.'

He looked about, as if to reassure himself of what he already knew, which was that no one was close enough or paying attention enough to overhear his response. Still, he kept every word beneath his voice, speaking cautiously. 'You got to understand something, C-Bird. In here, finding this guy that Miss Jones wants, with all the publicity and attention and maybe a state investigation and headlines and television stations and all that showing up, why, that would mean some people's careers. Far too many questions, getting asked. Probably tough questions, like why didn't you do this, or why didn't you do that? Maybe even have to have hearings at the State House. Lots of rocking the boat, and there ain't nobody who works for the state, especially a doc or a psychologist, who wants to be answering questions about how they let a killer live in the hospital here with nobody paying too much mind. We're talking scandal here, C-Bird. A helluva lot easier to cover it up, explain away a body or two. That's easy. No one gets blamed, everybody gets paid, nobody loses their job, and things go on day in and day out, just like before. Ain't no different from any hospital. Or prison, either, you think about it. Keeping things keeping on, that's what this is all about. Ain't you figured that part out for yourself yet?'

He had, he realized. He just didn't like it.

'You got to remember,' Big Black added, shaking his head, 'no one cares all that much about crazy people.'

* * *

Miss Luscious looked up and scowled when Lucy walked into the reception area outside of Doctor Gulptilil's office. She made a point of busying herself with some forms, turning to her typewriter and furiously starting to type, just as Lucy approached her desk. 'The doctor is occupied,' she said, her fingers flying over the keyboard, and the steel ball of the old Selectric banging away on a piece of paper. 'I don't have you scheduled for an appointment,' she added.

'This should only take a second or two,' Lucy said.

'Well, I'll see if I can work you in. Have a seat.' The secretary didn't make an effort to change position, or even pick up the telephone until Lucy moved away from the desk and plopped herself down onto a lumpy waiting room couch.

She kept her eyes directly on Miss Luscious, boring into her with intensity, until the secretary finally tired of the scrutiny, picked up the office phone and turned away from Lucy as she spoke. There was a brief exchange, and then the secretary turned and said, 'The doctor can see you now,' an almost comical cliché, given the circumstances, Lucy thought.

Doctor Gulptilil was standing behind his desk, staring out at the tree just beyond the glass. He cleared his throat as she entered, but remained in his position, not moving, as she hovered waiting for the physician to acknowledge her presence. After a moment or two, he turned, and with a small shake of his head, slumped down into his seat.

'Miss Jones,' he said cautiously, 'Your arrival here is most fortuitous, for it saves me the trouble of summoning you.'

'Summoning me?'

'Indeed,' Gulptilil said. 'For I have recently been in contact with your boss, the Suffolk County prosecutor. And he is, shall we say, most curious about your presence here, and your progress.' He leaned back with a crocodilian smile. 'But you have a request for me? That has brought you to this office?'

'Yes,' she replied slowly. 'I would like the names and files for all the patients in Williams, in the second-floor dormitory, and if possible, the locations of their beds, so that I can connect names, diagnosis, and location.'

Doctor Gulptilil nodded, still smiling. 'Yes. This would be from the dormitory that is in such upheaval now, thanks to your prior inquiries?'

'Yes.'

'The turmoil you have already created will take some time to settle down. If I do give you this information, will you promise me that before engaging in any other activities in that area of the hospital, you will inform me first?'

Lucy gritted her teeth together. 'Yes. In fact, I would like to have that entire location searched.'

'Searched? You mean you want to go through and inspect what few private things those patients own?'

'Yes. I believe there remains hard criminal evidence available, and I have reason to believe that some might be located in that dormitory, so I would like your permission to search it.'

'Evidence? And upon what do you base this supposition?'

Lucy hesitated, then said, 'I have been reliably informed that one of the patients in that area was in possession of a bloodstained shirt. The nature of the wound to Short Blond suggests that whoever committed the crime would have clothing marred with her blood.'

'Yes. That would make sense. But didn't the police discover some bloody items on poor Lanky when he was arrested?'

'My belief is that those modest amounts were transferred by another person to his body.'

Doctor Gulptilil smiled. 'Ah,' he said. 'Of course. Transferred by this latter-day Jack the Ripper. A criminal genius, no, sorry, I apologize. That's not the word. A criminal *mastermind*. Right here in our mental hospital. No? Farfetched and unlikely, but an explanation that would permit your inquiries to persist. And of this alleged bloody shirt . . . might I see it?'

'It is not in my control.'

He nodded his head. 'Somehow, Miss Jones, I anticipated your response to that question. So, were I to allow this search you request, would this not create some legal problems with any potential items seized?'

'No. This is a state hospital, and you have the right to search any area for contraband or any banned substance or item. I would merely ask you to engage in that routine, within my presence.'

Gulptilil rocked in his chair for a moment. 'So, now,

suddenly, you believe my staff and I can be of some assistance?'

'I don't know that I understand the implication in what you say,' she responded, which was, of course, a lawyer's lie, for she understood completely what he was saying.

Doctor Gulptilil obviously saw the same thing, for he sighed. 'Ah, Miss Jones, your lack of trust for the staff here is most discouraging. Regardless, I will arrange for the search, as you request, if only to help persuade you of the folly of your inquiries. And the names and the bedding arrangements at Williams, these, too, I can provide. And then, perhaps, we can conclude your stay here.'

She remembered what Francis had asked, and so she added, 'One other thing. Might I have the list of patients scheduled for release hearings this week? If it's not a burden . . .'

He looked askance at her. 'Yes. I can give you that, as well. As part of my efforts to support your inquiries, I will have my secretary provide these documents.' The doctor had the ability to easily make a lie seem like the truth, a quality that Lucy Jones found unsettling. 'Although, I am not sure what possible connection our regularly scheduled release hearings might have to your inquiry. Would you be willing to connect those particular dots for me, Miss Jones?'

'I'd rather not, not quite yet.'

'Your response doesn't surprise me,' he said stiffly. 'Still, I will get the list you request.'

She nodded her head. 'Thank you,' and started to leave.

Gulptilil held up his hand. 'But there is something I must ask of you, Miss Jones.'

'What is that, Doctor?'

'You are to call your supervisor. The gentleman that I had such a pleasant conversation with not so long ago.

Now, I would wager, would be a good moment for that call to take place. Allow me.'

He reached down and turned the telephone on his desk toward her, so that she could dial. He made no effort to leave.

★ ★ ★

Lucy's ears still rang with the admonitions of her boss. *A waste of time* and *just spinning your wheels* had been the least of his complaints. The most insistent was *Show some real progress promptly, or else get back here as soon as possible*. There had been an angry litany of the cases on her desk that were piling up, unattended, matters that demanded urgent attention. She had tried to explain to him that the mental hospital was an unusual place to try to conduct an investigation, and not the sort of atmosphere that lent itself to the usual tried-and-true techniques, but he wasn't very interested in hearing these excuses. *Come up with something in the next few days, or we're going to pull the plug*. That had been the last thing he'd said. She wondered how much her boss had been poisoned by his earlier conversation with Gulptilil, but it was irrelevant. He was a blustery, devil-may-care, hell-bent Boston Irishman, and when persuaded that there was something to pursue, was single-minded in his intensity, a quality that got him reelected over and over again. But he was just as quick to drop an inquiry, as soon as it hit his rather low tolerance for frustration, which, she thought, was a political expediency, but didn't help her much.

And, she had to admit, that the sort of progress that a politician could point to was elusive. She couldn't even prove the links between the cases, other than the style of murders. It was a situation that lent itself to complete insanity, she thought. It was clear to her that the killer of Short Blond, the Angel who'd terrorized Francis, and the man who'd committed the killings in her own district were the same. And that he was right there, under her nose, taunting her.

Killing the Dancer was clearly his work. He knew it, she knew it. It all made sense.

But no sense, at the very same time. Criminal arrests and prosecutions aren't based on what you know, but on what you can prove, and so far, she couldn't prove anything.

She realized that for the moment, the Angel remained untouchable. Lost in a tangle of thoughts, she made her way back to the Amherst Building. The early evening had a touch of chill in the air, and some vacant, lost cries reverberated around the hospital grounds, and Lucy was unaware that whatever agony was attached to any of these plaintive noises evaporated in the cooling air around her. Had she not been so wrapped up in the impossibility of her own beliefs, she might have noticed that the sounds that had so upset her when she first arrived at Western State had now disappeared within her into some location of acceptance, so much so that she was slowly becoming something of a fixture in the hospital herself, a mere tangent to all the madness that lived so unhappily there.

★　★　★

Peter looked up and realized that something was out of place, but couldn't quite put his finger on it. That was the problem with the hospital; everything was twisted around, backward, distorted or misshapen. Seeing accurately was nearly impossible. For an instant, he longed for the simplicity of a fire scene. There had been a sort of freedom in walking amid the charred, wet, and smelly remains of one fire or another, and slowly picturing in his mind's eye precisely how the fire was started, and how it had progressed, from floor to walls

457

to ceiling to roof, accelerated by one fuel or another. There was a certain mathematical precision in dissecting a fire, and it had given him a great amount of satisfaction, holding burnt wood or scorched steel in his hands, feeling residual warmth flowing through his palms, and knowing that he would be able to imagine everything that was destroyed as it had been in the seconds before the fire took grasp. It was like the ability to see into the past, only clearly, without the fogs of emotion and stress. Everything was on the map of the event, and he longed for the easier time where he could follow each route to a precise destination. He had always thought of himself like one of the artists whose duty it was to restore great paintings damaged by time or the elements, painstakingly recreating the colors and brushstrokes of so many ancient geniuses, following in the path of a Rembrandt or Da Vinci, a lesser artist, but a crucial one.

To his right, a man wearing loose-fitting hospital clothes, disheveled and unkempt, burst out into raucous, braying laugh, as he looked down and saw that he had wet his own pants. Patients were lining up for their evening medications, and he saw Big Black and Little Black trying to keep some order in the process. It was a little like trying to organize stormy waves that were pounding a beach; everything ended up in more or less the same place, but everyone was being driven by forces that were as elusive as winds and currents.

Peter shuddered and thought: *I've got to get out of this place*. He did not think himself crazy yet, but he knew that many of his actions could be seen as mad, and, the longer he stayed in the hospital, the more they would dominate his existence. It made him sweat, and he understood there were people — Mister Evil for one — who would happily see him disintegrate at the hospital. He was fortunate; he still clung to all sorts of vestiges of sanity. The other patients gave him some respect, knowing that he wasn't as mad as they. But that could end. He could start hearing the same voices that they did. Start shuffling, start mumbling, wet his pants and line up for medication. It was all right there and he knew if he did not escape, he would get sucked in.

Whatever the Church was offering, he knew he had to take it.

He looked around, eyeing each patient as they crowded forward, heading toward the nursing station and the rows of medications lined up behind the iron grating.

One of them was a killer. He knew this.

Or maybe one lining up at the same time, over in Williams or Princeton or Harvard, but moving to the same schedule, was the killer.

But how to pick him out?

He tried to think of the case as he would have an arson, and he leaned back against the wall, trying to see where it started, because that would tell him how it had gained momentum, took flower and finally exploded. It was how he processed every fire scene he was called to; work backward to the first little flicker of flame, and that would tell him not only how the fire occurred, but who was standing there, watching it. He supposed it was a curious gift. In olden times kings and princes surrounded themselves with folks who purportedly could see into the future, wasting their time and money, when understanding the past was probably a much better way of seeing what lay ahead.

Peter slowly exhaled. The hospital had a way of making one dwell on all the thoughts that echoed within him. He stopped in midthought, realizing that he had been moving his lips as he spoke with himself.

Again, he breathed out. Close. Almost talking to yourself.

He looked down at his hands, for no real reason other than to reassure himself that he was still intact. Get out, he told himself. Whatever you have to do, just get out.

But as he reached this conclusion, he saw Lucy Jones enter the corridor. She had her head down, and he could see that she was both deep in her own thoughts and upset. And, in that second, he saw a future that frightened him, leaving him with an empty, helpless feeling. He would exit, disappearing off to some program in Oregon. She would exit, returning to her office and the steady processing of crime after crime. Francis would be left behind, with Napoleon, Cleo, and the Moses brothers.

Lanky would go to prison.

And the Angel would find someone else's fingers to take.

26

Francis spent an unsettled night, sometimes laying rigid on his bunk, listening for any sound that was out of the ordinary in the dormitory that would signal the return of the Angel to his bedside. Dozens of these noises penetrated past his squeezed-shut eyes, echoing as deep as his own heartbeat. A hundred times he thought he felt the Angel's hot breath against his forehead, and the sensation of the cold knife blade was never far from his memory. Even in the few moments when he slid inexorably away from the night fears that had driven him to sweat and anxiety, into a semblance of sleep, his rest was disturbed by frightening images. He imagined Lucy holding up her own hand, mutilated like Short Blond's. Then, this image evaporated into one of himself, and he'd felt as if his own throat had been slashed and he was in his nether state desperately trying to hold the gaping wound together.

He welcomed the first morning light that slithered through the windowpanes, past the metal bars and grates, if only to signal that the hours when the Angel seemed to own the hospital were finished. For a moment he remained in his bunk, clinging to the oddest of thoughts, which was some half-finished notion that it was somehow wrong for the patients in the hospital to have the same fears of dying as the normal people outside the walls. Inside the walls, life seemed to be much more tenuous, it didn't seem to have precisely the same quotient as outside. It was, he thought, as if they didn't amount to as much, and were not quite as valuable and therefore shouldn't put such a high price on their lives. He remembered reading in a newspaper once, that the sum total value of the parts of the human body only amounted to something like a dollar or two. He thought to himself that the inmates of Western State were probably worth just pennies. If even that.

Francis went to the washroom and cleaned up, readying himself for the day. He felt a little comforted by the familiar signs of life in the hospital; Little Black and his huge brother were out in the corridor trying to get patients to make their way to the dining room for breakfast, a little like a pair of mechanics tweaking an engine, trying to get it to turn over and start running. He saw Mister Evil cruising the hallway, ignoring the entreaties from various folks about one problem or another. Francis wanted to embrace the routine.

And then, as quickly as this thought hit him, he feared it.

It was how the days slipped away. The hospital, with its compulsion for simply getting through time, was like a drug, even more powerful than those that came as pills or hypodermics. With addiction, came oblivion.

Francis shook his head, for one thing was clear to him: The Angel was much closer to the world outside, and he suspected that if he ever wanted to rejoin it, that was the mountain he would have to climb. He thought: Finding Short Blond's killer might be the only sane act left in the entire world to him.

Inside his head, his voices were a jumble of turmoil. They were clearly trying to tell him something, but it was as if they couldn't all agree on precisely what it was.

One warning did come through, however. All the voices agreed that were he to be left behind to face the Angel alone, without Peter and Lucy, he was not likely to survive. He didn't know how he would die, or precisely when. Sometime on the Angel's own timetable. Murdered in his bed. Smothered like the Dancer or throat slashed like Short Blond or perhaps some other way of killing that he hadn't considered yet, but it would happen.

There would be no place to hide, other than to descend into some greater madness, which forced the hospital to lock him up each day, all day, in one of the isolation cells.

He looked around for his two fellow investigators, and thought, for the first time, that it was time for him to answer the questions that the Angel kept asking.

Francis slumped up against the corridor wall. *It's there. It's right there in front of you!* He looked up and saw Cleo steaming up the corridor, arms waving, like a great gray battleship slicing through a regatta of timid sailboats. Whatever was disturbing her this morning was lost in an avalanche of obscenities muttered in tempo with the wildly swinging arms, so that each 'God-damn!' 'Motherfuckers!' 'Sons of bitches!' was issued like the stroke of a clock. Patients shrank aside as she cruised past, and in that second Francis saw something. *It's not that the Angel knows how to be different. It's that he knows how to be the same.*

When he looked up, in Cleo's wake, he saw Peter. The Fireman seemed to be engaged in a heated conversation with Mister Evil, who was shaking his head negatively, back and forth, as Peter inched first closer to the psychologist, then back. After a moment, Mister Evil seemed to dismiss what Peter had to say, and turned on his heel and cruised back down the corridor. Peter, left standing, raised his voice and shouted after Mister Evil, 'You need to tell Gulptilil! Today.' And then he quieted. Mister Evil kept his back turned, as if to refuse to acknowledge what Peter had shouted. Francis peeled himself off the wall, and quickly went over to the Fireman.

'Peter?' Francis asked.

'Hey, C-Bird,' Peter responded, looking up a little like someone who has been interrupted. 'What is it?'

Francis whispered. 'Peter, when you look at us, the rest of the patients here, what do you see?'

463

He hesitated, then responded, 'I don't know, Francis. It's a little bit like Alice in Wonderland. Everything is curiouser and curiouser.'

'But you've seen all the types of crazy that there are in here, haven't you?'

Peter hesitated, suddenly bending forward. Lucy was coming down the corridor, and Peter gave her a little wave, as he stepped closer to Francis. 'C-Bird sees something,' he said quietly. 'What is it?'

'The man we're looking for,' Francis whispered, just as Lucy hovered close, 'is no more crazy than you. But he's hiding by pretending to be something else.'

'Keep going,' Peter said softly.

'All of his madness, at least, the murdering madness and the finger-cutting madness, all that isn't like any of the regular craziness we have in here. He plans. He thinks. It's all about being evil, just like Lanky kept saying. It's not about hearing voices or being deluded, or anything else. But in here, he hides because no one would think to look at him and not see a crazy person, but instead see something evil . . . '

Francis shook his head, as if speaking the thoughts that were echoing inside of him was painful.

'What are you saying. C-Bird? What do you think?' Peter had lowered his voice some.

'What I'm saying is that we went all over all those admissions forms and conducted all those interviews because we're looking for something that connects someone in here with the outside world. You and Lucy, what were you searching for? Men with violence in their past. Psychopaths. Men with obvious anger. Police records. Maybe people hearing voices that order them to do evil things to women. You want to find someone who is both crazy and criminal, right?'

Lucy finally spoke up. 'That's the only approach that makes sense . . . '

'But in here, *everyone* has some crazy impulse or

another. And any number of them could be killers, right? *Everyone* is walking some sort of thin line in here.'

'Yes, but . . . ' Lucy was chewing on what Francis was saying.

Francis pivoted toward her. 'But don't you think the Angel knows that, too?'

She didn't reply to this.

Francis took a deep breath. 'The Angel is someone with nothing in his record that anyone could point to. On the outside, he's one person. In here, he's something else. Like a chameleon who changes color with his surroundings. And he's someone we would never think of looking at. That's how he can be safe. And that's how he can do what he wants.'

Peter looked skeptical and Lucy, too, wore a look that seemed to need more convincing. She spoke first, 'So, Francis, you think the Angel is faking his mental illness?' She let this question drag out and linger, as if in the word *faking* she had already implied the impossibility of that action.

Francis shook his head, and then nodded. Contradictions that seemed so clear to him weren't to the other two. 'He can't fake voices. He can't fake delusions. He couldn't fake being . . . ' Francis took a deep breath, before continuing, ' . . . like me. The doctors could see through that. Even Mister Evil would recognize that before too long.'

'So?' Peter asked.

'Look around,' Francis answered. He pointed across the hallway to where the large, hulking retarded man who'd been transferred from Williams was leaning against the wall, clutching his Raggedy Andy doll and crooning softly to the gaily colored bits of fabric with its jaunty hat and crooked smile. Then Francis saw a Cato standing motionless in the center of the corridor, eyes raised to the ceiling, as if his vision could penetrate the soundproofing, the support beams, the flooring and furniture on the second floor, straight through, past everything, right through the roof and up into the morning blue sky above. 'How hard,' Francis asked quietly, 'would it be to be dumb? Or quiet? And if you were like one of them, who in here would ever pay any attention to you?'

★ ★ ★

Howling, screeching, caterwauling noise like a hundred screaming feral cats scraped at every nerve ending in my body. Clammy, moist sweat dripped down between my eyes, blinding me, stinging. I was short of breath, wheezing like a sick man, my hands quivering. I barely trusted my voice to make any sound other than a low, helpless moan.

The Angel hovered next to me, spitting with rage.

He did not have to say why, for every word I'd written told him.

I twisted on the floor, as if some electric current were charging through my body. They never gave me electric shock treatment at Western State. Probably that was the only cruelty masquerading as a cure that I haven't had to endure. But I suspected the pain that I was in this moment was little different.

I could see.

That was what hurt me.

When I turned in that corridor inside the hospital and spoke those words to Peter and Lucy, it was as if I were opening the one door within myself that I had never wanted to open. The greatest barricaded, nailed shut and sealed tight door within me. When you are mad, you're capable of nothing. But you're also capable of everything. To be caught between the two extremes is agony.

All my life, all I wanted was to be normal. Even

466

tortured, like Peter and Lucy were, but normal. Able to modestly function in the outside world, enjoy the simplest of things. A fine morning. A greeting from a friend. A tasty meal. A routine conversation. A sense of belonging. But I couldn't, because I knew, right in that moment, that I would forever be doomed to be closer in spirit and action to the man I hated and the man that scared me. The Angel was giving in and luxuriating in all the murderous evil thoughts that lurked within me. He was a fun house mirror version of myself. I had the same rage. The same desire. The same evil. I had just concealed it, shunted it away, thrown it into the deepest hole within me that I could find and covered it up with every mad thought, like boulders and dirt, so that it was buried where I hoped it could never burst forth.

In the hospital, the Angel truly made only one mistake.

He should have killed me when he could.

'So,' he whispered in my ear, 'I'm here now to rectify that error in judgment.'

★ ★ ★

'There's no time,' Lucy said. She was staring down at the cluttered files spread across her desk in the makeshift office where her makeshift investigation was centered. Peter was pacing to the side, clearly sorting through all sorts of conflicted thoughts. When she spoke, he looked up, slightly cockeyed at her.

'How so?'

'I'm going to get pulled out of here. Probably within the next few days. I spoke with my boss, and he thinks that I'm just spinning my wheels here. He didn't like the idea of me being here in the first place, but when I insisted, he gave in. That's about to come to a sudden stop . . . '

Peter nodded. 'I'm not going to be here much longer,

either,' he said. 'At least I don't think so.' He didn't elaborate, but did add, 'But Francis will be left behind.'

'Not just Francis,' Lucy said.

'That's right. Not just Francis.' He hesitated. 'Do you think he's right? About the Angel, I mean. Being someone we wouldn't look at . . . '

Lucy took a deep breath. She was clenching her hands tightly, then releasing them, almost in rhythm with her breathing, like someone on the verge of fury, trying to control their emotions. This was an alien concept in the hospital, where so many people gave vent to so many emotions on a near constant basis. Restraint — other than that encouraged by antipsychotic medications — was pretty much impossible. But Lucy seemed to wear some sort of punishment behind her eyes, and when she looked up at Peter, he could see great waves of trouble behind her words.

'I cannot stand it,' she said, very quietly.

He did not respond, for he knew she would explain herself within moments.

Lucy sat down hard on the wooden chair, and then, just as swiftly, stood back up. She leaned forward to grasp the edges of the desk, as if that would steady her from the buffeting winds of her turmoil. When she looked over at Peter, he was unsure whether it was a murderous harshness in her eyes, or something else.

'The idea of leaving a rapist and killer behind in here is almost too much to imagine. Whether or not the Angel and the man who killed the women in my other three cases are one and the same — and I think they are — leaving him in here untouched makes my skin crawl.'

Again, he did not say anything.

'I won't do it,' she said. 'I can't do it.'

'Suppose you're forced to walk away?' Peter asked. He might as well have been asking the same question of himself.

She looked hard at him. 'How do you do that?' she

468

answered, a question to match a question.

There was a momentary silence in the room, and then, suddenly, Lucy looked down at the stack of patient dossiers on the desktop. In a single, abrupt motion, she swept her arm across the desk, dashing the folders against the wall. 'Goddamn it!' she said.

The manila folders made a slapping sound, and papers fluttered to the floor.

Peter kept quiet and Lucy stepped back, took aim with her shoe at a metal wastebasket and sent it skittering across the room with a well-placed kick.

She looked up at Peter. 'I won't do it,' she said. 'Tell me, which is more evil? Being a killer or allowing a killer to kill again?'

There was an answer to this question, but Peter wasn't sure that he wanted to say it out loud.

Lucy took a few deep breaths, before lifting her eyes to where they locked in on Peter's.

'Do you understand, Peter,' she whispered, 'I know in my heart one thing: If I leave here without finding this man, someone else will die. I don't know how long it will be, but sometime, a month, six months, a year from now, I will be standing over another body, staring down at a right hand that's missing four fingers and now a thumb, as well. And all I'll be able to see is the opportunity that I lost, right here. And even if I catch the guy, and see him sitting in a courtroom, and get to stand up and read off the list of charges to a judge and jury, I'll still know that someone died, because I failed here, right at this moment in time.'

Peter finally slumped down in a chair and lowered his own face into his hands, as if he was washing up, but he was not. When he looked up at Lucy, he didn't really address what she said, but then, in his own way, he did.

'You know, Lucy,' he said softly, as if someone might be listening, 'before I became an arson investigator, I spent some time hauling hoses. I liked it, you know.

Fighting a fire is just one of those things that has little ambivalence about it. You put out the fire, or else it destroys something. Simple, right? Sometimes, on a really big, bad blowup, you could feel the heat on your face and hear the sound that a fire makes when it is really out of control. It's an awful, angry sound. Comes straight from hell. And then there's this second when everything in your body says to you 'Don't go in there!' but you do, anyway. You go ahead, because the fire is bad, and because the other members of your brigade are already inside, and you simply know that you have to. It's the hardest easy decision you can ever make.'

Lucy seemed to consider what Peter said, and then asked. 'So what about now?'

'I think,' he said slowly, 'that we're going to have to take some chances.'

'Chances?'

'Yes.'

'What about what Francis said,' she continued. 'You think in here everything is upside down? If we were on the outside, doing this investigation, and a detective came to us and said we need to look at the *least* likely suspect, not the *most* likely, I would, of course, pretty much have that guy fired from the case. It makes no sense at all, and if nothing else, investigations are supposed to make sense.'

'Nothing in here really makes sense,' Peter said.

'Which is why Francis is probably right. He's been right about a bunch of things, anyway.'

'So, what do we do? Go over every hospital file again searching for . . . ' He paused, then asked, ' . . . Searching for what?'

'What else can we do?'

Peter hesitated again, thinking hard about what had happened. After a moment, he shrugged a little and shook his head. 'I don't know,' he said slowly. 'I'm reluctant . . . '

'Reluctant for what?'

'Well, when we shook up the Williams housing unit, what happened?'

'A man got killed. Except they don't think so . . . '

'No, beyond that, what happened? The Angel emerged. He came out to kill the Dancer — maybe. We don't know for certain. But we do know that he showed up in the dormitory room to threaten Francis with his knife.'

Lucy took a deep breath. 'I think I see what you're driving at.'

'We need to get him to come out. Again.'

She nodded. 'A trap.'

Peter agreed. 'A trap. But what would we use for bait?'

Lucy smiled. But it wasn't the sort of smile that implied something funny. It was more the devil-may-care look of someone who understands that to accomplish much, much needs to be risked.

⋆　⋆　⋆

Early in the afternoon Big Black collected a small squad of Amherst Building residents for a sortie out to the garden area. It had been some time since Francis had seen the results of the seeds they had planted in the hospital gardening area, before Short Blond's death and Lanky's arrest.

It was a fine afternoon. Warm, with shafts of light energetically bouncing off the white trim paint on the side of the hospital buildings. A light breeze that sent the occasional bulbous white cloud skidding across the expanse of blue sky. Francis lifted his face toward the sunlight, letting the heat enter him, and hearing a murmuring of satisfaction within his head that might have been his voices speaking, but just as easily could have been a small sense of hope creeping into his

471

imagination. For a few minutes he believed he could forget everything that was taking place around him, and luxuriate in the sunshine. It was the sort of afternoon that made all the darknesses of being mad seem a little distant.

There were ten patients on this particular outdoor trip. Cleo started out in the front of their lineup, having taken the lead as soon as they stepped out of the doors of Amherst, still muttering, but surging forward, with a purposefulness that seemed in opposition to the laziness that was part of the day. Napoleon at first tried to keep pace with her, but failed, and then complained to Big Black that Cleo was making them march too fast, which made all of them come to a stop on the pathway and created a bit of an argument.

'I should be first!' Cleo shouted out angrily. She lifted herself up haughtily, looking down at the others with a regal attitude that stemmed from some wayward thoughts within her. 'It's my position. My right and my duty!' she added.

'Then don't go so fast,' Napoleon countered, wheezing slightly, his portly frame shaking.

'We will move at my speed,' she replied.

Big Black looked exasperated. 'Cleo, please . . . ,' he started, and she pivoted to him.

'All applications are inappropriate,' she said.

Big Black shrugged and turned to Francis. 'You lead the way,' he said.

For a moment, Cleo stepped into Francis's path, but he looked at her with such a hangdog look of resignation that after a second, she snorted with imperial disdain and moved to the side. As he stepped past her, he could see that her eyes were aflame, as if her thoughts within her head were being singed by some out of control fire. He hoped that Big Black saw the same, but he wasn't sure, as the attendant was trying to keep the group in some semblance of organization. One man was already crying, and another woman was wandering off the pathway.

Francis stepped out and said, 'Let's go,' hoping that the others would follow. After a moment, the group seemed to accept Francis in the head position, probably because it defused a potential shouting match that no one particularly wanted. Cleo dropped into place behind him, and after urging him to speed up a few times, was distracted by catcalls and disjointed cries that echoed between the buildings.

They stopped at the edge of the garden, and whatever tension seemed to be building in Cleo's head, seemed to quiet for just one moment. 'Flowers!' she said in astonishment. 'We've grown flowers!'

Tangled clumps of reds and whites, yellows, blues, and greens all twisted together haphazardly through the muddy quadrant of the hospital grounds edge. Peonies, baby's breath, violets, and tulips had sprung from the murky soil. The garden was as chaotic as any of their minds, with sheets and slices of vibrant color heading in every direction, planted without order or organization, but flowering wildly nevertheless. Francis stared, a little astonished, reminded in that instant how drab their lives truly were. But even this depressing thought was shunted aside, in exuberant delight over the growth in front of him.

Within a few seconds, Big Black had distributed some modest gardening tools. They were children's implements, made out of plastic, and they didn't do particularly well at what the task at hand was, but still, Francis thought, they were better then nothing. He plunked himself down next to Cleo, who seemed barely aware of his presence, and started working at organizing the flowers into rows, trying to bring some order to the explosion of color surrounding them.

Francis was unaware how long they worked. Even Cleo, still muttering obscenities to herself, seemed to

473

put some of her stress on hold, although she occasionally sobbed as she dug and scraped in the moist loam of the garden, and more than once Francis saw her reach out and touch the fragile blooms of one flower with tears in her eyes. Almost all the patients at one point paused and let the rich, damp dirt dribble through their fingers. There was a smell of renewal, and vitality, and Francis thought the fragrance filled him with more optimism than any of the antipsychotic drugs they were forever ingesting.

When he rose, after Big Black finally announced that the sortie was over, he stared down at the garden, and had to admit that it looked better. Almost all the weeds that threatened the flower beds had been plucked out; some definition had been imposed upon the rows. It was, Francis thought, a little like seeing a painting that was still only half-completed. There was form and possibility.

He tried to dust some of the dirt from his hands and clothes, but only half-heartedly. He found he didn't mind the sensation of being filthy, at least not on that afternoon.

Big Black arranged the group into a single line, and returned the plastic gardening tools to a green wooden box, counting them at least three times as he did so. Then, as he was about to give the signal to start back down the pathway to Amherst, he stopped, and Francis saw the huge attendant's gaze focus on a small group that was gathering about fifty yards away, on the very edge of the hospital property, behind a wire fence.

'That's the cemetery,' Napoleon whispered. Then he, like all the others, quieted.

Francis could see Doctor Gulptilil and Mister Evans and two other senior staff. There was also a priest, wearing a collar and several workmen in gray hospital maintenance uniforms gripping shovels, or leaning on the shafts, awaiting a command. As the group gathered together, Francis heard a chugging, diesel noise, and he saw a small backhoe being driven over to where the group was standing. Behind the backhoe there was a single black Cadillac station wagon, which with a shock, Francis recognized as a hearse.

The hearse came to a stop, and the backhoe shuddered forward. Big Black muttered, 'Maybe we should leave,' but remained rooted to his spot. The other patients lined up to watch.

It didn't take more than a couple of minutes for the backhoe, making all the mechanical grunting noises of machinery at work, to carve out a hole in the ground and deposit a modest pile of dirt beside it. The hospital maintenance men worked at the sides with shovels, preparing the hole. Francis saw Gulp-a-pill step forward, examine the work, and signal the men to stop. Then, with a second wave, he directed the hearse to pull forward. It did, parking a few feet away. Two men in black suits stepped out and walked to the rear, opening up the back. They were joined by four of the maintenance men, and this motley group of pallbearers removed a plain metal coffin from the back. The late afternoon sun glistened dully against the coffin's lid.

'It's the Dancer,' Napoleon whispered.

'Motherfuckers,' Cleo said quietly. 'Murdering, killing fascists.' Then, she added, sonorously, in theatrical tones, 'Let's bury him in the high Roman fashion.'

The six men struggled forward with the coffin, which Francis thought was odd, because the Dancer had hardly weighed anything at all. He watched them lower it into the grave, then step aside while the priest said a few perfunctory words. He saw that none of the men had even bothered to lower their heads in mock prayer.

The priest stepped back, the doctors turned and headed up the pathway and the funeral parlor assistants had Doctor Gulptilil sign some paper before they returned to the hearse and drove slowly off. The backhoe followed with a chugging noise. Two of the maintenance men started shoveling dirt from the pile onto the coffin. Francis could hear the thudding sound of clumps of dirt hitting the steel, but even that faded after a moment.

'Let's go,' Big Black said. 'Francis?'

He realized he was supposed to lead the way, which he did, slowly, although he could feel Cleo's presence pressuring him to move quicker with every stride. Her breathing was coming in short, machine-gun–like bursts.

Their bedraggled parade had only made it partway back to Amherst when suddenly, with a sort of mangled half curse, half gurgle, Cleo pushed right past Francis. Her bulk swayed and jiggled as she rushed forward down the path, torpedoing in the direction of the back side of the Williams housing unit. She surged to a halt on a grassy spot, where she peered up into the windows.

The late afternoon light was dropping fast against the side of the building, so that Francis couldn't see the faces gathered behind the glass. Instead, each window frame seemed to be like an eye staring out of a blank, opaque face. The building was like so many of the patients; it gazed out flat and unaffected, concealing all the electric turmoil within.

Cleo gathered herself together, put her hands on her hips and shouted: 'I see you!'

This was impossible. The reflected light blinded her, as it did Francis. She continued, raising her voice further.

'I know who you are! You killed him! I saw you and I know all about you!'

Big Black pushed past Francis. 'Cleo!' he cried out. 'Hush! What're you saying?'

She ignored him. She lifted a single accusatory finger and pointed it up toward the second floor of the Williams Building.

'Killers!' she shouted. 'Murderers!'

'Cleo, Goddamn it!' Big Black thrust himself to her side. 'Shut the hell up!'

'Animals! Fiends! Motherfucking, fascist murderers!'

Big Black reached out and grasped the bulky woman by the arm, spinning her toward him. He started to open his mouth and shout into her face, but Francis saw the huge attendant stop short, regain some composure, and whisper to her, instead, 'Cleo, please, what are you doing?'

She huffed toward Big Black. 'They killed him,' she said, matter-of-factly.

'Who killed who?' Big Black asked, spinning her so that her back was to Williams. 'What you mean?'

Cleo cackled a bit, grinning wildly.

'Marc Anthony,' she said. 'Act four, Scene sixteen.'

Still laughing, she let Big Black lead her away. Francis stared up at Williams. He didn't know who might have heard the outburst. Or what they might have interpreted it to mean.

Francis did not see Lucy Jones, who was standing not far away, beneath a tree, on the pathway that led past the administration building to the front gate. She also had witnessed Cleo's explosion of accusations. But she did not give them much thought, because she was far too centered on the errand that she was about to run, which would, for the first time in days, take her on a brief excursion outside the hospital gates and into the nearby town. She watched as the single file of patients made its way back into the Amherst Building, then she turned and rapidly headed out, believing it would not take her long to find the few items that she needed.

27

Lucy sat quietly on the edge of her bed in the nurse-trainees' dormitory, letting the deep night creep slowly past her. She had spread out on the bedspread the items that she had purchased late that afternoon, but instead of examining them closely, she was staring off into the vacuum around her, as she had done for several hours. When she rose, she walked into the small bathroom, where she began to inspect her face carefully in the mirror above the sink.

She lifted her hair away from her forehead with one hand, and with the other, traced the ridges of the scar, stretching from just beneath the hairline, bisecting the eyebrow, skewing sideways slightly, where the blade had just missed her eyeball, then traveling down her cheek and ending at her chin. Where the skin had knitted together, it was just slightly lighter than the rest of her complexion. In a couple of spots the slice was barely noticeable. In others, painfully obvious. She thought that she had grown oddly familiar with the scar, and accepted it for what it represented. Once, several years back, on a date that had started with promise with an overly self-assured young doctor, he had offered to put her in touch with a prominent plastic surgeon, whom, he insisted, could fix her face so that so one would ever know she'd been cut. She had neither contacted the plastic surgeon nor ever gone out on another date with that or any other doctor.

Lucy thought of herself as the sort of person who continues to define existence every day. The man who had put the scar on her face and stolen her privacy had thought he was damaging her, she told herself, when, in reality all he had done was give her focus and purpose.

There were many men behind bars because of what that one man had done to her one night during her law school days. She told herself that it would be some time before the debt — that outrage to her heart and body was owed — would be paid in full. Single immense moments, Lucy thought, steered one through life. What made her uncomfortable in the hospital was how the patients weren't necessarily confined by a single act, but by great accumulations of infinitesimally small incidents, all of which sent them hurtling into their depressions or schizophrenia, psychosis, bipolar diseases, and obsessive-compulsive behavior. Peter, she recognized, was much closer to her in spirit and temperament. He, too, had let a single moment shape his entire life. His, of course, had been rash impulse. Even if justifiable, on one level, it was still the product of a momentary lack of control. Hers was far colder, far more calculated and, for lack of a more correct term: revenge.

She had a sudden, harsh memory, the sort that enters unbidden into one's imagination and nearly slices one's breath away: In Massachusetts General hospital, where she'd been taken after she had been discovered sobbing, bleeding, stumbling about haphazardly in a quadrangle between buildings by a pair of undergraduate physics majors coming home late from a lab, the police had questioned her closely, while a nurse and a doctor had performed the rape examination. The detectives had stood up by her head, while the physician and assistant had worked in quiet in a different realm all together, below her waist. *Did you see the man?* No. Not really. He wore a tight ski mask and all I could see were his eyes. *Could you recognize him again?* No. *Why were you walking alone at night across campus?* I don't know. I'd been in the library studying and it was time to go home. *What can you tell us that will help us to catch him?* Silence.

479

Of all the terrors that had been delivered to her that night, she thought the one that had undeniably stayed with her was the scar on her face. She had been almost comatose from shock, her mind fleeing from her body, separating itself from sensation, and then he had cut her. He did not kill her — he could have easily done that. Nor was there any overt need to do anything else. She was almost unconscious and lost, and he had more than ample opportunity to flee undetected and unobserved. But instead, he'd leaned down, marked her forever, and then through the fog of pain and insult, she'd heard him whisper a single word in her ear: *Remember*.

The word had hurt more than the cut across her beauty.

So she did, but not she thought, in the way the man that assaulted her expected.

If she could not put the man who had scarred her in prison, she could put dozens of similar men there. If she regretted anything, it was that the assault had stolen what remained of innocence and lightheartedness from her life. Laughter came much harder afterward and love seemed impossible to attain. But, she often told herself, she was likely to have lost those qualities soon enough anyway. She had become monklike in her pursuit of evils.

She stared into the mirror and slowly put all her memories back into the compartments where she kept them filed in an orderly and acceptable fashion. What had happened once, was finished now, she told herself. She knew the man she hunted in the hospital was as close to the one man who haunted her actions as any that she'd stared down across a courtroom. Finding the Angel would do much more, she thought, than merely stop a repetitive killer from striking again.

She felt a little like an athlete, centering herself on the single purpose of the moment.

'A trap,' she said out loud. 'A trap needs bait.'

She moved her hand through the cascade of black hair that framed her face, letting it drip between her fingers like raindrops.

Short hair.

Blond hair.

All four victims had worn hair that was styled noticeably short. They had all approximated much the same physical characteristics. They had all been killed in the same fashion, the same murder weapon used in each case and the throat slashed left to right the same way. The postmortem mutilations to the hands had been the same. Then their bodies were abandoned in similar settings. Even the last victim, there in the hospital, when she considered the storage room that had housed the nurse-trainee's last seconds, she could see the way that the killer had replicated the rural, forest locations of the other killings. And, she remembered, he'd compromised the physical evidence with water and cleaning fluid in the same way that nature had unwittingly abetted him with the first three homicides.

He was here, she knew this. She suspected that she'd even looked directly into his eyes, at some point during her days in the hospital, but hadn't seen him for what he was. This thought made her shudder, but also seemed to stoke the fury that was building within her.

She stared at the strands of black hair that she held like so many delicate spiderwebs in her fingers.

A small price to pay, she thought.

She turned abruptly and returned to the bed. The first thing she did was remove a small black suitcase from where she had stored it beneath the frame. The suitcase had a combination lock, which she dialed and opened up. There was a second, zippered pocket inside, and this she opened as well, drawing forth a deep brown leather holster which held a snub-nosed .38 caliber revolver. She hefted the pistol in her hand for a moment, feeling its heft and weight. She had fired this weapon less than a half-dozen times in the years that she had owned it, and it felt unfamiliar, but incisive in her hand. Then, with a single, determined motion, she scooped up the remaining items gathered on the bedspread: A hairbrush. A pair of barber's scissors. A box of hair dye.

Her hair would grow back in time, she told herself.

And the great sheen of black that she'd known for the entirety of her life would return before too long.

Telling herself that there was nothing permanent in what she was doing, but what could be permanent was not doing enough to find the Angel right then, right at that moment, she took all the items into the bathroom and arranged them all in front of her on a small shelf. Then she lifted the scissors and half expecting to see blood flowing, began to saw away at her hair.

★   ★   ★

One of the tricks that Francis had learned, over all the years since the first day in his childhood when he'd first heard voices, was how to find the one that made the most sense in the symphony of discord within his head. He had come to know that his own madness was defined by his ability to sort through everything that came rushing at him from inside, and make his path ahead as best he could. It wasn't exactly logical, but there was some practicality in what he had learned to do.

He told himself that the situation in the hospital was not all that different. A detective takes many disparate clues and pieces them together into a consistent whole, he thought to himself. He was persuaded that everything that he needed to know in order to paint the portrait that would become the Angel had already taken place, but somehow, in the wildly fluctuating, erratic world of the mental hospital, the context had been hidden.

Francis looked over at Peter, who was dashing cold water onto his face at a washbasin. *He will never see what I can see* Francis told himself. There was a chorus within him of agreement.

But before he could go any further with this thinking, Francis saw Peter pull himself off the basin, look up at himself in a mirror and shake his head, as if displeased with what he saw in the reflection. At the same time, Peter saw Francis hovering behind him and smiled. 'Ah, C-Bird. Top of the morning to you. We have survived another night here, which, upon reflection and on balance, is no small feat and an accomplishment that should be celebrated with a hearty, if not all together tasty, breakfast. What do you suppose this fine day will bring?'

Francis shook his head to indicate he was unsure.

'Maybe some progress?'

'Maybe.'

'Maybe something good?'

'Unlikely.'

Peter laughed. 'Francis, buddy, there's no pill and certainly no shot they can give you in here to reduce or remove a sense of cynicism.'

Francis nodded. 'None that can give you optimism, either.'

'Touché,' Peter said. He lost the grin he wore, and leaned toward Francis. 'We'll make some headway today, I promise.' Then he smiled again, and added, '*Headway*. That's a little bit of a joke. You'll get it soon enough.'

Francis had no idea what he was talking about, but asked, 'How can you promise that?'

'Because Lucy thinks a different approach might work.'

'A different approach?'

Peter looked around for a moment, then whispered, 'If you cannot bring yourself to the man you're hunting, perhaps you can bring the man to you.'

Francis recoiled slightly, as if pummeled by the noise within him of dozens of voices screaming danger. Peter did not notice the sudden shift in Francis's appearance, like the abrupt approach of a storm cloud on a distant horizon, as the younger man chewed over what Peter had said. Instead, he clapped Francis on the back and sardonically added, 'Come on. Let's eat soggy pancakes or runny eggs and see what starts to unfold. Big day, today, I'm guessing, C-Bird. Keep your eyes and ears open.'

The two of them stepped from the washroom, to where the men of the dormitory were starting to stumble and shuffle out of the doorway into the corridor. The start of the daily routine. Francis was more than a little unsure what it was that he was supposed to be watching out for, but any questions he might have had were instantly erased in that moment by the high-pitched, shrill and desperate scream that furiously echoed down the hallway, reverberating in the air around them with a complete helplessness that chilled everyone who heard it.

★ ★ ★

It is easy to remember that scream.

I have thought about it many times, over many years. There are screams of fear, screams of shock, screams that speak of anxiety, tension, and some even of despair. This seemed to mingle all those qualities together into something so hopeless and terrifying that it defied reason and comfort, amplified by all the terrors of the mental hospital rolled together. A mother's scream of danger closing in on her child. A soldier's scream of pain as he sees his wound and knows it speaks of death. Something ancient and animal that emerges only in the rarest and most fearsome of moments. It was as if something fixed firmly in the center of things was suddenly, abruptly gone, and it was too much to bear.

I never learned who emitted that scream, but it became a part of all of us who heard it. And stayed with us, no matter how much time had passed.

I pushed out into the corridor directly behind Peter, who was moving quickly toward the sound. I was only peripherally aware of some of the others, who were shrinking to the sides, hugging the walls. I saw Napoleon pushing himself into a corner and Newsman, suddenly not curious in the slightest, huddling down as if he could cloak himself from the vibrant noise. Peter's footsteps resounded against the corridor floor, as he picked up his pace, and hurried down the path of the echo toward the source of the scream. I caught just the smallest look at his face, which was set with a sudden harshness and clarity that was unfamiliar in the hospital. It was as if the sound had triggered some immense worry within him, and he was trying to outdistance all the fears that accompanied it.

The scream had come from the far end of the corridor, past the entrance to the women's dormitory. But the memory of the scream was as real in my mind as it was that morning in the Amherst Building. It curled around me, like smoke from a fire, and I grasped my pencil and wrote furiously on the wall of my apartment, fearing every second that the Angel's great mocking laughter would supplant it in my recollection, and I needed to get it down before that took place. In my imagination, I could see Peter, running headlong fast, as if he could outrace the echo.

★   ★   ★

Peter rushed forward, sprinting down the Amherst Building corridor, knowing that only one thing in the world could generate that sort of despair in a person, even a mad one: death. He dodged the other patients, who were shrinking from the sound, near panicked, unsettled, and filled with explosions of anxiety and fear, as they tried to escape a noise that terrified them. Even the Catos and the retarded men, who so often seemed oblivious to the entirety of the world around them, were pushing to the walls, trying to hide. One man was rocking back and forth in a squat, his hands held tight over his ears. Peter could hear the doleful drumbeat of his own shoes slapping hard against the flooring, and he understood that there was something within him that always drove him hard toward dying.

Francis was right behind him, fighting the urge to flee in the opposite direction, swept up and carried along by Peter's headlong rush. He could hear Big Black's deep voice, shouting commands, 'Get back, please! Get back! Let us through!' as the attendant and his brother raced down the hallway. A nurse in white uniform came out from behind the wire mesh station. Her name was Nurse Richards, but of course she was called Nurse Riches instead, but the elegance of her nickname was ruined by the look of unaccustomed distress and outright terror in her eyes.

By the entrance to the women's dormitory, a disheveled woman with wiry gray hair was rocking back and forth and keening to herself. Another was pirouetting about in circles. A third had put her forehead against the wall and was mumbling something in what Francis thought might be a foreign language, but might also have been gibberish; it was impossible to tell. Two others were wailing, sobbing, and had thrown themselves to the floor where they twitched and moaned as if possessed by devils. He could not tell if any one of the women he saw had issued the scream. It might have been any one of them, or someone else whom he had not seen. But it seemed to him that the noise of despair was still in the air around them, an unrelenting siren's call dragging them inexorably forward. Inside his own head, his voices were shouting warnings, trying to get Francis to stop, to retreat, to run away from danger. It took a strong physical effort to ignore them, and he tried hard to keep pace with Peter, as if the Fireman's sense of reason and understanding might actually carry him along as well.

Peter hesitated only for a moment by the doorway, turning rapidly toward the disheveled woman, and demanding forcefully, 'Where?' in a voice that bellowed authority.

The woman pointed toward the end of the corridor, to the stairwell behind what were supposed to be locked doors, and then burst out in a cackle and laugh, that disintegrated almost as swiftly into a series of wracking sobs.

Peter stepped forward, Francis directly behind him, and reached out for the handle on the large steel door. He pushed it open in a single, unafraid motion, then stopped.

'Holy Mary, Mother of God!' he burst out.

Peter gasped in a deep breath, then whispered the second part of the prayer, ' . . . Pray for us sinners in this the hour of our death . . . ' He started to raise his hand to make the sign of the cross, all that Catholic School training coming back to him in an instant, but he stopped in midmotion.

Francis craned past him, felt all the air drain from his chest and recoiled sharply. He stepped aside, as if to steady himself, suddenly dizzy. He thought there was no blood in his heart, and he worried that he might pass out.

'Stay back, C-Bird,' Peter whispered. He probably didn't mean this, but the words fell like some feathers caught in a gust of wind.

Big Black and Little Black stopped their own rush forward right behind the two patients, staring up, suddenly quieted. After a second, Little Black quietly said, 'Goddamn, goddamn . . . ' but nothing else. Big Black turned his face to the wall.

Francis made himself look ahead.

Hanging from a makeshift noose fashioned from a twisted dingy gray bedsheet, tied to the iron railing leading to the second floor, was Cleo.

Her chubby face was misshapen, blown up and inflated, twisted gargoyle-like in death. The noose fashioned around her neck had creased the folds of skin, cutting in like a knot at the bottom of a child's balloon. Her hair cascaded wildly around her shoulders in a tangled mess, and her blank eyes were open, but fixed ahead. Her mouth was cracked slightly askew, giving her an appearance of shock. She wore a simple, gray shift that hung from her sloped shoulders like a bag, and one gaudy pink sandal had slipped from her foot to the floor. Francis saw that her toenails were painted red.

He thought he was having trouble breathing, and he wanted to turn his face away and avert his eyes, but the portrait of death in front of him had a sickly, compelling urgency to it, and he stayed rooted in position, fixed on the figure hanging from the stairwell. He found himself trying to reconcile Cleo with her constant torrent of obscenities, her bouncing, energetic devastation of all challengers at the Ping-Pong table, with the lumpy, grotesque figure before him. The stairwell had a shadowy half light, as if the single uncovered bulbs that lit each floor were inadequate to hold back the tendrils of darkness that were eager to creep into the area. The air seemed musty and hot, as if rarely circulated, like inside an attic never visited.

He let his eyes sweep over her figure again, and then he saw something.

'Peter,' Francis whispered slowly, 'look at her hand.'

Peter's eyes dropped from Cleo's face to her hand and for a moment he was silent. Then he said, 'I'll be damned.'

Cleo's right thumb had been severed. A streak of crimson ran down the outside of her shift, and along the side of her naked leg, finally pooling in a black splotch on the floor beneath her body. Francis stared at the circle of blood, then gagged.

'Damn,' Peter said again.

The severed thumb was on the floor about a foot, perhaps two, away from the center of the small maroon circle of sticky blood, left there almost as if it had been discarded like some petty afterthought.

A thought occurred to Francis, and he surveyed the scene rapidly, looking for one single item. His eyes raced right and left, searching as quickly as he could, but he did not see what he was looking for. He wanted to say something, but instead kept his mouth closed. Peter, as well, had grown silent.

It was Little Black who finally spoke. 'There's going to be hell to pay over this,' he said glumly.

★   ★   ★

Francis waited over by the wall, sitting on the floor, while a number of things took place in front of him. He had the odd sensation that he wished that it was all a simple hallucination, or perhaps a dream, and that any moment he would wake up, and the usual day in the Western State Hospital would simply begin all over again.

Big Black had left Peter, Francis, and his brother in the stairwell, looking up at Cleo's body, and had dutifully returned to the nursing station and called Security, and then Doctor Gulptilil's office, and finally, Mister Evil's apartment number. There had been a

489

short lull, following the phone calls, during which time Peter had moved slowly around Cleo's dead form, assessing, memorizing, trying to fix it all firmly in his head. Francis admired the Fireman's diligence and sense of professionalism but he secretly doubted whether he would ever be able to forget any of the details of the death in front of him. Still, both Francis and Peter did as they had done before, when Short Blond's body was discovered, letting their eyes walk the entire scene, measuring, photographing, the way crime scene specialists might do, except that neither had any tape or camera, so they were left to form their own internal specifications.

In the corridor, Big Black and Little Black were trying to restore some calm to a setting that defied calm. Patients were distraught, crying, laughing, some giggled, some sobbed, some tried to behave as if nothing had taken place, others cowered in corners. A radio someplace was playing Top 40 hits from the 1960s, and Francis could hear the unmistakable strains of 'In the Midnight Hour' followed by 'Don't Walk Away, Renee.' The music seemed to make the whole situation even more demented than it already was, as guitar and vocal harmonies mingled with chaos. Then he heard a patient demanding in a loud voice that breakfast be served immediately, while another asked if they could go outside and pick flowers for a grave.

It did not take long for Security to arrive, followed in rapid succession by Gulp-a-pill and Mister Evil. Both men hurried with that half run, half walk pace that made them seem slightly out of control. Mister Evil pushed a few patients out of his path, while Gulptilil simply sailed down the corridor oblivious to entreaties and pleas from the nervous crowd of residents.

'Show me!' Gulptilil demanded of Big Black.

There were three gray-shirted security personnel standing in the doorway waiting for someone to tell them what to do, blocking his sight. None of the quasicops had done anything except stare up at Cleo's body since they arrived, and now they stepped aside to let Gulptilil and Evans enter the gloomy stairwell area.

The hospital director stepped forward, and gasped. 'My goodness!' he said, astonished. 'Oh, my, but this is terrible.' He shook his head back and forth.

Evans craned past him, also taking in the sight. His response, at least at first, was limited to 'Damn!'

The two administrators continued to examine the scene. Francis saw that they both absorbed the severed thumb, and the noose fastened to the stairway railing. But he had the curious thought that the two men saw something different from what he did. Not that they didn't see Cleo hanging dead. But that they were reacting differently. It was a little like standing in front of a famous work of art in a museum, and having the person next to him reach some opposing assessment, emitting a laugh, instead of a sigh, or a groan in place of a smile.

'What bad luck,' Gulptilil said quietly. Then he turned to Mister Evans. 'Has there been any indication . . . ,' he started, not truly needing to finish the question for the unit supervisor.

Evans was already nodding his head. 'I made a notation in the daily log yesterday that her sense of distress seemed to be increasing. There were other signs over the past week or so that she was decompensating. I sent you a memo last week about a number of patients who needed to be reassessed medically, and she was on it, right at the top. Perhaps I should have moved a little more aggressively, but she did not seem to be in such an immediate crisis that it was warranted. Clearly, that was in error.'

Gulptilil nodded. 'I recall the memo. Alas, sometimes even the best intentions . . . ,' he said. He added, 'Ah, well, it is difficult to anticipate these things, is it not?'

He did not act like he expected an answer to this question. Hearing none, he shrugged. 'You will take careful notes, will you not?'

'Of course,' Evans said.

Gulp-a-pill then turned to the three security guards. 'All right gentlemen. Mister Moses will show you how to get Cleo down. Bring a body bag and a gurney. Let's get her over to the morgue promptly . . .'

'Wait just a second!'

The objection came from behind all of them, and they turned to the sound of the voice. It was Lucy Jones, standing a few feet back, and staring past them all toward Cleo's body.

'My goodness!' Gulptilil said, almost breathlessly. 'Miss Jones? My lord, what have you done?'

But the answer to this, Francis thought, was utterly obvious. Her long black hair was gone, replaced by a sheet of streaky blond dyed hair, cropped closely, almost haphazardly. He stared at her dizzily. It was a little, he thought, like seeing a work of art defaced.

★　★　★

I pushed myself away from the words on the wall, scurrying back across the floor of the apartment a little like a frightened spider, trying to avoid a heavy boot. I came to a rest with my back against the opposite wall, and I stopped, taking the time first to light a cigarette, then pausing for a moment with my head up against my knees. I held the cigarette in my hand, letting the thin trail of smoke waft up toward my nostrils. I was listening for the Angel's voice, waiting for the sensation of his breath against the small hairs on the back of my neck. If he wasn't there, I knew he wasn't far. There was no sign of Peter or anyone else, although, for an instant I wondered if Cleo might not visit me in that moment.

All my ghosts were close by.

For a moment I thought of myself like some medieval necromancer, standing over a cauldron of bats' eyes and mandrake root, bubbling along, able to summon up whatever evil vision I needed.

When I opened my eyes to the small world around me, I asked her, 'Cleo? What happened? You didn't have to die.' I shook my head back and forth, closed my eyes, but in the darkness, I heard her speak in the gruff, rollicking tones that I had grown accustomed to.

'Oh, C-Bird, but I did. Goddamn bastards. I had to die. The sons of bitches killed me for sure. I knew they would, right from the first.'

I looked around to see her, but at first she was only a sound. Then slowly, like a sailboat emerging from the fog, Cleo took shape in front of me. She leaned up against the wall of writing, and lit her own smoke. She wore a frilly pastel housedress and the same pink flip-flops I remembered from her death. In one hand she waved her cigarette, in the other, as I should have expected, a Ping-Pong paddle. Her eyes were lit with a kind of maniacal pleasure, as if she had been set free from something difficult and troubling.

'Who killed you, Cleo?'

'The bastards.'

'Who, in particular, Cleo?'

'But C-Bird, you know. You knew from the moment you got to the stairwell where I was waiting. You could see, couldn't you?'

'No,' I said, shaking my head. 'It was so confusing. I couldn't be sure'.

'But that was it, C-Bird. That was it. It was all a contradiction, and in that, you could see the truth, couldn't you?'

I wanted to say yes, but I still wasn't certain. I was young back then, and unsure, and it was the same today.

'He was there, wasn't he?'

'Of course. He was always there. Or maybe he wasn't there. It's all in how you looked at it, C-Bird. But you saw, didn't you.'

I was still undecided.

'What happened, Cleo? What really happened?'

'Why C-Bird, I died. You know that.'

'Yes, but how?'

'It should have been with an asp held to my breast.'

'It wasn't.'

'No, alas, true enough. It wasn't. But still in my own way, it was close enough. I even got to say the words, C-Bird. 'I am dying, Egypt. Dying . . . ' which was satisfying.'

'Who was there to hear them?'

'You know.'

I tried a different tack. 'Did you fight, Cleo?'

'I always fought, C-Bird. My whole sorry goddamn life was a fight.'

'But did you fight the Angel, Cleo?'

She grinned and waved the Ping-Pong paddle in the air, rearranging the smoke from her cigarette. 'Of course I did, C-Bird. You knew me. I wasn't going down easy.'

'He killed you?'

'No. Not exactly. But sort of, as well. It was like everything in the hospital, C-Bird. The truth was crazy and complicated and as mad as we all were.'

'I thought so,' I answered.

She laughed a little. 'I knew you could see it. Tell them now, like you tried to tell them back then. It would have been easier if they'd listened to you. But then who ever wants to listen to the crazy people?'

This observation made us both smile, for it was the closest thing to the truth that either of us could muster in that moment.

I took a deep breath. I could feel a great welling loss,

494

like a vacuum within me.

'I miss you, Cleo.'

'I miss you, too, C-Bird. I miss living. How about a game of Ping-Pong? I'll even spot you a couple of points.'

She smiled before she faded away.

I sighed, and turned back to the wall. A shadow seemed to have slithered over it, and the next sound I heard was the voice I wanted to forget.

'Little C-Bird wants answers before he dies, doesn't he?'

Each word was confusing, a little like a pounding headache, as if there were someone banging against the door of my imagination. I rocked back and wondered if there was someone actually trying to break in, and I cowered, hiding from the darkness that crept through the room. Within my heart I searched for brave words to respond with, but they were elusive. I could feel my hand quiver, and thought I was on the verge of some great pain, but from some recess I found a reply.

'I have all the answers,' I said. 'I always did.'

But this was as harsh an understanding as any that had ever come to me unbidden. It frightened me almost as much as the sound of the Angel's voice. I pressed back, and as I cowered, I heard the telephone ringing in the next room. The jangling only added to my nervousness. After a moment, it stopped, and I heard the answering machine that my sisters had purchased for me click on. 'Mister Petrel? Are you there?' The voice seemed distant, but familiar. 'It's Mister Klein at the Wellness Center. You have not arrived for the appointment that you promised you would attend. Please pick up the telephone. Mister Petrel? Francis? Please contact this office as soon as you get this message, otherwise I will be forced to take some action . . .'

I remained rooted in my spot.

'They will come for you,' I heard the Angel say. 'Can't you see, C-Bird? You're in a box and you can't get out'.

I closed my eyes, but it did no good. It was as if sounds increased in volume.

'They will come for you, Francis, and this time they will want to take you away forever. They will think: No more little apartment. No more job counting fish for the wildlife survey. No more Francis walking the streets getting in the way of every day life. No more burden for your sisters or your elderly parents, Francis, who never loved you all that much anyway, after they saw what you would become. No, they will want to shut Francis away for the rest of his days. Locked up, straitjacketed, drooling mess. That's what you will become, Francis. Surely you can see that . . . '

The Angel laughed a little before adding: ' . . . Unless, of course, I kill you first.'

These words were as sharp as any knife blade.

I wanted to say 'What are you waiting for?' but instead, shifted about, and crawling like a baby, tears dripping down my face, crossed the floor toward the wall of words. He was right with me, every step, and I didn't understand yet why he had not seized hold of me. I tried to block out his presence, as if memory was my only salvation, and remembering Lucy's authoritative demand that seemed to cut across the years.

★   ★   ★

Lucy strode forward. 'No one should touch a thing,' she demanded. 'This is a crime scene!'

Mister Evans seemed confused by her appearance and stuttered some reply that didn't make immediate sense. Doctor Gulptilil, also taken aback by her outward change, shook his head, and stepped just slightly into her path, as if he could slow her pace down by forming some sort of obstacle. The security guards and Big Black and Little Black all shifted about uncomfortably.

'She's right,' Peter said forcefully. 'The police should be called.'

The Fireman's voice seemed to penetrate past Evans's surprise, and he pivoted toward Peter, saying, 'What the hell do you know?'

Gulptilil held up his hand and neither shook his head negatively, nor nodded in agreement. Instead, he shifted about in his place, as if switching his pear-shaped body amoeba-like from one position into another. 'I would not be all that persuaded,' he said calmly. 'Did we not just go through this sort of discussion with the prior death in this ward?'

Lucy Jones snorted. 'Yes, I believe we did.'

'Ah, of course. An elderly patient who passed away from sudden heart failure. Which, I recall, you also wanted to investigate as a homicide.'

Lucy gestured toward Cleo's misshapen body, still hanging grotesquely in the stairwell. 'This, I doubt, could be attributed to sudden heart failure.'

'Nor does it have the earmarks of your cases,' Gulp-a-pill replied.

'Yes it does,' Peter said briskly. 'The severed thumb.'

The doctor pivoted about and spent a few seconds staring at Cleo's hand, and then down at the macabre sight on the floor. He shook his head, as he often did, but replied, 'Perhaps. But then, Miss Jones, prior to engaging the local police, and all the trouble that act implies, we should examine the death ourselves, and see if we can reach some consensus. For my initial inspection does not suggest this is a homicide in the slightest.'

Lucy Jones looked askance, started to say one thing, then stopped. 'As you wish, Doctor,' she said. 'Let's take a look at the scene. As you wish.'

Lucy followed the physician into the stairwell. Peter

497

and Francis moved aside, watching them as they progressed into the small area. Mister Evil trailed after them, as well, after fixing Peter with a snarling gaze, but the others all hovered in the doorway area, as if getting much closer would somehow increase the potency of the image in front of them. Francis saw nervousness and fear in more than one set of eyes, and thought the portrait of Cleo's death managed to transcend the ordinary boundaries of sanity and insanity; it was equally unsettling to the normal and the mad, just the same.

For nearly ten minutes, Lucy and Doctor Gulptilil slowly walked around and through the small area, both sets of eyes reaching into every corner, surveying every inch of the space. Francis saw Peter watching them both closely, and he, too, tried to follow their vision, as if he could place their thoughts into his own head. And, as he did this, Francis began to see. It was a little like a camera out of focus, where everything was indistinct and fuzzy, but as he stood there, a certain sharpness slowly came to him, and he began to imagine Cleo's last moments.

Finally, Doctor Gulptilil turned to Lucy. 'So, tell me Madam Prosecutor, how does this measure up as a homicide?'

She pointed to the thumb. 'My perpetrator has always severed fingers. She would be the fifth. Thus, the thumb.'

He shook his head. 'Look about,' he said slowly. 'There are no signs of a struggle. No one has as yet stepped forward to say that there was a disturbance in this area last night. I would find it hard to imagine that your killer — or any killer for that matter — would be able to force a woman who possessed this bulk and strength, into a noose without attracting *some* attention to his efforts. And the victim here . . . well, what about this death reminds you of the others?'

'Nothing, not yet,' Lucy said.

'Do you imagine, Miss Jones,' Doctor Gulptilil said cautiously, 'that suicide is unheard of here in this hospital?'

And there, Francis thought, it is.

'Of course not,' Lucy replied.

'And was not the woman in question unhealthily fixated on the nurse-trainee's murder?'

'I don't know that for a fact.'

'Perhaps Mister Evans can enlighten us?'

Evans stepped out from the doorway. 'She seemed to take a far greater interest in the case than anyone else. She had had several significant outbursts, where she claimed knowledge or information about the death. If anyone is to blame, it is me, for failing to see how critical this obsession had become . . . '

He said this last mea culpa in a tone that implied the exact opposite. In other words, Francis thought, he thinks he's the least to blame. He looked up at Cleo's bloated face and thought the entirety of the situation surreal. People arguing back and forth about what had taken place literally beneath the feet of the dead woman. He tried to remember her alive, but had trouble. He tried to feel sad, but, instead, he was mostly exhausted, as if the emotion of the discovery was like climbing some mountain. He looked around again, staying quiet, and found himself thinking: *What did happen?*

'Miss Jones,' Doctor Gulptilil was saying, 'death is not unheard of in the hospital. This act fits a sad scheme that we are familiar with. It is thankfully not as frequent as one might imagine, still, it does occur as we are sometimes slow to recognize the stresses that drive some patients. Your alleged killer is a sexual predator. But here we have no signs of such activity. Instead, we have a woman who, in all likelihood mutilated her own hand as her delusions connecting her to the prior murder grew out of control. I imagine we will find scissors or a razor hidden among her personal items. In addition, my guess is that we will discover that the bedsheet that she fashioned into a noose comes from her own bunk. Such is the resourcefulness of a psychotic bent on taking his own life, alas. I am sorry . . . '

He pointed to the waiting security personnel.

' . . . We must get this residence hall back on some kind of routine track.'

Francis expected Peter to say something, but the Fireman kept his mouth closed.

'And, Miss Jones,' Gulp-a-pill added, 'I would like to discuss at your earliest convenience the impact of your, ah, shall we say *haircut*.'

With that, the hospital director turned to Mister Evil and added, 'Serve breakfast. Get the morning activities started.'

Evans nodded. He looked over at Francis and Peter and he gave them a small wave. 'You two, back to the dining hall, please,' he said. The words spoken carried polite tones but were as much a command as any issued by a prison guard.

Peter seemed to bristle at Evans giving him any sort of instructions. But instead he looked over at Gulptilil. 'I need to speak with you,' he said. Evans snarled, but Gulp-a-pill nodded.

'Of course, Peter,' he said. 'I have been anticipating that conversation.'

Lucy seemed to sigh, and take a last look up at Cleo's body. Francis could not tell whether it was discouragement that went through her eyes, or some other sense of resignation. It was almost as if he could see that she thought that everything was coming to an end unhappily, no matter what she did. It was the look of someone who believes that something is just beyond reach.

Francis turned back and stared at Cleo's body as well. He let his eyes survey the scene one last time as the security personnel moved to lower her to the ground.

Murder or suicide, he thought. For Lucy, one was likely. For the hospital director, the other was obvious. Each had his own needs for one outcome or the other.

Francis, however, felt an empty cold deep within his heart, because he saw something different.

Murder or suicide? he thought to himself. He stepped back from the stairwell door and took a quick glance into the women's dormitory. He knew Cleo's bed was right inside the door. He took notice that both sheets were intact, and there was no sign of a knife or blood, if that had been the place where she'd severed her thumb. He could hear echoes from his own voices shouting conflicting visions inside, but he shut them all away almost as if he could close the lid on their complaints. *Murder or suicide? How about both?* he whispered to himself, as then he turned and followed Peter back down the corridor.

28

Cleo's body was hustled out of the Amherst Building by Security at the same time that Big Black and his brother herded the distraught patients into the dining area for the morning meal. The last Francis saw of the sometime empress of Egypt was a great misshapen lump encased in a shiny black rubberized body bag disappearing through the front doors as he was being directed to stand in line by the serving counter. After a few moments, Francis found himself staring down at a desultory plate of French toast, dripping with sticky, tasteless syrup, trying to assess what had taken place in the hours that most of them had been asleep. He was joined at the table by Peter, who seemed in a deeply foul mood, and took to pushing his food about on his plate. Newsman wandered by, took one look at Peter, started to say something, only to stop when Peter said, 'I know what today's headline is. *Patient in Hospital Dies Hard. No One Gives a Damn.*'

Newsman looked as if he might burst into tears and hurried over to an empty table. Francis thought Peter was wrong, because there were a number of people who were upset by Cleo's death and he looked around as if to point these folks out to the Fireman, but instead, he saw the hulking retarded man first, who was having trouble cutting his toast into bite-size pieces, then his gaze traveled over to one of the other tables where three women sat, each indifferent to the meal in front of them, indifferent to each other, talking to themselves.

Another retarded man glared at Francis, as if there was something in the way he was sitting that made him angry, and so Francis looked away, back to Peter.

502

'Peter?' he asked slowly. 'What do you think happened to Cleo?'

The Fireman shook his head. 'Everything that can go wrong, did go wrong,' he said. 'She was filled with something evil, you know, where all the things that are supposed to connect up and keep us levelheaded somehow got short-circuited or frayed, and no one saw it or did anything about it and so there you have it. She's gone. Poof! Like a magic trick on a stage. Evans should have seen something. Maybe Big Black or Little Black or Nurse Wrong or Nurse Riches or even me, maybe, but someone should have seen something was happening. Just the same as Lanky, back before Short Blond's murder. All sorts of things happening inside his head. Hammers pounding, bulldozers, earthmovers, like a construction project going on by the side of the highway, except no one noticed. And then when they do take notice, it's too late.'

'You think she killed herself?'

'Of course,' Peter said.

'But Lucy said . . . '

'Lucy was wrong. Gulp-a-pill was right. No signs of a struggle. And the severed thumb — well, that was probably just her craziness coming out. Some utterly weird delusion. Cutting her own thumb off probably made some crazy sense to her right at the last moment. We just don't exactly know what her logic was and we'll never know.'

Francis swallowed hard, and asked, 'Did you really examine that thumb, Peter?'

The Fireman shook his head. 'I liked Cleo,' he said. 'She had personality. A character. She wasn't a blank slate, like so many people in here. I wish I could have gotten inside Cleo's head for just a second, to see how it all added up for her. There had to be some unique and twisted Cleo-like logic. Something to do with Shakespeare and Egypt and all of that. She was her own

503

theater, wasn't she? Belonged on a stage somewhere, I guess. Or maybe, turned everything around her into its own stage. Maybe that's the best epitaph for her.'

Francis could see churning within Peter some great storm of thoughts moving back and forth like tossed seas driven by wild winds. Nowhere in Francis's view, at that moment was Peter the arson investigator. Francis continued to ask questions, a little under his voice. 'She didn't seem like the type who would kill herself, especially after mutilating herself.'

'True enough,' Peter answered, sighing deeply. 'But I'm thinking that no one exactly seems like the type who would kill themselves, until they do, and then, all of a sudden everyone around here nods their heads and says, 'Why of course . . . ' because it seems so damn obvious.'

He shook his head. 'C-Bird,' he said, 'I've got to get out of here.' He took another deep breath, then amended this statement: 'We've got to get out of here.'

Then Peter looked up and saw something in Francis's face, because he stopped short and spent more than a few seconds simply staring at the younger man. After a long stretch of quiet, he said, 'What is it?'

'He was there,' Francis whispered.

Peter knit his brows and leaned forward. 'Who?'

'The Angel.'

Peter shook his head. 'I don't think so . . . '

Francis whispered. 'He was. He was in at my bed the other night telling me how easy it would be to kill me, and this night he was there with Cleo. He's everywhere, we just cannot see him. He's behind everything that has happened here in Amherst, and he's going to be behind whatever happens next. Cleo kill herself? Sure. I guess so. But who else would unlock the right doors for her?'

'Unlock the doors . . . '

'Someone opened the door to the women's dormitory. Someone made sure that the stairwell door was unlocked. And someone helped her get past the nursing station so that she wasn't seen . . . '

'Well,' Peter said, 'that's a good point. Actually, several good points . . . ' He seemed to chew this over for a moment, before saying, 'You're right, C-Bird about one thing. Someone opened some doors. But how can you be so sure it was the Angel?'

'I can see it,' Francis answered quietly.

Peter looked slightly perplexed, and more than a little doubtful. 'Okay,' he said. 'What do you see?'

'How it happened. More or less.'

'Keep going, C-Bird,' Peter said, lowering his voice a little.

'The bedsheet. The one that was fastened into the noose . . . '

'Yes?'

'Cleo's bed was intact. Sheets still on it.'

Peter said nothing.

'The thumb . . . '

The Fireman nodded encouragingly.

'The thumb wasn't dropped directly downward. It was like it had been moved a couple of feet. And if Cleo had sliced it off herself, well, there should have been something — scissors or a knife or something — right there. But there wasn't. And if it had been cut somewhere else, well, then there would have been blood. Maybe a trail of blood, leading out into the stairwell. But there wasn't. Just the single pool beneath her body.'

Francis took another deep breath, and then whispered again: 'I can see it.'

Peter was a little openmouthed, about to ask the obvious question, when Little Black hovered up to where they were sitting. He pointed an index finger at Peter, jabbing the air, interrupting the conversation abruptly. 'You're up,' he said. 'The big doc says for you to come over right now.'

Peter seemed to waver between questioning Francis more closely and the impatience that Little Black seemed to have just at the edge of his voice. So, what he did say was, 'C-Bird, just keep your opinions to yourself until I get back, okay?'

Francis started to respond, but Peter leaned forward and added, 'Don't let anyone around here think you're any crazier than you already are. Just wait for me, okay?'

The point Peter was making made some sense, and Francis nodded. Peter deposited his tray over by the cleaning station and dutifully followed the attendant out the door. For a moment or two, Francis remained at his seat, alone in the midst of the dining area. There was a constancy of noise — the clatter of plates and utensils, some laughter, some shouts, and one person singing off-key an unrecognizable tune that just didn't quite match up with the distant sound of a radio playing from back in the cooking area. The usual morning, he thought. But when he rose, unable to mouth another forkful of French toast, he saw that Mister Evil was standing in the corner eyeing him carefully. And, as he crossed the room, he had the sensation that there were other eyes watching him as well. For a moment, he wanted to turn, to see if he could spot the people tracking his path, but then he decided not to. He wasn't at all sure that he wanted to know who might or might not be taking notice of his movement around the dining hall. He wondered for a moment, as well, whether Cleo's death had prevented something from happening. He picked up his pace and started moving more swiftly, because it occurred to him that it might have been his own murder that had been planned for that night past, and interrupted only by another opportunity presenting itself.

★ ★ ★

When Peter, accompanied by Little Black, entered Doctor Gulptilil's waiting room, he could hear the high-pitched noise of the psychiatrist's voice, raised in frustration and barely restrained anger coming from the inner office. The attendant had only handcuffed him, having left the leg shackles off on this trip across the hospital grounds, so that Peter was, at least in his own mind, only a partial prisoner. Miss Luscious was behind her desk, but she only glanced in Peter's direction as he came through the door, gesturing with a nod of her head toward the waiting bench. Peter strained to hear precisely what Gulp-a-pill was so upset about — because he thought that a compliant medical director was one far more likely to help him than a furious one. After a second, he realized that the object of the doctor's wrath was Lucy, and this startled him.

His first instinct was to rise, and burst into the doctor's office.

He reined this urge in, taking a deep breath.

Then he heard, penetrating right through the thick wall and wood of the door, 'Miss Jones, I am holding you personally responsible for all the disruption here at the hospital. Who knows what other patients might be in jeopardy due to your actions!'

The hell with it, Peter said to himself, and he rose abruptly, and crossed the room before either Little Black or Miss Luscious were able to react.

'Hey!' the buxom secretary said, 'You can't . . . '

'Sure I can,' said Peter, reaching for the door handle with both his handcuffed hands.

'Mister Moses!' Miss Luscious cried.

But the wiry black attendant moved languidly, almost nonchalantly, as if Peter bursting into Doctor Gulptilil's office was just about the most routine thing in the world.

Gulp-a-pill looked up red-faced and startled. Lucy was sitting in the inquisition's seat in front of his desk, a little pale, but icy, as well, as if she had adorned herself with some hardened casing and his words, no matter how enraged were simply rebounding off of her skin. She remained expressionless, as Peter tumbled through the doorway, trailed by Little Black.

The medical director took a deep breath, regaining some composure, stared coldly across the room and said, 'Peter, I will be with you in a moment. Please wait outside. Mister Moses, if you will — '

But Peter interrupted. 'It's as much my fault as anyone's,' he said.

Doctor Gulptilil was in midwave, dismissing him, but he stopped, leaving his hand in the air. 'Fault?' he said. 'And how so, Peter?'

'I've concurred with every step she's taken so far. And clearly, to smoke out this killer here, some extraordinary steps must be involved. I've urged that from the start, so I'm as much to blame for any disruption.'

Doctor Gulptilil hesitated, then said, 'You ascribe much power to your choices, Peter.'

This oblique statement left Peter a little befuddled. He inhaled sharply and said, 'It is a simple fact of any criminal investigation that at some point dramatic steps must be taken to force the target to act in a way that will isolate him, and make him vulnerable.' This sounded, to Peter's ears, smug and sophomoric, and, he understood, wasn't actually all that true, but, he guessed, at least it was something to say right in that moment and he said it with enough conviction to make it at least *seem* to be true.

Gulptilil rocked back in his seat, taking a breath, pausing. Both Lucy and Peter looked over at him, and both thought more or less the same thing: What made the doctor a curiously dangerous person was his capacity to step back from outrage, insult, anger, or whatever passion was knocking so eagerly to emerge, and settle instead, into a quiet, observant mode. It unsettled Lucy, for she was more comfortable seeing people act out their rages, even if she was unwilling to do the same. Peter thought this a formidable capacity. It seemed to him that every conversation anyone had with the psychiatrist was really a little more like playing a hand of high stakes poker, where Gulptilil held most of the chips, and anyone sitting across from the doctor was betting money they didn't have. It seemed to both of them as if the doctor was calculating in his head. Little Black reached out and seized Peter by the arm, to pull him back into the waiting room, but now, abruptly, the doctor seemed to change his mind. 'Ah, Mister Moses,' he said, his voice returning to normal, the anger that had penetrated the walls dissolving rapidly. 'Perhaps that won't be necessary, after all. Actually, come in, Peter.'

He motioned to another chair.

'Vulnerable, you say?'

'Yes,' Peter replied. What else, he thought, could he say?

'More vulnerable, say, than Miss Jones has rendered herself with this childishly transparent attempt to mimic the physical characteristics of the victims that she is interested in?'

'It is difficult to say,' Peter responded.

The doctor smiled weakly. 'Of course it is. But would you say that if this person she pursues — this possibly *imaginary* killer — actually exists here within these walls, that she has done something which will, of necessity, gain his immediate and probably undivided attention?'

'I believe so.'

'Very good. I suspect so, as well. *If* this gentleman is here. So, we could postulate, could we not, Peter, that were *nothing* to happen to Miss Jones in the immediacy of time, that we could reasonably believe that this maybe killer of hers was not, in actuality present in the hospital? That the unfortunate nurse-trainee was in fact killed by Lanky in a fit of homicidal delusion, as the evidence indicates?'

'That would be a considerable leap, Doctor,' Peter answered. 'The man Miss Jones and I have been pursuing might have more discipline than we have come to believe.'

'Ah yes. A killer with discipline. A most unusual characteristic for a killer being driven by psychosis, no? You are, as we have discussed, pursuing a man who is *dominated* by his murderous impulses, but now that is seemingly a less convenient diagnosis? Or, if he is, as Miss Jones suggested upon her arrival here, some Jack the Ripper mythological sort, that might explain things. But, then, in the small amount of reading I've managed about this historical fellow, I have learned that he seemed to have precious *little* in the area of discipline. Compulsive killers are driven by immense forces, Peter, and ultimately incapable of restraining themselves. But that is a conversation for historians of these things to have, and concerns us little here, today. Might I ask the two of you: If the killer you are so persuaded is here were to be able to constrain himself, wouldn't that make it even more unlikely that you would ever discover him? No matter how many days, weeks, or even years you were to search?'

'I cannot predict the future any more than you can, Doctor.'

Gulptilil smiled. 'Ah, Peter, a most clever response. And one that speaks of your potential for recovery when we get you into this most progressive program suggested by your friends in the Church. That, I take it, was your actual reason for bursting into my office here today? To signal your desire to take them up on their most generous and thoughtful offer?'

Peter hesitated. Doctor Gulptilil eyed him closely.

'That was, of course, your reason?' he asked a second

time, his voice precluding any response but the obvious one.

'Yes,' Peter said. He was impressed with the way Gulptilil had managed to conflate the two issues: an unknown killer and his own legal problems.

'So, Peter wishes to leave the hospital for a new course of treatment and a new life, and Miss Jones has done something which she believes will encourage the reason for her presence to emerge so that she can bring him to justice. Is that not a fair assessment of the moment we find ourselves in?'

Both Lucy, who had remained silent, and Peter nodded.

Doctor Gulptilil allowed himself a small grin, just around the corners of his mouth. 'Then, I think, we can safely say that a small, but suitable amount of time will allow us to answer both these questions with certainty. It is Friday. I would think that on Monday morning I will be able to say farewell to both of you. No? That would be more than enough time to discover whether Miss Jones's approach might bear fruit. And for Peter's situation to be, well, *accommodated*.'

Lucy shifted about. She thought of several things she might say that could alter the doctor's deadline. But, as she squirmed slightly, she saw that Gulptilil was thinking hard, turning over one thing after another in his own head. She imagined that at the chess game of bureaucracy she would always finish second to the psychiatrist, especially as it played out on his own turf. So, instead, she replied: 'Monday morning. Okay.'

'And, of course, by putting yourself in this hazardous position, you will undoubtedly sign a letter absolving the hospital administration from any responsibility for maintaining your safety?'

Lucy's eyes narrowed, and her voice freighted the one word response with as much contempt as she could muster. 'Yes.'

511

'Wonderful. So, that part is settled. Now, Peter, let me just make a call . . . '

He pulled a small black leather address book from the top drawer of his desk. After casually flipping it open, he grasped an ivory colored business card. In short order, Doctor Gulptilil read a number off and dialed it. He rocked back in his seat, while the connection was being made. After a second, he said into the handset, 'Father Grozdik, please. This is Doctor Gulptilil at the Western State Hospital.'

There was a small pause, and then, Gulp-a-pill said, 'Father? Good day. You will be pleased to learn that I have Peter here in my office and he has agreed to the arrangements we discussed recently. In all regards. Now, I believe there is some paperwork that will need to be processed so that we can bring this unfortunate situation to a speedy close?'

Peter sat back heavily, realizing that his entire life had just changed. It was almost as if he were outside of himself, watching it happen. He didn't dare to steal a look at Lucy, who was also on the threshold of something, but was unsure precisely what, because success and failure seemed to have muddied in her head.

* * *

Francis walked down the corridor and into the dayroom, looking across past the disjointed knots of patients toward the Ping-Pong table. An old man in striped nightclothes and a cardigan buttoned up to his throat, although it was hot in the room, had taken up a paddle and was swinging it, as if he were playing a game, but there was no opponent on the other side, nor did he have a ball, so that the game was played in silence. The old man seemed intent, concentrating on each point, anticipating each return from the imaginary foe, and had a determined look, as if the score was in balance.

The dayroom was quiet, except for the muted sound of the two televisions, where announcers' and soap opera actors' voices mingled freely with the mutterings of patients who conversed primarily with themselves. Occasionally a newspaper or magazine would be slapped down on a table, and every so often a patient would inadvertently slide into the space occupied by another, which would prompt some words. But for a place that could see explosions, the dayroom was quiet. It was a little bit, Francis thought, as if the loss of Cleo's bulk and presence had stifled some of the usual anxiety in the room. Death as a tranquilizer. It was all an illusion, he thought, because he could sense tension and fear throughout. Something had happened that made all of them feel at risk.

Francis dropped himself into an overstuffed and lumpy chair and wondered how he had arrived at where he was. He could feel his own heart racing, because he thought that he alone understood what had taken place the night before. He hoped that Peter would return, so that he could share the observations, but he was no longer sure that Peter would believe them.

One of his voices whispered *You're all alone. You always have been. You always will be.* And he didn't bother to try internally to argue or deny the sentiments.

Then another voice, equally soft, as if trying to keep from being heard in the area beyond his head, added *No, there's someone searching for you, Francis.*

He knew who this was.

Francis wasn't precisely sure how he knew the Angel was stalking him. But he was persuaded that this was the case. For a second he looked around, to see if he could spot someone watching him, but the trouble with the mental hospital was that everyone watched one another and ignored one another at more or less the same time.

Francis rose abruptly. He knew one thing: He had to find the Angel before the Angel came for him.

He started to walk toward the dayroom door, when he spotted Big Black. An idea occurred to him and he called after the attendant. 'Mister Moses?'

The huge man turned. 'What is it C-Bird? Bad day today. Don't go and ask for something I can't give you.'

'Mister Moses, when are the release hearings scheduled?'

Big Black looked sideways at Francis. 'There's a bunch for this afternoon. Right after lunch.'

'I need to go.'

'You what?'

'I need to watch those hearings.'

'Whatever for?'

Francis couldn't quite articulate what he was really thinking, so instead he responded, 'Because I want to get out of here, and if I can watch what other people do in a release hearing, maybe it will help me not make the same mistakes.'

Big Black lifted an eyebrow. 'Well, C-Bird,' he said, 'that makes some sense. Don't know that I've ever had anyone else ever ask for that before.'

'It would help me,' Francis said.

The attendant looked doubtful, but then he shrugged. He lowered his voice. 'I don't know that I'm believing you fully on this C-Bird. But tell you what. You promise no trouble, and I'll take you over and you can sit with me and watch. This might be breaking some rule. I don't know. But seems to me that all sorts of rules been broke today.'

Francis breathed out.

A portrait was forming in his imagination, and this was an important brushstroke.

Light gray clouds were cluttering the sky, and a sickly, humid heat filled the midmorning air as Lucy Jones, Peter in handcuffs, and Little Black walked slowly across the hospital grounds. She could feel the rain that was an hour or two off. For the first few yards, the three were quiet; even their footsteps against the black macadam pathway seemed muffled against the thickening heat and darkening skies. Little Black wiped a hand across his forehead, glanced at the sweat that had accumulated there, and said, 'Damn, but you sure can feel summer coming about,' which was true. They took a few more steps, when Peter the Fireman abruptly stopped.

'Summer?' he said. He looked up, as if searching the heavens for some sunlight and blue skies, but they were obscured. But whatever he was seeking wasn't in the steamy air around them. 'Mister Moses, what's happening?'

Little Black also stopped and eyed Peter curiously. 'What do you mean 'What's happening?'' he asked.

'Like, in the world. In the United States. In Boston or Springfield. Are the Red Sox playing well? Are the hostages still in Iran? Are there demonstrations? Speeches? Editorials? Is the economy good? What's happening to the stock market? What's the number one movie?'

Little Black shook his head. 'You ought to be asking Newsman these questions. He's the one with all the headlines.'

Peter looked around. His eyes fixed on the mental hospital walls. 'People think those are to keep all of us in,' he said slowly. 'But that's not what really happens. Those walls keep the world out.' Peter shook his head. 'It's like being on an island. Or like being one of those Japanese soldiers stuck in the jungle who were never told the war was over and who thought year after year, that they were just doing their duty, fighting on for their emperor. We're stuck in some *Twilight Zone* time warp, where everything just passes us by. Earthquakes. Hurricanes. Upheavals of all sorts, man-made and natural.'

Lucy thought Peter was absolutely right, but still hesitated before speaking. 'You're making a point?'

'Yes. Of course. In the land of locked doors, who would be king?'

Lucy nodded. 'The man with the keys.'

'So,' Peter said, 'how do you set a trap for a man who can open any door?'

Lucy thought for a moment. 'You need to make him open the door where you can expect him.'

'Right,' Peter said. 'So, what door would that be?'

He looked over at Little Black, who shrugged. But Lucy plunged deep into thought, and then inhaled sharply, as if the thought that came to her had been astonishing, maybe even shocking. 'We know one door he opened up,' she said. 'It was the door that brought me here.'

'Which door do you mean?'

'Where was Short Blond when he came for her?'

'Alone in the Amherst Building nursing station late at night.'

'Then that's where I should be,' Lucy said.

29

By midday it had started to rain, an erratic drizzle, interrupted frequently by stronger downpours, or even the occasional overly optimistic light break that spoke of clearing, but which soon enough was swept aside by another line of dark showers. Francis had hurried along at Big Black's side, dashing between the dampness and sticky humidity, almost hoping that the attendant's huge bulk would carve a path through the gloomy weather, and that he could remain dry in the big man's wake. It was the sort of day, he thought, that suggested unchecked epidemic and rampant disease: hot, oppressive, sultry, and wet. Almost tropical in character, as if the usual conservative dry New England world of the state hospital had been suddenly overtaken by some alien, bizarre rain forest sensibility. It was weather, Francis thought, that was every bit as out of place and insane as all of them. Even the light breeze that swept rain puddles from the asphalt sidewalks had an otherworldly thickness to it.

As was the custom in the hospital, the release hearings were held in the administration building, inside the modestly sized staff lunchroom, which was reconfigured for the occasion into a pseudocourtroom. It had a thrown together, makeshift quality to it. There were tables for the hearing officers and for the patient advocates. Uncomfortable steel folding chairs had been arranged in rows for the hospital inmates and their families. A desk was provided for a stenographer and a seat for witnesses. The room was crowded, but not to overfilling, and what few words being spoken were whispered. Francis and Big Black slid into chairs in a row at the back. At first, Francis imagined the air in the room was stifling, then, upon reflection, thought perhaps it was less the air, than it was the cloud of eager hopes and helplessness that filled the space.

Presiding over the hearing was a retired district court judge from Springfield. He was gray-haired, overweight, and florid, taken to making large gestures with his hands. He had a gavel which he banged every so often for no apparent reason, and he wore a slightly frayed black robe that had probably seen better days and more important cases some years in his past. To his right was a psychiatrist from the state Department of Mental Health, a young woman with thick eyeglasses, who kept shuffling through files and papers, as if unable to find just precisely the right one, and to his left a lawyer from the local district attorney's office, who lounged in his seat, with a young man's bored eyes, clearly having lost some office pool which led to the assignment at the hospital. At one table, there was another young lawyer, wiry-haired, wearing an ill-fitting suit, slightly more eager and open-eyed, who served as the patients' representative, and across from him, various members of the hospital staff. It was all designed to give an official flavor to the proceedings, to couch decisions in conjoined medical and legal terms. It had the veneer of authenticity, of responsibility, of system and attentiveness, as if every case being heard had been carefully examined, properly vetted, and thoroughly assessed before being presented, when Francis immediately understood the exact opposite was the truth.

Francis felt a world of despair within him. As he looked around the room, he realized that the critical element of the release hearings had to be the families sitting quietly, waiting for the name of their son or daughter or niece or nephew or even mother or father to be called out. Without them, no one got released. Even if the initial orders putting them in Western State had long since expired, absent someone willing on the outside to take responsibility, the gate to the hospital remained closed. Francis could not help but wonder how he would be able to persuade his parents to open their door to him again, when they would not even come to the hospital to visit.

Inside his head, a voice insisted *They will never love you enough to come here and ask for you to be returned to them . . .*

And then another, speaking quickly, saying *Francis, you must find a different way to prove you're not crazy.*

He nodded to himself, understanding that what he hid from Mister Evil and Gulp-a-pill was crucial. Francis shifted about in his seat and slowly began to survey the people seated about the room. They seemed cut from all sorts of cloths, rough-edged, rough-hewn. Some of the men wore jackets and ties that seemed out of place and he knew that they had dressed up to make a good impression, when, in truth, the opposite was far more likely. The women wore simple dresses and clutched Kleenex, sometimes to dab away tears. Francis thought there was a great deal of failure loose in the room, and an accordant amount of guilt. More than one face carried the marks of blame, and for a moment he wanted to say *It's not your fault we turned out the way we did . . .* but then, he wasn't at all sure that that was accurate.

He heard the red-faced judge blurt out, 'Let's move on . . . ' as he pounded the gavel sharply two or three times and Francis turned to watch the proceedings.

But before the judge could clear his throat, and the psychiatrist with the files and confused look could read out a name, Francis heard several of his voices all at once. *Why are we here, Francis? We shouldn't be here at all. We should run, fast. Get away. Go back to Amherst. It's safe there . . .*

Francis pivoted first to the right, then the left, assessing the gathered people. None of the patients in

519

the room had noticed him come in, none were staring at him, none were eyeing him with malevolence, hatred, or anger.

He suspected that might change.

And he took a deep breath, for he knew that he was, if he was right, in as much danger right in that moment, surrounded by patients and hospital personnel, and even sitting in Big Black's shadow, as he'd ever been. Danger because of the man he thought was in that room with him. And danger because of what he was letting loose within himself.

He bit down on his lip and tried to clear his imagination. He told himself to simply be a blank slate, and wait for something to be written upon it. He wondered if his shallow breathing and sweaty forehead, or the clamminess he suddenly felt in the palms of his hands might be observed by Big Black, and with an immense force of will, he insisted to himself: *Be calm*.

And then, he took a deep breath, and inwardly spoke to all his voices: *Everyone needs a way out*.

Francis squirmed in his seat, hoping that no one, especially Big Black or Mister Evil or any of the other administrators could see how much turmoil he was in. He was pitched to the edge of his chair, nervous, frightened, but compelled to be there, and to listen, for he expected to hear something that day that was important. He wished that Peter was at his side, or Lucy, although he didn't think he could have persuaded her that listening was crucial. Francis at this moment was alone, and guessing that he was closer to an answer than anyone else might imagine.

★   ★   ★

Lucy came through the doors to the hospital's morgue and felt the chill of too much air-conditioning. It was a small, basement room, located in one of the distant buildings on the fringe of the hospital grounds that was generally used to house out-of-date equipment and long-forgotten supplies. It had the questionable virtue of being near the makeshift burial ground. There was a single, shiny steel examination table in the center of the room, and a bank of a half dozen refrigerated storage containers built into one wall. A glass paneled and polished steel bureau held a modest selection of scalpels and other surgical implements. A filing cabinet and a desk with a battered IBM Selectric typewriter were stuffed into a corner, and a single window was set into the cinder block wall, high up, looking out onto the ground, and only permitting a single shaft of wan, gray light to slip in past a crust of dirt. A pair of insistently bright overhead lights hummed like a matched set of large insects.

The room had an empty, abandoned quality, save for a slight smell of human waste that lingered in the cold air. On the examination table there was a clipboard with a set of forms attached. Lucy looked around for an attendant but no one was around, and so she stepped forward. She noticed that there were sluicing channels on the examination table, and a drain in the floor. Both wore dark stains. She picked up the clipboard and read a preliminary autopsy report that stated the obvious: Cleo had died by strangulation caused by bedsheet. Her eyes dwelt for a second on the entry: Self-Mutilation, which described her severed thumb, and for a moment on her diagnosis, which was schizophrenia, paranoid type, undifferentiated, with delusions and suicidal tendencies. Lucy suspected that this last observation had been, like so much else, added postmortem. When someone hangs themselves, their preexisting potential for selfdestruction becomes a little clearer, she thought.

She read on: No next of kin. There was an entry for *In case of death or injury please notify:* which was answered with a line through the space.

A medical examiner, a famous man in forensic circles, had once addressed her senior year class on evidence, and had, in most grandiose terms told all the law students that the dead spoke most eloquently about the means of their passing, often pointing directly to the person who had illegally helped them on their path. The lecture had been well attended and energetically received, but in this moment, Lucy thought it was ridiculously abstract and very distant. What she had was a silent body in a refrigerated cooler in the corner of a dingy, forgotten room and an autopsy protocol crammed onto a single sheet of yellow paper fastened to a clipboard, and she didn't think it was telling her anything, especially something that might help her in her pursuit of a killer.

Lucy put the clipboard back down on the examination table and moved over to the cooler. None of the doors were marked, so she pulled first one, then a second open, revealing a six-pack of Coca-Cola that someone had left behind to chill. The third, though, was hesitant, as if stuck slightly, and she guessed that it contained the body. She took a deep breath, and slid open the door a couple of inches.

Cleo's naked body was jammed inside.

Her bulk made it a tight fit, and when Lucy tugged on the sliding pallet that Cleo rested on, it wouldn't budge.

Lucy gritted her teeth, and got ready to pull harder, when she heard the door open behind her. She spun about and saw Doctor Gulptilil standing in the entranceway.

For a moment, he looked surprised. But he removed this look and shook his head.

'Miss Jones,' he said slowly, 'this is unexpected. I am not sure that you should be here.'

She did not reply.

'Sometimes,' the medical director said, 'even as

public a death as Miss Cleo's should have some privacy.'

'I would agree with that, at least in principle,' she said haughtily. Her initial surprise at the doctor's arrival was immediately replaced by the belligerence that she wore as armor.

'What is it you expect to learn here?' he asked.

'I don't know,' Lucy replied.

'You think this death can tell you something? Something that you don't already know?'

'I don't know,' she said again. She was slightly embarrassed that she couldn't come up with some far better response. The doctor moved into the room, his portly figure and dark skin gleaming under the overhead lights. He moved with a quickness that contradicted his pear-shaped figure, and for a second she thought he was going to slam the door to Cleo's temporary tomb shut. But, instead, he put his hand out and tugged; finally the dead woman slid forward, so that her torso was exposed on the slab between them.

Lucy looked down at the purplish red ligature marks that surrounded Cleo's neck. They seemed to have been absorbed by skin that had already turned a porcelain white. The dead woman had a faint, grotesque smile on her face, as if her death had caused some joke somewhere. Lucy breathed in and out slowly.

'You want something to be simple, clear, obvious,' Doctor Gulptilil said slowly. 'But, Miss Jones, answers are never like that. At least, not here.'

She looked up and nodded. The doctor smiled wryly, a little bit like the small grin that Cleo wore.

'The outward signs of strangulation are apparent,' he said, 'but the real forces that drove her to this end are shrouded. And, I suspect, the actual cause of death would elude even the most distinguished examination by the greatest pathologist we have in this nation, for the reasons are obscured by her madness.'

Doctor Gulptilil reached out and touched Cleo's skin for a second. He looked down at the dead woman, but he directed his words toward Lucy.

'You do not understand this place,' he said. 'You have not made an effort to understand it since you arrived, because you arrived here with the same fears and prejudices that most people who are unfamiliar with the mentally ill embrace. Here, what is abnormal is normal and what is bizarre is routine. You have approached your investigation here as if it were the same as the world outside the walls. You have looked for documentary evidence and telltale clues. You have searched the records and walked the hallways, just as you might have were this not the place that it is. This is, of course, as I have tried to point out, useless. And thus, Miss Jones, I fear your efforts here are destined for failure. As I have suspected they would be from the start.'

'I have some time remaining.'

'Yes. And you have invited a response from the mysterious and perhaps nonexistent target of your pursuit. Perhaps this would be an appropriate activity in the world you are accustomed to, Miss Jones. But here?'

Lucy fingered her shorn locks. 'Don't you think this is unexpected, and might work?'

'Yes,' the doctor said. 'But on whom will it work? And how?'

Again, she kept quiet. The doctor looked down at Cleo's face and shook his head. 'Ah, poor Cleo. I enjoyed her antics so much of the time, for she had a manic energy that was, when under some control, most entertaining. Did you know that she could quote the entirety of Shakespeare's great drama, line for line, word for word? She is, alas, destined this afternoon for our own potter's field. The undertaker should be here shortly to prepare her body. A life lived in turmoil, pain, and a great deal of anonymity, Miss Jones. Whoever cared for her once, and might at some point have actually loved her, has disappeared from our records and what institutional memory we have. And so, her years on this planet amount to very little. A most modest sum. It doesn't seem altogether fair, does it? Cleo was rich in personality, decisive in opinion, strong in belief. That all these were mad in nature doesn't diminish the passion that she had. I wish that she could have delivered a little mark on this world, for she deserved an epitaph larger that the notation in the hospital record that she will receive. No headstone. No flowers. Just another bed in this hospital, only this one will be six feet under. She deserved a funeral with trumpets and fireworks, elephants, lions, tigers, and a horse-drawn cortege, something fit for her queenliness.'

Lucy heard the doctor sigh. He looked up at her, pulling his eyes off the dead body. 'And so, Miss Jones, where does it leave you?'

'Still searching, Doctor. Searching right up to my last moments here.'

He looked slyly toward her. 'Ah, obsession. Single-minded pursuit in the face of all obstacles. A quality which you might admit comes closer to my profession than yours.'

'Perhaps *persistence* is a better word.'

He shrugged. 'As you wish. But answer me a question, Miss Jones: Have you come here searching for a madman? Or a sane one?'

He did not wait to hear her answer, which was slow in coming anyway. Instead, the doctor pushed Cleo's body back into the refrigerated unit with a grunt and a squealing sound of the runners complaining under her weight and said, 'I must go to find the undertaker, who is expected shortly and has a busy day ahead. Good day, Miss Jones.'

Lucy watched the doctor exit, his plump body swaying a little under the harsh overhead lights and she thought to herself that she was a little in awe of the killer who had managed to find the hospital. Even with all her efforts, she recognized that he was still concealed within the walls, and probably, for all she knew, utterly immune to her powers of investigation.

★   ★   ★

That is what you thought, right?

I closed my eyes, knowing that it was inevitable the Angel would be at my side within moments. I tried to calm my breathing, slow my racing heart, for I thought that every word from here on was dangerous, both for him and for me.

'Not only was it what I thought. It was true.'

I pivoted about, first right, then left, trying to see the source of the words I heard in the apartment. Vapors, ghosts, filmy lights that wavered and blinked seemed on either side of me.

'I was completely safe, every minute, every second, no matter what I did. Surely, C-Bird, you can see that?' His voice was rough-edged, filled with arrogance and anger and each word seemed to slap against my cheek like a dead man's kiss.

'You were safe from them,' I said.

'They did not even understand the law,' he boasted. 'Their own rules were completely useless.'

'But you weren't safe from me,' I replied. Defiant.

'And do you think you are safe from me, now?' the Angel said harshly. 'Do you think you are safe from yourself?'

I didn't answer. There was a momentary silence and then an explosion, like a gunshot, followed by the shattering sound of glass breaking into hundreds of shards. An ashtray, filled with cigarette butts had burst against a sidewall, thrown with lightning speed and force. I shrank back. My head spun drunkenly, exhaustion, tension, fear all vying for purchase within

526

me. There was a smell of stale smoke and I could see some dusty ashes still fluttering in the air next to a dark smudge against the white paint. 'We are closing now, Francis, on the end,' the Angel said, mocking me. 'Can't you feel it? Can't you sense it? Don't you understand that it is almost all over?'

The Angel's voice ragged me.

'Just like it was all those years ago,' he said bitterly. 'Dying time getting closer.'

I looked down at my hand. Did I throw the ashtray at the sound of his words? Or did he throw the ashtray to demonstrate that he was taking form, gaining substance, slowly returning to shape. Becoming real once again. I could see my hand quiver in front of me.

'You will die here, Francis. You should have died then, but now you will die here. Alone. Forgotten. Unloved. And dead. It will be days before someone finds your body, more than enough time for maggots to infest your skin, your stomach to be bloated and your stench to penetrate the walls.'

I shook my head, fighting as best as I could.

'Oh, yes,' he continued. 'That is how it will be. Not a word in the newspaper, not a tear shed at your funeral — if there even is one. Do you think people will come together to eulogize you, Francis, filling up the rows of some fine church? To make nice speeches about all your accomplishments? All the great and meaningful things you did before you died? I don't believe that's in the offing, Francis. Not in the slightest. You're just going to die and that will be it. Just a lot of relief by all the people who haven't cared a whit for you, and will be secretly overjoyed that you are no longer a burden on their lives. All that will remain of your days will be the smell you leave behind in this apartment, which the next tenants will probably scrub away with disinfectant and lye.'

I half gestured toward the wall of words.

He laughed. 'You think anyone will care about all your stupid scribblings? It will be gone in minutes. Seconds. Someone will come in, take one look at the mess the crazy man created, fetch a paintbrush and cover up every word. And all that happened a long time ago will be buried forever.'

I closed my eyes. If the words pummeled me, how long before his fists? It seemed to me, right at that moment, that the Angel was growing stronger every second, while I was growing weaker. I took a deep breath, and started to drag myself back across the room, my pencil in hand.

'You will not live to finish the story,' he said. 'Do you understand that, Francis? You will not live. I will not allow it. You think you can write the ending here, Francis? You make me laugh. The ending belongs to me, It always has. It always will.'

I didn't know what to think. His threat was as real at that moment as it was so many years earlier. But I struggled forward and thought I had to try. I wished Peter was here to help, and he must have been able to read my mind. Or perhaps I moaned Peter's name out loud, and wasn't aware of it, because the Angel laughed again. 'He can't help you this time. He's dead.'

30

Peter hustled through the Amherst Building corridor, sticking his head into the dayroom, pausing outside the examination rooms, taking a quick glance into the dining area, dodging clusters of patients, searching either for Francis or Lucy Jones, neither of whom seemed to be anywhere close by. He had the overwhelming sensation that something was happening that was critical, but that he was being prevented from witnessing. He had a sudden recollection of walking through the jungle in Vietnam. At war, the sky above, the moist earth beneath his feet, the superheated air and clammy foliage that caressed his clothes, all seemed the same as they were every day, but that there was no way of knowing, other than some otherworldly sixth sense, that around a corner there might be a sniper in a tree, or a waiting ambush, or perhaps just a nearly invisible wire stretched across the trail, patiently awaiting an errant step to trigger a buried mine. Everything was routine, everything was in place and ordinary, just as it was supposed to be, except for the hidden thing that promised tragedy. That was what he saw in the hospital world surrounding him.

For a moment, he paused by one of the barred windows, where an old man in a dull steel wheelchair had been left unattended. The man had a little white line of spittle meandering down his chin, where it mixed with a gray stubble. His eyes were fixed on the outside land beyond the window, and Peter asked him, 'What can you see, old man?' but he got no response. Rivulets of rain distorted the view, and past those haphazard streaks, it seemed there was little but a gray, damp, muffled day. Peter reached down and took a piece of brown paper towel from the man's lap and wiped his chin. The man didn't look toward Peter, but nodded, as if grateful. But the old man remained a blank slate. Whatever he might have been thinking about his present, remembering from his past or even planning for his future, was all lost in whatever fog had descended right behind his eyes. Peter thought there was little more of permanence to the man's remaining days than those raindrops dripping down the windowpane.

Behind him, a woman with long, unkempt, and wild gray-streaked hair flowing electrically from her head lurching from right to left down the corridor a little drunkenly, suddenly stopped, looked up at the ceiling, and said, 'Cleo's gone. She's gone forever . . . ' before putting her engine back into its never-ceasing gear and moving off.

Peter headed into the dormitory area. Not much of a home, he told himself. One day, he thought to himself. Two days. That was all it would take. A flurry of paperwork, a handshake or a nod of the head. A 'good luck,' and that would be it. Peter the Fireman would be shipped out and something different would take over his life.

He was a little unsure what to think. The world of the hospital did that to one rapidly, he thought. It engendered indecisiveness. In the real world, decisions were clear-cut and at least had the potential to be honest. Factors could be measured, assessed, and balanced. Decisions reached. But inside the walls and locked doors, none of that seemed the same.

Lucy had cut her hair and rendered it blond. If that didn't bring out the predatory urge in the man they hunted, he didn't know what would. Peter gritted his teeth for a second, grinding them together. He looked up at the ceiling, a little like a motorist waiting for the light to change from red to green. He thought Lucy was taking a chance. Francis, too, he thought, was walking a narrow line. Of the three of them, he understood, he had risked the least. In fact, he was hard-pressed to see how he had risked anything yet. Certainly, he hadn't put himself into any jeopardy that he could readily see.

Peter turned and left the room. When he exited into the hallway, he spotted Lucy Jones, hovering outside their small office, and he hurried in her direction.

★ ★ ★

One after another, the release hearings had progressed all morning and into the afternoon. They were a theater of the expected; Francis swiftly understood that if you had arranged all the factors necessary to qualify for a hearing, the likelihood was that you were going to be released. The charade that he was watching was a bureaucratic opera, designed to make certain that unforeseeable risks weren't taken and careers unnecessarily threatened. No one wanted to release someone who promptly descended into a psychotic rage.

The bored young man from the prosecutor's office reviewed any legal cases outstanding against the patients in a perfunctory fashion; everything he said was uniformly objected to by the equally young man from the public defender's office, serving as patient advocate, and who wore the ardent behavior of a do-gooder. More critical to the hearing panel was the assessment from the hospital staff and the recommendation from the young woman from the state Department of Mental Health, still hunting through her folders and notes, and who spoke in a hesitant, half-stuttering fashion, Francis thought, which made a weird sense to him, because she was really being asked whether it was safe to release someone, and she actually had no idea. 'Is he a danger to himself, or to others?' It was like a church litany. Sure it was safe, he thought, if they kept up their medications

531

and they didn't walk directly back into the same circumstances which had driven them mad in the first place. Of course, these were the only circumstances available, so that it was hard to be very optimistic about anyone's actual chances beyond the hospital walls.

Patients were released. Patients came back. A boomerang of madness.

Francis shifted about in his chair, still bent forward, listening intently to every word spoken, watching the faces of every patient, every physician, every parent, brother, sister, or cousin who rose to speak. Within his heart he felt nothing but turmoil and chaos. His voices threatened to send him spiraling into some dark, deeply pained place. They shouted desperately for him to leave. Insistent, screeching, pleading, begging, demanding — all equally fervent, almost hysterical in their desire. It was, he thought, like being trapped within the pit of some hellish orchestra, where every instrument played louder and more harshly, more utterly out of tune with every passing second.

He understood why. Occasionally, he would close his eyes, trying to get some rest. But it didn't help much. He continued sweating, feeling every muscle in his entire body tensed. That no one had as yet seen the struggle he was trapped within surprised him for he thought anyone who truly looked at him would see in an instant that he was teetering on some razor edge.

Francis breathed in hard, but thought there was no air in the room.

What can't they see? he asked himself.

The hospital is where the Angel hides. In order to be free to kill, he has to be able to come and go.

He looked across the room at the hearing board. *This is the exit door*, he reminded himself.

Francis stole a quick look at the gathering of family and friends surrounding the patients. *Everyone thinks that the Angel is a lone killer. But I know something they don't: Someone here, whether they know it or not, is helping him.*

And then: *Why did he kill Short Blond? Why did he draw attention to himself here, where he was safe?*

Neither Lucy nor Peter had asked that question, Francis heard himself say deep inside. As much as anything, it scared him. That he knew to ask this made Francis's head swirl and he felt as if a wave of nausea might overcome him. His voices resounded within him, warning him, cajoling him, insisting that he not venture into the darkness that beckoned.

They think he killed Short Blond because he had to kill.

He took a short breath of stale air.

Maybe so. Maybe not.

He hated himself in that second more than ever before. *You could be a killer, too,* Francis heard himself say. For an instant he thought he'd spoken out loud, but no one turned and paid any attention to him, and so he guessed that he hadn't actually uttered the words.

Big Black had wandered off, bored with the droning routine of each hearing. When he returned to the room, Francis made an immense effort to conceal the anxiety that pummeled him. The huge attendant slumped into the seat next to Francis and whispered, 'So, C-Bird, you got the hang of this yet? You see enough?'

'Not quite,' Francis replied softly. What he had not seen yet was what he both feared and expected.

Big Black craned forward to muffle his words. 'We've got to be getting back to Amherst. Day's almost finished. People gonna be looking for you pretty soon. There a therapy session scheduled for this evening?'

'No,' Francis half lied for he didn't really know the answer. 'Mister Evans canceled it after all the excitement.'

Big Black shook his head. 'Shouldn't be canceling those.' He spoke to Francis, but more to the world of

533

the hospital. The attendant looked up. 'Come on, C-Bird,' he said. 'We've got to be getting back. There's only a couple of these hearings left. Ain't gonna be any different from what you've already seen.'

Francis didn't know what to say, because he didn't want to tell Big Black the truth, which was that one was going to be quite a bit different. He looked across the room.

There were three patients still waiting. Each was easy to pick out in the remaining crowd of people. They simply weren't as well groomed. Their hair was either slicked down, or frizzy and uncontrolled. Their clothes weren't as clean. They wore striped pants and checked shirts, or sandals with mismatched socks. Nothing about them seemed to quite fit, not what they wore, or how they looked out at the proceedings. It was a little as if they were all slightly lopsided. Their hands shook and their faces twitched at the corners of their mouths — those were the different medications and their side effects. All three were men, and Francis would have guessed their ages to be between thirty and forty-five. None was particularly distinctive; they weren't fat or tall or white-haired or scarred or tattooed or anything that made them stand out. They wore their emotions inwardly. Outwardly, they seemed blank, as if the drugs had worn away not only their madness, but much of their names and pasts, as well.

None had turned aside and looked at him, at least that he could tell. They had remained stoic, almost impassive, staring ahead as each case had been heard throughout the long day. He could not quite see their faces; at best they were profiles.

One man was surrounded by perhaps four visitors. Francis guessed an elderly set of parents and a sister and her husband, who squirmed in his seat, clearly unhappy to be there. Another patient sat between two women, both far older than he, and Francis supposed a mother and an aunt. The third sat beside a stiff older man in a blue suit with a stern, unrelenting look on his face, and a much younger woman, a sister or a niece, Francis thought, who seemed unafraid and listened intently to all that was being said, occasionally taking down some notes on a yellow pad of legal paper.

The overweight judge banged his gavel down. 'What have we got left?' he asked briskly. 'It's getting late.'

The woman psychiatrist looked up. 'Three cases, Your Honor,' she said with a slight stutter. 'They shouldn't be difficult. Two of the men are here with diagnoses of retardation and the third has emerged from a catatonic state, and shown great progress with the help of antipsychotic medication. None have any current charges pending . . . '

'Come on, C-Bird,' Big Black whispered, a little more insistently. 'We've got to get back. Ain't nothing different gonna happen in here now. These cases are going to be rubber-stamped and out-of-here quick. Time for us to leave.'

Francis stole a glance toward the young woman psychiatrist, who was continuing to speak to the retired judge. ' . . . All these gentlemen have been committed and released on several prior occasions, your honor . . . '

'Let's go, C-Bird,' Big Black said in a tone that didn't leave room for debate. Francis didn't know how to say that what was about to take place was what he had spent the day waiting for.

He stood up and Francis realized that he wasn't being given a choice. Big Black gave him a little push in the direction of the door, and Francis stepped that way. He did not turn around, although he had the impression that at least one of the three remaining men had slightly turned in his chair and aimed a glance in his direction, his eyes burning into Francis's back. He could feel a presence that was both cold and hot all at the same time, and he understood that was what the killer felt, when he held sway with knife and terror over his victim.

For a second, he thought he heard a voice shouting after him: *We are the same, you and I!* but then he realized that there was no real noise in the hearing room, except the routine voices of the participants in the daylong exercise. What he heard was hallucination.

But it was real, and not real, all at once.

Run Francis, run! his own voices clamored.

But he did not. He simply walked forward slowly, imagining that the man they had hunted was directly behind him, but that no one, not Lucy, Peter, or the Moses brothers, Mister Evil, or Doctor Gulp-a-pill would believe him if he blurted this out. There were three remaining patients in that room. Two were what they were. One was not. And Francis thought behind that one false mask of madness he could hear the Angel laughing at him.

He understood another thing: The Angel seemed to like risks, but Francis might have slipped past the acceptable category. He would not leave Francis alive much longer.

Big Black held the door to the administration building open and the two of them stepped out into a haphazard drizzle. Francis turned his face skyward, and felt the mist flow over him, almost as if he could get the sky to clean away all his fears and doubts. The day was rapidly closing down, the gray skies fading to a washed-out black that heralded night. In the distance, Francis could make out the sound of some heavy machinery laboring hard and fast, and he turned in that direction. Big Black, as well, had pivoted about and was staring across the hospital grounds. Over by the garden, in the makeshift cemetery in the most distant corner of Western State, a bright yellow backhoe was dumping a final load or two of moist dirt onto the ground.

'Hold on, C-Bird,' Big Black said abruptly. 'We need

to take a minute here.' The huge attendant lowered his head down, and then Francis heard him whisper, 'Our Father, who art in heaven . . .' and the rest of the brief prayer.

Francis listened quietly. When Big Black lifted his head, the attendant said, 'I'm thinking that'll be just about the only words spoken over poor Cleo.' He sighed. 'Maybe she'll have more peace now. Lord knows, she had little enough while she was alive. That's a sad thing, C-Bird. A real sad thing. Don't make me have to speak a prayer over you. You hang in there. Things will get better, sure enough. You trust me.'

Francis nodded. He did not truly believe this although he wanted to. And, when he looked up once again into the darkening skies, hearing the distant noise of Cleo's grave being filled in, he thought right at that moment that he was listening to the overture of a symphony, notes and measures and rhythms that promised that there were surely still deaths to come.

★ ★ ★

It was, Lucy considered in reflection, the simplest, least adorned plan they could come up with, and probably the only one that held out any hope for success. She would simply take the late night nursing shift that had proven to be fatal for Short Blond. After taking up her position in the nursing station alone, she would wait for the Angel to show up.

Lucy was the tethered goat. The Angel was the man-eating tiger. It was the oldest of ruses. She would leave the hospital intercom open to the second-floor station, one flight above her, where the Moses brothers would wait for her signal. In the hospital, cries for *help* were pretty familiar and often ignored, so it was decided that if they heard Lucy say *Apollo*, they would race to her side. Lucy had chosen the word with a twinge of irony. They might as well have been astronauts heading for a distant moon. The Moses brothers did not think it would take more than a few seconds for them to descend the stairwell, which would have the added advantage of blocking one of the routes of escape. All Lucy had to do was keep the Angel occupied for a few moments — and not die doing it. The front entrance to Amherst was double-locked, as was the side entry. They all imagined that they could corner the killer before he was either able to slice Lucy or to fumble his way through keys and out into the hospital grounds. But even if he did flee, by then Security would be alerted, and the Angel's options would be rapidly narrowing. And, more important, they would see his face.

Peter had been particularly insistent on this point and one other detail. It was critical, he'd argued, that the Angel's identity be learned, regardless of what happened. It would be the only way to back build the cases against him.

He had also demanded that the door to the first-floor men's dormitory be left unlocked, so that he, too, could monitor the situation even if it meant a sleepless night. He argued that he would be a little closer to Lucy, and that the Angel was least likely to expect an attack from a door customarily locked. The Moses brothers had said that was true — but that they could not leave the door unlocked themselves. 'Against the rules,' Little Black had said. 'Big doc would have our jobs if he caught wind of that . . . '

'Well — ,' Peter started, only to be shut down by Little Black holding up his hand.

'Of course, Lucy will have her own set of keys for all the doors around here. What she does with them while she's at the nursing station ain't our business . . . ,' Little Black said. 'But it ain't gonna be my brother and I leave that door open. We find this guy, all is good. But

I'm not looking for any more trouble than we've already got coming.'

★ ★ ★

Lucy looked down at her bed. It was quiet in the nurse-trainees' dormitory, and she had the sensation that she was alone in the building, although she knew that couldn't be true. Somewhere there were people talking, perhaps even laughing over a joke, or sharing some story. Not her. She had laid out a white nurse's outfit on the surface of the cot. It was to be her costume for the night. Inwardly, she felt a little mocking laughter. First Communion dress. Prom dress. Wedding dress. Funeral dress. A woman laid out her clothes with care for special occasions.

In her hand, she hefted the small, snub-nosed pistol. She placed it into her handbag. She had not told any of the others that she had it with her.

Lucy did not truly expect the Angel to show, but she was at a loss as to what else she could do in the time remaining. Her own stay was coming to an end, her welcome long past expiration and by Monday morning Peter would be shipped out as well. That left this one night. In some ways, she had already begun to plan ahead, considering about what she would be forced to do when her mission ended in failure and she departed the hospital. Eventually, she knew, the Angel would either kill again inside the hospital or seek release and kill once he'd stepped outside the walls. If she monitored every release hearing, and kept a watch on every death at the hospital, sooner or later he would make a mistake and she would be there to accuse him. Of course, she realized, the problem with that particular approach was obvious: It meant someone else had to die.

She took a deep breath and reached for the nurse's

outfit. She tried to not imagine what that other, nameless, faceless but very real victim would look like. Or who she might be. Or what hopes and dreams and desires she might have. She existed somewhere in some parallel world, as real as anyone, but ghostlike. For a second, Lucy wondered if this woman out there waiting to die was a little like the hallucinations that so many of the patients in the hospital had. She was just out there somewhere, not knowing that she was next in line for the Angel if he did not show up at the first-floor nursing station in the Amherst Building that night.

With the full weight of that unknown woman's future resting on her shoulders, Lucy slowly began to dress herself.

★   ★   ★

When I looked up from the words to catch my breath, Peter was there in the apartment, standing nonchalantly up against the wall, arms folded in front of his chest, a troubled look on his face. But that was all that was familiar about him; his clothing was in tatters, the skin on his arms was seared red and black. Dirt and blood streaked his cheeks and throat. There was so little left of him that I remembered, I am not sure whether I could have recognized him. The room filled with a foul odor and suddenly I could smell the awful stench of burned flesh and decay.

I shook off a sensation of dread, and greeted my only friend.

'Peter,' I said, relief flooding my voice, 'you're here to help.'

He shook his head but didn't voice a reply. He gestured once to his neck and then his lips, like a mute signaling that words were lost to him.

I pointed back at the wall where my story was collected. 'I was beginning to understand,' I said. 'I was there at the release hearings. I knew. Not everything, but I was beginning to know. When I walked across the hospital grounds that night, for the first time, I saw something different, didn't I? But where were you? Where was Lucy? All of you were making plans, but no one wanted to listen to me, and I was the one who saw the most.'

He smiled again, as if to underscore the truth in what I was saying.

'Why weren't you there to listen to me?' I asked again.

Peter shrugged sadly. Then he reached out a hand that seemed almost stripped of flesh, like a skeleton's bony fingers reaching for my own. In the second that I hesitated, the hand reaching for me faded, almost as if a fogbank had slid between him and me, and after I blinked again, Peter was gone. Wordless. Disappearing like a conjurer's trick on a stage. I shook my head, trying to clear my thinking, and when I looked up again, filmy, slowly taking shape very close to where Peter's apparition had been, I saw the Angel.

He glowed white, as if there was some harsh, unblinking light within him. It blinded me, and I shaded my eyes, and when I looked back, he was still there. Only ghostlike, vaporous, as if he was opaque, constructed part of water, part of air, partially by imagination. His features were indistinct, as if they were slurred about the edges. The only thing sharp and distinct about him were his words.

'Hello, C-Bird,' he said. 'There's no one here to help you. No one left to help you anywhere. Now it is just you and I and what happened that night.'

I looked at him and realized that he was right.

'You don't want to remember that night, do you Francis?'

I shook my head, not trusting my own voice.

He pointed across the room at the story growing on the wall.

'Close to dying time, Francis,' he said coldly.

Then he added, 'That night, and this one, too.'

31

Francis found Peter outside the first-floor nursing station. It was pill time, and patients were lining up for their evening medications. There was a little jostling back and forth, a few whiny complaints about this or that, a shove or two, but mostly things were orderly; if there was anything to suggest that this was just the arrival of another night in another week of another month of yet another year for the majority of them, it was impossible to see.

'Peter,' Francis said quietly, but unable to hide the tension in his voice, 'Peter, I need to speak with you. And Lucy, too. I think I saw him. I think I know how we can find him.' In Francis's fevered imagination, all that was necessary was to pull the files of the three men who remained behind in the release hearing room. One of them would be the Angel. He was certain of this, and his excitement spilled into every word.

Peter the Fireman, however, seemed distracted, barely listening. His eyes were fixed across the hallway, and Francis followed his gaze. He looked over at the line and saw Newsman and Napoleon, the hulking retarded man and the angry retarded man, three of the women with dolls and all the other faces that filled the Amherst Building with familiarity. He half expected to hear Cleo's voice booming forth, with some imaginary complaint that *the goddamn bastards* had failed once again to address, followed by her unmistakable cackling laugh bouncing off the wire bars that separated the station from the corridor. Mister Evil was behind the counter, overseeing the evening dispensing of medications by Nurse Wrong, making notations on a clipboard. Every so often Evans would look up and glare in Peter's general direction. After a second, Evans reached down and grasped a small paper cup from an array in front of him, then exited the station and made his way through the lineup of patients, who parted like river waters to let him pass. He came over to Peter and Francis before Francis had had time to say anything else to Peter about all that was troubling him.

'Here you are, Mister Petrel,' Evans said stiffly, almost formally. 'Thorazine. Fifty mikes. This should help quiet those voices that you continue to deny hearing.'

He thrust the paper cup at Francis. 'Down the hatch,' he said. Francis took the pill, popped it into his mouth and immediately slid it with his tongue to a place behind his teeth, cheeking it. Evans watched him closely, then gestured for Francis to open his mouth. Francis complied, and the psychologist took a perfunctory glance inside. Francis could not tell whether Evans had seen the pill or not, but Mister Evil spoke quickly, 'You see, C-Bird, it doesn't really matter to me whether you take the medication or you don't. If you do, well, then there's the chance you'll get out of here someday. If you don't, well, take a look around . . .'

He gestured widely with his arm, finally bringing it to rest pointing at one of the geriatric patients, white-haired, fragile, skin as flaccid and thin as paper, an afterthought of a man locked into a dilapidated wheelchair that creaked as it moved. ' . . . And imagine that this will be home for you forever.'

Francis breathed in sharply, but didn't respond. Evans gave him a second, as if he expected a reply, then shrugged and pivoted toward Peter. 'No pills for the Fireman this night,' he said stiffly. 'No pills for the real killer here. Not this imaginary killer you keep searching for. The real murderer in this place. You.'

Evans's eyes narrowed. 'We don't have a pill that can fix what's wrong with you, Peter. Nothing that can make you whole. Nothing that can restore the damage you've done. You're going to leave us despite my objections. I was overruled by Gulptilil and all the other important folks who've been here to see you. A real sweetheart deal. Going to some fancy hospital and some fancy program a real long ways away to treat a nonexistent disease that fictionally plagues the Fireman. But no one has a pill or a treatment plan or even some sort of advanced neurosurgery that can truly fix what the Fireman has. Arrogance. Guilt. And memory. It doesn't make any difference who you become, Peter, because inside you will always remain the same. A killer.'

He looked closely at Peter who stood motionless in the middle of the corridor. 'I used to think,' Evans said with frigid bitterness in every word, 'that it was my brother who would carry the scars from your fire for the rest of his life. But I was wrong. He'll recover. He'll go on to doing good and important things. But you, Peter, you'll never forget, will you? You're the one who will be scarred. Nightmares, Peter. Nightmares forever.'

With those words, Mister Evil turned abruptly and went back to the nursing station. No one spoke to him as he passed by the line of patients, who perhaps were not aware of many things, but recognized anger when they saw it, and carefully moved aside.

Peter glared after Mister Evil, but contradictorily said, 'I suppose he's not entirely wrong to hate me. What I did was right for some and wrong for others.'

He probably should have continued with that, but he did not. Instead, he turned to Francis and said, 'What were you trying to tell me?'

Francis glanced around to make sure none of the staff were watching him, and he spit the pill out into his palm, sliding it into his pants pocket in the same motion. He felt pummeled by conflicting emotions, unsure what to say. He finally took a deep breath and asked, 'So you're leaving ... But what about the Angel?'

'We'll get him tonight. But if not tonight, then soon. So, tell me about the release hearings?'

'He was there. I know it. I could feel it . . . '

'What did he say?'

'Nothing.'

'Then what did he do?'

'Nothing. But . . . '

'Then how can you be so sure, C-Bird?'

'Peter, I could feel it. I'm sure.' The words expressed a certainty that wasn't matched in the doubtful tone Francis used.

Peter shook his head. 'It's not much to go on, C-Bird. But we should tell Lucy if we get a chance.'

Francis looked at Peter and felt a sudden surge of frustration and perhaps a little anger. He wasn't being listened to now, they hadn't listened to him yet, and he realized that they would never listen to him. What they wanted to pursue was something solid and concrete. But in the mental hospital, such things barely existed.

'She's leaving. You're leaving . . . '

Peter nodded. 'I don't know what to tell you, C-Bird. I hate leaving you behind. But if I stay . . . '

'You and Lucy will leave. You'll both get out. I'll never get out.'

'It won't be that bad, you'll be fine,' Peter said, but even he knew this was a lie.

'I don't want to stay any longer, either,' Francis said. His voice quivered.

'You'll get out,' Peter said. 'Look, C-Bird, I'll make a promise. After I go through whatever the hell this program they're shipping me to, and then, once I'm clear, I'll get you out. I don't exactly know how, but I will. I won't leave you here.'

Francis wanted to believe this, but didn't dare allow himself to. He thought that in his short life many people had made promises and predictions — and that precious few of them had ever happened. Caught between the two pillars of the future, one described by Evans, the other pledged by Peter, Francis did not know what to think, but he knew he was a whole lot closer to one than the other.

Instead, he stammered, 'The Angel, Peter. What about the Angel?'

'I'm hoping tonight's the night, C-Bird. It's pretty much our only chance. Last chance. Whatever. But it's a reasonable approach, and I think it will work.'

There was a distinct murmuring within Francis, as the chorus of voices all seemed to mutter at once. He was caught between paying attention to them or paying attention to Peter, who briefly described the plan for that night. It was a little like Peter didn't want Francis to have too many details, as if he was trying to move Francis to the perimeter of the night, keeping him from the center, where he expected the action to take place.

'Lucy will be the target?' Francis asked.

'Yes and no,' Peter replied. 'She'll be there, and she'll be the bait. But that's all. She'll be fine. It's all worked out. The Moses brothers will cover her on one side, and I'll be there on the other.'

Francis thought this was untrue.

For a moment, he hesitated. It seemed to him that he had almost too much to say.

Then Peter leaned toward Francis, bending his head down so that their words just flowed between the two of them. 'C-Bird, what is bothering you?'

Francis rubbed his hands together, like a man trying to wash something sticky from his fingertips. 'I can't be sure,' Francis said, although he knew this was a lie, because he was sure. His voice stammered, and he wanted desperately to endow it with strength, passion, and conviction, but, as he spoke, he thought every word that tumbled past his lips was filled with weakness. 'I just sensed it. It was the same feeling that I had when he came to my bed and threatened me. The night that he killed the Dancer with the pillow. The same I felt when I saw Cleo hanging there . . . '

'Cleo hung herself.'

'He was there.'

'She took her own life.'

'*He was there!*' Francis said, mustering all the insistence he could.

'Why do you think so?'

'He mutilated her hand. Not Cleo. The thumb was moved, it couldn't have just dropped in the location it was found. There was no pair of scissors or homemade knife anywhere to be found. There was only blood there, in the stairwell, nowhere else, so slicing off the thumb had to be done there. She didn't do it. He did.'

'But why?'

Francis put his hand up to his forehead. He thought he felt feverish, hot, as if the world around him had somehow been burnt by the sun. 'To join the two together. To show us that he was everywhere. I can't quite tell, Peter, but it was a message and one that we don't understand.'

Peter eyed Francis carefully, but noncommittally. It was as if he both believed and didn't believe everything Francis said. 'And the release hearing? You say you could *sense* his presence?' Peter's words were endowed with skepticism.

'The Angel needs to be able to come and go. He needs access to both here and there. The world inside and the world outside.'

'Why?'

Francis took a deep breath. 'Power. Safety.'

Peter nodded and shrugged, at the same time. 'Maybe so. But when all is said and done, C-Bird, the Angel is just a killer with a particular predilection for a certain body type and hair style, with a penchant for mutilation.

I suppose Gulptilil or some forensic shrink could sit around and speculate about the whys and wherefores, maybe come up with some theory about how the Angel was abused as a child, but it's not really relevant. What he is, when you think about it, is just another bad-acting bad guy, and my guess is we're going to catch him tonight, because he's a compulsive type, who won't be able to refuse the trap set for him. Probably what we should have done from the start, instead of spinning our wheels with interviews and patient files. One way or the other, he'll show. End of story.'

Francis wanted to share Peter's confidence, but could not. 'Peter,' he said cautiously, 'I suppose everything you say is true. But suppose it's not. Suppose he's not what you and Lucy think. Suppose everything that has happened so far is something different.'

'C-Bird, I don't follow.'

Francis swallowed air. His throat felt parched and he could barely manage more that a whisper. 'I don't know, I don't know,' he repeated. 'But everything you and I and Lucy have done is what he would expect . . . '

'I've told you before: That's what any investigation is. A steady examination of facts and details.'

Francis shook his head. He wanted to get mad, but instead felt merely fear. He finally lifted his head and looked around. He saw Newsman, who had a newspaper open and was studiously memorizing headlines. He saw Napoleon, who envisioned himself a French general. He wished he saw Cleo, who once lived in a queen's world. He fixed on some of the geriatrics, who were lost in memory, and the retarded men and women, who were stuck in some dull childishness. Peter and Lucy were using logic — even psychiatric logic — to find the killer. But, what C-Bird realized was that this was the most illogical approach of all, inside a world so filled with fantasy, delusion, and confusion.

His own voices shrieked at him: *Stop! Run! Hide!*

Don't think! Don't imagine! Don't speculate! Don't understand!

Right at that moment, Francis realized that he knew what would happen that night. And he was powerless to prevent it.

'Peter,' he said slowly, 'maybe the Angel *wants* everything to be as is it.'

'Well, I suppose that's possible,' Peter said with a small laugh, as if that was the craziest thing he'd ever heard. He was filled with confidence. 'That would be his biggest mistake, wouldn't it?'

Francis didn't know how to reply, but he surely didn't think so.

★   ★   ★

The Angel leaned over me, hovering so close that I could feel every cold breath attached to each frozen word. I shook as I wrote, keeping my face to the wall, as if I could ignore his presence. I could feel him reading right over my shoulder, and he laughed with that same awful noise that I recognized from when he had sat on the side of my bunk inside the hospital and promised me that I would die.

'C-Bird saw so much. But couldn't quite put it together,' he scoffed.

I stopped writing, my hand paused just above the wall. I didn't look in his direction, but I spoke out, high-pitched, a little panicked, but still, needing the answers.

'I was right, wasn't I. About Cleo?'

He wheezed a laugh again. 'Yes. She did not know I was there, but I was. And what was most unusual about that night, C-Bird, was that I had every intention of killing her before dawn arrived. I figured simply to cut her throat in her sleep and then point some evidence at one of the other women in the dormitory. This had worked just as I knew it would with Lanky. It was likely to work again. Or perhaps just the pillow over the face. Cleo was asthmatic. She smoked too much. It probably wouldn't have taken long to choke the air from her. That worked with the Dancer.'

'Why Cleo?'

'It was when she pointed up at the building where I lived and shouted out that she knew me. I didn't believe her, of course. But why take the chance? Everything else was going just as I imagined it would. But C-Bird knows that, doesn't he? C-Bird knows, because he is like me. He wants to kill. He knows how to kill. He hates so much. He loves the idea of death so much. Killing is the only answer for me. And for C-Bird, too.'

'No,' I moaned. 'Not true.'

'You know the only answer, Francis,' the Angel whispered.

'I want to live,' I said.

'So did Cleo. But she wanted to die, too. Life and death can be so close. Almost the same, Francis. And tell me: Are you any different from her?'

I couldn't answer that question. Instead, I asked, 'You watched her die?'

'Of course,' the Angel replied, hissing. 'I saw her take the bedsheet from beneath her bed. She must have been saving it for just that reason. She was in a lot of pain and the medications weren't helping her in the slightest, and all she could see ahead of her, day after day, year after year, was more and more pain. She wasn't afraid of killing herself, C-Bird, not like you are. She was an empress and she understood the nobility of taking her own life. The necessity of it. I just encouraged her along the path, and used her death to my advantage. I opened the doors, then followed her out and watched her go into the stairwell . . . '

'Where was the nurse on duty?'

'Asleep, C-Bird. Dozed off, feet up, head back,

snoring. You think they actually cared enough about any of you to stay awake?'

'But why did you cut her, afterward?'

'To show you what you guessed later, C-Bird. To show you that I could have killed her. But mostly, I knew that it would make everyone argue, and that the people who wanted to believe I was there might see it as proof, and the people who didn't want to believe I was there would see it as persuasive of their position. Doubt and confusion are truly helpful things, C-Bird, when you are planning something precise and perfect.'

'Except for one thing,' I whispered. 'You didn't count on me.'

He snarled and replied, 'But that's why I'm here now, C-Bird. For you.'

* * *

Shortly before ten PM, Lucy moved rapidly across the grounds of the hospital toward the Amherst Building, to take over the late-night solitary shift. The graveyard shift, as it was called in newspaper offices and police stations. It was an awful night, caught somewhere between storm and heat, and she lowered her head and thought that her white outfit cut a slice through the thick black air.

In her right hand, she carried a ring of keys that jangled as she quick marched down the path. Above her, an oak tree bent and swayed, rustling leaves with a breeze that she didn't feel and which seemed out of place in the still, humid night. She had thrown her pocketbook, with the loaded pistol concealed inside, over her right shoulder, giving her a jaunty look which was far from how she felt. She ignored an odd cry, something desperate and lonely, that seemed to float down from one of the other dormitories.

Lucy unlocked the two deadbolt locks at the door to

Amherst, and put her shoulder to the heavy wood, pushing her way into the building with a scraping sound. For an instant, she was taken aback. Every time she'd been in the building, either in her office, or making her way through the corridor, it had been filled with people, light, and noise. Now, not even late, it had been transformed. What had seemed jammed and constantly busy, energized by all sorts of misshapen madnesses and misbegotten thoughts, was now quiet, save for the occasional eerie shout or scream that lurked through the empty spaces. The corridor was nearly black; some light that faded a little bit of the darkness to a manageable gray came weakly through the windows from distant buildings. The only real light in the corridor was a small cone of brightness, behind the barred door of the nursing station, where a single desk lamp glowed.

She saw a form move at the nursing station, and exhaled slowly when she saw Little Black uncurl himself from behind the desk and open the wire door.

'Right on time,' he said.

'Wouldn't miss this for the world,' she said with a measure of false bravado.

He shook his head. 'I'm guessing you're just in for a long, boring night,' he said. He pointed at the intercom on the desk. It was old-fashioned, a small squawk box with a single on/off switch on the top and a dial to reduce squelch. 'This will keep you connected to my brother and I upstairs,' he said. 'But we really got to hear you sing out that Apollo word, because these things got to be ten, twenty years old and they don't work too good. The telephone, too, connects upstairs. Just dial two zero two, and it rings. Tell you what, if it rings twice and then you hang up, we'll take that as a signal, too, and come running.'

'Two zero two. Got it.'

'But ain't likely to need it,' Little Black said. 'In my

experience, inside this place, nothing logical or expected ever happens right, no matter how much planning goes into it. I'm pretty sure that the guy you're hunting knows you're gonna be here. Word gets around pretty good, if you say the right thing to the right person. Gets broadcast real fast. But if this guy is as clever as you seem to think, I've got my doubts that he'll walk into something he's got to figure is a trap. Still, never know.'

'That's right,' Lucy said. 'You never know.'

Little Black nodded. 'Well, you call. You call if something happens with any of the patients you don't want to handle. Just ignore anybody calling out for help or something. We generally wait until morning for dealing with most any nighttime problems.'

'Okay.'

He shook his head. 'Nervous?'

'No,' Lucy replied. She knew she was *something* she just wasn't certain that *nervous* described it.

'When it gets late, I'll send someone to check up on you. That'd be okay, right?'

'Always appreciate the company. Except I don't want to spook the Angel.'

'I'm not guessing that he's the sort that gets spooked by much,' Little Black said. He looked down the corridor. 'I made sure the dormitory doors are locked,' he said. 'Men's and women's. Especially that one right over there that Peter wanted me to unlock. Of course, you know that's the key, right at the end of that chain that unlocks it . . . ' He winked conspiratorially. 'My guess is, just about everyone in there is lights-out fast asleep by now.'

With that, Little Black shoved back and stepped down the corridor. He turned once and waved, but it was so dark at the end of the hallway, near the stairwell on that end, that she could barely make out his features, beyond the white attendant's suit he wore.

Lucy heard the door creak shut, and then put her

pocketbook down on the table, next to the phone. She waited for a few seconds, just long enough to let the silence creep over her with a clammy enveloping sensation, and then she took the key and went down to the men's dormitory. As quietly as she could, she slipped the key into the door lock and turned it once, hearing a distant click. She took a deep breath, and then went back to the nursing station and began to wait for something to happen.

★   ★   ★

Peter sat wide-awake and cross-legged on his bunk. He heard the *click* of the lock tumblers being turned, and knew this meant Lucy had unlocked the door. He imagined her in his mind's eye rapidly walking back down to the nursing station. Lucy was so striking, from her height, her scar, the way she carried herself, it was easy for Peter to picture her every move. He strained, trying to hear the sound of her footsteps, but was unable. The noise of the room filled with sleeping men, tangled up in sheets and various despairs, overwhelmed any modest sound from out in the corridor. Too much snoring, heavy breathing, talking in their sleep going on around him to pick out and isolate noise. He guessed this might be a problem, and so, when he was persuaded that all around him were locked in whatever unsettled, uneven sleep they were going to get, he, silently unfolded himself and gingerly picked his way past the forms of men and came to the door. He did not dare open it, for he thought that the noise might awaken someone, no matter how drugged they were. Instead, what Peter did was simply slide down, back against the adjacent wall, so that he was sitting on the floor, waiting for a sound that was out of the ordinary, or the word that signaled the arrival of the Angel.

He wished he had a weapon. A gun, he thought,

555

would be helpful. Even a baseball bat or a policeman's baton. He reminded himself that the Angel would wield a knife, and he would need to stay clear of the man's reach until the Moses brothers arrived, Security was called, and success had been achieved.

Lucy, he guessed, would not have agreed to her performance without some assistance. She had not said she would be armed, but he suspected she was.

The edge they had, though, was in surprise and numbers. It would, he imagined, be sufficient.

Peter stole a glance at Francis and shook his head. The younger man seemed to be asleep, which he thought was a good thing. He regretted that he was leaving Francis behind, but felt that probably, all in all, it was going to be better for him. Since the arrival of the Angel at his bedside — an event Peter still wasn't certain had actually taken place — it seemed to him that Francis had been increasingly flaky, and increasingly less in control. C-Bird had been descending along some route that Peter could only guess at, and surely wanted no part of. It made him sad to see what was happening to his friend, and be powerless to do anything about it. Francis had taken Cleo's death very hard, Peter thought, and more than any of them seemed to have developed an unhealthy obsession with finding the Angel. It was a little as if Francis's need to find the killer signaled something different and immense to the younger man. It was something well beyond determination, and something dangerous.

Peter, of course, was wrong about that. Obsession truly lay with Lucy, but he did not want to see that.

He leaned his head back against the wall, closing his eyes for a moment. He felt fatigue running through his veins, parallel to excitement. He understood that much was about to change in his life, that night, the following morning. Within him, Peter pushed away many memories, and he wondered what was next in his own story. At the same time, he continued to listen carefully, waiting for a signal from Lucy.

He wondered if, after that night, he would ever see her again.

A few feet away, Francis lay rigid on his own bunk, perfectly aware that Peter had silently moved past him and taken up a position near the door. He knew sleep was very distant, but death was not, and he breathed in slowly, steadily, waiting for something he could feel was utterly inevitable to occur. Something that was set in stone, planned and plotted, measured out, deciphered and designed. He felt as if he was caught up in a current, dragging him someplace far closer to who he was, or who he could be, and that he was helpless to swim against the tide.

★   ★   ★

We were all exactly where the Angel expected us to be. I wanted to write that down, but did not. It went beyond the idea that we had simply taken up places on a stage, and were feeling that last rush of anxiety before the curtain rises, wondering whether our lines were memorized, whether our movements were choreographed, whether we would hit our marks and follow our cues. The Angel knew where we were physically, but deeper still. He knew where we were in our hearts.

Except, perhaps, for me, because my heart was so confused.

I rocked back and forth, moaning, like a wounded man on a battlefield who wants to call for help, but can manage only some deep sound of pain. I was kneeling on the floor, the wall space dwindling in front of me, as were the words I had available.

Around me, the Angel roared, his voice like a torrent, drowning out my protests. He shouted, 'I knew. I knew. You were all so stupid . . . so, normal . . . so sane!' His voice seemed to rebound off the walls, gain momentum in the shadows and then pummel me like blows. 'I was none of those things! I was so much greater!'

Then, as I lowered my head and squeezed shut my eyes, I yelled out, 'Not me . . .' which made little sense, but the sound of my own voice contending with his gave me a momentary burst of adrenaline. I took a breath, waiting for some pain to be sent my way, but when it did not come, I looked up, and saw the room suddenly bursting with light. Explosions, starbursts, like phosphorous shells in the distance, tracers racing through darkness, a battle in the dark.

'Tell me!' I demanded, my voice raised above the sounds of fighting. The world of my little apartment seemed to buckle and sway with the violence of war.

The Angel was around me, everywhere, enveloping me. I gritted my teeth. 'Tell me!' I called out again, as loudly as I could.

Then a softly dangerous voice, whispered in my ear. 'You know the answers, C-Bird. You could see them that night. You just don't want to admit to them, do you, Francis?'

'No,' I cried out.

'You don't want to say what C-Bird knew in that bunk bed that night because it would mean Francis has to kill himself now, wouldn't it?'

I could not answer. Tears and sobs wracked my body.

'You will have to die. What other answer is there, C-Bird? Because you knew the answers that night, didn't you?'

I could feel spiraling agony throughout my body when I whispered the only reply I knew that might quiet the voice of the Angel.

'It was not about Short Blond, was it?' I asked. 'It never was.'

He laughed. A laugh of truth. An awful, ripping

noise, as if something was being broken that could never be repaired.

'What else did C-Bird see that night?' the Angel asked.

I remembered lying in my bed. Beyond stillness, as rigid as any catatonic frozen in some terrible vision of the world, unwilling to move, unwilling to speak, unwilling to do anything but breathe, because as I lay there, I saw the whole world of death that the Angel had woven together. Peter was at the door. Lucy was in the nursing station. The Moses brothers were upstairs. Everyone was alone, isolated, separated, and vulnerable. And who was most vulnerable? Lucy.

'Short Blond,' I stammered. 'She was just . . .'

'A part of a puzzle. You saw it C-Bird. It's the same this night as it was then.' The Angel's voice boomed with authority.

I could barely speak, because I knew the words I grasped right then were the same that came to me that night so many years earlier. One. Two. Three. And then Short Blond. What did all those deaths do? They inevitably brought Lucy to a place where she was alone, in the dark, in the midst of a world that was ruled not by logic, sanity, or organization, no matter what Gulptilil or Evans or Peter or the Moses brothers or anyone in authority at the Western State Hospital might think. It was an arctic world ruled by the Angel.

The Angel snarled and kicked at me. He had been vaporous, ghostlike before. But this blow landed hard. I groaned in sudden pain, and then struggled back to my knees and crawled back to the wall. I could barely hold the pencil in my hand. It was what I saw in the darkness that night.

★ ★ ★

Midnight crept closer. Hours that slowed to a crawl. Night that seized the world around him. Francis lay stiffly, his mind searching through everything he knew. A series of murders that brought Lucy to the hospital, and now, she was just beyond the doorway, her hair cropped short and colored blond, waiting for a killer. All sorts of deaths and questions, and what was the answer? It seemed to him to be within his grasp, and yet was a little like trying to pluck a feather out of the breeze that carried it past him.

He turned in the bunk and looked over to Peter, who was resting with his head down on arms stretched over his bent knees. Francis thought that exhaustion must have finally grasped the Fireman. He did not have the advantage that Francis did, of panic and fear that held sleep at bay.

Francis wanted to explain that it was all very close to being clear to him, and he opened his mouth, but no words came out. And in the silence of despair, right at that moment, he heard the unmistakable noise of the lock that had been opened earlier, clicking shut.

32

Peter's head snapped up at the sound of the door being locked. He shook himself to his feet, leaping up, wondering how it was that he could have dozed off and failed to hear muffled footsteps just on the other side of the wall. He slipped his hand over the doorknob and placed his shoulder to the door, hoping, in that second, that the noise that had stirred him was something belonging to some half-sleep dream, and wasn't real. The handle turned, but the door would not budge, and he could feel the deadbolt lock holding it in place. He released the knob and stepped back a single pace, filling with some wild torrent of emotions, something different from fear or panic, distinct from anxiety, shock, or surprise. He had been filled with simple expectations based on reasonable suspicions about how the night would pass, and abruptly he realized that whatever he'd imagined was going to take place had evaporated, replaced with some terrible mystery. He was initially unsure what to do, so he took a deep breath, reminding himself that more than once he'd been in situations that demanded calm when all sorts of danger suddenly buzzed about his head, or tugged at his clothes. Firefights when he was a soldier. Fires when he was a fireman. He bit down hard on his lip and told himself to keep his wits about him and remain quiet and then he thrust his face up to the small window in the door, and he craned his head, trying to see down the corridor. Nothing yet had taken place, he reminded himself, that made this night any different from any other.

Behind him, Francis had spun his feet out of the bed. He was driven to his feet by forces he did not completely recognize. He could hear his own chorus of

561

voices shouting *It's happening now!* but he could not tell what *it* was. He stood, almost statuelike, by his bunk, waiting for the next moment to arrive, hoping that whatever it was he was *supposed* to do would become clear within seconds. And that when he was called to do it, he would be able. He was filled with doubt. He had never managed to succeed at anything, not once, that he could remember, throughout his brief life.

★   ★   ★

Lucy looked up from behind the nursing station desk, peering through the wire mesh into the gray black darkness of the hallway, seeing a figure near the end where a few hours earlier Little Black had waved goodbye. It was a human shape, that seemed to have materialized out of nothing. She craned forward and saw a white-jacketed attendant pause by the men's dormitory door, then continue to saunter down the hallway to greet her. The man gave her a small wave, and she could see that he was smiling. He had a confident, unfettered manner about him — or, at the very least, he walked with none of the shuffling hesitancy that she recognized in the vast majority of the patients. They always moved with the burdens of their diseases. This man had a lightness to his step that seemed to put him into a different category. Nevertheless, she reached down and placed her hand on her pocketbook, reassuring herself that her pistol was close by.

The attendant came closer. He was not overly large, probably no taller than she was, but carrying a bit more weight in a trim, athletic build. Moving down the hallway, it was a little as if he were stepping free from a cloud, coming into shape, growing more distinct with each stride. He stopped and checked first one of the storage room doors, making certain that it was locked, then a second, the door that led down to the basement heating system. He jiggled the door, then produced a set of keys not unlike the ones that she'd been given for that night, and he slid one into the lock. He was perhaps twenty feet away from her, and she lowered her hand down so that it gripped the butt of the pistol. She started to reach for the intercom, but hesitated when the attendant turned back away from the basement door, and said, not unpleasantly, 'The idiots in Maintenance are always leaving these things open, no matter how often we tell them not to. I'm surprised we haven't lost a dozen patients down there in those tunnels by now.'

He grinned and shrugged. She didn't say a word.

'Mister Moses asked me to come down and check on you,' the attendant said. 'He said it was your first night, and all. Hope I didn't make you nervous.'

'I'm fine,' Lucy said, keeping her hand wrapped around the pistol butt. 'Tell him thanks, but I don't need any help.'

The attendant stepped a little closer. 'That's what I figured. Night shift is more about being a little lonely and a little bored and mainly about staying awake more than anything else. But it can get a little creepy after midnight, for sure.'

She looked carefully at the man, trying to imprint every detail of his presence on her imagination, comparing every feature, every inflection, with the image she had created within her mind's eye of the Angel. Was he the right height, the right build, the right age? *What does a killer look like?* She could feel her stomach knotting tightly, the muscles in her arms and legs quivering with tension. She had not expected a murderer to come sauntering down the hallway with a smile on his face. *Who are you?* she asked herself.

'Why didn't Mister Moses come down himself?' she wondered instead.

The attendant shrugged. 'There were a couple of guys in the upstairs dormitory got into it a bit right around lights-out, and he had to escort one of them up to the fourth floor and see that he was restrained, put in observation, and knocked out with a shot of Haldol. So he left his big old brother at the desk, and asked me to come on down here. But it looks like you've got everything under control just fine. Anything I can do to help out before I head back upstairs?'

Lucy kept her hand on her weapon and her eyes fixed on the attendant. She tried to examine every inch of him as he came closer. His dark hair was longish, but well combed. He wore the white attendant's suit trimly and tennis shoes on his feet that made very little noise. She took a long look at his eyes, searching them for the light of madness, or the darkness of death. She scoured the man's appearance, looking for some indication that would tell her who he was, waiting for some signature that would make everything clear. She gripped the gun tighter, and pulled it partway from her pocketbook, readying herself. She did this as surreptitiously as she could. At the same time, she looked down at the man's hands.

The fingers seemed long, almost exaggerated. Clawlike. But they were empty.

He stepped closer, now only a few feet distant, close enough so that she could feel a kind of heat between them. She thought this was merely her own nervousness.

'Anyway, sorry if I startled you. I should have called on the phone to let you know I was coming down. Or maybe Mister Moses should have called, but he and his brother were a little busy.'

'It's all right,' she said.

The attendant gestured at the phone by her hand. 'I

564

need to call Mister Moses, tell him I'm heading back up to the isolation wing. Okay?'

She nodded at the phone. 'Help yourself,' she said. 'You know, I didn't get your name . . . '

Now he was close enough to touch, but still separated from Lucy by the protective wire mesh of the nursing station. The pistol butt seemed to glow red-hot in her hand, as if it was screaming at her to pull it out of its place of concealment.

'My name?' he asked. 'Sorry. Actually I didn't give it . . . '

The man reached through the opening in the mesh where medications were dispensed and took the telephone receiver off the hook, lifting it to his ear. She watched him dial in three numbers, and then wait for a second.

A momentary icy confusion sliced through her. The attendant had not dialed two zero two.

'Hey,' she said, 'That's not . . . '

And then it seemed her world exploded.

Pain like a sheet of red exploded in her eyes. Fear stabbed her with every heartbeat. Her head spun dizzily, and then she felt herself plunging forward, as if her balance was gone, and a second blast of hurt slammed into her face, followed rapidly by a third, then a fourth. Her jaw, her mouth, nose, and cheeks all suddenly seemed aflame, waterfalls of instant agony pounding down upon her visage. She could feel herself on the verge of losing consciousness, a blackness grasping hold of her. With what little remained of her memory and her control, she tried to tug her pistol free. It seemed to her that she was in a cone of pain and head-spinning confusion; the confident, firm grip she'd had seconds earlier on the butt of the gun seemed suddenly flimsy, loose, inadequate. Her motions seemed impossibly slow, as if they were restrained by ropes and chains. She tried to lift the weapon toward the attendant while the last bit of presence she retained screamed *Shoot! Shoot!*, but then, just as abruptly, the gun and all safety was gone, clattering away from her, and she felt herself tumbling down, falling to the floor, slamming against the linoleum, where all she could taste was the salty residue of blood. It seemed the last sensation open and available to her, the others eradicated by torrents of hurt. Explosions streaked crimson before her eyes. Deafening noise destroyed her hearing. The stench of fear filled her nostrils, erasing all else. She wanted to cry out for help, but the words seemed instantly distant and unreachable, as if beyond some great canyon.

What had happened was this: The attendant had suddenly driven the heavy telephone receiver up with a short, brutal uppercut, slamming it against the underside of Lucy's jaw with the efficiency of a boxer's knockout punch, as he had simultaneously reached through the opening in the wire mesh, and seized hold of her jacket. Then, as she had rocked back, he'd savagely pulled her forward, so that her face crashed into the screen that was there to protect her. He'd pushed her back, then blasted her forward viciously into the mesh three times, and then tossed her down, where she'd hit the floor face-first. The gun, which he'd rather easily knocked from her hand with the telephone receiver, skidded across the floor and came to rest in a corner of the nursing station. It was an assault of blistering speed and efficiency. A bare few seconds of unbridled strength, a limit of sound that didn't reach beyond the narrow world they occupied. One instant, Lucy had been cautious, assessing, hand wrapped around the weapon she believed would keep her safe; the next, she was down, barely able to put one thought next to another, except for a single awful idea: *I'm going to die here tonight*.

Lucy tried to lift her head from the floor, and through the haze of shock saw the attendant calmly opening the door to the nursing station. She made a great effort to get to her knees, but was unable. Her head screamed at her to call for help, to fight back, to do all the things which she'd planned to do, and which earlier had seemed so easily accomplished. But before she could martial the strength or the will necessary, he was at her side. A savage kick to her ribs burst what little wind she had from her chest, and Lucy moaned hard, as the Angel bent down over her and whispered words that pitched her into a far deeper fear than she had ever known could exist: 'Don't you remember me?' he hissed.

The truly terrible thing in that moment, the thing that went beyond all the terrible things that had taken place in the prior few seconds, was that when she heard his voice pressed up so close to her with an intimacy that spoke only of hate, it seemed to vault across the bridge of years, and she did.

★ ★ ★

Peter pivoted back and forth, trying to see down the corridor of the Amherst Building, thrusting his face up against the small glass window that had wire embedded into it to reinforce it. He was surrounded by darkness, and all he could see was shadow and shafts of wan light, none of which held any sign of existence or activity. He pitched his ear up against the door, trying to hear something through the thick steel, but its solid bulk defied his efforts, no matter how hard he strained. He could not tell what was happening — if anything. All he knew for certain was that the door that was supposed to be left open was locked tight, and that just beyond his sight and his grasp something might be happening and that suddenly, abruptly, he was powerless to do anything about it. He grabbed at the doorknob and furiously tugged on it, making a small, impotent banging sound not even strong enough to awaken any of the other well-drugged men in the room. He cursed and pulled again.

'Is it him?' Peter heard from behind his shoulder.

He spun about and saw Francis standing stock-still, a few feet back. The younger man's eyes were wide with fear and tension, a stray slice of light from a distant barred and closed window making his face seem even younger than he was.

'I don't know,' Peter said. 'I can't tell.'

'The door . . . '

'It's locked,' he replied. 'It's not supposed to be, but it is.'

Francis took a deep breath. He was absolutely certain of one thing.

'It's him,' he said with determination that surprised him.

★   ★   ★

Webs of pain constricted her every thought and motion. She was battling to remain alert, understanding that her life depended upon it, but she was uncertain how. One of her eyes was already swelling shut, and she thought her jaw was broken. She tried to crawl away from the sound of the Angel's voice, but he slammed her with his foot again, and then abruptly dropped down on top of her, straddling her, pinning her to the floor. She groaned again, and then she was aware that he had something in his hand. When he pressed it up against her cheek, she knew what it was. A knife, much as the one that he had used to slice through her beauty so many years earlier.

He whispered, but it had the force of a drill sergeant's command: 'Don't move. Don't die too quickly, Lucy Jones. Not after all this time.'

She stayed rigid with fear.

He lifted himself up, casually walked back to the desk, and in two swift, vicious motions, cut the telephone line and the intercom.

'Now,' he said, turning back toward her, 'A little conversation before the inevitable takes place.'

She pushed herself back, and didn't respond.

He dropped back down on top of her, once again pinning her with his knees, holding her in place. 'Do you have any idea how close I've been to you, on so many occasions I've lost count. Do you know that I've been at your side every step you've taken, day after day, week after week, adding all those seconds into minutes and letting the years come and go, and always been right there, so near I could have reached out and taken hold of you any time, so close I could smell your scent, hear your breathing? I have never left your side, Lucy Jones, not since the night we first met.'

He pushed his face down next to hers.

'You have done well,' the Angel said. 'You learned every lesson you could in law school. Including the one that I taught you.'

The Angel looked down at her, his own face a mask of anger. 'There's just time for one more final bit of education,' he said. He placed the knife blade up against her throat.

★   ★   ★

Francis stepped forward, staring hard at Peter. 'It's him,' he repeated. 'He's here now.'

Peter looked back at the small window in the door. 'We haven't heard a signal. The Moses brothers should be here . . . '

But he took one more look at the mixture of fear and insistence that Francis wore on his face, and he turned and threw his shoulder against the locked door, grunting hard with exertion. Then he pulled back and slammed himself into the unyielding metal again, only to drop back with a solid, meaningless thud. Peter could feel panic lurking around within him, suddenly aware that in a place where time seemed almost irrelevant, seconds now mattered.

He stepped back and kicked hard at the door. 'Francis,' he said loudly, 'we've got to get out there.'

But Francis was already tugging hard at the metal frame of his bunk, trying to pull one of the stanchions free. It took less than an instant for Peter to recognize what the younger man was trying to do, and he jumped to Francis's side, to help rip free some piece of iron that might serve as a makeshift crowbar, so that they could attack the door. Peter had an unusual thought penetrate all the mingled fears and doubts about what was taking place right in front of him, but beyond his reach, that the sensation he felt right then was probably the same as a man trapped within a burning building felt as he faced the wall of flame that threatened to devour him. Peter grunted hard with exertion.

★   ★   ★

On the floor of the nursing station, Lucy fought desperately to keep her wits about her. In the hours, days, and months after she'd been assaulted so many years earlier, there had been an inevitable replaying in her mind of *what ifs* and *if I'd onlys*. Now she was trying to gather all those memories, feelings of guilt and recriminations, internal fears and horrors back to her — to sort through them and find the one that truly might help, for this moment was the same as that one was. Only this time, she knew more than youth, innocence, and beauty were about to be taken from her. She screamed at herself, thrusting her imagination past the pain and despair, to find a way to fight back.

She was facing the Angel all alone in a world

surrounded by people, as isolated and abandoned as if they were on some deserted island or deep in some dark forest. Help was a flight of stairs away. Help was down the hallway, behind a locked door. Help was everywhere. Help was nowhere.

Death was a man with a knife pinning her to the floor. He had all the power; she understood that an electricity born of planning, obsession, anticipation of this moment must have been coursing through the Angel. Years of compulsion and desire, just to reach that single moment. She knew, in a way that went beyond anything she had learned in any law school class, that she had to use his triumph against him, and so, instead of saying *Stop!* or *Please!* or even *Why?* she spit out between swollen lips, and loosened teeth a statement of complete fiction and arrogance. 'We knew it was you all along . . . '

He hesitated. Then he pushed the flat of the knife up against her cheek. 'You lie,' the Angel hissed. But he did not cut her. Not yet, and Lucy understood she had purchased herself a few seconds. Not a chance to live, but a moment that had made the Angel hesitate.

★   ★   ★

The noise of Peter and Francis savagely ripping at the bed frame, trying to pry loose a strip of metal, finally began to rouse the patients in the dormitory room from their unsteady sleep. Like ghosts rising out of a graveyard on All Hallow's Eve, one after the other, the men of the housing unit stirred themselves to wake, fighting off the deep seduction of their daily sedatives, scrambling, struggling, blinking their eyes open to the novelty of Peter's increasing panic, as he fought against the metal with every muscle he could gather.

'What's happening, C-Bird?'

Francis heard the question and lifted his head in the

direction of the sound. It was Napoleon. As Francis paused, at first unsure precisely how to respond, he watched as the men of the Amherst Building slowly lurched from their bunks, joining together in a haphazard, misshapen knot behind Napoleon, staring out through the darkness at Francis and Peter, whose frantic efforts were making some modest headway. He had almost managed to free a single three-foot section of the frame and he grunted as he twisted and pried at the reluctant metal.

'It's the Angel,' Francis said. 'He's outside.'

Voices started to murmur, a mixture of surprise and fear. A couple of the men cowered back, shrinking from the thought that Short Blond's killer might be close by.

'What is the Fireman doing?' Napoleon asked, his voice tripping over each word with a hesitancy stirred by indecision.

'We need to get the door open,' Francis said. 'He's trying to get something that will break it down.'

'If the Angel is outside, shouldn't we be blocking the door?'

Another patient murmured in agreement. 'We need to keep him out. If he gets in here, what's to save us?'

From the back of the gathered men, Francis heard someone say, 'We need to hide!' and at first he wondered whether it was one of his own voices. But then as the men wavered indecisively, he recognized that for once his voices were quiet.

Peter looked up. The sweat of exertion was dripping down his forehead, making his face glisten in the wan light of the room. For a moment, he was almost overcome by the craziness of it all. The men of the dormitory room, their faces already marked by the fear of something terribly out of routine, thought it would be better to block the door, than to get it open. He looked down at his hands, and realized that he'd torn open great gashes in his palms, and ripped at least one nail from a finger, as he'd thrashed with the bed. He looked up again, and saw Francis step toward their dormitory mates, shaking his head.

'No,' Francis said with a patience that defied the necessity for action. 'The Angel will kill Miss Jones, if we do not help her. It's just like Lanky said. We have to take charge. Protect ourselves from evil. We have to take steps. Rise up and fight. If not, it will find us. We have to act. Right now.'

Again, the men in the dormitory shrank back. There was a laugh, a sob, more than one emitted some small sound of fear. Francis could see helplessness and doubt in every face.

'We need to help,' he pleaded. 'Right now.'

The men seemed to waver, swaying back and forth as if the tension of what they were being asked to do — whatever it was — created a wind that buffeted them.

'This is it,' Francis said, his own voice filling with a determination that shocked him. 'This is the first best moment. Right now. This is the time when all the crazy people here in this hospital building do something that no one would ever expect. No one thinks we can do anything. No one would ever imagine that we could manage something together. We're going to help Miss Jones, and we're going to do it together. All of us at once.'

And then he saw the most remarkable thing. From the rear of the clutch of mental patients, the hulking retarded man, so childlike in every action, who never seemed to understand even the most modest, clearly stated request, suddenly stepped forward. He pushed himself through the knot of men, coming straight for Francis. He had a baby's simplicity about him, and it was impossible for Francis to tell how he had come to understand a single thing about what was taking place that night, but penetrating through the great fog of his limited intelligence was some notion that Peter needed help, and it was the sort of help he was uniquely capable of giving. The retarded man put his Raggedy Andy doll down on a bunk and strode past Francis with determination in his eyes. With a grunt and with a single huge forearm, the retarded man pushed Peter back. Then, as they all watched in rapt silence, he reached down, grasped hold of the iron frame and with a single great heart-bursting effort, tore loose the bar, which ripped free with a screeching sound. The retarded man waved it in the air above his head, broke into a wide, unrestrained grin and then handed it to Peter.

The Fireman seized the bar and immediately thrust it deep into the space where the door met the frame, adjacent to the deadbolt lock. Throwing all his weight into the makeshift crowbar, Peter pushed hard to break the door free.

Francis could see the bar bend, metal complain with an animal-like shriek and the door begin to buckle.

Peter let loose a great sigh, and stepped back. He worked the bar into the space again, and was about to throw himself into it, when Francis suddenly interrupted him.

'Peter!' he said, his voice filled with urgency. 'What was the word?'

The Fireman stopped. 'What?' he asked, confused.

'The word. The word. The word that Lucy was supposed to use to call for help?'

'*Apollo*,' Peter replied. Then he tossed himself at the door again. Only this time, the huge retarded man stepped forward to help him, and the two of them bent their backs to the task.

Francis turned toward the gathered men of Amherst, who were frozen in place, as if awaiting some release. 'Okay,' he said, marshaling himself like a general in front of his army at the moment of an attack, 'We've got to help out.'

'What do you want us to do?' It was Newsman, this time, who spoke.

Francis lifted up one hand, like a starter at a race. 'We need to make a noise that they can hear upstairs. We need to signal for help . . .'

One of the men immediately shouted, 'Help! Help!' as loud as he could. Then a third, 'Help . . .' that was lower in volume, fading away.

'It does no good in here to yell for help. We all know that,' Francis said emphatically. 'Nobody ever pays attention. Nobody ever comes. *Help!* is useless. What we have to do is yell *Apollo!* as loud as we can . . .'

Timidity, confusion, doubt turned the men into a reluctant chorus. A mumbling of *Apollo*s followed.

'*Apollo?*' Napoleon asked. 'But why *Apollo?*'

Francis said, 'It's the only word that will work.'

He knew this sounded as crazy as anything, but he said it with such conviction that any further discussion was erased.

Several of the men instantly cried out, '*Apollo! Apollo!*' but Francis shut them down with a quick wave.

'No,' Francis shouted sturdily, orchestrating, organizing. 'It has to be together, otherwise they won't hear it. Follow me, on the count of three, let's try it . . .'

He counted down, and a single modest, but unified *Apollo* emerged.

'Good, good,' Francis said. 'Only this time as loud as we can.' He looked back over his shoulder at Peter and the retarded man, both groaning with exertion as they struggled with the door. 'This time, we need to make it heard . . .'

He raised his hand. 'On my mark,' he said. 'Three. Two. One . . .'

Francis brought his arm down fast, like a sword.

'Apollo!' the men shouted.

'Again!' Francis yelled. 'That was great. Again, now, three, two, one . . .'

A second time, he sliced the air.

'*Apollo!*' The men responded.

'Again!'

'*Apollo!*'

'And again!'

'*Apollo!*'

The word rose up, soaring, bursting from the group of patients full bore, exploding through the thick walls and darkness of the mental hospital, a starburst, fireworks word, never heard before in the asylum, and probably never to be heard again, but at least, on this one black night breaking past all the locks and barriers, beating back every strand of earthly restraint, rising, flying, taking wing and finding freedom in sound, dashing through the thick air, unerringly racing directly to the ears of the two men above, who were to be its primary recipients, and who craned forward, surprised, at the designated sound resounding from such an unexpected source.

33

'Apollo!' I said out loud.

In mythology, he was the sun god whose swift chariot signaled the coming of day. It was what we needed that night, two things that were generally in short supply in the world of the mental hospital: Speed and clarity.

'Apollo,' I said a second time. I must have been shouting.

The word reverberated off the walls of my apartment, racing into the corners, leaping up to the ceiling. It was a uniquely wondrous word, one that rolled off my tongue with a strength of memory that fueled my own resolve. It had been twenty years since the night I'd last spoken it out loud, and I wondered if it wouldn't do the same for me this night, as it did then.

The Angel bellowed in rage. Glass shattered around me, steel groaned and twisted as if being consumed by fire. The floor shook, the walls buckled, the ceiling swayed. My entire world was ripping apart, shredding into pieces around me, as his fury consumed him. I clutched my head, pushing my hands over my ears, trying to drown out the cacophony of destruction around me. Things were breaking, crumbling and exploding, disintegrating beneath my feet. I was in the midst of some terrifying battlefield, and my own voices were like the cries of doomed men surrounding me. I buried my head for a moment in my hands, trying to duck the shrapnel of remembrance.

On that night twenty years earlier, the Angel had been right about so much. He had foreseen everything Lucy would do; he understood precisely how Peter would behave; he knew exactly what the Moses brothers would agree to and help arrange. He was intimate with

577

the hospital and how if affected everyone's thinking. What the Angel comprehended better than anyone else was how routine and organized and drearily predictable everything was that sane people would do. He knew the plan they would come up with would leave him with isolation, quiet, and opportunity. What they had thought was a trap for him was actually the most ideal of circumstances. He was, far more than they, a student of psychology and a student of death and he was immune to their earthbound plans. To take her by surprise required him only to not try to surprise her. She had willingly set herself up; it must have thrilled him to know she would do that. And on that night, he knew murder would be in his hands, directly in front of him, ready like some weed that had sprouted up, to be plucked. He had spent years patiently preparing for the time that he would have Lucy beneath his knife once again, and he had considered almost every factor, every dimension, every consideration — except, oddly the most obvious — but the most forgettable.

What he hadn't counted on were the crazy folks.

I squeezed my eyes shut with recollection. I was a little unsure whether it was all happening in the past or in the present, in the hospital or in the apartment. It was all coming back to me, this night and that night, one and the same.

Peter was shouting deep, guttural noises, as he bent the door from its lock, the hulking retarded man wordlessly straining and sweating at his side. Beside me, Napoleon, Newsman, all the others, were arranged, like a chorus, waiting for my next direction. I could see them quiver and shake with fear and excitement, for they, more than anyone, understood that it was a night unlikely to ever be repeated, a night where fantasies and imagination, hallucination, and delusion all came true.

And Lucy, so few feet away, but alone with the man who'd thought of nothing except her death for so long, *feeling the knife at her throat, knew that she needed to keep stealing seconds.*

★ ★ ★

Lucy tried to think past the cold of the knife and the sharpness of the blade as it dug at her skin, a terrible sensation that reached deeply into the heat of the moment, and crippled her ability to reason. Down the hallway she could hear the noise of metal being bent, as the locked door was savaged, groaning with complaint as Peter and the retarded man assaulted it with the bed frame. It yielded slowly, hesitant to open up and let loose rescue. But above that noise, rising into the air beyond, she could hear the word *Apollo* being sung by the men in the dormitory, which gave her a wisp of hope.

'What does it mean?' the Angel demanded fiercely. That he had patience amid the sudden arrival of noise in what had been such a sleeping world, frightened her as much as anything.

'What?'

'What does it mean!' he asked, his voice growing lower, harsher. He did not need to attach a threat to his words, Lucy thought. The tone was clear enough. She kept repeating to herself *buy time!* and so she hesitated.

'It's a cry for help,' she said.

'What?'

'They need help,' she repeated.

'Why do they . . . ' and then he stopped. He looked down at her, his face contorting. Even in the blackness of the floor of the nurse's station, she could see creases in his face, lines and shadows, each that spoke of terror. Once he'd worn a mask as he terrorized her, but now, she understood *he wants to be seen because he expects that he will be the last thing I ever see.* She gasped for breath, and she

579

moaned beyond the pain of her swollen lips and ravaged jaw.

'They know you're here.' She spit the words between blood. 'They're coming for you.'

'Who?'

'All the crazy men down the hall,' she said.

The Angel bent down to her. 'Do you know how quickly you can die here, Lucy?' he asked.

She nodded. She didn't think she should answer that question because her words might invite the reality. The blade of the knife bit into her skin, and she could feel her flesh parting ever so slightly beneath its pressure. It was a terrifying sensation, and one that she remembered with an awful intimacy from the first terrible night that she'd had with the Angel so many years earlier.

'Do you know that I can do anything I want, Lucy, and you are powerless to do anything about it?'

Again, she kept her mouth closed.

'Do you know that I could have walked up to you at any point during your stay here in this hospital and killed you right in front of everyone, and all they would have said was 'He's crazy . . . ' and no one would have blamed me? That's what your own law says, Lucy, surely you know that?'

'Then go ahead and kill me,' she said stiffly. 'Just like you did Short Blond and those other women.'

He put his head down closer, so that she could feel his breath against her face. The same motion that a lover would make, leaving his partner asleep as he went off in some early hour on some distant task. 'I would never kill you like them, Lucy,' he hissed. 'They died to bring you to me. They were simply part of a design. Their deaths were just business. Necessary, but not remarkable. If I'd wanted you to die like them, I could have killed you a hundred times. A thousand. Think of all the moments you've been alone in the dark. Maybe you weren't alone all those times. Maybe I was at your side, you just didn't know it. But I wanted this night to happen in my own way. I wanted you to come to me.'

She did not reply. She felt caught up in the vortex of the Angel's sickness and hatred, and she spun around, feeling her grip on life loosening with each revolution.

'It was so terribly easy,' he hissed. 'Create a series of murders that the hot-shot young prosecutor couldn't help but be attracted to. You just never knew that they meant nothing and you meant everything, did you Lucy?'

She groaned in reply.

From down the hallway, the door being torn at emitted a great rending sound. The Angel looked up, searching with his eyes in the direction of the noise through the darkness that hung in the corridor. In this moment's hesitation, Lucy knew her life hung in balance. He had wanted minutes in the deep of night to luxuriate in her death. He had seen it all, right from the way he'd approached her, to the attack, and then beyond that. He'd fantasized and envisioned every word he would speak, every touch, every slice, every awful cut along her path to dying. It had all been a hallucination, in his mind every second of every waking moment, that he was compelled to make real. It was what made him powerful, fearless, and every inch the assassin that he was. Everything in his being had been directed to that space in time. But it wasn't happening quite the way he'd perfected it in his mind, day after day, through every turn, planning, anticipating, sensing the deliciousness of death when he delivered it. She could feel his muscles tensing as he was caught in a contradiction between what was real and what was fantasy. All she had left to hope for was that the real would take over. She didn't know if there was enough time.

And then she heard a second sound, penetrating past all the terror that cascaded around her. It came from upstairs, and was the sound of a door being slammed, and feet pounding against the cement of the stairwell. *Apollo!* had done its job.

The Angel blasted out a great scream of frustration. It echoed down the hallway.

Then he bent back down. 'So, this night Lucy is lucky. Very lucky. I don't think I can stay here any longer. But I will come for you some other night, when you least expect it. Some night when all your fears and all your preparations will mean nothing, and I will be there. You can arm yourself. Guard yourself. Move to some deserted island or some forgotten jungle. But, sooner or later, Lucy, I will be there at your side. And then we can finish this.'

He seemed to tense again, and she could feel him hesitate. Then he bent down toward her and whispered, 'Never turn out the light, Lucy. Never lie down in the darkness alone. Because years mean nothing to me, and some day I will be there for you.'

She breathed in sharply, almost overcome by the depth of his obsession.

He started to step off of her, dismounting like a rider off a horse. But then he coldly added, 'Once I gave you something to remember me by every time you looked in the mirror. Now you can remember me every time you take a step.'

And with that, he plunged the knife blade into her right knee, twisting it savagely a single time. She screamed as pain far beyond any she'd felt so far in any moment of her life seemed to constrict her every muscle and tendon. Black unconsciousness swept over her, and she rolled back, only vaguely aware that she was alone, and that the Angel had left her beaten, wounded, bleeding, barely alive and possibly crippled and with a promise that was far worse.

★   ★   ★

The metal in the door screeched one final time and a sliver of darkness grew between the frame and steel. Francis could see the corridor beyond, gaping like some dark mouth waiting open. The retarded man, suddenly straightened up, tossing the makeshift crowbar down to the floor, where it clattered aside. He reached out and pulled Peter away, and then he took a few steps backward. For an instant, he lowered his head, like a bull in an arena, infuriated by the matador's preening, then he abruptly charged forward, bursting out with an immense cry of attack as he did so. The retarded man threw himself against the door, which buckled and gave way with a huge booming sound. Staggering, shaking his head back and forth, panting, a thin line of dark blood dripping down from the edge of his scalp, running between his eyes across the bridge of his nose, the retarded man retreated. He shook his head, and for a second time, he braced himself, his face set like iron with the singleness of his task, and then a second time he bellowed a great sound of fury, and charged the door again. This time the door burst open, swinging free, and the retarded man tumbled into the hallway, skidding to a halt across the dark gap.

Peter jumped forward, with Francis close behind him, followed by the rest of the crazy men, who were swept forward by the energy of the instant, leaving behind much of their madness as the need for them to step ahead became clear. Napoleon was rallying the men, waving his arm above his head as if he carried a sword, crying 'Onward! Charge!' Newsman was saying something about the next day's headlines and becoming a part of the story, as they all tumbled into the corridor, a flying wedge of men, bent on a single task.

In the momentary confusion of their arrival, Francis saw the retarded man rise up, dust himself off and steadfastly return to the dormitory room, his face wreathed in glowing glory. Francis caught a half glimpse of the man plopping himself down on his bunk, taking his Raggedy Andy doll up in his arms and then turning and surveying his destruction of the door with a look of utter satisfaction.

Then Francis turned away, and he saw Peter racing ahead, toward the nursing station, moving as fast as he could, sprinting with the necessity of the moment. There was a faint glow coming from the station's single desk lamp, and Francis spotted a figure stretched out on the floor. He instantly pushed himself in that direction, his own feet slapping hard against the floor, beating a drummer's pace of emergency. At the same moment, he saw the Moses brothers burst through the far stairwell door, and as they tore past the women's dormitory, cries from that room started to rise up, high-pitched notes that combined in a symphony of confusion and panic, with an allegro of unknown fear keeping the beat.

Peter had pitched himself down toward Lucy's form, and Francis hesitated for an instant, afraid that they were too late, and that she was dead. But then, through all the other noise that had suddenly overtaken the entire hallway, he heard Lucy groan in pain.

'Jesus!' Peter said. 'She's hurt badly.' He had taken hold of one of her hands and was cradling it, as he tried to guess what to do. Peter looked up at Francis, and then to the Moses brothers as they arrived breathless at the nursing station. 'We need to get her help,' he said.

Little Black nodded, reached for the telephone, and immediately saw that it was worthless, with its wires sliced. He seemed to think hard, surveying the entirety of the nursing station in a single long glance and then replied, 'Hang on. I'm going back upstairs, call for help.'

Big Black turned to Francis, his own face a mask of worry and anxiety. 'She was supposed to say the word over the intercom or on the telephone . . . it took us a couple of seconds when we heard all of you . . . ' He didn't need to finish what he was saying, because

584

suddenly the preciousness of those few moments seemed to be in the same balance as Lucy Jones's life.

Lucy felt rivers of pain flooding over her.

She was only peripherally aware that Peter was at her side, and that the Moses brothers and Francis were close by. They all seemed to her to be on some distant shore, one that she was struggling against tides and currents to reach, as she battled against unconsciousness. She knew that there was something important she had to say, before she gave in to the agony that enveloped her, and let herself fall blissfully into the abyss of darkness that beckoned. She bit down hard on a bloody lip, and squeezed a few words past all the hurt that had arrived that night, and all the despair that she'd known, thinking only of the promise that she'd been given a few seconds earlier. 'He's here,' she spit out softly. 'Find him, please. End it here.'

She did not know whether what she said made any sense, or whether anyone could hear her. She wasn't even sure that the words that she'd managed to form in her imagination had actually made it past her tongue. But, she understood, at least she'd tried, and with a deep sigh, she let unconsciousness take her over, not knowing whether she would ever emerge from its seductive grasp, but understanding, at the very least, that all the pain she felt would be swept aside, if only for a moment.

'Lucy, damn it! Stay with us!' Peter screamed in her face, but without great effect. Then he looked up and said, 'She's out.' He put his ear down to her chest, listening for her heartbeat. 'She's alive,' he said, 'but . . .'

Big Black threw himself down beside her. He immediately started to apply pressure to the wound in her knee, which was pulsing blood. 'Somebody get me a blanket!' he yelled. Francis turned and saw Napoleon heading into the dormitory on that task.

Down the hallway, Little Black reappeared, running. 'Help's coming,' he shouted. Peter stepped back slightly, still poised next to Lucy's form. Francis saw him look down, and both men spotted Lucy's pistol on the floor. It was as if everything in the Amherst Building was moving in slow motion to Francis right at that instant, and he suddenly understood what it was that Lucy had been saying, and what it was that she was asking.

'The Angel,' he said quietly to Peter and the Moses brothers, 'where is he?'

*　*　*

That was it, right then, that moment right there, when everything that I knew as my madness and everything that might one day make me sane coalesced in some great electric, exploding connection. The Angel was howling, his voice a din of angry noise. I could feel his grip on my own arm, trying to stop me from reaching out to the wall, scratching, clawing at the pencil in my hand, wrestling with me, trying to prevent me from putting down in shaky script what happened next. We battled, fighting hard, my body pummeled by his blows, over each word. I knew that his entire being was bent toward seeing me stop, fold up and die right there, giving up, falling short, a few feet from completion.

I fought back, scrambling to drag the pencil across the dwindling space on the wall in front of me. I was screaming, arguing, shouting at him, near breaking, like glass about to shatter and burst.

*　*　*

Peter looked up and said, 'But where . . . '

*　*　*

Peter looked up and said, 'But where . . . ' and then Francis turned and looked away from Lucy's prone form and surveyed the corridor. In the distance, he could suddenly hear the caterwauling of an ambulance, and he wondered wildly whether it would be the same ambulance that had brought him to Western State that arrived that night for Lucy.

Francis searched first one direction with his eyes, but he was in actuality searching his heart. He looked down the hallway past the women's dormitory, to the stairwell where Cleo had killed herself and then had her hand mutilated by the opportunistic Angel. He shook his head and told himself *No. Not that way. He would have run directly into the Moses brothers.* Then he turned and examined the other routes. The front door. The stairwell at the men's end. He closed his eyes and thought to himself: *You would not have come here this night unless you knew that there was an emergency exit. You would have thought about much that might go wrong, but far more important, of far greater concern, you knew that you needed to disappear so that you could savor the last moments of Lucy's life. You would not want to share these with anyone. So, you would need a place where you could be alone with your darkness. I know you, and I know what you need, and now I will know where you have gone.*

Francis rose and slowly walked over to the front doors. Double-locked. He shook his head. Too much time. Too much uncertainty. He would have had to pull out the two keys and let himself out where Security might have seen him. And lock the doors behind him, so as to not draw attention to his flight. *Not that way* Francis's voices all shouted agreement. *You know. You can see it.* He did not know whether they were crying encouragement or despair. Francis pivoted slightly, and peered down the corridor toward the broken door to the men's dormitory. Again he shook his head. The Angel would have had to pass by all of them, and that would have been impossible, even for a man who prided himself on murder and invisibility.

And then, Francis saw.

'What is it, C-Bird?' Peter asked.

'I know,' Francis replied. The ambulance siren was growing closer, and Francis imagined that he could hear footsteps on the pathways of the hospital ringing with alarm as they raced toward the Amherst Building. This was impossible, he knew, but still he imagined he could hear Gulp-a-pill and Mister Evil and everyone else rushing there as well.

Francis stepped across the hallway and reached out at the door that led down to the basement and the heating ducts beneath the ground.

'Here,' he said carefully. And like a slightly shaky magician at a child's birthday party, he pulled open the door that should have been locked.

Francis hesitated at the top of the stairs, caught between fear and some unspoken, ill-defined duty. He had never, in all his years, given much thought to the notion of bravery, dwelling instead on the mere difficulties getting from one day to the next with his tenuous grip on life still intact. But in that second he understood that to take a step into the basement would require some strength that he had never asked of himself before. Below him a single overhead bulb threw shadows into corners and barely illuminated the steps leading down into the subterranean storage area. Beyond the weak arc of light was a deep, enveloping darkness. He could feel a wave of stale, hot air. It smelled of musty age and filth, as if all the awful thoughts and destroyed hopes of generations of patients living out their madnesses in the world above had seeped down into the basement, like so much dust, cobwebs, and grime. It was a place that whispered disease and death, and he knew, as he paused before

588

descending that it was a place the Angel would be comfortable in.

'Down there,' he said, contradicting the voices that he could hear within his own head shouting *Don't go down there!* But he ignored everything that was being said to him. Peter was suddenly at his side. In the Fireman's right fist, he gripped Lucy's pistol. Francis had not seen the sleight of hand that had plucked it from the corner where she'd lost it and delivered it to Peter's possession, but he was grateful that Peter had it. Peter had been a soldier, and Francis realized the Fireman would know how to use the weapon. In the black region that beckoned them, they would need some edge, and Francis believed that might be it. Peter hugged the weapon close to his hip, concealing it as best he could.

Peter nodded, then looked back toward Big Black and his brother, who were trying to administer first aid to Lucy. Francis saw the immense attendant raise his head and lock his eyes upon the Fireman's. 'Look, Mister Moses,' Peter said quietly, ' . . . if we're not back in a few minutes . . . '

Big Black did not have to answer. He simply dropped his head in agreement. Little Black seemed to comply. He made a fast hand gesture.

'Go ahead,' Little Black said. 'As soon as help comes, we'll follow after you.'

Francis did not think that either man had actually taken note of the weapon in Peter's hand. He took a deep breath, tried to clear his heart and his thoughts of everything other than finding the Angel, and with a hesitant stride, started down the stairs.

It seemed to him that the tendrils of heat and darkness tried to envelop him with each step. It was impossible to move as quietly as he wished, uncertainty seemed to encourage noise, so that every time he placed his foot down on the ground he thought it made some deep, booming sound, when in truth the opposite was the case, his footsteps were muffled. Peter was directly behind him, pushing him slightly, as if speed was an issue. Perhaps it is, Francis thought. Perhaps we have to catch up with the Angel before he is absorbed by the night and disappears.

The basement was cavernous, wide, lit only by the single bulb. Cardboard boxes and empty canisters that had once held something or another, but had long been forgotten, created an obstacle course of debris. A thin layer of grimy soot seemed to cover everything, and they moved as quickly as possible through discarded iron bed frames and musty, stained mattresses, pushing ahead on a path that seemed no different from moving through a dense jungle of abandoned items. A huge black boiler rested uselessly in one corner, and a single shaft of light shed a little clarity on the immense heating duct that penetrated a wall, creating a tunnel that rapidly became a single black hole in the world.

'Down there,' Francis pointed. 'That's where he went.'

Peter hesitated. 'How can he see his way?' he asked. He indicated the unending, gaping blackness of the tunnel. 'And where do you suppose it will take us?'

Francis thought the answer to that question far more complicated than the Fireman intended. But he responded, 'It will come out either in another building, like Williams or Harvard, or else lead back to the power plant. And he doesn't need light. He only needs to keep moving, because he knows where he's going.'

Peter nodded. More than a few things had occurred to him. First, there was no way of telling if the Angel knew they were in pursuit, which he thought might be an advantage, but also might not be. And second, whatever path the Angel might have been taking on his prior trips to the Amherst Building, tonight would be different, because he was no longer going to be safe at the Western State Hospital. So this night the Angel meant to disappear.

But precisely how, Peter was unsure.

These things had occurred to Francis, as well. But he understood one additional thing: There would be no underestimating the Angel's rage.

The two men pushed forward, into the darkness.

It was tough to maneuver down the path of the heating duct. The tunnel hadn't been designed for anything except the equipment of steam, certainly not for men to use as an underground conduit between buildings. But even if not designed for that purpose, it still had that result. Francis could feel just enough space to half crouch, half stumble forward in a world better suited to the rats and other rodents that thought it a fine home. It was an antique space, built in a different era, left crumbling and ancient over all the years, its usefulness questionable to everyone except the killer who they trailed.

They traveled by touch and by feel, stopping every few feet to listen for sounds, their hands stretched out in front of them like a pair of blind men. It was oppressively hot, and sweat soon rimmed their foreheads. They both could feel themselves covered with grime, but they maneuvered on, penetrating farther into the tunnel, squeezing past any obstruction, clinging carefully to the side of the heating duct, an ancient tube that seemed to be disintegrating under their touch.

Francis's breath was coming in short, tense bursts. Dust and age seemed in every tug of wind that his lungs demanded. He could taste years of emptiness with each step forward, and he wondered whether he was lost or whether he was finding himself, with every stride down the tunnel.

Peter remained directly behind the younger man, pausing every so often to strain his ears and eyes, inwardly cursing the darkness that crippled the speed of their pursuit. He was overcome by the sensation that they were traveling half as fast, half as steadily, as they should, and he whispered urgently to Francis to move quicker. In the darkness of the tunnel, it was as if any connection they had to the upper world had been severed, and the two of them were alone in the chase, their quarry somewhere ahead, hidden, invisible, and very dangerous. He tried to force his mind to be logical, to be accurate, to assess and consider, to anticipate and predict, but it was impossible. Those were qualities that belonged in the light and the air up above, and Peter found he could not summon them any longer. He knew the Angel would have some plan, some scheme, but whether it was escape, or evasion or merely concealment, he was unable to grasp. All he knew was to keep moving and to keep Francis moving, because he had the awful fear that no jungle trail he'd ever walked, or any burning building he'd ever stepped into, was quite as dangerous as the path he was on. Peter made certain that the safety on the pistol was clicked off, and he tightened his grip on the butt.

He stumbled once and swore, then swore again as he regained his balance.

Francis tripped on some ill-defined piece of debris and gasped as he thrust out his arms to steady himself. He thought each step was as uncertain as a child's. But when he looked up, he suddenly saw the slightest yellow light, seemingly miles ahead. He knew that darkness and distance were tricky, and after a second, he understood that ahead of them was something different, and he tried to hurry himself toward the light, eager to emerge from the darkness of the tunnel, regardless of what might lie ahead.

'What do you think?' he heard Peter whisper.

'Power plant?' he answered softly. 'Another housing unit?'

Neither man had any idea where it was that they were

arriving. They didn't even know whether they had traveled in a straight line from the Amherst Building to wherever they were headed. They were disoriented, frightened, and filled with the unruly tension of the moment. Peter clung to the weapon, because, at least for him, that spoke of some reality, something firm in an unsettled world. Francis had nothing so concrete to rely upon.

Francis pushed ahead toward the pale light. With each stride it grew, not in strength, but in dimension, a little like some weak dawn rising over distant hills, battling against fog and clouds and the residue of some immense storm. He thought, at the least, that they were being drawn to it with the same determination that the moth has when it spots the flickering candle. He wasn't sure that they would be any more effective.

'Keep going,' Peter urged. He said this as much to hear his own voice and reassure himself that the claustrophobic, enveloping existence of the heating tunnel was coming to a conclusion. Francis, for his part, welcomed hearing Peter speak, even if the words came out of the darkness behind him, disembodied, as if spoken by some ghost that trailed just behind him.

The two men struggled forward, realizing that the wan yellow light that beckoned them finally was distributing some clarity to the path they traveled. Francis hesitated, holding up a dirt-streaked hand in front of his face, as if curiously unfamiliar with the sensation of being able to see. He stumbled again, as some misshapen piece of debris clung to his leg. Then he paused, because something terribly obvious hovered just beyond his reasoning, and he wanted to grasp hold of it. Peter gave him a small shove, and they approached the space in the wall where the duct emerged, and as they tumbled out into the weak light, welcoming the ability to see, Francis realized what it was that he was trying to understand.

They had traversed the length of the tunnel, but not once had he felt the sticky unpleasant touch of a spider's web, stretched across the dark space. Surely, Francis thought to himself, this was improbable. There had to be spiders in that tunnel.

Then he understood what it meant. Someone else had traveled that way, clearing them out.

He raised his head, and stepped forward. He stood at the edge of another dark, shadowy cavernlike storage room. As back at Amherst, a single weak bulb, stuck in a crevasse near a stairway on the far side provided a pathetic aura of light. Around him were the same piles of discarded material, abandoned equipment, and for an instant, Francis wondered whether they had gone anywhere, or whether they had merely turned in some bizarre circle, for the world was the same. He turned and examined the shadows around him, and had the odd sensation that it appeared that all the debris had been moved, creating a pathway ahead. Peter emerged from the tunnel behind him, brandishing the pistol, crouched over in a shooter's stance, readying himself.

'Where are we?' Francis asked.

Peter did not have time to respond, before the room suddenly fell into utter darkness.

34

Peter inhaled sharply, taking a step back, as if he'd been slapped in the face. At the same moment inwardly he screamed furiously to keep his wits about him, which was difficult in the abrupt wave of night that overcame the two of them. To his side, he heard Francis let out a small cry of fear, and he could sense the younger man cowering down.

'C-Bird!' he commanded, 'don't move.'

Francis, for his part, found this an easy order to follow. He was nearly frozen by sudden, total panic. To have felt the momentary relief of *some* light, after descending into the darkness of the tunnel, to defeat that enveloping danger, to emerge, and then, in a flash, to have that little clarity abruptly severed, terrified him beyond any location he had even known before. In his chest, he could feel every heartbeat, but they told him only that he was still alive, and yet, at the same time, every voice within him screamed that he was on the edge of death.

'Be quiet!' Peter whispered, as he stepped slightly forward, into the room, into the pitch-black, thumbing back the hammer on the pistol as he did so. He held out his left hand, just touching Francis on the shoulder, to register his position in the basement. The gun preparing to fire made a frightening *click* in the dark. Then Peter, too, held himself steady, trying not to move, or to make any telltale sound.

Francis could hear his voices screaming *Hide! Hide!* but he knew enough to realize that there was likely no hiding, not at that moment. He crouched down, trying to make himself as small as possible, his feet rooted to the cement floor, his breathing coming in shallow, nervous gasps, and he wondered with each whether it was the last he would take. He was only peripherally aware of Peter's presence, as the Fireman, his own nervousness contradicting his training, dangerously took another step in front of the two of them. His foot made a small clapping sound against the cement floor. He could feel Peter slowly pivoting, first to his right, then his left, as the Fireman tried to determine from which direction the threat would come.

Calculating fiercely, Francis tried to assess what was taking place. There was little doubt in his mind that the Angel had doused the lights, and was waiting somewhere in the black pit they found themselves trapped inside. The only difference was that the Angel was on familiar ground, and moving through intimate territory, while Peter and he had only a second or two's glimpse of their surroundings before being locked in the darkness. Francis could feel his hands clenching into fists, and then, like a waterfall's cascade within him, every muscle tensed, stretched to its limit, shrieking at him to move, but he could not. He was as locked into place as if the cement beneath their feet had been wet, and had solidified around their shoes.

'Be quiet!' Peter whispered. He continued to swing first one direction, then the other, holding the pistol in front of him, ready to fire.

Francis could feel the space between him and death narrowing with each passing second. The complete darkness of the room felt like a coffin lid had been slammed shut above him, and the only noise he could hear was the sound of clumps of dirt being shoveled on top. A part of him wanted to cry, to whimper, to shrink away and curl up like a child. The voices shouting within him wanted that desperately. They urged him to run. To take flight. To find some corner where he could huddle alone, hiding. But Francis knew that there was no safety anywhere, beyond the place where he stood, and he tried to hold his breath and listen.

A scratching sound came from his right. He turned that way. It could have been a rat. It could have been the Angel. Uncertainty was everywhere.

The darkness made everything equal. Bare hands, a knife, a gun. If the balance of weaponry had belonged to Peter carrying Lucy's pistol, then it had shifted in more than one way to the man silently stalking them in the basement room. Francis was thinking hard, trying to push reason past the reef of panic that threatened to overtake him. He thought to himself: *So much of my life has been spent in darkness, I should be safe.*

The same, he understood, might be true for the Angel.

Then he thought to himself, *what did you see before the darkness came?*

In his imagination, he reconstructed the few seconds of sight that he'd had. And what he understood was this: The Angel had sensed the pursuit, or else had heard the sounds of men trailing after him. He had then made a choice not to flee, but to turn and wait in hiding. He had left the light on just long enough to ascertain who was chasing after him, and then he had brought on the darkness. Francis strained to picture the room. The Angel would come for them down the route that he'd cleared and that he'd traveled before, on more than one occasion. He would not need the light, as long as he could feel his way close enough to deliver death. Francis built the room in his head. He tried to recall exactly where he stood. He craned forward, listening, thinking that his own breathing was like a bass drum; it was so loud that it threatened to obscure any other sound.

Peter, too, knew they were under attack. Every fiber within him shouted for him to take charge, to do something, to maneuver, prepare, seize the momentum. But he was unable. For a second, he thought the darkness a disadvantage to everyone, but then, he understood it wasn't. All it did was underscore his vulnerability.

He, too, knew the Angel had a knife. So it was only a matter of closing the space between them. In the world that trapped him, the gun in his hand seemed far less an advantage than he had thought it would prove.

He turned right and left. The nearing of panic, mingling with tension, blinded him just as surely as the pitch-black. Reasonable men, faced with reasonable problems can see their way through to reasonable solutions, he knew, but there was nothing reasonable about their circumstances. They were as unable to retreat as they were to charge forward. They could no more move than they could remain rooted in position. Dark like a box contained them.

Francis thought that the night accentuated sounds, but then, he abruptly understood, it obscured them and distorted them. He told himself *the only way to see is to hear* and so, in that second, he actually closed his eyes and lifted his head, turning it slightly. He concentrated hard, trying to reach past the Fireman's form, and gauge where the Angel was.

To their right, a few feet away, there was a thud.

They both heard it, and turned that way. Peter lifted his weapon, found all the tension in his body roaring into the pressure of his finger upon the trigger, and he fired wildly once in that direction.

The explosion of the gun deafened both of them. The flash of the muzzle was like a shock of electricity. The bullet screamed through the darkness, ricocheting into the cavernous room with deadly purpose and no effect.

Francis could smell gunpowder, almost as if the echo of the shot carried the smell. He could hear Peter's heavy, excited breathing, and listened to the Fireman curse softly. And then he had a single, terrible thought: Peter had just displayed where they were.

But before he could say anything, or peer back through the darkness in the other direction, he heard a small, alien sound nearly beside him, almost at his feet, and the next thing he knew, some iron form had burst past him, seeming to fly, as if not connected to the floor or the earth, but traveling through the air, smashing into Peter. Knocked aside, Francis fell back hard, stumbling against something, losing his balance, and then tumbling to the ground, hitting his head, all connection with where he was and what was happening disappearing in one disorienting second.

He struggled, fighting off a wave of dizzying pain and unconsciousness — and then realized that somewhere a few feet away, but beyond his sight, Peter and the Angel were suddenly locked together, their bodies entwined, rolling in the dust and dirt of decades, amid the litter and debris of the basement. Francis reached out with his arm, but the two men had pitched themselves away from him, and for a single, terrifying instant he was totally alone, save for the animal sounds of a desperate struggle taking place somewhere within reach, or perhaps miles away.

★ ★ ★

In the Amherst Building, Mister Evans was infuriated, busy trying to organize the patients and return them to their bunk room, but Napoleon, energized by all that had happened, was being difficult, obstinately insisting that they had their orders from C-Bird and the Fireman, and until Miss Jones was transported safely by ambulance, and C-Bird and the Fireman had returned from wherever they had disappeared to, no one was moving. This bit of bravado on the part of the small man was not altogether true, because while he was standing in the center of the corridor facing up to Mister Evil, Newsman at his side for support, many of

599

the other patients had begun to wander about in the space behind them. Down the hall the women still locked in their dormitory were crying out in unison any number of shouted fears — 'Murder! Fire! Rape! Help!' — more or less whatever occurred to them in the absence of any understanding of what was going on. The din they created made it hard to concentrate.

Doctor Gulptilil was hovering over Lucy's bleeding form, as two paramedics worked over her feverishly. One finally managed to get the bleeding in her leg stifled with a tourniquet, while another worked a plasma drip into her arm. She was pale, hovering on the edge of consciousness, trying to speak, but unable to find words that would work past her dry lips and beyond the pain. She finally gave up and allowed herself to drift in and out of reality, only peripherally aware that people were trying to help her. With Big Black's assistance, the two paramedics maneuvered her onto a stretcher, and lifted it. Two gray-suited security guards stood to the side, uncertain what to do, awaiting some instructions.

As Lucy was wheeled out, Gulp-a-pill turned to the Moses brothers. His first instinct was to loudly insist on an explanation, but then, he decided to bide his time. Instead, he merely asked: 'Where?'

Big Black stepped forward. His white attendant's jacket was streaked with blood from trying to staunch Lucy's wounds. Little Black was similarly marked.

'Down the basement,' Big Black said. 'C-Bird and the Fireman went after him.'

Gulptilil shook his head. 'Goodness,' he said, under his breath, but thinking that in truth the situation demanded obscenities far worse. 'Show me,' he demanded.

The Moses brothers led the medical director to the basement door. 'They went into the tunnel?' Gulptilil asked, already knowing the answer. Big Black nodded.

'Do we know where it comes out?'

Little Black shook his head.

Doctor Gulptilil had no intention of following anyone through the dark pit of the heating tunnel. He took a deep breath. He was reasonably confident that Lucy Jones would survive her wounds, despite the savagery with which they had been delivered, unless loss of blood and shock conspired to steal her life. That was possible, he thought, with professional detachment. At the moment, though, he didn't care much what happened to her. But it was abundantly clear to the medical director that someone else was likely to die that night, and he was already trying to anticipate the trouble that was likely to cause him. 'Well,' he said with a sigh, 'we can speculate that it either emerges in Williams, because that is the closest building, or else travels back to the power plant, so those locations are where we should look.' Of course, what he did not say out loud was that those destinations assumed that Francis and Peter successfully emerged from the tunnel, an assumption that he was not completely willing to make.

★   ★   ★

In the darkness, Peter fought hard.

He knew he was injured severely, but how badly was just beyond his understanding. It was as if each piece of the battle he was fighting was separate, distinct, and he tried to concentrate on each individually, to see if he could put together a defense that was whole. He could feel blood throbbing from a wound in his arm, and he knew that the weight of the Angel was bearing down on him. The pistol that he'd gripped so tightly had disappeared, easily knocked by the force of the Angel's assault into some black corner, gone from his touch, so that now what he had remaining to fight with was solely a desire to live.

He punched out hard, finding flesh, and he heard the Angel grunt, then followed it up with another blow, only to feel the knife slash at his arm, digging in sharply, furrowing his own skin. Peter shouted out some sound that wasn't a part of any language other than that of survival, and kicked as hard as he could with his feet. He battled against shadow, against the idea of death, as much as he did against the killer who was pressing him.

Locked together, blind and lost, the two men tried to find a way of killing the other. It was an unfair fight, for time and again the Angel was able to plunge the knife down, discovering purchase in Peter's body, and the Fireman thought he was going to be sliced to pieces slowly by the repeated blows. He lifted his arms, warding off strike after strike, kicking, trying to find some vulnerable spot in the utter black of the moment.

He could feel the Angel's breath, feel the man's strength and thought he would be no match for the deadly combination of the knife and obsession. Still, Peter fought hard, scratching, clawing, hoping for the Angel's eyes, or perhaps his groin, something that might give him a momentary respite from the knife that chopped at him. He thrust out his left hand, and it grazed against the Angel's chin, and in a burst of comprehension, knew that the killer's throat would be close by, so wildly he reached and suddenly felt skin and he closed his hand, choking the man who was trying to kill him. But, in the same instant, he felt the knife suddenly penetrate into his side, digging past flesh and muscle, searching for his stomach, hoping then to turn and rise upward and destroy his heart. Pain sheeted over his eyes, and Peter half gasped, half sobbed at the thought that he was going to die right there, right at that moment, in the darkness. He could feel the knife searching out death, and he grabbed at the Angel's hand, trying to slow what seemed like an inevitable march.

And then suddenly, like an explosion, an immense force seemed to slam into the two men.

The Angel groaned, knocked sideways, his grip on Peter suddenly halved, and the killer spat wordlessly in rage.

Peter did not know how Francis had managed to assault the Angel from behind, but he had, and now the young man clung to the killer's back, furiously trying hard to wrap his own hands around the Angel's throat.

Francis was shouting some great war cry, high-pitched, terrifying, one that combined all his fears and all his doubts into a single immense song. All his life, he had never fought back, never battled for something more important, never taken a true chance, never understood that this moment was either to be his best or his last, until this very second. And so he threw every ounce of hope into his fight, slamming his fists into the Angel's back and head, then grappling with the killer, trying to pull him back, off of Peter. He used every ounce of madness to buttress what muscle he had, letting every fear and rejection that he'd ever experienced fuel his battle. He gripped the Angel with a tenacity born of desperation, unwilling to let either nightmare or killer steal from him the only friend he thought he would ever have.

The Angel twisted and shook, struggling terribly. He was trapped between the two men, the one wounded, the other crazed with fear certainly, but more driven by something larger, and he hesitated, unsure which to fight, uncertain whether to try to finish the first battle and then turn to the second, which seemed increasingly impossible beneath the rain of blows Francis threw. Then he was stymied, when Francis suddenly grabbed hold of the Angel's arm, and twisted him backward. This abrupt change loosened the pressure that the Angel was putting on the knife in Peter's side, and with a reserve of strength that seemed to well up from some hidden spot within him, the Fireman seized hold of the Angel's hand with both of his own, neutralizing the pressure on the knife blade, arresting its drive toward his own death.

Francis did not know how long his own strength would last him. He knew the Angel was stronger in many ways, and if he was to have a chance, it would have to be right at that moment, right at the start, before the Angel could direct all his attention to him. He pulled as hard as he could, investing every bit of power he had in the desire to free Peter from beneath the Angel's figure. And, to his astonishment, he succeeded, at least in part. The Angel twisted back, off-balance, then slammed back farther, so that now Francis was caught beneath his body, under his back. Francis tried to wrap his legs around the killer, and he hung on with deadly determination, like a mongoose biting down on a cobra, as the Angel tried to find a way to beat off Francis's grip.

And in that second of confusion, the three bodies tangled together, Peter found that the knife in his side was free, and he wrapped his own hand around the handle and, screaming with red pain, he pulled it loose from his body, feeling his life chasing after it with every pulse of his heart. Summoning every bit of remaining strength, Peter grasped the knife, and thrust it forward, hoping that it wasn't Francis that he killed, searching for the man who he thought very likely had killed him. And when the point of the blade bit flesh, Peter threw all his weight behind it, because, he knew, this was the only chance he had, and all he could hope for was some luck.

The Angel, gripped tightly by Francis's last bit of strength, suddenly screamed. It was high-pitched, otherworldly, a noise that seemed to combine all the evil that he had done to so many, bursting forth and resounding off the walls, lighting up the darkness with death, agony, and despair. His own weapon betrayed him. Peter inexorably drove it into the Angel's chest, finding the heart that the killer never thought he needed.

Peter determined to use everything he had left in that final assault, and he kept all his weight bearing down on the knife blade until he heard the Angel's breath rattle with death.

Then he fell back, thought of a dozen, perhaps a hundred questions he wanted to ask, but could not, and closed his eyes to wait for his own end.

Francis, however, could feel the Angel stiffen and die beneath his grasp. He stayed in that position, holding the dead man for what seemed to him to be a very long time, but was probably only seconds. The voices he'd heard for so long seemed to have fled from him in that moment, taking their fears, their advice, their wishes and demands along with them, and he was only aware that everything was still dark, and that his only friend on earth was still breathing, but that it was shallow, labored, and closing in on some end that Francis did not want to consider.

And so Francis carefully unwrapped himself from the embrace of the Angel, whispered, 'Hang on,' in Peter's ear, although he did not imagine that the Fireman actually heard him, seized hold of his friend's shoulders, tugging him alongside, and a little like a baby let loose from his mother's grasp, slowly, tentatively, began to crawl through the pitch-black basement, searching for the light, hunting for the exit, hoping to find help somewhere.

35

The noise in my apartment had reached a crescendo, all memory, all rage. I could feel the Angel choking me, clawing at me, years of festering silence building, his fury unending, unlimited. I cowered down, feeling his blows batter me around the head and shoulders, tearing inwardly at my heart and at every thought I had. I was shouting, sobbing, my tears streaking my face, but nothing I spoke out loud seemed to have any effect, or make any sense. He was inexorable, unstoppable. I had helped to kill him that night so many years earlier, and he was with me now to exact his revenge, and he would not be dissuaded. I thought that it was probably fitting, in some perverse way. I'd had no real right to survive that night in the hospital tunnels, and that now he'd come to claim the victory that was truly his. In a way, I recognized, he had always been with me, and as hard as I'd fought then, and as hard as I'd fought this night, that I'd never really had a chance against the darkness he delivered.

I twisted about, throwing a chair across the room at his ghostly shape, watching the wooden frame splinter and shatter with a crash. I shouted defiance, measuring what little resources I had left, hoping that in the moments I had remaining, and the small space at the bottom of the wall that awaited my last words, I could finish my story.

I crawled, just as I had that other midnight, across the cold floor.

Behind me, I could hear pounding, a repetition of fierce demand, on the door to my apartment. Voices called out to me that seemed familiar, but far away, as if they came from a very great distance, across some divide I could never hope to traverse. I did not think they existed. I screamed out, 'Go away! Leave me alone!' not knowing whether the sound was real or fantasy. All these things had become jumbled in my imagination, and the curses and screams of the Angel filled my ears, blocking out whatever cries came from somewhere beyond the few square feet remaining in my world.

I'd pulled, half carried, half dragged Peter across the basement storage room, trying to get away from the killer's body remaining somewhere in the void behind us. I was feeling my way, pushing aside whatever obstacles tumbled into our path, dragging us both forward, not really knowing if I was heading in the right direction. I could sense that each foot traveled brought him closer to safety, but also to death, as if they were two convergent lines being plotted on some great graph, and when they came together, I would lose my struggle and he would die. I had held little hope that any of us would survive, and so, when I saw a door ahead of me open, and a small shaft of light tumble unheralded into the darkness that surrounded me, I swam toward it, gritting my teeth against all that had taken place. The Angel howled behind my head, but that was this night, for on that night he was dead, and I reached out toward the wall, and thought that at the very least, even if I were to die within the next few moments, I still needed to tell about looking up and seeing the unmistakable great wide shape of Big Black hovering in the tiny sliver of light, and the music of his voice, when I heard him call out: 'Francis? C-Bird? You down there?'

* * *

'Francis?' Big Black shouted, standing in the doorway leading down to the power plant's basement storage area and the heating tunnels that crisscrossed beneath

607

the hospital grounds, his brother close by his side, and Doctor Gulptilil only a foot or two to the rear. 'C-Bird, you down there?'

Before he could reach out and find a switch for the solitary light that might illuminate the rickety stairs, he heard a faint but familiar voice penetrate the darkness in reply, 'Mister Moses, please, help us!'

Neither of the brothers hesitated. The reedy, thin cry that seemed to slice up through the pit below told them more or less everything they needed. Bounding toward the sound, the Moses brothers raced ahead, while Doctor Gulptilil, still holding a little reluctantly in the rear, finally located the switch to give them some light, and flicked it on.

What he saw, in the faint glow from a yellowed, weak, exposed bulb, pitched him into action. Struggling through the debris and abandoned equipment, streaked with blood and grime, was a teary-eyed Francis. Right behind him, being dragged forward was Peter, who seemed to be near unconsciousness, though he held his hand over an immense wound in his side that had left a shocking path of red across the cement floor. Doctor Gulptilil looked up and was startled by the sight of a third patient deeper in the basement, eyes open in surprise and death, a large hunting knife lodged firmly in his chest. 'Oh my goodness,' the doctor said, as he hurried to catch up with Big Black and Little Black, who were already trying to administer some help to Peter and Francis.

Francis repeated over and over, 'I'm okay, I'm okay, help him,' although he was not altogether certain that he *was* okay, but it was the only thought that penetrated his exhaustion and relief. Big Black took everything in with a single immense glance, and seemed to understand what had taken place there that night, and he bent over Peter's form, pulling back the tatters of the Fireman's shirt, revealing the extent of his wound. Little

Black pushed to Francis's side, and quickly, expertly, did more or less the same, examining him for injury, despite Francis's headshaking and protests.

'Hold still, C-Bird,' Little Black said. 'I need to make sure you're okay.' Then, he whispered something else, as he nodded his head toward the Angel's body, 'I think you done good work here tonight, C-Bird. No matter what anyone else says.'

Then he seemed satisfied that Francis wasn't badly wounded, and he turned to help his brother.

'How bad is it?' Gulp-a-pill demanded, leaning over the two attendants, staring down at Peter.

'Bad enough,' Big Black answered. 'He needs to get to the hospital right now.'

'Can we carry him upstairs?' Doctor Gulptilil asked.

Big Black didn't reply. He merely reached down, and with two massive arms cradling beneath Peter's limp form, he lifted the Fireman from the cold floor and with a heave and a grunt, carried him up the stairs to the power plant's main area, like a groom carrying his bride over the threshold. He walked slowly, steadily to the front door, then gently knelt down just inside and lowered Peter's body. 'We need to get the Fireman help right away,' he said, turning to Doctor Gulptilil.

'I understand that,' the medical director was saying. He had already seized an old black rotary dial telephone from a desktop, and was dialing a number. 'Security?' he said briskly, when the line was connected. 'This is Doctor Gulptilil. I need another ambulance, yes, that's correct, another ambulance, and I need it immediately at the power plant. Yes, this is a matter of life and death. Please make that call instantly, if not sooner.'

Then he hung up the telephone.

Francis had trailed after Big Black, and was standing next to Little Black, who was speaking to Peter, urging him over and over to hang on, that help was coming, reminding him that this wouldn't be the right night to

609

die, not after all that had taken place, and what had been accomplished. His steady, reassuring tone brought a smile to Peter's face, which managed to reach past all the gathered hurt and shock he felt, and the sensation of his life dripping from his side. He didn't say any words, however. Big Black cradled Peter's head, and then took off his white attendant's jacket, folded it up and began to apply it to the gash in Peter's side. 'Help is on the way, Peter,' Doctor Gulptilil said, bending toward the Fireman, but whether the wounded man heard this or not, neither he, nor any of the others could tell.

Doctor Gulptilil took a deep breath, surveyed their solitude, and then started to calculate fiercely in his head, trying to assess the damage that had been done that night. That it was a mess, the medical director understood, was a minimalist's statement of the events that had transpired. All he could see was a dizzying array of reports, inquiries, harsh questions with perhaps some very difficult answers, all awaiting him. He had an out of control prosecutor on her way to the local hospital with terrible wounds that no emergency room doctor was going to remain silent about, which meant policemen at his door within hours. He was staring down at a patient of significant notoriety and of substantial interest to many people, bleeding on the floor, clinging to life mere hours before he was supposed to be shipped off to another state in secret. And then he had a third patient very dead, and just as clearly killed by this notorious patient and his schizophrenic companion.

He had recognized that third patient, and he knew that a hospital file existed with his own handwriting on the jacket that stated unequivocally: Severe Retardation. Catatonic. Prognosis Guarded. Long Term Care required.

He knew also there was a notation that the dead man had been released for several weekend furloughs in the

610

custody of an elderly mother and aunt.

The more he thought, the more he realized that his career hung in the balance of what he decided to do in the next few moments. For the second time that night, he heard a distant noise of sirens, which added urgency to his thinking.

Doctor Gulptilil breathed in sharply. He looked down at Peter and said, 'You will live, Mister Fireman.' He said this not knowing whether it was true or not, but knowing how important it was. Then he looked up at the Moses brothers. 'We need for this night not to have happened,' he said stiffly.

The two attendants quickly glanced at each other, then nodded.

'Going to be hard to make people not notice some,' Little Black said.

'Then we need to make them notice as little as possible.'

Little Black bent his head toward the basement, where the Angel's body remained behind. 'That body's going to make things tricky,' he said. He was speaking quietly, as if guarding his words carefully, understanding that this was a moment of some importance. 'That man back there, he was a killer.'

Doctor Gulptilil shook his head, speaking a little like he might to a grade school class, emphasizing some words. 'There's no real *evidence* to support that. All we know for certain is that he tried to assault Miss Jones earlier tonight. For what reason, we have no idea. And, more critically, what he has done on some other occasions, in other locations, well, that remains a mystery. It has no connection to us, here tonight. Unfortunately, what is not a mystery is that this patient was pursued and then was murdered himself by these two patients. Now, they may have been justified in what they did . . . '

He hesitated, as if waiting for Little Black to complete

his sentence. This, the smaller brother did not do, and so Doctor Gulptilil was forced to finish it himself.

'. . . But perhaps they were not. Regardless, there will be arrests. Headlines in the newspapers. Perhaps an official inquiry. Certainly a state inquest is a strong likelihood. Criminal charges are a possibility. Nothing is likely to be the same for some time . . .'

Doctor Gulptilil paused, watching the expressions on the two brothers' faces. 'And perhaps,' he added quietly, 'it might not be merely Mister Petrel and the Fireman who conceivably would face charges. The people who helped allow this disastrous night to take place, they, too, might find their jobs in jeopardy . . .'

Again, he waited, carefully measuring the impact of what he said on the two attendants.

'We didn't do anything wrong,' Big Black said. 'And neither did Francis and Peter . . .'

'Of course,' Doctor Gulptilil said quickly, shaking his head back and forth. 'Morally, certainly. Ethically? Of course. But legally? Everyone did the right thing, I'm quite positive. I can see that. But others, ah, that would be outside investigators, I'm less sure how they might perceive these quite terrible events.'

They were silent, then Doctor Gulptilil spoke quickly. 'I believe we need to think creatively. And as quickly as possible. We need,' he repeated, *for as little of this night to have happened as possible.*' And, as he said this, he pointed toward the basement.

Little Black could see this, as could his brother. Wordlessly, the two brothers seemed to comprehend what was being asked of them. Both men nodded.

'But if that man ain't dead,' Little Black said, 'then C-Bird, and the Fireman, why no one likely to look at them again. Or us, either, for that matter.'

'Correct,' Doctor Gulptilil said stiffly. 'I think we understand each other fully.'

Little Black seemed to think hard for a moment.

Then he turned to his brother and to Francis and said, 'You come with me. We've still got some work to do.'

He led them back toward the basement, turning once to Doctor Gulptilil, who now was bent over Peter, holding his hands over the Fireman's wounds, stanching the pulsing flow of blood with Big Black's jacket. 'You should make the call,' Little Black said.

The medical director nodded. 'Hurry,' he said. Then, as Francis watched, Doctor Gulptilil left Peter's side momentarily, and went back to the desk, where he picked up the telephone and dialed a number. After a second or two, he seemed to take a deep breath, and he said, 'Yes. State Police? This is Doctor Gulptilil at the Western State Hospital. I need to report that we have had one of our more dangerous patients escape from the hospital grounds this night. Yes, he appears to be armed. Yes, I can provide you with a name and description . . . ' He glanced back at Francis and he made a gesture with his arm, as if to urge him to hurry. Outside, in the distance, the sound of the ambulance accompanied by the security staff was getting closer.

★   ★   ★

Rain spit on Francis's face, seemingly contemptuous of what had happened. Or perhaps, Francis thought, as if determined it could wash away the past hours. He was unsure. A wild wind bent a nearby tree back and forth, as if it were shocked at the procession passing by in the middle of the night.

Big Black was in front, the Angel's body tossed over his broad back like a misshapen dark duffel bag. Right behind him, Little Black quick marched through the night, two shovels and a pickaxe in his arms. Francis brought up the rear, hurrying when Little Black urged him forward. Behind them, Francis could hear the arrival of the ambulance in front of the power plant, and

613

on a distant wall he could see the reflection of its flashing red emergency lights. A black security car had pulled in, as well, and its headlights carved a white arc out of the deep midnight world. But the three of them were out of the direct line of sight, and maneuvering through the darkness, using the weak residue of light to find their way deep into the corner of the hospital grounds.

'Be quiet,' Little Black said, although this was an unnecessary admonition. Francis looked up into the midnight sky above, and thought he could make out rich seams of ebony, as if some painter's hand had decided the night was not dark enough, and had tried to add even greater streaks of black.

When Francis looked back down, he immediately saw where they were heading. Not far away was the garden where he'd planted flowers at Cleo's side. Now he was at her side, once again. He followed the Moses brothers past the rickety metal link fence into the small cemetery, where Big Black grunted and swung the Angel's body to the ground. It thudded, and Francis thought he ought to feel sickened by the noise, but that, to his surprise, he wasn't. He looked at the man and thought that he might have passed by him in a corridor, in a dining room, on a pathway or in the dayroom a hundred times when he was alive, and never known who he really was until that night. And then, he shook his head in contradiction and thought this couldn't possibly be true, that if he'd ever once looked directly into the Angel's eyes, he was certain that he would have seen there what they had seen that night.

Big Black seized one of the shovels, and stepped to the side of the small mound of freshly dug dirt that marked where Cleo had been lain to rest the day before. Francis stepped to his side, took up the pickaxe, and without saying a word, lifted it above his head, and sunk it down into the moist ground. He was a little surprised at how easily they were able to carve away the soft earth of Cleo's grave. It was, he thought, as if she'd been expecting their arrival that night.

Behind them, out of sight, paramedics were fighting hard for the second time in the past few hours. It wasn't long before all three of them heard the urgent sound of the ambulance starting up, then racing across the mental hospital grounds, heading fast toward the nearest emergency room, precisely as it had done earlier, at the same breakneck speed, following the identical bumpy path.

As the noise of the siren faded, they were left with simply the muffled sound of their shovels and the pickaxe assaulting the muddy ground. The rain continued, soaking them thoroughly, but Francis was barely aware of any discomfort or even the suggestion of cold. He felt a blister forming on his hand, but ignored it, as he swung the pickaxe over his head time and again, and felt it bite into the earth. He had gone someplace well past exhaustion, into a locale dominated by what he knew he was trying to do that night and understanding that whatever chance anyone had, it would rest beneath the ground.

Francis was unsure whether it took an hour or longer to dig through the earth down six feet, to where the dull steel of the cheap coffin that held Cleo's body was finally exposed. For an instant or two, raindrops seemed to beat a drummer's tattoo against the lid, and Francis oddly hoped that the noise hadn't disturbed the queen's sleep.

Then he shook his head and thought *She would lik this. Every empress deserves a slave in the afterlife.*

Big Black wordlessly tossed down his shovel. F looked at his brother, and Little Black joined him lifting up the Angel's body by hands and fe Stumbling a little, sliding in the muddy ground, the attendants maneuvered over to the side of the gr

and then, with a push, dropped the Angel down upon the coffin top, with a muffled thud. Big Black looked up at Francis, who was standing at the edge of the hole, hesitant, and this time the attendant said, 'No need to say a prayer over this man because there ain't no prayer in this world strong enough to do him any good where he's heading.'

Francis believed this to be true.

Then, without hesitating, the three of them picked up their shovels and the pickaxe, and quickly began to fill in the grave, just as the first tentative dawn light began to creep over the far horizon.

★   ★   ★

And that was it, then.

I curled up, rolling myself into a ball, at the base of the wall.

I shivered, trying to shut out the chaos around me. From someplace miles away, I could hear shouts, and a great banging, as if every fear and doubt and ounce of guilt I'd concealed over all these years were beating against my door, threatening to burst the hinges and crash inside. I knew that I owed the Angel a death, and he was there to claim it. The story was told, and I didn't believe I had any more right to live. I closed my eyes, and as I heard loud voices and urgent shouts cascade down upon me, I waited for him to take his revenge, expecting any second to feel the ice of his touch. I squeezed myself into as small and insignificant a parcel as I could, and I heard footsteps racing frantically in my direction, as I calmly, sadly, waited to die.

Part Three

EGGSHELL WHITE, FLAT LATEX

36

'Hello, Francis.'

I squinted at the sound of a familiar voice.

'Hello, Peter,' I replied. 'Where am I?'

'Back in the hospital,' he responded, grinning, his old devil-may-care flash in his eyes. I must have looked alarmed, because he held up his hand. 'Not *our* hospital, of course. That one is gone forever. A new one. Quite a bit nicer than the old Western State. Take a look around, C-Bird. I think you'll see that the accommodations this time around are significantly improved.'

I slowly pivoted my head first to the right, then the left. I was lying on a firm bed, and I could feel crisp, clean sheets beneath my skin. An intravenous tube dripped some concoction into a needle stuck into the flesh of my arm, and I was dressed in a pale green hospital johnny. On the wall opposite my bed there was a large and colorful painting of a white sailboat being driven by a stiff breeze across some sparkling bay waters on a fine summer's day. A silent television set was hung by a bracket from the wall. And my momentary survey discovered that my room had a window, which gave me a small, but welcome view of an eggshell blue sky with a few wispy high clouds, which seemed to me to be curiously like the afternoon in the painting, repeated.

'See?' Peter said with a small wave. 'Not bad at all.'

'No,' I admitted. 'Not bad.'

I looked over at the Fireman. He was perched on the edge of the bed, near my feet. I looked him up and down. He was different from the last time I'd seen him in my apartment, when flesh had hung from his bones, blood had streaked his face, and dirt had marred his smile. Now he was wearing the blue jumpsuit that I recalled from the very first day we'd met, outside of Gulptilil's office, and he had the same Boston Red Sox cap pushed back on his head.

'Am I dead?' I asked him.

He shook his head, a small smile flitting across his face.

'No,' he said. 'You're not. I am.'

I could feel a wave of grief rising up within my chest, stifling the words I wanted to speak in my throat. 'I know,' I said. 'I remember.'

Peter grinned again. 'Wasn't the Angel, you know. Did I ever get a chance to thank you, C-Bird? He would have killed me for certain down there if not for you. And I would have died if you hadn't pulled me across that basement floor and got the Moses brothers to get help. You did real well by me, Francis, and I was grateful, even if I never got a chance to tell you.'

Peter sighed, and a little sadness crept into his words. 'We should have been listening to you all along, but we didn't, and it cost us a great deal. You were the one who knew where to search, and what to look for. But we didn't pay attention, did we?' He shrugged as he spoke.

'Did it hurt?' I asked.

'What? Not listening to you?'

'No.' I waved my hand in the air. 'You know what I mean.'

Peter laughed briefly. 'Dying? I thought it would, but if truth be told, not at all. Or, at least, not all that much.'

'I saw your picture in the paper a couple of years back when it happened. It was your picture, but the name underneath it was different. It said you were out in Montana. But it was you, wasn't it?'

'Of course. New name. New life. But all the same old problems.'

'What happened?'

'It was stupid, really. It wasn't a big fire, and we only

620

had a few crews working it, almost haphazardly; we all thought it was just about under wraps. We'd been digging firebreaks all morning, and I guess we were really only minutes away from declaring it contained and pulling everyone out, when the wind shifted. Shifted hard, and blew up something fierce. I told the crew to run for the ridge, and we could hear the fire right behind us, being blown along. It makes a roaring sound, almost like you're being chased by a huge runaway train. Everybody made it, except me, and I would have made it, too, if one of the guys hadn't fallen, and I went back for him. So, there we were, with only one fire cover between the two of us, so I let him crawl underneath where he had a chance to survive, and I tried to outrun it, even though I knew I couldn't and it caught me a few feet from the ridge. Bad luck, I guess, but it all seemed strangely appropriate, C-Bird. At least the papers called me a hero, but it didn't feel all that heroic. Just pretty much what I'd been expecting, and, I'm guessing, probably what I deserved. Like it was all in balance, finally.'

'You could have saved yourself,' I said.

He shrugged. 'I'd saved myself other times. And been saved, as well, especially by you. And if you hadn't saved me, then I wouldn't have been there to save him, so it all worked out, more or less.'

'But I miss you,' I said.

Peter the Fireman smiled. 'Of course. But you no longer need me. Actually, Francis, you never did. Not even the first day we met, but you couldn't see it, then. Now maybe you can.'

I didn't know about that, but I didn't say anything right away, until I recalled why I was in the hospital.

'But what about the Angel? He'll come back.'

Peter shook his head, and lowered his voice, as if to give weight to his words. 'No, C-Bird. He had his shot back then twenty years ago, and you beat him and then you beat him again after all that time had passed. He's gone for good now. He won't bother you, or anyone else again, except in some folks' bad memories, which is where he belongs and where he'll have to stay. It's not perfect, of course, or exactly clean and nice. But that's the way things are. They leave a mark, but we go on. But you'll be free. I promise.'

I didn't know if I believed this. 'I'll be all alone again,' I complained.

Peter laughed out loud. It was a wide, unadorned, unfettered laugh.

'C-Bird, C-Bird, C-Bird,' he said, shaking his head back and forth with each word. 'You've never been alone.'

I reached out to touch him, as if to prove that what he said was true, but Peter the Fireman faded away, disappearing from the edge of the hospital bed, and I slowly slid back into a dreamless, solid sleep.

★ ★ ★

None of the nurses at this hospital had nicknames, I quickly learned. They were pleasant, efficient, but businesslike. They checked the drip in my arm, and when that was removed, they monitored the medications I was given carefully, charting each one on a clipboard that hung from a slot on the wall by the door. I didn't get the impression that anyone could cheek any medication in this hospital, so I dutifully swallowed whatever they gave me. Every so often, they would speak with me, about this or that, the weather just beyond my window, or perhaps how I had slept the night before. Every question they asked seemed a part of some greater scheme, which was restoring me to some familiar level. For example, they never asked me if I liked the green Jell-O, or the red, or whether I might want some graham crackers and juice before sleep, or if

I preferred one television show over another. They wanted to know specifically whether my throat felt dry, I'd had any nausea or diarrhea, or whether I had a quiver in my hands, and most especially, had I heard or seen anything that just might not actually be there?

I didn't tell them about Peter's visit. It wasn't what they would have wanted to hear about, and he didn't return again.

Once each day the resident on the ward came by, and he and I would talk a little about ordinary things. But these weren't really conversations, like one friend might have with another, or even like two strangers meeting for the first time, with pleasantries and greetings. They belonged to a different realm, one where I was being measured, and assessed. The resident was like a tailor seeking to make me a new suit of clothes before I was to be set off in the great wide world, except that these were cuts of cloth that I wore within and not without.

Mister Klein, my social worker, came by one day. He told me I'd been very lucky.

My sisters came by on another day. They told me I'd been very lucky.

They also cried a little, and told me that my folks wanted to come visit, but were too old and unable, which I didn't believe, but I acted as if I did, and that really, I didn't mind, not in the slightest, which seemed to cheer them up.

One morning, after I had swallowed my daily dosage of pills, the nurse looked at me and smiled, told me that I should get a haircut, and then informed me that I was going home.

'Mister Petrel, big day today,' she said. 'Going to be discharged.'

'That's good,' I said.

'You have a couple of visitors, first,' she said.

'My sisters?'

She leaned close enough so that I could smell the

intoxicating freshness of her starched white outfit and shampooed hair. 'No,' she said, her voice just above a whisper. 'Important visitors. You have no idea, Mister Petrel, how much people here on this floor have wondered about you. You're the biggest mystery in the hospital. Orders from up high to make sure you got the best room. Best treatment. All being taken care of by some mysterious folks whom nobody knows. And then, today, some VIPs in a long black limousine to take you home. You must be an important person, Mister Petrel. A celebrity. Or, at least, that's what people around here are wondering.'

'No,' I said. 'I'm nobody special.'

She laughed and shook her head. 'You're too modest.'

Behind her, the door opened, and the psychiatric resident poked his head in. 'Ah, Mister Petrel,' he said. 'You have visitors.'

I looked toward the door, and from behind him I heard a familiar voice. 'C-Bird? What you doing in there?'

And then a second, 'C-Bird, you giving anyone any trouble?'

The psychiatrist stepped aside, and Big Black and Little Black stepped into the room.

If anything, Big Black was even bigger. He sported an immense waistline that seemed to flow like some great ocean into a barrel chest, thick arms, and steel pillar legs. He wore a three-piece blue pin-striped suit that to my uneducated eye seemed very expensive. His brother was equally dressed up, with leather shoes that reflected a sheen from the overhead lights. Both men wore some gray in their hair, and Little Black had gold wire-rimmed glasses perched on the end of his nose, giving him a slightly academic appearance. It seemed to me that they had set aside their youth, replacing it with substance and authority.

'Hello, Mister Moses and Mister Moses,' I said.

The two brothers pushed their way directly to the side of the bed. Big Black put out his massive hand and clapped me on the shoulder. 'Feeling better, C-Bird?' he asked.

I shrugged. Then I realized this perhaps wasn't the most positive of impressions to be giving, so I added, 'Well, I'm not wild about all the medications, but I certainly think I'm a lot better.'

'You had us worried,' Little Black said. 'Damn scared, really.'

'When we found you,' Big Black was speaking quietly, 'we weren't sure you were going to make it. You were pretty far out there, C-Bird. Talking to folks that weren't there, throwing things, fighting, shouting. Pretty shaky.'

'I'd had some rough days.'

Little Black nodded. 'We've all seen some tough times. You scared us plenty.'

'I didn't know it was you that came for me,' I said.

Big Black laughed, and looked over at his brother. 'Well, it's not the sort of thing we do a whole lot anymore. Not like the old days, when we were young guys working at the old hospital and doing what old Gulp-a-pill wanted. No more. But we got the call, and we hurried right over and we're just damn glad we got there before you, well . . . '

'Killed myself?'

Big Black smiled. 'You want to put it that bluntly, C-Bird, well, that's exactly right.'

I leaned back a little onto the pillows and looked over at the two men. 'How did you know . . . ,' I started.

Little Black shook his head. 'Well, we've been keeping an eye on you for some time, C-Bird. Getting regular reports from Mister Klein at the treatment center about your progress. Plenty of calls from the Santiago family, 'cross the hall. They've been helping us watch out for you. Local police, some of the local business men, they all pitched in, help keep tabs on C-Bird, year in, year

625

out. I'm surprised you didn't know.'

I shook my head. 'I had no idea. But how did you arrange . . .'

'Lots of folks owe my brother and me, big-time, C-Bird. And there's lots of folks who are always looking to do a favor or two for the county sheriff' — he nodded toward Big Black — 'or a city councilman . . .'

He paused, and then added: 'Or a federal judge who has a most genuine and mighty big interest in the man who helped to save her life one real bad night a number of years ago.'

★   ★   ★

I had never ridden in a limousine before, especially one driven by a police officer in uniform. Big Black showed me how to make the windows roll up and down, and then he showed me where the telephone was and asked me if I wanted to make a call — at taxpayer's expense, of course — to anyone, which I might have liked, but I couldn't think of anyone that I wanted to speak with. Little Black gave the driver directions to my street, and he held onto a small blue duffel bag that contained two sets of clean clothes that my sisters had given me.

When we turned down the narrow block that led to my apartment, I saw another official-looking car parked outside. A driver in a black suit was standing by the door, waiting for us. He seemed to know the Moses brothers, because when we got out of the limousine, he merely pointed up toward the window to my apartment and said, 'She's upstairs waiting.'

I led the way up to the second floor.

The door that had been burst from its hinges by the Moses brothers and the ambulance crew had been repaired, but was wide open. I stepped just inside my apartment, and saw that it had been cleaned up, fixed up, and restored. I could smell new paint, and saw that the appliances in the kitchen were new. Then I looked up, and saw Lucy standing in the middle of the small living room.

She leaned a little to the right, using a silver aluminum cane for support. Her hair shone, glistening, black, but with a little gray around the edges, as if she was showing the same age that the Moses brothers had. The scar on her face had faded further with the passing of the years, but her green eyes and beauty were still as breathtaking as the day I'd first seen her. She smiled, when I approached her, and she held out her hand.

'Oh, Francis,' she said, 'you had us so worried. It has been so long, and now, it is good to see you again.'

'Hello, Lucy,' I said. 'I've thought about you often.'

'And I about you, as well, C-Bird.'

For a moment, I remained rooted in position, frozen a little like I was the first time we'd met. It is always hard to speak, think, or breathe, at some moments, especially when so many memories are reverberating in the air, just behind every word, every look, and every touch.

It seemed to me that I had much to ask her, but what I said, instead was 'Lucy, why didn't you save Peter?'

She smiled ruefully, and shook her head.

'I wished that I could,' she said. 'But the Fireman needed to save himself. I couldn't do it. Nor could anyone else. Only him.'

She seemed to sigh and as she did so, I looked past her and saw that the wall where my words were collected remained intact. The rows of writings marched up and down, the drawings leapt out, the story was all there, just as it had been the night the Angel had finally come to me, but I'd slipped through his grasp. Lucy followed my eyes with her own, and half turned toward the wall.

'Quite an effort, C-Bird,' she said.

'You've read it?'

'Yes. We all have.'

I didn't say anything, because I didn't know what to say.

'You understand, some folks might be hurt by what you describe,' she said.

'Hurt?'

'Reputations. Careers. That sort of thing.'

'It's dangerous?'

'It might be. Always a little hard to tell.'

'What should I do?' I asked.

Lucy smiled again. 'I can't answer that for you C-Bird. But I have brought you several presents that might help you to make a decision.'

'Presents?'

'I guess, for lack of a better word, that is what you might call them.' She gestured with her hand at a simple brown cardboard box that was pushed up against the wall. I walked over to it and reached inside and took out some items collected inside.

The first was a package of large yellow legal notepads. Next to that was a box of Number 2 pencils with erasers. Then, below those, there were two cans of eggshell white, flat latex wall paint, a roller, a tray, and a large, stiff paint-brush.

'You see, C-Bird,' Lucy said carefully, measuring her words with a judge's precision and pace. 'Just about anyone could come in here and read the words you've put up on the wall. And they might interpret them in any number of ways, not the least of which is to wonder just how many bodies *are* buried in the old state hospital graveyard. And how those bodies happened to get there.'

I nodded.

'But, on the other hand, Francis, this is your story, and you have the right to tell it. Hence the notepads, which have a slightly greater permanence, and significantly more privacy to them than the words scrawled on the wall. Already those are starting to fade, and pretty soon, they are likely to be illegible.'

I could see that she was telling the truth.

Lucy smiled, and she opened her mouth as if to add something else, but then stopped. Instead, she simply leaned forward and kissed me on the cheek.

'It's good to see you again, C-Bird,' she said. 'Take better care of yourself from now on.'

Then, leaning heavily on her cane, dragging her ruined right leg with every step like a memory of that night, Lucy slowly limped from the room. Big Black and Little Black watched her for a moment, then they, too, wordlessly, reached out, shook my hand, and followed after her.

When the door closed shut, I turned back to the wall. My eyes raced over all the words there, and as I read, I carefully unwrapped the pencils and the pads of paper. Without hesitating for more than a few seconds, I quickly copied down from the very top:

Francis Xavier Petrel arrived in tears at the Western State Hospital in the back of an ambulance. It was raining hard, darkness was falling rapidly, and his arms and legs were cuffed and restrained. He was twenty-one years old and more scared than he'd ever been in his short, and to that point, relatively uneventful life . . .

The painting, I thought, could wait for a day or so.

We do hope that you have enjoyed reading
this large print book.

Did you know that all of our titles
are available for purchase?

We publish a wide range of high quality
large print books including:
Romances, Mysteries, Classics
General Fiction
Non Fiction and Westerns

Special interest titles available in
large print are:
The Little Oxford Dictionary
Music Book
Song Book
Hymn Book
Service Book

Also available from us courtesy of Oxford
University Press:
Young Readers' Dictionary
(large print edition)
Young Readers' Thesaurus
(large print edition)

For further information or a free
brochure, please contact us at:
Ulverscroft Large Print Books Ltd.,
The Green, Bradgate Road, Anstey,
Leicester, LE7 7FU, England.
Tel: (00 44) 0116 236 4325
Fax: (00 44) 0116 234 0205

THE ANALYST

John Katzenbach

'Happy fifty-third birthday, Doctor. Welcome to the first day of your death. You ruined my life. And now I fully intend to ruin yours.' Until the moment he reads those words, New York psychoanalyst Dr Frederick Starks has led a quiet and, so he believes, blameless life. But suddenly he is plunged into a dizzying battle of wits designed by a man who calls himself Rumplestiltskin. The rules: in two weeks Starks must guess his tormentor's identity and the source of his fury. If he succeeds, he goes free. If he fails, one by one, Rumplestiltskin will destroy fifty-two of Dr Starks's loved ones — unless the doctor agrees to kill himself . . .

3RD DEGREE

James Patterson and Andrew Gross

Detective Lindsay Boxer is jogging along a beautiful San Francisco street when there is a fiery explosion. A townhouse owned by an internet millionaire is immediately engulfed in flames, and Lindsay finds three people dead. A child is missing, and a mysterious message at the scene leaves Lindsay and the San Francisco Police Department completely baffled. Then a prominent businessman is found murdered, with another mysterious message left behind. Lindsay asks three of her friends to help her figure out who is committing these murders — and why they are intent on killing someone every three days. Even more terrifying, the four friends — who call themselves the Women's Murder Club — discover that the killer has targeted one of them . . .